Praise for **BONES**

"Bones is a tale of flesheating zombie terror. What separates it from the current
horde of undead drivel is the simple fact that the protagonist (and title character) is
a dog. Now, before your fragile mind breaks with bad memories of the insipid
original *Hills Have Eyes 2*, wherein a canine is not only featured prevalently but
even has its own flashback, rest assured that this attempt is handled with a greater
degree of subtlety and intelligence." --*Fangoria*

"Somebody needs to jump on Wheaton's Bones stories - a really unique zombie
tale that has a cadaver dog as the main character. It's like *Benji* and *The Dawn of
the Dead* (well, not really as Bones is no Benji, but he's totally lovable!)." --
Badass Digest

"As the story goes on, Bone's sense of smell becomes quite important as a tool for
the people in the story to find the undead menace, so he winds up in a series of
increasingly exciting and bloody set-pieces. It's a pretty graphic tale, full of
viscera and various grue, but that's what one expects from zombie fiction, and
Bones delivers. Bones is fine example of quality, independent horror literature. A
new take on the zombie outbreak story, it's a good, quick read, and well worth
your time." – *Jon is the Best Blog*

"I kind of like dry humor and oddities (like the whole funyun scene cracked me up
for some reason, yeah, so a kid died, whatever, he scored some funyons!). I'm not
so much for books that are so gory they make you wince. I like a good story. This
novella was perfect for me because it met all of those criteria. A great Halloween-
ish read!" – *Candy's Raves* [referring to *Bones*]

Praise for **FOUR NAILS IN THE COFFIN**

"Remarkably character-driven…Wheaton rather convincingly showcases his
talents as a writer of horror prose, taking his time to craft characters who are
thoroughly fleshed out and engaging without holding off too long on the
suspense…proves here to be a quite gifted storyteller undeniably worthy of an
interested reader's time and attention." – *Fangoria*

"These stories are all incredible. Easily worth your buck, especially *Sunday Billy
Sunday*, which is possibly the best slasher homage I've read." – *CHUD*

"The writing is fabulous. It flowed easily off of the page and was very enjoyable
to read. I also loved the premise for the first 2/3 or so of the book. I, quite literally,
could not put it down. I had to know what happened and what was going on and…
who and why and how and…This was a good novella. Pick it up and give it a
whirl." – *Candy's Raves*, [referring to *Last Tuesday*]

"Mark Wheaton is a T4000 horror writer. He brings a millennial aesthetic, a screenwriter's eye and ear, and an imagination as wide, sun-seared, and American as Route 66 to this quartet of novellas. This is muscular, original fiction that marks the debut of an exciting new voice in the speculative/dark fantasy genre." - Michael Rowe, author of *Enter, Night* and editor of the *Queer Fear* anthology series

"Genuinely twisted and engrossing...may just leave you shaken for days." – *Rue Morgue* [referring to *Sunday Billy Sunday*]

"His tales are visceral, intellectual, and often grisly, but Wheaton never forgets that touch of humanity and wry humor which allow true horror to cut that much deeper to the bone." – Ken Plume, author, *There's a Zombie in My Treehouse*

"A very entertaining and creepy story." – *Red Adept Reviews* [referring to *Sunday Billy Sunday*]

"Wheaton's writing is haunting. Days, weeks, even months later, you will find your mind returning to his worlds. Stephen King is no longer my only addiction." – Todd Farmer, screenwriter, *Drive Angry, My Bloody Valentine in 3D*

"Mark Wheaton is a magician. He misdirects you with accessibility while performing tricks of genius. Don't try to figure out how he does it - just enjoy the show. *Four Nails in the Coffin* is a shotgun blast to the brain. In a good way." - Gary Dauberman, screenwriter, *Swamp Devil, In the Spider's Web*

"This is an outstanding collection of interesting, original horror fantasy fiction. Clearly Wheaton works in Hollywood, as each story bursts with clear, potent visuals and is powered by a relentless narrative drive. Yet there's a definite political/social commentary running through the stories -- not enough to make them polemics, but enough to make you think. But Wheaton is mostly out to tell a ripping good yarn, and he delivers such in spades. Buy it now and have fun!" - Craig Perry, producer, *Final Destination I-V*

"Mark Wheaton's collection of novellas shows off a sharp sense of the uncanny. Here is a storyteller who can take us into the weirdest of scenarios through the eyes of characters who are, however offbeat, always believable. One part horror, one part suspense, *Nails* is a fully engaging and out of the ordinary reading experience." – Shara Kay, co-producer, *Mother's Day, Veronika Decides to Die*

"4 ¼ STARS. This novella opened well, roping the reader in with scenes from the lives of Daniel and Marcie Towne. The suspense is built pretty quickly...Daniel and Marcie were both extremely well developed characters. The descriptions were vivid and well done. The dialogue was realistic with good voice." – *Red Adept Reviews* [referring to *Last Tuesday*]

Praise for *CLEANERS: ABSENT BODIES*

"The Cleaners is equal parts police procedural, mystery, horror fiction, and sci-fi thriller. One might expect the combination of all these genres to result in a plot messier than one of Bellarmine's crime scenes, but "Absent Bodies" is quite tidily-written, or as least as tidy as could be expected of a this blood-spattered gorefest of a story. This is largely thanks to Wheaton's screenwriting experience, which is evident in the realistic dialogue and cinematic quality of the panel layouts and arrangements…a great read." – *NYC Graphic Novelists*

"This is a completely modern horror story that hinges on the age old fear of blood and the contemporary fear of what diseases lie within…The book really does dole out a healthy dose of paranoia and make you feel downright ooky upon reading it." – *Aint-It-Cool-News*

"The best first issue I've read in a long time. All I can say is 'wow'…I am at a complete loss for words when it comes to how impressed I am right now…What we have here is nothing less than one of the best new books of the year." – *Pop Syndicate*

"The writing is excellent. Feeling like a successful breed of TV crime shows Dexter and CSI, Cleaners does represent a good mystery comic where the details lead the reader along on a rollercoaster in the dark…" - *Fangoria*

"The way the story goes in depth about scientific knowledge on blood and disease reminds me of the dedication Chuck Palahniuk would take. If you're a fan of crime stories with a twist of supernatural…The Cleaners is a must." – *Bloody-Disgusting*

"Four stars" – *Comics Bulletin*

"I'm more excited about The Cleaners than I have been for any title in a long time…there's a sense of freshness here, of unexplored territory that has me anxious to see what comes next." – *CHUD*

"One believes what is happening is possible and well explained…the minute attention to details make this a rewarding read…the script is almost flawless. A powerful, yet careful voice. The story has more potential than any horror title since '30 Days of Night' made the scene." – *Broken Frontier*

"Check it out!" – *G4 TV*

"Gruesome. Odd. And quite disturbing. The Cleaners is a glimpse into the ugly underbelly of a violent society. But underneath all this muck and violence…lie good people…A great mystery." – *Blood of the Muse*

BONES

OMNIBUS

Mark Wheaton

Southbound Films – 2013

ISBN 978-1484887592

First Edition

Cover art by Stuart Cripps

Table of Contents

Introduction

Introduction

The Littlest Hobo was an asshole. Every week the wandering canine star of this Canadian TV show would trot into the life of some needy young child, befriend them, help them overcome their problems, then promptly fuck off out of their life. We never saw what became of the kids after their furry benefactor disappeared, but it's fair to say they learned an important lesson about the fleeting nature of relationships in that moment.

Bones, the canine star of Mark Wheaton's indescribable literary saga, is a lot like The Littlest Hobo. He's not Canadian, but he's a lot more honest about his assholery. He too wanders the country, passing from human to human, but when Bones moves on it's usually because the person in question is dead, killed by the zombie-like victims of a giant mutant sea anemone, devoured by rabid rats in a post-earthquake Los Angeles or murdered by a New York thug under the influence of a demonic Bull Mastiff.

But I'm getting ahead of myself. Trying to explain the Bones saga in a sound bite is all but impossible. Break it down into its constituent parts, and you'll end up with a soup of seemingly incompatible ingredients. Urban crime drama. Backwoods horror. Epic disaster thriller. Post-apocalyptic tragedy. Zombies. Mutants. Ghosts. Witches. Bigfoot. Put these elements in the hands of most writers and ask them to come up with something and you'll get a pungent mess, a lumpy broth that defies digestion. Like the sushi chef who knows how to serve the blowfish without poisoning his customer, you need a chef like Wheaton to make these flavors work.

And work they do. The Bones saga thrills in a way very few horror series can: by surprising the reader. It's a sad truth that most genre fiction ends up being, by its nature, generic. Bones is anything but. I've read all nine Bones stories – from the twisted early horror yarns, through the chilling apocalypse trilogy, and on to the head-spinning Bigfoot coda – and couldn't even begin to predict where the tale would go from one story to the next.

Even within the boundaries of each story, Bones chews up the rule book and leaves it shredded and slobbery. Freed from the predictable rhythms of narrative by his mute and reactionary lead character, Wheaton can introduce us to someone, immerse us in their life in a few deft paragraphs, let us follow them enough to share in their hopes and dreams, then destroy them utterly without pause or remorse. Through the impassive eyes of Bones, friend or foe alike, we're all just animals waiting to be hunted.

It's a ruthless world, and Wheaton doesn't soften its edges with cutesy-poo anthropomorphism. Bones has no interior monologue, only instinct. He's heroic only in that he does what he's been trained for. He'll bond with you, help you, but, hey, if your eye gets torn out of its socket by a rabid seagull, you'd better believe he's going to gobble it up. There's an emotional distance in these stories that would be nihilistic if it weren't grounded in the animal kingdom. Forget Simba – this is the real circle of life.

I spent most of 2011 and 2012 researching my book, *Tooth and Claw: A Field Guide to Animal Attack Horror Movies*, which meant 24 months of watching people being mauled, eaten and otherwise finished off by rats, snakes, sharks, bears and – yes – dogs. I'd foolishly challenged myself to try and watch every "natural horror" movie ever made, from the heights of *Jaws* and *The Birds* to the lows of the creakiest killer ant TV movie. I watched literally hundreds of the things, and saw what I assumed was every conceivable way animals could be used in a horror story.

Wheaton draws from the same well as those movies but his prose has a pace and pulse that, I can conclusively say, is utterly unique. That's not something you can say very often when talking about horror fiction. Indeed, the worst thing about this book is that its finality means that the saga is at a pretty definitive end. If you've never encountered Bones before, you're in for one hell of a treat. Keep a tight hold on the leash and don't let go.

Dan Whitehead
England, 2013

THE EARLY
YEARS

BITCH

The banshee cry of the midnight freight to Buffalo pierced the summer night. As the quaking of the railroad tracks sent most wildlife scurrying for the thicket, the horn was almost unnecessary. Still, a crossing was a crossing and federal law required a certain number of horn blasts when the train drew close.

The crossing wasn't much. A pair of steel ramps were propped on either side of the tracks, with a thick rectangle of rubber placed over the ties to keep vehicles from getting stuck or scraping their chassis on the rails. The rural western Pennsylvania lane serviced by the junction was called Bucks County Road even though Bucks County was on the other side of the state. Spurred off Route 36, on the north side of the tracks, Bucks County Road became a gravel track a hundred yards up from the crossing.

There were no houses down that way and a single hunter or forestry services truck might bump over the tracks a few times a week. But this mattered little to the train drivers who passed through the area every day. A dashboard alert signaling the need for the sounding of the horn (two long blasts followed by a short one and then a third long blast) was one of the few actions that still required a manual response from the driver when it closed to within a hundred yards.

A few minutes later, and the halo of the engine's forward headlight would ghost through the thick woods, illuminating sycamores, pines, and ash. Whatever moon or starlight managed to pierce the tree canopy would be eclipsed by the 300,000-candlepower lamp.

This night, the only other light emerged from a tiny wooden shack fifty feet from the south edge of the crossing. A sad structure that sagged with age, a passerby could be excused for assuming it long abandoned. Its roof and walls had endured decades of miserable weather without so much as a new coat of paint. Water damage had caused a part of the porch to crumble away, leaving a pile of broken planks in a heap alongside the building.

A building inspector would've condemned the place and called it a day, but one would have to venture that far into the sticks first. As the shack was a place of business, one that sold food and liquor at that, a health inspector might've weighed in as well. But this was just as unlikely. This was how the Bait-N-Booze remained open, catering to the needs of a handful of hunters, adventurous campers, and local backwoodsmen who hadn't the foresight to pick up supplies at a fourth of the price closer to the big city.

"Hot-shot's late again," Ferris scoffed, eyeing the beer company clock his store had been "gifted with" by a distribution rep a few years back. He jiggled an almost empty tallboy of the very brand as he stared out toward the crossing. "Second time this month!"

As Ferris lived alone, his comment was met with silence. He'd been married twice, but both wives were in the grave, one from suicide, one from drink. When he spoke of it, he always said they'd both killed themselves.

"Every chick Hitler stuck his dick in killed themselves, too," he was fond of saying, delighting in the ensuing looks of shock. "But the big difference between me and Hitler is that I'm fucking insane!"

Ferris Aaron was sixty-two. He only had about half his teeth left, with a couple more ready to fall out as well. He'd been razor-thin his whole life but now just looked like someone had stretched a dead man's hide over a skeleton. His squint, magnified by thick glasses and amplified by a sharp nose that directed a viewer's attention back up to it, gave him a rodent's countenance. That he let his fingernails grow out to sharp points only exaggerated this impression.

Though most who came across Ferris Aaron assumed he was part of the landscape, a lifer who likely had been born within shouting distance of wherever he could be found standing at any given moment, this was their mistake. In point of fact, Ferris had been all over the state as a guest of many of its detention facilities and penitentiaries. His proudest achievement was having been the subject of one of the state's intense and wide-ranging drug trafficking investigations, a case that landed him in the maximum security facility at Graterford for six years. When folks doubted his claim, he'd whip a crumbling newspaper article from his wallet. A front-page story, albeit from below the fold, it featured his booking photograph with his name in the caption, and highlighted the work of law enforcement in busting this "major criminal."

"See there? Biggest meth producer in the history of the state. *Boom.*"

Two months after he'd gotten out of Graterford, he was already back at it, building a new lab in a cargo container in the woods half a mile from his shack. In the pen, he'd met a major racketeer named Cuno who claimed to have the biggest problem with supply when it came to methamphetamine, though none with demand. Ferris swore that he'd never have that problem with him. When Cuno got out, he looked up his old cell mate, and they made a deal for the mobster to exclusively distribute Aaron's product in Pittsburgh. Aaron proved true to his word. Cuno never had a problem with supply again. Three times a month, a beer truck rolled up to the Bait-N-Booze to restock the meager supplies. Ferris handed over everything he'd cooked up since the last pickup and got paid for the previous shipment. Cuno had assured Ferris that the driver was reliable, as he was Cuno's son, Christopher.

Ferris settled into a quiet life out in the woods, cooking meth, consuming heroic amounts of alcohol, and doing so much of his own product that he sometimes stayed awake for days. Occasionally he indulged in a high-end prostitute he'd arrange through Christopher. The girl and her chaperone would arrive at the Bait-N-Booze thinking they were either lost or, at worst, had been suckered. But then Ferris would flash a smile and the right amount of cash. A moment later, he'd be leading the perplexed, but usually high, working girl back to his cot in the storeroom, where they'd drink, screw, and get fucked up for hours. When he started giving the girls the option to be tipped in cash or drugs, he became a favored client.

It was one of these girls who decided Ferris needed a full-time companion and brought him a tiny Yorkshire terrier on one of her return visits. Ferris hadstared at the Yorkie with its sleek, two-toned coat and thought the animal of just about the most impractical breed he'd ever seen. Out in the woods, a dog like that wouldn't last a day. Out of deference to his guest, he smiled and thanked her, agreeing to keep and feed her. When she then asked him what he planned to name her, he said he'd name the dog after her so he'd always remember who gave her to him. She seemed to like this, though Ferris had long forgotten her name. When she'd left, he grinned at the Yorkie as if he might bite her.

"Got to keep your head down around here, Bitch," he joked.

Apparently, the dog understood. She stayed close to the shack and even closer to Ferris. When he remembered to feed her, she ate quickly before any bugs or neighboring varmints came in the screen door to make a play for the Yorkie. She kept out from underfoot. And when hunters came into the store with their dogs off the leash, Bitch went straight for an overturned wooden box in the storeroom that was jammed so tight against the wall by a cabinet that no other animal could get to her. Eventually, Ferris nailed the box to the floor and stuck a blanket inside to give Bitch her own hiding place.

But when they were alone, which was often, Bitch would hop onto the store's counter and sit with Ferris as he stared blank-faced out the front door in a drug-induced stupor. When customers did come in, she learned to greet them with the same bemused suspicion as her owner.

If at first Ferris only tolerated the animal, he soon communicated with her in much the same way as he did his late wives.

"Wonder if they're having union trouble again," Ferris snorted, shooting back the last of his beer as the train drew near.

Bitch was napping in the corner of the store beside the ice machine, which Ferris kept running from spring until Christmas. It could be ten below, but there were still hunters who insisted on keeping their beer and meat on ice.

The sound of the empty tallboy clanking into a trash can woke the Yorkie. She glanced at Ferris and decided he was ready to head to bed. Getting to her feet, Bitch padded past the six recently stocked refrigeration units and hopped onto the counter. But Ferris had something else on his mind. He pointed to a bikini-clad Latina who had been showing her thong-divided ass to the patrons of the Bait-N-Booze from the cover of a low-rider magazine for almost six months.

"How hard do you think it would be to track that girl down?" Ferris asked, a mischievous look forming on his face. "The magazine's got to have something about her on file, even if it's just a tax form. For the right price, I'll bet I can get them to give me her agency's contact information. I call them up about some big job out here, drop the name of some pro photographer, offer to fly her in, put her up in some swanky joint in Pittsburgh, commission a shoot, et cetera, and it's just a matter of time, right? I just keep laying out the bread and watch as her eyes get bigger and bigger. Pretty soon, she'll be ready to negotiate."

Though Ferris had wandered along this train of thought several times over the last few months, it sounded like he was beginning to convince himself of how easy it might actually be.

A train of a different kind, the Buffalo-bound hot-shot, a hot-shot being a freight that didn't make any stops from disembarkation point to destination, blasted its horn two more times as it neared the crossing. The headlight's glow reached the porch of the Bait-N-Booze as the train decelerated slightly.

"Trains used to blast right past here at full speed, regs be damned," he jeered. "But it's all robots and computers now. They barely need a driver anymore with all the auto-pilot software that's been installed. Worse, the speed's monitored by remote. If they don't slow down at crossings, the eye in the sky busts 'em when they get where they're going."

Ferris scoffed, thinking something taking more time and becoming less efficient due to technology was pretty funny. He remembered hearing of a study once that concluded that people being watched and timed in their tasks actually worked faster. If they ever made *him* part of a study like that, he'd slow that shit down to "near nonexistent."

That's when Bitch's ear twitched. It was a barely noticeable movement, but one that had the effect of quickly sobering her owner. Ferris had learned that even a dog as small as Bitch could pick up the faintest sound coming in from outside. He reached under the counter and grabbed the sawed-off, pump-action shotgun that was seldom more than an arm's length away. He actually kept a cleaned and loaded .38 in his back pocket, but this was the decoy that he'd let someone take off him if they caught him unawares. There were few folks who knew he was out there alone, but he didn't put it past any of them to try to take advantage. They would also assume he was armed. The goal was then to have just a couple more guns hidden in propitious locations around the shack that could fall into his hands at the right moment.

Aside from the shotgun, he had two Heckler & Kock 9mm pistols under a false bottom in the cash drawer, a second .38 (this one a Colt snubnose), and then a shotgun over the door of the storeroom that he imagined reaching for if he was ever forced back there with his hands raised. In addition, he had two fairly new AR-15s under his bed should he get *really* lucky and find himself with the upper hand.

That said, the one thing Ferris hoped to guard against was having his arsenal lulling him into a false sense of security. If he'd had a Rottweiler or pit bull, he imagined any potential robber would find a way to work around that. But Bitch? No one would think twice, and her ears and instincts were just as effective as a larger, expensively trained watch dog.

"Ferris?!" came a voice from outside. "I know you've already got a gun in your hand, but it's just me. We need to talk."

The voice belonged to Christopher Cuno, who had only restocked the fridges with beer and the safe in the bathroom floor with stacks of cash days before. The racketeer's son had seldom come out to the Bait-N-Booze without ringing first to make sure Ferris was around, and he'd *never* had come at night. Ferris checked to make sure there was a shell chambered in the shotgun before taking the .38 from his pocket and placing it on the counter. The wooden counter looked as rickety as the shack itself, but Ferris had reinforced it with three heavy steel plates.

Combined, they would stop most anything short of an artillery round.

Ferris ducked low behind the register, angling the shotgun around until it was aimed directly at the door.

"You alone?" Ferris asked, hoping to buy time.

"I'll be the only one coming through the door, if that's what you're asking."

"Well, come on, then," Ferris barked, trying not to sound as resigned as he felt.

A moment later, Christopher entered with his hands on his head, fingers interlaced, wrists attached by handcuffs. His eyes found the shotgun barrel aimed at his face, and he looked nowhere else.

"Hey, there, Ferris."

Ferris was shocked by Christopher's appearance — the only reason he didn't immediately shoot the young man. A wide swath of dried blood coated the beer truck driver's T-shirt, starting at his neck and forming a "V" that came to a point just above his navel. His nose, broken at several points, looked as if it had been squished into place to prevent it from falling off. His left eye had swelled shut, giving him the appearance of a boxer who never learned to keep his hands up. Ferris hadn't noticed if Chris had slurred his words, but when the younger Cuno opened his mouth, the owner of the Bait-N-Booze saw that at least six teeth were now missing, and a couple remaining were little more than splinters.

All that damage, but the primary source of blood appeared to be the slab of glistening meat left in place of the twenty-something's missing ear on the left side of his head.

"What the fuck, Chris?" Ferris yelped, his voice rising in alarm.

"They've got Dad out there."

"Who is 'they,' *Chris*?"

The young man stalled, as if unsure of the answer himself.

"What the hell do they want with me?" Ferris asked.

"If you tell them where your money is, they'll let you go."

Ferris rolled his eyes. "Told you that, did they?"

"Yeah. I'm a dead man. But my leading them here buys my kids their lives."

"So why'd they bring your dad? Sounds like bullshit to me."

A desperate look of panic flashed across Christopher's face. Ferris realized that the young man really had believed everything he'd been told. That's when he heard the noise at his back door, the approach that Christopher's entrance was meant to distract him from.

"Sorry about your kids, Chris," Ferris sighed.

He picked the .38 off the counter and coldly drilled a bullet into the handcuffed man's already devastated eye. The blood-swelled protuberance of flesh erupted like a fast-opening flower, sending blood in every direction as the young man wheeled and fell, his bound hands unable to catch him as he face-planted into the doorframe. But before the dead man even slid to the floor, Ferris spun around and sent three rounds from the shotgun blasting down the hall to the back door.

Bitch had been cowering under the counter since Christopher walked in. This was due less to her own fear than what she sensed in her owner. When the driver with the familiar scent, a man who had occasionally brought her treats "from his own dog's stash," flopped to the floor, Bitch finally bolted from her hiding place behind two phone books to race toward the safety of the storeroom. Unfortunately this took her directly into Ferris's zone of fire. When he squeezed off the last of his three volleys, an errant pellet seared through the Yorkie's ear, slicing it in half.

With a yelp, she hit the floor, sliding to a stop when she hit the baseboard.

"Bitch!" Ferris cried, instinctively lurching forward to recover his dog.

But then everything around him began to explode as high-velocity machine gun rounds tore the place apart. Ferris lunged for the cover of the reinforced counter but caught a bullet in his left heel. The pain was intense, as if someone had wrenched off his foot and placed a red-hot poker on the stump. He forced the feeling aside and crawled for the cash register. Pulling the whole thing off the counter so it clattered violently to the floor, he yanked open the drawer and withdrew the two loaded pistols.

Even as he gripped the automatics in his fists, he knew it wouldn't be enough to save his life. Whoever waited outside had more than enough firepower to overcome Ferris's meager cache.

As several more high-velocity rounds tore the small shack apart, the sound of the Buffalo-bound hotshot clattering through the crossing was virtually drowned out. A single last blast from the horn, however, cut through the ballistic cacophony. It would be the last thing Ferris Aaron ever heard.

"Nothing but bad guys up here," the patrolman was saying. "Eight bodies in all, completely shot to hell. We think one of them is Demetri Cuno and another, the owner of the shack, Ferris Aaron, this big meth supplier. And get this, one of them is in handcuffs with all this ante mortem trauma."

"And the others?" asked Sergeant Billy Youman from the front seat of his white Ford Bronco.

"At least a couple are Cuno's goons. Still trying to get IDs. They're thinking Mr. Handcuffs is Cuno's kid, Christopher, a real fuck-up he kept on as a driver."

"So, what do you make of that?" Youman asked, reaching over to scratch between the ears of the large German shepherd sitting beside him on the passenger seat.

"Who knows?" The patrolman shrugged. The shack behind him and a pair of black SUVs parked in front were enveloped by swarming law enforcement officers wearing the uniforms of a variety of branches: local, state and federal. "Somebody was probably out to screw somebody else, it went bad, now they're all dead. When the detectives ID'd Cuno Sr., they were giddy. Said it felt like Christmas morning. How come they called in a K-9?"

It was Youman's turn to shrug. "There was a blood trail leading away from the scene. They think there might another body or two in the woods."

"Happy hunting."

Youman pulled the Bronco past the roadblock and looked for a place to park. There were at least two dozen vehicles spread around the perimeter, but he finally pulled into a space alongside a state trooper's sedan. He took the German shepherd, Bones, by the leash and led him out. As he closed the driver's-side door, a pair of familiar Allegheny County deputy sheriffs approached from the scene.

"Billy Bones!" called the lead deputy, smiling wide, clearly a man happy to be out of the office for the day.

"Aren't you a good two counties outside of your jurisdiction?" the dog handler asked.

"Nah." The deputy grinned. "Looks like a couple of the weapons used might've been boosted from a shop in Port Vue. We just might close a case today."

Bully for you, Billy thought.

Ten minutes later, Billy and Bones expanded their search radius to just over a hundred yards from the shack, crossing the railroad tracks at two points. The deputies had shown them where the blood trail began at the side of the dirt parking lot, but it just as quickly vanished.

"Got anything?" Youman asked the shepherd, expecting little.

But Bones just kept walking. So far, he hadn't alerted to much of anything other than the feces of other animals. But those he eyed quickly, then moved on.

"*Shit*," Billy exhaled, folding over a piece of gum before popping it in his mouth. When his dog looked up at him expectantly, the handler took a carob dog treat from his pocket and tossed it to Bones. "They're not going to like a loose end. Or hell, maybe they won't care."

The German shepherd scarfed up the carob treat, paying little attention to Youman's words. But then his ears stood straight up. Youman eyed him curiously and glanced around the woods.

"What do you hear?" the sergeant asked. "Somebody else out here?"

Two long blasts from an approaching freight train echoed through the woods. Billy sighed.

"Let's go."

"We're starting to put it together," a state trooper Billy knew offered when the handler brought Bones back to the shack. "We found a few texts between the concerned parties. It looks like Ferris Aaron and Christopher Cuno were trying to knock over Chris's dad to take over the business. We thought Aaron was this small-time player, but he seems to have had quite a few contacts dating back to his prison days. They lured the old man out here with this ploy about Aaron kidnapping the kid. Unfortunately for them, Demetri figured it out and came in guns a'blazing. Ballistics should tell us if we're missing anything."

Billy nodded, hoping to avoid having to say that he and Bones had come up dry.

"So, what're you thinking?" the trooper, who wore the stripes of a station commander, asked. "You want to head back? Or make another circuit of the woods?"

"Maybe one more." Billy nodded, figuring he shouldn't pass up an opportunity to redeem himself.

Bones barked. Not a woof of warning or concern, but one of alarm. The shepherd tugged at the leash, fighting to get inside the shack.

"Bones, what the fuck?" Billy cried, trying to get his animal under control.

A second yank, and Bones pulled free from the sergeant. Almost knocking over the troopers posted alongside the shattered back door, the dog burst into the shack and made a beeline for the storeroom. With Billy and the station commander close behind him, Bones went right for a wooden box nailed to the floor in a corner. The shepherd pawed at it and nipped at the edges. He shoved his snout between the one open side and the wall, but couldn't get inside.

"What's gotten into your mutt, Sergeant?" an ATF officer Billy recognized but didn't know asked from the doorway.

"One of your guys take a shit in the corner?" Billy shot back, trying to get a hand on Bones's leash. The dog pulled away a second time. Knowing a lost cause when he saw one, Billy unhooked the leash from Bones's harness and let him go.

"What'd you do that for?" the station commander asked.

"He's alerting to something," Billy said, "and if I don't let him find it, he's going to tear my hand off."

Bones jammed his nose back into the cubby, only to yelp and leap backward a second later. A whisper-thin trickle of blood oozed from a fresh cut to his snout.

"There's some kind of animal in there," the ATF agent suggested dully as Billy pushed his dog aside.

The handler grabbed a corner of the wooden box and yanked it upward. As the top split, Ferris Aaron's tiny Yorkshire Terrier, Bitch, scrambled out and made a break for it. Just as she was about to reach the door, the ATF agent kicked it closed. The tiny dog skidded to a stop, turned, and ran back toward the wooden box. However, a German shepherd easily twenty times her size now stood in the way.

"What is that?" the agent asked.

"A Yorkie," Billy shot back, eyeing the terrified dog. "She's been hurt."

It took a lot of coaxing to calm the Yorkie down. What finally did it was one of Bones's carob treats. Billy placed it about a foot in front of the small animal, and her hunger overwhelmed her fear. Even as she accepted the snack, the little dog's eyes never left Bones. When the shepherd finally padded over to the Yorkie, she looked like she might bolt away again. But as she was cornered, she finally allowed the bigger animal to give her shredded ear a quick lick. The terrier remained tense but didn't swat the shepherd away when he continued to clean her wound.

"Wait a sec," said the station commander. "Is he licking up dog's blood or people blood? Your canine could be destroying evidence."

"It'd be tainted anyway," Billy guessed. "Better just to calm her down."

The dog handler heard the others in the room scoff. He didn't expect them to understand what the little dog had gone through, much less care.

Billy tried to locate a leash among Ferris's things, but finally gave up and simply took the Yorkie outside on Bones's lead. He figured the shepherd could be trusted not to run off and was proven right. Whether it was out of concern for the Yorkshire terrier or loyalty to his handler, Billy didn't know. The sergeant had initially thought Bitch might be able to help with the blood trail, but after peeing against a tree, she promptly fell asleep at Billy's feet.

As the unlikely two-dog, one-handler trio sat on the porch, forensic techs came and went. Some were after fingerprints, others, DNA evidence. An entire squad of ballistics experts showed up, with property and evidence techs soon to follow. The last items to be tagged and hauled away were the two vehicles that had brought the doomed men to Ferris Aaron's doorstep the night before. As the two tow trucks departed for the Pittsburgh impound, the ATF agent stepped out of the shack and eyed Sergeant Youman.

"You're still here?"

"Figured we'd check for scents once the Yorkie woke up."

"Why? I think we're good here."

"My report's going to look pretty barren otherwise. Might as well pad it out to justify the trip up."

The agent chuckled and headed away. Billy looked down and saw that Bitch was awake.

"Let's take a walk. Don't make me look like an asshole."

The group set out for the woods. Billy could tell right away that the Yorkie was in no shape to play police dog. So he took it easy. He relaxed the circuit he and Bones made around the shack, and more or less took the pair for a walk.

"You get anything, I'm sure you'll let me know," Billy said quietly.

As if on cue, the Yorkie tensed. Its nose dove to the ground. There was a familiar scent in the grass after all. Bones moved next to the smaller dog, sniffing around as well.

"Don't tell me she found something you didn't," Billy scoffed.

But now the Yorkie was on the move. As she headed north toward the railroad tracks, her gait switched from a trot to a run. Though she was small, Billy still had a hard time keeping up once she was at a full gallop with legs extended. It was then that Billy heard the second electronic train horn of the day, this one coming from a train rolling westward toward Pittsburgh.

"Shit!" he hissed, double-timing it as he cursed himself for letting the dogs off the leash.

If he somehow lost an animal in his charge to an oncoming train, he prayed it was the Yorkie.

The horn sounded again, the time closer and with what Billy imagined to be with greater urgency. Bones was still close at his side, but as the Yorkie rabbited ahead, Bones accelerated as well, following the unseen trail. When the train finally came into view, it was less than fifty yards away. The sergeant had never been great at math, but even he could tell that the Yorkie and the locomotive were on a collision course. There was no question who would emerge victorious.

"Stop!" he yelled at the Yorkie, knowing it would do no good.

Sensing the danger, Bones broke from Billy. As he hurried protectively after Bitch, it looked as if the shepherd was soon to be struck as well. But then the Yorkie took a sharp right. Rather than cross the tracks or hit the train, she moved alongside it. As the freight train roared past, the Yorkie continued on her quest, sniffing at the air.

Billy wasn't sure what to make of the dog's movements. He was glad she hadn't been struck by the engine, but now he fretted the Yorkie might dart under its wheels. He didn't blame the dog for being messed up in the head, but if it led to his animal getting killed, he was sure to be suspended.

What came next happened so quickly that the handler wasn't able to process it until minutes later. The trail Bitch was following on the ground ended suddenly, and she turned and jumped at the train. Billy thought she would bounce right off, but instead she vanished. When the car passed the officer half a second later, he saw the reason: the freight car's door was open and Bitch just visible inside. The sergeant caught a brown flash in his peripheral vision. As he turned, he glimpsed Bones's tail disappearing into the open freight car, too.

"Bones! What the hell?!" he yelled.

But by the time the words were out of his mouth, the train's last car rumbled past his position, disappearing into the deep thicket.

The freight car Bones and Bitch leaped into was empty save for a few yellow straps, the kind used to rope cargo onto pallets. The steel walls, having baked in the sun all day, radiated heat, though a cold wind blew in through the open door. This combined to make just about any spot in the car unbearable.

Regardless, Bones chose a spot near the door and curled his body into a circle, his thick coat keeping himself warm. Bitch settled first into one corner, then a different one. After failing to locate a comfortable spot in the third, she moved next to Bones. When the shepherd didn't appear to mind, the Yorkie gradually scooted in close until she was cuddled up next to the larger dog.

Then they slept.

It was hours before they reached the Bessemer Yards on Pittsburgh's north side. The train eased alongside a warehouse where workers would offload the freight, much of it having crossed into Buffalo from Canada to then be sent off to destinations around the country. By the time any workers reached Bones and Bitch's car, the dogs were long gone.

The German shepherd let the Yorkie lead. At first, the little dog seemed as confused by her new surroundings as she was outside the shack. Then a new scent reached her nose, and she hurried across several tracks and under a two stationary trains. When they emerged on the far side of the rail yard, they found a break in the fence. Bones had picked up a human scent as well now, but stayed behind Bitch as she slipped past the fence and into a stand of trees.

"What do we have here?" thundered an old man's voice.

Bitch and Bones found themselves at the campfire of a squat man in a heavy coat. He had thick stubble on his cheeks and chin, but a recent haircut suggested he hadn't been fully away from civilization for that long.

"Henry," the man said by way of introduction, tossing slices of lunch meat to the two animals. "A couple of them call me 'Crazy Henry,' but that's just because they ain't got nothing nicer to say. You look like you got into some kind of trouble."

He was eyeing Bitch's torn ear. When Bitch wouldn't come any closer, Henry poured some water from an old plastic jug into an empty pie plate. This time, both dogs moved in, lapping it up quickly.

"I'll give you a little more in a minute," Henry said. "There's a tap down the yard a bit. Only, the yard bulls don't like us around, so we'll have to wait until dark."

He eyed the police harness on Bones.

"Is that real? Or did your owner have some kind of odd sense of humor?"

When Bones didn't answer, Henry shrugged and tossed the shepherd a few more pieces of meat. He then retrieved a tube of antiseptic cream from his backpack and rubbed a little on Bitch's torn ear. At first, she didn't like this at all. A couple of seconds later, however, she let him minister to the wound in silence.

"When I got divorced, I thought I'd had it," Henry explained as he worked. "I was unemployed, half the reason I found myself short a wife, and had no future to speak of. I was an addict then, but being on the streets has a way of making you clean up or spiral straight down. The day I finally woke up without the craving, I realized that was where God wanted me to be. It's no easy life, but occasionally I'll take the odd job, recharge for a couple of days in a motel, then head back out. Maybe I'll be ready to go back to the old ways one of these days. Right now, though, this is how I see my life."

Bones and Bitch kept eating, so Henry kept talking. He told them that he didn't plan to hop his next train until the sun went down but was concerned for anything heading east. There was meant to be some big summer storm gathering in that direction. He considered Fort Wayne, as people there treated guys on the road "less like hobos and more like a neighbors," but he was also thinking about going south toward Louisiana. He was born in Lafayette but had most recently lived in Tyler, Texas, This was where his wife, well, ex-wife, continued to reside.

"There are no stops in Tyler, but I've been on a line that runs from Memphis to Dallas that passes near Tyler. If the door's open and facing the right direction, I always look for my house or her car at a crossing, but I've seen neither. I don't know what I'd do if I saw her. Probably just smile."

When night fell, Henry led the dogs back into the train yard.

"Here's the faucet if you're looking for water," he said, turning it on. The appreciative dogs drank long and hard, Bitch needing to pee immediately afterward. But then they followed Henry toward the trains powering up for overnight travel.

"This one's on to Syracuse, this one's off to Philly, this one's on to New York," Henry said, indicating the different lines. "Can't tell you where this one's going, but maybe Wilmington? Hard to know."

Bones caught the scent of several other riders emerging from the surrounding hobo jungles on their way to the trains. Some eyed the trio curiously, but most kept to themselves. At first, Bitch didn't seem to notice the smells. But then the little Yorkie stopped short alongside an open freight car. Bones poked his nose up at the car, but Henry quickly pulled him back.

"Not your best idea, police dog," he cautioned. "See this chalk?" He pointed at a symbol marked alongside the door. "This car belongs to the BCRA, one of those gangland crews that uses trains to get around the country. They'll rob a place in Miami and be in Chicago by the next night, move drugs into Baltimore, then be in Kansas City before it even hits the streets. Hell, they've done hits that way. They catch anyone riding in their cars, they get stomped, beheaded, and thrown out. A couple of dogs? They'll probably eat you."

But both animals had alerted to a greasy smudge on the edge of the door. Henry eyed this before shying away.

"What did I tell you? *Blood.* Last thing you want to do is get in that car."

But even as Henry said this, the Yorkshire terrier was leaping inside. Bitch raced from one end of the car to the other, sniffing every inch. Having clearly rediscovered the trail she had picked up outside the Bait-N-Booze, Bones jumped in as well.

"Well, you guys seem bound and determined," Henry declared. "I will thank you for your company in passing the afternoon with me and wish you good luck out there."

Bones glanced back at Henry before looking away. The man smiled, taking this acknowledgement as more than it was. He went back to searching for the right train.

Inside the freight car, Bitch whined as she moved around the car. Every new scent bothered and repulsed her. Bones joined in, discovering even more blood. He soon identified the individual odors of six different people, the spilled blood belonging to two of them. The smell of death – feces and rot – was also in abundance.

The train didn't leave the yard for another half hour. When it finally did, it took about fifteen minutes to get up to speed and soon shot down the tracks like a rocket. Inside the car, without the sun heating the exterior, the floor, walls, and ceiling were soon as cold as a winter's night. Bitch and Bones again huddled together for warmth, but this time in the corner farthest from the door.

As the train pushed north and east, the exhaust fumes of the city melted into the distinct scent of pine. All at once, the odor of humans was commingled with that of deer, raccoon, possum, badger, and skunk.

The dogs inhaled all of this, seeking out the familiar. For a long while, there was nothing. But when the train slowed as it neared the Bait-N-Booze, Bitch got to her feet and moved to the door. The train sounded its electronic horn the mandated four times, the sound echoing through the woods as if memorializing Ferris Aaron.

The lights were still on in the shack, as two local deputies had been tasked with keeping looky-loos away. The press had gotten word of what went down just past noon. Bitch sniffed the air as the train rolled through the crossing as if trying to pick up any vestigial remnants of her old life. But as soon as any traces appeared, they were gone again. Another moment, and she returned to Bones's side.

It was forty-five minutes later when Bones smelled smoke. He clambered to his feet and moved unsteadily toward the door, the motion of the train wreaking havoc on his legs. Bitch was already at the open door, her nose bouncing up and down at the same scents. As the train neared the source, four large bonfires came into view just away from the tracks. In addition to the smoke, the dogs also smelled about three dozen people, the gasoline of several vehicles, a lake of booze, and a cornucopia of narcotics.

Bones glanced down at Bitch, but she was already gone.

"A quarter of a million dollars? That's crazy! Who keeps that much cash?"

"Somebody who went around the bend a long time ago and wasn't never coming back."

The man who asked the question, clad in a black suit and tie, had an all-business haircut that matched his demeanor. He first scoffed, but then nodded, as if recognizing the veracity of the comment. The man who had spoken those words looked like the suited man's idea of a necessary evil. His long gray hair flowed past his shoulders, and it looked like you could paint a barn with his thick, squared-off beard. He wore torn-up blue jeans, a black T-shirt, black handkerchief and slide, the leather cut with the sigils of the BCRA on the back, and black boots. Tattoos suggesting an aberrant personality crawled up and down his leathered arms.

"Anything on the radio from the cops?" the suited man asked.

"Worked out how it was supposed to." The tattooed man shrugged, his voice a growl. "They think it was all inside the Cuno clan. Ferris fucked 'em somehow, so they came and knocked on his door. The handcuffs have them thinking Christopher was involved, as they don't think Aaron could've delivered that kind of beating. They'll spend the next few weeks chasing that angle."

"Just like you said they would."

The tattooed man, born Arthur Bigelow but who had gone by Monster for as long as anyone could remember, smiled. The suited man almost shuddered at how aptly the dangerous-looking mouthful of teeth matched the man's nickname. Still, Monster and his boys had delivered. He nodded to a compatriot, who handed over two thick stacks of banded cash.

"Good work," the suited man proclaimed. "With the Cuno family out of the way, things should be looking up for *our* organization. We're looking to assume a lot of their old territories."

Monster let the suited man, whose name was Jacob Golen and who lived in the Bradford Woods section of the Pittsburgh metro area with his second wife and four kids, crow a bit more. When the fellow suddenly realized how much bluster he was unloading to a man who'd certainly seen a harder part of the criminal world than he had, he silenced himself with a squirm.

One of Monster's lieutenants, a prison-cut mountain of a man called Doyle, sidled up to his boss with the cash.

"We're good."

Monster shook hands with Golen and patted him on the shoulder.

"Safe drive back to the 'Burgh." Monster nodded.

After Golen and his crew of paid-for muscle took off in a pair of SUVs, Doyle turned back to his boss.

"Why didn't we just kill him and keep the money?"

"They trust us now." Monster shrugged. "Next time, our cut'll be twice as much. But there'll come a time when we get too expensive, and they'll start looking at us like a liability. By then, we'll know what they're worth to their enemies, and it'll be a seller's market."

Doyle nodded thoughtfully, but Monster knew the younger man had all the brains God gave a woodchuck. What Monster had just described was precisely what he'd just done to the Cuno family. That Golen had no idea how involved his rivals were with the BCRA told him all he needed to know about the man.

As the SUVs bounced out of the field and onto the dirt road that would eventually return them to the world they understood, Monster glanced around for a beer. As he did, he felt the same old peculiar feeling he got in his legs every time he spent more than a few hours on "dry land." Some of the other guys were already tinkering with the motorbikes their landlocked supply teams had hauled up on trailers, but this wasn't for Monster. He understood the appeal of bikes, but he'd taken to the rails for a reason. It was like a secret world constantly in motion away from societal mores. It was the last place other than the open ocean where he felt like a proper pirate.

The rails were home.

The men were in high spirits. They knew the killing of Ferris Aaron and the framing of the Cuno family had gone off without a hitch. Well, aside from the death of Knucklehead and the maiming of Webster.

Monster had seen some awful violence in his day. Perpetuated a bit, too. But seeing a bear of a man bleed out from a single well-placed bullet to the shoulder while a skinny kid got half his face and all his fingers shredded off by a shotgun blast and somehow lived to tell the tale? That was one for the books, all right. Sure, Webster had begged for death due to the blast sheering off half his face. But Monster knew Web's brother back at the camp, Ace, would've objected to having his opinion go unheard.

So Monster let the skinny kid writhe on the train car floor while they tried to save Knucklehead. Monster had hoped Web might kick off on his own on the ride up to the campsite, but despite his screaming and carrying on that each breath was his last, he made it all the way back. By the time they jumped off the freight car, the BCRA leader was at peace with Knucklehead's death and the younger man's survival. They fireman-carried Webster to camp, delivering him straight to their medic — really, the one ex-serviceman who remembered any first aid. But the moment Ace saw his brother, he threw up an afternoon's worth of beer, chips, and hot dogs.

It took hours to stitch up Web's stumps and remove the pellets from what remained of his face. One of the guys said it looked like Web's cheek, jaw, and eye socket had been replaced by a tall-stack pastrami sandwich. Monster forced himself not to laugh at this, due to Ace's presence and the fact that Webster was still conscious.

Now that the Golen meet had gone off without a hitch, Monster figured he owed the brothers a visit. He moved through the fire-lit field, nodding to the men who were blowing off steam for real now that the money had come through. As he reached the medic's, nicknamed Ratso's, all-weather tent, Monster plucked four beers out of a nearby ice chest. He popped the tab on the first as he entered, planning to hand it to Webster.

But when he pushed aside the tent flap, he found Ace and the medic already drinking, a somber pall over the proceedings. Webster's body was stretched out on the ground, two blood-soaked towels covering much of his face, save a single eye staring blankly at the tent roof.

"What happened?" Monster asked, sipping Webster's beer.

"Subdural hematoma," Ratso, a man who Monster thought resembled more the Cowardly Lion from *The Wizard of Oz* than a rodent, replied. "Bleeding in his brain, impossible to detect, really, without opening his skull. Brain herniated due to the pressure, and it killed him. If that was the case, however, there's no telling how much was left to save."

"What do you mean?"

"Hematomas can crush brain tissue, cut off circulation, limit the oxygen flow around the brain. He could've already been brain dead, and we wouldn't have known it."

Monster's eyes shot to Ace. If he thought his kid brother might've been saved if taken to a hospital, the incident could sow the seeds of animosity. But when Ace met Monster's eyes, he simply shook his head.

"He wasn't coming back from that, Monster, so I've got no beef with you or anybody else," Ace admitted, raising his hands. "To tell the truth, I doubt he'd have wanted to keep going on like that. I appreciate you bringing him back, respecting me as his brother, but this is on him. Not you, not Ratso, not me."

Monster acknowledged this by soberly raising his beer.

"He was the first motherfucker to the door, ready to kick ass," Monster pronounced. "Not naming names, but some of the guys were shitting themselves knowing what kind of guns Ferris had in there. Not Web. He was a Marine about it."

Ace nodded, patting his dead brother on the shoulder.

"Thanks for saying as much, Monster. The one thing I know for certain is that he wouldn't want to be buried in the city. When Luca died and we did that funeral pyre for him, I remember Web being like, 'Yeah, that's what I want for me.' You think that'd be..."

Ace's train of thought was interrupted by shouts from outside. Monster grabbed for his sidearm. But then Doyle burst into the tent, a silly grin plastered across his face.

"You ain't gonna believe this!"

Bitch had limped unseen into the camp. Her front left leg buckled as she stepped, the result of a poor landing moments before. Not that she knew this, but her left carpal bone was broken in two places, her metacarpus in one. But none of this would stop her now that the scent she'd been following for much of the past day hung so heavy in the air.

"Shit, is that a rat?" someone asked, drunkenly heaving a rock in her direction.

She'd stopped and tensed. When the rock landed safely more than two yards away, she kept steadily moving toward the bonfires, tracking the elusive scent.

As her features came into view, one of the men, a bullet-headed bruiser nicknamed Zig-Zag, recognized her immediately.

"Holy shit!" he practically shrieked, a drunken grin spreading over his face. "That's that bitch from last night!"

No one was quite sure what to make of Zig-Zag's outburst, but he was adamant.

"I was next to Webster when he took the shot to the face," he explained. "The dog was hauling ass down the hall. See? She even got winged on the ear."

"Are you serious?" someone else asked, peering through the darkness at the newcomer.

"Hell, yeah! Same damn dog."

"You mean she followed you guys all the way back here?" the drunk who heaved a rock at her asked.

"Sure what it looks like," replied Zig-Zag. "That's some real Oprah shit, huh?"

Bitch's eyes never strayed from the group as she edged closer to the fire. She would take a step, decide against it, then pull her paw back, a noncommittal chess player keeping her hand on the pieces. As she did this, more BCRA members gathered and made Zig-Zag repeat his story. Most were skeptical, but Zig-Zag considered the split ear incontrovertible evidence.

When Doyle led Monster over, he took one look at the Yorkie and signaled over a bushy-mustached gang member so fat his belly shoved his T-shirt halfway up his chest. His scent was the most familiar to Bitch, and she took a step back.

"She was at Aaron's place?" Monster asked.

The bushy-mustached guy, nicknamed Bulldog, ironically enough, started laughing, his jowls quaking as he placed his palms on his gigantic stomach as if fearing it might roll away.

"Yeah, that's Ferris's toy pooch, all right. Thing used to stay on his counter. When we scouted the place a couple of weeks back, he even let me pet her. You know what she's called? *Bitch*."

Monster shook his head, both at Ferris's sense of humor that outlived the man himself or the misfortune of the poor dog. He squatted in front of her, unable to hide his shit-eating grin.

"Hey, Bitch. I'm the one who put the final two rounds in your daddy. Hope you ain't too pissed."

He extended a hand for her to sniff, but she limped backward instead. Pinning her ears to the side of her head, the Yorkie bared her teeth and growled. It took Monster a moment to realize what she was doing, as the sound was barely audible. He hushed the others as she tried to look as fierce as possible. As he regarded the display, Monster's eyes lit up with amusement.

"That it? Hell, I guess just showing up here passes for tough as nails when you're that small, huh? Well, shit. Gotta respect that, huh?"

These were the last words Arthur Phillip "Monster" Bigelow would ever say.

That Bones was able to get so close to the camp undetected was a testament to the diversion created by the Yorkie, but also his naturally cautious approach to any situation. By the time he felt that Bitch was being threatened, he was only three feet behind her, albeit cloaked in darkness.

Monster's throat was only five feet away, easy enough for a German shepherd to cross in a single leap.

As Bones appeared out of thin air, closing fast, the gang leader had only enough time to raise his hands and shut his eyes. His face was contorted with annoyance, the kind of reaction he might have if discovering a prank was being played on him. But a second later, the shepherd having torn out his external carotid artery and superior thyroid artery with one bite, Monster's eyes flashed open in horror, knowing he'd completely misjudged the danger the presence of the Yorkie in his camp presented.

Blood burping out of his savaged throat in time to his dying pulse, Monster's body hit the ground, the gang leader clawing for his attacker. But Bones, recognizing a mortal wound, had already closed his bloody maw around Doyle's thigh, shredding flesh, muscle, and, most importantly, the femoral artery. As Monster's lieutenant now cried out in agony, Bones turned on Zig-Zag, sinking his teeth into the bald man's genitals. One jerk of the shepherd's neck muscles emasculated his victim in a single stroke.

Two more men were to hit the ground before any of the others reacted out of anything but terrified self-preservation. It was Bulldog who skinned his pistol first and fired the first of four rounds at Bones. Unfortunately for him, his shooting was bad enough when he was sober, and a little drink did nothing to improve it. The first three bullets were wasted in the dirt, while the fourth exploded into the foot of the dead Monster.

"*Shit*," Bulldog cursed, swearing to himself that he'd make the next one count.

As he scanned the darkness for Bones, however, he felt a searing pain in his leg, as if he'd stepped too close to the fire. He gasped, but then looked down and saw Bitch digging her tiny jaws into his Achilles tendon.

"Motherfucker!" he bellowed, violently shaking her off.

The tiny dog tumbled away, landing about three feet in front of Bulldog. He could've been blind drunk and still hit her. He aimed his pistol at her and squeezed the trigger, only to have the bullet go wide when the seventy-pound German shepherd landed on his back, sending him face first into the dirt.

"*Goddammit,*" he bayed, trying to roll over.

But that's when he felt Bones's hot breath on his neck. A second later, he gasped as his own breath was forced from his throat as the dog's iron jaws crushed his windpipe.

More shots rang out as the BCRA men finally realized it was their enemy that was outnumbered, not them. But with their senses dulled by alcohol, errant shadows thrown up by the fires drew as many bullets as the German shepherd. When rounds actually met flesh, it was human.

For his part, Bones continued to hunt his targets one at a time, unfazed by the mayhem. He chose at random, picking off whichever ones were close or slow. When a victim put up a fight, the shepherd upped his game, unleashing a fury that was more akin to a rabid or feral dog than one trained by law enforcement personnel. But this was just another aspect of his training, something drilled into him by his first master, Lionel Oudin, so many years ago. He was relentless in his attack and didn't stop until the threat was nullified.

Two of the smarter men found their way to the two pickup trucks that had pulled the bike trailers. But once they were inside, any brains they had slipped away as the booze and adrenaline blasting through their bodies gave the drivers a belief in their own god-like faculties. Rather than head away, both came to the conclusion that running down the dog was the answer. Both aimed their vehicles for the shepherd, stepped on the gas, and accidentally mowed down a handful of their comrades as they took single-minded aim at their furry enemy.

But as the two trucks closed in on Bones from different angles, they found each other first, with horrific results. The first truck, going sixty miles per hour, slammed into the second one, which was bouncing across the field at a mere forty-five mph. The impact rolled the slower truck over, directly onto one of the bonfires.

When the truck burst into flames a few seconds later, exploding a few seconds after that, the remaining BCRA members decided they'd had enough and fled the scene. But even then, the only one who managed to haul a motorcycle off one of the trailers smashed headfirst into a ninety-foot-high bitternut hickory tree a moment later, shattering his spine and snapping his neck.

He, a teen named Spider, would be the last to die.

The time between Monster's death and Spider's was only six and a half minutes. In that time, Bones would kill eleven men. The various stray bullets, vehicular assaults, and ensuing fires would kill another six while wounding more than twice that. Only a handful escaped unscathed.

Those who lived to tell the tale would never come to a consensus as to what happened that night. Most believed they'd either fallen victim to a rival railroad gang, likely the FTRA (even though they didn't typically operate that far east), a double-cross from Golen's group (despite the fellow having paid them their money and left), or retribution from some heretofore unknown associate of Ferris Aaron or the Cuno family (what the majority felt made the most sense).

To a man, however, none believed the responsibility rested on the shoulders of a single canine. When the dog was brought up in conversation, most denied having even seen it. The same men suggested those who suffered bullet wounds must have received them from other shooters, not their own comrades. In addition, they believed those in their own party with guns probably took down "at least a couple dozen" of the enemy.

It was eventually decided that their enemy was the one who fled, not them. When the BCRA members broke for the trees, it was only for cover. When they immediately circled back to return fire, the "chicken-shit ambushers" had already hightailed it away. No thorough police report or multi-part piece of investigative journalism into the bizarre incident that decimated their ranks could convince them otherwise.

It took Bones almost five minutes to locate Bitch after the last gang member had fled. The combined smells of blood, burning flesh, and gunpowder had cut into the shepherd's remarkable scenting ability. But then, there she was.

The Yorkie's body was on its side about two feet from Monster's corpse, a bullet drilled clean through her torso, having pierced her tiny heart. Bones gave her face a couple of licks, but there was no doubt that she was dead. The German shepherd nuzzled her open mouth with his nose for a moment before settling down next to her body, placing his head on his paws, his eyes downcast and hollow.

As the fires burned down and the night grew cold, Bones remained alongside the terrier for hours, alert for signs of predators. He never closed his eyes.

When morning came, a heavy mist descended on the meadow, giving the blood-soaked field a gauzy, ethereal appearance.

When the nearby railroad tracks began to quake with the coming of the day's first train, Bones slowly clambered to his feet. He leaned his snout back down to Bitch's corpse, her fur still warm from his own body keeping the Yorkie warm throughout the night. He inhaled her scent one last time and headed away.

As the train came into view, the shepherd trotted up to the tracks. He jogged alongside the train as he'd seen Bitch do. When the open door of a freight car passed, he hopped in. The car was colder than either he'd encountered the day before. He had to huddle in the corner farthest from the open door to keep warm.

It was a long ride back to civilization, the train's final destination of Akron several hours and almost two hundred miles away. But the cold and the scent of the dead Yorkie troubled Bones's attempts at sleep, keeping him awake almost the entire way.

HELLHOUND

Prologue

Devaris couldn't tell if the smell was something blowing in off the East River or boiling up from the sewers. As if the acrid stench wasn't bad enough on its own, the street lamps, yellowed by oxidation, cast the block in a dog's breakfast of bilious colors: toxic green, blood-piss orange, and the congealed gray of yesterday's oatmeal.

East Harlem near Jefferson Park was its own particular brand of hell on a midsummer's night. Too hot for anyone to get comfortable doing much more than fucking in a shower or getting high in a meat locker.

Devaris had already done the latter while double-shifting at Triple A the past sixteen hours. He was looking forward to doing the former once he found out if Ro was home. And if she wasn't, wasn't it about time he knocked on that girl Sheila's door over in Building 2?

He smiled as he turned the corner on 111th and 2nd. It may have been two o'clock in the morning, but Devaris Clark wasn't afraid of getting jacked. Everyone knew he was out of the game. If they didn't, he knew all the right scary names to drop.

Besides, he knew he didn't look like he was worth the trouble. A skinny guy with an empty backpack slung over one shoulder and a single Parliament jammed behind his right ear probably wasn't rolling in it.

It didn't hurt that he smelled like blood and dead animal flesh. Gloves, aprons, helmets, boots, and goon suits kept the blood off his T-shirt and jeans, but the smell of the Liberty Avenue slaughterhouse where he worked got in everywhere. It was under his fingernails, hanging in his eyelashes, and sweating out his balls. He'd seen its effect on animals here and there. A cat giving him a long cold look as if he'd smoked every other pussy in its litter before skinning its mother. The crows that would call to other crows to get a look-see. The dogs that went crazy, their eyes sparkling and their lips smacking like they wanted a taste.

But they all gave him room. How were they to know he wasn't willing to add a couple more victims to those three hundred hogs he'd killed that day?

"Heeey, you ready?" cried a voice from across the street.

Devaris looked over and saw a girl in booty shorts dancing down the steps to a waiting car, two girlfriends hanging out the window.

Damn, where were they *going?*

He stared at the girl's thighs where they met the straining-at-the-seams shorts. Half an hour from now, she'd be bouncing that thing over some brother at a club that wouldn't be him. He'd have to settle for the girl across the hall who'd give it up for little more than the time of day.

But one day things would be better. One day that better come soon.

He popped the ear buds into his ears and kept walking, turning up his iPod until the last word he made out from Booty Shorts was a reference to her pussy.

The Triborough Projects loomed large over in East Harlem. Also known as Neville Houses, they consisted of sixteen high-rise brick apartment buildings that wove across four square blocks. Designed by an architect who'd rookied in designing Texas prisons, Neville Houses was packed with thousands of people. There were families, old people, singles like Devaris, multi-generation immigrant clans, and then a handful of illegal squatters, the apartments rented out by Nigerian gang lords who filled up rooms with assholes fresh off the boat that they'd call INS on a day after they'd drained their last cent.

The buildings themselves were identical, but their relation to one another created a labyrinthine effect. Instead of being on a grid, the towers slanted at odd angles that, if seen from above, looked like some kind of modernist sculpture.

But if you were on the ground, or worse, had to live in there, you'd pack for minotaur any time you had to cross the threshold.

Devaris didn't mind. It was better than his brother's place in the South Bronx and a hell of a lot better than the streets, a shelter, or lockup. He'd had plenty of experience with all three.

That's why, when he felt the eyes watching him from the side-view mirror of the one car parked facing west in a row legally obligated to face east, he did nothing to adjust his gait. Only prey runs. When the doors of the car swung open and the footsteps approached him from behind, he couldn't help but tense, though he demanded his heart resist the temptation to accelerate.

"Hands out of your pockets!"

Devaris did as he was asked. The ear buds were popped out of his ears and a hand placed between his shoulder blades.

"Police. Turn out your pockets and put your hands on the wall."

Devaris turned to find two men, a black guy and a Latino, standing behind him. The black one was Phil Leonhardt, a ten-year veteran who'd done all his time in Harlem's notorious 22nd Precinct. The precinct had earned much of its reputation from two inglorious distinctions: one of the highest geographical concentrations of violent crime in the country, and then one of the highest rates of police officer suicide.

The Latino, Ramon Garza, was a five-year veteran who'd only recently transferred in from the 34th Precinct in Washington Heights.

"You ain't cops," Devaris grunted.

Garza pulled out a badge. "Got anything else to say?"

Slow as you please, Devaris turned to face the nearest wall, spread his legs, and placed his palms against the bricks. This apparently wasn't good enough for Garza, who kicked Devaris's legs apart even further, almost knocking him down.

"You think we've got all night, asshole?" the detective asked.

"You think I've seen your calendar?"

"Wow, you hear this guy?" Garza asked Leonhardt, slipping on latex gloves. "I don't know what you're heard, kid, but this is New York. Cops here have a pretty low threshold for assholes."

"I'll remember that."

Garza gruffly shoved Devaris's head back down before beginning his pat-down. "Anything in here we'd be interested in?"

"Dunno. Depends what you're into, I guess."

Leonhardt stifled a laugh. Garza scowled.

"Now you've gotten on my bad side," the Latino detective snapped.

"A real man would've hit me by now."

Leonhardt jumped in. "We're going to find you for something, kid. You won't be laughing when they set your bail."

"Yeah, right," Devaris retorted. "For what?"

"Vagrancy, resisting…" Garza spat.

"*Possession*," Leonhardt added evenly.

Devaris met the black cop's gaze, scrunching his brow. "Bullshit. I ain't holding."

"Oh, you must have something," said Garza. "My partner's a one-man K9 unit. If he says you're holding, you're *holding*."

From across the street, the men were being watched by two sets of eyes. As Garza searched Devaris's clothes, Leonhardt tossed the backpack. The watchers could see, could practically *smell* Devaris's sweat. Even better, the sweat was activating the blood the young man had rightly surmised was caked into every pore in his body. Within seconds, a new aroma joined the sick of the streets.

The watchers liked this.

Leonhardt turned the backpack inside out. He *knew* there was something in it, but its position was eluding him. As he searched the pockets yet again, he could see Devaris's body relaxing in his peripheral vision even as the detective's frustration grew.

When even Garza glanced over with concern, Leonhardt shrugged and handed the bag back. "It's clean."

Garza shot him a look of *are you sure?* Leonhardt glanced away. Garza slapped the backpack into Devaris's hands.

"Tomorrow night, then?" Devaris asked.

"It's a date, fucktard," Garza flung back, spittle ejecting from his mouth.

Devaris smirked, threw the backpack over his shoulder, and walked on down the sidewalk.

As soon as he was out of sight, Garza turned to Leonhardt.

"You slipping?"

"Nah, he had something. I just couldn't find it. It happens."

Garza grunted and moved back towards their car. Once the two were inside, the Latino detective gunned the engine and peeled away, as if hoping to wake up half the neighborhood.

Devaris watched the cops leave but then took off his pack. Pulling the right strap close, he withdrew a thin joint from a tiny hole in the seams. He lit up with a smile. The first puff tasted even better than he'd imagined it would.

He headed onto the Neville Houses grounds, trampled grass and rocks demarcating the lot borders better than the sidewalks. Building 7 was directly ahead of him and inside, Ro's ass just waiting to get fucked. He lowered the joint from his lips knowing that if he showed up with less than half, she'd pout, but he'd already gotten a buzz on.

It was going to be a lovely evening.

But that's when he heard it. The sound of running feet echoed down the walls of the buildings, causing Devaris to look up. All the way on top, he could just barely make out the form of a little kid running along the roof, his shiny jacket illuminated by the moon.

"Oh, *shit*," Devaris muttered before raising his voice. "Hey! HEY!! Get back from there! C'mon, man!"

But the kid didn't answer. Devaris even thought he heard a taunting laugh.

"Shit," he repeated.

Booking it into the building, he found the elevator broken. *Again.* Turning to the stairs, he shook his head.

"Kid, your momma better be an appreciative piece of ass."

Extinguishing the roach and stuffing it in his pocket, Devaris began making the long climb.

The view from the top of Neville Houses was nothing special unless you knew just the right angle. Taller buildings surrounded the projects except at the front corner where, on a clear day, you could see all the way to the river, to the RFK Bridge, and even to Randall's Island on the other side.

Devaris had never seen that angle and, busting a lung as he tried to catch his breath, wouldn't be doing so tonight. The stairs had taken it out of him. He wasn't happy by the time he burst out onto the roof.

"Kid? The fuck are you, you little prick?"

When there was no answer, Devaris made a circuit of the roof, looking everywhere for the little boy.

"Come out, come out, wherever you are!" Devaris joked, feeling just a little fucked-up. "Better get in before you trip your ass right over the edge!"

But as he kept walking, he saw no sign of any kid.

That's when he saw it: a paint stirrer propped up next to the ledge, a shiny and torn jacket hanging from the top.

"What the hell?" Devaris muttered, moving in close.

He picked up the paint stirrer, eyeing the jacket with its two arms jutting out either side. It looked like a scarecrow.

"Oh, fuck this," Devaris exclaimed, throwing it to the ground.

He didn't hear the footsteps this time, didn't even feel the push. As he tumbled over the edge of the building, the sensation Devaris felt more than anything was the rush of air being forced out of his lungs by the enormous pressure his own drag was building against his diaphragm. He couldn't breathe, his eyes looking in every direction as his body focused on only one thing: re-catching his breath.

Just when it looked like that might never happen, the action proved unnecessary as Devaris's body completed the sixteen-floor drop and smacked onto the pavement directly in front of Building 7. The instantaneous buildup and release of pressure within his body caused his skin to rupture in multiple places, muscles, sinew, and blood showering out of his corpse, deflating it like a balloon.

A motion-activated light flickered to life almost immediately, illuminating the body in a bluish-yellow halo for a full thirty seconds before, figuring its job done, it flickered back out.

The watchers emerged from the darkness then and moved over to where the body had fallen. A hand touched Devaris's crumpled forehead before its owner moved away, leaving half a shoe print in the slowly expanding pool of blood.

A moment later, the neighborhood was still.

I

"Bones?"

Sergeant Youman stared into the permanently trashed bedroom that was the German shepherd's domain. The bed had been shredded, newspapers laid down in case of "emergency" torn to ribbons, and countless allegedly indestructible dog toys eviscerated. If he'd been called to this scene on the job, the assumption would be domestic violence.

"*Bones*," Sergeant Youman repeated.

As if the animal hadn't heard him the first time.

"Goddammit," Youman swore.

This was the wrong day for him to lose his partner.

Bones had figured out the window latch the day he and Sergeant Billy "Billy Bones" Youman moved into their place at Westfield and Hampshire in Beechview. Using the tip of one claw, the shepherd had only to toy with the latch a couple of times before it popped free. They were on the second floor, but Bones had been trained for just this kind of thing. Once he was on the outside, he carefully made his way across a narrow ledge of brickwork like a wire-walker.

At the corner of the building, he balanced for a quick moment before leaping to the roof of the storage shack that stood beside his and Billy's apartment. The shack was made from the same quality of aluminum as siding and gave just as much when the gravity-aided weight of an eighty-five-pound German shepherd landed on it. After the first dozen or so such escapes, Bones's repeated battering of the roof created a dent that began to collect rain water. This began to rust.

The shepherd didn't notice.

It wasn't often that Sergeant Youman left Bones alone during the day, but when he did, Bones's routine was fairly set in stone. He would investigate the trash cans along the side of the building and continue on to the ones in the alley. On the rare occasions when he was able to slip up to a rat, the German shepherd would snap it up in his jaws, often devouring it with a single bite.

The rest of Bones's day would alternate between naps, more dumpster-diving, and the occasional jaunt all the way out to Mt. Washington or Grandview Park. There he would feast on picnic leftovers, the hoardings of the sleeping homeless, or even the occasional squirrel.

It wasn't like a massive German shepherd with a police collar wasn't noticed hauling ass across the various roadways of downtown Pittsburgh. Quite the opposite. Calls would go out to animal control, local police precincts, and even to 911 dispatchers. A truck *might* be sent out, but the phantom shepherd was never rounded up. The one time word had gotten back to Billy, he'd come home and found Bones right where he'd left him, so he'd forgotten all about it.

Today was different.

Billy had gotten the call from the assistant chief of operations the second he'd walked into the office. It was a paperwork day, hence leaving Bones at home for a change. When Billy's phone rang, he figured it was some administrator breathing down his neck about dignitary security for the pope's visit the following month. Apparently, the pontiff's detail had contacted the mayor's office and announced that PNC Park lacked even the most basic anti-terrorism defenses.

Yeah, well, don't come to Pittsburgh next time, ya prick, Billy thought.

"This is Youman," he said, already sighing into the receiver.

"Hold for the assistant chief of operations," came a voice.

Youman sat up straight. *What was* this *about?*

"Sergeant Youman?" barked the voice of what could only be a career bureaucrat.

"Yes, sir?"

"You're the K9?"

"Um, yes, sir."

"What's the name of your dog, or 'partner,' whatever you want to call it?"

Youman bristled. Half the department treated animal officers with the respect the sergeant believed was their due, likely because they'd worked with them in the field. The other half didn't see any difference between them and the family pooch getting fat on Alpo and shitting on anthills back home.

"Bones, sir."

"Bingo. You're to deliver him to the airport. He's being loaned to NYPD for a short-term operation. Human smuggling."

"I'm not going with him?" Youman asked.

"They've got a handler there. NYPD is short of K9 units due to budget cuts. They put out a search. Your animal comes highly-recommended."

"Is it dangerous, chief?"

"How the fuck should I know? Collect your dog. Get him to the airport. Pronto. You'll be contacted en route as to flight number."

The line went dead.

Billy slowly hung up the receiver, less than thrilled with the way he'd just been ordered around.

But that's when he remembered Mitzi.

Mitzi, the chick in the property room who never missed an opportunity to flirt with him whenever he swung by. Mitzi, who had her tongue in his ear and her hands so far down his pants at the Christmas party that he spent the rest of the season getting a hard-on every time he heard "Jesu, Joy of Man's Desiring." Mitzi, who was allergic to dogs and had never made good on her promise to ditch her husband for a night to spend an evening doing nothing but sucking his balls while he watched *Thundercats.*

Maybe ditching the roommate for a week or two wouldn't be the worst thing in the world.

So when Billy got home to an empty apartment, his frustration at finding Bones gone was compounded by a much greater factor than it might've been *sans* Mitzi.

"Bones!" Billy yelled in frustration.

He tromped over to the window and threw it open. Eyeing the ledge his shepherd must've used to further his escape, Billy couldn't help being at least a little impressed at his partner's ability. But his concupiscence-tinged indignation returned with a vengeance, and he set out to locate his dog.

Bones had watched this entire spectacle from the pigeon-shit-covered rooftop of the liquor store across the street. He had heard the familiar grumble of Billy's Bronco as it rattled up to the apartment and parked half a block up. But Billy was so engrossed in leaving a message on Mitzi's voicemail that he hadn't noticed the animal. A second later, when the window was thrown open, Bones had seen Billy again, this time his face colored by righteous fury.

The cop was soon out on the street, leash in hand, as he glanced down towards the shack Bones used as a stepladder. Deciding a promising lead might lie in the alley, Billy slipped between the buildings and disappeared in back.

Bones waited for Billy to return. When he didn't, the shepherd got to his feet, stretched, walked to the edge of the roof, and hopped off, descending down a pile of pallets to street level. Waiting for a break in the traffic, the furrier half of the K9 unit trotted across the street towards his building. Climbing on top of the aluminum shack, he leaped to the narrow ledge on the second story, eased around the corner to the front of the building, and disappeared back inside his apartment.

When Billy returned to his apartment four hours later, he found Bones asleep on the sofa. Furious, he resisted the urge to empty his service automatic, a Heckler & Koch 9mm USP, into the shepherd's torso. He knew the instant he pulled the weapon, his dog's sixth sense would trip him awake and, maybe, just *maybe*, the animal would tear his arm off before he'd gotten off a single shot.

Some days it was a short walk from "partner in law enforcement" to "that fucking dog."

"We're heading out, Bones," Billy said.

Bones hopped off the sofa and began trailing his handler around the apartment as Billy gathered up Bones's supplies for the trip. He almost couldn't find the extra-large pet carrier. It took up so much room in the apartment that he'd been using it as a table, covering it with magazines and mail. Shunting all that to the side, Billy tossed Bones's blue teddy bear inside, stuffed the paperwork he'd brought home from the precinct into the bag containing Bones's "handler history," and picked up Bones's leash.

"Let's go."

It was always a long trek out to the airport, but there was little traffic. Billy allowed Bones to sit on the passenger seat and flipped through radio stations as they went. As much as the sergeant wanted to pretend otherwise, his mind was already well past Bones's drop-off.

He'd Tivo'd Thundercats, *hadn't he?*

The thought made him smile. He accelerated towards the exit for Pittsburgh International.

The United Express flight to Newark lasted only an hour, but Bones fell asleep the moment he'd entered his carrier. And only when the crate was bumping along the ramp out of the cargo hold did he wake up. He knew that he was thirsty and hungry, in that order, but was also curious to see what would happen next.

"Bones?" came a female voice.

Bones moved to the wire cage door of the carrier and saw a young woman looking in at him. She was short, five-foot-nothing, Latina, and had her hair knotted up inside her policeman's cap tight as a drum.

"Sergeant Marina del Vecchio," the woman intoned. "I'll be your handler while you're attached to the NYPD."

She moved close enough so that Bones could get her scent. He smelled other dogs on her gloves, including one that was recently in heat. He also picked up the dank stench of human blood, sweat, and excrement. Snorting, he took a couple of steps back.

"Out of the cage or in the cage?" the sergeant asked.

Bones didn't move.

"I'm going to take that for *in*," del Vecchio replied.

She unlatched the cage door and reached in for Bones's collar. Attaching a black lead to his Pittsburgh P.D. harness, she scowled at the familiar checkerboard pattern of the out-of-town force.

"We'll have to get you fixed up with a loaner so no one thinks you're not local."

She tugged on the leash and Bones dutifully followed.

On the car ride to Manhattan, Sergeant del Vecchio talked to Bones the entire way, stopping only to yell at someone she seemed to know while going around the toll booths at the Lincoln Tunnel. She told him that she was born in Jamaica, Queens. She explained that her family had been there for years and, for a time, she dreamed of becoming an actress. When she was in high school, she'd seen the respect the Junior ROTC kids got and, despite her school having an over fifty-percent dropout rate, managed to graduate and went straight into basic training two weeks after she'd cleaned out her locker. It was there that she learned she had a natural ability with "MWDs."

"An MWD is what they call military working dogs," del Vecchio explained. "Once I got into the handler program, my first assignment was with a Belgian Malinois named Destry. He was just the sweetest dog. We trained together for months before deployment. We did three tours together in Afghanistan, but he was kept on after I finally cycled out. I really hope I can adopt him when he's on the other side."

As the sergeant continued describing her time in the military alongside Destry, Bones stared out the window, taking in all the new smells. The area was heavily industrialized, so the shepherd's olfactory senses were being assaulted by the acrid smells of wastewater treatment facilities industry, oil refineries, and any number of chemical plants, combined with the exhaust fumes of thousands of heavy trucks and commuter vehicles.

Bones came close to vomiting several times, though his mostly empty stomach would've discharged little.

The New York Police Department's Canine Team was part of the NYPD Emergency Services Unit, which was part of the even larger Special Operations Division. There was a training facility on West 20th across the street from the large kennels that housed active-duty dogs on operation days.

"The reason we had to bring you in, Mr. Bones, is because we're just stretched too thin and have had too many injuries lately," del Vecchio said, leading the shepherd out of her car on a lead. "My dog, Perseus, got shot on a narcotics raid in Staten Island a few weeks ago after being loaned out to those bozos. I'm still pissed on that one. So, when we go after these assholes today,

I'm going to have you in a vest. Pretty sure you're only being used on point. Detection, intimidation, possible pursuit but not likely."

The Special Ops division building was old and in desperate need of a facelift. A onetime precinct house, the place had been taken over by Special Ops in the late seventies. Year after year, renovations projects were budgeted and put forth to the city and, year after year, they were among the first things cut. It got so bad that a couple of officers had even come in with buckets of paint on their days off to at least make the first floor presentable. They made it an hour before a visiting administrator accosted them for a work order and shut them down.

So now, alongside curling linoleum, rat-eaten corkboard ceilings, and chipped doorframes, were four half-painted hallways, a reminder to all of the power and absurdity of police bureaucracy.

"That the Pittsburgh mutt?" called a uniformed tactical officer when he spied Bones and del Vecchio.

"This is the guy. Already told him if he felt like biting someone in the ass, O'Hara was just the douchebag to see."

"Oh, fuck off, del Vecchio," O'Hara snarled. "Ever wonder why no one buys your shit about gender bias in the division? Five minutes next to you and they know it's your mouth holding you back. And in an outfit as small as New York's finest, people talk."

"Fuck yourself," del Vecchio called. "But I guess you'll be doing that a lot now that your wife ran off with your son's LittleLleague coach."

O'Hara blanched. "How'd you…?"

"Like you said, people talk."

A smirk on her lips, del Vecchio led Bones towards the kennel in back.

"Problem is, he's *exactly* my type, *Huesos*. Six-foot, family of cops going back four generations, Irish drunken fuck, works out every day, probably going to be a captain one day, maybe even deputy chief. His whole life is policing. Kind of guy needs a cop-wife to keep him in line. I just might try to get in on that."

Bones picked up the scents of at least two dozen different enforcement dogs in the kennel, though there was only one being housed. Del Vecchio led him to the last enclosure, swung open the chain-link gate, and put him inside.

"We'll get you fed and watered. Take it easy. The operation's set for midnight, so we'll rally at ten. Got that?"

Bones looked at her for a moment and the sergeant nodded.

"Good dog."

II

The tactical team was relatively small. Twelve officers in all, plus Bones and the drivers of the two tactical vehicles. Four car units had been assigned to back up the SWAT officers, but the pervading belief was they would be unnecessary. The Spec Ops guys would breach with a lot of sound and fury, the targets would fold, and they'd call it a night.

For his part, though, Bones was attentive. He knew it was game time. The excitement pulsing through the officers had infected the shepherd as well. He'd spent most of the afternoon and early evening asleep, waking only to eat moments before he was brought onto the truck. Once he was there, his temporary handler quickly attached a camera apparatus to his harness.

"We're going to hit the lights in this place," del Vecchio explained. "We send you up ahead, around a corner, into an apartment, and you'll be our eyes. Got it?"

Bones hadn't replied.

"Some toy," O'Hara grunted from a few seats up as del Vecchio checked the camera feed on a handheld monitor.

"I'd let you borrow it, but I'm afraid of what I'd find on the memory stick when you gave it back," del Vecchio quipped, tugging the harness. "Besides, with your pecs you'd need something more in the realm of a 44 regular, am I right?"

Rather than be offended, O'Hara grinned.

"Post-raid plans, sergeant?"

Del Vecchio offered O'Hara a smile that was at least part invitation before turning back to her charge.

"Don't worry, Bones. My mind's totally on your safety 'cause I know your mind's on mine. I don't take that lightly."

Bones eyed del Vecchio expectantly, but she went quiet.

A second later, the captain at the front of the vehicle spoke up.

"Three nights ago, a Mr. Devaris Clark was thrown off the roof of the building we have business in tonight. We believe it to be the work of one Mr. Chiedozie, a Nigerian slum lord who lines up squats for incoming illegals and then calls INS once he's drained them dry. He keeps his neighbors quiet with threats of violence. We're here to round up him and his organization. Some of the people in your line of sight will probably be the victims of his fraud, while others will pretend to be. Not our job. We get 'em down, cuff 'em tight, slide them to booking, and go home. We're the dog catchers, not the Board of Records, present company notwithstanding."

He nodded to del Vecchio. She gripped Bones's lead a little tighter.

"All right. Let's hit the ground running."

The tactical vehicles turned onto East 112th and slowed at Neville Houses, but did not stop. The back doors flew open and the teams hopped off and moved directly towards the building.

Sergeant del Vecchio and Bones were the first ones out of the second vehicle. The dank scents that had polluted Devaris's nose only days before now ravaged Bones. But he had no time to investigate this piece of garbage or that fetid pool of rat piss. He was going where he was led, end of story.

"Here we go, Bones," del Vecchio whispered.

At that moment, Building 7 of Neville Houses was plunged into darkness as the power was cut half a block away by Con Ed employees. Anyone lingering around the courtyard had vacated the second the tactical vehicles showed up on the block, so the team had a clear path all the way to the front door.

"What happened to the lights?" came a voice from the lobby.

"Police!" the captain yelled back. "On the ground, now!"

Bones and del Vecchio moved past the captain to follow the other tactical officers up the stairs. They were heading for the sixth floor but were stopping on five to allow their four-pawed companion to take the lead.

"Ma'am? Please return to your apartment! This is a police matter."

Whoever the words were directed at seemed to take heed. Del Vecchio heard a door slam shut. She had on night vision goggles but was already staring into the handheld monitor as the image bounced up and down with Bones's quick steps. It was times like this that she envied not the shepherd's incredible sense of smell, but his ability to see in the dark.

"Easy, Bones," she whispered into her throat mic, her voice traveling into his ears via specially designed ear buds, a loan from the military.

They reached the fifth-floor stairwell and stopped. Del Vecchio waited for the command from the captain, checking and rechecking the view from the monitor on Bones's back.

"Send him in."

Del Vecchio took Bones off the leash and indicated the next floor.

"Okay, Bones. Search!"

Bones moved up the stairs and glanced down the dark hallway on the sixth floor. Seeing nothing, he walked down the hallway, sniffing at every closed door. A door cracked open up ahead. Bones looked up. As he did, del Vecchio glimpsed a large man peering down the hallway, holding a gun. She showed this to the captain, who nodded.

"That's our guy. Give the command."

"Take hold!" the sergeant barked into her mic.

Bones had a significant prey drive. He'd been silently sizing up the man since his hand had gripped the doorknob. When given the command to bite the fellow, it was like an invitation to play time. He would merely be doing exactly what domestication and training kept him from doing naturally.

The gunman sensed something coming at him from the darkness only seconds before Bones's jaws clamped down with an average 200 psi on his right arm. He'd made the mistake of trying to aim the gun at the unseen intruder at the last moment, giving Bones the moving target he was looking for. The shepherd hit the man so hard that he fell over, dropping the gun as he hit the ground.

Immediately, there were shouts, followed by gunfire.

On the screen, Sergeant del Vecchio counted a dozen pairs of glowing eyes. Fear raced up her spine, though it wasn't her own safety she was concerned for.

"First squad! Go!" cried the captain.

Six members of the tactical team swept up the stairs and onto the sixth floor. Del Vecchio, part of the second squad, stared at the monitor as muzzle flash repeatedly blinded the camera. When she could make something out, the image bounded around. Bones was clearly in attack mode. Her worry switched from the shepherd's safety to that of the tactical team.

"Bones! Out!!" she cried into her throat mic, unsure whether the dog could hear.

"Second squad! Go!"

Del Vecchio leaped to her feet and followed the others up to the sixth floor. She looked down at the monitor but couldn't tell if Bones had stood down. Just as she entered the hallway, she caught a glimpse of a man's eyes staring up at the camera in terror as Bones tore at his shoulder, already out of its socket.

"Bones! Out!" she repeated, panic in her voice.

This time, she knew he couldn't hear, so loud had the gunfire grown. That's when all other noise was blotted out by the sound of a gunshot so impossibly close to her head that she felt temporarily deafened. This was followed by a numb feeling behind her eye. She looked down at the monitor and saw its screen was now obscured by a thick greasy film of blood and brains.

Hers.

No one had heard the door to 632 open. The building's records had the apartment rented to one "Erna Fowler," aged eighty-two years. She'd been a resident since 1979 and lived alone. The idea that she would step out of her apartment with the small six-shot .357 she kept in a drawer and begin killing the officers in the hall with shots to the back of the head simply hadn't occurred to anyone in the planning stages of the operation.

As bullets flew, the chaos allowed Mrs. Fowler, married in 1951 to Archie, who died in 1993, to reload the weapon with a speedloader and continue shooting. She felled another two members of the tactical squad and was aiming at a third when a stray bullet from a MPK 9mm entered her left tear duct and exploded out the back of her head.

Still noticed by no one, she dropped to the ground directly beside the corpse of Sergeant del Vecchio, the .357 skittering down the hall before coming to a rest in front of 639.

Down on the street, Detectives Leonhardt and Garza stared up at the dark building as the distant, hollow report of gunfire continued, punctuated by intermittent flashes of light from three sixth-floor windows.

Leonhardt scrunched his brow.

"Weren't they only breeching 638?"

"That's what they said," Garza nodded.

"Then somebody's got their front door open."

"Fuck. Hope we don't have any civilian collaterals up there."

"We do, and everybody in the precinct will be looking over their shoulder for the next year. To say nothing of how the press will take it."

"Shit," scoffed Garza. "Any time these Special Ops assholes come up to 22nd Precinct, they've got to make things hard for the rest of…"

Garza was interrupted by a terrified voice over the radio.

"Something's happened up there!" someone squawked. "We have multiple officers down! We need emergency services and backup! Immediately!"

Leonhardt blanched. Garza popped a stick of gum in his mouth.

"You were saying?"

Becca Baldwin was nobody's fool and anyone would tell you that, or so she was fond of saying. With an agile intelligence, quick to backhand those who would question it with a taste of her biting wit, everyone knew Becca was going places. She was a favorite of the building and knew it. The grandmas loved her, the parents hoped their kids grew up to be like her, and those her own age accorded her the deference she felt she had earned and was deserved.

She lived with her one half-brother and her one brother-brother. The full brother was Kenny, aged twenty-four, who worked nights at a distribution warehouse for a grocery store chain. The half was Trey. He ran with a small time drug-slinging crew that seemed bonded less by entrepreneurial spirit and more by the desire to spend the whole day fucked up. Becca had no interest in working at a warehouse or selling drugs. No, she was going to go to college on a scholarship and be a lady scientist and never look back. She would get married, move to Chicago or San Francisco or Seattle or Minneapolis-St. Paul, and never look back. All she had to do was bide her time and get the right grades. That's what Mrs. Drucker told her, and she believed it.

She didn't remember her mom, a crack head now deceased, and when she saw her dad on the streets, he didn't remember her. She didn't care, though. They were weak; she was strong and determined. She had brains, and she read all the time. She read books by and about Frederick Douglass, the poetry of Umar Bin Hassan, and the theater of Amiri Baraka. She listened to classical CDs she'd borrowed from her music teacher and didn't get anything out of them but kept listening anyway.

Of the many other things Becca was, she was also twelve years old.

When the shooting started, she did what Kenny had always told her to do and hid in the hall bathtub. She pressed herself flat against the base, her nose touching the drain. The gunfire sounded far away, but she knew it was right outside the door. It alternated between machine gun fire and single shots, the singles sounding much louder than the others, echoing like thunder. She tried focusing on something else, finally settling on singing a song to herself. She ached to remember more than a couple of lines of this song or that and simply couldn't do it.

Finally, she settled on Tupac Shakur's "Keep Ya Head Up" and discovered that she could recite it from beginning to end. She did this four times.

By her final time through the song, the gunfire had stopped for a few minutes and she thought it safe to clamber out of the tub. She eased her way through the apartment to the front door. She could barely look through the peephole without standing on a chair but had no intention to do so. Instead, she was just looking for a better vantage point from which to hear the proceedings. She knew a stray bullet could still punch through the wall at any moment, but didn't think it likely.

The silence was broken by the sound of someone moving down the hall. Becca went to the door to try to figure out if it was a police officer or one of the bad guys. She paid attention to the goings-on in the building so far as she needed to avoid them. The people moving in and out of 638 didn't speak English, and she seldom saw any of them more than once. That is, except for Chiedozie and a couple of his crew. He'd glared at her a couple of times when she came up the steps, interrupting whatever conversation he was having with a "tenant." But she'd just glared back until, unable to get a read on the situation, Chiedozie had gone back to his chat.

When Becca cracked the door, it was his face that she saw first. Illuminated in dim light trickling in from his apartment windows, the Nigerian gangster was flat on his back, staring at the ceiling through dead eyes. Surrounding him were the dead bodies of several people, police officers and folks she took for Chiedozie's men alike.

That's when she saw movement at her feet. Looking down, she saw a large dog peering up at her, his snout black with blood.

"Oh, my God!" she cried.

Bones glanced up at her, took a couple of sniffs to register her heightened levels of fear, and resumed sniffing the gun that had landed on her doorstep.

When Becca saw that the dog wasn't particularly fazed by the goings-on, she bent down and offered him her hand to smell. Bones did so and followed it up with a quick couple of licks.

"It's not safe out there, boy," Becca whispered.

Bones looked up at her as she held the door open. The shepherd peeked in, took a couple more sniffs, and entered. Becca's gaze returned to the gun at her feet. When she suddenly heard voices on the stairs, she bent down, picked up the gun, and closed the door, locking it behind her.

She hadn't seen the pair of eyes at the end of the hall that had watched Bones's egress from the scene. In fact, no one had seen it, but this wasn't surprising, given the darkness.

But Bones hadn't seen the lurker, either. Hadn't smelled him, hadn't heard him, and hadn't detected him in any of the myriad ways his handlers over the years had used to support a claim that the shepherd had a sixth sense.

The lurker moved down the hall towards the fallen body of Mrs. Fowler, eyed it for a quick moment, but then disappeared just as the second wave of tactical responders appeared at the top of the stairs.

III

The lights were back on fifteen minutes later.

When the police came by knocking on doors to reassure residents that everything was "in hand" but to "stay in their apartments and let the paramedics do their jobs," Becca kept the door locked and didn't respond.

The knocker hadn't tried that hard anyway, giving up after two rounds of knocking and one shout of, "Police! Anyone inside the apartment?"

The little girl had taken the shepherd into the bathroom and washed the blood off his snout in the bathtub. She'd gone to get a bowl from the kitchen to fill with water, only to come back and find Bones thirstily lapping up the bloody water draining out of the tub. Making a command decision, she opened the toilet lid and urged the dog to drink. He did until the bowl was empty, so she flushed, and he drank that dry as well.

She eyed the apparatus on his back but wasn't sure how to remove it. In her search, she discovered his plastic name strip attached to his harness.

"Your name is Bones?"

Bones responded with a questioning glance and Becca nodded. "Bones it is. Are you hungry?"

Bones licked his chops. Becca smiled.

"Let me see what we've got."

Becca went back to the kitchen. The German shepherd followed.

The refrigerator was stocked with the same thing it was always stocked with: fruit and lunch meat, items Kenny brought home from the warehouse. For a long time, Becca worried that he stole it. But then, she'd learned to read the expiration dates and saw that the meats were almost always a couple of days past due and the fruit never less than ripe.

"They throw it away, can you believe that?" Kenny said every time he brought the stuff home. "Boxes and boxes and 'returns.' It would just go to a landfill somewhere. The night manager says anybody who wants it can take it so long as you don't call in sick after."

Becca sorted through the meat drawer. She found several packages of cold cuts now too rancid to eat, some having gone gray, others green. She finally came across a package of hard salami ringed with pepper that had only expired the previous Monday. Opening it, the little girl took out a couple of slices, and tossed them to Bones. He devoured them in one bite, so she simply placed the package on the floor and let the shepherd eat the whole thing.

When he finished it, he stared up at her expectantly, clearly wanting more. She went back to the meat drawer and selected the next most recently expired package.

"I really hope you don't throw up after this."

When the police rolled up to Neville Houses, Trey was smoking out with his friends Alvis and Pluto outside Building 3.

"5-0!" somebody cried out, half-ironically, but already hightailing it away.

"If they're after us, they're gonna be pretty disappointed we ain't holding," Alvis cried, hopping to his feet and tossing his joint away. "Still, locker room?"

"*Locker room*," Trey nodded.

Trey pushed the joint through a storm grate and followed. He was high as a kite and knew it, having been drinking since the afternoon. But he'd run in a fog before and knew to push all thoughts aside that didn't involve placing one foot in front of the other.

There was a maintenance locker room in the basement of four of the sixteen buildings that made up Neville Houses. The lockers served a dual purpose, giving the workers somewhere to change and keep their personal belongings, but also a place to lock up tools and equipment. Everything got stolen in Neville Houses, this much was understood, but no one stole from the lockers. If Granny on the ninth floor of Building 12 started flooding the place after clogging her sink, the right tool better be there or the neighbor downstairs was going to beat in some heads the next day. That's why the locker room itself was never locked: a reminder to would-be thieves to think before getting grabby.

The other thing about the locker room, the thing that appealed to Trey and his friends, was that there were four different ways to get in and out of it. One door that opened into the building, one that opened out into the courtyard, a service hatch that followed along the trash chute and let you out on any floor, and then a second hatch that took you under the building into the warren of water and gas pipes that connected the buildings. These service tunnels then had access points to the sewers for access by city workers. This made it possible to walk down the tenth-floor hallway, get into the trash chute service hatch, and slip down through and under the building unseen by anyone before popping up four blocks away.

Did this routinely make life that much easier for Trey and his crew? In a word, yes.

The three teens were already in the locker room of Building 3 when the shooting started. It didn't sound like much, just a distant knocking as if someone, somewhere was doing construction work or hanging a picture upstairs. But then a burst of automatic fire came along to sober Trey.

"What building is that coming from?" he barked.

"Dunno," shrugged Alvis.

"*Shit.*"

Though they'd come in via the outer door, Trey hurried through the storage area and bounded up the inside stairs to the lobby of Building 3. Gathered by the front door were a number of residents staring out at Building 7.

"What's going on?"

"Police raid. Think it's the Nigerians in 7. Squatters."

As Trey prayed it was anything but that, he counted up the windows to the floor where the muzzle flash was coming from.

Please don't be six, please don't be six, please don't be six…

"Sixth floor," one of the old-timers said, as if reading his mind. "You got people up there, son?"

"What do you know about it?" Trey scoffed, trying to scotch the worry from his voice.

Ken took off running the second word came over the radio. The warehouse was in the Bronx, usually about a twenty-minute ride on the 4 train.

Only tonight, he didn't have twenty minutes.

Normally, a black man running hell-bent for leather through the South Bronx was exactly the kind of thing that would get him stopped by a cop or tripped by some asshole, but maybe this night they saw his face and gave him a break. This was a man trying to stop time with the soles of his feet.

He finally spotted a cab at Morris and East 138th and beat on the driver's-side window.

"East Harlem, 111th," he cried.

Fearing the driver would wave him off, Ken was relieved when the fellow, wearing a bright orange turban, simply nodded and indicated the back seat.

The cab arrived at 115th and 2nd a few minutes later, but could advance no further. Police had cordoned off the block.

"Sorry for your troubles," the driver said to Ken as he paid him.

"Nothing's happened, man," Ken stated adamantly. "And that's just the way it has to be."

The driver nodded gravely and drove off.

Even with all the noise out in the hall, Becca still managed to fall asleep. She'd locked Bones in the hall bathroom first, figuring it would be easiest to clean up in there if he had to pee or puke. What she didn't count was the shepherd taking a quick nap, then getting up and opening the simple bathroom door with his teeth a few minutes later.

Bones walked around the apartment and got a clear aromatic sense of the place. He smelled Ken and the food he dragged in. He smelled Trey and Trey's friends and their drugs. The dog also picked up Becca's scent, figuring out pretty quickly which part of the living room she sat in to eat while watching television, what side of the couch she preferred, and which window she'd sit at to watch the neighborhood go by.

The floor was fairly crumb-free, so Bones headed for the couch. There he found broken chips, candy, chunks of bread, and pieces of cereal all buried between the cushions. He went after these with gusto.

But when that task was complete, Bones plopped down with his head on the armrest and stared at the noise coming from the hall.

It was a full hour before the voices neared the front door and stopped there.

"We'd ask that you stay indoors until we give you an all-clear, is that understood?" bellowed an authoritarian voice.

"'Understood?'" grunted Ken. "Shouldn't that be more like 'is that acceptable'? This is my house, man! My little sister's in there!"

"We sent officers door to door. No one answered here."

"Yeah, because she was probably scared shitless. Then you've got us waiting down there…"

"You couldn't call?"

There was a silence before Ken's voice replied, "Phone's disconnected."

"Well, that's too bad, then," said the cop, sounding triumphant. "You have a good night now."

Keys jangled in the door. A second later, it swung open, light pouring in from the hall as Trey and Ken quickly entered.

"Man, fuck that guy," Trey snarled. "He doesn't know I know he lives over there off Lenox."

"Oh, and what're you going to do about it?" Ken scoffed. "Go over and pretend you don't smell like a beer can with thirty roaches stuffed in it? He'd run you in so fast, you'd be crying."

Trey straightened up a little before rolling his eyes.

"Better than smelling like a grocery store dumpster. Rotten cabbage, rotten carrots, sour milk…"

That's when Trey's gaze traveled over to the couch and met Bones's.

"Oh, *shit!*" Trey shrieked.

He grabbed the front doorknob, but Ken had already set the door chain.

"Fuck, man!" he shouted.

Ken stared at the dog and realized there wasn't something right about it. He figured any other dog would leap to its feet and confront Trey. Dogs reacted to fear, right? But this one only sat there looking at Trey like he was just the latest attraction.

"Hold up, Trey. I don't think he's dangerous."

As if looking for the perfect way to punctuate Ken's assessment, Bones farted. Trey stared at the shepherd with incredulity before turning to Ken.

"I'm still way high, right?"

"What's going on?" Becca said in a too-sleepy-to-be-fully-awake voice as she walked into the living room.

"Becca! There's a dog!"

Becca eyed Bones, giving him a quick pat on the snout.

"How'd you get out of the bathroom, Bones?"

Bones seemed to know exactly what she was referring to and glanced backward at the bathroom without comment. Becca turned back to her brothers.

"Cops shot up the whole hallway going after Mister what's-his-name who's always having 'relatives' stay with him," she explained matter-of-factly. "Got a couple of the neighbors, too."

"Yeah, we saw. They took the cops down with him."

"No, that wasn't them," Becca claimed. "I heard the bullets. The cops came in, there was shooting, lots of noise, lots of machine guns, but then there was just that one coming up from behind them – *bang, bang, bang, bang.*"

Ken saw the look in Becca's eyes and shook his head.

"No way. You're not going down that road again, are you? Please say you're not. When are you going to stop this?"

"When are you going to believe me?" Becca countered. "You saw Mrs. Fowler's apartment door open?"

"Yeah," Ken replied, realizing he had.

"He was in there with her this time," Becca explained. "You know how she's always saying she got this gun. Well, here it is."

Becca went over and plucked the gun from its hiding place in the silverware drawer.

"Where'd you get that?" Trey said, grabbing it away from her.

"Bounced up to our doorstep after she got done killing all the police," Becca intoned. "Smell it."

Ken took the gun from Trey. Even without inhaling, he could tell from the heft that those were spent cartridges in the cylinder.

"Jesus," Ken said. "Why the hell did you pick it up?"

Becca shrugged, even though she knew the answer.

"I was scared. I knew he was out there in the hall somewhere just looking at me. Then this dog showed up and I figured it was going to be okay."

"Fuck, you stole a gun *and* a police dog?" Trey scoffed, checking out Bones's harness. "They're going to put you away for this!"

Becca walked over until she was only a few inches from Trey's face.

"You can laugh at me all you want, but first it was Mr. Preston, then Devaris the other night. Now it's a whole bunch of dead cops and Mrs. Fowler. It's that dog, Trey. That evil frickin' dog. And we gotta be ready for it because no one else is."

IV

Ken didn't bother going back to work that night, but he couldn't sleep, either. Sure, there'd been a string of bad luck in the buildings lately, but that was East Harlem. He'd worked night after night, week after week, month after month to get them out of there. He wasn't stupid. The young man knew that it was probably too late for Trey and one day he'd get a call that he was dead or in custody for something terrible.

But Becca.

She'd been through so much. He'd found a couple of houses in Queens, but that wasn't far enough away. He'd considered upstate and New Jersey with that killer commute, but that wasn't going to make it. That's when he'd remembered a cousin who drove trucks out in Colorado Springs. He called him up and was told that not only was housing cheap because of the real estate crash, but that he could get him a job.

"The money's not great until you own your rig," the cousin had said. "But once that happens, you're rolling in it."

It meant a lot of time on the road while Becca was at home, probably looked after by his cousin's wife, but they'd work that out. For some reason,

Ken just never figured Trey into the picture. He could see the conversation in his mind. He'd bring up Colorado, talk about the schools and the opportunity, Trey would start grinning, then start shaking his head. All Trey would be thinking about was how the move would screw up his plans.

What plans? Ken wondered, staring at the ceiling.

But now Ken wondered if it was too late. Becca had started with this dog-stuff a few weeks back, saying there was some kind of monster in the building. If she was five, that'd be one thing, but this wasn't an over-active imagination. So he'd treated it like a joke at first.

Mr. Preston had been a fall-down drunk. When he went to his cupboard, pulled a bottle of drain cleaner out instead of his Rémy Martin, poured it down his throat, and was dead minutes if not seconds later, no one was that surprised.

But Becca had said from the start that it was suspicious. She'd said that she'd seen Mr. Preston with a strange dog all of a sudden. He'd seemed out of it, like he barely recognized people he'd known for years. Then he was being carted out under a blanket of blue velvet with a funeral home logo in cursive flapping against the gurney.

As quickly as it had appeared, the dog was suddenly gone.

So when Becca told her oldest brother that she thought the animal had something to do with it, Ken assumed this was some kind of juvenile reaction to death. He told her that if this Devil Dog scared her, she should let it know that her brother was a much worse monster than anything it had ever seen and would kill it if it came around. He'd growled when he said it and made a face, hoping she'd feel better.

Instead, she just looked at him like he was nuts.

But now, she'd not only picked up what was apparently a murder weapon from the hall and brought it into the apartment, she'd also absconded with a police dog. He knew he'd have to start dealing with that in the morning but wasn't even sure where to begin. If he told the police what happened, suddenly Becca would be involved in all this. If they decided to start looking, might they start saying that he was trying to cover up for Trey? Then, he'd be roped into it.

It was at that moment that the door to his bedroom eased open and the police dog in question nosed its way in. It sniffed around for a second as Ken watched before hopping up on the bed next to him.

"Just make yourself at home," Ken cried, though he was intimidated enough not to shove the shepherd away.

He reached out to pet the animal, only to have his hand land on the harness. He felt something that didn't exactly feel like leash material and withdrew his hand.

"What is that, boy?" He turned on a lamp and eyed the thing before flopping back down on his pillow. "Aw, shit – a camera? *Really?*"

"Executions, every last one of them," Garza announced, joining his partner in the 22nd Precinct's empty briefing room. It was the one place where they thought they might escape the chaos erupting in every police station in the five boroughs but still have access to the latest on the case.

Detective Leonhardt pinched his sinuses. His head had been all right, but each piece of worse news increased the violence between his eyes. First it was that there were multiple officers wounded up on the sixth floor of Building 7. Then "mortally" became a prefix and every badge in a four-block radius began racing up the stairs, Leonhardt included. After that, it was a reporter the detective passed on the sidewalk who mentioned this would be the single greatest gun-related loss of life to New York law enforcement since Attica.

But *executions?*

When he'd gone up to see the carnage, it had looked like something out of an old *yakuza* movie. But the idea that each of the dead officers had been shot unawares in the back of the head, likely in the one spot not covered by body armor, was almost too much to take.

Detective Garza waited for Leonhardt to react, but should've known it would be all internal for his partner. He was a man who could make himself a magnet for blame, taking even imagined censure upon his back like a flagellant.

"Same gun?"

"Yeah. Something firing .357 caliber cartridges, possibly a Ruger SP 101."

"And they didn't find the gun?"

Garza shook his head.

"So," sighed Leonhardt, "somebody got away."

"I don't know. There were supposed to be eight in the room, five are dead, the other three wounded. We got Chiedozie, the big bad. No one's talking about a number nine."

"If you account for the weapons in 638 and of the Spec Ops guys, that leaves the old lady."

"Are you kidding me? She stepped out of her apartment at the wrong time and got shot in the eye."

"She walked halfway down the hall!" Leonhardt protested. "You think she couldn't tell what was going on?"

"It was dark. She might've been disoriented, she might've gotten pushed. You don't know what her bad luck was."

"No, but it *is* suspicious. I'd almost say someone knew we were coming and might've been waiting in her place to get behind everybody. How else do you account for somebody getting the drop on that many tactical officers?"

"I can't," Garza admitted. "All shot from behind, base of the skull while standing, pitch darkness. No one gets that lucky."

"They get anything off the dog handler's monitor?"

"No, the recorder was attached to the camera itself, not the monitor."

"Then where's the camera?" Leonhardt asked.

"You didn't hear? Dog's missing, too. They actually didn't notice right away. They think he panicked at the gunfire and bolted."

"An enforcement dog? That's the first thing they train out of them." Garza shrugged.

"Yeah, but that sound you're hearing is everyone from City Hall to 1 Police Place covering their asses."

Leonhardt sat for a moment longer, but then got to his feet, reaching for his coat.

"Up for a drive?"

"Sure, what are we doing?"

"Take your pick. Missing dog, missing gun, missing camera."

Trey had only been asleep a couple of hours when Ken shook him awake.

"What the hell, man?" Trey protested.

"That laptop," Ken hissed. "Where's the laptop?"

Ken refused to call the computer Trey had in his squat of a bedroom "his" laptop. Ken imagined the device, which just showed up one day about three months back, was anybody's *but* Trey's.

"Why?"

Ken held up the camera.

"This was on the dog."

Instantly intrigued, Trey rolled out of bed and began searching through piles of clothes. A minute later the laptop was open, a USB cord running from it to the camera. Ken figured it might require some kind of special rig only available to law enforcement or government types, but Trey indicated that the camera itself wasn't anything special.

"You can buy something like this on the corner for nothing," Trey said. "Cheap piece of shit, really."

"I'm impressed, tough guy. Can we see what's on it?"

A window popped up on the laptop screen asking if the user wanted to download the footage or simply view it. Trey hit "View" and a second window appeared and the footage began to roll.

"All right, Bones. Search!" came the disembodied voice of Sergeant del Vecchio.

Ken and Trey watched as the camera angled up the steps to the sixth floor. After a few fruitless sniff-arounds, Chiedozie appeared, coming out of his apartment. The camera lurched forward, galloping straight for the Nigerian slumlord. The man's face filled with terror as his unseen assailant tore into him.

Then the footage got interesting.

After the gangster was subdued, there was a flurry of activity from within apartment 638. Several armed men rushed at the camera and numerous shots were fired, but way over the dog's head, the shooters not yet realizing their leader's assailant wasn't human. The camera dove straight into these new attackers and began tearing them apart.

"Holy fuck, that dog!" Trey exclaimed. "He's a monster!"

"Quiet," Ken demanded.

At this point, the audio was all shouts, screams, and gunfire. The heavy footsteps of the tactical squad could be heard racing up the hallway. Bones wheeled around as the captain yelled out for the occupants of 638 to drop their weapons. By way of reply, they unleashed a torrent of machine-gun fire at the newcomers. For his part, the shepherd continued on, tearing into the bad guys even as Sergeant del Vecchio's voice could be heard calling him off in his ear buds.

But then the single gun shots began.

At first, the tactical officers looked as if they couldn't tell where the shots were coming from. The gunmen in the apartment took advantage of the distraction and pushed forward, shooting with near-suicidal disregard for their own safety.

As if finally hearing his handler's commands, Bones bolted through the crush of tactical officers firing from alongside the doorway. As he entered the hall, the camera immediately revealed the executions taking place in the darkness as the diminutive Mrs. Fowler quickly shot several officers from behind at point-blank range. It was a startling sight, an old woman methodically lining up shots aimed directly at the base of the officers' skull. She had a very serious, very determined look on her face as she pulled the trigger.

"Oh, my God!" Trey laughed. "Ms. Fowler going Scarface!"

"Shut up, Trey," Ken said, albeit toothlessly. He couldn't believe what he was seeing.

Mrs. Fowler's rampage lasted only seconds before the bullet caught her in the eye. She had no real reaction, as if the round had torn straight through her brain, closing her account before she knew what hit her.

As she sank to the ground, a new pair of eyes appeared behind Mrs. Fowler. Ken could just see the outline of an immense black dog, low to the ground, watching from down the hall.

"See, I told you," Becca said.

Trey and Ken turned and saw their little sister watching from the doorway with Bones.

"How do you know that's not Mrs. Fowler's dog?" Ken asked.

"Mrs. Fowler doesn't have a dog," Becca replied. "And if she did, you really think it would be some kind of monster like that one?"

"She's got you there, Ken," Trey said. "That thing would eat her alive."

On the screen, the dog stared back at Bones until the camera turned away. The shepherd had found Sergeant del Vecchio and was sniffing around her corpse. He nuzzled the dead woman's face though half of it had been blown away when the bullet had exited, taking her nose and right cheekbone with it. As the camera angle bobbed up and down, however, the eyes of the other dog remained fixed, as if staring directly into the lens. For a moment, Ken wondered if it wasn't a statue or some kind of taxidermy animal that Mrs. Fowler kept for one reason or another, so still did it stand.

But then it moved just a little, as if registering a sound on the stairwell. A second later, however, its gaze had returned to Bones.

"What is that?" Trey whispered, hypnotized by its gaze.

"I don't know," said Ken. "But since when do you have two dogs in the same place and neither one so much as gives the other a how-do-you-do?"

Ken looked back at Bones, wishing more than anything that the shepherd could give him the answer to that question.

They watched the rest of the footage, the dog making its way over to their apartment door and Becca letting him in. The shepherd didn't turn around once to see the other animal.

Trey popped the cord out of the camera and shook his head.

"Now that we know all this, what the hell do we do about it?"

Over on the eighth floor of Building 3, Vernon Lester ached all over. A mechanic, he'd never been too careful with his back or knees or elbows for the first thirty years on the job. But in the last five, it had all caught up with him. He couldn't find a comfortable position to sleep in anymore and used alcohol and pills to knock himself out more and more. Helen warned him away from this, but everybody at the bus yard had the same problem and even told him which doctor would give him the most substantial hydrocodone prescription.

Now, Vernon was often in haze throughout the day, time flying by as it never had before, which he didn't really mind at first. He'd take the pills during the week and drop off during weekends or holidays. This led to such a violent reaction -- he'd go from moody to furious anger to straight-up pitch-dark depression in the course of a handful of hours -- that he decided to take a few pills on the weekend, too. When even they didn't do the trick, he supplemented with alcohol.

Only, he'd woken up that morning to find that not only had he forgotten to refill his prescription, he'd also exhausted his supply of booze. He figured he'd be able to shower, dress, eat breakfast, and get down to the bodega on the corner for a couple of tall boys before it did too much mental damage. In the short term, however, the pain the pills were actually designed to suppress raged through his muscles. There were short sharp shocks just below the surface on the top of his feet and through his hands. But in his lower back, it was a dull throb that had him bent over and grabbing the sides of the shower stall to keep steady.

He knew at least one thing that would make him feel better, but he also knew Helen would see right through him it if he tried to get her to join him in the shower. She'd make a crack about not wanting to get her hair wet, then go back to doing whatever she found to occupy her mornings now that the bank had cut her hours to almost nothing.

"Hey, Vernon!" came Helen's voice from the hall. "You'll never believe what was sitting on our doorstep just now."

Got me there, woman, Vernon thought.

Vernon figured she had him there.

Helen entered the bathroom. Through the frosted glass, her husband saw that she was walking what he took for a massive black dog of an indeterminate breed.

"What the hell is that?"

"I don't know," laughed Helen. "But he sure was hungry. Found him nosing through the trash bag I'd put out there earlier. I gave him a piece of chicken and he smiled from ear to ear."

Vernon opened the shower door a little and saw the dog. He couldn't tell what it was. Maybe a mastiff of some kind, but with the upper body musculature of a Brahma bull. Vernon figured, if the thing put its mind to it, it could knock him straight to the ground.

"You planning on keeping it?" Vernon asked.

"Oh, no," Helen replied. "I'm sure it belongs to somebody in the building. Just reminds me of my dad's dog from when we were kids. He babied that animal."

Vernon nodded and eyed the dog a moment longer. It looked back at Vernon the way a hungry man might regard a turkey dinner just out of reach.

V

Leonhardt and Garza climbed the stairs of Building 7 in silence. For Leonhardt, each step sent a shiver up his spine, particularly as they neared the floor of the shooting. When he'd gone up only a few hours before with the other emergency responders, there'd been a task at hand. He could allow himself to get caught up in the situation. Now, it was revisiting a scene from which all traces of the crime had been removed, relying on Leonhardt's memory to fill everything in.

That corner? That's where he'd seen the captain slumped over, his half-open mouth drooling blood through shattered teeth.

That doorway? Where one of the Nigerians was sitting with his throat ripped to hell, though whether it was from gunfire or the missing police dog had yet to be determined.

The ceiling? Where Leonhardt had ducked under a congealing pile of hot brains blasted out through an officer's forehead, sticky stalactites of blood, brains, and spinal fluid only just beginning to form.

All of this had been scrubbed away by whatever trauma scene cleaners were on retainer to the buildings once the location was released by law enforcement. Leonhardt was never less than amazed at the work of these outfits, which could turn even the most heinous of abattoirs into a livable space within hours of a bloodletting. Just another thing New York did well.

All that said, the one thing they never managed to fully disguise was the smell. Chemical cleaners mixed with blood, shit, sweat, and flesh had such a peculiar odor that even a ventilated space, which the sixth floor of Building 7 clearly was not, would reek for days after.

The two detectives broke the seal on Mrs. Fowler's apartment and let themselves in. Flipping on a light, the pair were hit with a new but no less familiar scent.

"Yeah, an old lady lived here, huh?" Garza snarked, glancing from the cherry-finish console television to the curio shelves lined with blown-glass animal figurines.

The wallpaper was red, gold, and decades out of fashion. The carpet in the living room was thick and brown with threads of more gold woven in. The carpet stopped at the kitchen where peeling yellow-brown linoleum with a fleur-de-lis design took over. Like the rest of the apartment, the kitchen and breakfast nook looked like something re-created from a Sears catalog circa 1973. Nothing appeared out of place.

Leonhardt found what he was looking for on the counter: a silk lingerie bag with a drawstring. He knew the crime scene guys had given Mrs. Fowler's apartment the once-over. But as it was a victim's residence, not an actual site of violence, he wasn't sure they paid as much attention. She wasn't considered a suspect, after all. The detective picked up the bag and put it to his nose.

"Shit, man, what're you doing?" Garza scowled.

Leonhardt held it out to him.

"Gun oil. You know these old ladies don't keep their guns in a holster on the door."

"The missing weapon?" Garza asked, walking over.

"Couldn't have set the scene easier if I'd done it myself."

"Case closed! The little old lady got scared, walked out, popped off a bunch of shots, but then got popped herself."

Leonhardt nodded idly. That might fit. But that's when he spotted the dish on the floor. He stooped and saw the slick red-brown residue of dog food.

"She have a dog?"

Garza shrugged.

"Neighbors didn't say anything about a dog."

Leonhardt opened the fridge and saw a half-empty can of dog food with a pink plastic lid on top of it. Moving to the cabinets, he searched through until he found a bag of dry food and a stack of cans of the same brand. The label on the bag suggested the food was "specifically designed to meet the nutritional demands of a dog" between 175-200 pounds.

"Big dog," Leonhardt remarked.

"Maybe it ran off with the police dog."

Leonhardt plucked his phone out of his pocket and dialed a number.

"This is Detective Leonhardt. Animal Control came in to the Neville Houses shooting, maybe get a dog out of apartment 632? Can you double-check and call me back at this number? Thanks."

Leonhardt hung up and sniffed the air.

"What is it?" Garza asked.

"If it had been locked up in here for any period of time, it probably would've relieved itself. I don't smell anything."

"I'm pretty sure this isn't the clue that's going to break the case, detective," Garza snarked. "Want to keep looking around?"

"Yeah," Leonhardt replied absently

He was trying to imagine how the diminutive Mrs. Fowler managed to go up and down the stairs every time her massive pet needed to use the yard without a single neighbor seeing her.

"In closing, the reason I admire Benjamin Franklin so much is because he invented so many things and was so smart and knew how to miti...miti..."

"Mitigate?" asked Mrs. Cosmatos.

"*Mitigate* the differences between so many different people. Thank you."

As April took her seat, Becca did nothing to hide the rolling of her eyes. She took it for granted that the other students got help from their parents on their homework, but when it was an oral report? Well, it lessened her esteem for Mrs. Cosmatos that she let April by with such an obvious fraud.

"Becca Baldwin."

Becca picked the handwritten page up from her desk, "A Historical Figure I Admire" written across the top, and headed for the front of the classroom. She looked down at April's desk and, sure enough, her Ben

Franklin report was typed and printed out. Easier to hide one's accomplices that way, Becca thought, smug in her belief in April's inability to write even a one-page report. There were two roads in to the Carver Academy. Your name was picked in a lottery for places. Or you knew somebody.

As April's mom was not only head of the school's parent-teacher association and tended to air-kiss and wave - and hug and flail and embrace and cry – upon running into any number of the administrators or faculty, Becca figured April for the latter category. Having been there the night her name was pulled out of a bingo cage, Becca knew where she stood.

"The historical figure I most admire is Gordon Parks. He was born in Kansas in 1912. He moved to New York during the Great Depression. He wanted to be a songwriter and sold some songs but none hit big. Then he became a photographer. This made him famous. He took many famous photos during the 1940s. He took pictures of women in dresses for *Vogue* magazine and news for *Life* magazine. He made friends with Malcolm X and was godfather to one of his kids. He then wrote a novel called *The Learning Tree*. It got famous. He then directed a movie out of it. After that, he made a famous movie called *Shaft*. He directed *Shaft* here in Harlem. He also wrote poetry. His son, Gordon Parks, Jr., made a movie in Harlem, too, called *Superfly*. His son died in a plane crash. The reason I admire Gordon Parks so much is because he never stopped doing new things and being good at them."

Becca smiled.

Two grades ago, she'd been introduced to Parks when a teacher gave her *The Learning Tree*. This had led her to read one of Parks's autobiographies, *A Choice of Weapons*. She didn't think she could admire anyone more than she did Gordon Parks. The fact that he'd lived and worked in Harlem throughout his life only made it better.

It was then that Becca noticed no one else was smiling. Mrs. Cosmatos had a concerned expression on her face. The rest of the class had taken their lead from her.

"Becca, we have a fairly sincere honor policy in this classroom that we've all agreed to uphold. This includes excessive help from one's parents or, in your case, guardians."

"I didn't have any help from anybody!"

Mrs. Cosmatos fixed a skeptical look on Becca.

"Becca? I may need to have a word with your older brother. You haven't seen these movies you mentioned, have you?"

"I haven't," Becca admitted. "But I've read about them. And my old teacher, Mr. Newton, said *Shaft* was great."

"But all the rest of it?"

"I read about it in books."

Someone snickered. *Books.*

Mrs. Cosmatos gave a smile of incredulity.

"It's just, all of what you're talking about here is just a little too advanced for someone your age. You really thought you'd get away with it?"

Now everyone in the class sat staring daggers of bemused accusation at Becca. The little girl had no recourse but to fold her arms and stare back.

"Really, Mrs. Cosmatos?" she began. "I mean, what the *fuck?* How are you gonna go and accuse me of that shit?"

Ken had only just fallen asleep when the telephone rang.

"Hello?" he mumbled, just catching it on the fifth ring.

"Mr. Baldwin, this is Mrs. Drucker, the principal at Becca's school. There's been an issue with Becca today that we thought we should address with her guardian."

Ken knew who Mrs. Drucker was. He sat up straight, prepared for the worst. It was only then that he noticed Bones curled up on the floor by the foot of the bed. The dog was eyeing him expectantly as if thinking he might soon get fed.

"Um...what'd she do?"

"She used the f-word on a teacher after being accused of having help on her homework assignment from you."

Ken closed his eyes again, wishing he back asleep. "What was the homework about?"

"Excuse me?"

"What homework? And I'll tell you if I helped her."

Mrs. Drucker paused as if unsure how to respond to his candor.

"An essay on a person from history that she admired. She selected Gordon Parks."

"Mrs. *Drucker*, is it?" Ken began. "What you need to come around to understanding is just how much smarter Becca is than me or her other brother, Trey. I don't mean a little smarter, either. I mean, she could come down to my job and tell the *foreman* what he's doing wrong. The cursing? That's all me and Trey. I will have another conversation with her about what to ignore from the ignorance she hears coming out of our mouths in this apartment. But second, I've never heard of Gordon Parks. You say that's a name, I think that's what they're renaming the dog track down in Riverhead, feel me?"

The other end of the line went silent. Ken wondered if he'd overdone it. Sure, he'd *heard* of Gordon Parks. Becca had told him all about the guy when she started working on the paper. But he wasn't about to give this woman the satisfaction.

Finally, Mrs. Drucker returned to the line as if having first consulted with others in the room about how to respond.

"The shooting of the police officers last night, this was your neighborhood?"

Ken had to resist the urge to challenge an educator about how she could form a sentence like that.

"Neighborhood, building, and *floor*. Worse, Becca was here alone when it happened. I work nights and her brother was running an errand."

More silence. When Mrs. Drucker finally replied, her entire sentence a sigh.

"Well, I guess we can agree that the stress of something that dramatic might have impacted her behavior today."

"That's probably my fault," Ken said. "I wanted to keep her home today, but she insisted. She was so excited to share her paper on Gordon Parks."

No such exchange had occurred, but Ken figured if he was in for a penny, he might as well be in for a pound. Besides, it was literally the least he could do to help Becca out of a tight spot.

"I'll let Mrs. Cosmatos know. Thank you for your help and your candor, Mr. Baldwin."

"No problem at all, Mrs. Drucker." Ken set the phone back on its charger and looked down at Bones. "Well, if I'm up, I'm up. Want to hit the yard?"

"When'd you get a dog?"

Trey was half a second from replying that he didn't have no fucking dog, when through his mid-morning haze of drugs and alcohol, he realized what Alvis must be looking at from his tenth-floor window.

"Oh, you got Ken down there with a shepherd?"

"Big dog. Looks like he could bite your dick off."

"Oh, yeah…it was Mrs. Fowler's. We don't know what to do with it, so we're just taking care of the thing until her next of kin show up to claim it."

"Holy shit, you stole a dead woman's dog? That's cold!"

Everybody in the apartment, six or seven of the fellas and a handful of their girls, chuckled a little. This included Janice Gaines, the new girl in the building who Trey was still trying to get next to even though it'd been three weeks since she started hanging out with his crew.

"No, we didn't steal it," Trey scowled. "The thing got out and was nosing around our door. Becca let it in and fed it."

"Likely story," Janice snorted.

"All right, you got me," Trey nodded. "Times is hard. We figured no one would come looking for the mutt, so we were going to fatten it up with all kinds of shit and sell it to one of them Vietnamese restaurants over on Grand Street."

This broke up the crew, Janice laughing the loudest. Trey beamed. He thought that might push things with Janice over the finish line. He'd find a minute later when they were alone to close the deal. It would be a good day.

There was a knock at the door. Everyone glanced around as if checking to see if company was expected. Alvis got to his feet and moved to the door, glancing through the peephole. He turned back to the crew, a big grin on his face.

"It's Mr. Lester. Should I let him in?"

More out of curiosity than neighborly friendship, a verdict was reached and the door opened.

"Hey, there, Mr. Lester. What can we do for you?"

"You bitches holding?" Vernon asked, his voice raspy and strained.

"Who are you calling bitch, asshole?" Alvis replied, half-joking.

Vernon grabbed him by his throat and lifted him straight off the ground a good foot and a half. Trey leaped to his feet. He knew Alvis had a gun in his waistband but also one under the couch. He went for the latter.

"Sit down, Trey, before I wring your neck, too," Vernon croaked. "Now, *bitches*, who's got what? I've got money, but I obviously don't have your attention."

No one knew what to do. This was a school bus driver. Nicest guy in the projects. One of those big guys who laughed like you figured Santa Claus would. Trey remembered a time that he'd slow his bus so a kid could catch up, only to earn a horn blast from a taxi. Mr. Lester had lowered his window, flipped the guy off, and cursed him like no one had ever heard before. It was the kind of thing that could've gotten him suspended, but not a kid told on him. It just made them respect him that much more.

Figuring it was up to him, Trey went to the coffee table, reached under, and pulled up a wooden box that was taped beneath it.

"You looking for something specific?" Trey asked, making himself a calm sea for Mr. Lester to gravitate towards.

"Pills," Vernon spat. "What you got?"

Trey held the box out to Mr. Lester as the big man lowered Alvis. Alvis shot Trey a dirty look as he straightened his collar. Mr. Lester picked through the box, plucked out three bags with about fifty pills all told, and tossed five $100 bills back into the box, ten times what the pills were worth.

"You want change, motherfucker?" Alvis asked, still smarting.

Mr. Lester fired the back of his hand so hard across Alvis's face that the young man flew backward before crumpling to the ground, knocked cold. Trey stared at Mr. Lester, figuring the only time he'd seen someone punch like that was in a boxing match.

The older man nodded to Trey, as if the blow to Alvis's face hadn't happened at all.

"Thanks, Trey."

Trey nodded, having no desire to earn a punch to the face himself. Mr. Lester exited, disappearing down the stairwell at the end of the hall.

"What the fuck?" one of the other guys, nicknamed Pluto, asked.

"I think we just made a shitload of money. When Alvis wakes up, we should go celebrate."

Everybody liked this idea. Trey caught Janice's eye, seeing that she approved of the way he'd handled himself. Not only that, she was doing nothing to hide the fact that her gaze was melting the clothes right off his body.

This *would* be a good day.

VI

The girl was dead over a bag of chips. Shot through the neck, she wore in blue jeans and sandals, a white tank top, a reminder that summer was around the corner. She'd recently polished her nails. Her hair looked as if that's what she'd spent most of the morning on. Maybe she was on her way to see someone when she decided they were not only good enough for a couple of hours in front of a mirror, but a bag of chips, too.

Well, she'll never know, thought Leonhardt as he stared down at her dead eyes.

"What do we think, fourteen? Fifteen?" Garza asked.

Leonhardt handed over the girl's pink Hello Kitty wallet, momentarily wondering if she'd boosted that, too.

"Fourteen!" Garza announced.

"Check your math," Leonhardt muttered.

Garza eyed the date on the school I.D. again and whistled. "Thirteen. Shit. Jury's going to murder him."

Leonhardt looked over at the old Korean man sitting at the back of the tiny convenience store. Two officers were waiting for an interpreter to arrive from the courthouse on 121st to take his statement, but Leonhardt didn't imagine he'd be saying much then, either.

"Nah, he'll walk," Leonhardt said. "He's paid up."

"What do you mean?" Garza asked.

"Look at him. He's doing exactly what he's been told to do. Is that a look of guilt? How about worry? That's minor frustration at *most*. He's more pissed about the sales walking past his closed front door than the corpse he's got on the floor. I'll bet when we pull the tapes...."

"If there are any tapes in the machines," Garza interjected.

"Oh, I'll wager you a ten-spot there are," Leonhardt retorted. "Bet that's the first thing he checks every day, down to the second. Probably got a grandson who does it digital, so there aren't any tapes, but easily transferable digital files. Anyway, we'll see the girl come in, look around, wait for him to look away, then stash a couple of chip bags in her backpack. He'll confront her, things will get nasty – does she look like the type to take shit to you? Especially from an old man in a rundown bodega."

Leonhardt moved to where he imagined the two players would've been standing when this happened.

"Nah, he asked to look in her backpack, she got nasty, he made a grab – not for her, but for his property – and she probably took a swing," Leonhardt continued. "He'll sell it on the tape. He felt threatened. And then he waits, skitters backward, and waits to feel threatened a second time. If she was smart, she'd back up and leave. But she took one step towards him. Now, he's scared for his life. He pulls the .38 out of his back pocket and fires a single shot. He's lying in a prone position on his back and, if necessary, can claim it was meant to be a warning. His high-priced lawyer will paint a very specific picture of a man fearing for his life, not knowing if this girl had a weapon. The jury will buy it as his weeping family will fill the galleys every day for this, their sole breadwinner. Even if he has no family, they'll be there."

Leonhardt caught the shopkeeper's eye and realized he was listening intently.

"Wait, how's he going to pay for a high-priced lawyer?" Garza asked.

"He pays money to the Triad for protection. See that symbol behind the cash register?"

Garza glanced over at a small triangle with three dots in it over a letter in Chinese script.

"That's for the Heaven and Earth Society, the *first* Triad from a helluva long time ago," Leonhardt continued. "If you recognize it and come up in here, you know not to fuck with this guy. If you're not and you pull something, well, he can act with impunity, knowing some of the best lawyers on the East Coast will back him."

"For five bucks or whatever they rake in from this?"

"Nah, for the five bucks they rake in from everyone else for proving that their protection is worth the percentage. Smart business model."

"Jeez," Garza scoffed, looking at the old man. "Thought protection meant they'd burn you out if you didn't pay."

"Gotta keep current with demand. If this is what the people can use, this is what you provide."

Leonhardt pretended he didn't see the black-toothed smile emerge on the old man's face.

The next one will *bring a gun and you'll be the one on the slab*, Leonhardt thought, hoping the look on his face would reflect this idea.

The old man's smile disappeared.

The radio of one of the patrolman squawked.

"Domestic violence call, Triborough Projects," said the dispatcher.

The patrolman hit the black button on the side of the shoulder mic. "Shouts or shots?" he asked.

"Sounds like a guy choking his wife," replied the dispatcher. "Neighbor's listening through the wall."

The location of the incident gave Leonhardt pause, but hearing the method sparked the detective into action.

"Let's go," he told Garza.

"Since when do we respond to domestic violence calls?"

"Humor me. I've got a hunch about this one."

The sensation of murdering his wife was downright orgasmic for Vernon long after Helen had slipped into unconsciousness. How different were her initial choking cries of alarm from those of ecstasy? Even the look on her face had been curiously similar. She closed her eyes, her mouth open with her lips arched at an odd angle like a fish gasping for breath or someone about to cough. Her body quaked, unable to control its movements anymore. She slapped at him, but in the same ineffective fashion as when he used to go down on her and would keep going even when she'd clearly had enough.

All that said, part of him felt ridiculous over the fact that all this had given him an erection. He'd never been into any kind of extreme sex. For this to be the way his body informed him that it just might like tripping down such a particular garden path was bizarre.

Whatever the case, he shoveled another handful of amphetamines into his mouth and swished them down his throat with a beer. He placed his hand back on his wife's throat and continued squeezing. He'd heard once that strangling someone didn't always lead to death. The person being strangled usually passed out from lack of oxygen to the brain and the person doing the strangling walked away, only to have the victim revive. Vernon was determined to stave off oxygen long enough for the brain to die.

His neighbor, Mr. Jeffcoat, had been beating on the wall for a good ten minutes, shouting about calling the police. It only stopped when he apparently went to make good on that threat.

It wasn't until the pounding on the front door that Vernon realized time was short.

"Police! Open this door!"

Vernon raised his wife's unconscious body over the faux marble kitchen counter and brought it down with such fury that it not only snapped her neck, it also tore her flesh, nearly decapitating her. He stared down at her engorged tongue as it lolled out of mouth and then headed into the living room.

The mastiff was just sitting there by the television, having watched the proceedings without apparent interest.

"Worth the wait?" Vernon grunted at it.

The dog didn't so much as turn its head, much less bark. Its eyes stayed fixed on Vernon as he made his way to the window, unlatched its locks, and shoved it upward.

"This is your last warning!" bellowed a voice from the other side of the door. "Open this door or we'll break it down."

"Fuck yourselves!" Vernon called out as he stepped onto the fire escape landing.

He'd tied the rope to the railing a little while before. In fact, that's what Helen had been sticking her nose into when he'd decided to go ahead and finish his business. He slipped it over his head and tightened it around his neck.

See you soon, bitch, he thought.

As his doorframe shattered under the weight of a handheld battering ram, Vernon climbed to the top of the railing and leaped off.

The murder-suicide of Vernon and Helen Lester changed things at Neville Houses. Becca felt it the second she had reached the block as she walked home from school. No one was out in the courtyard. People in the businesses across the street stared and pointed, letting each customer know what had brought all the police and emergency services vehicles to the buildings across the street.

Becca had heard about the deaths at school. One of the students had been in the office when the news came in and heard teachers talking about it. Word traveled fast, particularly since it related to someone that some of the students knew or had known.

For Becca, the Lesters were just two more recognizable faces in the building. Since she didn't go to P.S. 108 or P.S. 30, she'd never ridden one of Mr. Vernon's buses. Still, she was aware of him. The fact that he'd killed his wife before killing himself couldn't help but trouble her.

It was the dog, she thought.

She didn't know how the dog got to the Lesters or, really, anything about its m.o., but it had lived with Mrs. Fowler, and now she was dead. Without a master, the animal must've wandered away. Not even twenty-four hours later, more death.

As Becca approached Building 7, a handful of officers tried to block her path.

"I live up there," she said matter-of-factly.

"We'd like to call up and have one of your parents escort you to your apartment, if that's all right," the officer said.

"My brother's up there asleep," Becca explained tersely. "He works nights. I'd rather you didn't wake him up, as you sure did a lot of that last night."

The officer was taken aback. He wasn't sure how to respond to this. That's when Trey walked up from across the courtyard and grabbed Becca by the shoulders.

"I got this. She's my sister."

"You got *what*, Trey? You think I can't handle this?"

Trey rolled his eyes.

"Give it a rest for a second, Becca. Ken's up, just went for a walk. He called in. Doesn't want us home alone tonight."

"It's the *dog*!" Becca exclaimed. "They have to get that dog!"

"Okay, Becca, they get it. You're crazy. Let's go."

Trey had just begun pushing Becca towards the building's entrance when a voice boomed after them.

"What dog?"

The half-siblings turned as Detective Leonhardt hurried up to them. He glanced from Trey down to Becca, as if attempting to divine Becca's credibility.

"What dog?" he asked again.

"The big dog that's been making people crazy," Becca replied urgently. "Mrs. Fowler had it last."

"A dog?" Leonhardt asked.

"Yes, a dog," Becca replied, exasperated at being made to repeat herself. "You calling me a liar?"

"Ma'am, I certainly am not."

Becca straightened a little, clearly delighted to be called "ma'am."

"Can you describe the animal?" Leonhardt asked, popping out a pen and pad of paper.

"It's a big black dog," Becca began. "Biggest dog I've ever seen."

"Tall? Like a Great Dane? An Irish wolfhound, maybe? With long hair?"

"No, muscular. Short-haired. Like a bull. We've got a picture...."

Trey squeezed Becca's arm and she cut herself off. Leonhardt noticed but pretended like he didn't.

"You have a picture?"

"We saw one online that looked like it," Trey said.

"But you saved it? She said 'we've got.' That could be really helpful."

Trey stared back at Leonhardt, knowing the detective was sending him every kind of warning in the book with his word choice and body language.

Don't make me go Bad Cop on you and your sister.

Trey was about to reply when Becca chimed in.

"We'll check the computer if you want. I don't want to wake up my brother, but I could email it to you."

Leonhardt looked from Trey to Becca and back again. She'd bested him, as if knowing nary a judge in New York would give him a warrant to seize or search that computer. He sighed and pulled out a card, scribbling his email address on the back.

"We're just trying to figure out who did this."

"And I told you," Becca said, matter-of-factly. "It was the dog."

Ken hadn't intended to walk Bones very far, but it had been awhile since he'd walked anywhere. It just felt like a good way to clear his troubled mind. He'd headed towards the water, crossing Harlem River Drive, where he turned north. The RFK bridge was only a few blocks away, so he led the shepherd to the pedestrian walkway.

"There are a bunch of parks on the Randall's Island side," he told the dog.

As they crossed the bridge, Bones seemed thrilled to be away from the cramped buildings and out in the sunshine. He cantered along, nose in the air, taking in the smells of the East River.

"There's a lot of bad shit down there," Ken joked. "Be careful what you're inhaling."

When they got to the other side, they followed something Ken saw labeled as the Harlem River Pathway. Now they were directly opposite the neighborhood, though Ken couldn't see his own building.

"Good-looking dog," someone said.

Ken glanced over and saw a woman in a tight jogging outfit nodding at Bones.

"Yeah, but he works out like crazy, only eats organic. You know the type."

The woman laughed and sidled up to Ken.

"You live over there?"

"Yeah, just off Jefferson Park," Ken replied, giving a thought to lying, but not caring enough to do so.

"Oh, Jeez," she replied. "You around for the shooting last night?"

"Nah, that was a couple of buildings over," Ken lied, not looking for pity.

"That's crazy. All those cops."

"Yeah, I know. Everybody in the neighborhood is freaked out," Ken replied while looking for a way to change the subject. "Where do you live?"

"Sunnyside, but I work here on the island. I use my lunch to do some running."

"Cool, where do you work?"

She shot a thumb over her shoulder.

"Psych Hospital. I swear I'm not an escapee."

Ken laughed.

"Well, maybe we'll get lucky and send you a couple of patients after all this sorts itself out from last night."

"Good thing you've got that dog."

"Good thing. I'm Ken. Dog's name is Bones."

"Catherine. Well, Cathy. Nice to meet you."

"You, too. If I see any lunatics on the trail, I'll be sure to send them your way."

"Do that," Cathy laughed. "You know how you can tell which are the crazies?"

"How?"

"They just say they work at the Psych Hospital and swear they're not escapees."

Ken laughed and gave her a little wave as she continued on her jog. It felt good to flirt, a reminder that, some day, he just might put his hands on a woman again. His life hadn't allowed for much socializing of late.

"Good boy, Bones," he said, scratching between the dog's ears.

That's when he heard the distant sirens carrying across the river.

"Hah, can't have more mayhem back home, can we?"

But the shepherd just looked up him confusedly, as if giving voice to skepticism.

"Shit, you're right," Ken sighed. "Way things are going, probably means the whole building's on fire."

VII

Upon encountering the police still conducting interviews on the Lester case in front of the building, Ken led Bones around the block. He came up to Building 7 from the rear, taking the back stairs up to his apartment.

"Where'd you go?" Trey asked, sprawled out on the sofa next to Becca, watching television.

"Randall's Island," Ken replied. "Felt good to get out."

He went straight to his bedroom and, a moment later, Trey and Becca could hear him on the phone.

"It'd just be for a couple of nights," Ken was saying. "You have to understand how bad things are up here."

"Shit," groaned Trey. "Bet he called Aunt Marta."

Becca held her breath. Their "Aunt Marta" was really "Great Aunt Marta" down in East Orange. Their mother's aunt, they'd only met her a few times. That entire side of the family had functionally abandoned them years ago, down to the absence of Christmas cards, which took a couple of years to be noticed.

Becca remembered being in Aunt Marta's house only once. It was large and filled with grandkids when they were there, but what Becca remembered most was being made to feel like a stranger. She'd gone off to explore the upstairs, only to be corralled by an older cousin or uncle who chewed her out for going in whichever mothball-smelling guest room she'd made her way to. To make things worse, when he'd brought her downstairs, he made a big deal out of implying that he'd caught her about to steal something. That this wasn't true in the slightest did little to assuage either Becca's guilt or her mother's humiliation.

"I would not be calling if this wasn't a life or death emergency," Ken said. He was silent for a moment, but when he spoke again, his exasperation was on the rise. "Turn on your fucking television! It's all over it! Whole team shot up. That was outside our front fucking door! Yeah, I'm mad! You…"

Trey and Becca could hear the other line clicking off from across the room. Ken walked into the living room and threw the cordless phone at the front door.

"You trying to ship Becca to Aunt Marta's?" Trey asked.

"Trying to ship both of you," Ken replied. "You hear the press conference earlier? They had the goddamn mayor, all these cops and borough presidents, all talking about what a great tragedy it was and how our police are all heroes. But they were talking about it as if it was this one isolated thing, this crime that happened, but is over. Mr. Lester today? Nothing to do with it. Devaris the other night? Same thing. Totally unrelated."

"So, you believe me about this dog now, huh?" Becca said.

"I didn't say that, but it's something. Mrs. Fowler, Mr. Lester, Devaris, Mr. Preston, and that dog. We know it's connected. They just think it's a crazy man on drugs, an old lady who got confused, a kid who got high, and a drunk who accidentally burned out his throat with acid. And that's all that matters to them. The easy answer."

Becca looked over at Bones who was sunning himself by the window. As Ken went to get something from the fridge to abate his anger, she sat next to the shepherd and began stroking his fur.

"Where's the other dog, Bones?" Becca whispered. "That's what we've got to know. Where's the other dog?"

The shepherd, now awake, eyed Becca curiously as she spoke, but then flopped back down to enjoy his tummy rub.

The afternoon passed into evening and eventually, the police and other first-responders left Neville Houses. Becca watched from her bedroom window, thinking she might spy Detective Leonhardt, but coming up empty. Bones came in to sit with her. Despite having slept most of the afternoon, he promptly fell asleep in her room as well.

Ken had come by to check on her a couple of times but didn't say anything. She'd heard him leave around six and watched him walk across the street to grab food from the corner grocery. He'd said he was going to stay home that night from work, but the phone had rung just as he was coming back. Even through the closed door, Becca knew it was his shift foreman.

"I just can't," Ken said. "You know those guys are just out drinking or whoring. I have a real reason."

When Ken hung up a few minutes later after not saying much, Becca expected the knock on her door.

"Hey," said Ken, trying to sound nonchalant.

"I understand if you have to go in," Becca said. "I'll keep the doors locked and the police dog close."

"Nobody knows what's happening here. I need to know that I can trust you to stay in here and not go out. Trey's going to do what Trey's going to do, but it's you I'm worried about."

"I'll be fine. I'll stay right here."

Ken looked hard at her, unsure whether to believe her.

"Did you really tell a teacher to 'fuck off' today?"

"You heard, huh?"

"You can't really do that and get away with it," Ken said. "Adults are already going to know you're smarter than them, which is strike one. Strike two is when you let them know that *you* know. Doing what you did is strike three, rubbing their face in it."

Becca smiled, knowing a compliment when she heard it.

"I'll be better."

"Okay, good. I bought some different kinds of dog food when I picked up supper. See what he likes."

"Okay."

Ten minutes later, the front door closed as Ken headed out. Becca waited another ten before exiting her room to make sure Trey was gone. She found a bag of dry dog food and a couple of cans and opened all of it, pouring the mess into a large sauce pan for Bones.

"Eat up, boy. We've got a long night ahead of us."

"What was your name again?"

"Trey, sir. I'm a friend of your daughter's."

Janice's dad stared at Trey with something resembling suspicion, though he was obviously too new to Harlem to recognize that Trey's intentions were absolutely one-hundred-percent counter to what he might want for his daughter. Seventy-five-percent, maybe. Possibly as high as eighty-five-percent. But there seemed to be a part of him willing to give Trey the benefit of the doubt.

Maybe it was the "sir."

As Janice's dad stepped back to retrieve his daughter, Trey made a mental note to beat the head in of anyone who "sir"ed him when coming by to collect any little girl he might have in his future.

"Hey, Trey," Janice said, coming to the door.

She wore the tightest orange T-shirt he'd ever seen, matched only by her jeans. He saw that her father was uncomfortable with this, but didn't say a word. Then he got it. Janice was one of those daughters who could do no wrong in their daddy's eyes. Girls always had daddy issues, but he knew that this brought on minefields all their own.

"'Sup, Janice? You ready to go?"

She nodded as Mr. Gaines stepped forward.

"Don't be out too late."

Oh, okay, Dad, said Janice's eye roll.

Trey smiled at her with understanding. He wondered how she planned to wrap him around her little finger as tightly as her dad.

After the fifth drink, Leonhardt's head slid to the cushioned corner of the booth and stayed there. He knew he could move it if he wanted to, but it just felt like too much effort. Besides, his eyes were fixed on a fight poster from over a decade and a half prior – George Foreman versus Lou Savarese – with a Budweiser logo and the date of the bout under it. He didn't know why the bar kept it up, but imagined it had been a freebie at some point and there weren't any after it.

Staring at this meant he didn't have to look at the other cops in the bar, all grim-faced with black bands over the badges, or the televisions showing the mayor and police chief's press conferences from earlier in the day. No, he could simply stare at Foreman's hard eyes and the soon-to-be-clocked-out gaze of Savarese looking back at him.

He remembered the fight. Before the first bell, the cabler who aired it had run a bunch of footage of each boxer to hype up the audience at home. They showed Foreman cutting down trees with an axe and pulling a Jeep up a hill, great chains around his chest. When they cut to Savarese, he was talking about being a vegetarian and writing poetry.

It was as if they were setting the Italian-American fighter who'd won a pair of Golden Gloves championships in New York up for a fall against returning heavyweight Foreman, the guy they knew everyone in the country was cheering for. The fight itself had been a straightforward affair. Savarese would land a few quick combinations on the lumbering forty-eight-year-old Foreman and would get a single punch in return. Unlike Savarese's hits, which were seemingly absorbed without comment by Foreman's thick frame, the shots from the older boxer caused the younger man's head to jerk back with tremendous force, as if yanked by a cord. Leonhardt's opinion of Savarese improved over the course of the fight as he kept coming back for more punishment.

Foreman won the decision, making the fight Savarese's first professional loss. But it made Leonhardt a fan. He watched the fighter win a few over the next couple of years, including a knockout against Buster Douglas. But a few losses, including a first-round knockout from Tyson, paved the way to a career-ending loss to Holyfield.

But Foreman would only fight one more time after Savarese. In a quirk of fate, another Golden Gloves champ from New York, Shannon Briggs, would defeat Foreman as if avenging his fellow New Yorker's earlier loss.

Leonhardt stewed in these memories, getting lost in the names, the dates, and the faces. He didn't want to think about anything, so he stayed with this. He'd been married then to Kara and they were already talking about the kids they'd have, a boy and a girl, to be named Micah and Anne-Marie. Amazingly, it worked out exactly as Kara planned, only her kids ended up coming by another man. She'd kept the names, though, as if that had been the idea all along and Leonhardt was a footnote.

He momentarily wondered what they were all doing tonight, but then scrubbed that thought from his mind to return to boxing.

"Hey, Phil, you know how much PCP they found in Lester's stomach?" Detective Garza said, sliding onto the bench opposite his partner.

"Thirty-five pills. I mean, holy shit, right? He would've been dead within the hour if he hadn't hung himself out to dry."

Leonhardt's dull gaze traveled over to Garza as the younger detective's facial expression turned from excitement in his news to disappointment in his comrade.

"You're kidding me? A couple of bad days, and suddenly you're every cop cliché in the book? Come on, man. Get yourself together."

"They found the dog yet?"

"Really?" Garza asked. "That's where your head's at?"

"I know they didn't find the gun," Leonhardt drawled. He nodded in the direction of the televisions. "It'd be all over the news."

"Fine. Nope, no police dog. And they haven't put it out on the nightly news, either, because it might be too much of an embarrassment with everything else. Still, I thought it would bite somebody by now and we'd get a call."

"Nah," Leonhardt scoffed. "Enforcement dogs are more on point than any soldier you'll ever see. Unless it gets told to grab somebody, it's not going to. They're great animals."

Garza gaze Leonhardt a look he usually reserved for vagrants as they invented tales of woe.

"You're going to need to do better than that, detective."

"Why? You heard them on the TV. The case is practically closed. Guns go missing all the time. The good thing about this gun is that, for all the police around, it was a civilian weapon. It's time to mourn our losses and celebrate our heroes. Isn't there even some kind of memorial march in the offing?"

As he'd barely masked his sarcasm or lowered his voice, Leonhardt's last remark turned a couple of heads by the bar. Garza glanced over, raising a hand to avoid trouble, but then kicked Leonhardt under the table like a recalcitrant fourth-grader.

"You don't believe that's the end of this any more than I do. Just because you're focusing on dumb shit like a missing dog…"

"*Dogs.*"

"…*dogs*, whatever, you know something's fucked-up over there. So, while you're thinking pooches, I'm thinking drugs. Who sold them to Mr. Lester? We sure Mrs. Fowler wasn't taking something? I mean, there's nothing about what she did that suggests rational little old lady behavior. And you were pretty certain that that Devaris kid was holding the night he took a dive. What if he wasn't pushed? Maybe he thought he was a friggin' bird. Are you starting to feel me?"

Leonhardt finally raised his head, staring dully back at Garza.

"Good. Then I think we should wander over there and take a look, don't you?"

Leonhardt nodded.

"Give me a couple of minutes in the bathroom. Have a coffee and a Diet Coke waiting for me when I get back."

"Done."

Alvis's apartment was in one of his sister's names. Only, she didn't know about it. Alvis wasn't old enough to rent an apartment in New York, didn't have any kind of credit, no previous addresses, etc. What he had was cash. And as long as the rent ended up in an envelope pushed into the building manager's office slot within the first five days of every month, no one said a word about a sixteen-year-old with his own apartment.

Even better, given the business Alvis conducted out of said apartment, his neighbors knew better than to complain about the drug dealer in Building 8. Returning the favor, Alvis's crew kept the buyers out of the building and, for the most part, kept the halls and stairwells crime-free. This was his territory and to rob or steal on it meant answering to him and his guys.

So, no one did.

The apartment itself was a kind of clubhouse-cum-crash pad for the crew. For the most part, they had other beds to go home to. But if they needed a place to stay or just wanted to keep hanging out, there were showers, beds, and food at Alvis's.

What it was used the most for, however, was sex.

"Oh, Trey, *goddamn*," Janice moaned as Trey went down on her.

It wasn't like she asked, but as soon as they had started making out, it was clear she needed some convincing. She'd been so surprised when he'd stripped off her pants that he was between her thighs, plucking aside her panties, before she could push him away.

By then, she was well on her way to her first orgasm of the evening.

The door was locked, but that didn't keep would-be onlookers from walking slowly as they passed on their way to the bathroom. For the most part, the crew respected the privacy of whoever might be screwing in one of the bedrooms. There had been one girl, whose name Trey had long forgotten, who wanted to take on the whole crew at once. This sounded like an interesting proposition at the time, but after the first two, they all decided the girl was crazy and kicked her out.

But tonight, Janice would be all his for as long as he wanted. With all the stress of the day on his shoulders, he planned on enjoying himself.

"Ah, Trey…right there…holy *shit*…"

Back in the Baldwin apartment, Becca was getting ready to head to bed. As much as she wanted to go all Jupiter Jones and the Three Investigators on the building, she knew how much trouble she'd be in if Ken found out. So, she locked the door, made popcorn, and watched television long after she normally would.

She was just padding back to her room, the shepherd trailing behind, when she felt the dog go absolutely still. His ears shot straight up and his nose was aimed towards the front door.

"What is it, Bones?"

In response, the shepherd whipped around and scrambled back to the kitchen. Watching him jam his nose at the bottom of the door and tear at the floor with his claws, Becca thought he was about to try to dig under it.

But that's when he got antsy. He pranced around, whining to get Becca's attention.

"What?" she asked quietly.

Someone pounded on the door, almost scaring Becca out of her skin.

"Hey! Trey in there?"

The voice of Alvis caused Becca to shudder. She tolerated most of Trey's friends, but actively disliked their ringleader. Trey had always liked to get high, but Alvis was the one who got him into dealing.

"He's not home!" Becca called out.

"You sure?" Alvis asked, not without menace.

"Yeah, I'm sure!" Becca spit back. "But I ain't letting you in to check."

There was a long silence. Bones continued to bounce around, obviously having picked up the scent of something that bothered him.

"Tell him to come find me," Alvis finally barked back. "Got it?"

"I got it," Becca replied, sounding as cowed as she felt.

She heard Alvis shuffle away. Bones continued to whine. He jammed his nose as hard as he could under the door, inhaling deep.

"You gonna take all day?" Alvis said, his voice distant now as he was calling from down the hall.

That's when Becca heard a guttural *woof* coming from the other side of the door. She ran across the room and slid down onto her stomach. Pushing Bones aside, she saw the black snout of the massive devil dog from the night before. It had been sniffing around a little, but now, in picking up her scent, inhaled long and deep.

A growl came next, deep and threatening, an animal ready to fight. It was only as she backed away from the door that she realized the sound was coming from Bones.

VIII

"Lord, that felt good," Janice said, settling back onto the pillow. "Who taught you how to fuck like that? You watch a lot of porn or something?"

"Maybe I just like pleasing women," Trey replied, trying not to sound smug.

"Ah, Mommy issues. Mother didn't love you enough, so you've got to go out and please women to feel good about yourself?"

Trey laughed, but a little too bitterly. Janice smiled.

"Don't worry. Mama will take good care of you, baby."

She put her arms around his chest and pulled his head down to her sweat-covered breasts.

Lord, get me out of here, Trey thought.

His thoughts were interrupted by the sound of someone screaming down in the courtyard.

"Did you hear that?" Janice asked, sitting straight up.

"The scream?"

"No, the gunshots!"

Trey then realized he had, but hadn't thought a thing about them. Two more shots followed. Trey raced to the window, carefully pulling aside the sheet that had long covered it. He didn't see a shooter, but several people across the street were scrambling for cover while pointing at the building Trey was in, Building 9.

That's when he realized the gun's report was familiar. *Very* familiar.

"Shit, where's Alvis?"

Becca had waited a few minutes before exiting the apartment with Bones in tow. She glanced up and down the dimly lit hallway, but saw no one. More than a little terrified, she shoved the German shepherd out first, though she kept his leash wrapped tightly around her right hand.

"Follow him."

Bones didn't have to be told twice. He moved quickly down the hallway towards the stairwell, half-dragging Becca behind him. His nose was moving fast, sniffing every square inch of floor as he strained at the leash. By the time they reached the stairs, he was ready to gallop.

"Slow *down!*" Becca commanded.

The shepherd half-listened.

A moment later, and they were in the lobby. Becca wasn't sure if Alvis had exited or maybe gone down to the subbasement. When she tried to angle Bones around to the stairs leading under the building, however, the shepherd pulled her to the front door.

"Are you sure?"

The dog was clearly certain. Whatever trail he had picked up on the sixth floor continued out into the courtyard.

"All right," acknowledged Becca, eyeing the darkness beyond the lobby doors with trepidation.

The passage of a few hours hadn't convinced anyone in Neville Houses that stepping outside was a good idea. For the most part, the scrubby network of courtyards between buildings was empty. As she eyed the shadow-cloaked corners, Becca tried to imagine what would happen if she was attacked. Would Bones, free of the leash, charge on down the trail? Or would he defend her?

She hoped she wouldn't have to find out.

The trail wove around a little, but soon it was clear that it led into Building 9. Becca realized this made sense, as this was where Alvis lived.

Duh.

But as they moved up the steps to the Building 9 lobby, Becca slowed. She was suddenly unsure of the plan. If they cornered Alvis somewhere, was she going to try and talk it out with the drug dealer? Warn him about the dog? What if he was already lost in the dog's thrall the way Mrs. Fowler or Mr. Lester had been?

Couldn't this end badly and *quick*?

Bones obviously wasn't taking any of this into consideration as he plowed ahead to the stairs. Becca thought this odd, since the elevator worked in this building.

Unless he's being led by the dog, Becca thought. *What do dogs know of elevators?*

With this strange thought in mind, the little girl followed the shepherd up the first couple of stairs. Taking the steps two at a time, she made good progress. Becca had just stopped to take a breather on the fifth-floor landing when she heard muffled gunshots from above followed by a distant scream.

She reached into the back of her pants and touched Mrs. Fowler's pistol. She didn't even know why she brought it. Without bullets, she could do little more than threaten. All the same, it made her feel safer.

"Shots fired, rooftop of Neville Houses on 111th."

Leonhardt grabbed the radio mic.

"Which building?"

"Building 9," replied the dispatcher.

"We're en route."

Leonhardt glanced at Garza, sobered.

"Pretty sure we're going to have to call the CDC and quarantine the whole block after this."

"Think some dealer decided to lace a whole batch of everybody's regular order with PCP or something? Somebody's idea of a joke?"

"If that's what's going on here, I'll be thrilled. *That*, we can contain. *That*, we know how to handle. So I'm hoping to hell you're right."

Garza didn't say anything as Leonhardt hit the gas, accelerating through a red light with the siren roaring, only three blocks to go.

Trey hurried through the apartment, seeing only Pluto smoking out in front of the television.

"You hear those shots?" Pluto asked, as if needing confirmation due to his altered state.

"Yeah, it's up on the roof!" Trey said.

"Oh, shit," Pluto grunted. "We know anybody with a beef?"

"No, but he's just shooting into the street. Anybody that walks by."

"Oh, *shit*," Pluto said again with even less emphasis than before.

Trey pulled the pistol from under Alvis's couch, checked the clip, and chambered the first round. Janice, having hurriedly gotten dressed, saw the gun and blanched.

"You're not going up there."

"Somebody's got to stop 'em."

Trey swung open the door in time to see something hurry past on the stairs. He barely glimpsed his half-sister, but knew it was her and their newly adopted police dog.

"Becca!" he yelled.

But she was already gone.

Alvis was annoyed. He'd imagined there'd be any number of passersby on the street below for him to shoot. But after unloading his first clip at a group of teenage girls on the corner, hitting none, he didn't see a soul. He heard the sirens of the approaching squad cars and knew his time was almost up.

"Fuck!" he yelled, then again. "FUCK!"

Then he had an idea. He aimed his gun at nearby Building 3 and started shooting out the windows on the higher floors. The pistol had impressive range, but it was near impossible to aim all the way to the street. But when shooting at the nearby building, he found himself nailing the windows down his sights.

A male voice screamed in agony, its owner struck by a bullet.

"Ha ha!" bellowed Alvis.

He emptied the gun and popped in a third magazine. He had just pulled back the slide when he heard the door to the roof swing open. He whirled around, ready to fire, but no one was there.

"Who's that?" he barked.

No one replied.

He stepped forward, holding the gun out in front of him.

"You'd better show yourself. Or hell, maybe I'll just start shooting."

He didn't even wait half a second before doing just that. Yanking back the trigger, he peppered the upper stairwell with sparks as bullets ricocheted off the door and wall. Unfortunately, the sparks and the muzzle flash only served to illuminate the fact that no one, in fact, was there hiding just within the shadows.

In any other circumstance, he would've had the presence of mind to count the bullets, leaving himself one in the chamber when switching out the magazine in case that was precisely what someone else was waiting on. But he was too addled this time, in too much of a hurry.

Instead, he simply dropped the empty clip as fast as he could and reached for another one from his pocket in the same motion. He was about to slam it home when a truly ferocious-looking German shepherd launched itself from the stairwell, jaws open and aimed at his throat.

"Fuc…"

He hadn't even finished the word before something much larger and faster than the shepherd intercepted the smaller animal in mid-flight. The two animals tumbled halfway across the roof before Bones smacked his skull on the short edge wall. Rolling over, he leaped to his feet, only to find himself face to face with the massive black dog that had so recently been sniffing around his doorstep.

The mastiff growled at Bones with such anger that the shepherd took a step back. The massive animal sounded more like a heavy tank rumbling over rough ground than anything that shared any kind of genetic common ground with Bones.

"Bones! Get him!"

Bones and Alvis both turned to the rooftop landing as Becca appeared. Alvis aimed his gun at the little girl, prompting Bones to launch himself at the young man. His jaws bit down into his arm in time to cause the drug dealer's first shot go wide. But while Bones tore into the young man's flesh, the black dog clamped his own teeth into the shepherd's right flank.

Bones whipped around, gnashing his newly bloodstained teeth at the monstrous black dog. Rather than engage the shepherd, the animal kept his teeth buried in Bones's meaty haunch. Blood flowed freely from several jagged punctures in the smaller dog's leg, turning his fur a deep red.

Alvis, meanwhile, was holding his savaged arm and yowling in pain. Through his anguish, he caught sight of Becca and raised the gun. She managed to duck away before he fired, but he pulled the trigger anyway.The bullet ricocheted off the stairwell ceiling.Alvis heard a dull groan.

He stepped over to the landing and looked down. In the dull light, he saw a body lying on the steps below, bleeding from the head.

Back on the roof, Bones continued to fight. Though limping, the shepherd managed to stay away from the larger animal's lumbering attempts to tear the flesh away from Bones's stomach. The shepherd attempted a few quick bites at his opponent's throat, but even when he connected for an instant, the flesh was too thick to penetrate.

It was like biting into a tightly wound rope.

But then the black dog batted Bones aside. His claws scratched at the shepherd's snout, drawing blood even then. Bones skittered backward, shaking his head like a fighter trying to clear his mind, the bell to end the round still too far away.

Before the shepherd could leap back into action, however, the black dog cocked its head at the sound of the arriving sirens. It then turned back to Bones, growling with tremendous violence. Bones, never one to back down, did so now. The shepherd moved back three steps to allow the larger canine a clear path to exit.

As the dog reached the stairs, it fixed its gaze on Bones one last time before disappearing into the shadows.

Trey didn't know what happened. He'd climbed up the stairs as fast as he could, the gun feeling light in his hand. He didn't understand what Becca was doing in Building 9, much less with Bones, and less than that, running towards the sound of gunfire.

"Becca! Hold up! Where are you going?!"

There was no response, only the sound of more footsteps. A few more flights, and Trey was downright winded. He slowed, grabbing the rail to propel himself higher. When he heard the flurry of gunshots flying into the stairwell landing above, he felt weightless, all the breath sucked out of his lungs at once. It wasn't until a second later, when he heard Becca command the police dog to attack, that he breathed normally again.

He kept going up the stairs, ready for anything as he reached the last flight to the roof. Though he still couldn't see Becca, he could now clearly hear the sound of the dog fight, followed, seconds later, by the screams of someone he recognized as Alvis.

"Is that Alvis?"

Trey turned in time to see Janice coming up the stairs behind him. Before he could answer, there was another shot and a spark he caught in his peripheral vision. Then he saw Janice's eyes go blank as she slumped to the floor. She hadn't made a sound, but as soon as he reached her, his fingers found the blood pouring from the side of her head.

IX

As Alvis moved into the stairwell, Becca realized that he hadn't seen her pressed up against the wall only a few steps down. She was trying to will herself invisible, and it seemed to be working. That's when she realized that Alvis was staring at something below her. She tried to see what it was, but was too afraid.

Something pushed into her, and she felt hot breath on her arm. Twisting her head, she saw the monstrous black dog, its snout inches from her face. Even with its mouth closed, she could see its canines poking out over its lower jaw. Its eyes were a wet black, as if ready to ooze out of the monster's skull. It licked its chops, a pink tongue splashing out like a snake's, thrilling at the opportunity to taste Becca's flesh.

But then it was gone.

Becca didn't dare turn her head as the dog trotted down the stairs.

"Aw, fuck, Trey," came Alvis's voice through the dark. "I didn't know you guys were down there."

At the mention of her brother, Becca's head jerked downward, and she spied Trey sitting on the steps below her. Cradled in his arms was the dead body of a girl she didn't recognize.

Alvis stepped past Becca, idly checking his gun.

"You at least get to bang her first?"

He'd made this remark in jest. Becca could tell that much from the lilt in his voice.

In response, Trey raised the gun he'd pulled from Alvis's couch, aimed it at its owner's face, and pulled the trigger once. The gunshot echoed down the stairwell even as Alvis's body was thrown backward, his head striking the wall before sliding down to the steps next to Becca. It was as if he'd finally seen her there and decided to settle in for a chat.

Becca found herself screaming at the top of her lungs.

Everything happened quickly after that.

The police arrived and swept through Building 9, finding Becca and Trey still in the stairwell next to the bodies of Janice and Alvis. They made the two survivors get on their knees, interlacing their fingers behind their heads. Becca had forgotten all about Mrs. Fowler's gun in her waistband until one of the policemen took it out, placing it on a step above her where she could easily see it.

The cops had deduced what happened and were going easy on the pair. Paramedics arrived, but it was clear neither of the victims could be revived. Janice was taken down first.

The residents of Building 9 had stayed behind closed doors during the shooting, but as soon as police were heard on the stairwells, they moved out into the halls to get a look. Janice was covered by a yellow sheet, but just enough residents had glimpsed her chasing after Trey to spread the word that she was one of the victims. By the time the body had been carried all the way to the ground floor, her father was waiting in the lobby to see if the rumors were true. When he saw it was his baby girl, he started screaming and wailing as if something sharp and terrible had begun spinning its way through his guts.

"I'll take this."

Becca turned and saw Detective Leonhardt coming up the steps towards her. For some reason, his appearance caused her to burst into tears, a truant child caught. Leonhardt already knew that they'd found his business card in her pocket with the gun, but wasn't sure if this made it better or worse.

She'd clearly considered calling him before going on this misadventure, but he hadn't made a strong enough impression for her to follow through.

"You okay?" Leonhardt asked, putting his arm around Becca as he offered her a handkerchief.

She nodded unconvincingly and they sat in silence for a moment.

"What're they going to do to my dog?" she finally asked.

"What dog?"

At that moment, shouts were heard from above followed by savage barking. Leonhardt looked up in alarm as several patrolmen hurried back onto the landing from the roof.

"There's a pissed-off dog up there!" one of the patrolman called down. "Looks hurt!"

Leonhardt eyed Becca.

"*Your* dog?"

"He saved me. You want the *other* dog."

Other dog, Leonhardt thought, reminding himself again that parenting a preteen girl was no one's idea of an easy time.

When the officers brought Trey down in handcuffs, Janice's father lunged for his throat. Rather than fight back, Trey allowed himself to be manhandled for a moment before the officers tore the grieving man off him. Just as Mr. Gaines made another attempt, Detective Garza stepped forward and calmly placed a hand on the fellow's chest.

"He didn't kill your daughter."

For a moment, Gaines looked confused. But then he saw that the guilt in Trey's eyes wasn't over Janice's death, but putting her in harm's way in the first place.

"Who killed her?" Mr. Gaines barked.

Garza shot a thumb over his shoulder to the stairs.

"Should be coming down any minute."

Janice's father eyed Trey one last time before the patrolmen led him outside.

Though a couple of officers wanted to shoot the German shepherd, Animal Control arrived shortly after Alvis's body was carried out of the building and took over. Despite having lost a significant amount of blood, Bones continued snapping at anyone who got close, including the men trying to slip the lasso over his neck. When they missed, the emboldened shepherd clambered to his feet as best he could and got in a fighting stance.

Rather than challenge the animal, the control officers deferred to a K9 unit trainer who booked it over from Garden City to handle the situation. Rather than a leash or prod, the trainer brought only a single tool: an old worn-out tennis ball. He sat cross-legged next to the door for a moment as the wounded shepherd backed away. After a few minutes, he got to his feet and, very animatedly, began waving the ball as if playing with his own pet in the park.

Without thinking, Bones got to his feet and began tracking the movements with his snout. For a moment, he was a different dog. The trainer gently bounced the ball over to the shepherd and, after a moment, it was returned. The trainer repeated this three times before calling for someone to bring water. A bowl was brought up and a bottle emptied into it. It took a few more minutes before Bones would take a drink, but by then, the trainer was already addressing him by name and stroking his fur.

When the trainer slipped a harness over the animal's neck, Bones barely seemed to notice. Still later, the shepherd was gently sedated and trucked off to a nearby emergency veterinary clinic in midtown utilized by the NYPD. New Yorkers seeing the police escort for an ambulance tearing down Broadway might've imagined a visiting dignitary had a heart attack or, worse, an officer had been struck down in the line of duty. After a fashion, this was precisely what had happened, but most would've been surprised to know what was lying on the stretcher inside.

"He'd lost some blood and we had to stitch him in a couple of places, but other than that, he was in pretty good shape."

Leonhardt smiled across his desk to Becca and gave her a thumb's-up. Though this answered her most repeated question of the past two hours, it didn't change the solemn expression on her face.

"You figure out what made the scratches?" Leonhardt asked.

"Likely another canine," the veterinarian reported. "Much, *much* larger than this animal. Anybody report seeing anything like that out there?"

Leonhardt looked over at Becca. She eyed the detective as if she could hear every word of his conversation.

"Nah, no one mentioned another dog," he said flatly, meeting Becca's gaze. "But everything went down before we got there. We'll ask around."

"You might want to. It might be somebody's pet, but it's clearly dangerous. If it's just some feral animal, it could get at some kid."

"I owe you one," Leonhardt added, though he didn't worry the vet would ever have any reason to collect. Hanging up, he turned back to Becca. "Bones is going to be fine. Did you know he's considered one of the best police dogs on the East Coast? You rescued a real hero."

Becca's eyes twitched at "rescue." Leonhardt took a deep breath.

"That's how I've decided to characterize your detention of the German shepherd," Leonhardt explained. "You knew it was police property, didn't you?"

Becca shrugged.

"Correct answer."

There was a moment of silence, the pair still trying to feel each other out. Just as Leonhardt was about to give up on the idea of getting anything out of the little girl, Becca spoke up.

"How much trouble is Trey in?"

"Some," Leonhardt admitted. "Depends on whose weapon that was. At the end of the day, though, he shot a man who had been firing willy-nilly into the street and other buildings, wounding a man through a window and then killing the girl in the stairwell."

Leonhardt's eyes flitted upward as he saw a severe-looking woman walk into the detectives' bullpen, only to be directed his way. Social services.

"If I'm the District Attorney's office, I'd plan to go pretty easy on the kid if I didn't want to get hung out to dry by the press."

"Can I talk to him?"

Leonhardt glanced up at the woman making a beeline for his desk.

"That might be complicated."

"What if I tell you everything you want to know about the dog?"

Leonhardt raised an eyebrow.

The negotiations between the woman from social services and Leonhardt were brief, tense, and eventually involved Becca inviting the woman to go to hell. As Leonhardt took Becca back to the interrogation room, the social worker took to her cell phone to hunt down her superior, Leonhardt's superior, or Becca's older brother.

As soon as they had settled into their chairs, Leonhardt opened his hands.

"The dog."

"Trey?"

"We've got a few minutes. But he's on his way, if that's what you're asking."

"It's a big black dog, but not like any I've seen before. His body looks like a big bulldog and his face looks like a normal ol' dog."

"Like the police dog?"

"Like Bones, yeah. Long nose."

"Snout."

"*Snout.*"

"You said you had a picture of him."

Becca looked down at her hands.

"The police dog had a camera on him when all the cops got shot."

"You *have* the camera?"

Becca nodded. It took all of Leonhardt's self-control not to exit the room and go to retrieve the camera immediately.

Get what you can from the girl, he told himself.

"What's the dog doing on the camera?"

"Watching. The police rush in, everybody starts shooting, Mrs. Fowler comes out and starts shooting, and the dog just watches."

"From the doorway?"

"I guess. It's just strange. The camera on Bones bounces up and down. He's fighting and running. This dog just stands still like nothing's happening. It's so weird-looking."

"What happens then?"

"Once everybody was dead, the dog just kind of walked away. Then, last night, he and Alvis came back around my apartment. It was sniffing under the door."

Leonhardt was cringing. That a girl this young could talk so easily about such grim, horrific violence was something he found unsettling.

"And it was on the roof with Alvis just now?"

"Yep, same dog. It attacked Bones."

"And before that?"

"Same thing. Just watching Alvis shoot, calm as you please."

Calm as you please. The girl sounded like Leonhardt's grandmother.

"And then it left again?"

"Walked past me on the stairs," Becca said, her demeanor shifting enough to tell Leonhardt this wasn't the whole truth. "I don't know where it went."

"Had you seen it before the shooting in your hallway?"

"Yeah. It was with Mr. Preston before he died and then was with Mrs. Fowler when she went crazy. It gets next to people and makes them kill."

"Who's Preston?"

"The first one. You guys just thought it was a suicide. The dog drove him to do it like it did Mr. Lester."

Leonhardt wasn't ready for this assessment, but pressed on.

"You think Mrs. Fowler killed Devaris Clark?"

"I know she did."

"But why?"

"Because the dog told her to."

There was a knock on the door and Leonhardt went to answer it.

"Got Trey," Garza said when he saw Leonhardt.

"You stay with them, but give the time they want," Leonhardt said quietly. "She earned it."

"What do you mean?"

"I'll fill you in later. I've got to get back to East Harlem."

They hadn't told anybody about the shoeprint in Devaris Clark's blood. The idea that anyone else had been involved hadn't leaked. The story was that he'd gotten high and fell. That was it.

That there had been a shoeprint. That a witness had seen Devaris flying up the steps. That the time between Devaris's interaction with the detectives and the first call about the body on the pavement left him no time whatsoever to have smoked out.

All of this had been held back from the press.

For his own peace of mind, Leonhardt had run the math a few times. The only way Devaris could've hit the ground at his time of death was if he left the detectives, ran back to the building, ran up the steps, and immediately ran off the edge. He might've slowed down for some of it, but it happened so quickly that the detective had actually wondered if somebody who had seen him and Garza stop the young man might imagine they had a hand in his death.

When Leonhardt entered the apartment of Mrs. Fowler for the second time in twelve hours, he didn't even bother turning on a light. He walked straight through her living room to the bedroom which smelled of rosewater and mothballs. He turned on the light in her closet and began going through her shoes. All were orthopedics, whether slippers, tennis shoes, or nurse's shoes, but none matched the printout he had brought of the partial shoeprint.

The apartment was so meticulous that he worried the shoes could only have been in the closet or on her feet during her last moments. If that was the case, the amount of bullshitting he'd have to do to get at them might be significant.

But then he realized that, if what Becca had said was true, Mrs. Fowler might not have been herself lately. So he moved into her bedroom and began looking around for the shoes there.

Then he saw them. They were beige with a slight quarter-inch lift from faux wooden heels. She hadn't even bothered to clean them. The blood stain matched the one in the print-out exactly.

Leonhardt sat down on the floor and stared at the wall. The ramifications of the discovery washed over him. They were planning to search Mrs. Fowler's apartment for PCP they could trace to Alvis's apartment. They'd already found a match there for what had been found in Mr. Lester's stomach. It would've made this one easy.

But now he was on telepathic dog duty. A dog that told people to kill.

That's when something rang a bell way in the back of his mind. It was an old memory and took some time to excavate, but after a minute or two, he had a name.

Harvey.

X

"Where's Ken?"

"Don't know. They said they were calling him. He's supposed to pick me up."

Trey nodded. He glanced up at Garza but then stared deep into Becca's eyes.

"You know what's going on in there. You *need* to communicate that to Ken. When you get home, you've got to throw some shit in a backpack and get the fuck out of Dodge. You walk in, you walk out. Got it?"

"Yeah."

"I don't mean to rain on your parade here, but she's going to need to stay in the area in case we need to question her," Garza interjected.

Trey regarded Garza for a moment before turning back to Becca.

"No. You're not listening to that guy. If you're not under arrest, they can't make you stay. You get the fuck out of here. Understood?"

"Hey!" Garza interjected. "You want us to put some kind of other charge on you?"

"Knock yourself out, dickhead," Trey said without looking. "You know how many people have died in my building the past few days? The numbers aren't great. You want to throw another charge on me? That just means I'm safely locked up out here away from all that for a couple more days. Not the case with my sister or brother, got it?"

Becca tried to hide a smile. It wasn't that Trey was defending her as much as him calling her his "sister" without qualifying it with some verbiage about "half-" or her having a different mom.

Garza considered a response, but then bit his tongue. Trey turned back to Becca, lowering his voice.

"There are going to be a lot of opinions about what you did. For me, I think it was pretty brave. I know you were scared, I know you weren't sure about what you were doing, but what you did know was that something bad was going to go down and you walked out the front door to do something about it. I don't care if you're nine or ninety, that's a rare thing in a person. I'm proud of you."

Becca had tears in her eyes as Trey reached out to touch her arm.

"Was that your girlfriend?" she asked.

"She might've been one day," Trey replied with what he thought a decent man would say in that situation. "She was pretty special. I think you would've liked her."

"I'm sorry."

"So am I. But that's on Alvis. I don't want you thinking about it twice, okay?"

"Okay," Becca said quietly.

Trey tightened his grip on her arm as she wept more freely.

Ken arrived a few hours later to find Becca asleep on a bench. His manager had given him shit about leaving him in a lurch, so Ken had quit on the spot and gone back home in the mistaken belief that Becca was home. He'd received several messages about the incident, but information about Trey's arrest hadn't been a part of it. The young man was in agreement with his younger brother, however, that the answer was to leave. He'd cashed out some savings and called a coworker about borrowing his SUV. By the time he got to the police station, he'd already called a hotel down in Ocean City on the Jersey Shore and booked a pair of rooms.

"I thought you might want some time to yourself," he explained to Becca, who was indeed grateful for his thoughtfulness.

Like Becca, Ken was allowed in to see Trey, but for a shorter amount of time. Trey told Ken exactly what happened. When Ken nodded to Garza, particularly when Trey mentioned running to get the gun from Alvis's couch, Trey shrugged.

"I appreciate you thinking I'm smart enough to come up with a good lie to get me out of here, but I'm stuck. The truth is probably the only thing I've got going for me."

Ken couldn't help but agree.

"You have enough money for the week?"

"It'll be tight, but yeah. You have some big stash I don't know about?"

"My cut of the money from selling Mr. Lester those pills," Trey offered.

Garza grunted from the corner of the room.

"Don't push it, kid."

Ken sighed.

"Do me a favor and call my phone every chance you get," the older of the brothers requested. "When you find out when you're getting out, call me. We'll be here to pick you up."

"I don't know what kind of bail they're going to set."

"We'll raise it. We're family. We're all we've got. Okay?"

"Okay."

The brothers embraced. A moment later, Ken collected Becca, signed a stack of papers presented to him by a new and less irate social services worker, and carried the tired little girl out to the car.

By sunrise, they were southbound on the Jersey Turnpike.

Two hours later, asleep in adjoining rooms two blocks from the beach.

"Morning, officer. We haven't met. I'm Detective Phil Leonhardt, NYPD."

Leonhardt extended his hand. Bones eyed the offering for a moment from behind the chain-link gate of his narrow concrete kennel, but then leaned forward and gave it a sniff.

"I know you're accustomed to being on the enforcement side of things, but you've become a witness on this case. Means that you might be pressed into service before you get to fully recover."

Leonhardt reached into a duffel bag he'd brought into the kennel with him. He extracted evidence bags, opening each and placing the contents on the floor in front of Bones.

"These were taken from the apartments of Mrs. Fowler and Mr. Lester," he explained, setting out two impromptu dog dishes as well as towels and blankets he'd collected off their respective floors. "I've always been told that I had a good nose, but yours is supposed to be legendary. Well, I need you to use it now."

Bones sniffed the items through the gate and became excited. Leonhardt had been told the shepherd would still be groggy from being put under the night before, but it was clear something to do with the items had gotten the animal's attention.

"Yeah, you know that smell, huh?" Leonhardt grinned. "They say there's nothing more suspect than an eyewitness account. But something tells me your nose is slightly more accurate than most humans' eyes. What do you say?"

Bones met Leonhardt's gaze. The detective smiled, taking this to mean the shepherd was looking for a rematch.

"Good. 'Cause this may not be your ordinary everyday dog."

Ten days passed.

That was how long it took Detective Leonhardt and Bones, quietly and with occasional assistance from Detective Garza, to search the buildings of Neville Houses from top to bottom. Officially, they were on the hunt for drugs, which is why they were allowed such latitude. The police department hadn't publicly identified a link between the deaths at the different buildings, but if Garza's theory about drugs held any water, they'd happily announce it from the rooftops.

But after ten days, Bones hadn't alerted to a single thing related to the mysterious missing dog. While he had led to a handful of minor drug arrests and the identification of four more squats used by illegals, this had nothing to do with what Leonhardt wanted out of him.

"Pretty sure it's half past time to pack it in on this one," Garza announced on day nine. "This just isn't getting us anywhere."

By then, even Leonhardt had to agree with this. They'd asked several residents to give them a call if they came across a strange dog in the area. So spooked was everybody that the calls came rolling in. Neighbors' pets were reported, stray cats were added to the mix, and one lady turned in her own pooch.

Twice.

But not a one successfully described the animal on the footage from the Fowler shooting.

With Trey's permission, his laptop had been recovered from the Baldwin apartment, as well as the camera. Threats were made about additional charges, but Leonhardt made sure that these went away as quickly as they were put forward.

"Jesus Christ," muttered Garza as he watched the video for the first time. "Nobody should ever see this."

"Wishful thinking," Leonhardt replied.

The truth was, as soon as it came in the door, copies of the digital recording were sent to the mayor's office, the office of the police commissioner, and the team tasked with investigating the shooting. Within the hour, however, duplicates made it into every precinct in Manhattan and quickly fanned out to the other boroughs. By evening, word would leak to the television news, and screen grabs would make it online.

"So, what now?" Garza asked on day ten, the day the lieutenant formally asked for their report. "Send the dog back to Pittsburgh?"

Leonhardt didn't have a ready answer.

"I mean, the dog's clearly gone, right? He's there in the video, I believe the little girl that he was there on the roof. Something whacked our fellow officer around. But that's the end of it."

"And the bloody shoeprint?"

"Mrs. Fowler was fucked-up on PCP."

"Even though her apartment was clean?"

"Repeat after me: Mrs. Fowler was fucked-up on drugs."

"What about the dog bowl and blankets in the Lester apartment?" Leonhardt retorted. "Bones alerted to them."

"Do me a favor and think like a detective…hell, a *rational human being* for a single second. Rather than believe it was drugs, you're going to go down the garden path of this being some killer dog. I went along with it when I thought there might be some dangerous animal in there, because something bad happened and searching those buildings was better than working any day. But, we didn't find anything. It's over. And you really need to come back to earth and see that."

Ocean City was so far removed from Becca's day-to-day existence that, at first, she wasn't sure what to do with herself. She'd been out to Coney Island a couple of times, which had a boardwalk and games, too, but Ocean City was so small in comparison. There were rows and rows of two-story wood frame and aluminum siding houses on narrow streets beyond the beach, but many seemed empty. Despite Ken advising her to stick close to the boardwalk when she left the hotel on her own, Becca had grown tired of it after only a day.

No, the neighborhoods were of more interest. Though the houses were very much the same in their construction, each had touches of personality. Becca liked to imagine who might live there, even part time. Was the faded windsock something with such sentimental value that even though it looked awful, it just couldn't be thrown out? Same for a coconut and bamboo set of wind chimes that looked brought back from an island vacation? What of all the little metal cats and roosters and pigs and every other animal under the sun propped up on porches and windowsills?

Becca would see how many streets she could go without seeing a living person. There would always be some car in the distance to ruin her fun, but occasionally, she'd go four or five blocks with nothing. No airplane overhead, no laughter echoing up from the beach, only the wind.

It was like being the last person on earth.

She hadn't wanted to bother Ken too much. He stayed in his room on the phone almost nonstop except when heading out for food or when checking on Becca.

"Trey met with the court-appointed lawyer this morning," he told her over breakfast on the third day. "There's some concern that the primary witness in his defense is his own sister, but enough people saw and heard you on the roof to put you there at the time of the shooting. The other good news is that the preliminary ballistics tests and crime scene reports all back up to a letter your and Trey's recollection of events."

"When will he get out?"

"They have to set bail, and that'll happen this week. They're going to try and get it set pretty low. I already talked to a bond company. I had to lie and say I hadn't quit my job. I just hope I get another one before they check up."

"Do you think you can find one?"

"You remember meeting Gus, the guy who came and fixed our plumbing that one day? He does maintenance in the building. I called him because he'd mentioned they were always looking for people. He said he'd put me in touch with Mr. Uribe, who runs all those guys. Said it's the easiest job in the world."

"What about school?"

"I talked to Mrs. Drucker. She understood. Said they could email you your assignments to print out if we got to a computer down here."

Becca scowled. Ken shook his head.

"None of that. You still need to be focused on your schooling. You know that. This isn't an excuse to let that slip. You fall behind even a little bit and that can cost you in the long run."

Becca understood, but the thought of being cooped up in her motel room with the sun and sand within reach sounded like torture. Ken seemed to recognize this and softened a little.

"Maybe we'll go find that computer tomorrow."

It had been a massive undertaking, but the New York Police Department had eventually digitized just about all of its records. The only problem with that was any time anyone sought out an older file, an electronic footprint linking the officer doing the search to said file was left behind.

What Leonhardt desired was the opposite. He wanted to peer into a file with complete anonymity. The file he sought was one of the most notorious in the history of the department, right next to John Gotti, Bernie Goetz, and the George Metesky, the Mad Bomber. The Criminal Records Section offices four blocks west of the former World Trade Center had become a real graveyard since the digitizers left. If you were assigned there, the question wasn't if you fucked up, but how much higher up the food chain was the person who got fucked because of your fuck-up. There was shit detail with little chance for advancement.

Then there was the prison cell of records.

"Vincent! Hey, Vinnie!"

Leonhardt banged on the cage leading into the closed-access archive. Vincent Harrell was back there somewhere as he was every day, either watching television or reading the paper. He'd actually petitioned the department for a larger television complete with DVR and gotten it a few years before. He was a nut for the Mets, having grown up on Long Island. During the season, he'd record the game from the night before (and whatever other game was being televised unless it involved a certain Bronx-Area rival that favored pinstripes) and watch it through once or twice during the following day. This meant his mornings had become downright ritualistic in his avoidance of learning the previous day's score. At first, it was a joke. Officers would look for ever more inventive ways to spoil his game.

Then he punched out a guy and got written up, called on the carpet, and almost kicked out. The attitude since then had become, *well, if he's THAT serious about it.* And he was left alone to enjoy his games.

"Vincent!! Come on, man! It's Leonhardt!"

After a couple more minutes, a mountain of a man appeared at the end of the hallway, so wide that he just about touched both walls at the same time.

"Phil! How the hell are you?"

"Good, man. On a bit of a mission."

"That doesn't sound good at all!" the officer scoffed as he unlocked the gate. "This about all that up in Harlem?"

"This isn't about anything, Vince. I was never here."

"Oh, shit! You're putting yourself in my debt here. That's something. What are you looking for?"

"Berkowitz."

"Jesus. You're not looking to sell something on eBay, are you? Getting bribed by someone writing a new book?"

"No. You were right the first time."

Vincent's face went blank, but then he furrowed his brow.

"That thing in Harlem?" he asked.

"That thing in Harlem."

XI

Fifteen minutes later, Leonhardt found himself pinching his sinuses, wondering if he'd finally lost his fucking mind.

The Berkowitz files, concerning the so-called .44 Caliber Killer while the manhunt was on, the Son of Sam after he was caught based on a moniker he gave himself, were massive. The main reason for this was that they contained every false lead and miscue compiled by the department during the year between David Berkowitz's first murder in July of 1976 and his arrest in August of the following year.

The Berkowitz case had been notoriously difficult to solve even after a massive task force had been assembled to locate the man using a .44 caliber Charter Arms Bulldog revolver to shoot young women. Even more notoriously, the case was solved because of a parking ticket left on the windshield of Berkowitz's car during the night of the final shooting, though he was initially sought as a potential witness.

There was no question of Berkowitz's madness. In several letters, he had described himself as "Mr. Monster" and raved about rising from the sewer to "please Sam," who he described as his father, by committing violent murder. After his arrest, he claimed that the "Sam" was his next-door neighbor in Yonkers, Sam Carr, but that really the one telling him to kill was Sam Carr's dog, Harvey, a black lab.

Though he stuck with the whole Satanic cult thing for as many years as the newspapers would print it, Berkowitz had long since recanted. In fact, he'd become a born-again Christian behind bars and even tried to pay restitution to his victims. The Harvey story was just that, a small piece of a massive fiction invented by a delusional lunatic and lapped up by a public unwilling to believe that such a horrific series of murders, six in all with a greater number wounded, could have a rational explanation. It had to be supernatural, or they couldn't sleep at night. It had to be the Devil, or what was preventing it from happening again tomorrow?

But as Leonhardt stared down at the facts of the case, everything from horrific crime scene and autopsy photos to photostats of the letters sent to police and *Daily News* columnist Jimmy Breslin, he realized that this had nothing to do with the deaths in Jefferson Park. He was just as desperate as Breslin's readers over a quarter of a century ago for that supernatural explanation.

The dog, Harvey, looked nothing like the black mastiff from Neville Houses. In two photographs, both showing the black lab with his owner, Sam Carr, the animal looked like what it was: the family dog.

Leonhardt sighed and closed the brown manila folder, doing up its rubber string tie, which had gone dry and rigid with age. He shelved it alongside the several other volumes of the same case file and made his way to where Vincent was watching television.

"You find what you were looking for?" Vincent asked. "Wait, don't tell me if you did. Plausible deniability."

"Came up dry," Leonhardt said anyway. "It was a shot in the dark."

"I thought you guys knew what happened up there."

"Yeah, yeah, I think we do," Leonhardt admitted. "Always the same with cases like these."

"But when they're so weird, you start looking for answers to all the unasked questions. That's just not a place you want to go."

The detective nodded.

"You got me there."

Ken got the job as a maintenance man in the building. The pay wasn't much better than the warehouse, but if he agreed to be on call at night, this could up substantially, as each call was time and a half.

Trey's bail was set at $100,000, the minimum for a case like this, and he was bailed out that afternoon. The ten percent Ken had to put up meant that he and Becca had to clear out of Ocean City, but then they received help from a surprising source.

"If it had been me standing there, I would've done the exact same thing," Mr. Gaines told Trey through his lawyer. "You did me a favor."

To that, Mr. Gaines put in $1,000. Half an hour later, Trey was out.

Though there hadn't been a single incident of violence at Triborough Houses since the shooting of Janice, Becca still shuddered as they approached the building.

"I'm going to park and drop off our stuff on the loading dock so we can use the service elevator," Ken said. "I'll have a key now, so we won't have to tromp up and down the stairs every day."

Becca nodded and climbed out of the borrowed SUV at the curb. She stared up at Building 7, wondering if anyone would notice if she turned around, caught the next train for Ocean City, and just found one of those empty houses to break into and live in until she was old enough to get a job.

As she entered the lobby, she remembered that the last time she'd been here, she'd had Bones by her side. It was, she imagined, like carrying a loaded gun. Everything seemed a little less daunting with a ferocious German shepherd waiting to go off next to you.

She took the stairs two at a time until the fifth floor and then single-stepped it to the sixth. Like on the Jersey Shore, the place felt oddly depopulated. In this case, everyone was at work, not simply absent until the seasons changed or the weekend arrived. When she got to her door, she located her key, turned the lock, and stepped inside.

The apartment smelled like pizza, and she soon saw why. Trey had beaten them home and had brought a couple of boxes with him from the place over on Lexington. He must've just arrived, as he was still in the shower when she walked in.

Okay, she thought. *Maybe I can do this.*

She dropped her keys on the counter, went to her bedroom, closed the door, and flopped down on the bed.

"He's looking pretty good," the police veterinarian told the kennel master as he checked over Bones's mostly healed wounds. "I'm ready to sign off on him for transport."

The kennel master rolled his eyes.

"I know he's been working up there in the 22nd Precinct. You got some kind of deal with the detectives?"

"I don't know what you're talking about," the vet replied. "You capable of getting his ass back to Pittsburgh? Or do you need a requisition?"

"I'll have him on the first plane in the morning. And good riddance. He smells."

"Yeah, that's his job," the vet snarked.

"Fine, he *stinks*," the kennel master sighed, disinterested in semantic wordplay. "Happy, asshole?"

"Always."

Bones watched this back-and-forth for a moment but then flopped over asleep.

The afternoon passed quietly in the Baldwin household. Trey sat on the floor of the living room watching television.Ken stayed on the phone. Becca came and went from her room. It was an unusual homecoming with everyone giving each other space but still checking on each other every few minutes as if to make certain no one had left.

Ken had to start his shift at six o'clock but was going to go down to the maintenance locker room early to get into his work clothes, a dull gray jumpsuit provided by the building.

"When I tell you to stay in the apartment tonight, I mean it," Ken told Becca, who was making one of her circuits of the living room. He turned to Trey. "And I'm going to ask you to stay home, but I don't expect you to listen. Just, it's our first night back and I'd love to know both of y'all are safe and sound. Is that asking too much?"

Trey shook his head.

"I'm staying in. I don't want to see anybody, I don't want anybody to see me. Just going to sit here, watch TV, and eat pizza until I pass the fuck out. Cool?"

Becca stifled a laugh. Ken rolled his eyes.

"Answer the phone if it rings, okay? A hundred people might be calling."

"Done," said Trey.

Ken grabbed his keys and headed out the front door. Becca was about to go back to her room when Trey waved at her.

"Hey, come here a sec."

Becca flopped down on the sofa behind Trey.

"Is Ken okay?" Trey asked.

"I think so. Why?"

"This is precisely the kind of thing that drives him out of his mind, you know? Sister in trouble, brother in trouble, job out the window, etc. He spends all his time worrying about providing for us and so little on himself. But he seems to be on an even keel, taking it all in stride."

"He spent the whole time in Ocean City on the phone dealing with all of this."

"Really?"

Becca nodded.

"Well, I guess that's something," Trey acknowledged. "But we've gotta pay him back by keeping things tight in the short term, cool?"

"Cool."

Becca wasn't sure she understood exactly what Trey was saying, but figured he might be announcing a hiatus from drugs, both dealing and using.

At least, in the short term.

Ken headed down through the building, a bounce in his step. Everything was falling into place. It had been rough going for a few days there and he had questioned whether things would actually work out. But now, as he walked down the endless stairs, he felt a certain lightness.

Reaching out, he ran his fingers along the bumpy wall. The paint was "graffiti-proof," but time and time again, this tagger or that had found just the right paint pen that allowed them the execution of their handiwork.

It felt plastic under his fingers, almost as if it had been dripped into place. He idly wondered what they would put in its place, if anything. Would they use the same building materials? Meaning cheap? Meaning designed for people who frankly didn't mean much to anyone who might feel otherwise?

Everything would be better with the arrival of the fire.

Becca had just drifted off when she heard the phone ring in the other room. It took Trey a couple of rings to answer it, so she imagined he'd fallen asleep as well.

"Hello?"

There was more silence, but then Trey shuffled down the hallway and lightly knocked on Becca's door.

"You awake?"

"Uh-huh."

Trey pushed the door open, his hand covering the mouthpiece.

"You know a Mr. Werden?"

"Um...," was all Becca managed.

"Says he's the guy Ken borrowed the SUV from. Did you guys borrow luggage from him, too?"

"What?"

Trey rolled his eyes and handed over the phone before disappearing.

"Hello?"

"Hey, is this Becca?"

"Yes."

"This is Cy Werden. You guys borrowed my truck."

"Yeah, I think Ken is going to take it back in the morning. He's at work right now. Is that okay?"

"Oh, yeah. He told me that. No, middle of the day yesterday, he came by to drop off my dog carrier. He left it with Patricia and I guess she didn't know any better, but the thing is torn to hell. The handle's off, something practically chewed through the metal gate, it's scratched to shit. We're going to have to talk about that."

Becca shook her head, trying to process this.

"I don't know what you're talking about. We didn't have a dog carrier."

"Um, yeah you did. He asked me for it specifically. It was in the back of the SUV when he drove away a week and a half ago. Dropped it off yesterday afternoon before driving back to Ocean City. Thing stinks something awful, too."

Becca searched her memory. When Ken picked her up from the police station, the SUV was pretty packed, but it was dark. She didn't see any dog carrier. But then, she hadn't really looked in the back. She'd climbed into the passenger seat and fallen asleep for the entire trip. When they got there, it was morning and…what? Becca struggled to remember.

And Ken immediately sent me to see how close we were to the beach and to buy a few bottles of water, Becca recalled. *By the time I got back to the parking lot, he was waiting with my bags and a room key.*

She hadn't thought about it twice. She'd taken took her bags, gone to her room, and slept until noon.

And then there had been that one afternoon.

She'd come back early from a day at the local library to knock on Ken's door. She could hear him on the phone, so she'd tried his door, only to be surprised when it opened. She remembered seeing the wild look in Ken's eyes as he saw her, bolted from halfway across the room, and half-slammed the door in her face.

"Don't you know I'm on the phone?" he had hissed.

Becca had gone back to her room, figuring this was the usual Ken. He was trying to get a job or was dealing with somebody on Trey's legal team. No other explanation had occurred to her.

"Can I have Ken call you back?" Becca asked Cy.

"Sure, but make sure he does. I'm not happy with…"

Becca hung up. She stared at the phone for a minute, unsure what to do. She moved over to her backpack and dug around until she found Detective Leonhardt's business card. She took a deep breath before dialing his number.

"This is Leonhardt."

"The dog's back, Detective Leohardt. And this time it has my older brother."

Down in the maintenance locker room, Ken quickly fed the mastiff. He'd left food for it the day before when he'd brought it down, but knew the food wouldn't last long. He had tried to steal away upon dropping off Becca at the front, but too many people were around and the animal was nowhere to be seen.

"That's a good boy. Eat it up. Been hungry, huh?"

The mastiff wolfed down the dog chow and then looked at Ken expectantly once the bowl was empty.

"Jesus! You're next to starving, huh?"

Ken quickly opened a second can and spilled its contents into the makeshift bowl, a bucket he'd found in the laundry room. The dog attacked this with the same verve as the first portion.

As the dog ate, Ken walked to a wall filled with clipboards hanging from hooks. Gus had said that each clipboard represented a work order that had to be filled. Ken scanned past all of these until he found the Triborough Houses master list. Every apartment number in every building appeared on it. Alongside them were the names of the tenants in each and their phone numbers.

But what interested Ken were the ones marked "unrented." He knew some of these were being used by squatters, but that's what his companion was along to identify. Taking that into consideration, he still estimated there to be about forty empty apartments spread across the sixteen buildings.

More than enough for his task. But he would need to start.

"Are we ready?" he asked the mastiff.

The dog looked up at him with a dull expression. Ken smiled and moved towards the stairs. The mastiff slowly padded along behind him.

XII

The kennel master didn't know what to say. The detective across the counter was staring at him like he was about to take a bite of his nose.

"Are you going to give me the animal or not?" Leonhardt repeated.

"You're not a handler, detective. I couldn't give you the animal even if I wanted to. Department policy."

"People are going to die, sergeant. *Die*, with a capital 'D.' Same as what happened a couple of weeks back up in Jefferson Park. Except they aren't going to be cops this time, but a bunch of kids or their families. You want that on your head?"

"Yeah?" blustered the officer. "What's a dog going to do about it?"

Leonhardt sighed and punched the man in the face, dropping him with a single hit.

"A hell of a lot more than you, asshole!" the fallen kennel master bellowed.

His hand instantly throbbing from one or more broken knuckles, Leonhardt vaulted the counter, took the kennel master's key, and let himself into the maze of kennels beyond a white door the kennel master had been ostensibly blocking.

"Bones!" Leonhardt called out.

Several enforcement dogs began barking at once. Leonhardt moved past a couple of Belgian Malinois and Dutch shepherds before reaching the one dog that hadn't barked once.

"That dog's back, Bones. We have to stop it. I don't know what it wants or what it's up to, but it's not good."

Bones just stared idly at the police detective while the one human in the room fumbled with the lock on Bones's gate. As soon as the gate was open, Bones stepped forward. Leonhardt raised a hand.

"No, we're going to have to do things my way," he explained, holding up a harness. "I know I'm not your regular handler, but we're going to have to make this work."

Bones allowed the harness to be placed around his neck and forelegs. Once it was snug, Leonhardt nodded.

"Let's get going."

On the way out, they passed the kennel master as he nursed his broken nose, a phone already propped up by his ear.

"I hope you're drunk, detective. In fact, I'll go easy on you and tell them you were toasted. They'll take your badge, but maybe leave you your pension."

"Don't do anything on my account," Leonhardt said as he reached the front door. "I sure wouldn't do it for you."

The first time Trey was ever arrested, he was put in front of a youth counselor with all these big ideas about change. The guy talked about growing up in a hard part of Baltimore surrounded by crime and drugs, but that he was able to overcome it and get out. Trey asked questions of his own and quickly found out that the guy's father had a small business and was able to sell it off to move the family. When the guy continued his crime wave in the new locale (little more than tagging and getting into trouble at the *private* school he attended), the father mortgaged the house and sent him to military school.

"So you see, anybody can pull themselves up by their bootstraps."

At the time, Trey had scoffed in his face, calling him an ingrate whose parents should've thrown him out on the street. Rather than become incensed, the counselor seemed pleased, telling Trey that now they could have an "honest dialogue."

Trey stopped cold and laughed in the man's face. He told him to go ahead and take him back to his cell, as it was clear an honest dialogue would be too much of a two-way street for the counselor to handle. The befuddled counselor did as he was told and began seeking out a more susceptible convert from Trey's peers.

But there was one turn of phrase the man had used that stuck with Trey. He said that when you "entered the life of a career criminal," the "mouth of your grave had opened." For Trey, it was a beautiful and apt image. It meant that he could die at any moment and the ground was waiting to take him. He'd heard the similar idiom that "someone was walking over their grave," but that wasn't the same thing. That was some future site that was being alluded to in the moment. Suggesting that somewhere out there was an open grave with his name on it felt like a constant, a debt waiting to be paid that hung over his head like a halo of vultures.

As he listened to his little sister explain why she believed their oldest brother was in the thrall of a devil dog, he got the same kind of chills.

This is it, he thought. *This just might be the moment of my death.*

"So, I called the detective and he's on his way…"

"You did what?" Trey asked, snapping out of his trance. "You bring in the cops, what if one of them decides to shoot Ken or something? You don't think they're going to be a little nervous walking back up in here?"

Becca hadn't thought of that, but quickly shook her head.

"It's just that one detective. I don't know if he's bringing anybody else. But I told him to bring Bones."

Trey thought fast. He glanced around the apartment, trying to remember if Ken had a gun.

"What do you think his plan is?"

"I don't know. With that dog, could be anything, right?"

Trey nodded. It was the "anything" that scared the hell out of him.

Apartment 302 of Building 5 had been empty for over a month. The problem was toxic mold and the management company had decided to keep a lid on it as they slowly had the walls and floors torn out and replaced. The hope was that, to avoid lawsuits, they could minimize the number of people who learned about it. It had been discovered inadvertently when a maintenance worker was replacing a sink after the previous tenants had moved away. This man had been given ten $100 bills to keep his mouth shut and he did.

Except to Gus Byrd, whom he liked working with and thought should know to avoid the apartment. Gus told Ken as an example of what their employers tried to get away with and what they expected their workers to ignore.

"If you can't look the other way, you shouldn't take this job," Gus had said. "It's not all peaches and cream."

Ken admitted that he had no problem looking the other way as he "just needed a damn job." But now, as Ken entered 5-302, he thought about where else in the buildings there were other problems like this. Tenants sucking bad air that was slowly killing them. He imagined where else in Harlem this was happening and figured it had to be hundreds of buildings, if not thousands. This plague masquerading as a city, the humans pretending to be something other than vermin. He thought of the potential lawsuits and couldn't help chuckling to himself. These people who couldn't get through a day without booze or drugs or insulin or handfuls of pills or fifteen hours of television suing a building because otherwise they'd be perfect physical specimens.

No, whatever cancer ate them from the inside out was probably born from a whole orgy's worth of fathers all taking turns at the same hole. They'd rot and rot and become even more of a drag on society as they grabbed onto anything they could on their way to hell.

From that point of view, Ken was doing the world a favor.

The mastiff moved through the bare apartment. The wallpaper and carpeting had been stripped away, leaving what looked like an empty cinder block in the middle of an otherwise completed building. The dog trotted towards the kitchen where the cabinets had been pulled away from the walls. The space where a refrigerator would stand was also bare.

But the mastiff seemed interested only in the stove. It was a crappy model, probably thirty or forty years old, with broken knobs and aluminum foil under scorched burners. It wasn't plugged in, but the plastic housing for the electronic display was cracked and didn't look like it worked.

It didn't have to. Ken grabbed the back of the stove and ripped it forward as hard as he could. The rubber having long molted off the metal legs, deep gashes were torn out of the linoleum floor as it was moved.

The electric cord had long been unplugged. The hose leading to the gas spigot had also been disconnected. The shut-off valve was perpendicular to the spigot, indicating it was closed. Ken reached down and gently turned the valve until it ran parallel to the spigot.

He inhaled deeply, filling his lungs with the gas.

The mastiff woofed a little, snapping Ken out of his reverie.

"You're right. Thirty-nine more to go, eh, boy?"

As they exited the apartment, Ken used the heavy electrical tape he'd bought in bulk the evening before to seal the edges of the front doors. He had worried that the silver of the tape would provoke curiosity from passersby. As he flattened it against the brown of the door frame, he saw that it was barely visible in the low light.

Perfect, he thought.

The mastiff had already started down the hallway towards the stairs. Ken pocketed the tape, then continued up the steps to the next floor.

Though he wasn't about to admit it to the kennel master, Leonhardt *was* drunk. In fact, he'd been drinking since he left the archive. When Becca called, it was like receiving a shot of adrenaline. He'd been shaking as he left the bar for his vehicle. Now, with Bones in the backseat, he was in a hazy mindset, as if driving on autopilot and praying that no one ran into the street ahead of him. He didn't have much farther to go, his siren wailing as he flew through intersection after intersection, but there were moments where he thought he might fall asleep.

As he crossed East 106th, a cab, figuring it could beat the cop through the intersection shot out in front of him. Leonhardt slammed on the brakes, sending the shepherd tumbling off the backseat and into the floorboards with a thud.

"Oh, shit! You okay, Bones?" the detective barked, sounding genuinely worried.

The shepherd rolled over, shaking its head before hopping back on the seat.

"Don't freak me out like that!" Leonhardt cried, flipping the bird at the cab driver as he passed him.

"Hello?"

"Your fucking partner just beat up the kennel master at the 13th Precinct and stole that working dog you guys had been using up in Harlem. Any idea where he might be heading?"

"Oh, Jesus," groaned Garza.

"Seriously," continued the lieutenant. "He apparently drove away like a bat out of hell. Figure we should rein him in, no?"

"Yeah."

"This ain't a sexual thing, is it?" joked the lieutenant.

"Not that I'm aware of," Garza replied dryly.

"Well, see what you can do. You've got an hour before I go ahead and okay his arrest on sight."

"Yep."

Garza hung up and climbed out of bed. His wife, now awake, too, pulled the covers up over her.

"You've got to get a new partner," she muttered.

"Yep."

Trey almost laughed when he found the empty dog food cans and makeshift dog bowl down in the maintenance room.

"Bro, I gotta teach you something about covering your tracks," he said aloud.

That's when he saw the boots.

The subbasement was actually divided into three rooms: laundry, lockers for the maintenance workers, and the supply room where the workers left the tools of their trade. It was in this third space that a pair of boots were visible. But rather than standing upright, they were leaned over on their backs but not on their sides. Clearly, something was still in them.

The something was Mr. Byrd, his throat ripped out.

"Oh no, Ken. That's…that's it for you."

Trey checked the body just to make sure there was nothing that could be done and then headed upstairs. He had no idea where to begin looking for Ken or the big black dog, but prayed he got to him before anyone else died.

Becca tried to keep busy in the apartment, but it was something easier said than done. She had turned the television on and off three times already. She'd called back Detective Leonhardt, only to get his voicemail.

She tried to read a book in her bedroom, but every time she heard someone on the stairwell or out in the hall, she would race to the door to look through the peephole. She never really saw another person until it was Ken.

She gasped, her hand reaching for the door knob. But then a sixth sense kicked in just as her fingertips touched brass. A second later, she saw the mastiff pad by behind her brother. It seemed to have grown, its massive head the size of a Halloween pumpkin. It stared straight ahead.

That is, until it reached the Baldwins' apartment.

As if feeling Becca's eyes watching it, it stopped in its tracks and moved over to the front door. Becca quickly moved away but saw its silhouette as it sniffed around the base. Frozen in place, the little girl kept waiting for the animal to move away, but it only seemed to press its head harder against the door. That's when she heard the wood begin to creak under its weight. She didn't think it would come off its hinges, but the sound was getting louder.

Taking a couple of cautious steps forward, she was only a few feet away when it began bashing its head full-force into the door. She knew she should be scared. She imagined that any sane person would run from the room and hide in the furthest closet of the furthest room.

But she found herself moving forward until she could reach her hand out and touch the shuddering door. The impact of dog skull on wood reverberated through Becca's body. It felt as if the entire room was shaking due to a jetliner passing only a few hundred feet above the building.

She closed her eyes to listen, the moment impossibly surreal. There was no way a dog could hit the door with this much force, but Becca knew the clatter she heard behind her was the dishes rattling in the cupboards. She glanced back and saw the window panes vibrating with each strike as well.

She sank down onto her knees, running her hands down the door until she reached the base. The pounding came to a slow halt. A moment later, Becca felt the hot breath of the devil dog on her hand, followed by warm spittle as it licked her fingers.

She recoiled as blood-black saliva trickled down to her palm. She stared at it in horror as it seemed to move by its own volition, tracing a pattern across her skin. She wanted to wipe it off, but felt paralyzed. She had what she wanted to do, but then there was what her body was allowing her to do.

"Hey!"

Becca almost cried out, so surprised was she to hear her brother's voice. It took her a second to realize that he was talking to the mastiff.

"Get away from there," Ken ordered.

From deep within the animal came a terrifying growl. It was marked with a furious anger aimed squarely at Ken. Becca listened for Ken's reaction, but she didn't hear movement.

Instead, he repeated his words.

"Get away from there!"

The growl slowly subsided. Becca gingerly rose to her feet and peered through the peephole. Ken stood only a few feet away, hands on his hips, eyes dark as night. The standoff continued only another second before Ken turned and walked away. She waited to see the head of the mastiff follow, but saw nothing.

Leaning back down, she looked back under the door. She expected to see the mastiff, but he wasn't there. Now terrified, she eased back up to her full height, took hold of the doorknob, held her breath, and turned it. Swinging it wide, fully expecting the mastiff to be waiting inches away, she was surprised to discover the hall empty.

She finally exhaled a second later. When she took in her next breath, a faint smell wafted up her nose. She looked over at Mrs. Fowler's door and saw the electrical tape wrapped around the frame. She walked over and took up a corner of the tape between her fingers. She tugged at it until she'd pulled the tape down four or five inches.

When she smelled the gas, her eyes went wide. She looked left and right, but didn't see a soul. As Ken's footsteps echoed down the stairs, Becca turned to follow.

XIII

The first 911 call was placed at 11:36 p.m. by an elderly woman named Ann Lobrano. A resident of Building 2, she reported smelling gas coming in through the ventilation ducts. The 911 operator was alerting the fire house on 3rd Avenue when a second call came in, this one from a woman in Building 5 just coming off her shift at the Metropolitan Hospital. At first, it was believed there had been some confusion as to which building it was in. But then the calls were played back and emergency responders dispatched to both locations in Neville Houses.

The first ladder (#14) unit was just clambering onto 1st Avenue when the next three calls came in. There was a second one from Building 5, but then came reports from Buildings 7 and 12. As this was being relayed, the floodgates opened. One call after another poured in until all the buildings of the Triborough Projects were represented.

"I don't know," one operator said, patching in her supervisor. "Could be the real deal."

The supervisor was about to reply when someone started screaming. He rushed over to her station, only to hear white noise on the other end of the line.

"What happened?!"

The explosion in Building 4 was felt twenty blocks in every direction and seen from as far away as Jackson Heights, Queens, an orange blossom of flame that flowered and died within seconds even as debris continued to tumble from the side of the housing tower. A steady stream of tenants had been exiting the buildings as word of gas leaks passed from apartment to apartment. After the explosion, panic reigned and a frenzied exodus began in earnest.

Detective Leonhardt had been in Building 7 evacuating people. The officer had smelled the gas upon arrival and had had a pretty good idea whose handiwork it was.

"Police! Gas leak!" he yelled as he pounded on the doors. "You've got to get out of there!"

When doors didn't open, he hit them harder. Bones, excited by all the activity, barked like crazy and almost flew through a couple of the newly opened doors, forcing Leonhardt to yank him backward by the harness.

"Bones! Keep with me!"

The problem was, the shepherd was completely discombobulated by the heavy smells. The stench of sulfur from the odorant added to the gas was going straight to his head. His prancing and shivers were attempts to clear his olfactory canals of the odor, but it wasn't working.

Then the explosion happened. Screams echoed throughout the building to the point that Leonhardt thought it might've gone off in Building 7.

"What's happening?!" an old man shouted, tears in his eyes as he opened the door to an equally panicked Leonhardt.

"Gas leak in the building. You have to get out of here."

"No, out there!" the man pointed to his living room window.

Leonhardt dragged Bones into the apartment and peered out the window, seeing that the building affected by the explosion was a couple away. Several residents who had been staring up at the conflagration were now being peppered by chunks of wall and other detritus raining down from above.

"Oh, fuck," Leonhardt sighed.

He didn't even want to think how many people might've been killed in the adjoining apartments. He wheeled the shepherd around and saw the old man still standing in the doorway of his own apartment, his hands extended plaintively.

"What do I do?"

"Go outside," the detective said quietly.

"But I'm scared."

"Don't think of it like that. Just like you were going to get groceries. Take your time. Go to the stairs and make your way down. There'll be people down there to help you."

The man nodded as if expected to, not because he understood, and turned to leave. Leonhardt followed him into the hall, but then shook his head.

"This isn't working. No more knocking. We have to shut this shit down!"

The job was finally done.

As he stood on the roof of Building 3, Ken waited for the second explosion. He knew it wouldn't be long in coming. The fire in 10 started by the first explosion was working its way through the walls and ceilings. However, Ken wasn't sure if it would soon encounter the sealed room on the seventh floor or the fourteenth first. The seventh was closer, sure, but as smoke poured out of windows on the eleventh and twelfth floors, he thought the intensity of the blaze had directed itself upward.

It would be an interesting experiment.

The second explosion, it turned out, wasn't much of an explosion. Rather, it came in the form of a fireball that blasted out windows across the sixth floor of Building 2. It was truly something to see. Shattered glass exploded outward from each apartment as what looked like an orange comet raced around the inside of the floor, a flaming wrecking ball setting alight anything in its path.

Ken didn't think he'd ever seen anything so beautiful or surreal. He looked back to the courtyard to wait for a third with the calm of someone watching the sky for falling stars. It was then that he heard the mastiff growl. The animal had been sitting a few feet away, its nose in the air as if merely taking in the rarefied scents of a cool evening. Ken turned to the stairwell and held up the bloodstained garden trowel he'd used to tear out Mr. Byrd's throat.

"Who's there?"

It took Becca a couple of seconds, but she finally stepped out of the shadows.

"You have to stop all this, Ken," she said as evenly as she could, trying to maintain what she imagined to be a commanding tone. "You have to stop it now."

"Oh, yeah, well... *that*," Ken began. "See, I'm not doing any of that. That's from people cooking their food, sparking up a joint, heck, lighting candles on a birthday cake. You want me to have a word with *all* of them?"

Becca eyed the mastiff. It stared at her, unblinking. Lit only by the nearby buildings, its size was masked by the darkness, making it appear even larger in Becca's mind's eye.

"It's the dog," Becca said. "The dog's making you do it."

Ken glanced over at the mastiff as if taking its measure. He turned a look of incredulity back on Becca.

"Is that what you think?"

"You don't sound a bit like my brother, so yeah."

Ken scoffed. The building shook.

Becca reached out to steady herself, but nothing was there. She found herself flying backward into the stairwell, a weightless feeling coming over her body born from not having any idea how close the ground was. For all she knew, she might fall forever.

Instead, she fell six feet, landed on her head, bounced up again, rolled down seven more steps, and smacked her face against the wall on the first landing. For a second, she thought she was only dazed. Another second and she had slipped into unconsciousness.

Back on the roof, Ken turned his attention back to Building 10. The fire had sped up its downward trajectory and was now visible in at least a couple of rooms on the seventh floor. But when it reached the sealed apartment on that floor, there was no explosion. Ken recounted the floors, wondering if he'd somehow focused on the wrong room.

That's when he saw the broken windows all around the floor. As he watched, someone hastily bashed out another window as the fire neared. His eyes narrowed. He could see the mastiff getting to its feet in his peripheral vision. It looked over the edge of the roof towards Building 10 and gave a little woof.

"Let's go," Ken agreed.

Leonhardt knew no trainer worth his salt would use Bones the way he was using him now. The odor of the gas drove the dog crazy, so the closer they got to an open valve like the one they found on the sixth floor of Building 7, an apartment Leonhardt was amazed to be entering yet again, Bones would just go *off.*

The good news was, he had found a pair of heavy woolen shirts in an open apartment and managed to soak both before wrapping them around his and the dog's mouths. Bones tried and tried to tear his off, but the detective finally tied it in such a way that the shepherd couldn't do a thing about it. They could still smell the gas just fine, worryingly so, but Leonhardt hoped it would be enough to keep them from passing out.

Mrs. Fowler's apartment had been picked over, the "family members" the police had been made aware of apparently coming in at some point to take a couple of photos and pieces of furniture while leaving much behind. The second Leonhardt had seen the tape around the doorframe, he figured what Ken's plan was. He kicked the door open with one strike.

The gas was just about overwhelming, but the detective felt lucky already knowing the apartment's layout. Closing the front door and dropping Bones's leash, he made a beeline for the kitchen and turned off the gas valve. He tore a drawer out of the kitchen cabinet and smashed it through the living room window. He did the same in the bedroom before circling back to grab Bones.

"We've got to find all the rooms like this. Sorry, boy."

After they'd cleared two more sealed apartments in Building 7, Leonhardt hurried off to Building 10. With the fires already raging there, the detective feared the flames reaching one of the sealed rooms and causing an explosion so big it might take down the building. Pulling the German shepherd behind him, the cop had to navigate through an intense crush of terrified human traffic to reach the burning building.

The smoke had an even worse effect on Bones than the gas. His romping and head shaking became whining and straining at the leash.

"We've got to do this, Bones," Leonhardt chided. "Doesn't mean I'm not sorry for your pain."

When they reached the seventh floor, they found smoke billowing out of one open apartment already. Seeing one of the sealed rooms up ahead, the detective realized they might be too late, the fire likely now reaching apartments filled up with gas. Kicking in doors, Leonhardt ran from room to room smashing windows. When he reached the sealed one, he double-timed it to the valve, shut it off, and then broke out the windows in this room as well.

He then re-wet and retied the shirts around his and Bones's mouths and noses before heading back out into the building.

Even as flames raged around them, Bones and Leonhardt continued to go from room to room. The detective kept fearing they'd find a body or two that had succumbed to smoke or gas inhalation, but they continued to get lucky. Floor after floor, they smashed out windows and tried to dissipate the gas even as explosions rocked the nearby buildings.

When they finally got to the fourteenth floor, however, a change came over Bones.

"What is it, dog?" Leonhardt asked.

The shepherd was more focused now, shaking off the smell of smoke and gas, and alerting to a door midway down the hall. Like the other sealed apartments, Leonhardt could see the electrical tape winding around the doorframe. But unlike the others, this door appeared to have been recently opened.

Without thinking twice, the detective pulled his gun. Pushing through the door, the first thing he saw was Ken standing near the closed living room window.

"Kid, what're you doing in there? Don't you know how dangerous…?"

Before the next words could leave his mouth, he felt something strike his neck with great force, followed by a sharp pain in his throat. It felt like a great hand had come and closed around his windpipe. He simply couldn't breathe.

He looked down and saw a length of clothesline extending from Ken's hand all the way to just below his own chin. He pitched forward onto his knees as his hands felt the trowel that had speared into his neck causing blood to geyser from his body like a shopping mall fountain.

He tried dully to pull the thing out, but he already didn't have the strength. That's when Ken yanked the line backward, causing Leonhardt to tumble forward with such force that his nose and jaw splintered as they struck the floor.

Bones, who had been at the detective's side, lunged for Ken, only to have his own leash snap back, having been wrapped around Leonhardt's wrist.

"You want him?"

The mastiff, which had been standing in the corner, moved to just outside Bones's reach and stared down the furious shepherd. Rather than be intimidated, Bones doubled his efforts to get at the larger dog.

But the body of the swiftly dying cop was just too heavy.

"Come on," Ken said to the mastiff. "The fire will be here in a minute. It'll take care of him."

The mastiff held Bones's ferocious gaze for a second longer, but then slowly padded in a wide circle around the shepherd until it was by Ken's side. As Bones blocked the front door, Ken moved to the window, opened it enough to let the mastiff and himself out. He then gave Bones a quick wink before descending the fire escape.

The chaos at Triborough Houses was nothing like Detective Garza had ever seen. Fire engines were parked for blocks. He counted at least four dozen squad cars. He slipped his badge onto a chain, left his vehicle in the middle of crowded intersection, and started running towards the buildings.

Smoke poured out of five of the towers, and flames were visible for blocks. What complicated matters for the first responders was the sheer number of people evacuating from the buildings. Thousands of residents choked off the streets and alleys, preventing firemen and police officers from getting anywhere near the blazes.

Realizing he'd have to try something different, Garza pulled out his cell phone and dialed Leonhardt's number. It rang and rang, but there was no response.

"Dammit, Phil, where the hell are you?"

When it finally went to voicemail, Garza hung up. He was just pushing his way to Building 1 when an explosion rocked one of the buildings in back. He looked over as flames plumed away from one of the highest floors of Building 10. As fire momentarily illuminated the tower's façade, he caught sight of a man and a large dog moving down a fire escape away from the blaze. They paused at the next floor and disappeared through a window into an apartment, having only been visible for a couple of seconds.

But this was all Garza needed. He knew the moment he laid eyes on the animal that it was the one from the police video.

"Jesus Christ, if you were right, you crazy motherfucker," he said under his breath, knowing Leonhardt would never let him live this down.

Checking his gun, Garza pushed past several paramedics and climbed on top of a fire engine in order to bypass a handful more as he fought his way forward.

XIV

Becca came to in tremendous pain. Her nose and lungs burned like fire, her eyes stinging as if beset by wasps. And this was while they were closed. When she tried to open them, the pain was so great, she had to squeeze them tight again to blot of the agony.

She finally remembered where she was and understood that the only way to safety was straight up and back to the roof. Climbing as best she could, she pulled herself up the steps, a new pain coming in the form of a throbbing headache where she had landed on her skull moments before.

It was only about a dozen steps, but it felt like an uphill mile. When she finally emerged onto the roof, she crawled to the edge and breathed in as deeply as she could.

A nearby explosion caused her to open her eyes and, like Detective Garza, she spied her older brother and the mastiff walking down the fire escape of Building 10.

She looked back at the stairwell and saw nothing but black smoke pouring out, as if she'd been passed out in a chimney. Turning back to the edge of the roof, she saw the fire escape a good floor below her. If she wanted to get onto it, she'd have to lower herself down the side of the building and then drop.

She couldn't imagine anything more terrifying.

Bones could smell the smoke and knew it was getting close. He chomped down on the leash that ran from his harness to Detective Leonhardt's wrist, but it held fast. He bolted towards the hallway, trying to drag the dead man with him, but the weight was just too much.

The German shepherd bit into the leash a second time, but then moved over to Leonhardt's wrist. At first, he tried bite through the loop around his hand, but this proved impossible. He played at it with his forepaws but then licked at the detective's hand a little.

Gingerly, Bones lifted the dead man's wrist into his jaws. He pulled at it for a second before digging his teeth into the soft flesh. Once he had a really good grip, he jerked at the man's limb with such force that the entire arm dislocated out of its shoulder joint at the same time that the elbow snapped.

Bones rolled over on the ground next, twisting the corpse's wrist until the flesh had been almost entirely flayed away. He then dug his teeth into the bones and cracked them just as easily.

A second later, Detective Leonhardt's severed left hand trailing behind him at the end of the leash, Bones skittered out the door towards the stairs. Before he'd gotten even one step down, the entire fourteenth-floor hallway exploded. As the stairwell collapsed around him, the shepherd raced to the darkness below as quickly as he could go.

As soon as Ken entered the maintenance subbasement, he could tell something had changed. Though he could still hear the sounds of chaos coming from outside, there was a new stillness in the locker room that he couldn't immediately identify.

That's when he walked over to the thick gas main that ran up the wall next to one of the water pipes and put his hand on it.

Nothing.

The show was over. The fire department had finally gotten to a master relay for the block and, with or without help from Con Ed, shut off the gas leading to Neville Houses. An inevitability, but Ken was surprised by how quickly they had managed to do it.

"Well, I guess that's it," Ken said simply.

If he was talking to the mastiff which had descended into the subbasement with him, the dog did nothing to acknowledge it. Instead, it moved to the back of the locker room. Once there, it worked its right forepaw around the edge of a service hatch that led below the building.

"Hey, where are you going?" Ken asked.

He hurried after the animal, but it was now actively fighting against the hatch's latch, trying to break it off its hinges in order to enter. Ken got over to it and put a hand on its back. The animal didn't turn, but a low rumble thundered up from its belly. Ken hesitated for a moment but then grabbed it by the mound of flesh at the back of its neck.

This time, the dog whipped around and snapped at his hand. Ken barely managed to get out of its way.

"Yeah, I don't think it likes that."

Ken whirled around and found Trey standing behind him with a gun.

"What're you doing here?"

"Came to kill the dog. Are you going to move and let me?"

"Are you kidding? I'm not going to let you shoot some dog."

"Not some dog," Trey said, darkening. "*That* dog. The one that's turned you into some kind of murderous lunatic. The one that, when I've put a bullet in its brain, will hopefully release you from whatever fucking spell it's got you under. You understand, don't you?"

The mastiff finally stopped doing what it was doing and turned around to face Trey. As it did, Ken stepped between it and his brother.

"You want to shoot this dog, you're going to have to shoot me, too."

"If that's the way it's gonna be, that's the way it's gonna be," replied Trey, raising the gun and pointing it at Ken's chest.

By the time Becca finally made it all the way down the fire escape to the courtyard, the panic had begun to subside. The fire teams were still putting out the major blazes, but as word went around that the gas had been shut off from afar went around, most assumed the danger had passed.

She'd run as best she could down the iron stairs and now had to push past folks milling about sheeplike on her way to Building 10. But as she arrived in the lobby, she was greeted by a peculiar sight, a group of middle-aged men dancing around the bottom of the stairwell, laughing though their faces betrayed horror at whatever they were looking at.

"Who the hell do you think that belonged to?"

"I don't know, but that's just about the most fucked thing I think I've ever seen. Who's got a camera?"

Somebody offered a camera phone. One of the men snapped a picture. Becca moved in close and saw a familiar German shepherd trying to exit the stairs, only to be blocked by the men.

"Bones!" she cried.

The men all turned, giving the dog the opening he was looking for. He barreled down the steps and began sniffing around the lobby. Becca raced over to him and picked up the leash, only to see the object of the men's incredulity: a severed hand still attached to the leash. Rather than deal with it, she simply unhooked the lead from Bones's harness and patted his head.

"Where is he?"

But the dog, its nose still filled with smoke and the scent of gas, looked around aimlessly, as if trying to find something he believed hidden that, in truth, was already long gone.

The standoff between Trey and Ken continued. Neither blinked nor showed any sign they might do so.

"I'm sorry, Ken, but I can't let that thing leave here. You know how many people have died because of it? Because of *you*?"

"You don't know what you're talking about," Ken scoffed. "You're really a fucking idiot, aren't you?"

"Am I?"

"You think this dog told me to do all this? That would imply that I needed to be told that our neighbors deserved this. That they had infested this place, that *we* had infested this place, and needed to be dealt with. Humans are a plague, Trey."

"Wow, you sound like the internet," Trey said dryly. "Now, why don't you move, let me take my shot, and we can go upstairs? Maybe I'll even let you borrow my gun, take a couple of shots into the crowd?"

"Why don't you drop that gun and we'll just agree no one's going to do anything?"

Trey and Ken turned as Detective Garza came down the stairs and into subbasement.

"Yeah, uh-oh. Police," Garza added. "By now, you know this is all over, right?"

"If it's all over, why is this motherfucker pointing a gun at me?" Ken barked.

"Just wondering that myself ," Garza replied, his eyes fixed on Trey. "Why don't we try lowering the gun?"

"I don't know what you think you're looking at, officer, but it's not what's in your head. This man is my brother. He's the one that's been going around pulling gas lines. You check his pockets, you'll find a shitload of keys and probably a list of vacant apartments."

"First off, I'm not an officer, I'm a detective," Garza began. "Second, I've seen your sheet. It's long. Hell, you shot a guy two weeks ago. Your brother, well, clean as a whistle. Also, you've got the gun. You'll forgive me if I make assumptions."

Trey finally looked nervous. He eyed the mastiff. Its expression hadn't changed. But then the young man remembered something.

"My sister called your partner about all this. She told him about Ken, told him about the dog. He was going to get the police dog, Bones, and come back. He knew all this shit."

Garza hesitated. Though he hadn't talked to Leonhardt, he knew something must've brought him here.

"I can't seem to get a hold of him."

"That's because my little brother here killed him up on the fourteenth floor of this building," Ken said. "You go up there and you'll find his body burned to a crisp. Becca called the detective about her brother, but she meant this one."

Trey stared daggers into Ken. He couldn't believe what he was hearing.

"Detective," Trey said. "You have to believe me. It's some fucked-up shit. You saw the video of Mrs. Fowler, didn't you? What about Mr. Lester? Whoever's in with the dog is the one causing this shit. You've *seen* it. You *know* this."

Garza turned to Ken and, for the briefest of moments, saw something flash across the man's face that looked disturbingly close to madness. His mouth opened as if to comment, but he was interrupted by the mastiff rising to its feet, pushing past Ken, and walking over to Trey where it sat at his feet, looking up at him expectantly.

"Oh, fuck you," Trey exclaimed, turning his gun on the dog.

He pulled the trigger, only to then see that his arm was still outstretched, the weapon still aimed at his brother. The bullet erupted from the muzzle, crossed the short distance between the brothers, and entered Ken's chest just above his heart. Trey's eyes went wide as Ken fell back. He turned to Garza in time for his vision to be momentarily blinded by muzzle flash as Garza fired two shots into his torso. The impact sent Trey flying, his gun dropping to the floor.

It had all happened in the briefest of moments, so fast that Garza almost didn't believe what he was seeing.

He hurried to Trey's side and checked his vitals, only to see that he was in the process of dying. The detective stared into the younger man's face as it looked like he was trying to speak. Garza leaned down, but Trey pushed him away.

"My *gun*," Trey hissed, blood misting out of his mouth as he spoke.

Garza turned. The last thing he ever saw was the wounded Ken aiming Trey's pistol at his face.

When the first gunshots echoed through the Building 10 lobby, no one moved. But when Ken emptied the magazine into Detective Garza's head at point-blank range, everyone scattered.

"Somebody's shooting!" they called out as they ran into the courtyard.

Everyone, that is, except Becca and Bones.

"Come on, boy!" Becca cried.

The German shepherd didn't need an invitation. Together, they hurried to the stairs leading to the subbasement and descended. What they found was easily Becca's worst nightmare.

"Trey! *Ken!*" she screamed, clambering down the stairs and over to them.

Detective Garza's head had been functionally obliterated, a mass of blood and ruined bones, so Becca had no idea who that corpse belonged to. But as she pushed it aside, she saw that Trey's eyed were fixed and beginning to dilate as they stared at the ceiling.

"No!" she wailed, the tears coming quickly.

She turned to Ken and, upon seeing the gun, wondered if he had been the one to shoot both of the others. She couldn't imagine Trey had shot him, but until this day, there were a lot of things she couldn't have imagined either of her brothers capable of doing.

She went over to Ken and found him unconscious, though still breathing, labored and shallow. She looked around the locker room, unsure what to do, until she saw Bones at the service hatch. He pawed at it, trying to unhook the latch.

"Is that where he went?" she asked breathlessly.

Bones glanced back at her for only a second before continuing to work on the door.

Becca picked up the gun next to Ken, but it felt light. She knew there weren't any bullets in it. She moved over to Trey, the gun that had taken his life sitting close by. It was heavier. She pocketed it and then moved with the shepherd to the service hatch.

"Okay," she whispered.

Swinging the hatch open, the unlikely duo exited the locker room and slipped into darkness.

XV

Becca had never been under the city before, but she understood that there was an endless labyrinth just below the streets. Trey had talked about the ways the various buildings of Neville Houses were connected by service tunnels and that some of these had access points elsewhere in the city, but she didn't always believe everything Trey said.

Trey.

She couldn't make the connection between the body she'd just seen in the subbasement and her brother. He couldn't be gone. Not him. She hadn't wanted to leave Ken behind, but part of her wondered if that was her brother anymore. She'd heard him on the roof. Something was inside him. Something, she feared, that couldn't be extricated until the dog lost its power over him.

That meant killing the beast. And that meant following it all the way to hell if necessary.

She wasn't sure what made her feel better, the gun in her hand or the German shepherd at her side. She didn't know why Bones was going after the mastiff. She knew there was nothing "personal" between the two dogs...or was there?

She eyed the dog. Bones's nose was pressed to the concrete floor of the dark tunnel. Becca had feared that it would be completely dark, but there were dull emergency lights glowing every thirty yards or so. They didn't do much, but they cut down Becca's terror.

Though she hadn't seen the mastiff since they'd entered the tunnels, she was confident that Bones was taking her in the right direction. He didn't stop moving, but kept right on going as if the trail was lit in neon. When they came to side tunnels or other passageways, the shepherd might lift his head to sniff the air a little, but then he'd go left or right or straight ahead without doubling back.

He knew exactly where the other dog had gone.

At one point, the environment changed. The tunnel, already cold, grew colder. The tunnel narrowed and the walls and floor became slick, as if Becca had somehow entered the throat of a living creature.

But as Bones pressed on, so did she.

She wondered how long they'd been underground, but the darkness played tricks on her perception. It might've been an hour, but if it turned out to be fifteen minutes, Becca would've believed it. She had long given up trying to determine which direction they were going, much less how long it would take to reach their destination.

Then it changed. The tunnel widened again and the air remained dank, but the walls no longer perspired, and she tasted fresh air. She could just make out a light source coming in from above. A ladder came into view, little more than iron rungs bolted into the wall, but Bones stopped in front of it and looked up.

"He climbed the ladder?" Becca asked in surprise, trying to imagine such a large animal ascending the steps with ease.

But then, as if making a point, the German shepherd placed its forepaws on one of the lowest rungs, sank back on its haunches, and then leaped forward, half-jumping, half-climbing to the surface.

As soon as the dog disappeared, Becca climbed up after it. When she reached the surface, she was surprised to find herself in the woods. The sun was just beginning to rise in the east. She realized she must have been underground a lot longer than she'd initially suspected.

Turning back, she saw the lights of Manhattan behind her. She walked towards the edge of the trees and saw that she had walked all the way from Harlem to Randall's Island, having taken a service tunnel under the East River.

She turned back to see where Bones had gone, but he was out of sight. "Bones?!" she cried, instinctively feeling for the gun in her pocket.

She hurried through the trees until she found herself in a large park. There were two soccer fields and a baseball diamond, all with bleachers. She'd been here, she realized, but only a couple of times with Ken. There'd been a neighborhood get-together and then a birthday party for a classmate once. She scanned the area, but saw no sign of the German shepherd.

What she did see was a single open gate at the edge of the park. She made a beeline for it, hoping that the animals simply hadn't hopped the nearest fence and gone off in a different direction.

Once she was on the other side of the fence, she found a long, curving road and began to follow it along the shoulder. The longer she went without seeing Bones, the worse she felt. She'd undertaken this mission, and now she had failed in it.

She kept going until she reached the far side of the little island, finding herself between two bridges that crossed the East River, emptying out into Queens. One was the continuation of I-278 to Queens, the other a much smaller bridge used by trains.

As she eyed the train bridge, she saw, silhouetted against the purpling sky, the shape of the mastiff as it made its way to the center of the bridge.

Her reaction was immediate and instinctual. She took off running. She moved as fast as her legs would carry her, almost tripping over her own feet as she flew down the rock-strewn shoreline towards the train bridge. She still saw no sign of Bones, but didn't care.

She had the gun.

She had the target.

This was going to end right now.

When she got to the bridge, there was no easy access at the waterline, so she had to go inland a few dozen yards to clamber up onto the train tracks and hurry onto the bridge that way. She could still see the dog. It had stopped walking and was now sitting dead center, staring down into the water. It looked like it was waiting for something or, stranger, about to jump.

She kept running, fumbling for the gun. She took out of her pocket and felt the safety, which was on. She knew a lot about guns for someone who had never fired one. She knew when a safety was off, when a gun was loaded, and when a bullet was in the chamber.

A second later, and all three of these things were true about the pistol in her hand. The mastiff still hadn't acknowledged her by the time she was only ten feet away. She stopped, held the gun in both of her hands, and aimed it at the dog.

"Hey, motherfucker!" she yelled, spitting her rage at this horrible beast.

As the mastiff turned to her, she realized that she wasn't looking at the black dog at all, but Bones, the German shepherd sitting there as calm as could be, staring out over the water.

"Oh, no," she whispered.

She felt the mastiff's hot breath on the back of her legs a second later. She didn't know how it had gotten behind her, but there it was, its teeth inches away.

"Bones?" she said, as calm as she could muster.

The German shepherd slowly got to its feet and turned towards Becca. The way its lower jaw hung down, its tongue lolling out between its bottom teeth, Becca thought the dog looked downright rabid.

"Come on, Bones," she said, tears welling up into her eyes. "Not you, too."

The shepherd moved up close and, when it was only a few feet from Becca, it began barking, its teeth bared. The little girl started to tremble as the shepherd stamped its front feet and lowered its head, clearly getting ready to pounce. Becca raised the gun and pointed it at the dog.

"Please don't make me do this, Bones," Becca begged. "I don't want to shoot you! Come on, boy. Don't come any closer!"

But the angry shepherd inched ahead, causing Becca to back up, her body pressing up against the mastiff. As she felt its weight on her skin, something changed in her mind, a synapse fired, a connection made where one hadn't been before. She'd seen Bones try to fight the dog before and it hadn't worked. The shepherd hadn't been able to get so much as a tooth into the other animal's thick hide.

She turned and faced the mastiff, looking into its soulless eyes. It stared back at her as dully as the night sky, without concern. She pointed the gun directly between the mastiff's eyes only to feel a slight shift in her vision. Everything looked the same, but it was that same warped perspective, the same feeling that what was in front of her was an optical illusion.

Even more indicative was the subtle shift in the direction from which Bones's barking came. He should be behind her, shouldn't he? Then why did it sound like the barks were coming from something mere inches from her gun?

She turned back around and the optical illusion seemed to fall away. She was now facing Bones, but the sound of his barking was still coming from directly in front of her.

She turned and looked over the side of the bridge to where she thought the mastiff had been looking. Directly under her, she saw something black deep within the water. At first, it appeared to be moving, but then she realized it was an optical illusion. She moved her head one way or another, and the shape disappeared. Then she'd find it again, a large patch of darkness like a shadow at the bottom of the river.

"What is that?"

She turned from the angry shepherd to the impassive mastiff, but then back to the water. Everything about this was wrong. She ran through her options, finding little to recommend. But then a new one appeared. As Bones continued to inch forward, she tumbled over this new idea in her mind and finally made a decision.

"I'm sorry, boy," she said to the shepherd.

And jumped.

Though the bridge was hardly the highest in New York, when Becca hit the surface of the water, it still felt like she'd been in a car crash. Her head shot back, all the air was forced from her lungs, and her legs felt as if they'd been torn off her body. The fact that the water was frigid was something she only noticed after a few seconds had passed and she'd clawed her way back up to the surface.

She had only been up for a moment before she came face-to-face with Bones, hurtling downward from the bridge, his snarling jaws aimed directly for her throat.

She took a deep breath and forced herself back under the dark waves. *Come on, Bones*, she thought.

She swam towards the dark shadow on the riverbed below. Even as she got closer, she still couldn't tell what it was. There was a part of the river bottom that she could just make out, rocks and ridges, mostly, and then a part she couldn't: a gaping maw with ill-defined edges, albeit vaguely in the shape of a circle.

She pushed herself deeper and deeper, feeling the burn in her lungs not unlike what she'd so recently encountered in the smoke-filled stairwell. She glanced back and saw the German shepherd still coming towards her, a trail of air bubbles floating away from his clenched jaws.

Even in the lowlight, she saw the fire in his eyes. She was his target. He wouldn't stop until he'd killed her.

Keep coming, boy. Keep coming.

She was within a few dozen yards of the black pit when she began to feel lightheaded, her arms and legs going to jelly as her strength began to ebb. She tried to see into it, but saw only darkness. Nothing lay beyond its mouth but black.

But still she pressed on. She forced her fingers to claw forward, raking the water aside as she went deeper. Her vision began to blur as well. She knew it wouldn't be long now.

She turned and saw Bones approaching, but similarly running out of steam. He stretched his neck as if trying to take a bite out of her leg. She kicked a little harder and moved ahead, but that was the last of her energy. She was almost to the shadow when she felt herself going limp. Her momentum slowed as her body gave up. It was a welcome feeling, a weightlessness that swept all cares away.

She curled around and tried to see Bones one last time, but her eyes failed her.

That was okay, she thought.

Then nothing.

"Kid! *Kid*! Wake up! Come on!"

There was a distant light, there was blue, there was a sick feeling, and then Becca threw up. Her eyes opened as water belched out of her lungs. She tried to hold herself up with one arm, but the strength wasn't there and she collapsed back down, only to vomit again.

"Oh, my God!" cried a panicked woman's voice. "Oh, my God!"

Becca felt a hand go under her back and lift her into a seated position. Her eyes finally began to focus, and she saw a woman in running clothes staring back at her.

"Oh, my God," the woman repeated a third time, Becca having the presence of mind to think it a bit much. "Are you okay?"

Becca tried not to scowl. She thought this a ridiculous question.

"I saw you go into the water. Do you fall off the bridge?"

"Bridge?" Becca asked.

The woman pointed. "The Hell Gate. The train bridge."

Becca stared at it for a moment before everything came back to her at once. "A dog! Did you see a dog?"

"Yeah! It jumped in after you. Tried to save you. I saw it when I dove in to fish you out. It was swimming for you. But then I lost track of it. Was that your dog?"

"Yeah," Becca said.

"I'm really sorry," the woman said. "He was a really brave dog."

Becca nodded before looking back up to the bridge.

"You didn't see a second dog, did you?"

Epilogue

Bones was found a week later in Queens. He'd been skulking around behind a row of restaurants on Roosevelt, eating rats and garbage, when one of the local business owners finally had enough and called animal control.

It took a couple days, but a sharp-eyed veterinarian's assistant who volunteered at the local shelter had heard from a friend about a police dog who'd been stitched up after a dog fight a couple of weeks before in the exact same area where this animal had been. She made a couple of calls and the presumed-dead shepherd was brought back to Manhattan. Once his identity was confirmed, he was put on the next plane back to Pittsburgh.

"Jesus Christ, Bones!" Sergeant Youman said upon picking up his partner at the airport. "You look like shit. That's the last time I entrust you to the NYPD. Hope you slept on the flight. Got a guy downtown who claims he buried a couple of bums in Point Park. Pretty sure that'll kill most of the morning."

Bones just stared up at the sergeant until the officer sighed, jammed a fist into his pocket, and brought out a half-eaten bag of pretzels.

"How the fuck did you know? *Prick*."

Bones licked his lips. Billy tossed him a couple, the shepherd swallowing these without chewing. The sergeant sighed and poured the rest of the bag into his hand.

"Here."

The shepherd scarfed them up then followed his handler out of the airport to where Billy had parked his truck at the curb.

"I dare airport security to give a ticket to a K9 officer. Seriously, you'll bite their balls off if I ask you to, right?"

Bones glanced up at him expectantly.

"Ah. You'd do it for more pretzels. Well, let me see if I've got any in the glovebox."

A minute later, they were on the Penn Lincoln Parkway, making good time back to the city.

"What happened to the dog?"

"I don't know."

"You didn't see it?"

"No. It was on the bridge when I jumped off. It was gone when I came back."

Ken sighed.

"And you didn't see it in the water?"

"Not at all."

Ken nodded from his bed only a few hundred yards from the exact spot Becca had been pulled out of the river by one of the nurses at the hospital for the criminally insane that was currently housing the young man. It had taken two weeks of petitioning by social services to get Becca in to see him. It wasn't until the threat of certain deviations from policy in Detective Leonhardt's handling of her and her family coming to light were made that the police relented and allowed this one visitor.

"They said that you're probably never getting out," Becca said quietly.

"Do you know how many died because of me? Worse, you know that I killed two police detectives, right? They've got me dead to rights on both of those. Oh, yeah. That maintenance guy, too. Used the same thing on him as I did the detective."

"Stop it!" Becca protested.

Ken shrugged.

"What? Should I feel sorry for myself? I'll have plenty of time for that when they put me in Riker's or wherever they stuff folks like me. Right now, my entire focus is on finding you the right home."

"Did you talk to Mrs. Drucker?"

"I did. She said all the right things. Just like you'd think she would."

"And that's a bad thing?"

"Did I say that?"

Becca went silent. There was only one thing she'd wanted to bring with her to show Ken in the hospital, the *New York Post* cover story on the discovery of Bones, a banner headline reading: *Drowned Hound Found!* She thought it would make Ken laugh, but the social workers who had driven her there said that it would be confiscated, so she should leave it in the car.

"What matters to me is what *you* think of living with your principal for the next few years?"

"I guess it's okay," Becca said. "I've been there a few days now. It's all right."

"Where is she?"

"Down in Chelsea."

"She rich?"

Becca shrugged.

"What do you want me to tell her?"

"That you're okay with me living there. I think she's afraid of you."

Ken snorted. "Maybe it's better that way. She won't fuck with you as much."

Despite every doctor, orderly, social worker, and cop telling her she wasn't allowed to do so, she reached over and hugged her brother tight.

"Excuse me, miss?!" one of the officers growled.

Becca hugged Ken for a second longer as if she hadn't heard, but then broke away. "I'm sorry. I forgot."

"Can we swing by the bridge?" Becca asked as the social worker's car pulled out of the hospital parking lot.

"You really want to do that?"

"I think it would help with the healing process, don't you?"

The social worker scowled, but took a right instead of a left out of the parking lot.

The actual bridge wasn't accessible by road, so they had to park and walk over to it. Becca moved to climb onto the tracks, but the social worker shook her head.

"It's dangerous up there."

"Yeah, I know. I've been."

"You can't go up there!"

But Becca was already hurrying along the tracks at a deliberate pace. The sun was high in the air as she walked, reaching the bridge just as the social worker stumbled up onto the tracks behind her. Becca broke into a jog until she reached the center of the bridge. Once there, she stared down into the water.

"Wait!" cried the social worker, already panting. "Don't jump!"

Becca tried in vain to see the dark spot under the waves, but she couldn't see an inch below the surface. The sun was angled in such a way that the black of the river worked as a mirror, reflecting the bridge, the shore, the sun above, and the girl's tiny silhouette.

The social worker reached the little girl and grabbed her shoulder so awkwardly that she almost pushed her over the side.

"Jesus," the woman muttered. "What're we doing here?"

Becca eyed the water one last time before turning away.

"Nothing," she whispered. "We can go."

With that, she turned around and began walking back down the tracks. The social worker stared after her, hopelessly confused, but could do little but follow her back to the shore.

Becca reached the car and waited, the woman unlocking the doors with a remote key. Without a word, the little girl climbed into the backseat. As they drove away, she stared out the window at the passing trees.

"Why's it called the Hell Gate?"

"I actually know that," the social worker replied proudly. "It's Dutch. *Hellegat.* Only, it has two meanings. *Helle* in Dutch means 'bright' and *gat* is 'hole' or 'tunnel.' But, of course, *helle* is also 'hell,' so it's either a passage to hell or a passage to bright light, like heaven. When the first explorers discovered it, they didn't know what was down that river. Eventually, *Hellegat* became Hell Gate."

"That's really messed-up," said Becca. "Why don't they change it?"

The social worker shrugged. "Do you know how many maps they'd have to change? How many street signs? Sometimes, people just let it go."

Becca nodded idly, wondering how people could just "let go" of a place in the river named after an entrance to hell, but then thought, *Yeah, New York*.

She let her mind wander to her planned outing that afternoon with Principal Drucker. They were going to a ballet studio that Becca had selected almost randomly from the list of activities the eager-to-please woman had offered up in an attempt to "make inroads."

Becca didn't particularly like ballet, but it was geographically the farthest from both the Carver Academy and the Drucker apartment. If Becca signed up, there'd be all kinds of leeway with the time spent getting down to it and getting back home.

Time for herself.

More than anything else, this was what Becca wanted right now. She sank back into the seat as the car crossed the RFK Bridge back to Harlem. She felt the river on either side of her in a way she never had before. This time, she refused to look. A shiver traveled up her spine and made her scalp tingle. Her level of fear rose and rose until it was all she could do to keep from screaming.

She closed her eyes tight and waited until for the sound of the car bumping along the bridge to even out to the smooth of the road on the other side of the water. The sound seemed to go on forever, getting louder with every beat. She pressed her hands over her ears, tears now forming in her eyes as she felt herself beginning to hyperventilate.

Only a few more feet, a tiny voice in the back of her head whispered. *Only a few more feet...*

But soon even that voice was blotted out by the piercing wail rushing through Becca's body like a banshee. She screamed and screamed, the social worker almost slamming into a truck in the adjacent lane.

"What is it?! What happened?" she cried, pulling the car over to the shoulder of the bridge, right under a sign that read: *No Stopping On Bridge*.

The social worker threw on the hazard lights and ran around to the backseat of the car. She opened the door and tried to pull Becca's hands from her ears.

"What's the matter, Becca? Talk to me."

But even as she tried to sound calm, the sight of the little girl in complete hysterics terrified her.

The cars behind them began to slow, a couple of drivers hitting their horns. The ones who could see what was going on silenced theirs, waiting for the disturbing spectacle to ebb. Drivers in the opposite lane braked to better rubber-neck and, inevitably, shake their heads. Even those with their windows up and radios on couldn't help but hear the terror in the little girl's screams.

They eventually drove on, but Becca's voice hung heavy in their eardrums and, for some, would continue to do for days to come. A couple would even check the news or try to look it up online.

But the little girl who couldn't stop screaming was never to be found.

CUR

"Shepherds ain't the best fight dogs," the man with the black widow neck tattoo scoffed. "Pits, rotts, mastiffs like the Canario, some Dogos, maybe a Boerboel, even an Akita or a Kangal, *those* are dogs bred for the ring. German shepherds? They just don't get pissed off enough. They're not born ready to kick ass."

The tattoo moved and flexed as the fellow spoke. Billy couldn't take his eyes off it any more than the dog currently being derided at his heel could. When the man's monologue finally ended, the police sergeant glanced down to his purebred German shepherd, Bones, who sat placidly with his tongue out in a pant. It was true. There really was nothing about the animal that shouted "born to kick ass."

"But this guy's a monster," Billy enthused. "I've seen him tear through junkyard dogs, English bulldogs, even a *pit*. I wouldn't waste your time."

Black Widow Tattoo, whose real name was A.J. "Playboy" Vickers, was unmoved. The bent-lip snarl that had been on his face since the temporarily undercover cop had approached the fight check-in table moments before, shepherd at his side, remained firmly in place. He now crossed and uncrossed his boot-clad feet as if waiting for Billy to get the message and shove off.

But the officer didn't budge.

Instead, he reached into pocket, pulled out the entry fee of twelve twenty-dollar bills and a single ten-spot, and laid them on the table. Then he waited. Vickers let his gaze drop from Billy back to Bones. This time, he decided there was something he didn't like about the shepherd's face.

"Fine. You've got a hard-on to watch your dog get killed in the ring? We can accommodate you. Just don't come around here again with a non-fight breed. Got it?"

Billy nodded. Vickers made a show of counting the money, as if looking for one last excuse to turn him away or at least beat him to a pulp. The officer tried to remember what he could of Vickers' record. There were drug charges and arms charges, a robbery conviction, and a slew of early misdemeanor arrests that went nowhere.

Hardly on par with plotting to assassinate a sitting president.

As much as he'd like to haul Vickers in and see if there was anything outstanding they could pin on him, Billy knew he had to leave him alone. Him, and any of the other criminal types frequenting Timothy Knippa's dog fight compound outside Blairsville that night. No, Billy and Bones had one job: locate Henry Knippa, Timothy's older brother. Though it was Timothy, a skinny young man born and bred in Indiana County, who'd made a name for himself as the breeder of some of the most ferocious fight dogs in the state, Henry was currently considered the greater threat. This despite having a rap sheet hardly as ostentatious as his notorious sibling.

"Timothy's like some kind of mad scientist," Secret Service Field Supervisor Antonio Michaels had explained to Pittsburgh Police Sergeant Billy Youman earlier that day in a monologue that made Billy's blood boil. "To make the dogs last longer in the ring, he experiments with all kinds of performance-enhancing drugs, mostly different kinds of crystal meth, but also PCP. One of his animals could have its leg hanging by a tendon, but, feeling no pain, it fights on 'til the death. This is why he's starting to draw real crowds. He's built up his events into some kind of gladiatorial spectacle. And since he's also a breeder, he breeds the perfect dogs to go with the perfect drug cocktail. One of our guys even wondered which came first, the drug combo or the dog to go with it? Chicken or egg?"

Billy seethed.

"Why are we finding out about this now?" he demanded. "You know some guy is out there doing this shit, and you just let it ride?"

Michaels glanced at Billy's superior, a retiring sort named Bob Zusak. Though the look was clearly a request for the lawman to rein in his charge, Zusak said nothing.

To his credit, Billy thought.

"Timothy Knippa is what the FBI refers to as a 'shit magnet,' which is why they had a guy in with his organization in the first place," Michaels explained. "He attracts the worst shitbags in the state, pulling them out of Philly, Pittsburgh, Allentown, Erie, and bringing them together in Blairsville. There, they can be I.D.'d and checked out. The amount of information gathered due to this guy's operation is staggering."

"So if I see him, you're saying I can't cave in his skull for all dog-kind, right?"

"That's *exactly* what I'm saying, Sergeant," Michaels hissed, more than a little perturbed. "The target is Henry Knippa, and *only* Henry Knippa. He's the priority above all others. You understand that, right?"

Even if he didn't want to admit it, Billy understood one hundred percent.

The President was coming to Pittsburgh, and that meant the Secret Service knocked on the doors of everyone who'd sent a threatening letter, made a threatening online post, or just in general implied in some forum that they would like to kill the commander-in-chief.

"There's a class of psychos that just get fixated on the President," Michaels had explained when Billy was first brought into the meeting room. "Doesn't always matter who's in the White House, either. It's what the office represents; it's somehow come around to being identified as the source of all misery. And with the current guy, the number of threatening letters and posts online is through the roof. This helps us do our job, as it's easier to I.D. the lunatics. I mean, they really believe we're not monitoring the bug-fuck websites? So, we track all these people down and pay them a visit in person, like you called that number for a free Book of Mormon. Nine times out of ten, they're shocked to see us, like how could we have found them on the vast World Wide Web? In those case, it's often an isolated incident, somebody blowing off steam. Dad just got fired, the kids need braces, so let's do the craziest thing imaginable. But the reason doesn't matter. We let them know they're on a list forever, and if they do it again, it's jail. When the President's in town, we knock on that door again, just so they know we haven't forgotten and they should consider staying away from this list of venues. Doesn't matter if they're locked up even and couldn't get near the President if they tried. We still make the visit."

"So, this Henry Knippa wrote a letter?" Billy asked.

"He *didn't*, which is why we're a little more worried than if he had," Michaels explained. "No, we were alerted to it by the FBI. Their informant who runs with Timothy Knippa heard that Timothy's brother was this deranged lunatic looking to shoot the President through the eyes. The guys joked about it, but the informant could suss out that Henry had the means and motivation. So he made it so that he ended up at Henry's place one night. In his house, Henry had multiple guns, a rough layout of the President's schedule for the Pittsburgh union meet, and a shitload of video files on multiple hard drives showing various recent presidents moving in and out of speaking engagements."

"Laying out Secret Service protection procedures," Billy surmised.

"Exactly."

"So you heard about this, got a warrant, and Henry rabbited before you could make an arrest?"

"Worse," Michaels sighed. "We hit the house when he wasn't there to try and lock up the guns. It was in a residential area, after all. But then he never came home. A few hours later, we found the informant with his brains blown out on a river bank. Also, at least half the guns the informant told us about were missing."

Billy didn't need a calendar to remind him the President was set to arrive in less than thirty-six hours. There wasn't a dog handler on the force who didn't know they were expected to pull double duty over the three days.

"Can't you tell the President to stay away?"

"If the President altered his schedule to accommodate every credible and imminent threat, he'd never leave the residence. So I hope this gives you a window into the pressure and time constraints we're facing. We need to get Henry Knippa into custody, and we're grasping at straws to make that happen. Will you help us?"

When it came down to it, what bothered Billy wasn't just that the FBI and U.S. Secret Service were so cavalier about letting a horrific dog fighting enterprise operate with impunity in order to keep tabs on crooks. It was that once Billy had said he'd go along with their operation, they'd laid out the shittiest, most half-assed, and undercooked plan he'd ever heard.

"I mean, they want to just send a fresh face into the lion's den with a non-fight dog a week after a paid federal informant takes one in the ear?" Billy complained to Bones once they were back in Billy's apartment, preparing for their first mission as undercovers. "They can talk all they want about how close our tactical backup'll be, but if shit goes down, it's our ass, not theirs. We'll be dead before they get out of their trucks."

But if the German shepherd was intimidated by the mission, he didn't show it. Instead, the dog ate his dinner and settled down next to Billy's bedroom window to watch the gray winter clouds roll in.

"I mean, who knows who's going to be in there, right?" Billy continued, tossing on a faded Megadeth T-shirt, blue jeans, and work boots, hoping they didn't scream "costume." "No one's checked out the place. Plenty of guys know my face, not just from some lowlight collar, but sitting there staring at me in the witness box as I testify against them. This isn't the way undercover work's supposed to go."

As he made this final statement, Bones raised his head and eyed his handler's outfit before settling back down and going to sleep.

At seven o'clock, Billy loaded Bones into his Bronco and made the hour-long drive to the town of Derry. Derry was only fifteen minutes from the Knippa farm. The plan was to use the local Pennsylvania State Police barracks parking lot as a staging area before splitting up and moving out.

The Secret Service agents were there, as well as a tech on loan from the FBI. As the tech approached the dog and his handler, he held up what looked like two silver threads.

"These are your mics," the tech on loan from the FBI told Billy and Bones as he came over, holding what looked like two silver threads. "One is for the dog's collar and one for your shirt. I just have to make a quick incision in the material, and in it goes."

Billy leaned down, allowing his shirt to be operated on, but then removed Bones's collar for the tech to work on.

"I'm not saying he'll bite you, but he hasn't bitten anybody for a couple of weeks now. I can tell he's getting the itch."

The tech scoffed.

"If I didn't think you could control your animal, would I be standing here?" he drawled, pouring the Bronx over his accent.

But when he looked down at the shepherd for some kind of reassuring *we're all friends here* tail wag, he received nothing but a cold, closed-mouth stare. It was as if Bones was weighing his options; bite him in the leg? Or in the balls?

Billy grinned and stroked Bones's head.

"Looks like he's gonna let you off easy. Guess he figures he'll get to bite a whole bunch of folks later."

Being forty miles east of Pittsburgh off Route 22, the Knippa farm was two counties away from Billy's Pittsburgh jurisdiction. To get around this, the Secret Service, coordinating through the local FBI field office, had the dog handler and his animal formally assigned to the federal investigative team. Billy knew this typically took weeks of paperwork and red tape, and assumed the fast turnaround came from his chain of command covering their collective asses in advance should he or Bones get shot or killed. Even Indiana County officials, initially reluctant to allow a Pittsburgh cop and his dog on their turf, changed gear once they realized a few signatures absolved them of any and all responsibility.

"We'll have men in the woods, but you won't see them on your way in," Michaels told Billy in the Derry parking lot. "We gave you the sheets on all the players we know will be there, but we anticipate there being at least six or seven times that number. But these additional participants have no loyalty to Knippa and won't stick around if things go bad. We've also heard a local recording artist and his entourage may be in attendance. They may be armed as well, but they're to be left alone."

"Are they?" Billy asked witheringly.

"*Yes*," stressed the field supervisor. "Part of what motivates would-be assassins is the media attention. The perceived infamy. The less the press and public know about this operation, the better. If we can control the narrative and characterize this as a drug bust, that's a big win for us. Any questions?"

Billy tilted his head as if considering whether all his bases had been covered, but then scoffed.

"How far from the main house is your nearest man? How much time will it take him or her to get to the house in case of an emergency? It's supposed to snow again tonight, so how will that affect their time? Will this person be listening in and have discretion when it comes to rendering aid, or will they have to wait a few seconds – or even minutes – for the order to come down the chain of command? If they come in guns a'blazing after I make a positive I.D. on Knippa, how much time have they had with my photograph to know not to shoot me? As my dog is mic'ed, but won't be able to point out the target in court, will he be given the same no-shoot priority as me, given the number of other animals inside?"

Michaels glared at Billy but said nothing before stalking off, shaking his head. The police sergeant understood, though. When it came to matters like this, he was supposed to feel an overwhelming sense of patriotism to carry him past any of the niggling details. For a guy like Michaels, giving a lowly cop the opportunity to *sacrifice* for the greater good was a gift. Only for some reason, this dog handler wasn't playing ball.

Billy supposed that was what happened when you're a branch of law enforcement most judged on its failures rather than its successes.

Still, this didn't mean a hill of beans to Billy as he left Derry for the short drive to Blairsville. Derry was to the southwest, so he would reach the city itself, then cut back west on Route 22 to reach the farm. He had to remember that in case anyone asked him where he was coming from, as it wouldn't look like Pittsburgh.

"I'll tell 'em I got lost," Billy snarked to Bones as they bumped along the unmarked gravel road that left the highway and went about a half mile into the woods before reaching the farm.

Billy had been afraid of getting the Bronco stuck out in the snow or mud. But the way the slush had been packed down by the previous vehicles made it easy to stay in their tracks. It also told the cop he and Bones were among the last to arrive.

Though almost entirely obscured by trees, the Knippa compound was actually quite large. There was a large two-story Queen Anne–style Victorian farmhouse nearest the road, but as massive as it was, it was dwarfed by the barn behind it. Both structures were easily a hundred years old, the age showing in the sagging roof of the barn and the crumbling porch of the house. A newer building with cinder-block walls and a steel roof ran alongside the barn, looking like a long warehouse.

All three buildings were drab in color, which Billy took for camouflage. Even the roof of the warehouse had been painted a dull gray, which would've read as dirt from above. Billy figured the state police did the occasional flyover, looking for meth labs, but wouldn't be low enough even in helicopters to see much more than an old dirt track heading off to nowhere from the main highway. He idly wondered if they changed the paint depending on the season.

There were about forty other cars and trucks parked in front of the farmhouse, including an imposing black Yukon Denali alongside a tricked-out Rolls Royce Phantom.

The recording artist and entourage, Billy surmised.

"Think they like watching dogs get torn apart?" Billy asked Bones. "Or just betting on the outcome?"

Billy parked and clambered out of the Bronco. He pulled on Bones's leash to get the shepherd to hop out after him. The officer hesitated, the cold winter air harsh in his lungs. But then he looked down at the shepherd, whose features were taut and alert. Bones was all business, spoiling for a fight.

"Let's get to it."

"There it is again!"

Henry Knippa stormed around the small upstairs bedroom as if ready to explode. His brother Timothy, standing in the doorway, had hoped he'd run out of steam by now. Instead, he'd only spun himself into more of a tizzy.

For Timothy, this was familiar. Henry's behavior had defied logic since they were kids. But as he got older and bolder and "realized" his medications were an attempt by the "social hierarchy" to "control him biochemically," the younger brother had to come to terms with having a full-bore loony on his hands.

"This isn't normal," Henry continued. "Somebody out there's got all kinds of equipment. It's completely messing with my system."

"Come on, Henry," Timothy sighed. "We've got a full house back there. I finally even got Lil' Mwerto and his posse out to look at the dogs. We get a little of *his* shine on this place, and we're not just some backwoods operation anymore. I need you to quit winding yourself up. Have a beer."

He held out a can of Old German, their late father's brand going way back. But Henry just shook his head and pointed at the ever-growing pile of electronic equipment strewn around his childhood bedroom.

"You just don't get it, do you, Timothy?" Henry said, shaking his head as if *he* was the sane one.

Though Henry had left Blairsville at eighteen, living first in Philly and then Baltimore, he'd returned to the Knippa compound after getting locked up on a battery charge. This involved a woman Henry had referred to several times as his girlfriend. In fact, Timothy had spent hours upon hours over the months leading up to the arrest listening to Henry on the phone telling him what a "vile bitch" she was. But after Henry entered the woman's apartment and roughed up both her and a young man she'd brought home, Timothy learned the truth.

"She said she'd never seen him before in her life," the arresting officer had told him. "If I had to guess, I'd say he was stalking her, but had all these delusions that it was reciprocal."

"Couldn't she be one of those crazy chicks just looking to get him busted?" Timothy had pressed. "I've heard him talk about this bitch for months."

"Trust me, we get plenty of those," the cop agreed, more sympathetic than Timothy'd expected. "Hell, wouldn't be Bawlmore if we didn't. But this woman was scared out of her mind, while your brother couldn't even come up with her real name."

"Catherine-something?" Timothy offered, figuring it would be fruitless. "Catherine Gilmartin?"

"Anna Dominguez. We finally got it out of him that 'Catherine Gilmartin' was the real name of some porn star he'd fixated on."

"Aw, fuck me," Timothy managed before hanging up the phone.

After a disastrous psych evaluation, Henry was moved from Baltimore City Detention to the Clifton T. Perkins Hospital in Jessup for further observation. Once those doctors got Henry talking, Timothy could tell his brother was in danger of being put away for some time. So he paid the right lawyer to convince the judge to release Henry into his brother's care.

This after paying off Anna Dominguez to the tune of $50,000 to drop all charges.

Unfortunately, the new boyfriend, Clay-something, who Henry also roughed up, came sniffing around for a payoff of his own. Tired of being treated like an ATM, Timothy had a couple of his guys drag the aggrieved fellow out to the northern branch of the Patapsco River to show him where they'd dump his bullet-riddled corpse if he kept at it. To the boyfriend's credit, even then he tried to negotiate, offering to take half of his original request for $25,000. Over a cell phone held by his goons, including Vickers, Timothy offered the man $5,000 and his life.

The offer was accepted.

But not long after Timothy had installed Henry in a rental house in Blairsville near St. Simon & Jude Church, the young man started hearing stories about Henry raising hell and making trouble. Timothy went out to talk to Henry, inviting him to stay at the farm, take a job working the dogs, even have his pick of the girls Timothy ran from time to time, but Henry would have none of it.

"Don't you see?" he'd say. "These are the things you use to keep the truth *away*. I don't have any use for them. I'm not afraid like everyone else is. I see what's coming, and I know it's the end. I just wish you could see it, too."

Timothy endured several dark nights of the soul in which he considered putting a bullet in his brother's heart. But he didn't need to see the future to know he wouldn't be able to live with himself afterward. He'd be plagued with questions: What if Henry got better? What if there was some turn in the road up ahead where he recognized what he'd become and rejoined civilization?

As long as there was that chance, he couldn't kill his only brother.

This was before Henry went off and shot Jim D'Leo. Timothy had told his brother a dozen times that the rat-faced fuck was an informant and that he should leave him alone while the organization figured out what to do about him. When word got back that D'Leo was found dead in the very spot they'd threatened to dump Clay-something, Timothy wondered if he'd waited too long to deal with Henry.

That was less than a week ago. Now the fight dog entrepreneur just had to get through that week's event before settling on a course of action.

"All right, Henry," Timothy said, a calming tone in his voice. "Run it by me one more time."

Henry sighed and smiled condescendingly, the teacher having to explain a simple problem to a recalcitrant student for a third time.

"These are parabolic mics and radio receivers," Henry said, indicating the various pieces of equipment. "You aim one of the mics at anybody within five hundred yards and you can hear what they're saying, same as if they were in the room with you. The radios pick up cell phone transmissions almost anywhere in the county. I know before you do when anybody gets close. Even better, I know what your men say when they're talking shit about you behind your back, but don't think anyone's around."

Maybe there is something useful in Henry's mania, Timothy thought.

"You open a window around the Washington, D.C., say, at the Hay-

Adams Hotel, a building that faces the White House, and a mic like this is the first thing the Secret Service spotters on the White House roof aim in your direction. They want to know if you're taking a shot at the President, so they listen in."

But as soon as I think that, it's this President-thing again, Timothy sighed inwardly.

"Get to the point," he prodded.

"Well, about fifteen minutes ago, a helluva lot of radio equipment showed up on Route 22," Henry enthused. "At first I figured it was folks coming to the fight."

"It wasn't?"

"The signals split up, half rolling into place in the east woods about a quarter mile up and the other half to the north. Now it's just sitting there. I was just trying to figure out why when I picked up even more interference from the parking lot and ended up following one of your dog fighters into the barn."

"Wearing a wire?"

"Bingo."

Shit.

"You're sure about this?" Timothy asked.

"Sure as I am standing here. Even better, I can use this stuff to point him out to you."

"That was my next question."

"All right, you're good," Vickers told Billy, the money counted and placed in an envelope. "The kennel's that concrete outbuilding beside the barn. Drop off your dog and grab a Bud. They'll call you over the speaker when it's time to bring your dog to the fight pit. Cool?"

"As a witch's tit," Billy replied, giving Bones's leash a tug.

Vickers offered a final scowl before the police sergeant walked off.

As they walked to the kennel, Billy got a look inside the barn, its two sliding doors wide open. Spectators were already gathered on risers around three of the building's four walls. In the center was the fight pit, which Billy assumed was a converted cellar, its ceiling removed. Though the floor would be a good ten to twelve feet down, it would keep the dogs from leaping into the crowd while still allowing the crowd a good view of the action.

As he and Bones moved on to the kennel, the police sergeant glanced toward the woods. He wondered which Secret Service agents or local sheriff's deputies had him in their sights at that moment. He wished he could get some kind of sign off them, though it would be worse in a moment. With Bones at his side, he still felt invincible, the biggest weapon in the woods by his side and at his command. But putting the dog in the kennel was akin to turning in his gun and stripping naked. Four dozen armed men guarding his back from the woods didn't make him feel an iota less vulnerable.

Though he'd seen the kennel when he parked, Billy only now realized how deceptively large it was. It might have only been a single story high and about twenty feet wide, but it extended back into the trees more than twice that.

"Checking in a dog," Billy told the young man at the door. When the fellow looked up, Billy recognized him from Michaels' files as Paul Amis, whose first run-in with law enforcement came a month before his twelfth birthday when he'd stabbed another kid on his front lawn. For the rest of his teen years, Amis was in and out of state facilities until he met one of Knippa's crew while awaiting trial in Latrobe. After that, the arrests petered off. He was being mentored by a better class of criminal.

"That a shepherd?" Paul scoffed, eyeing Bones.

"Nah, an Irish setter."

"Name?" Paul sneered.

"Bones."

"Cute!" Paul laughed, bending down to the shepherd. "You're about to get your fucking heart ripped out, Bones? That cool with you?"

Bones didn't flinch. Even better, it didn't even look like he'd considered it, which made Billy smile. He'd taken Bones through crowd-control training exercises a few times. They'd spent days with instructors taunting them without Bones batting an eye. The dog proved unflappable.

In this instance, it just angered the one doing the taunting.

"Put him in 19," Paul scowled. "Then get the fuck out of here."

Billy pushed past Paul and into the kennel, only to have the bright fluorescent lights blazing inside nearly blind him as he entered. But even more than the volume of luminescence, the wave of sound waiting for him on the other side of the door just about knocked Billy on his ass.

Long as the building was on the outside, it was clear once inside that it was divided in half. The room Billy and Bones had entered was filled to the ceiling with steel cages on every wall, mirroring the barn with its risers. But instead of drunken spectators, these cages were filled with furiously barking dogs across several breeds, mostly mixed. There were pit bulls and Rottweilers, Dobermans and mastiffs. An English bulldog barked at an Akita ten times its size while the Akita growled at a sleeping pit one cage over. The sound of it all was deafening.

"It looks like the damn *Brady Bunch*," Billy joked to Bones, the reference coming from the cages being stacked three high with a different face peering out of each, staring out at its neighbors.

There was a metal ramp with rubber edges nearby, mats bolted onto the surface. Billy surmised it was a ramp that allowed the animals to descend from the second- and third-level cages, the mat to keep the dogs from slipping. But the empty cage "19" turned out to be on the ground floor, so no ramp was necessary.

As he led Bones to the cage, Billy flinched half a dozen times as this dog or that turned its fury on the newcomers. The closer he got, the more he could see the dogs' battle damage. There were heavy scars and missing fur, broken teeth and misshapen limbs that hadn't been set properly after being broken. Almost worse than this, however, were the steroid cases. It was most obvious on the pits, their beefed-up muscles giving them the appearance of overstuffed body builders. They were freakish. Some of their mouths were so misshapen that their teeth were prominent and bent, but then Billy wondered if this was a desired effect.

For Billy, who'd fallen into dog handling in the Army, only to come out loving dogs above most humans, it was a devastating sight. These dogs were beyond help. Even if law enforcement managed to shut down a ring like this, these animals would surely have to be put down.

"Fucking hell, Bones," Billy muttered as he ushered the shepherd into the empty cage. "I'm sorry about this."

But Bones seemed to barely notice. He clambered into the cage, turned around, and faced Billy with an expectant look on his face. Billy hesitated before closing the cage, but then didn't slide the latch all the way in place.

"Just in case," he whispered, tapping the unused lock. "One good hit, and you're sprung."

Bones took a sniff before lying down on an old crusty towel on the bottom of the cage. Billy wondered how many dogs had spent their last moments on that piece of cloth before he banished the thought from his mind.

"See you on the flipside," he said, though he didn't know if the dog had heard him.

When he exited a moment later, the sergeant marveled at how soundproof the building was. What was a commotion so loud he couldn't hear himself think one minute was completely muted the second the heavy door closed shut, sealing in the din.

"Evenin', everybody!" Timothy barked through a megaphone to the crowd in the barn. "You stone-cold bastards ready to see some hardcore fucking bloodshed?"

The crowd, seventy-some-odd people all told, roared their approval. Most were drunk or high, the smell of marijuana hanging in the air. In addition, more than a couple had taken up offers from some of Timothy's girls wandering the barn for a quick blowjob or fuck in the nearby sealed-up stables. Timothy knew these girls came equipped with meth, ecstasy, GHB, and occasionally ketamine, but as long as they gave him a cut and maybe threw a couple of freebies at his boys, he knew they were great for business.

"Now, for anybody that ain't been to our dog pit before, you might be thinking, 'Dogs hate *cats*, dogs hate *squirrels*, dogs'll fuck up a *burglar*, but what about other dogs?'" Timothy continued, hamming it up for the crowd. "Don't they just like scrapping and barking at them? *Naaaaah*. I think it was Herodotus who told us that the Greeks could get all pissy and precious about fighting others, but when it came to fighting other Greeks, they'd *fucking tear them to SHIT*!"

The crowd laughed, though Timothy didn't think they had any idea who Herodotus was. Hell, he hadn't until Henry made him read *The Histories*, suggesting he might learn something about being a leader.

"Dogs are like Greeks in that respect," Timothy added, though everyone had already gotten the punch line. "So when we put one of these canine killers in the ring, don't feel sorry for the furry little shit. This is what they were born to do — fuck up another member of its own race. They *live* for this shit, and they'll fucking die for it, too. Wait…what the hell are we waiting for?!"

More laughter and applause. Timothy plucked the first two slips out of his pocket.

"Now, will the handlers of Jinsky and Titus bring your animals to the pit?"

A fat, fifty-something redneck with a bushy red beard and coveralls stood up as those around him cheered their champion. In another section of the same risers, a Hispanic man of about the same age also rose, drawing as much if not more applause. The pair disappeared out the barn door, and the other spectators began the countdown to the night's first event.

Next to the pit, Timothy glanced up into the rafters. He could just make out where Henry sat, headphones on, a small electronic device in his hand that he aimed from one spectator to the next. He entertained a passing thought that if Henry fell and broke his neck, his problems would be solved, but he just as quickly banished it.

Henry saw him looking and shook his head, as if to say, *No luck yet.* Timothy sighed and waved back.

The entrance of Titus's and Jinsky's owners to the kennel sent the caged dogs into a tizzy all over again, waking Bones, who'd fallen asleep. The shepherd got to his feet and eyed the two fight dog handlers with curiosity as they retrieved their animals.

"Jinsky's never lost a fight," the redneck bragged. "I knew he had it in him when he killed his own mother. That's just not natural, especially not in dogs!"

The redneck clearly expected, if not hoped, to be taunted in return, but the other man said nothing. Rather, he walked straight to a cage near the door and ushered out a Kangal so big it looked like it took up the entire cage. The redneck's eyes went wide.

"Jesus fuck," he whispered.

Going to the cage of his own animal, he brought out a stubby gray pit bull that hadn't stopped slobbering or barking since Bones had entered the room. When Jinsky saw the Kangal being led to the same door it meant to exit, the smaller dog unleashed a flurry of barks that seemed to threaten nuclear annihilation.

"Yeah, Jinsky's ready to tear out your doggy's belly," the redneck said, starting up again. "Wonder if 'Titus' knows he's only got a few seconds to go in life."

The Kangal turned to Jinsky at that moment, bared its teeth, and growled, low and guttural, its meaning clear. The pit took two steps back and unloaded a pile of shit onto the floor. The Kangal's handler offered the redneck a withering look and then exited the door. Jinsky's handler shook his head in disappointment.

"You stupid motherfucker," he spat. "I've got money on you. You lose, you're dead, you know that? This ain't no fucking game!"

The redneck jerked Jinsky's chain and hauled him after the Kangal. Bones watched until the door closed again, but then settled back down on the floor of his cage, head nestled on his front paws.

Bets were allowed from the moment the dogs were placed in their chutes under the barn floor until the second before they entered the ring. The timing was decided by Timothy, who generally made sure everyone who wanted to lay money got the chance before signaling the judges' table to sound the bell.

The odds for each fight were decided by an elderly man Timothy referred to as "Uncle John," who wasn't related to him, but had been a friend of his and Henry's father. Uncle John sat beside the judges, who tonight included Lil' Mwerto, who'd accepted Timothy's invitation to do so. Beside him was a stern-faced Irish fellow named Cookie Moran who Timothy thought looked like a *Killing of a Chinese Bookie*–era Ben Gazzara. Cookie was a friend of Uncle John's.

Rounding out the trio was a skinny twenty-year-old kid getting a veterinary degree at Delaware Valley College in New Britain. He'd impressed Timothy and the others the first time he came around with his fight dog knowledge and his ability to handicap the dogs. When the regulars got wise and refused to take the kid's bets, Timothy offered to pay him $10 a fight as a judge. The student, named Derek, agreed. Each time Derek entered the barn, his gaze never strayed to the handlers, spectators, other judges, or Timothy himself. Instead, they stayed fixed on the fight pit, whether there were dogs in it or not.

At the end of the night, when all the dogs were either dead or crowned champions and all the bets had been paid, Derek exited without a word, Timothy having Vickers pay him as he passed the check-in table by the parking lot.

But for the first fight of the night, Jinsky v. Titus, the judges earned their ten bucks without being asked for a decision, so clear was the victor. Jinsky had won the fight in forty seconds, having broken the Kangal's leg in his very first attack. When the larger animal reared back, the pit dove for Titus's belly, tearing out a chunk of flesh before scrambling around onto its back. As the wound on its underside bled, the Kangal struggled to flick off the much smaller dog, but Jinsky had burrowed his teeth into his opponent's scruff, the pit's preferred kill spot. The pit rode the mastiff like a rodeo bull, shaking his head violently to inflict more damage, teeth shredding skin and muscle all the way to the bone.

Finally, the blood loss was too great, and, with a strangled whine, the Kangal flopped onto its side, wheezing out its last breaths.

The redneck leapt to his feet as the spectators cheered the unlikely victor.

"Hell, yeah!" Jinsky's handler bellowed, sounding as surprised as he was relieved.

Only, the celebration turned somber a second later as Derek nodded to the redneck.

"You've got to put him down," he advised. "He's in bad pain."

All eyes returned to the ring as the dying whimpers of the Kangal were drowned out by the keening cries of the pit as it struggled to move, its back legs dragging uselessly behind it. Its back was broken, the mastiff having landing awkwardly on the pit when it smacked to the ground.

The redneck handler looked stunned, standing stock-still even as his friends collected their winnings from the other spectators, their tone now muted. Jinsky's handler slowly made his way to the pit, hopped down, cradled his champion in his arms, hesitated a moment longer as the pit gave his master a familiar lick on the arm, then gingerly placed the dog's neck in the crook of his elbow. He finished the victorious fighter off with a swift backward twist of his right forearm.

As the handler, tears now streaming down his face, carried the dog out of the pit, Lil' Mwerto pulled Timothy's microphone close to his mouth.

"A round of applause for my boy, Jinsky," he drawled, clapping his hands.

The spectators followed, applauding solemnly for the fallen pit bull as his distraught owner tripped on the stairs and almost fell on his ass. With a helping hand from Cookie Moran and Uncle John, he finally staggered out of the arena and made his way to the door. Once he was gone, Timothy searched the crowd for the Kangal's owner.

"We got Titus's handler here?" Timothy asked, nodding toward the remaining corpse.

"He left," someone called back. "Think he's getting another dog from his truck."

Timothy nodded, understanding the man's desire to try to win back some of the money he'd inevitably bet on his own animal. He signaled a couple of his guys, who hauled the Kangal out of the pit and took the corpse out back, where it'd be incinerated the next day with any other unclaimed losers. Timothy didn't begrudge any handler who didn't want to go home with a dead dog in their ride, particularly if it meant avoiding unwanted questions from law enforcement in the case of a traffic stop.

That's when he suddenly remembered Henry and looked up. The scowl on his brother's face suggested he'd been waiting for Timothy to turn his attention back to the more important matter at hand.

"*Him*," Henry hissed, pointing at a thirty-something man in the risers wearing a Megadeth T-shirt.

Timothy eyed the man. He hadn't seen him before, but he didn't think the fellow looked like law.

You sure? Timothy mouthed back to the roof.

Henry nodded vigorously, holding up the electronic device gripped in his right hand.

God, let my dumbass brother be useful for once, Timothy thought, climbing past the judges and waving to get Megadeth T-shirt's attention.

At first the handler looked away, as if he hadn't seen Timothy draw near. But this only made the fight operator lean in closer.

"Sir?" he said in a sharp, officious tone. "They're telling me your dog got all fucked up in its cage. Like, it was trying to get out and its paw got caught. You need to get over there."

"Shit, really?" Billy said, taken aback and truly surprised. "Sorry about that. He's a moron, my dog."

"Yeah, well, you should check on him," Timothy sniffed. "Make sure he can still fight."

"You got it."

The police sergeant rose and headed for the door. He knew Timothy Knippa was staring at him as he walked, but he didn't dare turn around. He tried to re-create Timothy's face in his mind's eye. Had he seemed suspicious? Or was that just indifference?

Whatever the case, the second he was out of the barn, he jogged the short distance to the kennel.

"Heard my dog got fucked up?" he said to Paul, still manning the door.

"Hell if I know," the young man shrugged, jutting a thumb over his shoulder.

As soon as Billy was inside, his eyes found Bones. The shepherd, in fact, looked just fine, standing in his cage, the one dog not barking in a sea of furious canine faces. Billy thought he looked fine, realizing only too late that this had been a ruse and he had fallen for it.

Henry Knippa, would-be presidential assassin, leaned against a stack of nearby cages, eyeing Billy.

"Goddamn, Megadeth sucks," Henry scoffed, slashing the coiled-up leash in his hand across Billy's face.

The impact was severe enough that it sent the cop sprawling backward. As blood gushed from Billy's mouth, nose, and a cut under his eye, he felt a cool wind coming in from outside as Timothy, Paul, Vickers, and a couple others walked in.

"Where?" Timothy asked.

Henry pulled a knife and quickly worked it into the threads of Billy's shirt collar. A moment later, he smiled triumphantly as he tugged a near-invisible wire from the lapel. He held it up to Timothy, who thought it looked more like a thick dog's hair than a transmitter.

Until he saw the tiny teardrop-shaped microphone at the end.

"Now who's the crazy one, brother?" Henry grinned.

"Was that Henry Knippa?!" Field Supervisor Michaels shouted, his voice practically shaking the surveillance truck. "We've got vocal samples to compare it to, right? Somebody tell me if that was Henry Knippa!"
The techs on either side of him worked as quickly as possible, but their computers proved sluggish.

"The cold's doing a number on our machines," one of the techs sighed. "It'll be another minute or two."

"Another minute, and my man could be dead," Zusak, who had come along at the last moment in an unofficial capacity, retorted.

"Another minute, and we know if we can move in with deadly force or if this is just one more bullshit extralegal raid," Michaels shot back. "Your man was the one who wanted to fuck these guys up for the whole nine. Remember, he's technically a fed right now. They harm a hair on his head, and they'll spend the rest of their days behind bars."

"I'm sure Billy'll appreciate that when the mortician's sliding him into his dress blues," Zusak snapped.

Michaels huffed, voicing his displeasure at the remark even if he didn't have a satisfactory reply.

"This is about the President?" Timothy groaned, incredulous at Billy's admission. "Not because we're running girls and drugs and dogs in here? Not because he shot some asshole who'd been feeding you whatever I told him to? But because my dumbass older brother made some kind of *threat*?"

Billy, roped to a chair with dog leashes, nodded weakly. It had taken four more strikes to the head from Henry's makeshift blackjack to get him to talk, even though he'd mentally accepted that he'd soon give in after the first two. He was in a sort of doctor's office–looking room, complete with a surgical suite adjacent to where the dogs were held. There were multiple operating tables, cabinets filled with instruments and supplies, a couple of large refrigerators humming against the far wall, and shelves and shelves of drugs. Some looked like vitamins, but others were in tiny single-shot bottles like vaccines. The cop remembered Michaels referring to Timothy as a mad scientist and realized this must be his lab.

"How did they know?" Henry piped up, his face a mask of calm.

It took Billy a moment to realize Henry was addressing his brother and not the police officer.

"Ask yourself that, Timothy," Henry continued. "You think you're running this airtight ship, but other than me and you, who knew about my problems with the White House?"

"Fucking everybody, you idiot," Timothy screamed. "The guys *know* you're a crackpot! They talk all the time! How come those wonder-mics of yours never picked *that* up?"

"Maybe I didn't realize how sophisticated they'd become," Henry surmised. "Could they be talking in code now? Maybe they know I'm listening. So they say one thing, but it means something else, something maybe they've got on paper. There's probably a way to crack it. I mean, I record everything on the mics…"

"You record *everything*?" Timothy asked. "Everything that's said here?"

"Of course! You never know when something just like this might warrant going back over a few hundred hours of tape. You're lucky that I…"

Before Henry could finish his sentence, Timothy pulled Vickers's pistol (and old .357 Magnum he bought with one of his first paychecks day-shifting at a chemical plant) from his belt and fired a single bullet into his brother's heart. The older man didn't even have time to shift his facial expression, flopping straight down like a puppet whose strings had suddenly been cut. Everyone in the room gasped, looking as if they fully expected Henry to stand back up and the two brothers to admit the whole thing was staged. But as blood pooled away from the dead man's body, they knew he wouldn't be coming back.

"Yeah, well…," Timothy began, before trailing off, the argument warring on in his head reaching a conclusion.

Billy stared at the corpse in horror, wondering if the Secret Service or sheriff's deputies outside heard the shot. But then he remembered how soundproof the kennel was and figured they hadn't.

"Your turn, cop," Timothy said, opening a wardrobe-sized cabinet where hundreds of thin binders lined multiple shelves. "Each of these binders represents an individual dog. We record their parents' prenatal regimen, what protocols were followed while they were in utero, and what has continued after they were born. To a lot of people, the word 'cur' is synonymous with 'mongrel' or 'mutt.' But it's a breed, too, just like a pit bull or a shepherd. Only, it's hard to define exactly what a purebred cur *is*, so most people don't try. But that's what I build."

He pulled out one of the binders, holding it up for Billy's inspection.

"This dog has the body of a Rhodesian ridgeback, but the brain of a wolf and the stamina of a malamute. Her name's Akka, and she's just about the most dangerous war machine I've got in this club. But she's a daddy's girl. I'm not letting her in the ring. No, I've got to have an animal on me at all times. Better than a gun. Especially one that's already tasted human blood."

Timothy nodded to Paul. The young man opened the door to the kennel and headed inside, the barking as loud now as it had been before. Billy thought he heard Bones's voice amidst the chorus but wasn't sure. Maybe it was wishful thinking. Paul returned a second later with a massive ridgeback. The animal stood at attention when brought before Timothy.

"No dog's going to attack you while you're all tied up," Timothy said, moving on Billy with the knife his brother had used to pull out Billy's wire. "But if cut these leashes and kick you out the back door, you think your survival instincts are going to let you stand in one place? Or are you going to run for it, hoping to beat a dog you cannot outrun to your backup, to your car, to the house, wherever?"

"Come on, man," Billy whispered. "Henry's dead. Let's call it a day. I'll tell 'em whatever you want. You shot him because he was going to kill me or something."

"Nah," Timothy shrugged. "I know you mean that now, but you'd change your tune in a week or so. Nothing personal, happens to everybody. Seen it before, is all."

He cut the last leash and kicked over the chair. Billy was sent face first into a lake of Henry Knippa's blood.

"Now we know she won't lose your scent!" Timothy enthused, though the cocky edge to his voice was fading. "Akka loved her Uncle Henry, didn't you, girl? Smell his blood on that bad man?! Yeah, not saying anything, but maybe that's the guy who did him."

Akka bent her head low, her eyes staring straight into Billy's. The police sergeant shivered in terror. A man like Timothy was one thing, someone you could talk to or reason with.

But this creature looked like an emissary of death, bred to do but one thing. Her eyes were unlike that of any dog Billy had ever seen, those of a monster straight out of a childhood nightmare. He saw nothing of the kindness or even consciousness he so often recognized in the animals of his trade. Its dull gaze was more akin to that of a cobra calmly waiting to strike than anything that smacked of an intelligent, trainable mammal.

Billy shivered, already anticipating the feeling of the beast's ferocious jaws stabbing into his flesh. He hoped it would be over quickly.

From the moment Henry Knippa had struck Billy in the kennel, Bones had been pounding against the cage door. But among the sergeant's recent sins, he'd underestimated the strength of the latch keeping Bones's cage door in place. In fact, the hook stayed put with no give whatsoever.

But Bones didn't stop, the shepherd single-mindedly bashing its full weight against the door like a madman smashing his head against a padded cell wall. When Paul opened the door to the lab and the scent of not just Billy, but Billy's *fear*, wafted in, Bones doubled his efforts.

The latch refused to give, however, and it was the hinges themselves that finally clattered to the floor. As the dogs around him bayed louder, the shepherd leaped from the cage and raced to the lab door. Bones tried to bash and claw his way through this as well, but it was solid steel and held tight.

Bones doubled back, circling the room as he searched for another way out. But then the front door swung open as the next round of dog handlers entered to retrieve their fighters, including a member of Lil' Mwerto's entourage who'd brought a Rottweiler named C.J.

"Holy shit! That dog's loose!" were the man's last words before the shepherd leaped at his face and tore off his nose and part of his cheek.

As the young man fell back onto the snowy ground, the shepherd raced around to the back of the building. The second handler pulled a pistol and fired after the dog, but missed him completely in the dark.

"We have shots fired," a voice crackled over the surveillance truck radio, one of the deputies in the woods calling in.

Michaels sighed, knowing the mission was beyond repair.

"Everybody move in," he ordered. "Find Henry Knippa. Take him alive if possible."

Inside the barn, the gunshots were a surprise. The spectators all froze, waiting for more.

"Sounds like they're putting another one down," Lil' Mwerto joked into his microphone.

There were a few titters, but the crowd remained anxious. Then one of Lil' Mwerto's boys ran into the barn, swinging a pistol.

"Some dog fucked up Hilly."

But before anyone could respond, the back door of the barn was kicked in. Several sheriff's deputies swarmed inside.

"Indiana County Sheriff's Office," called the first one through the door. "This is a raid. Everybody's hands where we can see them. No sudden moves. No weapons!"

"Come on, Akka. Let's get this over with."

The ridgeback took a step forward. Billy flinched and blinked, feeling the lonely terror of the condemned.

Fuck it, he thought.

At the moment he'd surrendered himself to the inevitable, however, the back door swung open, and two federal agents hurried in, carrying assault rifles.

"U.S. Secret Service!"

The words had barely left the lead agent's lips before Akka turned her attention from Billy to the newcomer. Though his machine gun was raised, its butt planted against his shoulder, the lead agent was so surprised by the dog now racing straight for him that he actually looked like he might drop his weapon. By the time he'd recovered his senses, upon seeing that the dog's jaws were wide and aimed at his throat, it was too late.

The impact of dog against agent was so forceful that the man flew backward through the still-open door and landed in the snow six feet back. A moment later, his hands clutched at his neck as all the air was pushed from his lungs by the weight of the animal standing on his chest, but escaping through the gaping hole in his windpipe rather than his nose or mouth. It took mere seconds for him to die.

Akka then turned on his partner, who fared slightly better, getting off a single shot from his assault rifle before the ridgeback sank her teeth into his arm. But she hardly stopped there. Yanking backward with the force of a Mack truck, the dog popped the agent's arm from its socket and, with a twist of her head, snapped his humerus and clavicle. He screamed, but then grabbed his gun with his good hand, ready to shoot the dog in the face.

Before he could, however, Timothy stepped over, again with Vickers's pistol, and fired a single bullet into the agent's face. The man's head thudded backward as chunks of brain and skull splattered the snow behind him.

Akka looked up at her master as steam rose from the dead men's wounds. He sighed and waved her away.

"Do better than your daddy," he joked, pointing to the woods.

She hesitated a moment longer, but then he aimed the gun at her. Knowing what this meant, she raced off into the snow.

Timothy walked back into the lab and nodded at his men, including Billy in his gaze.

"Part of it is knowing when you're beaten," he said.

Without defining the "it" he referred to, Timothy put the pistol into his mouth and pulled the trigger. Billy momentarily thought there were two shots, but then realized the second sound he heard was the bullet smacking into the room's steel roof after exiting Timothy's head.

Vickers stared at Billy in surprise, as if realizing how in over their heads Timothy's guys had gotten within the last ten minutes.

"I'm sorry, man. Call your guys. We're done. We'll surrender. This is fucked."

But without thinking, he picked up his .357 and was about to put it in his pocket when a sheriff's deputy came through the door from the kennel. Vickers turned, gun still in his hand, and the deputy blasted him almost in half with a shotgun.

"Don't move!" the deputy cried as Vickers's corpse thudded to the ground.

Paul and the others raised their hands, and the deputies relieved them of their weapons. When they got to Billy, still on the ground, Billy shook his head.

"I'm unarmed. But I'm Sergeant Youman, the inside guy."

"Jesus Christ!" the deputy cried, having leveled a shotgun at Billy. "Sorry about that."

"Call Michaels," Billy said, his voice unnervingly calm to everyone in the room. "Tell him Henry Knippa's dead. Positive on the identification. Youman witnessed the shooting as well as the deaths of two of his agents and Henry's brother, Timothy, which was by his own hand."

"Who killed Henry?" the deputy asked. "In case he asks."

"Timothy Knippa," Billy said, pointing to the accused's corpse. "Tell him it wasn't pretty, and he owes me a beer."

The killing wasn't over.

Though everyone in the barn had initially complied with law enforcement, one man, high on pills and booze, made a break for it, however comedically. In doing so, however, he drew a gun from his waistband, though it wasn't clear if he meant to use it or if he was just afraid it might discharge as he ran.

A sheriff's deputy opened fire and struck the man three times in the back. Only, two of the bullets emerged from the fellow's chest, striking a second spectator in the face. As this man fell, Lil' Mwerto leaped to his feet.

"Holy shit, man!" he exclaimed.

A deputy turned his weapon on the singer, but before he could shoot, Derek, the college veterinary student, pulled out the .32 he kept in case he needed to off one of the dogs himself and shot that deputy in the neck and a second in the head. Both fell back into the fight pit.

"You're welcome," Derek said to Lil' Mwerto.

The recording artist didn't look a gift horse in the mouth. He signaled his entourage and raced for the door. More sheriff's deputies and more heavily armed Secret Service agents quickly followed, now opening fire on the remaining crowd. Several of the spectators reached for guns of their own, and soon bullets flew in both directions.

Out in the woods, Akka ran. But despite the violence she'd just witnessed, she thought only of the wealth of smells now filling her nose. Since she'd grown up in the kennel, the rich, inviting textures of trees, plants, soil, and the other animals of the forest were only there and gone. She breathed deeply, pulling the cool night air into her lungs and exhaling puffs of steam that soon trailed behind her.

She was soon panting, her heart pounding.

That was when she heard a new sound. She stopped and listened, but had known immediately it was a pursuer. She sniffed the air, recognizing a canine scent she'd smelled on the scared man in the laboratory.

She stopped running. She knew the other dog must smell her, too, and turned to wait. She planted her feet, her spine going taut as she readied herself for the coming fight. She growled and bared her teeth as saliva wet her mouth. When the animal emerged from the woods, she would pounce first.

But seconds passed, and nothing came. No dog or human. The smell was still there, but it was already beginning to fade. She whipped her head to the left, lifting her nose to the air in hopes of catching her enemy's scent in case it had tried to flank her. But again, nothing. She tried the right side without any more luck.

Simply, her pursuer was gone, the animal either having lost the trail or given up.

Akka hesitated not a second longer and hurried off again. A moment later, and she was once more enjoying the cold night air as it replaced the taste of blood still warm on her tongue.

Someone had called the press. That was the only explanation for why a news van had managed to reach the scene less than five minutes after the first shot echoed through the woods. Curiously, however, they'd sent a young female reporter whose beat was celebrity gossip, not crime scenes. Even as her crew unloaded their equipment for their first stand-up, she saw the first of a line of corpses, had a panic attack, and wouldn't be coaxed out of the van.

Still, the cameraman caught Lil' Mwerto and his entourage fleeing the scene. However, the sheriff's deputies pulled their cruisers up behind his Phantom in time to keep him from leaving. They were all arrested, and the images would make the rounds of the Internet within hours, the front page of tabloids worldwide by the morning.

Secret Service Field Supervisor Michaels, however, demanded the news crew tell him how they knew about the operation. The driver swore up and down that he had no idea. What he did know was that they'd received a tip Lil' Mwerto was having a surprise pop-up concert in Blairsville that night and would have several A-list guests with him. They confirmed this and sent a van.

That was it.

When Michaels continued to fume and fuss, the driver suggested further queries could be made at the station.

Billy watched this back-and-forth from the front steps of the Knippa house. He knew Henry Knippa's blood still drying on his face would prevent the cameraman from aiming his lens at him, much less request an interview. Still, he doubted the man's producer would recognize his voice anyway. It had taken calls to three different news stations before someone took the bait on the Lil' Mwerto story, Billy amping the lie each time to try to make it irresistible. It was only after one segment producer, who knew somebody in Mwerto's entourage, texted this contact to ask if he was "in Blairsville that night" and received a "Shhh…" in response, that Billy knew he'd hooked somebody. The man's delight at nabbing a scoop about a local recording artist just beginning to break nationally swept away any questions about Billy's credentials.

"We'll get a van out there. You're sure about the address?" the producer had asked.

"Yep, just off 22," Billy had replied, then hung up, knowing the dog fight pit would be shut down for gone.

"This your dog?"

Billy turned as a sheriff's deputy, hand gripped on Bones's collar, led the shepherd to his handler.

"Yeah, shit," Billy said. "His cage was empty, but he's got a tracker chip, so I knew the fuzzy bastard wouldn't get far."

"He was out by the woods. I think he ran at the first sound of gunfire."

"This guy?" Billy asked, snapping a leash on the collar. "He's not afraid of shit. Was probably chasing one of the bad guys."

"And then gave up?" the deputy asked, but then turned and left before

Billy could respond.

Billy patted Bones's head as the dog settled in next to him.

"Should've bitten that asshole," he said, nodding to the deputy.

When Bones sniffed the blood on his handler's clothes and stood to get a better angle, Billy just sighed.

"Told you it was going to be a shitty night."

INJA

Prologue

"Sir? There's been an incident in A2."

"Assassination?"

"Still trying to get confirmation."

"Witnessed on camera?"

"One of the wardens reported it."

"Only one?"

There was a telling silence. Charles sighed and sank back into his pillow. Barbara and the boys were up in Johannesburg. It was one of those rare weekends when he had the house in Green Point to himself.

He glanced at the clock. It was just past midnight. There was no waiting for one of the assistant chief wardens to arrive in the morning.

"I'll be right in. Assemble a medical response team, and call me on my cell when they're ready."

"Yes, sir." The guard sounded relieved.

South African prison policy had it that if an incident of violence happened after lights out, guards weren't allowed to enter the cell block, much less send in paramedics, without authorization from the prison's chief warden.

This authorization had to be delivered on site. At one time, the chief warden, then called the governor, and his family were made to live on the prison's grounds, but this hadn't been the case for the last couple of decades. The prisoners knew that locating the chief warden after hours was sometimes difficult, so that's when most attacks were carried out. In the time it took to dial the warden's home line, only to be told by his wife to try his cell, only to have to leave a message, then to wait for the man to ring back, a prisoner's entire lifeblood could exit his body.

But even if the chief warden had only been a block away, authorization was hardly a given. If the perpetrator was still loose on the block, the fear he might injure or kill those sent to investigate was real, despite the likelihood that a paid-off guard was how the prisoner got out of his cell in the first place. However, there wasn't a guard, bent or otherwise, who knew that a bribed man one minute could become a liability the next. It didn't help that Pollsmoor Prison was one of the most brutal lockups in a country already notorious for having one of the highest violent crime rates in the world.

The only good news, Charles knew, would be if it came back that it was an assassination rather than an argument that escalated or a spontaneous settling of scores. The century-old Number gangs ruled the prison, and assassinations had already gone through a complicated approvals process. An aggrieved party would approach the leaders of the 28s with his complaint, and the issue would be debated. If blood was called for, the killing would be handed off to a member of the 27s, not the offended individual. This way, any motive might be obfuscated in the ensuing investigation, and the real reasons behind a prisoner's death might never come to light.

Charles hated to think that the gangs took advantage of what amounted to a nighttime "grace period." But he also hadn't risen through the ranks of the correctional services without an understanding of the uneasy détente between prisoners and guards following decades of savagery on both sides. Worse, any attempt to disrupt the status quo could also mean political suicide, given the number of parliamentarians in the pockets of gang leaders these days. Should he intervene, a summons from the Minister of Correctional Services to come up to Pretoria and explain himself would surely follow.

No, better on this night for the chief warden to get out of bed and make the drive, if only to make good on the details of whatever "we regret that, last night, a prisoner in our care…" statement was released to the press the next morning.

"I'm going to have to cut this short," Charles called to the bathroom. "Can I offer you a ride?"

The dark-haired girl had left the room when the phone rang. She stepped back into the doorway, sending an unexpected thrill through Charles when he saw that she was still naked. She was small in stature, her hair descending almost to her waist. When he'd first seen her face at the Union Bar in the Table Bay Hotel, a place he actually favored for its muted lighting, he could still tell that she was utterly gorgeous, better almost than any other girl the agency had ever sent along. There hadn't been much preamble, as the plot had it that they have a drink and strike up a conversation, and, if she was acceptable, he'd slip her his address, where she was to meet him within the hour. He'd known right away that she was perfect.

Even so, looking at her now, despite having had sex for the better part of the last hour, he felt like he was seeing her for the first time. Maybe his lust had blinded him to anything more than the basics, though he imagined he could be excused for feeling distracted.

The previous week, Jacob Mpambani was murdered in broad daylight. The crime lord had been driving his armored Mercedes SUV on the N2, heading into the Cape Bowl. Four men on motorcycles approached from behind, pulled up to the driver's side, and began firing. Mpambani had acted quickly, slamming the SUV into one of the bikers, sending him careening into a truck. But over a hundred bullets, fifteen of which entered the gangster, finally brought the vehicle for a standstill as a dying Mpambani spun the wheel in a vain attempt to get away and ended up flipping the vehicle onto the shoulder. Ironically, it was the crash that killed him, the engine block shoving the steering wheel into Jacob's chest with enough force to send half a dozen splintering bones directly into his heart.

Charles could hardly have called Mpambani a friend. But when the gangster had been in Pollsmoor and a part of the ruling 28s, the then-guard had always found him fair and easy enough to deal with, a respected man. The killing, thereby, came as a shock. If somebody on the outside had a beef with Mpambani, it would be his lieutenants who were targeted, not the man himself. He'd earned that. What it suggested to Charles was that a fringe player looking to make a name for himself had foolishly gone after the crime lord. But instead of recognition, the shooters and their minders would earn a bullet to the head.

What worried the chief warden of Pollsmoor was that the score settling would overflow into the prison. He now wondered if the midnight assassination pulling him from his bed was the first of it.

Another glance to the girl, whose name he couldn't recall though it was the first question he always asked, filled him with greater regret. The opportunities were so fleeting, and he wanted to take full advantage, knowing it would have to keep him going for weeks, if not months. But now he drank up her visage, trying to commit every curve and nuance to memory. Her perfect, slender legs, her immaculate breasts, the smoothness of her skin under his fingertips from moments before. He knew, however, that it would be only days before mere flashes remained.

One of those flashes, he knew, would be the way she gamely arched her eyebrow back in the bar when he'd slipped his address to her. Of course, her coming home with him was a foregone conclusion. But they'd still gone through the motions of subterfuge, as if this had been the first time they'd met. So his bold proposition was still treated as such, the girl feigning hesitation and surprise, as if unsure whether she should be offended or tempted by his chutzpah.

Dare I? that raised eyebrow seemed to ask.

He had responded by offering her a warm smile, then rising to exit the bar.

The sex had been great, but it was none of his doing. It took the woman, the *girl*, if he was honest, only a few minutes to assess the balance between sophistication and innocence he required of her, and she proved worthy of RADA in her subsequent effort. She was so charmed by him, so turned on, so surprised at her own susceptibility. That she kept this going when he asked her if she needed a ride, even though the night was clearly over, impressed him that much more.

She looked a little embarrassed, as if worried that it was her performance that had cut things short. He knew this sort of thing was drilled into the girls for a reason. He'd known plenty of pimps and flesh traffickers in his day. The goal was to ensure that no client was able to divert his mind and consider the girl's actual circumstances, breaking the fantasy. That training was the difference between a street walker in Langa that would cost only a handful of rand versus the thousands Charles would pay to punt those thoughts forward a few hours.

"I know your driver isn't due back here until two," Charles said, breaking script for the sake of expedience while realizing he hoped to sound gallant. "But that's an hour and a half away. I can't have you waiting around here until then or until we can get in touch with him. So, if you just give me an address you wish to be dropped off at, I'll get word to your…" He struggled to come up with a word other than pimp, "…*patron*, that there were extenuating circumstances and your early egress had nothing to do with you."

She affected a demure stance for a moment longer. Or, as demure a post-coital pose could be now that Charles had flipped on the bright overhead fluorescents. But then she nodded and offered an address in Clifton.

Charles was surprised. Clifton was a tony, oceanfront neighborhood. If he'd been made to offer an opinion, he would've expected her to reside in the Cape Flats on the other side of Table Mountain. Manenberg or some place. But then he realized that the Clifton house was likely by her syndicate and probably housed several girls. He wondered if it was actually some kind of brothel that he could potentially try out during the day.

But it was good news. Clifton was on the way to Pollsmoor. If he'd had to drop her in the Flats, it would mean taking the N2 around the mountain, then weaving overland to whatever district she called home. From there, he'd have to figure out the best way to get over to the M3 and from there, the prison. Clifton meant a straight shot down the M6 and then crossing the range on the M63. It would be a quiet drive this time of night with the occasional pleasant view of the South Atlantic.

Charles took a two-minute shower. Though his guest offered to join him, he was all business now and declined. When he exited the bathroom, he found her dressed and waiting at the foot of the bed. Even then she had a look of expectation on her face. It was as if she'd mentally prepared herself to learn that all this hubbub was actually in service of some still-unfolding sex game. The chief warden wondered if powerful men really did arrange such things; *the country's economic future depends on me making this meeting, but…what's one more shag?*

He could see at least a couple of the nation's new captains of industry getting off on that.

Once they were in the car, the woman said not a word. His mind was already crafting an exit strategy that would get him out of the prison as quickly as possible, but he caught himself stealing glances at her. Wearing last night's cocktail dress, she looked smaller, as if playing dress-up. He wondered what her concerns might be. Did she expect a row when she showed up unannounced in Clifton? Worse, did she fear her pay might be docked?

He was just considering whether she might have a child at home when he felt her hand on his leg. But rather than the soft touch he remembered from the bedroom, it was one tensed, as if with alarm. He glanced down to it, just as something new appeared in his peripheral vision. He couldn't have been distracted for more than a second.

The first bullet hit the windshield with such force that Charles thought he'd struck a person. The safety glass spider-webbed, then collapsed inward, folding in on itself as the warden slammed on the brakes. It was only after realizing the dull throb in his chest came not from the tightening of the seatbelt that he noticed he'd been shot. A large hole had been blasted into his chest, though it was another instant before he felt as if his entire body had been set aflame.

The fusillade began in earnest now, high-powered rifle bullets punching through the car's chassis like cannonballs through cake. Within seconds, the shredded vehicle came to a halt, almost entirely disassembling, blood and oil commingling in a long smear across the pavement.

1

"Fuckin' *Africa!*"

Pittsburgh Police Sergeant Billy Youman writhed in agony. Even though it was over a hundred degrees outside, he'd woken up around four that morning, his teeth chattering and his limbs quaking. His sheets were now completely soaked through with sweat despite him finding it quite impossible to get warm.

"Goddammit!" he croaked, reaching yet again for the television remote. "What the *shit*?!"

Of course, he'd been warned. Don't drink the water; don't eat fruits and vegetables, as they had likely been washed in local water; don't order drinks with ice cubes; brush your teeth dry, but then don't wash the brush under the tap.

He tried to recall any moment over the past twenty-four hours that he might've slipped up. Did he not wipe the lip of the Coke he'd had with lunch? Had his breakfast yogurt been properly sealed? Was the barbecue they'd picked up at the braai actually cooked to within an inch of its life?

What could it *be*?

A memory.

It was only a flash. Less an image, more a feeling. Something moist on his lips. It wasn't food. It was…

"Oh, God," Billy realized, a new attack sending him into convulsions. "That *motherfucker*. Oh, God…"

Before he could even conjure the image of his assailant, his bowels seized. He had mere seconds to reach the bathroom. Racked with now violent tremors, he threw himself out of bed and hurried to the WC. With one hand he unbuckled his belt as his other slapped on the light switch.

A second later, as he evacuated the little bottled water he'd tried to keep down fifteen minutes earlier, his bare feet hovering just above the frigid linoleum of the bathroom floor, the picture of his saboteur formed in his mind. It was an animal, a German shepherd who was allegedly his partner. In his mind, he watched the vile creature give him an enthusiastic lick across the face only the afternoon before.

Moments after he'd drunk from a bowl shared by all the animals at the training grounds.

"That *motherfucker*," the sergeant repeated, though the sound of his chattering teeth drowned out his voice.

The object of Sergeant Youman's enmity was at that very moment lapping thirstily from the same community water dish at the South African Police Service's training facility in Muizenberg. The dog had been running since before first light, an endless series of exercises that would've exhausted all but the most committed canines, with a temporary handler. But rather than challenge the massive German shepherd, said temporary handler, a recent graduate of the Metro Police Training Academy named Moosa Xabanisi, thought it exhilarated him.

"Great time, Bones!" Moosa said, stroking the dog's back. "I've never seen one of our dogs get through the course so quickly."

Bones seemed to delight in the praise, the New Mexico–born police dog twisting his neck around to give Moosa a quick lick on the lips. Residual flecks of water from the community dog dish bounced from Bones's whiskers and tongue to Moosa's mouth. The South African trainer playfully feigned disgust.

"Careful, Bones!" Moosa cried. "You don't want the other dogs to think I'm fraternizing with the competition."

But the police dog kept licking anyway. In the absence of his American handler, he was happy to have found a new playmate.

"We heard anything new from Youman?" barked a voice from a few yards away.

Gabe Eachus was from Chicago, a middle-aged fitness nut with twenty-one years in the Illinois State Police. His jaw looked as if it could absorb hammer blows. He stalked over to the more slightly built Moosa as if planning to pound him into the ground.

"No, sir," Moosa replied, getting to his feet. "Not since he called in this morning."

"We all got the same vaccinations," the cop remarked, his accent straight out of a Hollywood movie. "Think he's faking? Maybe went on a bender last night?"

"I can't speculate." Moosa shrugged. "Everyone's natural immunity is different. There's no telling when it comes to stomach viruses."

Moosa waited for the big American to reply, perhaps say something else negative about the host country as the foreigners had been doing all week, sometimes overtly, though mostly when they thought no one was listening. But it appeared Eachus was already losing interest. The Chicago handler's dog, Brutus, a Belgian malinois, hadn't done particularly well that morning and had fallen asleep before finishing his breakfast. Moosa imagined that the reason Eachus pushed his animal so hard was because he took Brutus's achievement, or lack thereof, as an indicator of his own ability as a law enforcement officer. This had led to muscle fatigue in Brutus's legs, and he was already sore before the sun had even climbed that high in the sky.

Of all the dogs brought over for the joint U.S.-South African K-9 exercises, Moosa hadn't pegged Brutus to be particularly delicate, so he sympathized with the dog's plight. He was sure the dog wanted to make his handler happy, but his body wouldn't let him. Bones, however, had reportedly been incontinent, not only on the flight from Washington, D.C., where the dogs had all gone for a pre-trip checkup by army vets at Fort McNair to earn quarantine wavers from the South African government, and then to Paris, he'd also made a mess of his carrier on the way down to the Cape. Because of this, Moosa had pegged the Pittsburgh animal as the least likely to succeed.

But now, as he looked over at Brutus asleep under a tree even as Bones anxiously waited to run the course again, he realized how wrong he'd been. Brutus was friendly, seemed loyal, and was certainly alert, but that made him perfect for a family in the market for a pet/watch dog. What Bones had that separated him from the pack and made for the best enforcement animals was motivation. A normal dog had to be cajoled or bribed into continuing on even when an exercise got rough. A police dog had an inherent *need* to go to hell and back for even the slightest praise from its handler.

This was Bones.

"So, which do you want to tackle next?" Moosa asked the shepherd, continuing to scratch its ears. "Another run through the obstacle course? Or are you ready to try and clear the two-story training house in under five minutes?"

From the look on Bones's face, Moosa figured the dog's vote was "both."

"Christ, it's not even noon on a Wednesday, and he's already got an insatiable taste for pussy?"

Gauche as the old Afrikaaner police sergeant's question might've sounded in the panel van, it was one that had occurred to Inspector Leonard Moqoma on various occasions. He'd been on stakeouts where he'd watched morning commuters get off a bus downtown, walk to an ATM, take out a wad of bills, and then head directly to a massage parlor for a pre-workday session. Hell, he'd seen johns saunter into brothels on their lunch breaks, coffee breaks, or even after they'd gone home for the night, only to invent some innocuous-sounding post-dinner errand. It was worse after the bars closed, worse still on holidays. What he never got used to seeing were the men stopping in on their way home from church, still in their Sunday finest. Even the Zion Christian Church members, for all their external show of piety, were not immune to paying for sex. At a certain point, Leonard had wondered why the brothels closed at all.

Leaving money on the table, he thought, then chuckled at the irony.

"Can't we just go in?" one of the regular constables asked.

None of the man's three comrades, the sergeant, the colored constable, or the other black constable, seemed to have any idea.

"Then we should go! The trail's getting cold."

"Not yet," Moqoma replied, and four faces that had seemed to have forgotten that he was even in the vehicle with them turned to stare at him. At least of couple of the stares quickly became scowls.

"Why the hell not?" the sergeant, despite being lower in rank than

Moqoma, shot back.

"I don't know if I can say," Moqoma said, allowing himself a show of cheek, though he quickly kicked himself for it.

"Why don't you let me be the judge of that, Lieutenant?" the sergeant snapped back.

There was no fight Moqoma would win with these men, and everyone in the van knew it. He still thought of himself as an "inspector," but that was the old rank structure before they switched over to a more military format. Gone was a hierarchy that included "inspector," "superintendent," "director," and various levels of "commissioner," to be replaced by "lieutenants," "majors," colonels," and "generals." Moqoma had been an inspector, but it wasn't because of this that he earned their acrimony. Nor was it that he was colored. If the challenge from the white Afrikaaner sergeant had escalated into a fight, neither the black nor colored constables would lift a finger to help him. Worse, their versions of events, when retold to their superiors, would almost certainly sympathize with the sergeant.

"All right," Moqoma relented, though part of him wished he'd chosen to stay in his Land Rover a couple of blocks up. "I was merely trying to shield you from having to explain this in court." A couple of the constables shifted uneasily. "But do you see that black BMW at the corner up there?"

Everyone looked. The sergeant nodded.

"Yeah?"

"That belongs to Norman Nyawuza." Nyawuza, as everyone in the car knew, was a member of Parliament. "When I saw it, I informed the Lieutenant Colonel, adding that when I have surveilled this residence previously, he never stayed for longer than twenty minutes. I was told to wait until he left to avoid embarrassment."

In fact, prior to his being reassigned to the South African Police Service (SAPS), Moqoma's work with the Directorate of Special Operations, nicknamed the Scorpions, had brought him to this cliffside brothel several times. Although the place was located in a small exclusive neighborhood among several of the coastline's most expensive homes and views, the cover story of a group of young, hip, twenty-something girls leasing a house together passed muster with the other residents. Moqoma imagined that they, also members of Cape Town's moneyed elite, were likely encouraged to look the other way with bribes or favors. However, since so many were crooked themselves, he also figured some said nothing out of professional courtesy.

This was enough to silence the sergeant and two of the constables. It was the colored one who continued to look troubled. Moqoma returned his gaze with a hard stare of his own until the young man looked away. No time but the present to learn that, despite chunks of the chief warden of Pollsmoor's neurocranium lying in pieces across a coroner's table somewhere, protecting those who paid for the privilege still took priority. No one was going to bring Charles van Lagemaat back to life, but the fury of a parliamentarian caught with his willy in someone who wasn't his wife or mistress? Could cost a man his career.

Five minutes later, Nyawuza exited the building.

"Everybody ready?" Moqoma asked.

Without waiting for a response, he pushed out the back door. As Moqoma was the only one not in uniform, Nyawuza glanced at him for only a second before turning back to his cell phone. When the four officers followed Moqoma up the sidewalk, the parliamentarian blanched and almost tripped.

"Colonel Kjölsrud suggests you get in your car and you drive away."

"Y…yes, thank you," Nyawuza stammered before scurrying to his vehicle.

Moqoma didn't wait for the man to drive away before pounding on the frosted-glass front door of the brothel. Almost the entire ocean-facing side of the building was glass, affording its residents astonishing views, he imagined.

"Sibulele?! Are you in there?"

Moqoma caught the sergeant's queer look at the lieutenant's familiarity with the place, but he ignored it. He pounded his fist on the door a second time.

"Sibulele! It gets worse if we have to raise our voices."

He saw the outline of someone approaching. She seemed to eye him through an unseen peephole. She was joined by a second person, who quickly waved them away. As the short and stout Sibulele, a colored woman from not just the same district, but the same *street* as Moqoma's own mother, opened the door, the detective just glimpsed the departure up the stairs of a coltish young woman wearing nothing more than a G-string.

"What is it, Moqoma?" drawled Sibulele, affecting exasperation, though he knew she was less a madam and more a low-paid live-in caretaker for the girls, like a house mum in a dormitory.

"According to the chief warden's phone records, one of your girls was with van Lagemaat last night. You missing anybody?"

Surprise wasn't something Sibulele allowed herself that often, so it was hard for her to hide it when it came naturally.

"The papers said he was alone in the car."

"The papers didn't know one of his neighbors just installed security cameras on their outer wall. We checked, thinking he might've been tailed. Instead, it led us inside his house where it was obvious they'd just…well." He paused, as if not wishing to be indelicate. "We checked his phone. He'd arranged for her through your boss, Mr. Knosi."

Sibulele flinched. This visit had gone from an annoyance to one of grave portent.

"So, *Auntie*," Moqoma continued, "I ask again. Did one of your little pigeons not come last night?"

At this point, Moqoma and his comrades were invited in and offered the unlikely name of "Li."

"She'd only been here a few weeks, but we don't get girls who stay for much longer than that," Sibulele explained, leading the men to a room at the rear of the brothel's first floor. "I don't believe her English was very good, and she kept to herself."

"She was Asian, then?"

"Yes, many of them are," Sibulele continued. "But Chinese, Japanese, Korean? I don't know."

Moqoma nodded. He had a good idea which.

Sibulele led the group into the tiny room, two child-sized bunk beds, a chest of drawers, and a dresser the only furniture. There were no windows. Judging from the hook-ups Moqoma spied peering out of the back wall, this was designed to be a laundry room.

"Hers is the bottom one on the left," Sibulele said, indicating one of the beds. A thin blue blanket rested over an empty mattress with a small off-white pillow at the top. "The second to lowest drawer of the chest was hers, and she kept a couple of dresses in the closet. I don't remember her having too many personal belongings."

Because she was probably kidnapped in the middle of the night, Moqoma kept himself from saying.

As they'd walked through the house, the other constables had glanced up to the curious faces looking down at them from the second floor with the awe of adolescent boys. If they'd known that the prostitutes assumed they were there to be bribed with sexual favors, he wondered if they would have smiled back so broadly.

"Why they gotta pack 'em in here so tight?" one of the constables asked. "Must have a bunch of bedrooms upstairs, right?"

Though the question was shot at Sibulele, Moqoma stepped forward, sparing her the explanation.

"Those are for the clients," Moqoma remarked. "Different rooms, different themes. None of them include whore's private bedchamber."

This shut up the constable. Moqoma moved to the dresser and opened the drawer Sibulele had indicated as Li's. Inside were a pair of pants, three thin cotton shirts, three pairs of panties, a single pair of socks, and a thin chemise. He went through the other drawers and discovered much the same thing in those. The uniformity of the clothes likely came from them being purchased all in the same place. He went to the closet and didn't have much better luck. The dresses were the kind of interchangeably slinky nightwear that would only be considered suitable by trade or those desiring to appropriate their look.

"Send in one of her roommates."

A moment later, a tall, thin woman of Asian descent whom Sibulele introduced as "Mai" entered. Rather than be cowed by the panel of official inquisitors, she affected nonchalance.

"Which dresses did Li wear?" Moqoma asked.

"This…and *this*," the woman said in English, indicating first a short red dress, then an equally revealing white one.

The sizes jibed with the small stature of the woman seen in the security footage. Moqoma looked over the dresses, hunting for tags. The labels were in Chinese.

"Purchased in China?" Moqoma asked. "Was she here legally?"

Mai shrugged and glanced to Sibulele.

"They were probably bought on a shopping trip to one of the China Towns, either the one in Ottery or that newer one in Century City," the non-madam suggested. "The girls go there all the time."

The speed at which Moqoma crossed the room took everyone by surprise, particularly Sibulele, the object of the detective's fury, who raised her arms defensively. Moqoma stopped, his face centimeters from Sibulele's.

"You've decided to start lying?"

"I…I wasn't sure…"

"*Bullshit.* You know the comings and goings of the girls. The *only* time they leave is on calls, and those require chaperones. Don't sell me the fiction that they have the ability to come and go as they please. I know there's a house full of armed men down the block right now waiting to see how long we're in here before calling up Mr. Knosi's boss. The girls take one step out of this building, and there's a bullet waiting. Don't treat me like I'm some kind of *doos.*"

Sibulele was trembling now. Moqoma knew she'd been a prostie herself decades earlier, but all that toughness melted away in an instant.

"Now, what I do know is that her passport is somewhere in this building."

"If it's not in this room, I don't..."

Moqoma smacked his hand against the doorframe. The sound erased the rest of Sibulele's sentence.

"You want the *skollie* cop?" Moqoma shouted. "These men all think I'm bent. You think they'll care if I knock you around?"

Sibulele's features hardened even as the angry gaze of the other officers burned into the back of Moqoma's neck.

"Your mates don't look so sure," Sibulele remarked as bravely as she could.

"But you'll notice that none have stepped forward," Moqoma shot back.

Sibulele hesitated, then softened.

"Come with me, Moqoma. But only you. As you say, everyone knows you're the *skollie* cop. Your word means nothing."

Sibulele led Moqoma through the first level of the house. The living room, just off the foyer, ran almost the length of the residence and had twelve-foot ceilings, which gave it the appearance of a banquet room. As Moqoma had suspected, the view of the South Atlantic was unbelievable. But it occurred to him that he'd never seen a single soul in this room when watching from the street. Johns would enter the frosted glass front door, move directly up the steps to the bedrooms, also behind frosted glass, and the tableau went wasted except for Sibulele and, likely on rare occasions, the girls.

"Come along," Sibulele snarked. "Don't fall in love with the pretty vista."

They passed through a large dining room and kitchen before arriving in what Moqoma realized was the current laundry room. Sibulele reached behind a dryer and felt around the back of it. After a moment, she came back with a stack of passports rubber-banded together. But before she could even take off the band, Moqoma had them in his hands.

"Oh, you know who you're looking for, then?" Sibulele asked.

Realizing she was right, Moqoma handed them back with a scowl. Sibulele made a show of stripping off the rubber band and sorting through the passports, opening each carefully as she looked at the photos. She stopped at one with a maroon cover.

"Here she is," Sibulele announced. "Li, Hui-Ling."

Growing up, Moqoma had only occasionally encountered the small population of Chinese immigrants who had settled in the Cape. When he'd joined the SAPS, he was informed that most of the illegal abalone smuggling originating from South African ports was done by the Chinese.

Though mostly ignored by locals, abalone was a valuable delicacy in Asia. Since democratization and the beginning of the post-apartheid era, the Chinese interest in South Africa had grown exponentially. Only a few years on, there were formal trade agreements between the government, mining concessions originally granted to European companies passed to the Chinese, and immigration had exploded. The last time Moqoma had flown into Johannesburg, half the tourist bureau ads in Tambo were in Chinese and showed Asian people happily taking in safaris, the wineries, or sailing out in Algoa Bay.

Moqoma turned the passport over in his hand. Little was written in English, other than "People's Republic of China" and "Passport" on the cover. On the identity page, however, he found two dates he thought useful. One, three years in the future, seemed to be when the passport expired. The other, seventeen years in the past, he took for Li's birthday.

"I'm taking this with me."

Sibulele said nothing, having expected as much. Moqoma turned to exit, but then heard the woman slipping the rubber band back around the stack. He did a silent calculation.

"How many girls you got here?" When Sibulele didn't respond, Moqoma whipped around, lip turned up in a snarl. "How many *girls*?"

Before she could respond, the detective's hand flashed forward, grabbing the remaining passports from her hand.

"Just a minute!" Sibulele yelled, suddenly realizing, despite her initially cavalier attitude, that she'd made a grave error in judgment.

But Moqoma was already into the kitchen, stripping away the rubber band and opening one passport after another. Having cased the brothel quite a few times before, he had known the answer to his question before he asked it. An alarm had sounded in the back of his head when Sibulele didn't fight him for taking the passport, but he'd let it slide, figuring she'd conceded once he threatened her. But it was the sound of the rubber band stretching around about twice the number of passports as there were girls that stopped him in his tracks.

"What do you think you're doing?!" Sibulele roared, chasing after him. "Now it'll be me calling up Mr. Knosi and giving him your name!" Moqoma was halfway through the stack when he found the first double. A short-haired girl with the last name of Zheng appeared in a Chinese passport, aged eighteen, only to appear again in a blue-jacketed American one under the name Wong. In this one, her birthday had been pushed back three years, and her birthplace was given as Vancouver, British Columbia.

He found two more doubles in the red jackets of Great Britain, but it was within the familiar forest-green cover of a South African passport (the newly updated coat of arms of SA always throwing Moqoma for a loop) that he found Li staring back at him. Only now she was Ana Leung, she'd been aged up to nineteen years, and her birthplace was listed as Durban, South Africa.

The fury on Moqoma's face when he returned to the foyer took the waiting officers by surprise.

"We're going to need a dog."

II

In Moqoma's mind, the presence of the Chinese passport was far more worrying than that of the South African one. When he'd been at his previous job with the DSO, South Africa's first attempt at a modern FBI-style national enforcement agency, the then-inspector came across his share of human trafficking cases. For the most part, they were as seedy as the media enjoyed indicating: Girls were lured from their home cities and villages with the promise of cash, thrown on a boat, nearly starved in the crossing, then dropped into a new level of hell and degradation when they landed on foreign shores. Plied with drugs and informed of how disposable they were every step of the way, the women either OD'd, were killed when they were no longer serviceable to even the lowest-paying client, or, in some cases, took their own lives. A handful, and it was debatable to say that these were the lucky ones, might escape into the night and end up on the street somewhere, almost inevitably tricking again, but for themselves.

Very few had any type of happy Hollywood ending, and none made it back home.

But the first thing a trafficker did was burn any documentation that would allow their girls the chance to get back home. A second set of IDs would then be established, typically one that ginned up a story "proving" that the girl was a local or from some other country who'd come to, in this case, South Africa looking for legitimate work and had ended up in the sex trade. If arrested, the result of an indictment would likely be a fine and, for foreigners, deportation. The girl would then be packed on a plane and sent "home," where a trafficker would be waiting at the airport to squire her to the next destination.

So why have a South African passport *and* the Chinese one? It was too pat. If discovered by local law enforcement, a group that took stage direction as easily as an ingénue, no one would question which was fake. Someone had set the scene knowing the death of Charles van Lagemaat would lead here.

And Moqoma had a pretty good idea who was behind it.

"Moosa, it's your brother," the voice barked over the cell phone. "I need a dog."

Moosa sighed. Not only was Inspector Moqoma not his brother, he often regretted being one of the few the ostracized cop still called for favors.

"Sorry, my friend," the handler replied, trying to sound resolute. "All dogs on the course are currently assigned. If you get an order from your captain, I can put in for a temporary transfer of a handler's assignment."

"I don't need the handler," Moqoma persisted. "Just the animal. I have the training."

"You know that's not the issue."

Moqoma sighed. "It's the van Lagemaat shooting. I don't have time for all the red tape. The trail is hot *now*."

Moosa considered his fellow officer's request. If it had been anyone else, he probably would've found the animal. But Moqoma? In a police force rife with bad apples, he was considered rotten to the core.

"It's two phone calls, Inspector. You're in your car, aren't you? By the time you get here, it could be lined up."

"It's 'Lieutenant,' now, but you knew that," Moqoma fumed, before lowering his voice. "And I didn't want to bring this up, but there are bigger issues in play here. I'm just now learning who might be involved and how far this goes up the chain of command. Discretion is the watchword."

Moosa knew what Moqoma was implying but wouldn't have put it past him to use a reference to the delicate nature of a case to get what he wanted. But Moosa was one of the few SAPS who believed the DSO/Scorpion anti-corruption task force that Moqoma had been a part of had gotten a bad rap. Parliament formed them to root out malfeasance in government. After a two-year search, they had uncovered a vast number of crimes leading straight to the top. But before they could file charges, they themselves were accused of being corrupt. Though no charges were ever filed, the unit was dissolved, and all the officers who'd been elevated to these lofty positions were scattered back into the regular police force, but at their DSO pay grades.

This only drove the wedge between the regular SAPS and the disgraced Scorpions deeper, which was clearly what the government desired.

"I'm telling you, Moqoma. We've got no dogs for anything."

Moqoma went silent, as if considering whether he should deliver the last piece of information.

"What if I tell you a girl's life may depend on it?" he intoned.

Moosa could hear two things in Moqoma's voice: desperation, but also the unmistakable ring of truth. Even if Moosa was skeptical a girl's life could be saved by a dog while investigating the van Lagemaat killing, the inspector certainly believed it was so.

"What girl?"

"There was a prostitute in the car with the chief warden when he was ambushed, but her body wasn't at the scene, leading me to believe that the shooters took her away. She's a living witness or a missing corpse. Either way, we find her, and we may just find the shooters. I know where she was living and was going to bring a dog on site. Only, the trail is growing cold by the minute. What I fear most is the powers-that-be shutting me down for fear of embarrassing the memory of the dearly departed."

Though this was a blend of half-truths and exaggerations, Moqoma could tell by Moosa's silence that he finally had him.

"What if someone else calls up for a dog?"

"I only need him for a few hours," Moqoma added quickly. "He'll be back in his kennel before anyone even knows he's gone."

Moosa sighed. He stepped outside the training house where he'd taken the call and eyed the nearby kennel.

"I may have one for you. But if anything happens to this canine, no joke: It'll be both our heads on a platter."

"An American police dog?" Moqoma shouted when he arrived at the training grounds. He stared at Bones through the kennel wire. "Are you *befok?*"

"I thought you were desperate," Moosa protested. "'Any animal will do,' right? Well, here's 'any animal.'"

Bones regarded the two men with curiosity, having woken from his nap to the sound of their approaching feet. His ears were at attention and his head cocked, as if listening for any clue as to their business with him.

"What about his handler?"

"His handler is sick and a bit of a dope anyway," Moosa explained. "If anybody comes by, I can say that he was accidentally sent back into the city with our dogs or that he got sick and is at the vet, but it's just dehydration and he'll be fine. And I will keep to that story as long as you have him back here by tonight."

Moqoma considered this a moment longer. He didn't know how long he'd need the dog, but he didn't want to alienate one of his few remaining allies.

"What's his name?"

"Bones. He's whip-smart and driven. One of the best animals I've seen."

"But trained in the States?"

"This one seems to know what it's doing." Moosa shrugged.

Moqoma regarded the shepherd one last time. The animal rose to all fours, expectant and at attention.

"You have a chain?" the inspector asked.

Moosa placed one in Moqoma's hand and nodded at the dog. "It's all right, Bones. Moqoma may seem like a bad guy, but that's for the humans. I've never seen him look cross-eyed at a dog."

Moqoma stepped forward and clicked the leash onto Bones's collar. He bent down and looked the dog in the eyes as he stroked his snout.

"I need this nose for a few hours. I also may need you to be an intimidating *brak*. But then back here to treats and relaxation and fun. Acceptable?"

Bones stared back at the inspector without moving. Nonetheless, he seemed to be giving off the tense, kinetic energy of one ready to be fired from a cannon.

"Good enough," Moqoma replied.

By the time the inspector and his new partner made it back to the oceanfront brothel, several more officers had arrived and were milling about. Though a couple were higher on the food chain than Moqoma, he parked, off-loaded Bones, and hurried into the house with no explanation. Sibulele was in handcuffs now, but it appeared that the girls had been allowed to leave. He imagined they hadn't gone too far. When Sibulele caught sight of him, she offered up her weariest look, wanting him to know that management had deemed her expendable. Moqoma turned away.

Sorry, ugogo.

He ushered Bones to Li's bedroom and was gratified to find it empty. As he suspected, however, all of Li's clothing and that of her roommates had long since been bagged and removed. This was a big case now, though it had little to do with the shooting of the Pollsmoor chief warden. A brothel this connected with the underworld meant a lot of handouts would be forthcoming to get the genie back in the bottle. Given the circumstances of van Lagemaat's death, no widow was likely offering a reward for the apprehension of his killers.

For his part, Bones seemed to be enjoying the field trip quite a bit. There were all new smells to smell, sights to see, and people to interact with. After being out in the country for so long, the bustle and move of activity excited him.

"All right, Bones, get over here," Moqoma quietly instructed, indicating Li's lower bunk.

The shepherd obeyed as Moqoma pushed the blanket aside and slowly stripped the sheets and pillowcase.

"Unfortunately, this is as good a scent article as we have to work with. The upside is that the clothes were probably just washed before they were put away and smell more of detergent than the target, while it's clear no one's washed the sheets for weeks."

Bones disinterestedly sniffed the sheets and pillowcase, seeming to isolate a scent. His nose bobbed from wrinkle to fold, as if trying to locate a hidden source.

The sight recalled to Moqoma the last dog he'd worked with, a shepherd named Robin. German shepherds in South African law enforcement recalled to many the bad old days of apartheid when white authorities would use the shepherds on blacks and coloreds, much the way they were used in the American South during the Civil Rights movement and, of course, in the concentration camps of Nazi Germany. Still, when the opportunity to become a handler arose, Moqoma leapt at the chance, as he'd already had more than his share of personality conflicts with his first human partners.

But Robin was special, a keenly intelligent dog with better instincts than half the officers on the force. They'd worked together for three years and helped crack several cases. Many had been drug-related, Robin discovering caches of narcotics or weapons, but they'd also used her like a bloodhound to resolve missing persons cases.

Then Moqoma made a decision he would regret for the rest of his life: He took a vacation. Really, it was just a seven-day leave to take a training course in Pretoria. He found out on day three that Robin was dead, killed in a raid on a hijacking ring while Robin was temporarily attached to the robbery squad.

When Moqoma returned, no one would tell him who Robin's handler had been that day. He never was to find out. But the shooter was arrested the day of the raid. Moqoma hunted the man down in his cell, asking for "five minutes" with the prisoner. The man seemed to know who Moqoma was but didn't have any idea as to what would come next.

Moqoma quickly went to work.

He thought of Robin's terrific speed and shattered the shooter's leg in three places. He remembered the dog's amazing sense of smell and shattered the man's nose. He recalled her ability to isolate sound and punched the man hard enough in the side of his head to deafen him in one ear. He was reminded of Robin's intelligence and heart, and began kicking in the fellow's ribcage and skull.

Though the shooter's jailers knew what to expect, the violence the then-sergeant inflicted on the prisoner was out of bounds. Still, they let it go on for a few more seconds before rushing in to pull Moqoma out and away.

To Moqoma's knowledge, the prisoner's injuries were never reported, and he soon disappeared into the prison system. The next time Moqoma even heard the man's name, it was when he was being transferred between Pollsmoor to Goodwood Prisons to make way for the inspector when he arrived, allegedly a "dirty cop," but actually undercover with the DSO. By that point, the story of his attack on the young man was leaked anyway as part of his cover. Dirty cops were always ending up in prison, but it was never bad to go in with a violent reputation.

A day behind bars hadn't gone by that Moqoma didn't see himself as atoning for the death of Robin. As he worked to ingratiate himself to the target of his investigation, a low-level 28 inside Pollsmoor who was a major crime lord outside named Mduduzi "Roogie" Mogwaza, the lying and betrayal came that much easier knowing he was doing it for Robin.

As Bones finished sniffing the pillowcase, Moqoma was hit by a wave of melancholy. All that duplicity and deception for Robin, only to have the DSO disbanded under the same brand of lies and betrayal. And here he was again, trying to reach the outcome in a case that many would probably wish remained a mystery if not tied up with the simplest, most media-friendly resolution imaginable.

The dog eyed him expectantly again, as if reading his thoughts.

"Let's go for a drive, Bones. See if my hunch is right this time."

Jianguo Qin's Camps Bay compound was modest by some standards. The main house was a six-bedroom affair, but with a conventional design that suggested a golf course–adjacent timeshare rather than the home of Cape Town's most visible Chinese gangster. Though he had never so much as spent an hour in court, he had been implicated in an impressively diverse series of financial crimes involving South African real estate, banking, mining, shipping, and manufacturing interests. In one notorious and oft-cited incident, Qin found fourteen out of fifteen charges that were being prepared against him dropped, only to have the Justice Department pursue the fifteenth. It was the least of the allegations and related to environmental damages inflicted on a beach near a construction site. Qin was a majority shareholder in not only the firm doing the building, but also in the hotel whose resort was being built.

The infraction was minor and the fine negligible. Still, the Deputy Director of Public Prosecutions wanted to send a message that she would go after Qin wherever and in whatever capacity he was related to a crime. Qin sent a message of his own, but quietly. Out of nowhere, a bill was introduced in Parliament that would change the law in Qin's favor. Before the Justice Department could even file a protest, it had been voted on and approved, soon to be signed into law. Though Qin's name was never mentioned in connection with the bill, the primary and most immediate effects of which would be felt in Durban, there was no mistaking who was behind it.

When the Deputy Director was asked to resign a few months later after a slew of public failures, she did so without protest.

Meanwhile, Qin continued to live in his modest home, suggesting the lifestyle of a successful immigrant perhaps a couple of generations removed from tremendous wealth. In fact, the only thing that alluded to an unorthodox piece of property was the vast, walled-in backyard that took up three times as much space as the house. Rather than fill it with signs of status, there was a small pool and a guesthouse, but the rest was scrub. Though tended by a gardener, it was still an odd sight, particularly surrounded as it was by eight-foot walls.

But Moqoma understood its purpose from the moment he first saw it.

To begin with, it made the house look even smaller, as if the land had been bought before the price of construction was tallied. It appeared as if the builder, in this case Qin, had made a mistake or simply overextended himself. Who would suspect a man like that of everything the Justice Department accused him of?

Second, and perhaps more importantly, it kept any neighbors at a remove. Qin's property took up almost an entire block. The nearest house to the east was at least a hundred meters away. To the west, easily fifty meters. There were a couple of houses across the street, but the main house was far enough back on the property that there were a good forty meters between Qin's front door and the houses it faced.

This meant that no one could easily see in through Qin's windows or over his walls unless they wanted to climb the sheer cliff face that the back of the property abutted.

Even so, as Moqoma and Bones clambered out of Moqoma's Land Rover, the detective could tell without looking that the backyard and house were filled with guests. Cars were parked three and four blocks away; the sound of children playing echoed over the walls; and, most peculiarly, the smell of gunpowder, the sight of smoke, and what sounded like low-caliber gunfire emerged from inside the compound.

Bones's raised his nose, took a few sniffs, and then shook his head violently as dozens of thin, individual wisps of smoke clawed into the sky above the backyard.

"What the hell is all this?" Moqoma muttered, not expecting the shepherd to answer.

As they approached the house, two suited security-types moved to the edge of the driveway, clearly meaning to head them off. Moqoma held up his badge and ID card and made to push right past them. Both guards, large Asian men with heads like artillery shells, squared their shoulders and let Moqoma see the submachine guns hanging from their shoulders on bandolier straps. Only, this was South Africa. The armored car men picking up the week's receipts from the neighborhood gas station carried more firepower, and there'd generally be twice as many.

Moqoma wasn't intimidated.

When the detective's smirk told the guards just that, they changed tack.

"Sir? May we ask your name and your business here?"

"My name is Lieutenant Inspector Leonard Moqoma. My business is with your master, Mr. Qin."

He expected a rebuke, subtle or physical. But the guard merely bowed, as if having received a compliment.

"Today is a holiday, and he has guests here. I will inform him of your arrival, but it may take a couple of minutes. Would you mind waiting inside the house?"

"The dog comes with me," Moqoma replied challengingly.

"Certainly." The guard nodded.

The first man nodded to the second, who raised a phone to his lips and spoke a few words in Chinese. Moqoma assumed they were looking for Qin but didn't want to leave the driveway unattended. A third guard, this one slightly older, emerged from the house, a stern look on his face. He gestured to Moqoma to follow him into the house. When he saw the German shepherd accompanying the investigator, his lack of reaction suggested he'd followed the exchange from just inside.

As the trio entered the home, Moqoma glimpsed the backyard festivities. Around a hundred well-dressed adults chatted and ate as their children ran around the yard, a merry afternoon garden party. But this party was accompanied by the setting off of fireworks and the burning of what looked like money.

"It is Qing Ming Jie," the stern-faced functionary, who had given his name as Xiang, said. "Tomb Sweeping Day. We honor our ancestors by burning items they might find useful in the afterlife."

"You're kidding me," Moqoma scoffed. "Like what?"

"Money, incense," Xiang genially responded. "One of the families brought a large paper house to burn. My own son was able to purchase a paper iPad and cell phone to send to his grandmother this year."

Xiang ushered the pair through the house's large, two-story living room to a stairwell, Bones's toenails clicking against the marble floor as they walked. Moqoma managed a second glance out the bay windows in back and could more clearly see the various items set to be burned.

"Where can you buy stuff like that?"

"China Town." Xiang shrugged. "You can buy them in every stall this time of year. All variations of the same."

They reached the second floor, and suddenly the décor became more ostentatious. There were a few paintings downstairs and a statue of a crane, not dissimilar to ones Moqoma saw in slightly higher-end gift shops. Tourist junk. The upstairs, however, took on the appearance of a museum of Chinese antiquities. Though hardly a customs officer, the investigator had seen more than his share of valuable property stolen from the wealthy and picked up a sixth sense for authenticity. The biggest surprise was how easily the rich were duped into buying into, and more importantly, paying insurance premiums on, fakes.

Xiang led Moqoma and Bones through a hallway lined with statuary and drawings dating back centuries. What really caught the detective's eye was all the jade. He knew that much of it was strictly banned from export, and he assumed Xiang or Qin knew this before deciding where he was to be received. It occurred to him that they might be planning to kill him and the German shepherd right there, though he doubted it.

Qin's study, in the corner of the second story of the house farthest from all neighbors, had a high ceiling, at least five meters.

"Please wait here," Xiang said, before turning on his heel and quickly disappearing back down the hall.

Moqoma was surprised to be left alone among the most valuable pieces, which dotted this room, but he considered that it was to appeal to his lesser angels. Maybe being surrounded by all this finery would be like dropping Ali Baba in the cave of the Forty Thieves. He would decide that some of it should come home with him and, while left waiting, would calculate the bribe he would attempt to extort from Qin.

But Moqoma wasn't in the mood. He turned his attention from the most valuable pieces to the more curious decorative choices, which included several shelves of old books, more Chinese relics, but a cache of African trinkets as well. Though he had no doubt as to the value of the Chinese artifacts, the African ones keeping them company suggested a collector who wanted only to represent the most extreme examples from his adopted continent. There were masks and skins, but the masks were a ragtag blend of the completely sacred and the child's toy, while half the skins were fake.

All the hallmarks of an émigré paying lip service to a place he had no interest in understanding or adapting to.

"*Soutpiel*," Moqoma sneered.

"What's that mean?" came a voice from behind him.

Moqoma turned to find a young Chinese woman in the doorway. She was in her thirties and, though dressed casually, carried herself with a professional demeanor. A guest at the backyard party, Moqoma presumed.

"It is a rude thing," Moqoma admitted. "I should not have said it."

"You think I will blush?" the woman asked, already sounding exasperated. Though her accented English suggested that she'd learned the language in China, it was already inflected with enough Africanisms that Moqoma knew she'd been in RSA a while already.

"You might at that," he said, almost flirtatiously.

"Then I can't wait to hear it," she demanded. "Please, go on."

"'Soutpiel' is Afrikaans for 'salt penis.'" Moqoma shrugged. "Explain?"

"It refers to someone who has one foot in South Africa and another in their country of origin, leaving their penis to hang down into the ocean. As I said, a rude term."

"You think Mr. Qin is a *soutpiel*?"

Moqoma stared at the woman for a beat. If she was at Mr. Qin's party, she was likely acquainted with the man and could be baiting the detective into saying something he'd regret. But the casual way she asked the question made him think she was simply curious as to how he might answer.

"I have never met the man face to face. But this…" Moqoma indicated the room, "…is symptomatic of a case."

The young woman scoffed, but she seemed to do so in order to hide a smile. Moqoma was intrigued.

"My name is Nina Zhu. I'm a member of the Ministry of State Security."

Moqoma was taken aback. She had pronounced the name of China's vast foreign intelligence service, the equivalent to Israel's Mossad, Great Britain's MI6, or the United States' CIA, as casually as one might announce their employer as British Airways or Coca-Cola.

"Leonard Moqoma, South African Police Service."

"And how have you and your companion come to serve us today, Leonard Moqoma?" The question was carved from ice.

"Well, there are two things, one that was brought to my attention and one that was brought to the attention of, as you say, my companion," Moqoma began, feigning obsequiousness. "First, your Mr. Qin owns several properties, I believe. One these includes a beautiful oceanfront house in Clifton. We have discovered, I mean, the South African Police Service has discovered, just this morning that it is being used as a brothel."

The Chinese agent seemed genuinely surprised by this, but maybe she was just a good actress.

"We were sure that Mr. Qin would want to be advised personally of this before word might slip out and potentially ruin his good name."

"And the other thing?" Nina Zhu asked.

"The way we learned was in following the clues surrounding the assassination of Charles van Lagemaat, of which you surely have heard," Moqoma continued. "When he was killed, he was in the process of driving one of the prostitutes back to this residence. She has since gone missing, and, for reasons that should be self-evident, we would like to find her in hopes she might prove useful to our investigation. Now, to my friend here."

He indicated Bones.

"He was given her scent at the brothel. Do you know what it means for a detection dog to 'alert' to something?"

"I don't know the term, but I can deduce," Zhu replied, piqued.

"Well, he has spent the last ten minutes 'alerting' to traces of the missing girl's scent in this room, in the hallway, and in the lobby. Though it's different from dog to dog, some suggest animals can follow a trail even five days old. I would submit that it's a lot less, maybe as much as twenty-four hours, little more."

He made a grand gesture of checking his watch.

"So, if she was in this room before or after last night's incident, it would be useful for us to know why. Would you not agree?"

The agent's mouth opened, but no words escaped. As she looked from Moqoma to Bones, the detective could tell that what had been, in her mind, only a dog moments before had attained new status.

"I need to make a phone call."

"Please do. We will wait here."

A nod. But then the special agent was gone.

III

Moqoma and Bones were made to wait half an hour. The shepherd took up a position alongside the windows, allowing himself a nap in the sun. Despite the occasional explosion of fireworks from the backyard, the dog never woke.

For his part, Moqoma strolled to the bookshelves. What first caught his attention was a shelf full of H. Rider Haggard novels. Of all the imperialist/colonialist adventure writers, Haggard was somewhere below Conrad and Kipling, closer to Edgar Rice Burroughs, and guilty of presenting a less-than-nuanced view of "the dark continent" to the world that created perceptions and stereotypes that lasted into the twenty-first century. Moqoma believed his government's embrace of China had at least something to do with them positioning themselves as "a fellow post-colonial power."

Moqoma had just pulled what appeared to be a first edition of Haggard's *Elissa, The Doom of Zimbabwe* from the shelf when Special Agent Zhu returned with Cordell Hofmyer, the Regional Head of the Department of Justice and the likely successor to the current Deputy Minister. Moqoma was most alarmed to see that Hofmyer was smiling.

"This is an amazing piece of detective work you've assembled, Lieutenant Moqoma," Hofmyer began. "The kind of thing that makes us very proud of the Service."

"Thank you, sir," Moqoma replied automatically.

"As you surmised, Mr. Qin was completely unaware of what was happening in his house in Clifton, primarily because it was a rental property," Hofmyer divulged. "We have traced the renters back and identified a connection to Roogie Mogwaza's Yankee Boys."

"Oh?" Moqoma asked.

"This coincided with a report just delivered that the ammunition used in the shooting of van Lagemaat matched a load of armor-piercing rounds the Yankee Boys took possession of in a hijacking last year."

Convenient, Moqoma thought.

"Due to the complexities of our relationship with the People's Republic, it was very wise of you to use discretion and bring this directly to Mr. Qin."

Moqoma allowed his gaze to flit toward the window. The party had carried on outside, uninterrupted by the news he'd delivered in the study.

"What of the missing girl?" he asked.

Hofmyer looked annoyed, as if hoping the detective would simply nod and exit. But Zhu handed Moqoma a printout of the identity page from Li's Chinese passport. The first thing the lieutenant noticed was that the date it was set to expire was different from the one he'd seen in Clifton. This one would expire in only a couple of months.

"She was here, yesterday, in fact. She wanted Mr. Qin's help in arranging a visa for herself to travel to Macau to see her mother."

"Mr. Qin arranged such things?" Moqoma asked, receiving a quick look of reproach from Hofmyer.

"Among the many parts he plays in your country, some are official," Zhu replied. "In his role as a consular attaché here in Cape Town, he would be someone to see about a visa."

Moqoma couldn't tell from Zhu's facial expression whether she was frustrated with answering a local cop's insipid questions or simply didn't enjoy lying. But Moqoma knew he'd pushed things as far as they could go.

"It sounds as if everything is in order, then," Moqoma said, reaching for Bones's leash. "I'll make sure the two of you receive copies of my report."

"Thank you, Lieutenant Moqoma," Hofmyer replied. "But please direct it to the Deputy Public Prosecutor. I think it's going to be a big day for them, and once the dust settles, they'll need to start pulling all the pieces together and make sure it's all airtight."

Moqoma pulled up short. It was as if a pile of numbers that had been bouncing around in his head suddenly had begun to form an equation. The answer was still murky, but he saw clearly where the unknown quantities were yet to be filled in.

"Why's it a big day for them?" he asked.

"You hadn't heard? They think they've finally got enough on Mogwaza to take down his entire operation, soup to nuts."

"This shooting?"

"The shooting and the prostitution are enough to arrest all the boys at the top. Then it becomes about getting them all to start implicating each other in the shakedowns, security scams, clubs, and hijackings. They're taking down the drug labs, the chop shops, *everything*."

Moqoma felt a dull hot throb behind his eyes. He stared at Hofmyer, searching the man's eyes for signs that he knew what was happening. Seeing nothing, he turned to Zhu. She was more inscrutable. Instead of a blank look, she seemed to be reading Moqoma even as he tried the same thing on her.

"Come on, Bones," Moqoma said, hurrying on his way. "Let's get you back to the kennel."

Once they were back in the Land Rover, Moqoma's mind raced. There was no such thing as a coincidence, was there? Moqoma knew Roogie. The *last* thing he'd do with ammunition from a hijacking was use it. In fact, he seemed to remember that case specifically. The Yankee Boys got the bullets, put them on a boat, rounded the Cape, landed at Durban, and were sold up country, likely to the Sudanese.

But maybe, they were actually selling them to a Triad.

That was, Moqoma knew, the type of criminal organization Qin sat at the top of. Traditionally, a Triad wasn't like the Cosa Nostra or some other traditional emigrant-organized crime groups where homage is paid to the groups back home. A Triad was established within a new community of Chinese expatriates. In recent times, however, this had changed with the arrival of the so-called "snakeheads," Triad members who would leave China (or Hong Kong, or Singapore), arrive at a new destination, set up shop, and then act as a sort of travel agent for human trafficking, typically illegal immigrants who paid a certain amount to be slipped into the country of their choice. In the United States, those who brought illegals over the southern borders from Central and South America were called "coyotes." Snakeheads served much the same function.

There was no doubt in Moqoma's mind that such an operation was going on in Cape Town, but Qin's connection to the Consulate and the girls brought in as prostitutes confirmed this. But though he was involved in several shady legitimate businesses, it was clear that he now meant to move on the Western Cape's indigenous criminal outfits, starting with the most powerful and the most connected, Roogie Mogwaza's Yankee Boys.

Mogwaza did not come up in a gang, as so many had. Instead, he'd grown up in a fairly successful family – well, successful for the apartheid era – in which the father owned a handful of buildings around the Cape Flats. *His* father had been a collections man for a white slumlord who never wanted to see one of his tenants face to face. So he hired Roogie's grandfather to collect rents. Rather than be the hard-ass the slumlord thought he'd be, Roogie's grandpa would often cover those who couldn't pay and allow them to "catch up" on rent later. Because of this, he built a reputation among the community and was favored by many despite their sometimes squalid living conditions. No one blamed Roogie's grandfather. He was the go-between. But he didn't make things harder than they needed to be.

By the time the slumlord figured out what Roogie's grandfather was up to, the old man, already a father of nine children, had saved up enough money to build a handful of houses in Langa. Naturally, people fought to be his tenants. Others with money approached Roogie's grandfather about investing in more homes, and he built these, too.

When Roogie's dad took over the business, the family owned several commercial and residential properties in the Flats. This was in the mid-eighties, when Botha began to relax certain strictures of apartheid, the ownership of property being one of them. The use of subterfuge and white fronts went away, and the family emerged as one of the more successful in the Western Cape.

But this wasn't enough for Roogie.

No, he wanted a bigger piece of the pie — in this case, the commercial real estate game in the Cape Bowl downtown where the whites played. With a stroke of genius now characteristic of his family, Roogie bribed his way into a job as a building inspector. He spent five years opening every door in the Cape Bowl. He learned which buildings were the most desirable, which were crumbling, whose name was on the door, but who actually built and controlled the structure, and most importantly, the sort of unteachable instinct for the commercial real estate business that allowed one to gather inside information without needing to seek it out.

All this meant Roogie was in the perfect position to cash in when the building boom of the Mandela years hit in the mid-nineties. But Mogwaza knew from the start that he'd never be happy with the income of a "successful businessman" and had been growing the criminal side of his business as well. Roogie had a cousin named Thembi in the Yankee Boys. Roogie had long been a fixture at Yankee Boys events, but it wasn't until he'd made a name for himself in business that he began to hire them for jobs.

The "security scams" referred to by Hofmyer were one of Roogie's specialties. A new business would move in at an address in the Cape Bowl, and a legitimate security firm – bodyguards, locks, cameras, etc. – owned by Roogie would come by and pitch its services. If the owner refused, a few weeks would go by, and then the Yankee Boys moved in. During business hours, they'd go in and make trouble, harassing the workers, then daring them to call the SAPS. After hours, there'd be break-ins and vandalism until the owner threw his hands up. Nine times out of ten, a neighbor clued him in to what was happening, and he would go ahead and hire Roogie's firm. That one in ten who tried to raise a ruckus, employ gangsters of his own, go to the police, or try to rally the other business owners against Roogie? These men were soon victims of Cape Town's notorious carjacking rings, a bullet to the head for their wallet, vehicle, and cell phone.

The message was clear, and soon Roogie not only owned several buildings around the city, but he also ran the largest commercial security company in the Western Cape. A number of people suggested he go into the equally lucrative home security field, where, with his brand name, he could've made money hand over fist. But Roogie, a nickname that came from the old slang for a 50-rand note, had no interest in this. It was money without power.

When Moqoma met Roogie, it was almost a decade since he'd been on top. Having spent years coasting on his reputation, he'd made himself and the Yankee Boys soft targets for other gangsters looking to get a leg up. When he inevitably retaliated, he did so with the violence of a wounded lion, all bravura while hoping that he had a slugger's chance of knocking out his opponent with one blow. It was his connection to an execution-style killing of a rival gang leader, a bullet to the head and the body dumped into the bay for the great whites to devour.

But everybody knew Roogie was behind it, and the SAPS couldn't look the other way anymore. So he was arrested, stood trial, and was convicted on a ridiculously lesser charge that earned him two years in Pollsmoor. Moqoma believed from the start that Roogie knew he was an undercover officer but didn't threaten him in any way. They were both intelligent, interested men who had several things in common. Though Moqoma never admitted to being a detective and Roogie never admitted to wrongdoing, they spoke often and took their meals and exercise together. Moqoma didn't know it for sure, but he believed that Roogie's unofficial protection kept the undercover alive while on the inside.

And now that man, whom Moqoma felt he owed a debt, was likely soon to die. Worse, it wasn't at the hands of another *tsotsi*, but the police, and part of their justification for doing so would come from his zeal in pursuing van Lagemaat's killers.

That's when Moqoma glanced at Bones. *The girl.* If they could find her or her body, there was still a chance they could tie it back to Mr. Qin and his mysterious organization. But would the damage already be done?

"Bones," Moqoma said grimly, accelerating toward the Cape Bowl. "For what it's worth, I hope I'm not leading you into death and danger. If so, I apologize in advance."

Moqoma glanced to the animal, searching for any sign the shepherd understood his words. The dog seemed only to register that his temporary handler's mood had darkened and had become alert, if not eager.

"All right. Time to make a phone call."

Mduduzi "Roogie" Mogwaza was behind his desk when the head of his security team burst in, announcing that a heavily armed police tactical unit was swarming up three of the building's four stairwells.

"There are several more taking up positions in the surrounding blocks," the man continued, winded from his run.

It wasn't that Roogie hadn't believed the rumors that they were going to try to pin the chief warden of Pollsmoor's assassination on the Yankee Boys. He just didn't think the reaction would be so swift. He reached for his cell phone, but the security man shook his head.

"No time."

Roogie ignored the man and began dialing a number. But then a pair of assistants in his commercial business firm came running in. They looked terrified.

"We heard shots."

Roogie tensed. He'd anticipated being frog-marched out of his office in handcuffs. The reality of the situation, however, began to dawn on him.

"You sent men downstairs?" he asked.

"Two unarmed teams," the security man replied.

"Try them."

The security man hit the "call" button on his radio. "Alfred? Judas? What's going on down there?"

Static.

The security man shook his head. Roogie nodded and quickly moved across his office to a narrow wood panel alongside his bookshelves that ran from floor to ceiling. There was a sound of distant thunder, as if someone had thrown a barrel down the fire stairs and it was gaining speed as it rolled through the building.

Their mistake was tipping their hand, Roogie thought. *If they'd come to kill him, why announce their intentions by killing his guards?*

He pulled the wood panel back to reveal a service elevator. On all other floors, the elevator was obscured in a building-wide redesign. Anyone who might've remembered that it existed in the first place would be hard-pressed to remember where it had been located.

For Roogie, it was an insurance policy.

The car door was already open, and Roogie stepped inside. He nodded to his chief of security, who seemed to understand his grave new role as temporary stop-gap and nodded back.

With that, Roogie touched the only button that still worked in the car and began his descent. As he went, he idly wondered why the police hadn't cut the power and decided they probably didn't think it necessary. Regardless, the elevator could be operated manually for a single descent, so he wasn't worried, only curious.

He felt for his phone, only to feel it vibrate. He plucked it from his pocket and saw the number of a gatsby stand in Fresnaye on the caller ID. It was one of the dozen or so public numbers he'd established to be used only in an emergency. He then provided this information to only one other man.

"*Awe*, is this El Zayde?"

"*Ja*, El Zayde here. Howzit Lazarillo?"

Roogie exhaled. "Not great. We have guests."

"You've had guests before," Moqoma offered.

"These are more insistent. Far more."

"I hate to be the bearer of bad news, but I've heard in cases like this that it gets worse before it gets better."

"What're you saying?" Roogie asked, apprehensive.

"What they want is to make things unlivable. They flushed you out of your own house, and they've got you right where they want you."

Roogie cursed under his breath. He knew what Moqoma was telling him, that the police must know about his elevator and were potentially waiting for him at the exit, hoping he'd try to get away. They wanted blood, and only his would do.

"Suggestions?"

"Don't drive away. Put down stakes. Dig in."

Roogie knew the detective couldn't possibly mean stay and fight. Then he figured it out.

"I'll see you there?"

"Might take me a minute to find you, but I'll be along."

Roogie hung up. He didn't consider for a moment that Moqoma was in on it or was baiting some further trap, though he wasn't sure why. He'd be suspicious of almost anyone else. But Moqoma was an odd fellow, a Cape Flats boy who watched his father get burned alive for refusing to side with either the ANC or the Inkatha during the violence leading up to the '94 elections. Roogie had always believed the young man had become a cop to exact revenge on those who did the job, but then he did nothing of the sort. Rather, he was a peacemaker, a cop with a sense of fairness who understood there would always be a dirty side to things and let certain things slide. He wasn't driven by a strong sense of justice or moral duty, but more a belief that everyone was in this together, and sometimes the bullies taking advantage had to get sorted.

It occurred to Roogie that the young Moqoma put on the gun and uniform out of a sense of fear, a need to feel the weapon close to him and know that if he used it, it would be assumed he was in the right. But this wasn't it, either (though he'd met plenty of SAPS who fit that profile). No, Moqoma did the job because he understood that someone had to, and that person might as well be him.

When Roogie reached the fourth sub-level parking garage, he emerged from the service elevator with trepidation. There was the work truck, gassed up and waiting for his egress, but he knew from Moqoma's words that the police were stationed at every garage exit. So he bypassed the truck and headed straight for a service door against the far wall. Though it was covered with signage alerting passersby to its danger, suggesting live wires behind it, that was camouflage. In reality, the locked door opened into the city's oft-derided and disease-ridden sewer system, a descent into which many might feel was worse than electrocution.

Roogie took the key from his wallet, one of the only ones he had on him at all times, and unlocked the door. He stepped inside and closed it behind him.

He hadn't been down there since he was a teenager, using it as a quick escape after holding up businessmen hunting their cars in dark parking garages at the end of a long day, but the horrific smell seemed a thousand times worse than his memory.

He wasn't sure if Moqoma meant him to head away from the building, but he decided to regardless, choosing a corridor that led west to the Victoria & Alfred Waterfront. The stench of oil and seawater would soon overpower that of the city's raw sewage.

He didn't think there were any officers beside Moqoma in the sewer with him, but he had two guns on him that he intended to use if they appeared. He pulled his favorite, a Heckler & Koch HK P30 with virtually no recoil, and checked the magazine. Even in the dull light of the sewer's work lights, he could make out the full double-stack of fifteen 9mm bullets. Rather than put it back in his waistband, he held it in his hand as he ran, giving him an additional feeling of comfort.

But then a new feeling gripped Roogie: *fear*.

There was a tingling at the top of his spine as he felt the presence of something else in the tunnel with him. Something *moving*. He slowed a little and pulled the second gun from his trousers.

"That you, El Zayde?"

He was answered by silence.

Roogie began to run. He imagined this was precisely what the person or persons in the dark wanted him to do, but it didn't slacken his pace. Instead, he grew angry at himself for being afraid. He gritted his teeth, imagined coming face to face with his tormentor, and pictured himself taking *them* by surprise, placing his twin gun barrels directly into their eye sockets and pulling the trigger.

The image of an enemy having their face, brains, and skull pulped by his bullets, so much so that they appeared to have been beheaded, calmed him immensely.

Suddenly, the sixth sense was replaced by a sound as he heard someone coming up behind him. He turned the gun down the tunnel, dropped the safety, and aimed into the darkness.

"That you, Lazarillo?"

When no one replied, he fired. The muzzle flash lit up the entire tunnel like a strobe. Though he could see something moving at him in still images, he couldn't make out what it was. There was something off about it, as if it was a man ducking the oncoming fire but still coming much faster than any man could.

Before he could adjust his fire, the magazine was spent. He went to reload, only to feel a sudden change in the air around him, a rogue breeze cooling his exposed skin.

An instant later, he was on his back, having been struck by something massive and fast-moving. He tried to beat his assailant with the pistol, but what was clear to him now as an animal had caught his wrist at just the right angle, and he couldn't pull it around. As the creature continued to twist his arm around, he involuntarily dropped the gun, though the noise it made as it clattered to the ground was drowned out by his own angry shouting.

"Jesus Christ, get off me, you motherfucker!" he snarled, rolling his body back and forth.

But then he heard footsteps and glimpsed a man jogging down the tunnel.

"Bones! Get off him, boy! *Now!*"

The German shepherd released Roogie immediately. The gangster scuttled a few meters away before picking up his empty pistol, slapping a new clip into it, and aiming it at the dog.

"Roogie, no!" Moqoma shouted. "He's American. You want to get in real trouble?"

Roogie couldn't help but smile, as much as he wanted not to. The dog, now sitting nearby, stared idly at him as if waiting for the command to attack again.

"Why do you have an American dog, Inspector?" Roogie asked,

matter-of-factly.

"It's 'Lieutenant' Moqoma now, Roogie, but don't get attached to it. It'll be 'Convict' Moqoma soon enough."

"You didn't have to come after me." Roogie shrugged.

"No shit, I didn't, *bru*, but it's a lot worse than you think."

Roogie eyed the river of water and shit that flowed past them.

"Yeah, worse than that," Moqoma nodded. "So you best come with me so maybe we start winning a few points for our side, okay?"

"Sounds like a plan," Roogie grunted, clambering to his feet and following the detective and the German shepherd back through the sewer.

IV

Bones stared out the window as the Land Rover bounced out of the underground parking garage onto Riebeek Street. They were eight blocks away from the building in which Roogie's company occupied the top three floors, but they were still only just on the other side of the massive police cordon.

Though Roogie slouched into the back floorboards to avoid being seen by passersby, Bones's nose was happily pressed against the window. There were so many new smells in the thicket of buildings that made up downtown Cape Town: Street vendors sold food on corners, they passed an open-air market with at least four spice dealers hocking their wares on a side street, and there was the cacophony of human traffic in general. Businesspeople moved between buildings, tourists on foot swept from the nearby luxury hotels to the beaches and waterfront, and laborers from the Flats, moving quickest of all, wove in and around all others.

All of these rich scents pushed into the shepherd's olfactory canal, the foods causing him to salivate. He opened his mouth and licked his lips. Drool spilled onto the armrest, and spittle from his tongue dotted the window.

"You ever feed this mongrel?" Roogie asked, eyeing Bones's display with disgust.

"I haven't," Moqoma admitted. "I know a Lebanese place over on Kloof if you want to run in for carry-out."

Roogie rolled his eyes and stayed put. "So what's the plan?"

As he said this, the Land Rover pulled through an intersection. Roogie could just glimpse the police barricade still roping off the heart of the city.

"You don't even want to know what's going on?" Moqoma asked.

Roogie shrugged. "They're putting van Lagemaat on me and the Boys. What else do I need to know?"

"That Qin's Triad is behind it. They fixed it with the government to take you down. I don't know what the *iRiphabliki* is to receive in return, but it's probably a fair trade."

"*Qin?*" Roogie exhaled. "What does he want with me?"

"What else? Less competition, likely on the underworld and legit business front. Someone's going to need to shake down all those Euros coming down here with a dream of opening some franchise bistro."

"Don't push your luck, Moqoma. You let me keep my guns, remember?"

"And I kept you from being dead, *remember*? These past fifteen minutes you've still been breathing? I own them all. Now, are you ready to get to the bottom of this?"

Roogie was. Moqoma explained to him the timeline of the van Lagemaat assassination, but also that of his own investigation since. When he brought up his belief that Li might still be alive, Roogie scoffed.

"He would've killed her immediately. No question. She's in the water."

"But so soon?" Moqoma pressed. "They know they have to bury her pretty deep, even if she was in on it. They're not going to risk some fisherman or cop spotting them doing their dirty work."

"You think she was in on it?"

"There was the hit at the prison. That drew van Lagemaat out. Then there was the matter of taking her home. He didn't want to leave her in his place, so of course he'd take her back to Clifton. Without her, they're not a hundred percent on his location the whole time leading up. She's got eyes on him."

Roogie thought for a moment, hesitant to buy into Moqoma's version of events, if only because he hadn't come up with them himself.

"So, say she *is* alive, where do you think she'd be?" Roogie asked.

"That's why I've got you in the car," Moqoma admitted. "Qin has to have some stash house somewhere, the kind of place that he could put her, put some guys with guns around her, and know she was safe. If she's just some girl, the killing might've scared her, too, so she might be looking to rabbit. This keeps her under his thumb until he can send her back to China or wherever."

Roogie thought for a long moment. It even looked like Bones was awaiting his response. At first, he didn't have a single idea. But then a tiny piece of information floated to the front of his mind, a house in the middle of nowhere a couple of his boys had suggested was being used by smugglers. And when Moqoma brought up Qin, it dawned on him who might be the smuggler in question.

"He's got a house in Hout Bay," Roogie announced. "If they're trying to hide her, it's way off the beaten path. If they're going to bury her, where better than in the foothills above the water? If they're going to dump her in the ocean or smuggle her back to China, you've got the boats right there."

"Hout Bay it is," Moqoma agreed, making a sharp right onto Buitenkant and heading for the M62.

Hout Bay was a quiet fishing village down the coast from Cape Town on the shores of a small harbor tucked between two hills. Its primary notoriety came from being the home port of a large fishing fleet that provided the restaurants and markets with its fresh catch on a daily basis, including three eateries right there on the pier. The fleet would leave before first light and often return before lunch, allowing locals and a few brave tourists the experience of sampling the catch – hake, Cape snoek, yellowtail, dorado, sole, Cape salmon, and sometimes even longfin tuna – within hours of it being plucked from the depths. The most popular restaurant, Snoekies, was constantly busy, fish being offloaded from the place's own boats, rolled on carts to the back door, and in the fryer as soon as it could be washed, skinned, and deboned.

Its other source of notoriety came from its more recent emergence as a way station for the import of pharmaceuticals used in the manufacture of methamphetamines, known locally as *tik*. Customs officials at the waterfront had cracked down on smuggling in recent years, making it more and more difficult to bring in illicit goods in large quantities from overseas. Rather than give up or try a different method, smugglers decided to adapt, seeing as how only one end of the supply line was fouled up. The container ships would continue to be loaded with contraband and sent off to South Africa with their legitimate cargo. But as the ships neared the Cape, they would surreptitiously drop their unlawful freight into the sea lanes with GPS transponders and floatation devices attached. These would then be picked up by a couple of the fishing boats in on the scam and brought back to the docks. There, the watertight packages would be palleted and loaded on the same trucks that delivered fish all over the city.

For their part in the chain, the fishermen were paid the equivalent of about $600 to split four or five ways. If caught, they could face a decade in prison and a lifelong ban from commercial fishing, often their only source of income.

These fishermen, for the most part, along with the others who worked on the wharf (packing trucks, working the ice chutes, etc.), lived in the row upon row of rundown houses that lined the foothills overlooking the bay. Stacked on top of one another, the "houses" were little more than shacks, though there were a few multistory cinder block structures hanging down the hillside as well. From the street below, a tourist could be forgiven for believing they were looking at a shanty town or squatter's village. If they'd risked the drive up into the uniquely South African favela, their suspicions would've been only confirmed as they encountered mud roads that acted like quicksand to vehicle tires, endless piles of trash, and packs of roving dogs.

Moqoma eased the Land Rover onto the road that led up to the houses. Roogie, who kept low but was now seated on the back seat next to Bones, eyed the various buildings.

"Which one is it?" Moqoma asked.

"That one," Roogie said, pointing to one of the multistory block houses.

The building was midway down the highest row of houses on the facing hillside. The one good thing, Moqoma realized, was that there wouldn't be anyone above the structure looking down. But besides that, there was no question the place had been selected for its defensibility. All four floors had windows facing in every direction. With so few cars in the area, particularly when most of the neighborhood's inhabitants were at the pier, Moqoma's Land Rover would be spotted before it got within a hundred meters of the building.

And if no one inside happened to be on sentry duty, Moqoma imagined at least a few other watchers in the surrounding houses. A couple of rand and a free cell phone was probably all it took for a neighbor to ring up when strangers appeared in the area.

"We're going to have to drive past, maybe park at one of the restaurants on the pier, and walk up," Moqoma announced.

Roogie nodded in agreement but then eyed Bones.

"Going to have to be careful around here, Bones," the gangster warned. "You may be hot shit in American, but in Hout Bay, you're just another *inja*."

They parked and pretended to circle the restaurant, checking the menu. There was already a line at Snoekies, so it appeared perfectly natural that the two men and their dog might walk around a little instead. A few seconds later, they slipped across the street.

The houses on the hillside were arranged on something of a grid. A single road led straight up, and then individual streets broke off from it at perpendicular angles like the tines on a fork. This meant that whoever lived at the end of these blocks, should they have had a car, would have to drive all the way across the hill to the one road before descending to Harbour Road. So that pedestrians didn't have to do the same thing, makeshift wooden stairs ran up the hill alongside every third dwelling or so. In the early hours, the workers streamed down these stairs and then back up every night. During the day, however, the steps went virtually unused except by packs of children and packs of dogs.

Moqoma banked that the guards around Qin's house kept their eyes peeled for vehicles. He doubted they would pay much mind to a couple of colored men walking their dog up the stairs, particularly if they'd seen them park across the street. City boys looking for a view.

If they paid them a second thought, it might be to decide if they had anything worthwhile to steal.

The plan Moqoma had originally outlined kept Roogie in the car. He would point out the house, and Moqoma and Bones would scout the place, searching for signs of Li. If they found anything, they'd return to the vehicle and call in the cavalry, albeit specific members of the cavalry who would be told a particular story. When they arrived and just so happened to come upon Li, Moqoma would step in, pull rank, and take the girl into custody himself.

But then Roogie demanded to come along.

"I stay down there, someone's going to see me. My picture's on the front page of the paper every other day, and you know they're wrapping fish with my face in there right now."

Moqoma almost laughed but then saw Roogie was dead serious. He wasn't spoiling for a fight but feared that, should they be spotted by Qin's men, there'd be no way out *sans* bloodshed. Moqoma also knew if he was seen on his own in this area, having a known hard-ass like Roogie Mogwaza with him might be a good thing.

They had four guns between them, Roogie's two pistols, then Moqoma's automatic and a shotgun he had in the back of the Land Rover. And then there was the German shepherd.

Obviously, Moqoma hadn't seen the animal in action, but Bones clearly took his cues from his handler. When they were in the brothel in Clifton, the dog had been perfectly at ease. But once they'd entered Qin's compound in Camp's Bay, it was as if he'd recognized Moqoma's apprehension and tensed up, ready for action. It was an unexpected response, but one the detective now appreciated.

As they climbed the stairs, the two men tried to appear as nonchalant as possible. They moved slowly, taking in the view, and worked to convince anyone whose sightline they happened into that they were tourists.

They had chosen the stairs all the way at the end of the block, the ones that would afford the best view to those in search of one. But as they neared the top of the hill, Roogie shot a glance to the multistory cinderblock.

"They don't have anyone outside."

"If it's Qin's gang, from a practical perspective, don't you think they'd stay indoors? Maybe move in and out at night?"

"Why?"

"You don't think a bunch of heavily armed Asians out here in the middle of nowhere wouldn't attract at least some attention? No matter who they bribed?"

Roogie thought about this for a moment but then nodded. "So, what, you want to just walk past the front door?"

Moqoma shook his head and pointed to the road two levels below the top one. "We stop there, cut right, and walk through the neighborhood. When we get below Qin's house, we take the stairs and see what we see. We'll be close enough that unless they're looking straight down, they're not likely to see us."

Roogie was impressed. "You were a pretty good cop before going rogue and crooked, weren't you?"

Moqoma snorted and kept moving.

When they reached the third road from the top, Moqoma continued his pantomime, suggesting to Roogie with his hands that they should stop their ascent and head down the road. Bones helped out, having found an interesting scent to follow. Nose to the ground, he took the two men past the first couple of houses.

A familiar nervous exhilaration filled Moqoma. He preferred going it alone, away from the strictures and prejudice that came with group missions. Roogie and the American enforcement dog made for strange bedfellows, but he somehow still felt the invincibility that often accompanied the excitement. This was his day to win.

They reached the stairs and began climb. Moqoma hastened his gait a little and Bones followed, at least until they reached the road directly under the Qin house. The stairs here passed between two houses that couldn't have been greater opposites. One was a shack or, really, a series of shacks made from three cargo containers that had been formed into a "C" to allow for a small garden in the center. Its opposite number was a one-story cinder block that had two open-air floors built up on top of it. It looked like a house of cards, the sunlight shining through the thinner slats and pieces of plastic to illuminate the block in a halo of mismatched colors.

The stairs that went between them and up the hill passed directly alongside the Qin house.

"We head halfway up, look to the bay, glance back up as if distracted, case it as best we can, then drop right back down. We need to take a second look, we go to the next stairs."

Roogie was about to protest that the next stairs were three houses down, but Moqoma didn't wait for a reply before heading up the steps.

As they ascended, the detective was careful to keep one eye out to the water, still selling the illusion of trying for that perfect angle. Bones had been good about falling in step with this, but as they neared the halfway mark, the shepherd's demeanor shifted. Rather than keep at Moqoma's side, he lunged higher, straining at the leash.

"*Bones*," Moqoma hissed, yanking the dog backward. But then he chanced to look up to the house.

Framed in the window, for the briefest of moments, was a young woman. She'd appeared like a ghost, a quick image and then gone, as if pulled away. Moqoma barely glimpsed her beyond her long black hair and the terrified expression on her face. Still, even from that briefest of looks, he knew it was the girl from the security camera footage.

"Christ, was that her?" Roogie asked.

"Pretty sure. Time to go."

But Bones continued to pull at the leash, fighting to get up the steps. Moqoma had to grab the lead with both hands to pull him backward.

"What's gotten into you, dog?!" he cried.

That's when two new faces appeared in the window. One was a stranger to him, a young Asian man who was either bald or shaved his head on a near-daily basis. The other was Xiang.

Both held machine guns.

"Shit!" yelled Roogie, grabbing for his pistol.

The first bullets came not from the window where Li appeared, but from open ones nearer the top floor of Qin's building. As they were fired directly downward, the gunmen's aim was scattershot, bullets ricocheting all around rather than meeting flesh. But Moqoma knew what it was meant to do: panic them.

"We have to get out of here!" Roogie snapped. "Now!"

"No! They're trying to get us to go back down, as then they'll have a clear shot. We'll be out in the open. We have to go up!"

"Are you crazy?!" Roogie shouted over the weapon fire, incredulous. "They'll just shoot us straight through the windows."

"Not if we're fast. We get to the road and cut left. It's all rocks and scrub over the Sentinel. We'll have a head start and can make it back down following the water."

Roogie hated this option. Realizing it was the only one on the table, however, he pulled his second pistol and yanked back the slide to chamber a round.

"I get shot, I'm suing the SAPS," he said, then hastened up the stairs.

Moqoma hurried after, pulling the shotgun that he'd carefully concealed down the leg of his pants and dropping the safety.

As the trio hurried up the steps, bullets whizzing by overhead, Moqoma noticed that Bones wasn't affected by the noise or threat. He wondered if the dog had ever participated in some kind of live-fire exercise. He figured he must've had *some* kind of training like that, or he'd be potentially useless to a partner. Still, the dog's seemingly innate bravery took him by surprise.

A second later, they were alongside the lowest floors of the hillside house. A flurry of movement behind the windows betrayed the location of Qin's gunmen. But before they could get into position, Roogie turned both pistols on the windows and unleashed twin volleys of fire.

"Who do ya think you're dealing with, *moegoes*?" Roogie snarled, sounding every bit the Hollywood gangster.

Moqoma followed, a job made easier by the enemy hitting the deck to avoid Roogie's fusillade. Only once did one of the gunmen leap back up, gun in hand. Moqoma responded by blasting the man in the face with his shotgun at a range of less than six meters.

But rather than immediately break left and away from Qin's house once they'd reached the top of the stairs, Roogie went right, heading straight for the building's front door. Qin's men might have been firing from the lower floors, but Moqoma knew they'd be racing up the building's stairwells to intercept their attackers on the street. A few lucky shots notwithstanding, they were clearly outnumbered.

"Roogie!" Moqoma shouted, but his voice was drowned out by the pop of AK-47 fire.

He wheeled around, blasted the shooter, who was half hanging out a window to get a decent shot, and then went after Roogie. By then, however, Roogie had disappeared around the front of the house.

To his credit, Bones had stuck closest to Moqoma and not Roogie. But as they crested the stairs, the dog's nose went back to the ground, circling the area directly in front of the house.

He smells the girl, Moqoma thought, slamming more shells into the breech.

Roogie ran to the front door, emptying both pistols into the thin particle board as he came.

"You ready for this, assholes?!" he shouted like a war cry, then kicked in the door.

He was already inside and out of sight by the time Moqoma and Bones reached the door. Expecting to see his one-time block mate in a pool of his own blood in the foyer, Moqoma was surprised to find Roogie quickly disarming three corpses there instead.

"I think this idiot was looking through the peephole!" the gangster said, pointing at a young man in an Adidas T-shirt with his eye blown out the back of his head.

Roogie slung one AK-47 over his shoulder, jammed several magazines in his pocket, and reloaded a second. He offered a third one to Moqoma, who raised his shotgun.

"I'm good with this. But you've proved your point. Let's get out of here."

"These fuckers sent me into the sewer this morning. Least I can do is massacre the shit out of their guard post."

With that, Roogie raced down the stairs, the sound of heavy machine gun fire and expletives echoing back up as he went. Moqoma turned to Bones with a shrug.

"How many more could there really be?"

The answer turned out to be thirty-six. By the time they'd fought their way to the bottom floor, an experience Moqoma likened to battling a burst fire hydrant spewing gangsters with machine guns rather than water, Roogie was wounded in three places, Moqoma in one, his bicep where a hot round grazed his skin. As he continued to fight, he blocked out the pain by focusing on the smell of burning flesh. That scent he associated with the final moments of his father so many years before.

He didn't get shot a second time.

For his part, Bones was no slouch. The gunmen weren't expecting a dog, particularly one trained to kill. So when they went to shoot him, Bones did as his training commanded and attacked. As the shepherd aimed at whatever was moving, this usually meant his would-be shooter's arms or legs. A second later, his canines buried deep into the screaming fellow's limbs, Bones would twist and jerk, the move of a crocodile in water, bashing its prey senseless. Only, this animal was doing it to free the appendage from its socket.

But once the man collapsed in pain, Bones went for the fellow's throat, tearing it out quickly and efficiently. As blood showered out of the wound, the shepherd, his task with this target complete, moved on to the next one.

So when the trio reached the bottom floor, they looked as if they'd fought through Hell to get there. Or at least a slaughterhouse. Bones's face was a mask of blood, the rest of his fur streaked with it, his paws saturated. Similarly, Moqoma's hands and forearms were dripping red, as if he'd gutted his opponents rather than shot them at close quarters. For Roogie, the blood splattered across his body came from the wounds to his hand, shoulder, and hip as much as from his enemies.

When they found themselves opposite Xiang and Li, the last two people in the house, they reveled in Xiang's shock at their appearance. Qin's henchman had been holding a gun to Li's head even as Moqoma and Roogie burst in, but his grip loosened and he took a step back when he saw them.

"My God," Xiang gasped, aghast at the carnage.

"You know, she's good to us dead or alive," Roogie remarking, catching his breath and raising his pistol.

"Roogie!" Moqoma shouted, knowing what the criminal meant to do.

But it was too late. Roogie pulled the trigger and sent a bullet flying into Xiang's left eye. Though he had held Li a little ways out in front of him, her height made her less than an opportune human shield. Still, Moqoma was startled by Roogie's confidence in his aim.

As Xiang, a surprised look frozen on his face for all time, flopped backward, dead the moment the bullet tore out the back of his skull, Moqoma rushed to Li's side.

"Are you okay?" he asked, though she was flecked with the newly dead man's blood.

"I think so," she nodded.

But as he put his arms around her, Moqoma could tell that she'd been terrified. Her skin was tense and cold to the touch. He imagined she'd been imagining herself seconds from death when they'd come in.

"Roogie, we've got to get her out of here."

Roogie nodded, even though he was busy sifting through Xiang's pockets. Taking the man's gun, three cell phones, and wallet, he then raised Xiang's car keys.

"It has a BMW logo on it. Think I saw one out front. Should we use it to get out of here?"

Moqoma's knee-jerk response was to say "no," but then he realized it could get them back down the hill to the Land Rover a lot faster and unseen than on foot. The SAPS would be on their way. He had to think about the story he'd present to the colonel before he was caught with Roogie and van Lagemaat's nighttime companion.

But when he turned to Li, he froze. She was staring at Roogie with such intensity that it chilled him to the bone. She had the appearance of a lioness, her eyes wide and still, waiting for the wildebeest at the watering hole to edge just *too* close to her hide in the tall grass.

No, *not* a lion. More like a...

"Roogie?" she suddenly asked. "Roogie Mogwaza?"

Roogie eyed her suspiciously, holding Xiang's pistol tighter as he rose.

"Who wants to know?"

There was suddenly a new sound in the room. Or, it had been there for a few minutes already and Moqoma hadn't noticed, as his ears were still ringing from all the gunfire. It was the low, guttural growl of a furious dog.

At the base of the stairs, barely a meter into the room, Bones stood with his feet planted, his head and tail low, and his eyes fixed unblinkingly on Li. His teeth weren't bared, but his message was clear. This person was a threat.

"Bones, chill out," Moqoma ordered but knew the shepherd wouldn't respond to such a command.

He turned back to Li to apologize for the dog but then saw something alarming. Her face had undergone a subtle shift. Her eyes, which he'd thought brown only moments before, were now bronze with a thin gold band encircling her retina. The skin along her arms rippled, as if something was moving just below the epidermal layer. But just as Moqoma was trying to figure out what was causing the motion, the tiny waves froze as they crested, becoming peaked and rigid. The skin on her face tightened to her skull like a death mask. Her black hair, once long and straight, stiffened as well, matting itself to her neck until it looked as if she had no hair at all.

As Roogie and Moqoma watched this mad transformation, Li's body extended, raising her to a full height of almost three meters. Her now alien head curled downward to accommodate the ceiling.

"*I must thank you, Lieutenant Moqoma, for bringing the elusive Mr. Mogwaza to me,*" Li hissed, revealing a red tongue, forked in the middle. It slipped between two saber-like fangs curving down from her upper jaw. "*We knew he had his methods for escaping the police service's net. So imagine our delight when it proved so easy to direct you to the house in Clifton. Sibulele did well for us. She will be rewarded with a quick death. As will you.*"

Bones's growls became loud, savage barks. His entire body shook as he roared angrily at the snake-woman. Saliva flew off his teeth in every direction. This was enough to shock Moqoma out of stasis, and he launched himself toward the stairs. But Li's first target wasn't Moqoma or Bones, but

Roogie.

The gangster's jaw dropped as the snake-woman struck, a motion so quick that it was a blur to human eyes. The last thing Roogie saw were the long bone-white blades slashing into his throat like twin daggers.

V

The force of Li's attack was devastating. The tips of her fangs caught just under Roogie's clavicle, and, as she pulled backward, this had the effect of tearing his upper torso in half. His head had been virtually severed by the first strike, but now he didn't even look human as his life's blood splashed from his body as if from a popped water balloon.

All of this took the snake-woman less than a second to accomplish. Moqoma was only two steps up the carpeted stairway when Li turned in his direction. But this time there was a second flash of movement, this one brown with several more teeth than the serpent.

Bones landed on the snake-woman's back and immediately gripped the nape of her neck in his jaws. As she changed course, whipping around like a rodeo bull, the shepherd held on. But Moqoma could see that the dog's teeth had barely pierced the snake-woman's thick hide. Only the tiniest trickle of blood descended from both.

Knowing he had less than a second to react, Moqoma reached for his recently acquired AK-47, checked the magazine, and aimed at the snake-woman.

"Bones! *Down!*"

He didn't know if the German shepherd would react in time but pulled the trigger anyway. As the bullets struck home, blasting into the snake-woman, the dog did either leap or was thrown free, slamming into the far wall. As the snake-woman thrashed around, Moqoma emptied the entire magazine into her.

It was only when he'd fired every round, smoke drizzling from the hot barrel, that Moqoma saw that not a single bullet had done much, if any, damage. In fact, the barrage seemed only to have enraged the snake-woman.

"*Fuck!*" Moqoma shouted, managing to lunge upward just as the serpent's head struck the stair the detective had just been seated on.

Moqoma's survival instincts took over. His hands grasped at the stairs and pulled him up even as his feet sought holds to push off from. There was no fighting this thing, only escape. He climbed, crawled, and ran up the steps even as he felt the snake-woman's hot breath a mere few centimeters behind him. When he made it to the top of the steps, he just kept going. There was no collecting himself, no plotting a better route.

Only ascent.

Even when he made it to the second floor from the top, he didn't allow himself a moment of relaxation. He still ran out of white-hot fear.

When he burst through the front door and out onto the street, he kept going. He didn't look twice at the small gathering of onlookers. He didn't glance back to the house to see the looks on their faces as the snake-woman flew past them, or even if she did in the first place, but just ran and ran and ran.

It was almost dusk by the time Moqoma slowed to a stop, completely winded and in desperate need of water. The day had been turned upside down. A case that he had meant to break in order to save the day had revealed itself to be…*something*. Something he couldn't rationalize, no matter how much he tried to. Worse, he'd led the man he was trying to save into, literally, the jaws of death.

This actually produced an impulse to laugh. That's how he knew he needed to stop. He was clearly going mad.

"What *was* that?" Moqoma said aloud. "What the *FUCK* was that?"

As he slowed down, he realized the muscles in his legs were on fire. He could barely stand. Also, his feet were torn and blistered. He still wore the heavy boots he always took when the possibility of kicking in someone's face or through a door was on the table, as they'd been that morning. Now he was the one on the run.

He had made it all the way to the top of the Sentinel, the peak that rose up over Hout Bay, and finally had a great view out to the South Atlantic, the sun setting far on the horizon. There would still be about another hour of daylight, but even though he'd put significant distance between himself and Qin's house as he ran, he wanted to be twice as far when night fell. This was someone else's problem, not his.

When he heard something moving in the brush behind him, he almost wilted. He knew it was the snake-woman. She was just waiting for him to slow in order to strike. She'd been there the whole time, just as he'd imagined.

"Go on," he whispered.

But then he felt only the wet nose of a German shepherd touch his hand and begin to lick.

"Jesus Christ, *Bones*!"

He sank to one knee and threw his arms around the dog, partly out of joy, but also from the guilt of having left his partner behind at his moment of greatest need. Still, he didn't think he'd ever been happier to see anyone, human or otherwise, in his entire life.

"You got away without a scratch?" he asked, searching the dog's body for wounds. Bones made no reply, but Moqoma's hands continued over the animal's body, finding nothing. "You lucky chop."

Special Agent Zhu had just sat down to dinner when her cell phone rang. It had been an eventful day, particularly given the strange goings-on at Mr. Qin's house. Zhu had no love for Qin, really, just another over-entitled fat slob of a businessman who provided the face for a vast conglomerate of businesses with ties back to the mainland. He'd also made endless remarks about her obviously being some sort of prostitute on the Ministry's rolls, as otherwise, why would anyone employ a woman? When he'd made a weak attempt at putting his hand up her skirt at a local function the previous year, she'd almost snapped his wrist in four places.

Even so, he was back at it the next time she encountered him, this time at a trade agreement signing when Party Secretary Jia had visited South Africa, the first time such a high-ranking politician had set foot on the continent. It was a day that filled Zhu with pride, only to have Qin's infantile pawing at her breasts in an elevator ruin her exuberant mood. She punched him so hard in the groin that she thought he'd pass out.

Instead, he laughed.

"One day, my daughter," he'd croaked in broken English.

But now he needed her, and her superiors would be very unhappy if she didn't succeed in deflecting the South African government's attention from one of China's citizens. She knew Qin was likely guilty of everything he was routinely accused of, but that didn't mean she thought he'd receive a fair trial in Cape Town. She watched how easily the local government and constabulary could be bribed and knew that could lead Qin directly to jail. Of the many tasks of her overseas posting, keeping its people out of foreign prisons was a priority.

So when she answered her phone and heard the harried voice of Lieutenant Moqoma on the other end, she greeted it with mixed feelings. There was something about him in that study in Camp's Bay. He'd handled it perfectly, putting her in a position where deflection wouldn't work. He was a smooth operator and clearly wanted to get to the bottom of the van Lagemaat killing. She wasn't *as* certain he cared that much about the missing girl, even if he said he did, but it didn't matter. He'd been stonewalled by superiors of his own, and she figured that would be the end of it.

But now here he was with her private number.

"How can I help you, Lieutenant?" she replied, as icily as she could muster, letting him feel her aggravation.

"It's the missing prostitute, Li. The passports were both forgeries. She's not some poor country girl being run into this country or that for sex work. I have a feeling she's up in the Triad, big-time. Bigger than Qin."

Zhu paused. This was a ludicrous accusation, and she wondered what Moqoma could gain by making it. When she could determine no angle, she sighed.

"What're you getting at, Lieutenant? Have you found her? Did she reveal something to you?"

"I found her, all right. Her and three dozen dead men, including Qin's number two, that guy Xiang. They're all dead, but they were just bait in the trap. She wanted Roogie Mogwaza."

Zhu knew who this was. "And why would she want him?"

"To kill him herself. If she and the Triad were using the cops and local government to push out their biggest rival gang, Roogie's, then it must've had some kind of significance for her to kill Roogie herself."

Yes, in fact, Zhu thought. Going back centuries, the Triads had made a show of killing their rivals, particularly with beheading. But she couldn't say that to Moqoma.

"And how do you think she'll accomplish this?" Zhu asked.

"It's already been accomplished. I watched her do it. Roogie's dead, his body just about ripped to pieces."

Zhu went cold all over. She searched Moqoma's words for a sign that he was lying. When she determined that there was none, she felt even more afraid.

"So why call me? Isn't this the definition of a local matter? Particularly a murder on your shores?"

"Of course, but you saw how tied in my government is to Qin, who is probably just the front for the Triad down here anyway."

This could be true, Zhu thought. "Again, I must ask: Why call me? Couldn't I be just as tied in?"

Moqoma went quiet for a moment, but then he returned with a sliver of his rakish charm. "I'm a cop, madam. I saw you in there when they were tying this up with a bow. You know it stinks."

"So you expect me to immediately fly in the face of my own superiors as you are undoubtedly doing, upset a few apple carts, and allow justice to be served?"

"That would be optimal, yes."

Zhu fell silent again. "And barring that?"

"Figure out who Li really is. They had a clock on this. There's a reason it all went down today. I don't think she's going to be in South Africa much longer."

"You don't?"

"Nah, I get the feeling her profile means that she has to move around a lot. I'm starting to think I really wasn't meant to see that South African passport of hers in Clifton. That's the kind of forgery she could get on a plane with tonight or…."

Moqoma realized. *A boat.*

"What?" Zhu asked.

"Nothing. But see what you can find. This is some dark shit."

"What're you going to do?" Zhu found herself asking.

"You remember my dog-friend?"

"Of course."

"Well, he's got her scent good now. We're going to track her down. You know how we kill snakes in Africa?"

"Wait, what? How?"

"Same as everywhere else. We cut their fucking heads off."

"Lieutenant Moqoma, you'd better not do anything that rash…"

But Moqoma had already hung up. Zhu stared at the phone, knowing that calling him back would be fruitless. Similarly, calling his superiors. She'd have to figure her next move on her own.

And what had the detective meant by *snakes*?

There were six three-story buildings at the edge of Hanover Park that everyone knew better than to go near. They were arranged in two parallel lines of three and were bracketed by a small parking lot and the buildings themselves, and their windows were completely painted black, hence the compound's nickname, "Black Windows."

Along the eastern side was a field that extended all the way to the highway. The road that ran along the western side and the twin parking lots acted like invisible barricades, suggesting to all that crossing that particular minefield would be hazardous to one's health.

But just in case, someone spray-painted "The Gates of Hell" on the side of the building closest to the neighborhood it ran up against in tall black letters. Now even strangers to the area would know it was the property of the Yankee Boys. And for those who poked fun at the names of the various Cape Flats gangs – The Junkie Funky Kids, Total Pipe Killers, The Firm, The Sexy Boys, The Globe, The Hard Livings, The Naughty Boys – one only had to point at the literally thousands of casualties in their ongoing and endless turf wars to know that they were as savage as they were ruthless. Human life meant very little to the most dangerous members of each gang, and the Yankee Boys were no exception.

Earlier in the year, three school-age kids from a smaller, barely rival gang stepped from Hanover Park onto the grounds of Black Windows. Whether it was on a dare, a show of bravado, or a disastrous error in judgment, the result was the same. The trio was chased five blocks before being gunned down on the lawn in front of a shebeen. Though the shebeen was closed at the time, three men leaving a mosque next door heard the attack and rushed over. They later told the SAPS that they hadn't seen the boys' killers, but Moqoma found that believable, as the mosque was surrounded by a wall too high to see over.

Moqoma had been on the grounds a few times, though only in his capacity as an undercover cop just after his "release" from Pollsmoor. But as very little changed within the buildings — the workers inside produced *tik* twenty-four hours a day, seven days a week, utilizing pharmaceutical products smuggled in from China and India, — there was little reconnaissance that needed to be done. If one of the gang members was to be arrested, the SAPS typically waited until they were anywhere else than a spot surrounded by dozens of armed men, all high off their own product.

As Moqoma rolled up to the buildings behind the wheel of a workman's truck he'd stolen in Llandudno, he found them eerily quiet. He saw that almost every door had been kicked in and several of the windows kicked out. There were a couple of recent pockmarks in the courtyard and alongside the windows suggesting a minor firefight, but nothing more. Everyone had been cleaned out and taken away earlier that day during the raids on Roogie and the Yankee Boys' operations, but no SAPS appeared to have been left behind to guard the millions in drugs inside. But Moqoma knew it wasn't the crime scene tape across the doors and official citations posted on the frames that were keeping onlookers away.

Everyone knew Roogie's men would eventually be back.

Moqoma led the shepherd to the middle building on the eastern side. Ushering the dog inside, he ducked under the tape and entered, finding the place almost pitch-black. The windows on the first floor had survived the gun battle and continued doing their job of keeping out all light while disallowing outsiders a view in.

The detective momentarily wondered if the Yankee Boys had had the wherewithal to leave any traps behind. The chemicals used in the making of *tik* were volatile enough that it wouldn't take much to rig them to explode. He then realized that, in their haste to clear out their prisoners, the SAPS might've left some product cooking on the proverbial stove without realizing the potential result. A trap by design or an accidental one would yield the same result.

Another reason why he was glad to have Bones along.

"This shouldn't take long, boy," he coaxed. "There is one man in this building. Only, he will smell like a rat. When your nostrils fill with the scent of rodent, take him in your jaws and drag him out to me."

But even as Moqoma spoke, the harsh smells of the numerous

chemicals were so heavy that the shepherd was having a hard time isolating any scents at all. He'd only been inside for a few seconds, and already his nose burned. He shook his head and pawed his tearing eyes, but the odor was overpowering.

"Come on, Bones," Moqoma said quietly. "The sooner you get this guy, the sooner we can go after the snake-woman."

For some reason, this bit of language seemed to resonate with the dog. He raised his head, turned toward the stairs, and ran straight for them.

Moqoma had chosen this building, as he'd been privy to its many renovations through the years. While the other five structures all fit the same model – the top floor was the *tik* factory, second floor was storage and supplies to keep the factory up and running, and the bottom floor was the barracks and kitchen – the sixth one was mostly for show. Sure, they mixed chemicals and ran a small production line on the third story, and there was some storage on the second, but very few gang members were allowed to stay on the first. Part of this was because there wasn't anywhere near as much room as in the other buildings, even though, from the outside, it seemed to be the same size.

For years, the Yankee Boys had stockpiled weapons. For the most part, these were the kind of junk machine guns that filtered down from the conflicts in the Sudan, Uganda, Rwanda, the DRC, and elsewhere. But in recent years, they'd managed to get a hold of heavier firepower smuggled out of the Middle East. American-made, military-grade firepower. Not many pieces, certainly, but with European customs officials always on the lookout for stolen U.S. munitions, smugglers had an easier time moving them out through the Persian Gulf, into the Arabian Sea, around the Horn of Africa, and down to Durban. Though Jo'burg gangs took possession of many of these, enough trophies filtered over to the Western Cape to familiarize Moqoma with the various makes and aftermarket modifications done by the American armed forces' own gunsmiths.

But rather than keep this cache hidden in different locations around the Flats, the Yankee Boys had decided to turn one of the buildings at Black Windows into an armory. There would be a constant twenty-four-hour presence by their guards. Everyone knew to keep away. And, as the elaborate armory was constructed by widening, deepening, and raising the walls, floors, and ceilings of the building, no one making a quick inspection, as the SAPS likely had that day, would be the wiser. Moqoma, however, had once chanced to see the rows and rows of gun racks that could be made to easily disappear behind panels in almost every room.

He marked it in his mind not so much to warn others off the Yankee Boys' arsenal — he knew they didn't have the right ammunition for about ninety percent of the guns — but because he figured the false panels would make for extraordinary hiding places in a pinch.

And his target was just the man to think to utilize them. Moqoma knew he'd had advanced warning of the raid anyway. It was just a matter of determining where he was hidden. Also, there was no fear that he'd already made a break for it. Not knowing whether even a token force had been left downstairs, the man would've stayed put until after dark.

The detective followed the German shepherd upstairs as the animal paused on the second floor. The smells were stronger there, likely from the numerous men and some women who had been working there earlier in the day. But Bones never alerted to anything for very long. He'd stop at a pallet filled with pharmaceutical-grade table salt, one of the many components of *tik*, but then he'd move on. After a few minutes, the dog returned to the stairs and moved to the third floor.

The top floor was a nightmare of overlapping scents: marijuana, sweat, leftover food, smoke, propane gas, and then the numerous bottles, both empties and ones still filled with chemicals of every stripe. The shepherd stuck his head in every closet and around the corners of every chest of drawers. But beyond the scents of rats doubtless inches away behind walls and under floors, he found not another living creature.

Until.

It began as if something scented from outside. Bones's head jerked around, aimed at the upper corner of the room. Moqoma, right behind him, looked as well. There was a false panel there, too, high above the darkened fluorescent lights, just beside the ceiling.

"*Bones*," Moqoma whispered.

Needing no further prodding, the shepherd launched himself toward the panel. There was a stack of boxes against the wall, empties that were filled with spent bottles before they were taken downstairs, loaded onto trucks, and burned off-site. Bones was up at the boxes in a flash, ending at the top of a stack of crowded wooden shelves alongside the panel. He barked and pawed at the panel with tremendous ferocity. Immediately, Moqoma heard movement from the other side of the wall, including the sound of a magazine being inserted into an assault rifle.

Moqoma raised the shotgun he'd picked up from the weapons locker he kept at his house two neighborhoods over, and jerked the slide to chamber a round. The cinematic *click-clack* echoed over the cacophony created by Bones.

"Thembi! You pull that trigger, and you'll die in there, *chana*."

There was silence. Then: "Moqoma?!"

"Damn right. Now, let me call off my dog and I'll let you ease out of there alive."

Another silence, but following this, the panel opened a couple of centimeters. Bones saw an opening and shot his snout into the gap, forcing it wider.

"Moqoma!" Thembi shouted, his voice filled with terror.

"Bones! Come back!"

The shepherd waited a couple of seconds, extending Thembi's panic, but then broke away as quickly as he'd just ascended, rejoining Moqoma on the floor. The detective kept his shotgun aimed into the vague darkness as the target of the search emerged.

"You're alone?!" Thembi asked, his grip tightening on the gun he was about to toss aside.

"That a chance you're willing to take?" Moqoma replied, pointing the shotgun at Thembi's face.

Thembi hesitated, then set the gun back in the crawlspace before climbing down.

"All right, you found me, *skollie cop*," Thembi smirked. "What do you want?"

"This is from Roogie," Moqoma said.

Then bashed Thembi in the face with the butt of the shotgun, breaking the man's nose and sending him to the floor unconscious.

VI

Thembi woke up in a kitchen, his hands cuffed behind him. He vaguely recognized the location, knew it wasn't in Black Windows, but didn't think he'd been moved far. But when he heard the sound of MC Solaar wafting in from the other room, he shook his head.

A mistake, as the blinding pain that followed almost made him pass out again.

"Hey, what's new, Thembi?"

Thembi angled his head around and saw Moqoma sitting near the door alongside the German shepherd who'd found him at Black Windows.

"This is Bones. He's a badass, no?"

Thembi exhaled. He saw that his shirt was covered in drying blood.

"The fuck's wrong with you, Moqoma? You're a dead man for this."

"You mean like your cousin Roogie? Who you sold out to Qin's Triad? Or, should I say, the snake-woman's gang?"

Thembi blanched. He had no clue how Moqoma knew all this, but he realized too late that his reaction confirmed all of it if the detective had merely been fishing.

"What did they promise you?" Moqoma scoffed. "Some kind of position in their new organization?"

"What's it to you?"

"If it's anything like what they offered to the woman who fronted one of their brothel's out in Clifton, you're not going to fare much better than Roogie. He's dead, by the way. I watched her turn him inside out. Pretty sure she'll be doing that to you, too."

The old man, Nkopane, who ran the shebeen where Moqoma had taken Thembi, which had also been where the Yankee Boys had killed the three school kids a few months back, came in with a plate of food. Thembi's eyes lit up. He was starving.

"You think that's for you, *mompie*?" Moqoma laughed. "That's Bones's reward for finding your unwashed ass."

"You want anything?" Nkopane asked the detective as he placed the food in front of the shepherd. He asked with such nonchalance that Thembi wondered if police brought beaten suspects into his kitchen on a daily basis. "Cokes?"

"No, but thanks, man."

Nkopane nodded and exited. Moqoma turned back to Thembi. "Now, the reason we're here. Who was your contact inside the organization?"

"How'd you know it was me?" Thembi countered.

Moqoma sighed. "The dog just got his meal. I can take it away from him and feed him your testicles."

Thembi stared Moqoma down, then relented.

"His name's Chan."

"That's original. Let's have another."

"That's the name he gave me, you *dof kont*. You telling this story?"

Moqoma sank back into his chair, letting Thembi finish.

"Chan was in shipping. He'd buy every single part of a car we'd bring him, as long as it was completely dissembled. Didn't matter the model or the condition. He'd take a look, offer a shitty price, then open his garage door."

"Where'd these transactions take place?"

"He runs a shop at the Sable Square China Town. Custom rims, lights, radios, decals – the works. Cheap plastic junk he pulls in from South Korea. His real money comes from smuggling auto parts back to Asia. He'd send them all over. China, Malaysia, Korea, Indonesia, even Australia."

"He told you that?"

"The little shits that worked for him would tell my guys."

"And you never thought they were working you?"

"Fuck off."

"What else about Chan?"

Thembi shrugged. "Nothing. He'd always meet us with a big roll of tape and a black marker. We'd tell him what each piece was, and he'd write it on the tape, tear it off, and place it on the part. If it was an exterior panel like a door, fender, or mirror cover, he'd freak out if one of his guys put the tape on the painted part. It had to go under, on the unpainted side."

"And he approached you personally about selling out Roogie and the Yankee Boys?"

Moqoma expected a scowl, but Thembi was defiant. "My cousin had two feet out the door. He was done being a big-shot criminal. He'd bought all this land up and down the coast over the years, and was a few weeks away from selling it off to a single buyer. Word was, he planned to take the money and leave Cape Town for good. Maybe head to South America."

Argentina, Moqoma thought.

He remembered Roogie saying that if he ever cashed out, he wouldn't head to Europe or the States, but somewhere on the Pacific Rim where he could still see the water. Though he'd never been to Argentina, a couple of travel documentaries he'd watched once convinced him that was the place to be.

"And you couldn't just let him go? After all he'd done for you?"

"What about all I'd done for *him*?" Thembi erupted. "He treated me like gutter trash while he lived the high life."

"If the shoe fits," Moqoma spat.

Thembi lunged for him, but Bones was on his feet in a flash, teeth bared and hair stiffly raised. Thembi sank back down, his cuffed wrists no match for the angry shepherd.

"Sorry about his temper," Moqoma offered. "You know how Americans get. Now, what do you know about the snake-woman?"

"The snakehead?" Thembi asked. "She's the boss. The *real* boss, not Qin. But she's behind the scenes. They're all scared shitless of her, but only because she's got some kind of supernatural thing going on. Remember that famous bandit in India who had everybody thinking he employed supernatural means of escape? That's her. They think she's got magical powers, so they don't fuck with her."

"She does, *baas*."

Thembi scoffed. "You sure they didn't drug you or something? That's part of it. They get their guys all amped up when they fight. Maybe you got some kind of contact high."

"I saw what I saw. So did the dog."

"Whatever you say, *domkop*."

"So, when were you supposed to get your big reward? And remember, I'm doing you a favor by keeping you away from there."

"There's a meeting tonight. Before you ask, I don't know where it's to be. I wasn't going to find out until the last minute."

"Chan was going to call?"

Thembi nodded.

"She's leaving, isn't she?"

"How'd you know?" Thembi asked, genuinely surprised.

"I don't think she sticks around long. Too easy to be exposed. She's off to blaze new trails."

Moqoma nodded and got to his feet. Bones had finished his meal. Thembi's cell phone had been on the counter, and the detective picked it up.

"You're a thief now?" Thembi challenged.

"Guess so."

"What's to happen to me?"

"Word's going to get around about what you did to Roogie." Moqoma shrugged. "Once I start spreading it, I mean. If your conscience bothers you, maybe you'll try and explain it to the boys once they start getting released from jail. If not, getting out of the country would be my choice. Only, I doubt you'll get that far."

With that, Moqoma and Bones exited.

On his way to the Sable Square China Town, Moqoma took a mental inventory of his weapons. He had his backup shotgun from home that he'd brought into Black Windows and a backup pistol, an old uppity Glock that loved to jam. But he also had the two AK-47s he'd liberated from the Yankee Boys' cache. There were more advanced weapons, but he had no experience firing them and wanted something he was comfortable with. He'd also skirted the traditional curved-type magazines most associated with the weapon that the Yankee Boys had stacks and stacks of in favor of a couple of high-capacity drums. Despite resembling an antique straight out of an old gangster movie, the drums held seventy-five rounds to the banana clip's thirty. Though the danger with a fully automatic meant that he could go through the entire magazine in seconds, he needed stopping power. He'd taken six drums, as many as he could carry, and checked the bullets. Once satisfied, he loaded them into the stolen work truck next to Thembi's unconscious body and drove the short distance to Nkopane's shebeen.

So now he had 450 assault rifle bullets, a couple dozen shotgun shells, sixty-eight bullets for the Glock stretched across four magazines, and again, the German shepherd.

He didn't imagine it would be enough to stop Li or whatever forces she might have with her at the "meeting," but he hoped it would make a big enough splash that the subsequent press and governmental interest would be enough to blow the lid off the Triad's activities. He thought exposing the collusion between the Ministry of Justice and the Chinese in killing Roogie and dismantling the Yankee Boys was too much to hope for, but if he knew the spineless men and women who ran the prosecutor's office, the same people who had disbanded the Scorpions and humiliated him and his fellow officers when their own malfeasance was brought to the fore, he knew how quickly they'd throw the Chinese under the bus.

He also knew that this was a suicide mission.

He didn't mind so much his own death in the line of duty, but he was upset that he was dragging Bones down with him. The dog had proven to be nothing but the most exemplary enforcement dog he'd ever worked with, maybe even more skilled than Robin.

He glanced to the German shepherd standing on the backseat. Bones had slept for part of the drive in from the Flats, but as they'd left the highway and entered the more urban area of Century City, he'd awoken and began to look excitedly out the window.

Century City was as far removed from the Flats as could be. There were new roads, new housing developments, and forests of apartment complexes and condominiums that had only begun construction a year before. Moqoma hadn't had much reason to go into Century City, which was relatively low-crime, but every time he had, he marveled at how different it was from the area he remembered seeing as a child.

That was one of the biggest changes to the landscape post-apartheid. It wasn't the abandoned place and street names, apartheid-era heroes abandoned for those of the new South Africa. It wasn't the influx of modern goods in the market or equipment in the factories after the various trade embargos were lifted.

No, it was the influx of non–South Africans who suddenly wanted to live in South Africa and the need to supply them with housing and services.

Hence, the construction of Century City.

The Sable Square China Town in Century City was indicative of this change. The old one in Ottery was a rundown, crescent-shaped strip mall surrounded by a parking lot that stayed empty almost year-round. There were a couple dozen stalls that resembled large mechanic's shops, down to the massive garage doors that were pulled down and locked at the end of the business day. Though Moqoma had only been a couple of times, he'd found it difficult to tell one store from the other. They all seemed to sell the exact same cheap linens, DVDs, clothes, and housewares in every stall at the same prices. The decision to purchase wares from one versus another seemed to be determined mostly by which was closest to the shopper's parking space.

The new China Town was completely different. It was an actual shopping center, built on a square around an equilateral, open-air cross. In the four corners created by the cross were spaces for eight stores with different floor plans. The shop windows of the largest faced the surrounding parking lot, while the entrances to the others were accessible by the pedestrian walks that ran through the center of the square. In the middle of the complex was a large traditional Chinese arched gate called a *paifang*, a replica of one found at the Summer Palace in Beijing.

Though Moqoma hadn't spent much time there, either, he'd been surprised to see these new stores filled with the exact same products at the same prices as their counterparts in Ottery. However, the surroundings were more appealing, and the shopping center was closer to the apartments of Century City, where many of the Chinese immigrants had chosen to live.

As he pulled the pickup truck into the parking lot, he spotted a map mounted behind transparent plastic near one of the shops. He parked, raised a silencing finger to Bones, and hurried over to it. As best he could tell, there was only one auto parts shop in the shopping center with the helpfully descriptive name of Car Time.

He determined where the shop stood in relation to where he was now and returned to the truck. He pulled around to the far side of the shopping center and turned off the vehicle.

"Now we wait," he advised Bones.

Very few customers entered or exited the center over the next half-hour, though a steady stream of employees made their way to their cars and drove away. The stores didn't all seem to close at the same time, which surprised Moqoma, given their uniformity in other areas. One by one, the lights of the shops turned off, until only the lamps hanging over the sidewalks and parking lot were lit.

It was then that the cell phone in Moqoma's pocket buzzed.

Extracting it, Moqoma saw a single text: *Duncan Dock, 30 minutes*. Moqoma didn't have to guess what lay in wait for Thembi at Cape Town's deep-sea container terminal. He only wondered whether they planned to let his family recover a body at some point or if Thembi's corpse was destined for the shark-infested waters off Sunset Beach like so many before him.

Moqoma thought about texting back but realized he hadn't asked Thembi if there was any kind of shorthand he used with Chan. Deciding it didn't matter, Moqoma turned off the phone and tossed it on the dashboard.

A moment later, the service entrance alongside Car Time opened, and four men exited. Three were the same kind of young toughs Moqoma had been seeing all day. The fourth, however, was a stooped man with a gray comb-over and matching sweater vest. He looked to be in his eighties. The group moved to a waiting SUV, the three younger men deferring to the older as they opened the passenger-side front door for him, helped him inside, and waited to leave until he was settled.

As the SUV drove away, Moqoma saw the man straighten a little, and his gaze, rather unfocused a moment ago, sharpen.

"That's a good cover," Moqoma said, grinning at Bones.

He waited for the SUV to clear the parking lot before starting the truck. He counted slowly to fifteen, then followed.

VII

One of the most popular bits of apocrypha concerning Cape Point, the southern tip of the African continent about fifty kilometers south of Cape Town, was that one could see Antarctica from it. In truth, the Princess Astrid Coast of Queen Maud Land, East Antarctica, the nearest point on the ice-covered continent, was still 4,000 kilometers away. Another popular myth was that it was one of the only places on the face of the earth where one could witness the meeting of two oceans, the South Atlantic and the Indian. Again, in truth, the oceans met a few miles east at Cape Agulhas, despite what innumerable tour guides told their charges on a daily basis.

What was true was that the Portuguese sailor who first rounded the point dubbed it "Cabo das Tormentas," the Cape of Storms. Though this was later changed to the friendlier-sounding Cape of Good Hope, the weather had changed not at all. The final bit of land overlooking the cape was marked by a lighthouse atop a high, rocky promontory, this itself a part of a large national park that extended all the way back up to Table Mountain. There was only one road into the park, and, as the park closed at sunset, this highway was virtually empty after dark.

So as the SUV he was tailing passed Noordhoek Beach, Sunnydale, and even Ocean View, its destination becoming clear, Moqoma turned off at Scarborough, waited five minutes, then continued his pursuit with his headlights off. He knew this was an incredibly dangerous way to drive along the winding cliff-side roads leading to the Point, but any other way and there was no question he'd be seen.

As he neared the park entrance, really a toll plaza that blocked the road, he realized that there would undoubtedly be Triad men waiting there to shoo away anyone who wandered down. So, when he was about a quarter of a kilometer away, he pulled to the side of the road, parked the truck, and clambered out.

"We're on foot from here, Bones," Moqoma said, gathering the guns and slinging the ones with straps over his shoulder. "Means we may run into a troop or two of baboons, but I'd ask you use discretion in your dealings with them."

Bones made no indication that suggested he understood the detective's directive as his nose bobbed up and down in the air, having detected several new and unusual scents. The pair hurried the couple hundred meters to the fence, which was little more than a dilapidated wire affair, and crossed, Moqoma lifting the shepherd over before following. Bones was off the leash now, but the cop kept him close.

Though there was barely a moon and the ground was uneven, they made good time. They were out of sight of the road soon enough, Moqoma leading them toward the sound of the ocean. Though he had no idea where the Triad meeting was, which he now surmised to be some sort of ritualistic handoff of power between Li and Qin (or someone else meant to stay behind), he felt it would be near the water if Li was leaving by boat.

The starscape above their heads reminded Moqoma of walking home from his auntie's with his father as a boy. Though his "auntie" was by all accounts a kind and generous neighborhood woman who cared for children while their parents were at work, Moqoma hated her. Other kids got to go home at the end of the school day. Not Leonard Moqoma. He had to go to the old woman's house with several other unfortunates and play all afternoon. Though it was hardly taxing, it still felt to him like a double dose of school. When his father finally came by to pick him up, it was generally after dark. Though he would occasionally feign anger toward his dad over this grave injustice, he now looked back at those starlit walks, since Manenberg was just barely wired for electricity at the time, as one of his fondest memories.

What would his father think of his current mission? Moqoma wondered if the old man would think it remotely worthwhile, getting involved with political crimes and their attendant monsters. But Moqoma's feared it was his father's reticence that eventually led to his death, tragic as it was.

If Moqoma was to die, he would do so on his feet, fighting for his chosen side.

That's when he spotted the dark sea on the near horizon. More importantly, he saw the silhouette of a large container ship created by the absence of stars out past the breakers. A few more steps forward, and he could just make out the point where the water met the beach, the sand a dark gray in the dim light. There were at least forty people standing around, some facing the water, others, their stances rigid, facing the surrounding scrub.

Moqoma considered that he had only minutes to live. He gripped the AK-47 tightly in his hand and turned his thoughts to Roogie and all the men the snake-woman had callously sacrificed in order to bring the gangster to her feet. What was the lesson there? Perhaps that these men knew their purpose was to die for their otherworldly leader.

Moqoma took Bones's collar in his hand and held him back.

"Easy, Bones."

It was like this that they edged closer to the beach. Neither the AK-47 nor the shotgun had much. If he just started shooting, he might wound a couple, but so what? Death had followed the snake-woman to Cape Town, but he wouldn't let it leave. Blood would answer for blood.

He would have to get closer.

Moqoma dropped to his stomach and commando-crawled ahead, the dirt giving way to sand. Bones followed suit, keeping low to the ground as he inched forward as well. But as they neared, the shepherd became agitated, alerting to something he picked up on the wind.

"What is it?" Moqoma hissed, following Bones's gaze.

That's when he spied the diminutive form of Li moving among the men. As she passed, each bowed deeply to her. The detective thought he recognized Chan's stoopless posture as well as that of Qin. But when he saw who was moving along behind Li, his blood went cold.

It was Xiang.

Moqoma stared at the man in horror before noticing the eye patch over his left eye. Beyond that, however, there was nothing to suggest he'd had a brush with the abyss earlier in the day.

"What in Hell's name?" Moqoma whispered.

Over the sound of crashing waves, the whine of an engine echoed over the dunes. One of the container ship's lifeboats, a large, motorized self-rescue model with a fiberglass shell, approached the shore at speed. Moqoma squeezed the trigger guard of the AK-47 with his finger, knowing he had to make a decision.

"Fuck it," he said, getting to one knee and aiming the assault rifle at the nearest of the Triad gunmen. "Get ready, Bones."

The detective had misjudged the range of the drum-fed AK. As he fired fully automatic bursts of high-velocity rounds at the heads and torsos of the armed silhouettes, the bullets were drawn like magnets to their targets. He watched as heads exploded from the barrage and those nearby panicked as they were showered with blood and grue.

But just as quickly, he stopped shooting and quickly rolled a dozen meters to his left. As the Triad gunmen brought their weapons around, aiming where they'd last seen muzzle flash, Moqoma opened fire again, the spent cartridges popping out of the chamber at almost the same rate he was seeing the bodies of his enemy hit the ground.

When he rolled again, this time forward ten meters, he noticed that Li, Xiang, Qin, and Chan all seemed to have vanished. He searched the beach as he blasted a few more of the gunmen off their feet, but then he saw movement on the ground.

"Oh, shit," he managed to say, just as a half-man, half-snake erupted from the sand in front of him and attacked.

Miraculously, Moqoma managed to hang onto his assault rifle even as the serpent slammed him to the ground, then coiled its body around him like a boa constrictor. He fired into the creature's belly at close range, but the bullets glanced off its scales like a tank being shelled by a group of children with slingshots. The snake-man opened its mouth, revealing its massive fangs. It tongue flicked against Moqoma's face even as it raised up, ready to strike.

Expecting the icy feeling of the sharp blades diving into his torso, the detective was then surprised when he instead felt something land on his back, only to launch off again. Almost immediately, the bone-crushing grip the snake-man held him in began to relax, and Moqoma fought his way out. When he could get a good look at his would-be killer, he saw that Bones had landed on the thing's head, his teeth dug deeply into the monster's forked tongue. The shepherd appeared to be trying to yank the soft organ straight from its mouth.

A second later, he succeeded.

The amount of blood that erupted from the serpent's mouth was incomprehensible. It was as if the dog had popped the cork on a bottle of champagne, releasing the same frothy discharge, albeit black and steaming as it splashed onto the sand. The serpent bobbed away as if drunk, but then sank to the ground. As it slowly returned to a fully human shape, Moqoma could see that it was Chan.

That fucking dog, Moqoma thought. *Sitting there figuring out that thing's weakness and not even giving me the heads-up.*

He grinned, swung the second assault rifle off his shoulder, shoved a second drum on the first, and turned just as a second snake-creature launched itself from the darkness, jaws open and aimed for his face. This time, however, Moqoma was ready.

The sheer number of bullets he fired into the serpent's gaping maw would've been enough to kill fifty men. But as the red-hot lead chipped away at the top of the monster's mouth while others punctured its tongue, Moqoma was happy to merely draw blood. The snake-man reared up, closing its mouth even as blood poured over its jaws. Moqoma saw that one of its eyes was destroyed and knew it must be Xiang. He pulled the Glock from his belt and emptied the entire clip into Xiang's remaining eye. The security guard hissed and thrashed blindly as blood pulsed from his ruined eye socket. Moqoma brought the shotgun around, and, as Xiang's head swung by, he blasted the creature twice in its gaping mouth, shredding its tongue.

Xiang's head thudded heavily onto the ground, sending up a cloud of sand, blood seeping out of his head like pulped tomatoes sluiced through a colander.

Two down, Moqoma thought.

He wheeled around, chambering another round in the shotgun, and saw Bones tussling with another of the snake-creatures. The shepherd was having a harder time with this one, as it was sliding around quickly, keeping its mouth shut while trying to use its tail to coil around the dog. Just as the detective hurried over, the serpent succeeded in gripping the enforcement dog in its lower torso. As it pulled its muscles tight, Bones let out a yelp.

But then Moqoma swung both AK-47s around and unloaded two hundred rounds into the creature's face.

The snake flopped over but kept its ever-tightening grip on Bones.

The cop grabbed at the tight coils, trying to pull the dog free, but the serpent had the strength of ten men. Even as it lay stunned and possibly dying, its body reacted to the indignity by fulfilling one last task: the execution of the German shepherd.

"Dammit, Bones!" Moqoma cried, trying to free the dog.

He could see the pain on the shepherd's face as his body contorted under the reptilian coils. The air was being squeezed from his lungs even as his ribs were seconds from splintering like toothpicks.

Moqoma threw his arms around the snake's body, straining every muscle to pull it away. But it wasn't enough. He saw the light dimming in Bones's eyes as the dog's mouth opened, his tongue flopping out.

"NO!" the detective shouted.

But then a familiar voice cut through the darkness.

"Stand back, Lieutenant."

Moqoma looked up and saw Special Agent Zhu and a handful of men wearing the silver laurel and commando knife badge of the South African Special Forces, known as Recces. The detective rolled away as the one nearest the dying serpent carefully inserted a fragmentary grenade in the creature's mouth. When it exploded a second later, rather than contract in death, the coils relaxed immediately, sloughing away from Bones like a cut anchor line.

But as soon as they had fallen aside, the German shepherd collapsed.

"Bones!" Moqoma shouted, hurrying to the dog's side.

He put his head on the dog's furry chest and detected a faint heartbeat. He began gently massaging the animal's side and snout.

"Come on, boy. You're tougher than that."

But Bones's eyes were cloudy and his jaws still. Zhu squatted down next to them.

"Lieutenant. You've done all you can."

As Moqoma watched the light go out of the German shepherd's eyes, the dog sinking into unconsciousness, he got back to his feet.

"Where's Li?"

"We're afraid we might've arrived too late."

Moqoma turned to the water. The lifeboat bobbed up and down with the tide about fifty meters from shore. A large object moved through the waves straight to it, its body rippling in a serpentine motion to propel it along.

"Nope," said Moqoma.

He looked along the row of soldiers until he saw one with an M-16, the optional M203 grenade launcher attached just below the barrel.

"I need to borrow that, soldier."

The young man shot a questioning glance to Zhu, who had clearly been put in command of this detachment, and she nodded.

With the weapon and several grenades in his hands, Moqoma raced to the water's edge in time to see the snake-woman board the lifeboat as a serpent, then slowly return to her human form. Moqoma aimed the machine gun at the boat, then adjusted slightly up. He shoved a grenade in the launcher and fired.

The first grenade made a direct hit atop the lifeboat's hard plastic shell, shattering it into thousands of pieces in a fiery explosion. From Moqoma's vantage point, he could just see a couple of the people on board, now set aflame and screaming, hurry to throw themselves overboard. He calmly reloaded, and this time, with the cover obliterated, aimed at the engine. The grenade made a loud pneumatic "pop" as it exited the launcher. It whistled through the sky, slowing like a softly hit baseball, before missing the lifeboat's engine by an inch, albeit landing on the watercraft's twin reserve gas cans instead.

This time the entire boat exploded, a great fireball rising into the night sky, illuminating the dark water all the way to the shore. This time there were no screams, even as severed body parts flew into the air before raining back down into the water.

That'll bring the sharks, Moqoma thought.

But even as he imagined Li, in her snake-form, being torn apart by South Africa's finest great whites, he loaded another grenade, aimed for the smoldering wreckage, and fired again. The explosion was smaller this time, but no less satisfying to the detective.

He loaded another grenade, aimed, and fired again.

Epilogue

By sunrise, almost the entire Cape Town police force was down on the beach. Cape Point had, needless to say, been closed for the day, though Moqoma didn't envy the officers tasked with turning away visitors and tour groups any more than he did the guides who would have to return their meager fees to angry foreigners back up in the City Bowl.

The detective had stayed on the beach all night, pacing up and down while scanning the waves for any sign of the snake-woman. When there was movement, he immediately zeroed in on it with a night scope one of the soldiers had provided, only to see that it was indeed sharks drawn to the area by the bloodbath.

Only once had any of the officers combing the sand called over to him. As he hurried over, he saw something massive washed up on the shore, almost twenty feet in length. When he got to the officer's side, he saw that it was the corpse of a great white shark, its head almost severed by what looked like twin scythes.

He stared back out at the waves, a thrill going up his spine every time a new dorsal fin pierced the water, moving quickly, as if bearing down for the kill.

He didn't leave until almost sunset, having been awake for over thirty hours straight. Special Agent Zhu had left much earlier to sleep, make a full report, and tie up a few loose ends within her own department. When she returned, Moqoma was getting ready to leave.

"What're they saying?" Moqoma asked. "My people, I mean."

"That you're a hero. That you singlehandedly brought down a criminal organization that had made significant inroads to both the Western Cape and the South African government, all while pursuing the assassin of Charles van Lagemaat, the identity of whom you also discovered."

Moqoma stared at Zhu with incredulity. "Come on."

She smiled wryly. "Fine. They're saying there was some gang fight out on the beach with a couple of deaths, but that it was just a bunch of teenagers. They found evidence in Roogie Mogwaza's office tying him to van Lagemaat's assassination and, after locating the corpse, announced that he'd been killed by his own men over money."

Moqoma laughed out loud. Zhu glanced down, her smile replaced by a troubled look.

"What?" Moqoma asked.

"Part of the reason I wanted an overseas posting was to get away from those sorts of lies and political intrigue."

"Then South Africa was the absolute *wrong* choice, madam," Moqoma replied, returning to his feigned obsequiousness.

Zhu's smile returned. "Thank you, Lieutenant."

"No trouble, Special Agent. I'll see you around the Cape, then?"

"Looking forward to it," she replied, but then remembered something else. "Did you hear about the dog? The American?"

Moqoma looked surprised. He'd forgotten all about Bones in his determination to locate the snake-woman. He realized he owed Moosa the mother of all apologies, but that his explanation of what happened would never pass muster, given the cover-up to come.

"No, what about him? He died, yes?"

"That's what they thought, but as they were loading him in one of the police trucks, he woke up and immediately bit the officer in the wrist. They dropped him, and he bit the second one. It took four officers and two soldiers to get a leash on him and force him into the truck. They drove him to the vet's office in the city, where he was sedated and checked out. Would you believe it, he was *fine*. A couple of broken ribs and some dehydration, but that was it."

Moqoma sighed, a great weight he didn't know was there lifting from his shoulders.

"That crazy *inja*," he said, shaking his head.

"That crazy *inja*," Zhu agreed.

When Billy Youman returned to the training compound in Muizenberg two days later and saw Bones's taped ribs, he stared at Moosa with incredulity.

"Wait, *what* happened to my dog?"

Moosa shrugged. "He had a fall. He was up in the training house, ran through a door, and, I suppose, didn't realize it was on the second floor. They took him to the vet and taped him up good, though. He could've broken his neck."

"Shit, well, how am I supposed to work him out the rest of the week?" Youman asked.

Moosa shrugged again. "You can't. He needs rest and relaxation. In fact, we've heard from on high that he's to be treated with the greatest of care as he rehabilitates."

Youman shook his head, as if trying to wrap it around this new information. But he finally shrugged, jamming his hands in his pockets.

"So what am I supposed to do for the rest of my time here?"

"Take in the sights," Moosa suggested. "This is Cape Town, man. We've got the best beaches, the most beautiful views from up on the mountain, great wine, great girls. Good food. You're on your department's dime, right? If I were you, I'd head right back to the city and look at it like a nice holiday, eh?"

Youman hadn't thought of it that way. He'd seen a handful of the gorgeous ladies Moosa was referring to when he'd arrived at the airport. He'd even heard the name of the clubs they were looking forward to hitting now that they were back home.

"Yeah, too bad about Bonesy," Youman said, adding resignation to his tone. "Take care of him, all right?"

"Will do," replied Moosa.

Moosa waited until Youman had left before ambling over to the kennel where Bones slept. He saw that the shepherd had devoured the massive steak sent over by a few members of the Recces. They'd also sent a unit patch with a note designating Bones an honorary member. The trainer slipped into the kennel and checked the tape on Bones's ribs, seeing that it had started to wear away as Bones twisted and moved. He was just in the process of changing the bandages when the dog awoke with a start, his jaws making for Moosa's hand.

But the trainer was too quick and raised it in enough time for Bones to take a sniff and remember whose company he was in.

"Easy there, Bones," Moosa said calmly, stroking the dog's neck as the shepherd flopped back down. "I hear you've got a real taste for snake meat, and I'm just a local. I won't do for a creature of such discriminating tastes."

Bones turned and stared at Moosa, as if wondering what his words meant. Moosa sighed.

"Just rest, Bones. I hear there are more steaks coming for you from a couple more units that saw you in action. You sound like quite a hero, but even heroes need to take time to recover. By the way, one of our breeders said he's got at least a couple of bitches in heat right now, and do-we-have-any-studs-we're-looking-to-sire? If you're up for it, I don't think anyone'll protest if I put your name in the hat."

Moosa waited for a reaction, but the shepherd had already fallen back asleep.

"Ah, that's okay, Bones. I'll make all the arrangements. You rest. You've earned it, my man."

With that, the handler finished changing the tape on the shepherd's ribs and left the kennel. Bones sank into a deep sleep, his chest gently rising and falling as the last memories of the past couple of days fell away. He would dream of pursuit and capture and reward and wake refreshed.

MONGREL

"Wow, they really did a number on him, huh?"

Lionel grunted. He hated it when enforcement officers sounded like the police on TV, as it never failed to make him wonder if that's why they reached for a badge in the first place.

"What do you think happened?" Lionel asked.

The ATF agent, Oliver Mattis, glanced around the warehouse, gazing up into the rafters, rusted copper after years of disuse, and then back down to the dead man chained in a sitting position to a steel chair in the middle of the room.

"It's hard to say," Mattis replied. "I mean, obviously they tortured him, but it's difficult to know if they were torturing him because they wanted information or torturing him once they found out who he was."

Lionel hesitated and looked down at the third member of their party, a four-year veteran of the Doña Ana County Sheriff's Department named Bones who, despite being a German shepherd, was one of the most sought-after members of the force, particularly by visiting federal task force agents assigned to do something about drug trafficking on the New Mexico border.

"Oh, they tortured him for fun," Lionel said, as if Mattis had misunderstood his question. "Look at his feet. If they wanted information, the burns wouldn't be so uniform. They'd cook the sole but then turn up the dial so the pain would get incrementally worse. This guy, they were just fucking around. They burned his feet, burned his fingers off, tore out his teeth, probably with pliers, since they don't look cracked out as if they'd used a screwdriver, torched his groin, then shotgunned his kneecaps, shotgunned his belly, and finally shotgunned his face."

Mattis looked from Lionel to the corpse seated in the chair and was amazed at how easily the sergeant was able to piece that together. "What else can you tell me?"

"It happened last night, it wasn't done by his own gang, and he probably died screaming."

"How do you know it wasn't his own guys?"

"He's still wearing his cut," Lionel said, pointing to the leather vest the dead man was wearing, the word *FURIES* stitched into the back in red on white. "That's the first thing they'd do."

"So it was the Mexicans."

Lionel said nothing as he stared at the burned-out husk of a man, an ATF undercover agent named Jacob Hillenbrand, aka "Mongrel," who he'd met over a year and a half ago three counties over when he and Bones had been part of a massive tri-agency drug bust that had netted fifteen tons of marijuana worth about $10 million to the cartels. He looked down at Bones, who continued to sniff at the air, and then glanced back to the warehouse entrance, where the sound of approaching vehicles could be heard.

"Oh, I think the cavalry's here. I'm gonna wander Bones back to the kennel and start my report."

Mattis nodded absently and Lionel led Bones out of the building.

It was a long drive back to Las Cruces in Lionel's old Chevy Blazer, a vehicle that was now officially a law enforcement ride, as cutbacks at the Sheriff's Department meant that the sheriff, a whiskery old stick in the mud named Bob Shivers who Lionel would go hunting with anyway, was forced to be okay with it. Lionel got a lot of thinking done in the truck, idly listening to whatever country station currently seemed to be ignoring music (though Lionel was loath to call it that) that had come out after 1985. With no station to be found this day, he chugged the one working cassette he still owned,

George Strait's *Does Fort Worth Ever Cross Your Mind,* into the deck and turned his mind to the discovery of Mongrel's body. Shivers had rung Lionel himself sometime around four in the morning, saying they'd gotten a tip about a body out at an abandoned manufacturing complex in Perry that was popular with local teens. The timing and location garnered interest from ATF Special Agent in Charge Mattis, who had informed Shivers that one of his undercovers had gone missing under suspicious circumstances, and he arranged to meet Lionel at the front gate to check it out.

Sheriff's Deputy Oudin looked over at the German shepherd taking up much of the passenger seat, another enforcement no-no that Lionel chose to overlook, as every time he had tried putting the dog in back, the animal would whine and bay the whole trip, as if having suffered a grave injustice.

"What do you think, Bones? Think that was the Mexicans? Or are we being suckered?"

Bones looked up at Lionel as if needing more information, and the handler grinned.

"You're absolutely right. Only one way to find out."

The Furies' clubhouse had once been a two-farm chicken slaughterhouse out on Route 28, and the current occupants didn't let anyone come through the door without letting them know as such. It was often the first Furies anecdote anyone ever heard, the second usually having to do with chapter president Arthur Lankershim's dime he served in an Arizona pen. While there, he made his name for two things: prison boxing heavyweight champ six years running and longest consecutive time served in solitary in the history of the New Mexico corrections, 262 days.

For Lionel, the clubhouse was officially off limits, as he and the sheriff's department routinely rousted the place after fights or reports of drug dealing. Each time they left, it was made clear with a string of epithets that it would be dangerous for officers to ever show up "by their lonesome," though they were "certainly welcome to do so."

But it was still daylight by the time Lionel wheeled the Blazer into the lot and counted eight bikes alongside the building. He parked the truck, checked his weapon, and clambered out of the truck, figuring he'd be fine. Lionel was ex-military and looked like he was carved of granite, a fact that made at least a handful of suspects think twice before engaging the man in a fight. If they got a closer look and realized his somewhat advanced age and reversed that decision, they were introduced to Bones.

"Come on, boy," Lionel said as he opened the passenger side door and ushered the shepherd out, momentarily considering a leash but then deciding against.

When the pair came through the front door of the clubhouse, the bikers inside pretended not to notice. Four were occupied at two different pool tables and one sipped a beer at the bar and watched a replay of the previous night's Diamondbacks game, while another stood behind the bar, loading long-necks into a small, glass-fronted refrigerator.

"Sir, this is a private club and you need a membership to drink in here, as we do not carry a liquor license," the bartender said. "Also, we do not allow dogs, since it violates county sanitation ordinances."

"I'm not drinking and this is a work dog, so he's exempted," Lionel said, clocking reactions. He knew the men had been watching him since the second he rolled off the highway and caught furtive glances from the pool-playing men, reflected in a mirrored beer advertisement in the back of the room. "But, truth be told, I'm here about another dog you've had in your clubhouse. Name of Mongrel."

The room went ice-cold. Lionel watched as Bones stiffened, eyeing a door at the opposite end of the room, and knew who must be standing behind it.

"So are we going to keep pretending like we're all a bunch of assholes, or are you going to tell me if Arthur's here or not?" Lionel continued. "If I need to, I can go get him at his mother's place. I saw his bike out there, but I know she got the Chevelle out of the shop last week and he's been seen driving it, listening to Crystal Gayle."

The back door opened and Bones dropped his head, shoulders, and rear haunches, ready to spring, as a giant, wild-haired bruiser of a man covered in black-ash tattoos stepped out, wearing a leather vest, blue jeans, and rattlesnake cowboy boots.

"What the fuck you got against Crystal Gayle?"

"When she sang 'Cry' on the radio, it was a crime against God," Lionel replied. "There's only one version of 'Cry,' the Johnnie Ray version, and she ain't Johnnie Ray."

"Fuck yourself. What's this about Mongrel?"

Lionel turned serious. "Your friend Mongrel is not only an ATF undercover being run out of the Albuquerque office, he's also dead. They're looking at you for it."

"Yeah? Why the fuck would they do that?" Arthur asked.

"Because you're an easy target with serious priors," Lionel said. "And, well, the guy who actually killed him was Mongrel's supervising agent."

This statement sucked the air right out of the clubhouse. All eyes turned to Lionel. Arthur stared hard at him, wondering if he was being put on. "Says who?"

"Says my fucking dog," Lionel retorted. "Now, are you going to offer me a beer, or do I have to send my dog to pee in every pocket of your pool tables?"

Though the bartender offered to put Bones out in a fenced-in area behind the clubhouse, Lionel smiled in a way to suggest that that wasn't going to happen. The pool players were sent out to walk the perimeter while Arthur, the other man who'd been in the back office (a morbidly obese fifty-something with scraggly gray facial hair who Arthur referred to as "Tubby"), the bartender, who went by "Weevil," and Lionel took seats around a table as the man at the bar, who went unnamed but who Lionel recognized from some past rap sheet, continued sitting and drinking. Lionel saw that he had two Heckler & Koch 9mm pistols in his belt and, within easy reach of his right hand, a pump-action shotgun hanging under the bar over his knees.

"Do you believe in luck?" Arthur asked Lionel, as the sheriff's deputy poured a glass of water Weevil brought over into a dish for Bones, who appreciatively lapped it up.

"Not particularly."

"Neither do I," the biker replied. "So when people I know should be going away get off, I figure they found themselves in a jam and jumped right into the feds' pocket, offering to snitch to keep on the streets. When a bunch of those guys all gang up to vouch for a newcomer who I sure as hell never heard of, in this case Mongrel, I get a sixth sense about him."

"Then how come you let Mongrel in here?"

Arthur grinned. "If I kick him out, it looks like I've got something to hide. So I just let him in with a big smile on my face, treat him like any brother rider, and he ends up with nothing to report week after week. How long do you think the feds are going to spend taxpayer dollars on an operation like that? And after 'Mongrel' ends up 'moving on to San Antonio' or something, how long before any investigator will get operational funding to run another possibly fruitless undercover op against my club?"

Lionel said nothing but knew the chapter president was making a good point that, sadly, showed a real understanding of law enforcement.

"So you're admitting to me you knew he was an undercover but denying you had anything to do with his murder?"

"We ever have trouble, me and you?" Arthur asked. "Serious trouble, I mean? You think I'm going to murder an undercover cop?"

Lionel didn't reply, letting it hang out there that it wasn't outside the realm of possibility.

"Well, I guess you answered that by walking in here like that, knowing you weren't gonna get a bullet in the head," Arthur said. "You know us. We get caught, we do our time. We've never asked for special favors, and we've never tagged a cop. We're not going to start now."

"Which leads me to my next question," Lionel said. "You have any idea why ATF would want him dead?"

"You mean other than to justify their expenditures here by showing the big, bad Furies are capable of murder?"

"Wouldn't justify a thing if they couldn't make it stick," Lionel replied.

"Good point," Tubby said, his first words of the powwow, eliciting an annoyed glance from Arthur.

"You got anything going down soon that the ATF would be interested in?" Lionel pressed.

Weevil shifted uncomfortably as Arthur stared back at Lionel. Over at the bar, the unnamed man with all the guns stared intently at an ad for dishwasher detergent. Finally, Arthur sighed and rose from the table.

"Come on, then."

Arthur opened a trap door behind the bar and had turned to descend a ladder when Lionel brought Bones around the corner.
"You serious?"

"He goes where I go. But don't worry. Doubt he'd mark his territory anyplace that smells like this."

Arthur sighed and continued down the steps, followed by Lionel and Bones. Once they were at the bottom, Arthur pulled the chain on a naked bulb overhead, which illuminated a small room filled with cases of beer stacked to the ceiling. Arthur waved for Lionel to follow him through the narrow room to a large steel locker against the back wall. Lionel glanced around at the boxes, listing with their heavy contents, and imagined that it would be pretty easy to get crushed down there.

As they walked, Lionel watched Bones's reaction to the myriad of smells, a cacophony of scents from stale beer to intense body odor, but the shepherd wasn't detecting another human party lurking somewhere in the dark. Figuring he was safe enough, Lionel followed Arthur to locker, but as the biker opened it, he pushed aside the back panel to reveal that it was a doorway leading to a second room beyond.

"Pretty cool, huh?" Arthur said.

"I've seen better," Lionel scoffed, rankling the biker. "Bones?"

Bones immediately darted past the two men, surprising the biker as the shepherd disappeared into the far room. Lionel also slid the nylon retention strap off his pistol holster noticeably enough for Arthur to see.

"Still don't trust me?"

"You almost beat the brains out of a bank manager in Tucumcari not so long ago that I haven't seen the photos. You don't engender much trust."

Arthur shrugged and followed Bones in, flipping a switch this time to turn on lights that illuminated a much larger space than where the beer was stored. When Lionel entered, he almost gasped.

Around the room, on shelves, and stacked on the ground were machine guns all of a uniform make and model. There were so many of them that it looked like a factory showroom, except for the fact that they were so lazily and haphazardly stacked that Lionel knew the action on probably a quarter of them would suffer. Despite this particular weapon being a favorite of the U.S. military, it could be as dainty as a teacup when subjected to real-world conditions as simple as being improperly stacked or having heavy objects on top of it. It looked more like the way somebody who didn't care that much would store firewood after enlisting a couple of buddies to run the loads up and down the ladder between beer runs.

The job had been done with haste instead of care.

Lionel looked from where Bones sniffed the weapons up to the proud biker gang leader and decided not to say anything about their condition. He was mentally going over the past few months, trying to remember even the briefest mention of an armory robbery at an army base, but it didn't ring any bells. He didn't have to pick one up to know that these weren't civilian models stolen from a factory or dealer. These had army mods that were done in-house, typically by DOD contractors when they arrived at the base.

He did a quick count and estimated he was looking at just over two thousand weapons.

"Aren't you gonna ask where I got all these?" Arthur asked.

"More interested in who is going to get them next," Lionel replied. "I assume they're going across the border?" When Arthur said nothing, Lionel nodded. "Well, I don't think they're going to who you think they are."

"Does it matter?" Arthur asked. "You've still got big gangs running things down there, and sometimes they come over the border. They kill our guys, they kill your guys. We sell them some heavy firepower, maybe those drug-runnin' bastards'll just kill each other."

Lionel nodded, remembering that this was the excuse various white supremacist organizations used to gun-run to the cartels.

"That's not what I'm saying," Lionel added. "I think you're selling to *federales* down there. And I think they're planning to kill you for your trouble and just blame it on the gangs."

Arthur looked from Lionel to Bones with surprise before shaking his head. "I've heard some crazy theories in my day, but that's about the craziest."

Bones's nose was a marvel. The dog himself wasn't the sharpest tool in the drawer and no one claimed he was, but his olfactory epithelium where the sensory neurons of his smell receptors were housed should have been bronzed and sent to the enforcement dog equivalent of Cooperstown when all was said and done, in Lionel's estimation.

So when Bones had circled Special Agent in Charge Mattis early that morning when they'd met in the manufacturing complex's parking lot in a pattern that only Lionel knew, one that Bones traced when he smelled burned flesh, he figured Mattis might already have a good idea where they would find the dead body of Special Agent Jacob Hillenbrand, aka Mongrel, and that they'd find it extra-crispy. Lionel went along with the charade, as he had no idea why Mattis had committed the murder of the then only missing agent and then tested him with his observation that the dead agent hadn't been tortured.

Though an audio recording would not have revealed much, Mattis' body language immediately registered his fear at having possibly overlooked a detail in his "perfect murder." Bones, the walking fear-and-lie detector, reacted to Mattis as trained: He sat down and looked in the opposite direction. Only Lionel held the Rosetta stone to translate Bones's reactions to certain behaviors, and he'd never written it down. Bones was an extension of himself, another tool in the chest that elevated the dog from mere body locator/enforcement animal to a detective in his own right.

"You looking to bust us for these guns?" Arthur asked Lionel with just a hint of menace as they headed back to the ladder.

"The second I do that, the ATF man'll know I'm onto him," Lionel shrugged. "I've got one case, the death of Mongrel, and that's the one I'm working. Who am I to stand in the way of free enterprise?"

Arthur grunted. With that, Lionel and Bones headed back up into the clubhouse and exited the premises.

Lionel figured that, despite his protestations to the contrary, Arthur would believe part of what had been told him, and he'd try to solve the problem with an increase in firepower. Lionel kept tabs on the Furies and the activities around their clubhouse for the next couple of days as riders from two other New Mexico chapters rolled in, as well as four bikers from a chapter in Shreveport who came with a trailer full of weapons.

The sheriff's deputy also did some investigating into the weapons he'd seen, and it only confirmed what he'd suspected: there were no missing guns out there, at least not in that quantity. Lionel realized that Arthur and his dumb-ass compatriots had likely secured the large cache from some "trusted" fence who had sworn he'd come into a couple thousand machine guns and was willing to move them for rock-bottom prices.

So much for not believing in luck, Lionel thought.

So, night after night, Lionel and Bones would trek out to the desert and wait until some new flurry of activity might suggest the guns were on the move. He'd seen little of Agent Mattis since the discovery of Mongrel and chalked that up to the fact that the SAIC knew exactly when the buy was going to be and hardly needed to pound the pavement to tie up the loose ends of his case.

The only thing that concerned Lionel was his fear that the ATF and the Mexican federal police would get away with this. The way he had it figured, the U.S. government or maybe just Mattis (however unlikely) had decided to help the escalating drug wars by unofficially supplying some real firepower to the federal cops. Back channels had probably become necessary on both sides of the border for a horde of reasons. These included fear of reprisals on American soil from the "north side" chapters of the Mexican gangs and the fact that it would become a political hot button if the U.S. was actively involved in supplying weapons to aid another country's mess. Also, announcing to the gangs that a large shipment of weapons would soon be crossing the border might prove too enticing a hijacking target once they got to the Mexico side.

Lionel realized that Special Agent Mongrel probably had figured it out, too, and wondered if the undercover's downfall had been thinking that a group of "innocent" bikers would be taking the fall. He hoped Mongrel had been smarter than that and that his only real mistake had been in taking the matter straight to the wrong person, the fellow who had been overseeing the entire operation in the first place.

Lionel brooded over this in his Blazer, Bones at his side, night after sleepless night as the George Strait tape played endlessly into oblivion. He'd been so focused on the problem at hand that he didn't notice for an hour that the tape deck had finally eaten the cassette alive, silencing the truck halfway through the appropriately titled, *I Should Have Watched That First Step*.

He was still thinking about this at two in the a.m. five days after his initial confrontation with Arthur when about forty motorcycles showed up outside the clubhouse and men began filling bike trailers with guns loosely wrapped them in blue tarp. After the second gun fell out of its makeshift packaging, Lionel started to feel sorry for the clearly inept bikers.

"Should we just ring the state police and have them do a pull over, search and seizure?" Lionel asked Bones. The sleepy shepherd didn't seem to have an opinion, so Lionel sighed. "Yeah, you're right. They'd just find another way in a few months, and it'd be just as bad for somebody else."

Once the bikers had left the clubhouse, Lionel pulled his Blazer off the fire road ridge he'd used as an over-watch position, slunk down the bad road without headlights, and headed in the direction of the convoy of motorcycles.

By the time Lionel got down to Route 28, the highway was empty and black as far as the eye could see. Most took Interstate 10 down south towards

Texas and Mexico as it was faster, and the 28 had long stretches in various states of disrepair and really led nowhere except to a handful of farms and dead-end dirt roads. He figured the bikers would be riding without lights, so he kept his off, too. Dark roads like this made for easy ambushes, as a couple of men could drop off the road only about twenty feet out in the night and be completely invisible to traffic passing by on the road.

Lionel had his service revolver with him, a .38 he liked for the combination of stopping power and lighter weight in his holster. The entire department had switched to automatics years ago, but Lionel wasn't a fan. He thought they led to problems in gun actions involving officers, since men would use four bullets instead of one and still miss, as they were over-relying on the fact that their full clip of fifteen to seventeen bullets would allow a miss or two. Lionel had six in his chamber and that was it, but on at least one occasion he had shot six different men with it without reloading.

Others in his department couldn't put down six guys with three clips.

Of course, Lionel also had Bones, who was, as they say, "good in the pocket." Bones was fairly normal as enforcement dogs went, but Lionel had done all sorts of additional training with him over the years. If Lionel or any of Bones's handlers were in trouble, Bones would respond with prejudice. He was just over a hundred pounds and, when motivated, he could tear off a man's arm or rip out a throat. Lionel had seen Bones in action a number of times but, more importantly, had seen the reactions of those Bones attacked. Nothing took the fight out of a man like seeing a pissed-off German shepherd's jaws snapping only inches from his jugular.

But Lionel had really developed a couple of "settings" for Bones. One command was all show, shock and awe. Bones attacked, went all vicious, but was there to pin or hold the suspect. Another command was the opposite. When he got that one, Bones went in and killed his target as quickly, quietly, and efficiently as possible, like hunting prey.

So when Bones's nose told Lionel to turn off on a side road, the trail of forty-something bikes a pretty easy trail to follow, Lionel was able to ascertain which of those two commands he'd probably be delivering when they heard the calamitous thunder of distant guns accompanied by sparks of muzzle flash about a mile ahead.

"Looks like we almost missed the party," Lionel said and peeled off the road.

He knew this was dicey, given the rough ground and possibility of rocks and cactus ahead, but figured that the shooters would have one eye on the road and wouldn't welcome interlopers even if they were preoccupied with a gunfight.

When he was within a hundred yards, he finally picked up his radio mic.

"Shooting out in the desert off Route 28 and Afton," he said, more to cover his ass than anything. "Deputy Sheriff Oudin responding. Request immediate backup."

Without waiting for a response, he dropped the mic, stopped the truck, and stared out the windshield at the continuing firefight. Though he and Bones had missed the beginning, there seemed to be a lot of people still shooting.

"All right, Bones," Lionel said, sliding out of the truck cab and indicating for the shepherd to follow. Bones did so and kept a foot behind the sheriff's deputy as they both hurried through the night to close in on the action.

When they got closer, they could see that about twenty-five men were lying face down in the sand, some wounded, some dead. The bodies were between a large group of parked motorcycles and then three pickup trucks, both sets of vehicles now being used as cover by the surviving bikers and what Lionel took for the Mexican federal agents, though they were dressed in civilian clothes. Lionel wondered where the snipers had been, as he assumed the Mexican agents had brought some out equipped with night vision scopes, since it looked like Arthur and his guys just rode up in full force, thinking they'd come off as intimidating, as opposed to group that played its entire hand before the game had even started.

That's when Bones's head snapped left and Lionel recognized that the dog had picked up on someone getting close to them in the dark.

"Bones," Lionel whispered. "*Meat.*"

In an instant, Bones became a different dog. He left Lionel's side, moved towards the spot where he had detected movement, soon saw that it was indeed a man with a sniper rifle complete with Starlight scope. Bones flanked the man before coming up directly behind him. Though his eyesight during the day was fine for a dog, Bones's vision was downright eagle-eyed by night.

The sniper, actually a member of the elite Marines Amphibious Reaction Force (*Batallones de Comandos Anfibios*), unofficially on loan to the federal police, had just picked up Lionel in his crosshairs when he heard the sound of Bones's approach. He whirled around in time to see the shepherd lunge at him through the dark and clamp his jaws directly around his face. Bones then bit down hard and broke the man's jaw. As he began to scream, a sound drowned out by the near-constant gunfire nearby, the dog angled his snout down and tore out the man's throat.

Maw now soaked in blood, Bones slipped away from the sniper and continued moving around the action.

Lionel spotted Weevil against one of the motorcycles and moved close enough to signal the fellow, only to get a gun aimed in his direction.

"Dammit, I'm on your side, asshole!"

When Weevil saw who it was, semi-illuminated, since Lionel was in the multiple headlights, some broken, continuing to keep the gun battle bathed in an eerie light, he signaled the deputy over. When Lionel got alongside the biker, he saw that Weevil had been shot in the same leg twice and was losing blood.

"Where's Arthur?"

"He was the first one dead," Weevil said, shaking his head pitifully. "Bullet out of the night. He didn't even see it coming."

"You guys walked into a trap. One I warned you about."

"We thought it was part of a setup. Some ATF guy came down and said that he knew you'd talked to us but that Mongrel was dirty and had been informing on the Furies to the Mexican police, who killed him when he asked for more money. He said if we went ahead with the sale, we'd be protected."

Lionel nodded dumbly. He wondered if he'd ever meet a criminal whose IQ was higher than 100 or, failing that, one who had anything in the way of deductive reasoning skills.

"Well, how many of you guys are left, and how many of them?"

"We got about ten guys that can still shoot. Maybe the same on their side. They were holding back a little, staying with their trucks. When it all went down, they let their snipers do the work, so we never knew how many there were."

A small swarm of bullets whizzed by overhead and slammed amongst a nearby motorcycle, peeling back strips of metals and shredding the tires. Lionel looked out into the dark and tried to see where the shot had come from, but there wasn't a second one. But then he caught sight of another man rising behind the truck next to it and, just as that man fired a couple of rifled rounds their way from a large pistol, Lionel aimed at the man's head and fired. His bullet struck pay dirt, and the air was momentarily misted with blood and jellied brains as the corpse sank back behind the truck.

"Wow, that was some shooting," Weevil said.

"It's called 'drawing their fire,'" Lionel replied. "They're getting bored and bunkering in. Give them something to shoot at, and they'll start popping up like jackrabbits."

Lionel's point was proved a second later as a hail of bullets poured in, splattering around Weevil's impromptu hiding place. Lionel flinched wildly as if shot and spied one of the shooters checking to see if he'd landed a bullet. Lionel instantly raised his gun and blasted the man in the eye before then rolling over a couple of feet, catching a lucky angle on a second man, and shooting him in the side of the head. The man vomited a stream of blood and teeth as he sailed to the ground.

"Time to find a new hide," Lionel said, nodding to Weevil as he began crawling away.

"Wait, what?" protested Weevil. "What about me?!"

"You have a gun. Shoot back."

Out away from the lights, Bones was tearing out the throat of the second sniper when a familiar smell entered his nose. As the dying man gurgled and clutched at the ragged flesh around his neck, Bones stepped away and sniffed at the air, trying to clear the heavy stench of fresh blood from his nose. He picked up something over to his left, the third spot on a half-circle that had arched over the *federales'* position, their trucks having been parked in a way to make the area directly in front of them a perfect kill zone for the snipers.

Bones trotted over to where the third and final sniper had been and saw that he was already dead, having been shanked in the kidneys multiple times from behind. Though the smell of cordite still hung heavy over the man's position, his rifle was gone. Bones turned towards the desert and detected a man hurrying away into the night.

Wheeling around, the German shepherd bolted after the fellow.

Lionel shot five more of the *federales* before the last two surrendered. Both were astonished to see that they had been trading bullets with a county sheriff's deputy.

"We were warned about you," one of the men said in Spanish.

"Yeah, I'll bet," Lionel replied in the same language. "You know how fast your government's going to disavow you and say you were dirty and in with the gangs?"

The men said nothing, but Lionel's words had rung true.

"Good. Then you're going to cooperate and help me get the guy who tortured and killed a Federal undercover. Oliver Mattis?"

"Oh, he was here. The ATF man? He was here."

Lionel suddenly looked out over the desert, wondering how he could've missed him.

Bones pushed farther and farther into the low desert scrub, the running man easy enough to track, as he carried three unmistakable scents with him as he went: the dead sniper's blood, the burned powder of the recently fired rifle, and then a thick sheen of fear in the man's own sweat. It could've been a burning four-story building made of cinnamon (a particular Bones *bête noire*) instead of a desert, and the shepherd would've still been able to track the man.

But the agent was making good time. He was in great shape, and his fear was just beginning to give way to optimism. He knew it was still hours before sun-up, so even if local law enforcement got a helicopter in the air, he'd have long since hitched a ride back into Las Cruces with plausible deniability written all over his face when he "learned" of the debacle come eight o'clock.

He still wasn't sure where he'd gone wrong. The scene some poor local was to have found the next morning was meant to be simple: a bunch of dead bikers in the desert, tire tracks leading to Mexico. Mattis had not anticipated the arrival of Oudin but didn't think one man would have been able to turn the tide as he had. But after the deputy shot his first two men and the snipers didn't seem to be able to pick him up, Mattis decided to hedge his bets by getting the hell out of there. He'd ridden in with the *federales* and was cursing himself for leaving not so much as a rental car half a mile down the highway, but knew there'd be traffic on the 28 when he got there.

When he was about three hundred yards from the action, he finally stopped for a moment and wheeled the sniper rifle around, aiming the night scope towards the gunfight. He hadn't heard a shot for a couple of minutes and wondered if somebody had finally knocked down the pesky cop. Instead, he saw that the two *federales* had surrendered to the man and were probably in the process of giving him up.

"*Motherfucker,*" Mattis cursed before checking to see if there was still a round in the chamber.

When he saw that there was, he drew a bead on Lionel's chest and was about to pull the trigger when he picked up movement a few feet in front of him. He angled the scope down and saw Bones less than six feet away. He switched his aim, led the dog with the gun's muzzle, and as the bounding shepherd filled up the scope, he pulled the trigger.

As the shot rang out over the desert, Lionel stared out into the darkness, suddenly worried for Bones. The two *federales* looked a little more nervous than they had a moment before, and Lionel shrugged when the bullet didn't fly anywhere near them.

"We're all lit up here. If that rifle was aimed at any of us, we'd be dead. Besides, I've got a silent partner out there I failed the mention."

Lionel realized that he had said that in English and knew it was his concern for Bones speaking. He translated for the *federales*, and they nodded and relaxed, since there wasn't a second shot. The sheriff's deputy put handcuffs on both and could do nothing but wait.

A moment or two later, a long stream of flashing roof lights appeared out on the 28 and began racing out to the scene of the shootout. When he saw that they were indeed a phalanx of local and state cops, Lionel finally stepped away from his prisoners and looked out towards the source of the shot. As the first officer pulled up, Lionel quickly turned the scene over to her and then hurried out into the desert, calling back that he feared there might be an officer down out in the scrub.

Truthfully, he didn't believe that would be the case. Bones could handle almost anything. But there was a lingering feeling of doubt as he hurried through the darkness. He wouldn't admit it was fear, but there it was.

Though Lionel knew he might be inviting a gunshot, he shouted out into the darkness. "Bones!!"

There was only silence, but then a weak voice came from somewhere out in front of him.

"Oudin....call off your fucking dog."

Lionel slowed and could make out the weak green light of the battery-powered Starlight scope in the dirt attached to a rifle just ahead. He picked it up, looked through the scope, and spied a dry wash about twelve feet in front of him. He walked and saw SAIC Mattis lying on the hard, cracked ground of the wash bed, looking like he'd broken his leg. Bones, alongside the man, looked up at Lionel, his eyes flashing bright white on the scope. Lionel could see that the shepherd had torn a large bloody gash through the agent's arm, almost severing it, which probably caused the man to stumble backwards and fall into the arroyo. Blood, which showed up black in the scope, had pooled around the wound, and Lionel knew if he'd gotten there only a couple of minutes later, Mattis would've already bled to death.

Setting down the rifle, Lionel clambered down into the creek bed, pulled off his belt, and tied off Mattis' arm. "You're gonna lose this, I'm afraid."

"Yeah, 'cause of your fuckin' dog, Oudin," the agent replied ruefully, spitting blood.

"You hear they're looking to repeal the death penalty in this state?" Lionel replied. "Might do you a disservice. Not gonna be an easy thing, a one-armed ex-fed in the state pen."

Mattis went silent and then leaned back on the hard ground.

"Your fuckin' dog."

"Good day of work, Bones," Lionel told the shepherd as they drove back to Las Cruces a few hours later, the sun now painting the desert floor in pinks and orange.

But when he looked over, he saw that the shepherd, clearly exhausted, was curled up asleep on the passenger seat.

Lionel snorted, thought about when he might get some rest himself. With a sigh, he rolled up the driver's-side window, not wanting the noise of the passing traffic to disturb his snoozing partner.

THE APOCALYPSE SAGA

BONES

Homo homini lupus

Prologue

Roberto DeMatteis had seven species of animal named after him. Though most people think of an organism's scientific name, its binomial nomenclature, as solely derived from a combination of the two Latin words for its genus and species, *Homo sapiens*, *Drosophila melanogaster*, *Ursus arctos*, etc., there's an optional third part to the name that may designate its discoverer. Types of aloe vera plants include *Aloe arborescens* Mill (named for eighteenth-century botanist and chief gardener of the Chelsea Physic Garden, Philip Miller), *Aloe myriacantha* Bowie (named for nineteenth-century explorer James Bowie, who discovered a number of new aloe plants in his explorations of the southern tip of Africa), and *Aloe perfoliata* L. (for Swedish botanist Carl Linnaeus, who created binomial nomenclature in the first place in 1735; why he's prominent enough to need only an "L."). In the case of DeMatteis, his namesakes were seven sea creatures that he'd discovered living in the geothermally heated abyssal zones around Arctic hydrothermal vents, including the *Riftia pachyptila* DeMatteisii and the *Paralvinella sulfincola* DeMatteisii, as well as five more whose scientific names could all be additionally suffixed with the honorific, "DeMatteisii."

Roberto was proud of many things in his career as a marine biologist, but nothing compared to the uncovering of these seven animals, placing him in a line that stretched back to men like Linnaeus, Charles Darwin, John James Audubon, even Jacques Cousteau, whose television programs first got DeMatteis interested in the sea (though he was more apt to fabricate stories of seafaring great-great-grand-whatevers). Despite being routinely hailed for his groundbreaking books, lectures, and research in the lab, Roberto would describe his classification of these animals in terms most akin to how a mechanical engineer might refer to the patents of drill bit configurations he or she had invented, something to hang on the wall and be praised. Only instead of having made his breakthroughs utilizing a design computer, only to then hand them off to someone else to manufacture who would then hand them off to someone else to implement, Roberto made the endless dives to secure his treasures and a place in scientific history himself. These dives primarily took him to the vents along the Gakkel Ridge, an oceanic mountain range that ran under the Arctic Ocean from Greenland to Siberia. Each discovery, he figured, had been there for millennian merely awaiting the first human being to ever reach that earthly frontier before revealing itself. Space exploration? Feh. There were still plenty of places on the home world left unexplored, enough to sate anyone's sense of discovery. Space was just easier, Roberto would claim. Type something into one of those design computers, build a boat with sealed portholes, and chuck it high enough into the air, and they'll put your name alongside Magellan and Columbus. Sailors both, he would add.

But sink deep into the cold seas of the Arctic to decipher the secrets of your own planet's evolutionary history, and you had to bow and scrape for funding. The only way around this was to bring something back from the abyss you could claim as your own – an important new discovery – that you could then present to a society's fellowship committee and say, "See?! This is where your money went. This is hard science. This means something."

And as they ooh-ed and ahh-ed, you eased your way into their checkbooks, plucking out just enough for the next trip.

On his most recent voyage, one that had lasted fifteen amazing weeks, Roberto had discovered species numbers eight, nine, and ten, an unqualified, unparalleled bonanza. Even as he was bringing them to the surface, he imagined these three little creatures keeping him going for years, maybe even decades.

Because of that, he had refused to allow the specimens, being transported in large, temperature-controlled saltwater tanks, to leave his sight for more than even a few minutes and had blown out the rest of his department's annual discretionary budget chartering a flight that would take him from his ship's disembarkation port in Tromso, Norway, over to Heathrow for a refueling stop and then on to Pittsburgh International Airport. From there, they would then be packed into a refrigerated truck for transport 158 miles down the US-22 and up the I-99 back to Penn.

His worst fear wasn't a plane crash or temperature gauge malfunction but an auto accident out on the highway. To this end, he had arranged to escort the truck the whole way utilizing a rental, a Toyota Prius, he would pick up at the airport. He imagined himself spotting a runaway tractor-trailer hurtling the wrong way down the road straight for his prized catch and wondered if he'd have the wherewithal to angle into its path with the Prius. He'd even taken the insurance rider for the first time in his life, just in case, though it was $30 a day extra.

However, the entire trip turned out to be hopelessly uneventful, and the moment he arrived in University Park, he had a grad student run the car back to a local franchise of the rental agency. Relieved, he brought the portable specimen tanks into the lab to transfer each of the organisms into their new permanent homes. But his sense of security was misplaced. He couldn't know what his precious seawater tanks, the result of a relentless, eleven-year grant-writing campaign, had been used for in his absence. How the department head had loaned them out to the Agricultural Soil Science Department in exchange for Lady Lion basketball tickets. How a trio of grad students had been using them in their soil survey experiments for months now. Or how the work study associate whose job it was to clean the tanks had been using a solvent suitable for cleaning containers of soil or fertilizer, but one that would prove to be disastrously inappropriate for something that might later be used to hold any kind of living creature, particularly one capable of polymorphic mutation.

Disastrously inappropriate.

I

Bones stood up as the old Bronco bounced along the muddy, tree-lined road, its tires spitting gravel when it listed too far off the trail blazed through the mud by the heavy-use vehicles that made up the only traffic the old road ever saw. There were no houses on Spur 790, and the two mailboxes - one business, one residential – for its one address were way up by the highway, saving the postman a daily twenty-minute round trip in good weather. A day like today, with the sky pissing buckets, would've taken even the most intrepid mail carrier upwards of an hour.

"*Shit!*" cursed Billy.

He grabbed the steering wheel to prevent the truck's back tires from fishtailing over the rise on the right shoulder of the road. If they lost control and slid out of the tracks, that could mean plowing backwards the next six feet into a culvert, and it would be hours before they'd get out.

"You holding on back there?" Billy asked, half-joking.

Bones stared up at the uniformed man behind the wheel but made no reply.

"Almost there, buddy," Billy said, reassuringly turning up the radio as if to mask further turbulence.

Bones turned away from the rear speaker. He didn't like the propulsive rock music Billy insisted on blasting when he drove, but it didn't bother him enough to whine about it. Besides, as soon as Billy's hand had reached for the volume, Bones could see their destination out the window, surrounded by the usual, familiar activity - flashing lights, people in uniform moving about, a battalion of awkwardly parked squad cars, etc.

Billy pulled the truck up behind the last police car in what he estimated was a line of eight or nine, momentarily wondering how they'd reverse their way out of there when they were done. He spotted two SWAT vans among the vehicles and realized that this must be serious.

The police activity was centered on the entrance of a large junkyard that seemed out of place this far off the beaten track and so near the woods. It appeared that the yard might have been a relatively modest business at first, a few cars, a handful of old, now-rusty appliances, but as time passed, it had been expanded into the neighboring forest. Rather than cut down trees, the owners had simply extended the high chain-link fence – topped with twin strands of interwoven razor wire – into the forest, where old refrigerators, freezers, and washing machines now stood alongside the trunks of towering eastern hemlocks. The original part of the yard was now filled with hundreds of rusting chassis from cars and trucks of every make and model dating back forty years.

Billy climbed out of the cab, his boots immediately sinking into the soft mud.

"Christ," he muttered. He slammed the driver's-side door and opened up the back door where Bones stood on the seat, panting, staring back at him. "Ready to get to work?"

Bones, seeing Billy giving him an expectant look, gave a little woof in response. Billy grinned and reached in, grabbing the large German shepherd's leash, and then held it out and up, the indicator for Bones to hop out of the Bronco. The pads on Bones's feet touched the cool mud, which became the first smell that filled his nose, penetrating to the two hundred million scent receptors (one hundred ninety-five million more than a human) buried deep within his mucous membrane. Almost immediately, the smell of wet earth was overpowered by the stench of oil and exhaust fumes. Bones scrunched his nose, snorted a little, and then brought it down directly onto the ground, his eyes focusing on the grubby earth. Forcing aside the manmade smells to focus on the ground underfoot, Bones could soon smell the familiar scent of natural decay. Plants mostly, but also animals, alive and dead. The dead included a deer, likely killed through predation, as well as a rabbit who probably met a similar fate. Both gave off the harsh scent of rotting flesh and tissue, though a second rabbit, a more recent kill, came with the smell of vegetation rotting in its stomach, as the body itself had not yet begun to decay.

"Billy Bones!" came a booming voice from up by the junkyard entrance.

Billy, whose last name was Youman, bristled at the alliterative nickname for himself and his cadaver dog. But seeing that it came from George Zusak, the Zone 2 commander, he bit his tongue and faked a smile.

"Glad they sent you and not Lowe and his mutt," Commander Zusak said, extending a hand, which Billy shook. "That dog couldn't find a donut in an empty attic."

Billy bit his tongue a second time at the idea that Robot, Sergeant Perrish Lowe's Belgian Malinois, was any kind of mutt (except perhaps in comparison to Bones) and simply smirked as he figured it was what Zusak wanted him to do.

"What we got?" Billy asked, nodding towards the junkyard.

"Detective?" Zusak said, turning and nodding to a man who was already walking over. Billy clocked the guy's outfit, a garish, light blue suit that even an eight-year-old would burn rather than wear to church, and figured the guy either had to spend all his clothing allowance on alimony like he did or had a sideline in robbing funeral homes.

"Missing person, possible homicide," the detective said after introducing himself as Detective Nessler. "The suspect's name is Wayne Chapas, drives a tow truck for his father's company. Girlfriend, Tracy LeShoure, went missing over a week ago."

"Uh-oh," Billy said.

"We've got him dragging his wrecker out here twice this past week," Nessler continued. "Owner of the yard, guy named Dewberry, led us to the vehicles, but they were clean. We think he used the wrecks to drive her out here but then stashed her in another vehicle."

Billy nodded but then looked down at Bones. His partner's nose had already sifted through the myriad of junkyard, forest, and cop-related smells and had isolated the one he was trained to find, all in the time it took for this conversation to happen.

Billy grinned to himself, proud of his buddy. He could be an utter fuck-up, an off-duty drunk with two – count 'em, *two* – ex-wives docking his paycheck, but his dog's laser-guided missile of a nose made Billy invaluable to the force. Once a target was painted, there was nothing stopping Bones from leading his handler right to it. Billy knew that Bones's training was 99 percent of the battle, but he felt it was good for his standing in the department to make it seem like their consistent success had at least something to do with him, too.

"You ready to follow your nose?" Billy asked, addressing the shepherd as the detective and commander watched.

Bones looked back up at Billy with incomprehension, having already tugged at the leash to indicate that he knew precisely the direction in which their quarry lay. Billy turned to Zusak and Nessler, and nodded.

"He probably just smells the junkyard dogs right now," Billy lied. "Once we're in there, he'll get to it. C'mon, boy. Stop fucking around."

Billy gave the leash a light flip, and Bones surged forward to the gates of the junkyard, leading him past the other officers as they went.

"If you guys could just stay out here while we're inside?" Billy insisted to the patrolmen. "I don't want to confuse Bones none if he catches a whiff of one of you or, more accurately, what kind of meat might be rotting in your over-fed stomachs."

Rather than take offense, to a man the officers nodded solemnly as Billy and Bones passed through the junkyard gates and soon disappeared from view in the labyrinth of cars and trucks.

It took them forty-five seconds to locate Tracy LeShoure.

She'd been repeatedly bashed in the face; "beyond recognition" was an understatement. An I.D. wasn't going to be 100 percent without prints, but Billy figured how many other week-old corpses could there be in this junkyard? He stared down at her broken body, which hadn't been stuffed in the trunk of a car heading straight for the compactor as was more typical but actually crammed inside the twenty-gallon fuel tank of an S10 Blazer. Chapas would've had to know what kind of vehicle had such a large tank, had to have brought the tools to remove, then replace it once he'd placed Tracy's body inside, and probably figured the residual smell of gasoline would cover up any potentially incriminating odor in the time it would take to get through the queue to the compacter. All of this strongly suggested premeditation, which meant Murder One. It was the kind of arrest that led to bonuses, commendations, and weekends off for everybody *but* Billy, and he knew it.

"Here," Billy said, tossing another chunk of partly melted carob to Bones -- the shepherd's favored reward -- as they sat a few feet from the body. Billy knew he couldn't take in the stillness of the yard and surrounding woods for much longer. Soon they'd have to go back, announce their triumphant discovery, lead the detectives to the dump site, and then be shunted to the side so that the "real police" could take over the scene before the news cameras got there.

Billy popped the last square into his mouth and got to his feet. He half-brushed, half-smeared the remaining carob onto his jeans, then picked up Bones's leash.

"Good day of work, Bones," he said, stroking the thick fur between the shepherd's ears. It wasn't his fault the department sucked. "Good boy."

Bones rose to his feet, flecks of mud hanging off his belly fur, even more on his haunches and fore paws. Billy led him through the automobile maze back to the front of the yard, but as Bones trotted alongside his partner, a new scent filled his nose, taking him by surprise. The cadaver dog wheeled around towards the northeast corner of the junkyard, his whiskers aloft and playing in the breeze.

"Whatcha got, Bones?" Billy asked, glancing at the trees.

Bones hesitated for a moment, bobbing his nose up and down in the air. But as quickly as the scent had arrived, it was gone. Bones turned back towards the entrance and pulled Billy forward.

"Crazy dog," Billy muttered under his breath, however affectionately.

When they reached the gates, Billy announced the discovery to Commander Zusak and Detective Nessler, but neither of them looked surprised or even particularly impressed, which annoyed the human half of the K-9 unit. Instead, they simply asked to be led back to the body, and after Billy and Bones had done just that, the pair was effectively dismissed from the scene, just as Billy knew they would be.

"Asshole," Billy said, loud enough to be heard if anyone had still been around as he opened up the back door of the Bronco. "Up, up."

Feeling the flick of the leash, Bones jumped in back, and as he did so, Billy tossed the leash inside with him before closing the door, being careful not to catch Bones's tail or paws in it in case he turned around quickly. Then he climbed into the cab and slammed the driver's door shut.

Once he'd fired up the truck, Billy got an idea. He slapped the Bronco into reverse, backed up a couple of feet, and then executed a three-point turn to head back down Spur 790 to the highway. As he did, he took advantage of the mud and angled his rear tires perpendicular to Commander Zusak's sedan and hit the gas with just a little too much force, shooting mud across both the commander's driver's-side doors.

Satisfied, Billy finished executing the turn and headed away from the junkyard.

"You know what, Bones?" Billy asked, though the dog's eyes were closed, as he was already napping. "If I was going to kill somebody, there'd be *nothing* left of that body. I'd chop it up, soak the parts for three days in ammonia, and then encase it in cement. After that, I'd drive the whole concrete block to fucking Mexico and shove it into the ocean in one of those fishing coves that's off-limits to scuba divers. Then I'd burn the house down where I did the killing."

Billy hesitated when he said this last part, though, knowing how badly burn sites affected Bones's nose. As so many different materials were burned in your typical house fire – paint, insulation, plastics, chemical sealants, you name it – the noxious combination of smells always served to give Bones what Billy figured was the doggy equivalent of a really bad migraine, as it was his job to inhale all that without any kind of filter just to see if there were any bodies amidst the ashes.

"All right, so maybe not the house fire," Billy said. "For you, I'd clean it real good, then leave unwrapped Snickers bars all throughout the house but in places only you could…"

These were Sergeant Billy Youman's last words.

A burning '92 Ford Taurus, at a speed approaching ninety miles an hour, slammed into the side of Billy's truck with the force of a locomotive. The angle was such that it bowed the truck inward, like the top and bottom halves of a running back getting nailed by an oncoming safety. The truck's roof effectively decapitated Billy as it was torn in half, though his heart had been stopped milliseconds before when the steering wheel was driven through his ribcage by the engine block and his collapsing ribcage squashed his heart like a rotten peach.

The force of the impact also served to blast the back door on the driver's side open, and Bones was fired out like a furry cannonball. He woke up immediately during his short flight, just long enough to process that something was terribly wrong. But as he began to register alarm, the shepherd smacked headfirst into a patch of muddy grass and was knocked unconscious. The collision had occurred just as Billy was reaching the highway, though the Taurus had been traveling in a grassy area between the highway's gravel shoulder and the woods a few feet away, setting alight the odd clump of grass when a piece of flaming debris dropped off and landed in the car's wake. There was no indicator as to what caused the car to be on fire, but it continued to burn, the flames soon leaping over to the Bronco and engulfing it, too.

Bones was out for six or seven minutes. When he came to, the fire was still crackling across both cars with great heat, but the gasoline had burned off rather than exploded, since the truck's tank had ruptured and poured the less than a gallon Billy typically kept aboard onto the wet grass. His nose full of mud, smoke, and burning flesh, Bones was groggy from a concussion, and he tested each leg as he tried to rise. His body ached, particularly his snout, which he'd bashed pretty well against the ground. Though blood was seeping out of a number of small cuts on Bones's torso, it was his right eye that was giving him the most trouble. A large welt had risen on his brow, which effectively squeezed the eye shut, giving him the appearance of a boxer who'd taken too many shots to the face.

But, by some miracle, Bones's legs appeared not to have been broken, so he managed to walk a couple of steps before collapsing again. When he lifted his head back up, he got his first whiff of Billy's scent coming from inside the burning truck. Pulling from a healthy reserve of strength built by years of conditioning, Bones lifted himself back up onto his feet and made his way to the truck.

Billy's body was torn to pieces, and even though he couldn't see it through the smoke, Bones's nose told him plenty. Billy's head was sagging over what was left of the dashboard, hanging on to the rest of his body by about half an inch of skin and sinew. His bones were completely shattered, as the collapsing truck had had the effect of a coffee press on his body, flattening it to match the contours of the wreckage it would now be forever encased in.

Bones filled his nose with Billy's scent, staring at the truck for a few moments. Finally, he turned away and walked around to the Taurus, where he had picked up the smell of two more dead bodies. The passenger-side door had been torn open, and Bones nosed around inside. What looked like a blonde woman in her forties was in the driver's seat, her head having spider-webbed the windshield, compacting and exploding her skull into a bloody mess of hair and brains. A much older man was lying across the back seat, but he, too, was dead. The only problem was Bones's nose telling him that the man had actually been dead for hours *before* the crash.

Bones was about to move away from the car when, suddenly, the body of the old man began to move. Bones jumped back in surprise, reflexively barking at the corpse as if to call Billy over to check it out, forgetting that his master was dead. But as the old man continued to rise, Bones couldn't help but react with a stream of confused barking. His nose was telling him that the old man was dead, a corpse, but his one good eye and his ears were telling him that the man was beginning to slide out of the back seat of the car and move towards him in a threatening way.

Bones kept barking, refusing to give up his ground even as he was mightily confused. The old man didn't speak but seemed completely focused on the dog in front of him. As soon as he got a little leverage on the car door, the man lunged at Bones, his mouth open and his hands splayed outwards, as if clumsily trying to grab for his neck. Bones scampered backwards, but even though he was a little worse for wear, the shepherd felt threatened enough to retaliate by pushing forward and sinking his jaws into the old man's right arm.

Rather than react in pain, the old man simply punched at Bones, flinging him aside. Bones's weakened jaws released the old man's arm as the dog careened into the grass, causing his entire body to quiver in pain as the stiffening muscles of his back and sides punished him for his lack of reflexes.

Deeply dissatisfied with this result, Bones immediately rolled over into a crouch, coiled back onto his haunches, and sprang forward. Before the old man could raise an arm in defense, Bones's jaws were clamped tightly around his throat. With a quick twist of his neck, Bones tore the man's throat out, the body flopping to the ground, once again lifeless.

Bones stared at the old man for a moment, but once satisfied that he would not be getting back to his feet, Bones walked away from the car and started following a distant, yet familiar scent on the wind, that of Commander Zusak and Detective Nessler. Pretty soon, he was back on the muddy road, effectively backtracking to the junkyard.

As Bones walked, or rather, *limped* along, the scent of Billy's body began to fade away in the distance. At one point, Bones slowed down and stopped, turning and looking back towards the highway, but the wreck site was long out of view. Bones turned and kept walking.

As he got closer to the junkyard and the parked police vehicles, Bones realized that the smells he'd been following were changing. There were more people now or, actually, more *cadavers*. Stranger, the familiar scents, those of Zusak and Nessler, seemed to have either dissipated or been diluted in some way. They were still there, but something was different. Bones had his nose high in the air, trying to pick out these scents, when he heard a strangled cry:

"No! No! *A-NO!!!* NO! NO!"

Bones lowered his nose and trotted in the direction of the police cars to investigate. What he saw when he arrived were two men tearing at the flesh of a third, a police officer in uniform, face down in the mud, struggling to get to his feet. It was at this moment that the officer managed to lift his head and see Bones.

"Bones!" the man cried.

Upon hearing his name, Bones snapped into action and ran towards the officer. As he did, the injuries he suffered on the road hammered on him with every step, but he still managed to close the distance in less than three seconds and clamped his jaws down onto the leg of one of the two men tearing at the fallen officer. The second he did so, the same scent of death he'd received when he'd bitten the old man in the Taurus filled his nostrils. If seventy percent of taste was smell, Bones's well-trained nose ratcheted that up to about eighty-five, making the grip he had on this man particularly unpleasant.

Though his intention was to drag the man off the officer, the sheer force of Bones's attack had done the job for him, shoving the cadaverous fellow back and smacking his head against the door of one of the squad cars. But no sooner had Bones done this than the man got back to his feet, raised his arms angrily at Bones, and let out a deep, angry, guttural growl from behind teeth hanging with bloody strips of flesh.

"*Gnnnnnnh…!!!*"

II

Bones had originally been trained as a police dog at a small facility outside of Las Cruces, New Mexico. Once he'd become a full member of the Doña Ana Sheriff's Department, he'd been used in exercises all up and down the U.S.-Mexico border by the local police in concert with the ATF, the INS, and the Border Patrol. The job primarily called for sniffing out drugs and illegals from cars and trucks at the Puerto de Anapra and Puerto Palomas border crossings. His secondary training as a cadaver dog was primarily utilized when anonymous calls about dead illegals out in the Chihuahuan Desert came in -- usually, it was believed, from the very coyotes who took them out there.

After a nationwide call went out for cadaver dogs needed in Allegheny County, Bones and his partner/trainer – an older fellow and longtime veteran of law enforcement named Lionel Oudin who had raised Bones from a pup – moved up to Pennsylvania. There, they went to work for the Pittsburgh Bureau of Police, doing double duty at the K-9 school attached to the training academy on Washington Boulevard (with plenty of heavy woods across the street for "extracurricular" training), and then assisting with homicide and missing persons cases across all six of Pittsburgh's new policing "zones." Only two years into the new position, Lionel took early retirement. When the department asked if they could keep Bones on ("Bones" being the name given to him by Lionel's now-grown daughter, Amy, despite most figuring it was a vocational nickname), Lionel said "yes" without a second thought. It wasn't as if he wouldn't miss his near-constant companion of almost seven years, but he knew how much Bones enjoyed his work and didn't think he'd adjust so well to sitting on a "doggie bed" all day watching the paint peel.

That's when Bones was introduced to Sergeant Billy Youman, only his second partner.

Billy couldn't have been more different from Lionel. Decades younger, unconcerned about his often slovenly appearance, and, counter-intuitively, something of a ladies' man though anyone in the department would be hard-pressed to describe one of Billy's typical Friday night hook-ups as a "lady." For Bones, Billy's smells were those of a late twenty-something man who sweated fast food and soft drinks, a 180 from Lionel, who patted his face with harsh-scented aftershave and preferred Latin American cuisine, which he'd taught himself to make in his own kitchen. When Bones first walked into Billy's apartment, he spent days giving every inch the nose-over. When they'd first come up to Pittsburgh, Lionel had rented an old house on the outskirts that had retained pungent smells going back its eighty years. Billy's apartment had been around for less than fifteen and smelled primarily of the pets that had come before Bones, as the complex was one of the few affordable buildings in that part of Polish Hill that allowed animals. The department paid the pet deposit, though it took Billy three months to push all the paperwork through.

Unlike an officer, whose schooling primarily ended at graduation from the Academy, aside from a few annual and required refresher courses along the way, Bones was constantly in training at the K-9 school. While these workouts were more to train future K-9 officers as well as to get regular cops comfortable and familiar with the K-9 units it might eventually have to work with, it served to keep Bones in an almost permanent state of readiness. He may have known the obstacle courses by heart, but when doing scent training, Billy and the other trainers made sure to change up the exercises to make it ever more difficult for Bones to discover his quarry. It had been decades since thieves rubbed ammonia on their shoes and tossed steaks to throw off police or guard dogs, and TV cop procedurals had taught a generation of criminals how better to cover their tracks.

Now the trick that impressed visitors to the K-9 school the most was watching Bones discover rotten meat that had been buried three or four feet *underwater*, something dogs were allegedly unable to do. Bones would slosh through the training pond, stand on the bank, and then run back and forth to try and catch even the faintest scent of his target long after any residual smell of the burial detail had evaporated. When he inevitably locked in on it and leaped back into the pond to mark the exact spot, the visitors' eyes would go wide, their jaws would drop, and they would applaud with the same fervor one might reserve for a virtuoso violin performance.

As part of his training, Bones had also learned the finer points of various takedown strategies. This meant grabbing a suspect at the wrists or ankles and holding them long enough for a human officer to arrive and make the arrest. Police dogs were not weapons, as usually the threat of a dangerous animal was all one needed in the enforcement of public order, the primary mandate of a K-9 unit. They weren't fight dogs, counter to the public perception, and were not trained to kill.

But Bones was different.

Almost immediately after Billy had taken over as Bones's handler, he saw evidence of the shepherd's feral instincts and tendencies lying just below the surface, something you wouldn't see cultivated in an otherwise domesticated animal. It seemed to him that Lionel had wanted to make it so that, in an emergency, Bones was like having a .38 in an ankle holster or a collapsible baton in a hidden pocket. It's not like Bones was some kind of ticking time bomb ready to explode at any moment, but Billy could tell there'd been some "auxiliary" training from the way Bones would react in this real-life situation or that. The thing was, it only made him feel more comfortable with his dog than less (as long as he never had to draw down against retired Sergeant Oudin, he'd joke to himself). If he ever had his back up against the wall and it was life- or death, he was confident that Bones would step in and defend him to the death.

But back out in front of the junkyard on Spur 790 about forty-five minutes north of Pittsburgh, the police man on the ground outside his cruiser in the mud and muck had no way of knowing this, which was why it came as a surprise when Bones had applied the canine equivalent of a forward tackle to the man who had been tearing at his flesh.

What was probably even more surprising, maybe even *terrifying*, was then watching as the same dog tore the man's hand off at the wrist, then proceeded to bite his neck in two. Terrifying, but useful, given the circumstance.

"Bones!! Over here!!" the officer cried, before thinking – for the briefest of instances – that Bones might mistake him for a target, too.

Bones turned away from the now-dead-a-second-time fellow and ran back towards the officer, grabbing his assailant at the ankle and dragging him off the young patrolman. Again, Bones sensed immediately that there was no fear in this man. A typical response to a police dog pulling at a person's foot was that the person whose foot it was would stop what they were doing, panic, and try to pull away from the dog, turning it into a game of tug-of-war, which Bones quite enjoyed and had the jaws to win. In this case, the man seemed to barely notice the dog and continued tearing at the officer's throat.

"*Bones!!!*" yelled the patrolman as the dead man's fingers, skin flayed to the point that they'd become sharp, skeletal pincers, punctured his windpipe while his teeth tore at his throat.

Bones finally managed to yank the man off the officer to the point that the attacker realized Bones was enough of an obstacle to what he was hoping to accomplish that he'd better deal with the dog first. The man turned and lunged at Bones with a feverish growl.

"*Grrraaaahhhh!!*"

This gave Bones the opening he wanted and he launched himself at the man's neck, repeating the quick, reflexive motion to sever the man's head, a move that was becoming surprisingly rote through its repetition. Still, the taste of dead flesh in Bones's mouth from the two men he'd just killed was abhorrent to him, the reason Billy had learned to just walk into a supermarket, pluck a steak straight out of the butcher's case, and feed it to Bones in the parking lot, blood and all. Fresh or the illusion of fresh was all Bones needed to be happy. Anything else was like eating paint.

"*Booonessssss...*" gurgled the mortally wounded patrolman. Blood drooled out of his mouth and throat as he called for a familiar face to look at, even if it was a dog's, while he died.

Bones wandered over and sniffed at the patrolman, who moved weakly, only to finally pass a few seconds later, his pupils quickly becoming fixed.

Filling his nose with his scent, Bones gave the face of the just-dead officer an optimistic lick, but there was no response. Though the scent of the living quickly became the scent of the dead, in the actual instant of death, it was relatively similar. So Bones continued giving the man's face and hands a couple of friendly, encouraging licks before the body began to cool and Bones recognized it as a corpse. Bones took a few steps back from the body, but that's when he heard a sound coming from the other side of the cars. A *snapping* sound, like a broken branch.

Bones padded around to the other side of the line of parked police vehicles and looked towards the junkyard. Just inside the gate, he saw a number of other people – men *and* women – tearing apart the dead flesh of the police officers who had gathered out here to search for the body of Tracy LeShoure. They all had the same death-stench as the men whose throats he'd just torn out.

Bones started barking, a sharp, alarm-filled bark that again was meant to call out to any other human who might respond to this and know what to do. This was what Bones was trained to do, sure, but it was also the instinct of a domesticated canine. Instead of feeling threatened, the flesh-eaters all turned towards Bones, eyeing him with unmistakable hunger. Intimidated, Bones jumped back just a step but then squared off against them to continue barking. The flesh-eaters, ten in all, gradually rose from the bodies they were devouring, and started moving towards Bones.

That's when Bones experienced something he hadn't felt in a lifetime: *fear.*

He kept barking and started prancing around on his injured legs like a giddy faun, but was unwilling to give ground. The flesh-eaters, some shambling, some at a half-jog, got closer and closer to Bones until it reached the point of fight or-flight, and he glanced towards the woods, marking his escape route. He'd just about made the decision to bolt when a pair of hands reached out from behind and grabbed at this throat.

Bones yelped and leaped away. When he turned back around, he saw the dead patrolman whose life he had defended only moments before now crawling towards him, teeth bared and hands outstretched. The patrolman looked purple and gray, as if blood had pooled in his face, and Bones knew from one sniff that he should be dead. But, of course, he was not.

Having had enough of this, Bones turned and launched himself towards the woods, only to find his path blocked by one of the other flesh-eaters, who managed to get close enough to half-grab, half-fall on the now-panicked cadaver dog. Though Bones quickly feinted and dodged the attack, the falling flesh-eater landed on his injured right haunch, causing the shepherd to twist it badly. As Bones scrambled to get to his feet, he found himself boxed in. Two more flesh-eaters came around the back of the line of police vehicles and effectively flanked any escape Bones could make. He had nowhere to run.

Tail between his legs and the fight-or-flight decision now made for him, Bones turned towards the nearest flesh-eaters, flattened his ears to his skull, and began to growl a warning, long, low, and increasing in volume, leading up to a savage bark. This did nothing to dissuade the flesh-eaters, and the largest of them lunged for Bones...

BLAM!!

When it was merely inches away from Bones's neck, the large flesh-eater hit the ground and didn't move. Bones, unaware of what had driven it into the mud, immediately went for its throat, only to find that it was now permanently dead, having been shot directly in the forehead. Bones whirled around as the other flesh-eaters moved closer to him, ignoring the fate of the first-mover. Just as quickly, they joined him face down in the muck as the gunfire continued.

Like tin ducks in a carnival shooting gallery, every last one of the flesh-eaters tumbled to the ground, blood splashing out of wounds from a couple of them but noticeably absent from others, particularly those in greater states of decay. Bones had to skirt and dive to avoid all of the falling bodies, but then he found himself alone.

Click.

Though the odor of fresh corpses was heavy in the air, Bones quickly picked out the scents of living people and turned towards the woods, where he saw a trio of human males emerge carrying hunting rifles: a stout middle-aged man with wisps of brown-gray hair over his ears; a pale, skinny, blond-headed teenager wearing a green John Deere ball cap; and a second, shorter, brown-haired boy with an open, trusting face who couldn't have been more than nine or ten. The middle-aged man raised his rifle and aimed it at Bones, but the teenager shook his head.

"I don't think he's one of 'em, Mr. Arthur."

The middle-aged man – Mr. Arthur - eyed Bones carefully but didn't lower his rifle.

"Be that as it may, he's still a wild dog," the man said. "Good chance he'll try and attack us anyway. He looks pretty spooked."

Bones, still panicked, started barking, which did little to help his cause. Mr. Arthur took one step closer to get a better shot, but then the younger boy moved in front of him, setting down his gun as he walked.

"Ryan!" the teenager cried. "Don't be stupid!"

But the youngster – Ryan - kept coming, dropping to one knee when he was about eight feet away from Bones. He stared at the shepherd for a moment, his eyes traveling to the bright black-and-yellow collar around his neck.

"I think he's a police dog," said Ryan. "You can get in a lot of trouble shooting a police dog."

Bones noted the semi-relaxed expression on the little boy's face as he stuck out his hand, inviting the dog to come over and take a sniff. Bones was still pretty agitated but found the solemnity of the child calming. Besides, he knew the child didn't smell of death and, under the circumstances, thought this was a good sign. He took a couple of tentative steps forward, climbing past one of the twice-dead flesh-eaters, and took a sniff of Ryan's hand. He snorted once as if having inhaled pollen, then took a step back and peered into the boy's eyes.

"You're okay, boy," Ryan said, rising and slowly reaching for Bones's head. "You're okay."

Bones allowed the boy to stroke the hair between his ears, though it was matted with wet earth and blood. Bones ran his nose up and down the little boy as well, inhaling a healthy odor of blood, from what seemed like a host of different human sources. It was on his shoes and jeans and blended with the distinct smell of dried urine coming from inside his pants, creating a record of the past few hours of the boys' life as it wafted into Bones's olfactory canal.

As Mr. Arthur and the teenaged boy walked over, Ryan eyed the collar around Bones's neck.

"Is your name Bones?" Ryan asked. Bones looked up upon hearing his name, and the little boy smiled, turning to his human compatriots. "He's a K-9 officer of the Pittsburgh Bureau of Police."

"And he's the only one that survived this?" Mr. Arthur said. "Doesn't say much for our chances. Jesse – see if there's anything worth having in any of these police cars. Shit, where were these assholes a couple of hours ago?"

The teenager, Jesse, ran to the different squad cars and saw that they were, for the most part, unlocked. "They've got shotguns, but they're all racked in. Keys must be in their pockets."

"Make sure you give each of them a couple of slugs to the head before you get too close," said Mr. Arthur, walking over to the patrolman who had tried to grab Bones. "Looks like this one's got a Heckler & Koch 9-millimeter. Our tax dollars at work."

Mr. Arthur reached down and secured the man's weapon, placing it in his belt, and then grabbed a couple of extra magazines and the man's handcuffs. He couldn't find the cuff keys but kept the cuffs anyway.

Bones moved away from the hunting party and walked back towards the junkyard where the bodies of Detective Nessler and Commander Zusak were lying, just beside the trailer home that served as the yard's office. Zusak's head had been torn clean off, his weapon still in his hand, though much of the rest of his body had been devoured. Nessler, on the other hand, looked perfectly normal, almost as if he had just lain down for a nap -- unless you looked below his shoulders or above his belly button, as his entire chest had been hollowed out by the flesh-eaters who had snapped through his ribcage and torn out his heart, liver, lungs, kidneys, and intestines.

The flesh-eaters had dug through his torso so viciously that claw marks could be seen in the mud under the body, as if they had believed there was even more of Nessler that had somehow sluiced into the ground on which he was lying. Just as Bones began to move away, he caught sight of Nessler's fingers flexing and his eyes glancing around.

Immediately, Bones jumped back and started barking. Ryan, noticing the same thing, stepped forward, aimed his rifle at Nessler's head, and fired.

Ryan's gun was a single-shot, bolt-action .22, so he could only fire one bullet at a time, since a metal plate had been screwed over the slot where a magazine would be placed; a child's training rifle. As soon as he had fired, Ryan pulled back the bolt, ejected the spent shell, and inserted a bullet from his pocket that he jammed with his pointer finger into the breach. Once it was snug, he pushed the bolt forward, chambering the round, and locked down the bolt handle. He aimed for Nessler's head and fired a second time, his reload time being less than four seconds.

The impact of the second bullet caused Nessler's skull to fragment, sending pieces of cracked bone in a number of different directions while the rest of his life's blood slipped away into the mud. Bones had continued to bark at Nessler throughout all this and kept at it even as Ryan moved away.

"C'mon, Bones," called Ryan.

Bones barked a few more times at the dead detective but then followed Ryan back out of the junkyard and over to one of the squad cars. Jesse was trying different keys on a shotgun's trigger guard, having freed it from the driver's-seat gun rack. He finally wiggled the key in just right, and the troublesome guard snapped off. After all that, when he checked the breach of the shotgun, he found it unloaded.

"Cops are such *pussies*," Jesse scoffed, reaching for a box of shells he'd earlier uncovered in the driver's seat armrest. He proceeded to load the shotgun with shells and prime a round into the chamber. The cinematic kla-*klack* of the forestock made Jesse smile. "Let's see them come at us now!"

Mr. Arthur came around the car after walking off a perimeter and only offered the teenager a bemused grimace. He'd been through too much that morning for shows of bravado.

Bones padded around in a semi-circle a little ways away from Ryan, keeping his nose in the air. All he could smell was the dead, and he was having a hard time differentiating between the corpses that lay all around him on the ground and any more of the flesh-eaters that might emerge from the junkyard or woods. Still, he kept trying, pacing in circles and sniffing the air.

Once it looked like they'd collected anything useful from the police cars, Mr. Arthur nodded to the boys.

"We should keep heading towards the highway," he said. "We just have to flag somebody down and get into the city."

"But if these guys were already out this far, don't you think they'd have reached Gainey by now?" Jesse asked, indicating the pile of dead flesh-eaters. "That's right in our path."

"It's unfortunate for them, but these cops probably slowed them down a bit," Mr. Arthur suggested. "They're not going in a straight line. They're running into people on the road, people on the farms, and each time, well...taking their own sweet time at the trough."

Jesse nodded silently, as if recalling a troubling thought. Mr. Arthur recognized this and didn't continue along this train of thought.

"Come on, now," Mr. Arthur said, indicating for the boys to follow him. "Time's a'wastin'."

Ryan walked up alongside Jesse but then glanced back at Bones, who was still sniffing around the police cars.

"Come on, Bones. You'll be a lot safer if you come with us."

Bones watched the three humans walk away and knew he didn't want to be left behind. He trotted after them, quickly pulling up the rear, though his right haunch still caused him to limp, which was made worse by the soft mud. Every time one of Bones's left feet sank into the muck, he reflexively caught himself with his right haunch for balance, sending a shooting pain through his entire body. When he yelped the first time – really, more of a "yip" than a full cry – Mr. Arthur turned, scowling.

"*Shh!* Quiet, dog."

Bones knew what "shh" meant and moved along in silence, a little more gingerly now.

III

It was only a few minutes' walk before the three spotted a thin plume of black smoke rising into the sky up ahead. Mr. Arthur indicated for the boys and Bones to move off the road, closer to the woods to avoid being seen, but when they got down to the wreck of Billy's truck and the beige Taurus, he relaxed again.

"Pheeew-eee!" Mr. Arthur said as he walked around the smoldering cars and dead bodies, including that of the old man whose throat Bones had torn out. He turned to the shepherd, a little surprised. "Your handiwork?"

Bones looked up, as if confirming Mr. Arthur's suspicions.

"Who is that?" Jesse asked, peering at the body. "I think I recognize him."

"Charles Harvey!" Mr. Arthur reported with what sounded like satisfaction after he took a closer look. "One of the assholes-in-chief of the local HUD branch. Loved to screw with people by executing foreclosures first thing in the morning before most people even had their coffee."

But then, Mr. Arthur's face changed as he looked into the front seat of the Taurus.

"Hell," he muttered. "Means that's probably his daughter, Joyce. She was every bit the peach he wasn't. Sorry, darling."

Meanwhile, Bones was sniffing around Billy's truck, but the smell of his one-time master had all but vanished, as the fire had not only cooked him but also the vinyl upholstery, which obfuscated all other scents. Ryan followed Bones around the side of the immolated Bronco and saw the official police markings as well as the "K-9 Unit" designation on the wrecked door. He could just make out enough of the remains of Billy Youman in the driver's seat to realize there had been a person there at all. He nodded to the police dog.

"I'm sorry, Bones. He was your master?"

This time, Bones didn't turn when he heard his name. He completed his sniff-around of the truck and then moved away to sit in the nearby grass.

Mr. Arthur looked up and down the highway, scanning for vehicles, seeing none. Overhead, a jumbo jet flew in a northeasterly direction, leaving no contrails in the gray sky, the only sign of life.

"Guess we have to hoof it for now," said Mr. Arthur. "The good news is it might mean word's gotten out and traffic's been blocked from coming out of the city."

"And back there?" Jesse asked, pointing in the direction they'd come in from.

Mr. Arthur shook his head. "If we see a car coming from that way, I think we find a good firing position in the woods and take steady aim."

The group began moving down the shoulder of the highway, Bones walking a line between the paved shoulder and the grassy, gravel-strewn fringe that bled out to the neighboring woods. He kept his nose to the air, though they were walking into the breeze, making it easier on anyone coming up behind them. Even so, Bones's ears, while nowhere near as perceptive as his nose, were still sharp enough to hear a twig snap anywhere within a fifty- to sixty-yard radius, and in his heightened, hunting state, Bones was listening for just that.

The farther they walked, though, the more Mr. Arthur nervously glanced behind them, as if needing to be constantly reassured that they weren't being followed. Even though they appeared to be well in the clear, it was obvious he wasn't going to feel safe any time soon. Jesse seemed to be similarly nervous but drew a lot of confidence from the rifle clutched tightly in his right hand and the shotgun clutched in his left. Ryan, for his part, gained the same feeling from his proximity to Bones.

"That looks like it hurts," Ryan said, eyeing Bones's beaten-up face. Bones glanced at Ryan but then looked back ahead, whiskers twirling a little in the breeze. "They killed my dog. She was just trying to keep them from getting in our house, but they got her. It was one the neighbors. After they came in through the door, the lady-one bit her in the neck. Then they got in the kitchen and then the bathroom and they got my mom and my sister…"

By the time Ryan said this last part, his voice was quivering. Jesse saw this and walked over, giving him a kind of half-hug, half-nudge.

"Enough of that," said Jesse. "You know who got out? *You.* Now, you've got a reason to revenge yourself on these assholes. Keep that anger in you. It'll keep you alive, man."

Ryan nodded, but half-heartedly. Bones looked back at Ryan again, but halfway through the motion he noticed Mr. Arthur stopping in his tracks.

"Boys."

Jesse and Ryan followed Mr. Arthur's gaze and saw a large farmhouse appearing up on the left. Very quickly, everything got quiet.

"Think they'd have come this way?" asked Jesse.

"No telling," replied Mr. Arthur, seeing no sign of life at the farm. "If they'd come through the woods…"

Mr. Arthur looked over at Bones, who had also gone completely still. His nose pointed straight ahead, and it was obvious that the German shepherd had picked up on at least something from the farmhouse, though what was unclear. Bones took a tentative step forward, as if stalking some newly detected prey, his ears straight up and down, his shoulders rigidly upright and squared towards the house.

"What is it, boy?" Mr. Arthur whispered, tightening his grip on his gun.

Suddenly, the woods just beyond the farmhouse erupted with muzzle flash. Leaves were clipped, branches snapped, and bullets began splashing against the gravel and asphalt around Mr. Arthur and the boys.

"Shit!" cried Mr. Arthur as a bullet winged his left tricep. "Get down, boys!!"

Jesse tried to hit the deck but immediately caught two bullets, one in the calf, one in the elbow, and screamed as he was thrown back.

Ryan managed to flatten himself on the ground as Bones bounced around, barking like mad at the incoming fire. Amazingly, he wasn't hit.

"What the *fuck!?!*" screamed Mr. Arthur from his prone position on the road. "We're *human*, you assholes!!"

The fusillade kept coming, though, and it was a full ten seconds before it finally abated. As the trio stayed on the ground, trying to catch their breaths, a voice came booming out of the woods, amplified by a bullhorn.

"Toss your weapons away and stay on the ground! Move an inch, and we won't hesitate to shoot."

Mr. Arthur did as he was told, pushing his rifle away from him. Ryan did the same, but a quick glance back at Jesse suggested he was already halfway into shock and couldn't be made to do a thing. Luckily, his rifle had been thrown a few feet away after the first bullet hit, and the shotgun was momentarily obscured behind his body.

"All right! We're unarmed!" yelled Mr. Arthur. "You've got an injured child over here. Maybe two."

A group of black-clad, helmet-and-gas-mask-wearing SWAT team members emerged from the woods, guns aimed at the little group of survivors. An oddly shaped gun was aimed at Bones, who continued barking at the approaching officers, standing his ground between them and Ryan. The team leader nodded at the man with the gun.

"Knock him down."

The gunman nodded, stared down the iron sight at Bones, and *fired*.

"*No!!*" cried Ryan, but the rubber bullet was already in flight, smashing Bones in the shoulder before Ryan had finished shouting. Bones smacked into the ground and rolled over but was getting ready to jump right back up as if it was nothing when a second officer with an animal-control pole and lanyard raced over and tossed the loop around Bones's neck. As he pulled it tight, like a noose, a second officer looked over and stopped short.

"Bones?" said a voice filtered through layers of plastic and charcoal.

But Bones was already back on his feet, gnashing at his tether as the officer at the other end of the pole kept the shepherd at a distance, prodding him ahead by what now looked like a spear jutting out of his neck. The officer who had recognized Bones walked over and took the pole away from the other officer.

"It's okay," he said. "I've got this."

The pole officer bent to one knee, keeping Bones at a distance but inviting him to look his way.

"Bones? *Bones.* Hey, boy."

Bones, giving the air a sniff, managed to ignore the leash long enough to manifest some sort of recognition. The cop pulled the pole closer to him, allowing Bones to get within a foot.

"Bones, hey," the officer said, raising a hand to his gas mask, as if to take it off. "I'm a friend. We're on the same team. We trained together."

"You keep that mask on, Purnell!" cried the team leader, a little incredulous.

"Yeah, sergeant – I forgot," the officer – Purnell - said but then waved the sergeant over. "But sir, this is *Bones*. He's Billy Youman's better half in the K-9 unit."

"No shit?" grunted the sergeant. "Guess we know what happened to Commander Zusak and the others out on 790, then."

Mr. Arthur stared up at the men as they checked him over for additional weapons.

"You can quit with the stormtrooper act now," he grunted, though he was still in pain. "You can see we're not one of them."

"One of who?" asked the sergeant, as if having not a clue what Mr. Arthur could be referring to.

"Do I have to spell it out for you?" grunted Mr. Arthur. "Come on. You've seen a movie, read a comic book or two. You got cannibalistic dead guys running around the western Pennsylvania countryside."

"Sir, all we know is that we're dealing with an outbreak here," the sergeant replied. "For all we know, the three of you and maybe the dog, too, are infected."

"Are you kidding me?" asked Mr. Arthur as a medic bandaged his wound. "There's a big damn difference between me – *us* – and what we've been fighting out here all morning while you assholes sat on each other's dicks. Do I look dead to you?"

"At present, you may be merely a carrier, but should your 'status' change, you would express the characteristics of what we're currently labeling the 'Stage 2,'" the sergeant explained.

"Oh, you say that like it wasn't almost you guys who just about changed my 'status,'" Mr. Arthur bellowed. "So I guess if you'd shot me dead and then I'd gotten up and run over there to bite your head off, that would've been considered what – friendly fire? I'm sure you would've gotten a medal for it, but you'd still be dead."

The sergeant stared at Mr. Arthur through the shaded black eye holes of the gas mask and shook his head angrily.

"Sir, we probably have less of an idea of what we're dealing with out here than you do. You three are the first survivors we've come in contact with, and we have our orders. I'm sorry if that conflicts with your idea of due process, but right now, 'containment' is taking precedence. Maybe you'll come around to understanding that."

With that, the sergeant turned and headed away, deciding there was no need for further debate. Officer Purnell watched this exchange with a satisfied grin but then turned back to Bones, discreetly taking off one of his gloves and giving Bones a pat.

"You've probably been through hell, huh, boy?" Purnell said. "Shit, man. Bet this means Billy's bought it, huh? He wasn't too bad a guy."

Bones gave Purnell's hand a friendly lick. Ryan, being led towards the farmhouse alongside a patched-up Jesse, saw Bones and cried out. "That's *my* dog, you jerk!"

Purnell was a little startled by this outburst but then sighed as Ryan scowled at him. He shook his head as he turned back to Bones, stroking him between the ears.

"Sorry, kid," he said, though out of earshot. "But this guy's property of the Pittsburgh Bureau of Police. You'll just have to find another."

IV

Ten minutes later, a pair of police vehicles drove away from the farmhouse and headed back down the highway in the same direction Mr. Arthur, the boys, and Bones had just been going, only now they were in custody. Bones rode in the back seat of the lead vehicle, a patrol car driven by Officer Purnell, while Jesse, Ryan, and Mr. Arthur were stuck in the back of a paddy wagon, driven by a pair of SWAT officers with a third riding in back with the "prisoners." The convoy was making good time, as both lanes of the highway were clear. Purnell set the pace up around eighty miles per hour and kept it there.

When Bones climbed into the back of the car, he had lain down almost immediately, exhausted. Purnell poured a little water from a plastic bottle into a Styrofoam cup that he tore the top half off in order to create a small bowl, which Bones promptly drained in one gulp. Purnell emptied the rest of the bottle into the cup and snagged a second one, continuing the routine until Bones had drunk his fill.

"Now you're going to have to hold it all the way to the city," Purnell joked from the front seat as they hurtled down the highway. "Think you'll be okay?"

Despite his fatigue, Bones was too keyed up to fall asleep and eyed Purnell through the steel-cage prisoner partition as they drove. Purnell grinned at the dog in the rearview, but then his nose inhaled a big whiff of wet dog.

"Jeezus!" Purnell exclaimed. "No offense, Bones, but you smell like you're carrying about three miles of bad road in your coat back there." Bones didn't look offended. Purnell reached over to the dashboard and fiddled around with the air conditioner, switching it from closed to open circulation to bring in fresh air from outside.

Two seconds after the first outside air swept into the car, Bones leaped to his feet, his nose bouncing up in down in every direction as he looked all around. A second later, he started to bark, loudly and forcefully.

"Bones!!" cried Purnell, a little alarmed. "What the hell?! Have you gone crazy back there? Quiet down!"

But Bones continued barking, sounding panicked now.

"What's gotten into you?" Purnell asked, glancing back at the antsy German shepherd. But then, he turned back around in time to see precisely what had been troubling Bones's nose. "Oh, *shit…*"

Like rising floodwaters, a vast horde of flesh-eaters, easily numbering in the hundreds, poured out of the woods on both sides of the highway and launched themselves at the convoy. A slow-moving vise, the monsters massed towards the vehicles in a collapsing V-formation until they completely blocked the road.

"Jesus Christ!!!" Purnell said, instinctively spinning the wheel to avoid the attackers, but as they were suddenly everywhere, it only served to skid the car into the flesh-eaters at an odd angle, causing them to go flying as they bounced off the hood, roof, and windshield like bowling pins.

Purnell finally managed to slam on the brakes, stopping the car dead in the middle of the highway, the sudden halt throwing Bones off the seat. Behind him, the paddy wagon did the same, screeching to a stop about ten feet behind Bones and Purnell. The flesh-eaters immediately threw themselves against both vehicles as Purnell made a mad scramble for the door locks. Finding them secure, he grabbed the radio.

"Charlie, Purnell," he cried, trying not to sound as frantic as he felt. "You guys all right in there?"

He craned his neck around, seeing the driver of the paddy wagon – Charlie - reaching for the radio as he signaled Purnell from behind the reinforced windshield.

"Yeah, still in one piece," came Charlie's voice, crackling over the speaker. "The vehicles are secure, but I'm not sure what the play is here. These are citizens of the Commonwealth of Pennsylvania. If we start mowing them down and there turns out to be some kind of cure, we're suddenly Katrina doctors euthanizing patients."

Purnell snorted but figured the same thing.

"Besides," Charlie continued. "We roll over too many of them, and we'll start losing our tires."

Purnell laughed at this, his voice as jittery with adrenaline as Charlie's, but then replied, "Yeah, this wasn't exactly in the *Patrol Guide*, so whatever we do, we're the ones whose asses are on the line. Look, I'll radio the sergeant back at the command post and at least let them know they've been flanked even if they don't know it yet. Should keep them from sending anybody else back down this road."

"Sounds good," squawked Charlie on the radio, his voice almost washed out by the sounds of flesh-eaters pounding on either side of the paddy wagon.

"One question – we have any idea who all these people are?" asked Purnell.

Charlie sounded ready to answer with a verbal shrug when Purnell heard another voice from inside Charlie's wagon, which spoke for a few seconds. Then Charlie came back on the radio, sounding incredulous.

"One of the residents of Duncan we've got on board said he thinks it's the entire town of Gainey," said the paddy wagon driver. "Said he recognizes one or two of them. One had on a booster T-shirt for the high school soccer girls soccer team, if you can believe it."

Purnell flipped on his GPS and toggled around until he found Gainey, only a few miles away.

"Gainey's a little south, then directly east of here," Purnell exclaimed. "Christ, there's no telling how far they've gotten *and* all on foot. This is why we have to get some air support up here. We're going to be telling our grandkids about this day."

"Yeah," came Charlie's reply, as if momentarily uncertain whether "grandchildren" were still in his future.

Bones continued barking as the flesh-eaters pounded on the doors and the windows, though they hadn't managed to even chip the reinforced-glass windows or dent the riot-proof roof. Still, the constant battering was driving the shepherd nuts, and his barks now included actual strikes, biting into the air at invisible targets.

"All right, my dog's going cocoa-bananas in here," Purnell said. "I'll give you a horn honk if there's any kind of break in the flood, but maybe the play here is we just have to wait it out. They're going to get tired of this at some point, right? Over and out."

Purnell hung the radio mic on its hook and waved back at Charlie, who nodded from the paddy wagon. Purnell then turned back to the undulating mass of flesh-eaters squashing themselves up against the windows of the patrol car.

"Jesus Christ," he said, getting a much more close-up view of the creatures than he was comfortable with, but then he noticed something *different.*

That morning, Purnell had come out with the rest of the SWAT unit with little knowledge in the way of what was actually going on out in north Allegheny County, but after they'd encountered an entire family of flesh-eaters in the farmhouse, his team had wised up fast. What he was looking at here wasn't the same thing. The flesh-eaters back at the farm were clearly dead, some gravely wounded, others in various states of decay. The ones he was looking at now were oozing a greenish-black suppuration through reddish-brown sores that appeared all over their skin, something he figured he would have remembered seeing earlier. It was a gruesome sight, but what made it even worse was seeing that this grotesque substance was acting as a sort of adhesive, gluing together various parts of the flesh-eaters when they got too close to one another.

Well, was "gluing" the right word? It looked more like a scab, as if the substance was excreted from one body to scab over an open wound on another, but then they were stuck together. Purnell saw one trio that appeared to almost be a single organism, though each of the three bodies was trying to push and pull it in different directions.

He had the presence of mind to reach into his pocket, pull out his camera phone, and take a couple of photographs of the difference.

"Nasty," he exclaimed, looking at the pictures on the phone.

He tried to e-mail them back to the SWAT forward command post – specifically to his closest friend on the team, a guy named Sobel, who he thought would know the right person to forward them to, but there wasn't enough of a signal for them to go through. Giving up, Purnell just sank back into his seat with a sigh, wondering how long they were going to be stuck there.

In the back seat, Bones continued to bark at the many faces that pressed themselves against the windows, some baring their teeth in a mawkish way. As he kept it up, his voice became weaker and weaker as the day's events took a toll.

"C'mon, Bones," Purnell said. "You're not doing yourself any good, and these guys sure don't seem to care."

Whump.

This was the second time in one day that one of Bones's handlers was interrupted by a hit to the side of their vehicle, though this one with far less fatal results. Purnell was slammed against the steering wheel and Bones jolted against the back of the front seat as a sudden surge of bodies rammed into the front of the patrol car with great force.

"Fuck! What are they doing?" Purnell yelled, jamming down the parking brake.

The shapeless mass struck the car again with such force that Purnell found himself scanning the bodies in front of the car, figuring they must have a makeshift battering ram hidden amongst their number. The parking brake continued to hold the car in place, but Purnell didn't know for how much longer that would be the case. The radio buzzed to life.

"Purnell, what the hell are they doing to your car?"

"I don't know," Purnell radioed back. "Whatever it is, it's not going to work. They're just going to pound themselves flat."

This time, the flesh-eaters' impact was such that the mic tumbled out of Purnell's hand and landed on the floor of the vehicle. As he reached down to pick it up, he felt the car beginning to shift not backwards but sideways on the road.

Then rise up.

This time, the car buckled as it bounced upwards a good two or three feet, as if being carried off by a flash flood. Purnell and Bones were suddenly up over the action, the attacks having been used to get the bodies of flesh-eaters under the wheels of the car, which then bucked upwards like a primitive hydraulic jack.

"Fuck!! What the hell?" Purnell cried, the car rising and falling like a boat on the ocean. "Are they trying to carry us off somewhere? This is nuts!"

In the back seat, Bones began barking like mad. At first, Purnell thought this was out of surprise and fear, but when he looked back at the shepherd, he saw that Bones was no longer barking at the windows but straight down at the floorboards.

"Bones?" Purnell asked, sobering. "What is it?"

Bones's bark became a growl as the sounds of dozens of hands tapping around the undercarriage of the car became audible. In the front seat, Purnell stared down at the steel floorboards and blanched as he heard the piercing *scccrrrreeeeeecccchhhh* of tearing metal.

"Oh, *shit!*"

Purnell yanked his 9mm from his holster as the floor of the passenger side was ripped downwards and away. A bloody-faced flesh-eater appeared in the empty space just below it, the creature's mouth looking like it had taken a shotgun blast, which is how Purnell realized that the bottom of his car hadn't been torn away by fingers alone but also teeth. Purnell aimed his pistol at the flesh-eater and blasted it twice in the forehead.

BLAM-BLAM!

"FUCK!!!" Purnell screamed as the body fell away. He grabbed the radio mic and hit the button. "They're coming in through the floor of the car!"

Another flesh-eater popped its head up through the floorboard, and Purnell shot that one in the head, too, and then returned to the radio.

"You hearing me over there?" Purnell cried as he looked back towards the paddy wagon in the rearview. "They must have been testing every part of the car until they found a weak spot."

As the squad car rocked back and forth, Purnell looked back and saw that the flesh-eaters were shaking the paddy wagon as well, the van tilting like a jetty in rough seas.

"I think they're getting under us over here, too!" cried Charlie over the radio, his voice sounding dangerous, like he was losing it. Purnell could hear a familiar *tink-tink-tink* in the background and then Charlie screamed, "Shit – they're coming up!"

This sound was followed by a couple of gunshots before Charlie took his finger off the button. Purnell looked back towards the paddy wagon and watched as Charlie fired it up and slammed on the gas out of panic.

"Oh, crap!" Purnell cried, trying to turn on his own car, but it was too late.

CRUNCH!!!

The paddy wagon *slammed* into the back of the patrol car, decapitating a flesh-eater just as it was lunging at Paul, the torn floorboard flying forward just under its chin at the right angle.

"Shit!" Purnell yelled again as he smacked into the steering wheel.

In the back, Bones watched as hands viciously tore at the back seat floorboard. The smell of leaking oil and gasoline heavy in the air, a flesh-eater's face appeared, and Bones instinctively launched himself at it, locking his jaws at either temple and working to tear the head clean off the body.

In the front seat, Purnell tried to get the patrol car to start, but too many of its vitals were now lying on the highway. Cursing, he grabbed the radio, but then saw in the rearview mirror that Charlie was still dazed from bashing his head into the steering wheel after plowing the wagon into the rear of the squad car.

"Charlie – get it together!" Purnell roared. "Come on, man! They're just waiting for us to give 'em an opening!"

But as Purnell watched, something yanked Charlie out of his daze and he looked down, as if realizing there was something below him. Charlie and the officer in the passenger-side seat snapped into action and began fighting against the unseen assailants. Purnell even saw a couple of muzzle flashes before both men were yanked below the dashboard and disappeared under the car. Seconds later, he saw the flesh-eaters carting Charlie's body away from the paddy wagon, literally tearing him apart as they walked.

"Aw, man, Charlie," Purnell exclaimed, disgusted at what he realized might soon be his own fate. He turned back to Bones, who continued lunging at any flesh-eater that popped through the back floorboards, his teeth bared.

"I'm sorry, Bones, but I don't think we're going to get out of this one," Purnell said, unlocking the shotgun from its rack and sliding it down off the muzzle plug. "If you see an opening, take it, buddy."

He loaded the shotgun and aimed it at the passenger-side floorboard as flesh-eaters tried to squirm up into the hole but only got in each other's way. When the larger of the two forced the other aside and popped up, Purnell took satisfaction in rewarding it by blasting its head to pieces.

For Charlie, he thought.

But then he began to feel movement under his own feet, fingers rapping, drumming, and scratching at the metal plates, looking for any edge to get a finger-hold on. Purnell quickly lifted his feet from the floor and scrambled up on his seat, aiming the shotgun straight down between his legs.

"C'mon, you fuckers," Purnell said, training the barrel of the gun directly at the sound but knowing one blast wouldn't do much good.

Suddenly, a flesh-eater launched itself up from the hole in the passenger side and managed to grab Purnell's foot, yanking him to the side with great force, which smashed the back of Purnell's head into the driver's-side window. Stunned, he wheeled the shotgun around and fired in a panic.

BLAM!!

But at the last moment, the flesh-eater had jerked Purnell's leg to the side, trying to get a better grip to drag him under. This had the effect of pulling his leg directly into the shot pattern as it left the barrel, the blast instantly shredding his boot, pant leg, and flesh, all the way to the bone.

"*Gaaaaah!!!!!*" Purnell screamed, his face contorted in pain. "Fuck!!"

Emboldened by this, the flesh-eater, who only received a couple of shot pellets in the cheek, immediately sank his teeth into Purnell's exposed, blood-soaked calf.

"*Aaaaahhh...*" This time, Purnell's cry tapered off to a whimper, his teeth gritting in agony. "*Shiiit.*"

With great difficulty, he primed the shotgun, placed the barrel against the flesh-eater's forehead as it gnawed on his calf, and pulled the trigger.

BLAM!!

As the flesh-eater instantly fell away, the patrol car began to quake again.

"Oh, God," whimpered Purnell, who grabbed for the nearest seatbelt.

A few seconds later, the entire vehicle was jerked skyward by a large collection of flesh-eaters and rolled over first onto its side, then onto its roof, dog and man going flying. It finally crashed down on asphalt and flesh-eater alike, the roof lights exploding in a hail of plastic and glass. With the floorboards suddenly facing skyward, the flesh-eaters momentarily fell away to regroup and remember that their creatures inside were still accessible, just from above now instead of below.

Inside the car, Purnell was lying in a fetal position on the ceiling of his own car and turned to see Bones, who was already back on his feet after being knocked over. The dog's eyes met his through the prisoner partition cage, and Purnell just shook his head.

"This is that opening, dickhead," Purnell grunted, indicating the ripped-out floorboards. "Get out of here."

Bones was up and out of the hole before Purnell even finished his sentence. Once atop the overturned patrol car, Bones looked back towards the damaged paddy wagon, seeing the literally hundreds of flesh-eaters working to knock the wagon on its side as well. They finally managed to get it high enough off one side's tires and then...

WHAM!!

As soon as the paddy wagon smashed down on its side, the flesh-eaters began tearing apart its undercarriage. The few flesh-eaters that had been climbing on top of the overturned patrol car were momentarily distracted by the activity at the paddy wagon and Bones looked away to the nearby woods. He was about to race away when:

"Bones!!!"

Bones's ears pricked up as he heard his name coming from inside the overturned paddy wagon. Over the din of the flesh-eaters, Bones could hear a loud, metallic banging coming from within the wagon. Then, a second:

"Bones!!"

The shepherd launched himself off the patrol car, landing in the middle of the flesh-eaters. He quickly raced around to the back of the paddy wagon, slipping through the legs of the flesh-eaters so quickly they didn't have time to make a grab for him.

When Bones reached the paddy wagon, he saw that the twin doors in back had bowed outwards when it was slammed to the ground, cracking them off their hinges. From inside, Mr. Arthur was trying to kick the doors off or at least bend them enough so that he, Jesse, Ryan, and what appeared to be an additional SWAT team member lucky enough not to have been in the cab could get out. The officer looked like he had taken a pretty bad fall when the truck toppled and was currently too out of it to be of any use to Mr. Arthur.

As Mr. Arthur kicked at the doors, a flesh-eater launched itself at him through the narrow space he'd been trying to expand with his kicking.

"Fuck!" he gasped, horrified, and reached for the SWAT officer's automatic rifle. He wheeled it around as the flesh-eater pulled himself into the van, only to be immediately yanked back out from behind. Mr. Arthur squinted through the broken doors in time to see Bones moving his jaws from the dead man's thighs up to his larynx, which he promptly tore out.

Mr. Arthur exhaled a quick sigh of relief and then bent the doors the rest of the way open with his hands before launching himself out onto the asphalt, rolling over, and getting back to his feet. Finding himself completely surrounded by flesh-eaters that appeared surprised at the sudden appearance of a living being in their midst, he smiled, clicked the safety off the rifle and began drilling each of the nearby flesh-eaters in the head.

"Fuckers!!!" he screamed, for good measure. As a couple dozen twice-dead flesh-eaters were blasted back onto the others of their number, causing many to pivot over like dominos, Mr. Arthur turned the machine gun towards the woods and began blasting an escape path through the shambling undead.

As another six flesh-eaters ate asphalt, Mr. Arthur put in a fresh clip, now satisfied that he could use the gun to create a reasonably safe retreat. He turned and nodded at the rest of the paddy wagon passengers, who were watching him from the cracked doors.

"Gotta go while the going's good!" he cried. "Come on!

Ryan nodded to him and helped the injured Jesse get out through the hole, followed by the dazed SWAT officer, who still looked like he wasn't quite sure where he was or what was happening. When he finally looked up and saw the sea of swaying flesh-eaters, his body tensed with dread.

"Oh, God," he cried, stumbling to the asphalt, only just able to catch himself with his hands. Unfortunately, both hands landed squarely in the bilious muck that had exploded out of the head of one of Mr. Arthur's most recent victims.

"We've just got to reach the woods," cried Mr. Arthur, pausing to let Ryan and Jesse catch up. "Then we'll be safe!"

With the rifle at shoulder level now, the din in his ears tremendous, Mr. Arthur blazed as best a trail through the flesh-eaters as he could to the forest, mowing them down with a series of well-aimed, semi-automatic headshots. Soon the woods were only about twenty feet away.

"Bones!" called Ryan, suddenly noticing that the police dog wasn't with them. "Come on, boy!"

Bones, who had been busy tearing the leg off a nearby flesh-eater, saw that Ryan and the others were retreating and galloped ahead to join Mr. Arthur.

Pulling up the rear, the SWAT officer had worked a collapsible baton out of his pocket and was viciously beating away his would-be devourers. Though he wasn't landing all kill shots, some of the strikes had the effect of shattering a couple of skulls, which sent the flesh-eaters down just the same. It looked like he was even starting to enjoy the task, his concussed mind feeling as if it suddenly had some power over the situation again.

But then, suddenly, he came face to face with one of his former comrades. It was the officer who had been riding shotgun alongside Charlie, now a flesh-eater himself.

"Christ!" the officer screamed before whipping the baton down across the man's face, sending him reeling away. The surprise of seeing the familiar face, however, had the effect of dropping the officer back a step – just enough for a couple of flesh-eaters to get between himself and Mr. Arthur. Though intimidated, the officer raised his arm for another strike, doubling his efforts to beat back the tide. "Die, you bastards!"

When Mr. Arthur reached the edge of the woods, he scanned through the trees and saw no flesh-eaters in front of him. Ryan and Jesse were still a few feet behind him, so he whipped around and started firing over their heads, picking off the undead as they massed towards the escaping boys.

That's when he, like Purnell, saw a couple of the "conjoined" flesh-eaters, three arms where there should be four. Two heads on what looked like a single body. Thick, dripping excretions pouring forth from their numerous sores.

"Disgusting," Mr. Arthur said, blasting one of the two heads, only to have the flesh-eater remain upright, the jaws of the second head still opening and closing in hunger. Mr. Arthur just shook his head at the sight and shot the second head between the eyes.

Ryan and Jesse reached Mr. Arthur just as he was reloading, pulling his last remaining magazine from his pocket. He slammed the clip home, drew a chamber into the breach, and nodded at the boys.

"All right, I'll cover your retreat," he cried. "Whatever you do, don't look back, keep running, and if I don't catch up to you, just keep running. Do *not* come back for me."

Ryan was surprised but saw the dead serious look on Mr. Arthur's face and nodded. Helping Jesse along, the pair limped into the woods. Bones, who had been with the boys, went with them for a few feet but then came back alongside Mr. Arthur, who smiled.

"I appreciate the assist, Bones," he said. "You see that idiot SWAT officer, you'll drag his ass back over here, won't you? *If* he's still alive, mind you?"

Bones wasn't paying attention, instead barking at the mass of flesh-eaters. Mr. Arthur sighed and raised the gun, firing a few more rounds into undead foreheads. It was easy shooting, but there were just so many of them. He'd had nightmares like this from his hunting days -- one afternoon the turkeys finally rose up and fought back. He had to suppress a grin at the memory but then kept shooting.

That's when a flesh-eater emerged from the woods behind him and bit down squarely on both his carotid artery and jugular vein at the same time with a mouth wide enough to make any dentist proud.

"ARRRGGH!!!" screamed Mr. Arthur as he immediately sank to his knees. Hearing this, Bones wheeled around and quickly tore the flesh-eater's throat out, but it was clearly too late for the middle-aged former resident of Duncan.

"The *boys*..." Mr. Arthur managed to whisper to Bones, who immediately got the message. The Shepherd turned and went after Ryan and Jesse, leaving Mr. Arthur to die.

As the flesh-eaters moved closer, Mr. Arthur figured he had a single bullet left and raised the gun as he leaned against the trunk of a tree. He momentarily considered taking his own life but figured one more dead flesh-eater was more pressing. Suddenly, one of the mass lunged for him and Mr. Arthur squeezed the trigger, blasting the final bullet directly into the forehead of the surprised, still living but only for a nanosecond more SWAT officer, who had just escaped the cannibalistic horde only to now be blasted directly back into their arms.

This ended up being the last thing Mr. Arthur ever saw.

"*Crap.*"

Meanwhile, Bones was galloping through the forest, able to easily follow the scent track of Ryan and the wounded Jesse. But as he went, he suddenly heard a voice saying his name from just behind him.

"*Boooones.*"

Bones looked around and saw Officer Purnell approaching, limping through the underbrush on the devastated stump that was once his foot. Bones recognized the now-twin smells of the officer, the remnants of the once-living man but also that of the corpse he had now become. Bones whipped around and launched himself at Purnell's throat, tearing it out in a single motion. Before the officer had even sunk to the ground, Bones was back charging after Ryan and Jesse.

V

The boys and their canine companion had raced along as best they could for a good twenty minutes before Jesse finally collapsed alongside a dry creek bed. These flesh-eaters weren't very fast, particularly the ones now bound together, and the boys had put a good couple of miles between themselves and their attackers. Unfortunately, the jostling hadn't done Jesse much good, as the two bullets still lodged in his body made each step impossibly painful. Despite this, he still protested when Ryan laid him up next to a tree.

"Why are we stopping?" he asked, though he slurred the words.

"You're bleeding again," Ryan replied simply, pointing at the teen boy's wounds.

"*Shiiiit...,*" cried Jesse as he rolled up his tattered jeans and sleeve, seeing that both wounds were trickling blood through torn scabs, soaking his shirt and jeans.

"Don't worry," said Ryan, trying to sound reassuring. "We have to be pretty close to people by now."

Meanwhile, Bones was sniffing a wide perimeter around the boys, finding nothing at first but animal scents: a deer, a few rabbits, a possum or two, a bobcat and its two kittens, and what may have been a raccoon. But then he caught the scent of humans, live ones, and followed it a little ways away from the boys, through the dense underbrush, newly lush and green from the morning rain after a long dry spell.

Bones emerged from the woods onto an old logging trail, twin tire track gutters bending the grass into a road as they cut through the forest. Bones sniffed in a southeasterly direction,, and the human scent strengthened. He turned and ran back into the trees.

"Bones?" Ryan asked as the dog came jogging back to the creek bed. Bones stopped, turned around, *woofed* once, then turned around again and cantered back up in the direction of the logging trail. Unmistakably, he wanted to show them something.

"Can you get up?" Ryan asked Jesse.

"Probably?" Jesse replied, a little unsure, though he'd managed to staunch the blood flow with strips torn from his shirt. "The second I walk anywhere, it's going to move those bullets around, and I'll start bleeding again. Wherever we're going has to be close."

"Well, we can't stay here," Ryan said. "I think they can smell us. We have to keep moving or we'll get caught…like Mr. Arthur."

Neither boy had mentioned him since they'd fled the highway, but as Jesse ripped apart his shirt for bandages, each had kept on eye in the direction they'd come from, hoping, by some miracle, that he'd show up. It was obvious, however, that this wasn't going to be the case.

"We don't know what happened to Mr. Arthur," began Jesse, tightening the strip of cloth tied around his wounded elbow. "But if something like that happens to me, you make sure you don't let it happen to me, because if they really *can* smell us, then I'd probably come right after you. You understand?"

Ryan nodded quickly but couldn't find the words to reply with. Jesse got to his feet, patted Ryan on the shoulder, and started limping after Bones. A second later, Ryan hurried over to him, giving him an arm to hang onto.

It only took a few minutes for Bones to lead the boys to the logging trail and made the decision for them as to which direction they were going to go, leading them towards the human smells. But when Jesse looked down the trail, he blanched.

"This could go for miles," he protested. "They might have even cut it to go around any town. We could be out here for hours."

Ryan just looked at him for a moment with a *you've-got-a-better-plan?* kind of baleful expression but then began following Bones and the tire tracks. It wasn't ten minutes later that they could see the break in the dense trees up ahead and, a few minutes after that, the first couple of houses. Ryan shot a proud look at Bones, which he then turned on Jesse. Jesse, however, wasn't so certain and moved forward with suspicion.

"Bones?" Jesse nervously queried the dog, hoping for some kind of reassuring response as to the flesh-eater-free makeup of the homes ahead. Bones kept walking, sniffing the ground and sniffing the air without any hint of alarm, which Jesse finally took as a good sign.

They soon moved off the logging trail and onto a paved road, emerging at the back of a subdivision. They figured out which direction the highway was in and decided to head the opposite way. But as they passed by the eerily empty houses, they didn't see any more signs of normal humans than they did flesh-eaters.

"If they think there's food on the road, then they're going to stay out there," suggested Ryan. "And once that's gone, they'll probably head for the city."

Jesse nodded, though it was hard to tell if he believed Ryan or not. The trio took a right at the intersection of Bayless and Rohmer, finding another long street of houses that exhibited a strange, post–neutron bomb kind of feeling. It was as if the entire populace had gathered elsewhere for some sort of city-wide event, which, in effect, they had.

Ryan looked over at Jesse and noticed that his wounds were starting to bleed again.

"There's got to at least be a Band-Aid in one of their bathrooms," Ryan said, pointing at the houses. "We should just pick one and go in."

Jesse was about to roll his eyes at this suggestion but then realized that if there was a Band-Aid, there might be other medical supplies.

"All right," he nodded.

Jesse looked down the row of houses, his eyes hunting for one that seemed to suggest it belonged to a family that probably made regular trips to the drugstore for such supplies, and settled on the only two-story home on the block. He limped over to Bones, took him by the collar, and slowly led him to the house.

"We're going in here, Bones," Jesse whispered as Ryan followed behind, looking every which way for company. "But we're going to need you to make sure the coast is clear first."

They reached the front door of the house and found it locked, but then Ryan ran around to the side and found that not only was the garage door open, the door leading into the house from the garage was unlocked. Jesse took Bones to the door, pushed past Ryan, and opened it before half-leading, half-shoving Bones inside. Then Jesse, quickly as he could manage, stepped back out into the garage and slammed the door behind him.

"What are you doing?" Ryan asked, wide-eyed with surprise.

"If he's in there and somebody else is in there, he's going to find them in like two seconds," Jesse explained. "So if he goes crazy and starts barking, we need another house. If he doesn't, then we're okay."

"But if he starts barking, that means he's in trouble and we should have a plan to get him out of there," Ryan countered.

"Of the three of us, I think Bones has proven he can best take care of himself," Jesse said.

Ryan seemed to accept this and they fell silent for a couple of minutes, their eyes glancing around the well-stocked garage. Jesse finally had the good idea to at least close the garage door and did so. Though they didn't comment on it, they both noticed that a family's worth of bicycles were leaning up against the side of the garage between a faded red Civic and the wall. Absent appeared to be a second car, as there was an empty car-sized space alongside the Civic, complete with oil stains on the concrete.

As they waited, Jesse looked around the garage for a weapon, as they only had Ryan's rifle between them. He spotted a rubber mallet but deemed it too soft; a sledgehammer, too unwieldy; and even an edge trimmer, which he thought would be a fun way to dispatch a flesh-eater, though he also knew it would require an extension cord. That's when he picked up a simple claw hammer off a cobweb-covered workbench and put it through one of his belt loops, though Ryan immediately gave him a chastising look.

Jesse shrugged. "Hey, you were the one who suggested raiding some guy's bathroom for Band-Aids."

The pair finally figured it had been enough time and turned back to the door leading into the house, falling silent as they tried to hear Bones on the other side.

"I wonder if he's gone upstairs yet," Ryan whispered.

"You hear anything?" Jesse asked. Ryan shook his head and shrugged.

Jesse carefully pressed his ear to the door, as if fearing that somebody or some-*thing* might be doing the same on the other side. He paused, listened intently, but then turned back to Ryan, shaking his head.

"I don't hear him," he whispered.

Ryan put his hand on the doorknob, worried for Bones, but Jesse raised a hand. Ryan hesitated; Jesse took a deep breath and then nodded dramatically. Ryan turned the knob and swung the door wide...

...only to find Bones standing just on the other side of the door, looking up at them expectantly, his tongue lolling out of his mouth as he panted. Jesse rolled his eyes.

"Let's get that Band-Aid."

The two boys pushed past Bones, carefully closed and locked the door to the garage, and proceeded to raid the house. They started in the master bathroom with the medicine chest, Jesse pouring an entire bottle of hydrogen peroxide across his two wounds, only to get a surprise when one of the slugs fell out of the wound and bounced onto the floor with a metallic click, having worked its way out of the entry wound as they walked.

"Gross," was all Ryan could find to say.

They hit the kitchen next and found that a grocery run had probably been made as recently as that morning. They started gorging themselves, having had no idea how hungry they were until the sight of endless food was placed in front of them.

While the boys did this, Bones padded around the small living room and wandered into the master bedroom, hoping to avoid the smell of an ever-present throughout the house vanilla-flavored air freshener. Unfortunately, it was just as bad if not worse in the bedroom, which was decorated in pink with large, garish flowers on the drapes and bedspread with noisy bronze-colored carpeting to go with it, as if designed to clash. There were at least a couple of masculine touches: a nightstand with a dusty digital clock, a plaque announcing some kind of achievement in quarterly sales, and a dark wood chest of drawers, though in its reserve it only served to highlight the near-luminescent white dresser directly across from the foot of the bed covered with pink perfume bottles, jewelry with a similar bent towards the pink, makeup containers (again, in shades of pink), plastic jars for cotton balls and Q-Tips, and then a great number of family photographs, some framed but also a number tucked into the frame of the dresser's mirror.

Bones sniffed around the dresser, but the scent of the perfumes blending with the smell of the vanilla air fresheners was so overpowering that the shepherd eventually had to leave the room and head for the stairs to try to shake it off.

"Hey, Bones – want some food?" called Ryan, spotting the dog as he walked through the living room. Bones stopped and eyed Ryan, as if considering this, but only for a second before the dog turned and ascended the steps to the second floor.

The stairs led straight into a second-floor hallway with three open doors. Bones glanced in the first one, a bathroom, but then wandered into the second room, a bedroom for a little boy probably around Ryan's age. The shepherd sniffed around the boy's desk, closet, and bed and discovered a half-empty jumbo bag of Funyuns and a box of mini-donuts half-hidden under a pile of laundry. Bones dipped his nose into the box of donuts, scarfing up the contents and collecting powdered sugar on his snout in the process, which he greatly preferred to the stinging perfume that had saturated it for the last couple of minutes. He then used his claws to tear apart the Funyuns bag and ate the two dozen or so left of those as well.

The crinkling of the bag mixed with the crunching of the Funyuns in Bones's teeth meant that it took him a moment before he heard Ryan screaming for his life.

"*NOOOO!!!!*"

Bones whipped around and galloped out the bedroom door. He barreled down the stairs and into the living room, where he saw Jesse, prone on the floor, being torn apart by the mistress of the house, her jaws pulling meat directly from Jesse's now skin-free ribs as he lay prone on the floor. Ryan, meanwhile, was bashing away at the man of the house with a skillet as the flesh-eater cornered him on the sofa against the living room wall, Ryan's barrage having little effect.

Between the parents were two child flesh-eaters, torn between their desire to join in the attack on Ryan or to devour the already safely disarmed Jesse. The decision was made more difficult by the fact that all four of them were connected as a single, four-headed organism made up of four torsos, eight legs, and, effectively, five arms, as that was one of the primary areas where their bodies were fused. When the father went to strike at Ryan, his left arm was the same as his oldest child's right arm, meaning that he virtually had to pull the whole creature forward with him in order to attack the boy. This fact was probably the sole reason Ryan was still alive.

As Bones stared at this bizarre sight, a whole host of new smells filled his nose, and he recognized, for the first time, that there was a subterranean component of the house.

A *basement*.

Though the woman was clearly dead, her perfume was still thick in the air, serving to mask the cadaverous odors coming off her body and the bodies of the rest of her family, though the fresh scent of Jesse's blood, suddenly made to oxide into the air, was stronger yet. Bones could tell there was something *else*, too; he just couldn't make out what…

"Bones!!" screamed Ryan, terrified. "Help me!!"

Bones snapped into action and leaped at the dead father, jaws sinking into the arm he shared with his oldest son and forcefully yanking him back from the sofa. Unfortunately for the shepherd, this brought on an attack from the younger child – a daughter – who kicked at Bones and leaned down to try and bite him in his wounded shoulder. It was only the fact that she was still attached to her feasting mother that kept Bones from being bitten.

Ryan leaped off the sofa and ran for the fireplace, grabbing a poker. The father-end of this strange creature wheeled around after him, the mother finally realizing a fight was on and momentarily leaving Jesse to join in.

"You killed my friend!" Ryan screamed at the four-headed monster, waving the poker around like a sword.

All four mouths moved at once in a great half-hiss, half-growl, which Ryan answered by jamming the poker directly into the open mouth of the father. As the poker snapped teeth aside, stabbed through his upper palate, and entered the dead man's brain, the flesh-eater flailed wildly with his one free hand, staggering backwards and comically taking the rest of his family with him as he tumbled to the ground.

From just behind them, Bones prepared to make his own move, a lunge straight for the woman's throat, but he suddenly got a second whiff of the one scent he couldn't quite pin down. Sensing an approach, he turned and came face to face with a pair of house cats, one gray and one tiger-striped brown, which had joined their masters as denizens of the recently deceased. The cats were moving straight for Bones, their fangs bared and backs arched.

Bones immediately started barking as the undead felines crouched, preparing to attack.

The gray cat leaped straight for Bones's back while the tiger-stripe went for his throat. Bones was bigger than both cats combined but didn't have the same level of craven bloodlust on his side. He backed up quickly, trying to throw off the gray cat as it sank its claws into his already wounded shoulders. The attack made Bones yelp in pain, and he jerked his head around, clamping his jaws on the one part of the gray cat he could reach – its face – and flinging it off.

Bones turned his attention to the tiger-stripe just as it reared up and was lunging at his face, the claws of both forepaws flared. Bones ducked down and arrowed his snout directly into the cat's soft underbelly but then angled his head around at the last moment like a shark and clutched the cat around its torso in his jaws. Crunching down *hard*, the angry shepherd managed to snap the feline completely in half. Still hissing and "alive," the top half of the cat still swung its claws and tried to bite Bones, but he'd already moved away from it.

"Bones!!! Help me!!" cried Ryan.

Bones turned and saw that the family of flesh-eaters had finally regrouped enough that they were able to somewhat encircle the boy. Though it should've been dead, the father-end was still staggering around, the poker bashing into anything it got close to. The mother-end, however, was pursuing Ryan with a tremendous fury, one shared by her two children. They'd backed Ryan into a corner, and now the mother reached out and grabbed Ryan by the shoulders to pull him in for a bite.

"NO!!!" screamed Ryan, hitting at her but closing his eyes as he anticipated the sensation of her hot breath and sharp teeth on his neck.

When he got hot breath and no teeth, he opened his eyes and saw Bones standing on the nearby cabinet, having snapped the mother's head off with his jaws at the last moment.

"Oh, my God," said Ryan, tears bursting into his eyes.

The two child flesh-eaters were pulled to the ground by their falling mother but grabbed at Bones's tail and haunches as he hopped off the cabinet.

"*Gggnnnnhhhh!!*" the two juvenile flesh-eaters railed angrily at Bones.

If Bones heard the threat in the flesh-eaters' voices, he didn't react, but simply stood on each of their chests and tore their throats out. With the second death of the two children, the father, poker still jutting out of his face, finally died as well.

"Bones!!"

Bones turned just in time to see the gray cat, who had recovered from its toss across the room, leaping onto the coffee table to attack him again. Bones barked loudly and angrily at the cat, who jumped at him fearlessly. Bones reared up on his haunches and batted the cat to the ground with his forepaw, which he then used to hold it flat to the carpet. Bones's jaws shot forward, and he quickly dispatched the animal, making for four kills in less than sixty seconds.

Though the tiger-stripe half-cat continued to mewl angrily and wave its forepaws in front of the family's big flat-screen TV and surrounding entertainment center, which took up almost all the space against the living room wall, the house had suddenly gone quiet. Ryan, who was heaving mightily, stared down at Bones, still sniffling.

"Where were you?" he whimpered, accusatorily.

Bones was panting now and looked at Ryan but then turned, walked around the sofa, and went to Jesse, who he sniffed all over. The smells were quickly changing. There was the familiar scent of Jesse himself, the food he'd only just put in his mouth that now sat in his now partially exposed stomach, the rank odor of blood, but then, around his wounds, Bones could smell the saliva of the female flesh-eater…but also something else. He pushed his nose close into the open wounds as the juices of the two people began to mingle. Though Jesse smelled of death, the scent was beginning to change into the more acrid odor of a flesh-eater before Bones's nose.

"He's going to turn into one of them, isn't he?" Ryan asked quietly, indicating the dead family of flesh-eaters nearby. "It's what the driver was telling Mr. Arthur. He said it was some kind of virus that spread from one infected person to the next. If one of them killed us, we'd be like one of them, too, and keep spreading it until everybody got it."

Bones sniffed around Jesse's neck as the strange new smell made its way from the wound up through his body and all the way to his brain. Bones recognized the smell as the same bilious stench that had emerged from the leaking sores of the fusing flesh-eaters on the highway.

Suddenly, Jesse began to stir; just a movement in his feet that could've been misinterpreted as the result of a death rattle in any other circumstance. Bones jumped backwards and began barking at the corpse. As

Jesse continued to wake, Bones cautiously moved forward, still barking, with the goal of tearing the teen boy's throat out.

"Bones – *no!*" ordered Ryan.

Bones turned and looked at Ryan with confusion, wondering why he was being called off, but Ryan gave him a hard stare before uttering a second, sharp, "*No!*"

Bones held his ground but did as he was told. Ryan gave him one more harsh look before heading into the kitchen. The shepherd stared at Jesse's body as it started to re-animate and began barking at it again. Ryan came back in, this time carrying his gun, and aimed it at Jesse's head.

"Get back, Bones," Ryan said, waving Bones away with the barrel of the gun.

Bones stepped backed a few paces as Ryan tried to stop trembling, the barrel of the gun moving around violently as his body was wracked with tears.

"I'm sorry, Jesse," he whispered, almost sobbing.

The first bullet drove past Jesse's head, directly into the floor, where it made a dark, smoky hole in the carpet. Ryan yanked back the bolt, ejecting the spent cartridge, then inserted and chambered a second bullet. This time, Ryan said nothing but held his breath and aimed.

"*Gggnnnhhh…*," Jesse began under his breath, though his eyes were still closed, as if dreaming. "*Gggnnnhhh…*"

Jesse's brains exploded all over the carpet behind his head as the bullet entered his skull, instantly causing such a buildup of pressure that the ballooning matter's only recourse was to get blown out the back following in the wake of the exiting .22 projectile. Jesse's body became instantly still. Bones stared at it for a moment, anticipating a cautious approach, when he was startled by a second shot that was aimed elsewhere in the living room.

Bones looked over and saw that the "half-cat" was now a smoldering, bloody streak on the carpet as well. Bones barked at it a couple of times for good measure but then turned back to Ryan, whose tears had finally stopped. He ejected the spent cartridge, chambered another round, and lowered the weapon.

"Let's go, Bones."

VI

But they didn't leave -- not yet anyway.

As they were heading through the kitchen, Ryan cast a look back at Jesse's body, a look that then traveled over to the dead father-end of this new, strange multi-flesh-eater organism. Despite being impaled through the brain, he continued to fight on, a fact that was weighing heavily on Ryan.

He went to the kitchen cabinets and looked around for something, didn't find it, and went to the garage. As he did, Bones stayed in the kitchen, taking a couple of sniffs down the basement stairs, having to step over the pile of chairs and other debris that someone (a neighbor? another family member?) had stacked in front of the door to keep the man, woman, and presumably the cats at bay to give them enough time to escape. When Ryan came back in from the garage and saw what Bones was doing, he snapped angrily at the dog.

"Get away from there, Bones."

Bones did as he was told, following Ryan into the living room, where the boy stood over Jesse's corpse. In his hands, he held two things – a long cardboard tube filled with fireplace matches and a blue-and-white squeeze bottle of starter fluid for the barbecue. Setting down the matches, Ryan popped the nozzle up on the starter fluid and began spraying it onto Jesse's body but also around the room in general, getting some on his shoes and pants leg. Slowly but surely, he was able to empty the entire bottle, which he tossed on the sofa. He then picked up the day's newspaper and shredded it into a number of long strips, which he then twisted together and jammed into Jesse's pockets, the crooks of his arms, his shoes, and even his mouth and the hole in his forehead.

Once there were seven or eight of these wicks placed around the body, Ryan struck the first of three matches, lighting all of them until they began burning down towards the lighter fluid–soaked corpse.

Inhaling the scent of burning newspaper mixed with the harsh odor of the liquid accelerant, Bones got agitated and started whining. Ryan, watching the flames until they were well on their way to the body, finally turned when the first fire touched the starter fluid, immediately engulfing Jesse's left foot in fire.

"Come on, Bones," Ryan whispered under his breath, picking his rifle off the sofa and heading back towards the kitchen.

They exited out to the closed garage, and Bones took a couple of sniffs of the air. Nothing seemed to alarm him, so Ryan went ahead and opened the garage door. The fresh air began to quickly scrub away the scent of the house's many perfumes, the corpses, the burning Jesse, and everything else that had been filling Bones's nose, allowing his most powerful of senses to slowly recharge.

Ryan stared at the pavement below his feet as he walked, carrying the rifle in such a way that the steel barrel bounced off the concrete a couple of times, scraping the finish. He obviously didn't care; damaging the gun he had just been forced to use against another boy who'd been saving his life all day was having a soothing effect on his wounded conscience.

Bones trotted along next to him, inhaling the scents of the area dogs that had been marking their territory here for years but were now distinctly absent. A couple of times, the shepherd spotted a squirrel or a bird that momentarily distracted him, breaking the silence with a chirp or chatter, but the vague scent of humans and flesh-eaters alike continued to permeate the air, suggesting a horrific catastrophe that the boy and dog had missed by several hours. Bones was far from relaxed.

"Where are we even going?" asked Ryan dejectedly. "They're going to be pretty much anywhere, and we've got to sleep sometime."

Bones kept walking, panting lightly as he went, but he wasn't tired. Well past the point of exhaustion, he probably wouldn't have been able to sleep if he tried.

"Mom's dead, Jilly's dead," Ryan said. "I'll bet Grammy's dead, too. Uncle Norman is probably dead. Aunt Ronelle. Albert. Maggie. Miss Glover is probably dead."

Ryan scoffed at this, not altogether unhappy that his teacher might not have survived the apocalypse, but then his scowl returned.

"Mr. Harris is probably dead," he continued, wallowing in his despair. "Ms. Heartfield. Mr. Birdwell. Miss Hogan. Pastor Coleman. Dr. Rayburn. Dr. Holly. I guess I won't be getting braces now."

The rifle bounced off the concrete again. Bones hopped a step to avoid it coming down on him.

"All the kids on my street. All the kids on my bus. All the kids in my class," Ryan said as he kept walking, not noticing that Bones had stopped *dead* in his tracks. "All the kids at daycare, all the kids at the allergist's office…"

Ryan finally looked over and saw that his four-legged companion was no longer at his side. "Bones?"

He turned around and saw Bones standing stock-still, staring straight ahead. With great trepidation, Ryan turned to look where Bones's eyes were fixed, and soon understood why.

Standing at an intersection directly in front of them were a dozen flesh-eaters, but not massing in some mob or on the move. Instead, they were simply lined up shoulder to shoulder, similar to the family of flesh-eaters back in the house – fused at the shoulders, hips, hands, legs, thighs, calves, and even feet – but *unlike* the family, they weren't trying to pull each other in different directions. No, what had been disorganized about earlier incarnations of this fused undead monstrosity seemed to have been worked out in this version, the difference between a helpless newborn baby and a three year-old toddler, able to communicate, move, eat, and in general function as an individual entity.

The creature stared at Ryan, but with eighteen eyes instead of twenty-four, as three of the twelve bodies were *without heads*, though were still fused at the arms and legs. This meant nine mouths revealed their rows of teeth, many broken from hours gnashing through muscle into bone instead of a dozen. Eighteen ears heard it when Ryan gasped at the sight, and nine noses inhaled his scent of fear as twelve chests rose and fell in the exact same rhythm, the bodies breathing completely in unison.

Ryan knew when it stepped forward, it would do that as one, too. Probably when it ran as well. But this wasn't foremost in his mind. Even though the father flesh-eater was part of a longer chain and had been up on its feet after receiving a poker to the head, Ryan figured that that was the anomaly. He still fervently believed the one thing for certain about the flesh-eaters that had murdered his entire family was that a head shot equated death. Bullet to the head, *bang* – you're dead, like he'd had to do with Jesse. But now that comforting fail-safe was gone. The flesh-eaters had not only found a way around even this, but they seemed stronger for its execution. The living nightmare was only getting worse.

That's when the mouths of the nine bodies with heads opened wide and roared at Ryan and Bones.

"*RAAAAAAHHHHH!!!!*"

The noise was tremendous, like a phalanx of Ottoman Janissaries preparing to charge across an ancient battlefield with the sole intention of massacring their enemy to a man. Deep and guttural, the sound chilled Ryan to the bone, his eyes going wide with fear. Bones barked back and viciously bared his teeth as the free arms of the line of flesh-eaters began to gesticulate wildly, also in unison, readying their attack. The bodies hunched down, like a row of sprinters on their starting blocks, all eyes on Ryan and Bones.

"Shit-shit-shit-*shit*," inhaled Ryan as he quickly raised his rifle.

Before he could aim, the creature launched itself forward, its legs moving together like some kind of great, side-turned centipede. Startled, Ryan pulled the trigger, and his first shot went completely wide, the bullet whizzing skyward well over the head of the left-most flesh-eater on line. He went to reload, but unlike the other flesh-eaters, this monstrosity had the ability to use its multiple legs to really *run* and was quickly cutting the distance between itself and its would-be meal.

"*Bones...?!*" Ryan cried urgently, as if seeking permission to flee. He didn't have to wait long for Bones's reply.

Without so much as a woof, Bones suddenly broke to the left and Ryan followed, the creature changing its course to pursue them both. Ryan saw a narrow path between the back fences of two houses.

"Through there!" he yelled to the dog. "Over there!"

With Bones at his heels as they entered the alley, Ryan looked back, hoping to see that the flesh-eaters wouldn't be able to follow. But then he watched as the undulating creature rolled the segmented bodies that made up its form together into a more aquiline, insect-like version of itself and used its limbs to not just run across the alley floor but also to accelerate by galloping its hands across the fences on either side, pushing itself ever faster. Like a tunneling mole, the creature didn't seem particularly bound to directions up or down and was much quicker when pushing itself off against three surfaces than just one.

Though he was just behind Ryan, Bones hadn't been running at full speed, just fast enough to keep up with the boy or maybe a little faster to speed up his pace. But as the dog glanced back, his nose filled with the peculiarly dank smell of this new creature, a scent that differentiated itself from simply that of a cadaver but was an entirely new animal with its own, now-living smells.

Ryan looked back again as well, seeing that the creature was gaining on them. He turned and saw that the end of the alley was still about two house-lengths ahead. So panicked was Ryan, that he didn't see the couple of upside-down paint cans directly ahead in his path.

"*Oof!*" cried Ryan as his right foot kicked into the cans, sending him sprawling forward and landing with a *splat* against the grass. Behind him, the creature immediately arched itself up, its various arms and legs allowing it to straddle both fences and rise above the prone boy like a cobra readying to strike.

"I'm sorry, Mom," spat Ryan as he looked up at the creature, the first two flesh-eaters in the segmented chain being raised in the air, their bodies – arms and legs positioned around like mandibles - freed from the fences in order to be brought down like the jaws of a mantis.

But at the last second, Bones grabbed at Ryan's shoulder, yanking him towards a nearby open gate. The creature drove its front flesh-eaters forward, a couple more segments along with it making four bodies swooping down together, and smashed itself into the ground where Ryan had just been, the arms and legs of the flesh-eaters churning at the dirt and grass on the floor of the alley in a motion that suggested they would have easily torn Ryan to pieces given the chance. When they spotted his escape, however, the flesh-eaters all hissed in unison at the retreating boy and dog as they clambered through the gate into the backyard of the neighboring house.

"Thanks, Bones!" Ryan cried breathlessly.

The backyard had a pool, and as Ryan got to his feet on the other side of the fence, he momentarily considered jumping in, wondering if this new, efficient construct of flesh-eaters could swim. But Bones had already circled back around to the gate, barking his head off as the creature raised itself over the top of the fence, gazing into the backyard of their escape. As soon as its many eyes fixed on Bones and Ryan, its many arms and legs grasped the fence, and it swarmed itself over like a platoon of fire ants chained together at the waist.

Ryan abandoned his plan to jump in the pool and simply bolted for the back door of the house as Bones followed. He turned the knob but found it locked.

"*Shit!*" he cursed, looking around for other options.

Seeing that the gate extended around the side of the house, Ryan followed a brick pathway to the corner of the home and saw that the fence went the length of the house and ended with a gate that presumably opened up into the front yard. Glancing back to where the segmented creature was now slithering across the ground around the edge of the pool, Ryan figured it was his only chance.

"Come on, Bones!" he cried as the dog did double duty following him but also hurling warning barks back at the oncoming monster. Hearing his name, Bones turned and chased after Ryan, following him down the side of the house with the creature hot on their heels.

It took Ryan maybe thirteen steps to reach the gate, only to find that locked as well.

"*NOO!!!*" he cried, shaking the gate with all his might.

He grabbed onto its wood frame and realized that there were just enough toe- and hand-holds to pull him over, and he began climbing. He was halfway up the fence when he looked back and saw Bones, who was trying to follow him but clearly couldn't get over the fence in his wounded state. Just behind the dog, the flesh-eaters were skittering crab-style after him, their mouths open and drooling.

Ryan made a decision and climbed off the fence, getting back down to the ground alongside Bones as the shepherd, realizing he wasn't going to be able to climb the fence, turned and began frantically barking at the creature.

"I won't leave you, Bones," Ryan said quietly as he knelt down next to the dog and put his hand reassuringly on the fur between Bones's shoulder blades.

As Bones's barks became higher-pitched and more obviously filled with fear, Ryan looked up at the creature as it did another of its cobra-moves, arcing high above the two of them with teeth bared and pseudo-mandibles flared like an owl about to swoop down on a cornered mouse.

Suddenly, the creature exploded in a flurry of sparks, flesh, bone, and black, bilious blood, chunks of flesh, bone, and sinew splattering against the house, fence, and grass. Ryan had to cover his ears to block out the cacophony.

The tone in Bones's bark changed immediately as if he had called in the mysterious air strike himself. He seemed to be happy, working his jaws as if looking for a way to join the fight but seemingly realizing it was best to stay on the sidelines.

Just as suddenly as it had started, the violent racket came to a halt – at least, some of it did. What turned out to be a barrage of machine gun fire was replaced by the steady *whup...whup...whup...whup...* of an Apache attack helicopter that was hovering just over the front yard of the neighboring house. Ryan stared at it in awe, his jaw almost down to his chest.

"Holy shit, Bones. Are you seeing that, too?"

But Bones just kept barking, even as heavily armored Army Rangers bashed through the gate and hands reached in to extract the pair.

VII

It took some convincing of the Special Forces response team, specifically a Captain Willingham, for Bones not to be left behind to fend for himself in Gainey or, worse, shot. But after Ryan showed them Bones's collar and explained that he was a trained Pittsburgh police K-9 who now had more experience sniffing out and fighting against the flesh-eaters than any dogs they might have brought with them, the captain realized how valuable such an asset might be.

"All right, kid," Captain Willingham had said. "We'll treat you like a matched set."

After a visit to the company medic, who patched them up as best he could in the field, Bones and Ryan were loaded onto an Army CH-47 transport helicopter and whisked out of the combat zone. As soon as the helicopter was aloft, Bones fell asleep. He may have still been hungry but only accepted a quick drink from a soldier's canteen before closing his eyes.

The longer they'd stayed on the ground, though, the more antsy Ryan had become. His debriefing by the captain, who wanted to know in detail where he'd been and what he'd experienced, had repeatedly been punctuated by machine gun fire from both the Apache's forward cannon as well as troops on the ground exterminating flesh-eaters both near and far. So, when the helicopter was finally airborne and putting serious miles between himself and Bones and the scene of so much death that morning, Ryan was finally able to relax. His first reaction had been to break down and cry, but he was too dehydrated, and no tears came. Instead, his body merely racked with sobs as he tried to hide the fact from the soldiers in the chopper.

"We didn't know how wide it had spread until we started rising above the action," a Sergeant Lopez told Ryan, handing him a pair of headphones, figuring conversation might help the troubled kid. "It seems to have started around Duncan but quickly spread to Gainey, past Scottsburg, and into Hammond, Warsaw, and Belton. They'd turned the city into Fortress Pittsburgh, thinking that was the next place they'd go, but then *nada*. They'd all changed direction and started heading back out to the north."

Though he had winced at the mention of his town, "Duncan," Ryan liked that the man didn't talk down to him, and when he said as much, Lopez smiled.

"Judging from what you told the captain, you've had a lot more experience fighting these things than anybody else in my unit. You and your pal there have earned the respect of a lot of American servicemen today."

Ryan liked how that sounded. He glanced over at Bones, who was tethered to one of the seats of the helicopter by a nylon web belt a soldier had attached to his collar. The shepherd looked half-dead, so exhausted was he.

"What were those things that attacked us?" Ryan asked Sergeant Lopez. Sgt. Lopez sighed, as if Ryan was bringing up the one sore subject on the day.

"That's just it – we have no idea," he replied. "We're calling them 'Stage 3s' or 'MBNS' – Multi-Body Non-Sentients, which is one of the most laughable bits of bureaucratic-speak I've heard. We just call them Multipedes, just, well…because. Whatever the virus or parasite or whatever it is that's been infecting people has been mutating throughout the day, causing their hosts to mutate as well. Tissue samples they took off the first Stage 2 bodies that came in are night-and-day different from ones they took off Stage 2s that came in as little as an hour later. What they're really afraid is, well, these multipedes might not be the end of it. No one knows what they're looking for out there."

Ryan nodded and looked out the window of the helicopter as they flew over first Allegheny, then Butler, then Armstrong Counties. He could see smoke rising from a couple of fires in the distance, as well as a great number of helicopters heading off in multiple directions, some in lines of six or seven, like great aerial convoys.

As they went, they also passed over a great many neighborhoods just like the one -- until a few hours ago -- Ryan lived in. When he looked down into them, he couldn't see a single moving vehicle, a single person, or a single flesh-eater, just empty houses, streets, and yards as far as the eye could see.

Pretty soon, the sun began to set, and Ryan grew tired. It wasn't long before he joined Bones in sleep.

Some hours later, Bones awoke on a metal table. Everything around him was white, and the air was heavy with the scent of antiseptic cleaner meant to mask a lingering smell of blood and tissue, all human. A hand was laid gently on his neck and, though groggy, Bones immediately twisted to bite it but didn't have the strength.

"Easy there, Bones," came the voice of a tall, wispy-haired man in a military uniform who stood alongside the table. "I'm a friend."

Bones licked his chops, his mouth desert-dry. The man removed his hand and walked over to a sink, where he filled a kidney-shaped metal tray with water. He brought it back to Bones and placed it on the table. When Bones couldn't raise himself to get his tongue into the tray, the man put his hands under Bones's head and lifted it up enough for the shepherd to drink.

"To hear your buddy Ryan tell it, you've had a heck of a day," the man said. "Unfortunately, that included being exposed to a lot of pathogens. We had to run some tests on you, which is why you were knocked out. The anesthetic is why your mouth is so dry."

Bones continued lapping up the water and then tried to move again, this time attempting to get to his feet, but his already-clumsy paws couldn't get a grip on the slippery table and slid out from under him.

"Careful, boy," said the man, placing his hand on Bones's torso to discourage movement. Ignoring this advice, Bones immediately tried to get to his feet again with a similar result, this time almost tumbling off onto the floor. The man's voice turned grave.

"If you keep doing this, I'm going to have to put you under again."

Finally, Bones sank back down on his side, panting a little as he recovered his bearings. The man stroked his fur, gingerly avoiding Bones's wounds as he rubbed the dog's head, then patted the fur along his back.

"You'll be all right, boy. Just take it easy."

It was less than a minute before Bones fell back asleep.

When he woke up the second time, Bones found himself in an animal cage, lying on a towel. In a different room now, this one with windows that revealed it was the dead of night, Bones picked up an entirely new range of smells. Instead of human ones, these were all chemical and emanated from literally hundreds of plastic bottles lining rows of shelves alongside the cage. The combined scents were so heavy that Bones almost threw up as they pounded at his nose. Whoever stuck him in there had no idea what they were inflicting on him.

Bones *woofed* a couple of times but then lay back down and buried his nose in the towel. The towel, at least, had the smell of a geriatric old man, which was better than the pharmacological attack he was currently weathering.

Outside the room, he could hear a great deal of activity, people hurrying back and forth through the hallways with confusion and panic in their voices. Nothing sounded business as usual, even when someone was just asking directions to an office or particular wing. Bones kept his eyes on the translucent window in the door where the shadowy silhouettes of people could be seen. Having slept for hours and hours, Bones wasn't tired anymore, though his muscles were aching more now than they had. On top of that, he was pretty hungry by now but didn't bark, preferring to stay silent and sink his nose into the towel as he waited to be discovered again.

It was about an hour later that a group of silhouettes came right up to his door, talking fast as one of them fumbled with keys to unlock it.

"He's in here unless they moved him," said a young soldier who entered the room first, followed quickly by four officers; no sign of the wispy-haired man. The soldier spotted Bones and smiled. "Here's your man, sir."

The ranking officer walked past the soldier and stood over the cage, his hands on his hips as Bones looked up at him, his wounds seeming to give the officer pause.

"He looks like shit."

Bones's eyes flitted from the officer to his cohorts, then back down again.

"He's probably starving," offered the soldier.

The officer squatted down and looked closely at Bones. The German shepherd got slowly to his feet and met him at eye-level, then stuck out his nose and gave the fellow a sniff.

"You think you can help us out?" the officer asked Bones. "A lot of my officers think you're our best shot, 'the little police dog that could.' While you've been out of commission, well, things have taken a turn for the *fucked*, and we're hoping you might be able to help us *un*-fuck it."

Bones stared at the officer expectantly, still wondering if this contact would result in food. After another moment, the officer turned back to the soldier.

"Get him fed. Check his wounds. Get him out to the helipad in five minutes."

As the sun began to purple the eastern sky, Bones found himself on the move yet again, this time airborne and headed north-northeast. He was accompanied by a four-person team of MPs that obviously had a lot more experience with law enforcement dogs than anyone else Bones had run into since the death of his handler twenty-four hours before. More than anything, this was meted out by the fact that they'd simply treated him like a dog instead of a person, a confidante, a savior, or a soldier.

With them, in twin cages, were two military police dogs - a Belgian Malinois named Asra and a second German shepherd, Thor - but Bones was enjoying the privilege of flying cageless at the feet of a Sergeant Mickey Celek, a square-jawed, sandy-haired farm boy of an MP who had assumed primary control of Bones.

"Bet you're pretty sick of all the travel, huh, Bones?" Celek asked, keeping a hand between Bones's shoulders, while petting him at the base of his neck instead of on his head with his other hand. "This'll probably be the longest ride you'll take today but then – with a little luck – you'll call it a day."

Bones, lying on the floor of the helicopter, glanced from Celek to the one female MP, Sergeant Connie Holt, who was eyeing him, too.

"You really think he can figure out where these things went?" she asked skeptically.

"It was Colonel Daniels' idea, and even he said it was a long shot," replied Celek with a noncommittal shrug. "But have you seen this guy's record? Even before today, he was one of the best cadaver dogs in the state, if not the whole northeast. You've got a hell of a sniffer, huh, Bones?"

Celek reached down and stroked Bones's snout. Bones looked from Celek across to the other two MP Sergeants, Edwin Plume and Darryl Moore. Moore was either asleep or meditating, but Plume was eyeing Bones back, what looked like a thin smile on his face either of incredulity at the team's desperation or of optimism that they might finally have a workable solution to the current problem, though he said nothing.

"You believe what that kid said about the dog killing the Stage 2s?" asked Holt. "Made it sound like he'd torn through over a hundred."

"Kid's probably full of shit," Sgt. Moore suggested.

"You have any idea how many different blood and tissue samples they found in this guy's jaws?" retorted Celek. "Hell, in his fur? That kid walked out of Ground Zero alive, and it's not because he's some junior Quick Draw McGraw. He had help."

Sgt. Holt looked at Bones for a moment, meeting his gaze as she wondered if this one animal could be responsible for all that was being attributed to him, but then shrugged.

"Well, we're not asking him to fight anything, just borrow whatever he's got of a scent-memory," she said finally. "Probably won't get to see him in action."

She glanced back to Bones as he licked his chops, as if getting hungry even at the memory of fighting flesh-eaters.

The helicopter set down about an hour and a half later, just as the sun was beginning its morning arc in earnest. The landing zone was up in the Allegheny Mountains just outside the small hamlet of Coughlin, a coal mining town of about four or five hundred residents tucked a couple of miles off the Grand Army of the Republic Highway, U.S. Route 6, which one could take all the way to California or Massachusetts, depending which way they were so inclined (though locals suggested that CA and MA were both pretty much full of assholes).

While there were no signs of even a single local, the population had still increased exponentially that day, as a thousand or so National Guardsmen and women were swarming the place, some having arrived by helicopter but many more in canvas-backed trucks and armored vehicles from Fort Indiantown Gap in Annville. On top of that, there were also a couple hundred

Army Rangers who had been quick-deployed up from Fort Benning, Georgia, in C-130 transports that had landed in Erie the previous night and were then trucked down. These were the men who had recovered Ryan and Bones the afternoon before, utilizing twin Apache helicopters from the Air National Guard base in Johnstown, but who were now miles from their mop-up assignment in Gainey.

When the MPs disembarked from the helicopter, Sgt. Celek walking Bones on a leash, they were immediately met by an officer who, after returning four salutes, introduced himself as Major Buntin.

"You've been briefed on what you're going to be looking at?" Maj. Buntin asked.

"Yes, sir," came the unified response.

"Then follow me."

The four military policemen and their three K-9 cohorts were led to the outskirts of the small village – little more than a post office, a motel, a diner, and a handful of small wood-frame houses and even fewer trailers that stretched up into the foothills. While it looked like there was also a structure originally constructed to be a church, it had long since been boarded up. It took only four minutes to walk from the motel parking lot, which had been deemed suitable for helicopter take-offs and landings, all the way across town to the Coughlin city limits. A single one-lane gravel road separated the community from the woods. But as the three dogs neared the first tree line, they all picked up on what brought them there at once as their noses went into overdrive.

"Christ on a cracker," muttered Plume, the humans getting a nose-full as well. "What *is* that?"

It was only a few yards into the trees that they saw the source of the stench. Or, at least, one small part of it. Just within the woods, marked off by yellow tape and surrounded by armed sentries, was a trail of human bones arranged haphazardly as if they'd been gradually dumped off the back of a four-wheeler. In some places, there'd only be a femur, a skull, or a clavicle to mark the path, but at other points, it was as if that same four-wheeler had hit a bump and dropped four or five skeletons' worth in one spot. On top of that, the bones appeared to be covered in some sort of sticky brown glaze. The MPs stared at the sight with incredulity and horror, Sgt. Holt finally having to look away, as she felt sick to her stomach. That's when she saw it was actually a lot worse than she could have imagined.

"Look," she said, nodding left and right.

The group turned and saw that what they'd been looking at was only one trail of several dozen. Yellow "no crossing" tape could be seen wagging in the light breeze throughout the woods, marking bone trails fanning out as far as the eye could see.

"Do you know what kind of numbers we're looking at, sir?" Sgt. Celek asked the major, ashen-faced.

"We've been working off a human skull count, and right now, we're up around twenty thousand," Maj. Buntin replied gravely. "The numbers are starting to match the combined populations of Duncan, Hammond, Gainey, Coughlin, Belton, Scottsburg, and Warsaw – the towns primarily affected by this morning's outbreak. We have no idea what left these bones here or why they were arranged like this. Some of the bones show the kind of fusing we witnessed in the Stage 3s, which must have gone all the way down to the skeletal level, but we haven't been able to determine where the rest of the creature has disappeared to."

"You specified a 'human' skull count?" asked Sgt. Holt.

"We've found a number of other animal skulls in the mix – elk, bear, possum," Major Buntin replied. "Yesterday's assessment of the Stage 2s and 3s as being only cannibalistic, I feel, can be dismissed. Whatever these things are becoming, well, we can anticipate a different sort of ossification structure, to say the least."

"Couldn't this be it?" offered Sgt. Holt. "Maybe whatever this mutation is has a limited life cycle, and we're looking at the end stage."

Major Buntin offered Sgt. Holt a look filled with condescension but then shook his head.

"I don't think anyone believes that's what we're looking at here. They're still out here in the woods, and they're all moving in the same direction to some specific location. We need your dogs to find them because, if not, who knows where they'll show up next. This has to end. Now."

Sgt. Celek allowed Bones to move closer to the bone trail and get a good whiff. It was almost too much for the shepherd, who snorted loudly and shook his head, immediately backing away from it.

"So much for Wonder Dog," Sgt. Moore scoffed.

But then Bones turned his nose away from the bone trail and to the grass alongside it, then to the air, separating out the smell of the dead humans in order to pick up the fading trail of whatever left them behind. After a long moment, he finally began moving forward, heading into the trees.

"Here we go," Sgt. Celek said, inhaling sharply.

Sgt. Holt nodded and joined the small group following a few yards behind Bones, a company of National Guardsmen flanked by a platoon of Army Rangers falling in line behind them. Slowly but surely, Coughlin and the tree line disappeared behind them as they wandered farther and farther into the woods.

VII

Bones, flanked by Thor and Asra, led the phalanx of about a hundred military policemen, soldiers, and Rangers for more than two hours, deep into virgin forest. Several times, the MPs had to cut trail just to keep up with the dogs as the trees and underbrush grew impenetrably dense. The bone trails had continued for over a mile, which the army had been able to mostly ascertain from the air, but now the soldiers on the ground had to rely solely on the dogs' senses of smell to continue leading them forward towards the retreating multipedes, wherever they might be hiding in the vast and circuitous Allegheny Mountain range.

Bones alternated between keeping his nose in the air and then back to the ground. He routinely paused after finding traces of the sticky substance that had decorated the human bones on nearby rocks and trees, which he sniffed around on, and in one instance even urinated on, before continuing.

"We have any idea what that stuff is yet?" asked Sgt. Moore, indicating the brownish-red resin that hung like thin webs of molasses.

"It's organic, full of human blood and tissue but also a lot of other stuff," said a Lieutenant Nelson, the second female in the group after Sgt. Holt and the ranking officer of one of the National Guard platoons. "They're still trying to determine what the rest is, but what makes it different from animal blood is that there's very little oxygen or other gasses within it, as well as no hemoglobin, which you'd expect to find in a mammalian circulatory system."

Sgt. Celek let this process for a moment but then looked back down at Bones, who seemed to have found something next to one of the trees.

"Whatcha got, Bones?" Celek asked, leaning down.

Bones moved aside, and Celek pulled on a latex glove he extracted from a pocket. He reached over and picked up what looked like a long, smooth tree branch, completely stripped of not only leaves but any kind of buds or bumps. Instead, the surface had a bright, almost metallic sheen the same color as the sticky substance that had covered the bones.

"Hey, any idea what this is?" he asked, handing it back to Lt. Nelson.

She stared at it for a moment, weighing it in her hands, but was unable to render a verdict.

"It looks organic but feels manmade, like a piece of pipe," she offered. "But that can't be it, can it? Not way out here."

As she looked closely at it, a similar – albeit larger – branch-like object of the same type swept out from a tree branch above her and lopped her head off. It bounced onto the ground in front of the surprised MPs and rolled until it came to a stop against the trunk of a tree, her hair immediately getting stuck to the sap-like substance Bones had been using to trail the multipedes.

There was one more millisecond of quiet as the soldiers stared at the severed head, but then all hell broke loose.

"Holy shit!!" yelled Sgt. Moore, as he and a number of the other troops looked up and saw literally hundreds of the so-called "multipedes" descending on them from the deciduous tree canopy above. "Get 'em!"

As one, the soldiers raised their weapons, dropped their safeties, and began firing rounds up at their swarming attackers, but the minute amount of time it took to complete this simple task was still too long for a handful of troops who found themselves impaled on the long, sword-like mandibles of the fastest multipedes. Their comrades, staring in horror at the fallen men, so quickly and easily dispatched, found their panic levels rising and translated this into more erratic firing patterns. The multipedes, however, remained eerily calm, going about their slaughter – even as many of their number were blasted to pieces – with a cool, methodical attitude that only made them more frightening to behold. If they weren't afraid of this, what *did* they fear?

As the tremendous firefight exploded around him, Bones began barking like crazy and lunged at any multipede that got near, easily tearing off a few legs. The other enforcement dogs did similarly, though the Malinois – Asra – only managed a couple of yips before a giant multipede dropping from a branch several stories up landed two feet away from them and cut her and her handler, Sgt. Plume, in half with its mandibles.

As Sgt. Celek methodically fired away - picking a target, blasting it apart and then choosing a new one - it became quickly evident to him that this creature they were fighting was not the same as the multipedes back in Gainey but a further mutation of the Stage 3s. Instead of human faces, body shapes, arms, and legs, these creatures were far more snake-like and elastic after having shed their skeletons, and pulled themselves along with much shorter, stick-like legs that gave them the appearance of worms as they slithered around trees. In fact, the only thing that confirmed that these were even of the same species was that the body segments, while becoming uniform, still had the look of several humans fused together like vertebrae, all in fetal positions.

"This must be a completely new stage," Celek bellowed out to the other MPs between bursts of his machine gun, the overlapping muzzle flash like lightning through the trees. "The Stage 2s merged bodies to become Stage 3s. Then they dumped their bones and mutated into these worm-things."

Despite their vastly superior firepower, it was less than a minute before the hundred-man-strong force was halved. Arriving in a hail of broken branches and leaves, the multipedes had swept down, already working their mandibles forward in a chopping motion, resulting in a maelstrom of severed arms, legs, heads, and torsos raining down on the forest floor, followed swiftly by the human bodies to which they were once attached. Blood erupted, splashed, poured, oozed, and seeped from the now dozens of corpses soaking the ground.

But after a few minutes of this, the heavily armed and well-trained squad of Rangers and MPs (it was the Guardsmen with their lighter weapons that seemed to have fallen first) quickly improvised a workable defense and gathered almost back-to-back, laying down cover fire for each other as guns were reloaded and reset before being turned back on the enemy. But for every one multipede that was blasted away, two more seemed to take its place.

"How many are there?" cried Sgt. Holt, sidled up next to Sgt. Celek, blasting up into the trees as the multipedes swarmed back among the branches in an attempt to find new angles of attack against their pesky targets.

"Looks like hundreds," Celek replied, shredding the tree above him with bullets. He pointed at the thick, sticky substance that exploded out of the multipedes whenever they were hit. "That's why the dogs didn't start barking. The scent they've been tracking all morning is the same as what's coming out of the multipedes. I'm sure even their sniffers have a saturation point."

"But what are they doing out here?" asked Sgt. Holt. "Before they dumped their skeletons, they were rampaging all over the place, completely disordered. Those trails implied some kind of order, and now even their attack patterns are coordinated. They were *waiting* for us."

Like with a hive mind, thought Celek, but he didn't give voice to the opinion. He didn't like how what he was seeing completely changed the day's equation all over again.

For his part, Bones found fighting these new multipedes easier than the ones back in Gainey. Before, when he would crunch into a Stage 2 or 3, they could flail and beat him away with their bony limbs, which would eventually extract a toll. Now, without skeletons, it became a muscle game, and as the multipede would try to pull itself from Bones's jaws, all the shepherd had to do was lock in its jaws and wait for the creature to tire itself out. Then he'd bite off its head.

In doing this, however, he became quickly covered in the sticky blood of the multipedes and kept trying, in vain, to pull it off his fur by rolling on the grass during breaks in the action. While he was doing this, a thick, rich smell cut through the odor of the blood that had been filling his nose for some time. It was a new smell, and Bones momentarily ignored the multipedes and followed the scent, only to find that it was coming from straight down, the rich aroma of old, dry soil from deep within the ground, the kind that was seldom exposed to the air and elements, so that it could never be mistaken for topsoil. Somehow over the ceaseless machine gun fire, Bones also heard a new sound, one that seemed to be coming from…

Immediately, the shepherd began jumping around on the spot, barking and pawing at the dirt. At first, none of the soldiers noticed, but after a couple of seconds, Sgt. Celek finally saw what his charge was doing and ceased firing for a moment to watch, wondering what had gotten into him. It was then that he realized the vibrations he had been feeling for the last few seconds weren't, in fact, from having switched his AR-15 from semi- to full-auto.

"Everybody look down!!" he shouted. "I think something's com…"

But then the ground opened up and there was no need for him to continue.

Dozens of the worm-like multipedes erupted out of the ground like geysers, launching skyward a few feet before descending directly on top of individual soldiers whose positions they had easily navigated to due to the vibrations of their machine guns. The panicked troops began shooting wildly, only to have their fire chew into their nearest human comrade, so desperate were their fire patterns. The multipedes took easy advantage of their shock and horror to slice through the momentarily stunned friendly-fire soldiers, sending them to join their fellow corpses on the ground.

Sixty seconds later, there were only a dozen humans still standing, the forest floor an endless abattoir of corpses and spent shells.

Sergeants Celek, Holt, and Moore, who had managed – in the millisecond before the underground attack – to ready their defense and fend off the first wave, now found themselves the target of the surviving multipedes as they slithered in a circular pattern, flanking the survivors.

"What now?" Sgt. Holt screamed over the roar of her machine gun as her bullets cut through another multipede. "We don't have enough ammunition to kill all of them!"

Sgt. Celek knew she was right. At a certain point, the multipedes, by sheer force of numbers, would overwhelm them. But then he looked around and saw both Bones and Thor tugging apart the torso of one of the multipedes.

"I've got an idea," he cried. "Get over to Bones."

The MPs and a couple of the other surviving soldiers edged over to the two shepherds until Celek could get his hand on Bones's leash. He pulled him close as the other troops gave him cover.

"Go home, Bones!" he cried, pointing away from the action. "Find us a hole. *Go!*"

It took him a moment, but then Bones understood what was desired of him and bolted away, leading the group up a nearby rise and deeper into the woods but away from the multipedes.
Sgt. Celek watched him for a moment, then nodded to the others. "Come on! This might be our shot!"

The survivors chased after Bones as best they could, Thor leading the way after Bones escaped from view. The multipedes rushed after them in the trees and overland, their mandibles launching forward after their heels, but they weren't as fast as the soldiers on open ground, the element of surprise being their primary advantage. Some burrowed back underground as if hoping to flank those retreating, but they couldn't keep up, either.

Soon the multipedes were far behind, but this did little to slow Celek and the other survivors. They kept running, putting as much ground between them and their dead as they could.

"Central command, this is Wolf Team, over. Central command, this is Wolf Team, over. We *need* assistance!"

Even though Sgt. Moore continued trying to raise their commanders, it was obvious to everyone that the field radio had been too badly damaged in the attack to function. The handful of communication devices still carried by the others, mostly cell phones and walkie-talkies, satellite-enabled though they were, were having similar problems with signals bouncing around the high rocks of the Alleghenies, so high were they. That said, the soldiers figured they were much safer among the rocks, hoping the multipedes couldn't drill through black shale.

"What the hell, those things looked like worms or caterpillars or something, man," declared one of the surviving Rangers, a corporal who had introduced himself as "Romeo" when they'd slowed down enough to catch their breaths. "The ones we shot up outside Gainey still looked like people. These were like...*animals*. We sure they're even the same thing?"

"I don't know what to tell you," said Sgt. Celek, shaking his head. "Whatever's going on here keeps mutating every time we get a handle on how to fight the previous incarnation. Now we have to worry about it *digging*, for Chrissakes. The only good news is, if it's organized and can think, it'll be easier to fight than the randomness of the Stage 2 flesh-eaters, as we can try to predict its moves."

"Yeah, but the bad news is, we don't know how many more of them there are or how soon they're going to start popping up in Allentown, Scranton, Reading, or hell, downtown Philly to ring the goddamn Liberty Bell to add to their numbers," said Sgt. Moore. "And we'd been worried there might be a Stage 4 before, so now that we know there is, what's to say there's not some Stage 5, 6, or 7 out there that can really turn our lights out? What if it gets out of Pennsylvania? Over to Europe? Look how much damage it's done in twenty-four hours alone. Twenty thousand people? I'd say it's a lot more than that by now."

Sgt. Celek could only nod as Sgt. Moore outlined his worst fears. He glanced over at Sgt. Holt, who looked shell-shocked, and then moved over alongside her.

"You okay?" he asked.

"Not even close," she replied. "But I figure if he can keep going like it's nothing, who am I to complain?"

Sgt. Holt nodded over towards Bones, who was wandering around on the rocks, still shaken by the attack but for completely different reasons than the soldiers. While the smell of the Stage 4's blood was pretty bad, it wasn't all-consuming. It was the hot breath of the cordite exhaled by a hundred smoking machine guns that had burned itself into Bones's nose for the time being. Nothing messed with a cadaver dog's nose like a smell of burning, and Bones was having a particularly hard time shaking it off. Thor seemed to be having similar problems as he padded alongside Bones, the two animals moving in tandem as if Bones's actions back in the woods had well-established him as an alpha to be followed.

"That dog's some kind of a survivor," Sgt. Celek agreed. "If I'd been through everything he'd been through, I'd be curled up in a ball in a corner somewhere by now."

"Good thing for us you're not, then," replied Sgt. Holt, attempting a joke. "But do you really think he can walk us out of here? I have no idea where we are, and we're completely without support. If there's another attack like that last one, we're not going to survive more than a few seconds."

Sgt. Celek didn't have a reply for this. He looked back over at Bones but saw that the shepherd was suddenly standing still, his snout pointed straight ahead like an arrow, finally smelling something different. As Sgt. Holt shot Sgt. Celek a worried look, Bones *woofed* but just enough to get his handler's attention, then trotted ahead a few feet before stopping again, Thor close behind. Celek, fearing the worst, rose to join them.

"Bones? You got something, boy?" Celek asked, the other soldiers seeing what was happening and tensing. Hands reached for weapons that had only just cooled.

Bones, now with Celek at his side, stood still for another moment but then *woofed* a second time and moved forward, climbing across the rocks. Realizing that Bones didn't appear to be intimidated so much as curious, Celek relaxed a little, nodded to the others, and began following after Bones.

The group trailed Bones across the mostly treeless cliff side for a tenth of a mile before finally reaching the end of the rocks. Bones moved to the edge and looked straight down. Sgt. Celek, a few yards behind, indicated for the soldiers to fan out around the rocks in case something was waiting for them just under the lip but then joined Bones at the ledge.

"Oh, shit...," Celek whispered.

After crossing all those rocks, they were now dead-ended, overlooking an expansive coal mining operation. Appearing like a low volcano in the middle of the forest, the mouth of the mine pit was easily half a mile across, the crater floor several hundred feet straight down. On the floor of the pit were two large yellow earthmovers as well as an angled conveyor belt that carried freshly mined coal many stories up into the air before launching it into a massive coal pile on the east side of the pit, where two steam shovels waited to load it onto dump trucks. A zigzagging road led up the side of the pit, allowing trucks access from the base to a single road on the opposite side from where the soldiers stood. The road cut through the forest towards what Celek presumed must be a railroad spur that would then whisk the coal to civilization. The conveyor belt, empty of coal, was still chugging along, the electric whine of its heavy generator being the only sound emanating from the otherwise deserted-looking job site.

But everyone's eyes were focused on one thing – the eight or nine mine shafts at the base of the black shale walls that descended deep into the earth. The same thought had occurred to everyone at once; this is where they all went, and this is where they were all hiding.

"We seeing any signs of life?" Sgt. Celek quietly asked the other survivors, referring to people or multipedes.

Everyone nervously scanned the operation, from a pair of double-wide trailers – one up top near the service road, one down at the base of the pit – that served as the mining outpost's offices to the cabs of the large construction vehicles to the mouths of the mines themselves, but they didn't see movement. There were some relieved sighs, but not many.

"Check this out," said Sgt. Holt, waving Celek over after returning from a quick reconnoiter of the cliff's edge. They hurried to her, and she pointed down to a spot on the pit wall smeared with the now telltale blood substance they associated with the multipedes. "They're down there.

Sgt. Celek leaned over the edge of the cliff and was able to pick out multiple blood smears running all the way down. Bones followed his nose over to the ledge, drawing in the familiar scent.

"What do you think, Bones?" he asked. Bones's sniffing increased, followed by a snort.

Celek and the other MPs walked back to the surviving Rangers. "They're down there, people," Sgt. Celek reported. "Maybe all of them. Doing what, well, that's anyone's guess."

"How many is 'all of them'?" one of the Rangers asked.

"Thousands? Tens of thousands?"

This piece of information caused a few stomachs to leap into throats. The surviving soldiers looked around at each other nervously, knowing how close they must be to a potentially devastating enemy.

"So, what do we do about it?" asked Romeo, turning up the volume on his radio to reveal it still echoed with nothing but static. "Can't really call in an air strike, can we?"

"With the rate these things are mutating, by the time an air strike got out here, there's no telling if they'd even accomplish that much anyway," replied Sgt. Celek. "We have to come around to the fact that we may be the only thing standing between these monsters and everybody else on the Eastern seaboard. I'm afraid we're going to have to go down there and check it out."

"And do what?" asked Sgt. Moore incredulously. "Start the world's shortest firefight?"

"It's a mine, and where there's a mine, there's blasting equipment," Sgt. Celek countered, indicating a shed at the base of the pit alongside the office trailer. "If they're in there, we can send explosives down the shafts, blow them remotely, and sink this thing with all of them inside. That should buy the air force enough time to come in and mop up. They'll just have to follow the smoke."

"Doesn't sound like a plan with much of an exit strategy," another Ranger said. "What happens when they see the 'remote' explosives coming down the shafts and decide to see who sent them? How fast you think we can climb out of there when we're surrounded?"

Sgt. Celek shrugged. "I thought you guys got up in the morning looking for some noble mission to sacrifice yourselves on. Well, this is it, and here you are."

A couple of the Rangers chuckled but then – to a man – nodded at Celek and gathered their gear to head down into the pit.

"All right, then," said Sgt. Celek.

Bones had been inching closer to what appeared to be a narrow service/emergency trail cut down the side of the pit accessible only by workers, no trucks, and Celek moved over alongside him. Bones looked up at him and Celek nodded, giving Bones permission to start down the cliff-face trail, pausing only a couple of times on the way to let the soldiers catch up.

When they got to the base of the pit, the soldiers eyed the dark shafts nervously, but after nothing emerged for the first few minutes, they relaxed a little and double-timed it over to the explosives shed. The mine had been running when whatever Stage had descended laid waste to their workers, made evident by blood spatter on the tools and machinery that hadn't been visible from the cliff face, so the blast shed was unlocked and open, as if just waiting to be drained of its dynamite. Celek, Holt, and a couple of the Rangers began walking crates of the stuff out into the pit as Romeo pored over the track controls to determine how to send flat-bed carts down the various shafts remote but found most of the control board in pieces.

While this was happening, Bones and Thor, followed by Sgt. Moore, walked the pit's perimeter. Whenever Bones stopped cold and his nose rose from the ground and began sniffing the air, Moore couldn't help but tense his trigger fingers around the trigger guard of his machine gun. Inevitably, Bones would sink his nose back down, and Sgt. Moore could once again relax.

"You keep doing that, you're going to give me a heart attack, dog," Moore said, shaking his head.

But moments later, Bones did it again, stopping and sniffing the air but not so much of the pit, more a nearby mine shaft. Thor moved in next to Bones and started doing the same, both dogs becoming increasingly alarmed as they inhaled whatever was coming from deep within the mine.

"Thor, what is it?" asked Moore, hurrying over to join the dogs. As he stood in the mouth of the mine shaft, the sunlight only afforded the sergeant a view a couple dozen feet inside. But it hardly mattered as, even with the pervading darkness, Sgt. Moore could suddenly *hear* what the dogs were getting so anxious about.

Back at the explosives shed, Romeo was shaking his head over the track controls.

"What is it?" asked Sgt. Celek.

"All the electrical's been shorted or torn out," Romeo complained. "We're not going to get a one of these down into those shafts from up here."

Celek stared back at Romeo, realizing what was implicit about this statement. Romeo returned the grim stare and was about to continue when he was interrupted by a frantic cry.

"Guys!! *Guys!!!*" Celek and the others turned as Sgt. Moore, Bones, and Thor came galloping back over to them, completely out of breath. "Something's down there, maybe people! You can hear them from that shaft in the northwest corner."

"Why people?" Sgt. Celek asked, surprised.

"You can hear machinery," Sgt. Moore replied. "Whatever's making that noise is a hell of a lot bigger than any of those multipedes or multi-worms or whatever. The ground's getting chewed up down there – rocks, boulders, you name it. Maybe some people survived underground and just didn't get the memo about what's been going on topside."

Nobody thought this sounded all that plausible, but no other answer made itself readily available.

"Well, it might not matter," Sgt. Celek began. "Corporal Romeo was just explaining to me that the flat cars can't be sent down there remotely, so we're going to have to split up into two-man teams and escort them down into the shafts ourselves anyway."

This was met with incredulity. Celek continued.

"If there *is* somebody down there, we'd have to at least try to get word to them before the whole place goes up anyway," he suggested. "Since this was my idea, I'll lead the car that's going down that shaft."

Though a couple of Rangers suggested this had even less of an exit strategy than the first plan, acceptance of the inevitable came relatively quickly, and the soldiers moved to finish loading the flat cars with the last remaining explosives, now enough to blow the top of nearby Blue Knob Mountain if need be. Romeo then gave everyone a quick lesson in the application of blasting caps and the use of civilian trigger detonators as the six mobile bombs were lined up and readied for departure in front of their respective shafts.

"I'm coming with you, if that's all right." Sgt. Holt nodded at Sgt. Celek. "You and Bones are still a package deal, right?"

"I'm game if he is," replied Celek, glancing over at Bones.

The shepherd didn't look back, if he had even heard his name. Ever since he'd returned from the northwest mine shaft with Thor and Sgt. Moore, he'd stared at its black maw, as if hypnotized by the scent of the dark machinery that lay below.

IX

It was established that each team would trigger their explosives precisely ten minutes after their descent into the mines, as it was felt that communication would be impossible once they were "under." After a grim round of "good lucks" and a synchronizing of watches, the six teams of two descended into their assigned mine shafts, Thor riding shotgun with Sgt. Moore and Cpl. Romeo, Holt with Celek and Bones, and the other four platforms divided up amongst the surviving Rangers.

By now, Bones was tired but more importantly, thirsty and a little hungry. Sgt. Celek had given him some water, but his canteen had been practically dry when he poured what little liquid remained into the cap to offer it to the shepherd. Once they were in the mine, Bones located a few rivulets of water snaking down the inner walls of the shaft and lapped at them in passing, but had to keep breaking away to keep up with his two human companions and the flat car they were manually wheeling down the long iron track. Celek's hand stayed firmly on the brake as he and Holt pushed from behind, though gravity did much of the work. They were illuminated only by a dim tinted light at the tip of a metal pole attached to the side of the car, which cast everything in the shaft in an eerie green glow.

Bones's nose was beginning to recover from the cordite, and he inhaled the scent of cool rocks, the sweat of workmen, the oiled wheels of the mine cars, and coal dust, which didn't so much have a smell as it did work its way into Bones's nostrils and lungs, making it increasingly difficult to breathe. Bones was able to continue drawing in new smells, however, and kept his nose ahead, constantly on the hunt for the now-familiar scent of the multipedes.

Confirming Sgt. Moore's claim, as soon as the trio had gone five steps into the shaft, they could hear the distant sound of breaking rocks and moving earth. The only thing was, as they got even a little closer to the source, it was obvious to both Celek and Holt that the noise wasn't coming from anything remotely man-made.

"Way too big to be a machine," whispered Sgt. Holt as they descended deeper and deeper into the mine shaft, a sign they passed reporting that they were passing the point of 200 Feet. "But no way those are multipedes."

Sgt. Celek silently agreed.

Though he was still sniffing around for water sources, Bones's ears were also picking up the sound from below as it increased in volume. It wasn't long before all kinds of new smells began reaching his nose, and he moved ahead of the two MPs.

"Look at Bones," Sgt. Holt whispered, hand reaching for the manual brake.

In the green haze of the flat-car light, Sgt. Celek looked at the German shepherd, whose ears were now straight up and down like radar antennae, his eyes peering ahead and his nose squarely facing front. He held that pose for a moment but then crept forward, head still held high but the rest of his body a little lower to the ground. Sgt. Holt set the car's parking brake, and she and Sgt. Celek quietly followed after Bones from just a few yards behind.

As Bones moved forward, the air grew decidedly cooler, the ground wetter. A breeze blew past the shepherd as he neared the source of the great sound up ahead. As his eyes peered into the darkness, Bones could see that the floor, walls, and ceiling of the mine shaft he was padding down were quickly coming to an end, replaced by a wide open black space that seemed to go on forever. The source of the great sound was somewhere in that hollowed-out space.

Two more steps and the mine track ended along with the rest of the shaft, the iron ends bent down as if snapped by some great force that had crashed through the tunnel from above, smashing everything in its path like a giant cannonball crashing through the earth.

Which is precisely what had happened.

"Oh, my God."

Sgt. Holt's words were almost lost in the wind as she and Celek joined Bones at the edge of the cliff created by the destruction of the mine shaft. The cacophony, tremendous and foreboding, was coming from directly in front of them in the darkness, though they had no idea how far away it might be. The distant sound of rocks crumbling out of the walls and crashing to a rocky base far, far below could be heard, but any sense of size or scale was absent.

With a trembling hand, Celek reached into his belt and extracted a flare and a flare gun that he'd taken from the explosives shed. Sgt. Holt's heart skipped a beat, knowing that as soon as he lit it, they would not only see whatever great monstrosity was making the sound, but it would also – assuredly – see them. She still had the remote detonator in her hand and, without alerting Celek, armed it with the flick of a thumb switch. Just in case. No light came on, no sound emerged from the flat car a few yards back, but Holt had felt the quick vibration within the trigger that announced an electrical current now on the move and ready to send a signal back to the network of blasting caps on the dynamite if she so much as flinched. She turned to Celek and nodded.

Celek jammed the flare into the flare gun, twisting the cap to arm it, and aimed it skyward. He hesitated one last second before firing it into the darkness, sparks belching out of the muzzle. The flare arced high into what was obviously a truly massive space, dribbling white phosphorescence behind it as it went before it finally exploded in a hail of stars.

At first they could see nothing, as their eyes needed a moment to adjust to the light. But then the flare began to halo out its illumination, revealing a great, cylindrical cavern literally a few miles across in diameter and easily twice that in depth, a space large enough to hold all the skyscrapers of Manhattan like French fries in a cardboard cone. But the trio on the cliff's edge was hardly interested in the dimensions of the newly created cave, no matter how impressive. No, their eyes were fixed squarely on the thing in its center that had obviously created the cavern and was continuing to expand it straight down.

From one glance, it was clear to the two soldiers that what they were looking at was a giant sea anemone. The fact that it was the size and even somewhat the shape of the Astrodome didn't sink in immediately, so entranced were they by how the light from the flare played through the translucent blue and white skin of the anemone's body and attendant segmented tentacles, of which there were easily a hundred, each the length of a football field. Within the tentacles were much thicker finger-like creatures that appeared to be a different species altogether, though it was grafted on to the anemone. These wormy protrusions were of a different color (off-white with thick red bands around its body, giving it the appearance of a necktie or candy cane), but instead of coming to a finger-like tip at the end like the tentacles, these each had great mouths that were currently being plunged into the rocks below the anemone, where they used row upon row of teeth to drill.

As the flare began to fade, its arcing descent bringing it closer and closer to the area being tunneled, Sgt. Celek felt Sgt. Holt reach over and take his hand.

"I can't believe what I'm looking at," she whispered.

Sgt. Celek couldn't, either. It didn't look monstrous in the slightest, not like anything they'd seen throughout the day at all. In fact, it was quite beautiful, just simply out of scale, like seeing a sugar ant poised to fight a giant tarantula. It was also absurd, like coming around the corner of a zoo to find the woolly mammoth enclosure (*Mammuthus primigenius*). It just didn't compute. Celek didn't understand how it had gotten there or what it was trying to accomplish, much less why it existed in the first place.

Just as the flare faded away for good, he caught sight of one of the anemone's tentacles and managed to get a good look at just how they were segmented, much the same way as the multipedes. That's when it hit him, the sheer enormity of the events of the past thirty-six hours or so. This creature was made out of the combined flesh of literally tens of thousands of human beings fused together by an out-of-control, multi-stage mutation that had created a whole new organism. There had never been anything like it in the history of the planet, but as with anything else, it had always been a possibility lying dormant.

This was when Bones started barking.

At first, the two MPs didn't compute what they were hearing, but then Bones's thunderous alarm started echoing across the vast cavern inhabited by the anemone, and they blanched.

"Bones – *quiet*," Sgt. Celek bellowed, and the shepherd quickly silenced himself and turned to the two MPs. The two humans held their breath.

"Do you think they...*it* heard?" asked Sgt. Holt, scanning the darkness.

"I don't know," Celek replied, his breathing accelerating as adrenaline raced through his body. The pair waited in silence, Celek's hand firmly on Bones's collar. The sergeants' eyes peered out into the cavern in hopes of detecting any kind of movement but got nothing except a cool breeze.

"It didn't seem to see the light, so maybe it can't hear, either," suggested Sgt. Holt, allowing a modicum of optimism to infiltrate her voice.

On cue, they felt a sudden change in the breeze, something rushing through the darkness towards them and, half a second later, one of the giant tube worms had plunged its mouth - over twelve feet across - onto the end of the mine shaft, its teeth drilling in a circle a mere few inches from the MPs' faces. It churned rocks and dirt from the surrounding rock walls, blasting it in towards the soldiers and dog with gale-force intensity.

"Run!" screamed Sgt. Celek, who stumbled backward but was grabbed by Holt, who kept him on his feet. Bones let out a few terrified barks at the worm and bent down on his forepaws as if trying to convince the thing he only wanted to play. After getting struck by a couple of rocks, the dog did a quick 180 and sprinted after the MPs as the ground, ceiling, and walls around them began to quake, showering them with pulverized shale.

Bones's nose went into overdrive as silt and coal dust clouded into it, now pouring down from the crumbling ceiling like a heavy rain. What would've been most curious to Bones if he could have such a thought was that the tube worm and its symbiotic anemone gave off no smell whatsoever, despite its earlier stages carrying with them such distinctive, cadaverous scents. No sooner had he and his party gotten just past the flat car, about twenty feet up the shaft, than the downpour of dirt became a hail of rocks and the tunnel caved in all around them, burying them under hundreds of pounds of earth.

Back in the cavern, the symbiotic tube worm, detecting no more heat from the targeted mine shaft, returned to its task, drilling deep down into the earth. Like the anemone and the other worms, the nerve endings on this worm detected a very faint, yet incredibly intense heat signature coming from below the earth's surface, the greatest heat it could fathom. The worm kept digging, churning up black and red shale, sand, and limestone as it got closer and closer to its destination, a few hundred feet a minute, down, down, down, deep into the earth.

It was only a few minutes before Bones woke up, covered from head to toe in rocks and dirt. His sides hurt, his head hurt, his paws hurt. But the good news was, he could move. Sure, the ceiling of the mine shaft had collapsed, but above that was hard, solid (for now) rock that hadn't been affected by the attack of the giant tube worm. Though the exit was now blocked, Bones had managed to find himself in a small open pocket during the cave-in.

A little tentative still, Bones staggered to his feet, shook off as much of the dust and dirt as he could, then looked around. The dim light of the flat car could still be seen glowing through layers of collapsed rock, still at the shattered mouth of the mine shaft but virtually unreachable. Bones put his nose to the ground and began sniffing around, the smells of the tunnel now hanging heavy with death.

"*Booones*," came a voice from nearby.

Bones trotted over, recognizing the scent of Sgt. Holt, though mixed with the harsh smells of blood and human shit. Bones leaned his nose down to her hand and gave it a couple of quick licks. It was already starting to get cold. Bones caught the faint scent of Sgt. Celek as well, but it came from deep under a solid mountain of rocks.

"*Bones*," Sgt. Holt said, her voice weak and barely audible. "Help me..."

Bones saw her arm move and could tell that she was trying to dig herself out from under the dirt. Bones's training kicked in, and he began digging around her arm until it was completely free. Feeling ambitious, Holt then tried to move the rest of her body, only to shriek in agony. It took her a couple of moments to recover her breath after this attempt, but then she turned back to the shepherd.

"I'm paralyzed," she said, more to herself than the dog. "But I can almost reach the detonator switch."

She pointed out to the small, gray trigger that had tumbled clear of her during the cave-in, now sitting just a few feet away. Bones continued to dig around her torso with his claws, but in doing so caused more dirt and rocks to rain down over her.

"*Guuuhhh!!*" she groaned as pebbles slipped into wounds opened up on her back and neck, bouncing against shredded muscle and nerve tissue. Tears exploded up into her eyes. "Bones. Please…"

She pointed at the trigger. Bones looked at her oddly for a moment, but then she pointed again.

"*Bones*," she said, attempting a sharp tone in her voice. "There. Retrieve. Bring that to me. Come on…get it!"

Bones glanced over at the trigger, then back at Sgt. Holt, who waved her hand in the direction of the detonator, making Bones look back at it again.

"Get it, Bones," she tried. "Bring it to me. Wait, how about this one: *fetch*."

This was, in fact, one of Bones's commands. He turned, walked over to the detonator, picked it up in his jaws, and brought it back to her, though he dropped it just beyond her reach. As it fell, Sgt. Holt gasped, afraid it might set off the explosives, but then it clattered harmlessly to the mine shaft floor just beyond her fingers.

"*Jesus*, Bones," Sgt. Holt sighed, a little relieved that somehow it hadn't blown them up, though on some level she knew she'd be dead soon, whether it came from the explosion or her own life's blood draining away through her wounds.

She stretched out her fingers until they just touched the detonator. It took a couple of agonizing tries, but she finally managed to slide it close enough to pick up.

"That's a good boy, Bones," she said to the dog, who padded around, looking worried. "You're a good boy."

Sgt. Holt looked up at Bones and knew that the dog had no idea what was coming next. She also knew that, after all he'd been through, he didn't deserve it, either. She craned her neck around but saw that the mine shaft leading back up to the surface was completely blocked off, with no way out. She then looked back towards the dull light on the flat car and could hear the ongoing work of the monstrosity in the cavern. That's when she knew she was going to have to die alone.

"*Go*, Bones," she cried, pointing as best she could towards the light. "Get out of here. Go!!!"

When she flicked her wrist one more time, Bones flipped backwards, as if expecting to see that she'd lobbed something for him to retrieve – another game of fetch - but she hadn't, and he turned back to her, confused. That gave the sergeant an idea. She picked up a rock and threw it, albeit weakly, at Bones's head. It lightly connected, causing Bones to snort and back away.

"*Go!*" she screamed as loud as she possibly could. "*Get out of here!!*"

She picked up a second rock and threw it at Bones, this time hitting him in his injured shoulder. Bones let out a *woof* this go-round, still thinking it was playtime. Sgt. Holt gave up on the rocks and simply tried another gesture.

"Come on, Bones," she said, waving him away. "Just go…"

For some reason, this did the trick. Bones, mouth still open in a pant, wheeled around and climbed over the rubble leading to the flat car. As he did so, his hind legs started a small avalanche that dropped a handful of rocks over the opening he'd just used, effectively sealing Sgt. Holt in, all alone.

She stared at the space where the dull light had come in from only a second before, but then grasped the detonator in her hand. Taking a deep breath, she checked the switch to make sure it was still armed and then gently pressed the trigger.

"One-Mississippi, two-Mississippi…," she began.

On the other side of the collapse, Bones made his way to the flat car, which had been knocked over and half-buried in the tube-worm attack. He gave it a quick sniff-around but then walked to the gnarled edge of the mine shaft and sniffed out into the darkness. He could hear the gigantic beast out in front of him but couldn't see a thing. The lack of smell didn't help, which only confused the shepherd. But then, like a miracle, he picked up another smell nearby. It was the rich, dry soil he'd smelled earlier in the day, both during the underground multipede attack but also as he'd just descended into the mine. It represented the layer of earth that was near enough to the surface that any scent of it this far underground must have been coming in courtesy of another mine shaft, one that represented a way *out*.

Bones sniffed around the cavern wall alongside the mouth of the devastated mine shaft, his whiskers detecting that it was covered with small, jagged outcroppings made by the descent of the great, cacophonous engine currently plowing its way to the earth's core in the center of the cavern. Bones took a first, tentative step out to one of the rocks, found it solid enough to take his weight, then took a second step, then a third, and then a fourth out onto the sloping wall, using his whiskers to plot a course as best he could. The journey was treacherous, and Bones was continually off-balance as he went, finding himself less than sure-footed in the dark. But he went slowly, making the first dozen feet or so, gingerly stepping from outcropping to outcropping.

Then the ground beneath his feet gave way.

With a startled yelp, Bones tumbled down the side of the cavern wall, along with a cloud of rocks and dust he kicked up as he went. He scratched at the slope to regain his footing, but gravity kept pulling him back down until he was finally rolling head over heels a good hundred feet. Then he finally stopped after bouncing into something soft, like a rubber cushion.

Bones leapt back onto his feet and knew at once that what he'd struck was alive, *the anemone*, and started barking, his whiskers twirling against the fleshy creature's outer layer. The noise of the creature's digging was so loud that Bones's barking could hardly be heard. But then he felt something moving through the air directly towards him and leaped out of the way at the last second.

This time, the attack was two-fold, tentacles and tube worms both, bashing themselves into the rocks where Bones had just stood as he bounded away. Even though he couldn't see his attackers, Bones's other senses could feel their approach, and he began a pattern of dives and feints as he dodged out of the way, the ground erupting directly behind him with great force as the creatures zeroed in on his warmth.

Bones's nose caught the scent of that dry near-surface soil again, and he made a beeline for its source. Even though it was steep and would inevitably slow his progress, Bones leaped onto the rocky wall of the cavern and struggled to ascend. All around the shepherd, the worms and tentacles plunged after him, causing minor earthquakes that continually knocked Bones off his feet. Some of these proved fortuitous, since Bones would be thrown in a different, unpredictable direction, out of the firing line of an incoming worm.

But Bones was also starting to feel the touch of the tentacles that just missed him as well as the heat emanating from the mouths of the predatory worms. It was only a matter of time…

That's when a great light suddenly illuminated the cavern, followed by the roar of an explosion that was louder even than the machinations of the anemone. All of the worms and tentacles instantly retracted from Bones's location and moved to this new heat source, only to be ignited by the ensuing, fiery devastation and battered under a hail of boulders. Behind Bones, the anemone was visible again, looking even more monstrous than before as its tentacles caught fire, throwing long shadows across the main body of the monster as it flailed around in desperation.

Even with the smell of burning flesh in his nose, Bones could still pick out where the mine shaft was ahead of him and raced forward towards the source. As he ran, a *second* explosion from the opposite side of the cavern – another mine shaft - showered the anemone with super-heated rocks and earth. This was immediately followed by a third, coordinated blast that had the effect of shaking the entire cavern, which began caving in on itself.

With the ground shaking beneath his feet, Bones raced up the side of the cavern and finally reached an open mine shaft. The smell of the soil, tinged again with the oil and grease of mining equipment, filled Bones's nose as he galloped up the pitch-black tunnel. Behind him, a fourth explosion went off, quickly followed by a fifth, then a sixth. The roar of the drilling tube worms was soon drowned out completely by the tremendous din of the collapsing mine.

X

It was afternoon by the time Bones clambered out of the mine shaft, now solid black in color, so covered in coal dust was he. A jumpy National Guardsman almost shot him when he appeared, walking out of the mine, panting, but then Corporal Romeo spotted him and gave up a cheer.

"Bones!!"

Romeo raced over to the police dog, who gave him a couple of sniffs, followed by a friendly lick on the hand. The Guardsman, who a second before had almost shot him, stared at the dog, shaking his head.

"That's the fucking wonder-dog?" he asked, incredulous.

"Bones," Romeo said. "His name's Bones, and he's got more lives than a goddamn pussy cat. Don't ya, Bones?"

Bones looked up at Romeo, happy to be petted but thirsty and desirous of water to wash out his throat and help recharge his nose. After Romeo had gotten to his feet to announce the discovery of the dog to the others, Bones noticed some rainwater that had gathered in the wheel well of a nearby truck and went over to drink it.

It turned out that the interest in Bones was mostly short-lived, as the military operation over the mine had bigger fish to fry at the moment. A pair of servicemen were tasked with leading Bones out of the mine pit, where he was placed on a truck and, luckily, given a big bowl of water and a couple of energy bars. He devoured each in a single bite. No longer hungry, he lay down with his head resting on his paws as hundreds of National Guardsmen and army regulars were marched past and into the pit.

Bones was asleep within seconds.

"You've had a hell of a day, huh, Bones?"

Hearing the most familiar of voices, Bones's eyes opened, and his nose inhaled the most familiar of smells. He looked up from the hospital blanket that had been placed on the floor for him and saw retired police sergeant Lionel Oudin looking down at him from a stool. Bones, half-covered in bandages, with parts of his fur shaved away to allow for a couple of surgeries, excitedly got to his feet and licked Lionel's hands before planting his paws on his old master's knees and raising up to lick his face, too. Lionel chuckled.

"Easy there, Bones. You're a lot more hurt than you realize."

Bones didn't seem to notice or care. He continued to lick at Lionel's face, and Lionel let him. After a moment, the old man climbed down off the stool and sat on the linoleum floor next to Bones, running his hands over the dog's back, shoulders, forelegs, haunches, paws, throat, snout, and even tail, hunting for injuries the doctors might have missed. Lionel frowned when he felt the dozens of small cuts in the pads of all four of Bones's feet but was gratified to find that a large one over his right eye was already beginning to heal, which he felt boded well for the others. When he'd finally finished his inspection, he shook his head.

"You're a real hard case, you know that, Bones?" Lionel said. "It's guys on the force like you who made me retire when I did; figured your gung-ho, rushing-in-where-angels-fear-to-tread bullshit was going to get me shot. But you did a good job of work today. That thing was apparently trying to drill straight down to the earth's core to get to the heat. It wasn't even supposed to be here. Some idiot pulled it up from a hydrothermal vent under the Arctic. Only then Mr. Einstein accidentally brought it in contact with some heavy-duty industrial macronutrient fertilizers and then took them home with him for the weekend."

Lionel turned to Bones with a wry grin. *"Whoops."*

"They said it's some kind of big chemistry set down there and that all life on Earth probably originated around hydrothermal vents, but I told them they were lucky their little monster decided to wreak havoc on land, 'cause my dog doesn't like to swim and they'd have been fucked, eh, Bones?"

Bones was now lying at Lionel's feet. It looked like the exertion of his greeting had wiped him out all over again. Lionel smiled.

"Well, you get some more rest, Bones. Officially, Pittsburgh, the military, everybody else, they're going all Three Mile Island, saying it was some kind of gas cloud and oh-what-a-tragedy. 'Unprecedented.' More safety regulations on the mining industry, etc. Upshot is, the mayor's not going to be giving you a medal in front of the courthouse any time soon. Sorry about that. Worse, they're going to retire you just because they're assholes. Well, mainly because your injuries are so bad but also because they're assholes. They asked me if I could take you, but I told them the truth; I'm an old man now. They'd find you eating my fingers in a few months when I had a stroke in the shower. I think we're cooking up another solution, though. You might find it appealing."

Lionel looked down at Bones for his reaction, but the shepherd was already fast asleep.

Ryan knew the rules. Don't tell the other kids or teachers what you saw or did because they won't believe you and they'll just freak out. Uncle Norman and Aunt Ronelle know some but not all of the story, and it'd probably be better to keep it that way. If anyone puts two and two together of where you're actually transferring in from and starts asking questions, the best thing to do is say that you got knocked out during the "toxic event" and only remember things beginning after you woke up in the hospital.

As he got ready for his second week of school, now in Morgantown, three counties away from Duncan and just across the state line into West Virginia, Ryan ran through everything the government social worker, Mr. Wieseltier, had told him back at the hospital about how things were going to be once he got out. He had told Mr. Wieseltier that all he wanted to do was go home, get his things, bury his dog. See his mom and sister. Mr. Wieseltier had gone silent for a moment but then told Ryan that they would make arrangements for him to do this, but it might take time.

Ryan knew this meant never.

"Ryan? You're going to miss your bus," came the voice of Aunt Ronelle from downstairs.

Ryan gathered his books – math and a social studies reader – and stuffed them into his backpack before remembering his spelling homework, which was still on his desk. He grabbed it, added it to the mix, and headed downstairs, stepping funny when he turned back around. He winced and started to grab for his leg, but then just took a deep breath and let the pain recede away. He hadn't noticed when it happened, but when the flesh-eaters knocked the paddy wagon he was riding in over onto the highway, Ryan had been launched off the steel bench he'd been sitting on, only to bash his leg into the bench on the opposite side of the van. By the time he had reached the hospital that would be his home for the next couple of weeks, doctors told him that the wound had cut deep enough to cause damage to both the soleus and gastrocnemius muscles in his right calf as well as a handful of nerves. It was so bad, in fact, that once it healed completely, Ryan was scheduled for at least two skin graft operations.

"Coming, Ronelle," Ryan called down, then headed towards the stairs.

As soon as he reached the first floor, though, he saw through the front window that the yellow school bus had just pulled away from the curb. His aunt, having seen the same thing, was walking in from the kitchen with an exasperated look on her face, which she instantly transformed into a smile when she saw her nephew.

"That's okay, sweetie," she said, reassuringly. "Just let me find my keys, and I'll give you a ride."

"Nah, I'll walk," Ryan replied, heading for the back door.

"Oh, honey, I don't know if that's such a good idea. Your leg."

Ryan took a couple of practice steps to show that his leg was just fine.

"I think I can manage. I'm supposed to exercise it, right?"

Ronelle looked him up and down for a moment but then nodded in agreement.

"Okay. You won't get lost, will you?"

"I'll be fine," Ryan said, managing a smile.

Ryan walked out the back door, slinging his backpack over his shoulder as he headed to a fenced-in enclosure at the back of the yard. Even though the entirety of the large, suburban backyard was fenced in, there was a separate, smaller, dog-run-style section closed off against the back fence, complete with a doghouse. In front of the house was Bones, lying down with his nose in the grass. When Ryan approached, he quickly got to his feet.

"Missed my bus. Want to walk me to school?"

Bones eyed Ryan expectantly. Ryan smiled and opened the gate. Bones quickly bounded through it, and the pair headed for the side gate that led out to the driveway.

As they walked through the neighborhood, Ryan kept an eye on Bones, who sniffed this hedge or that, urinated on a couple of telephone poles, and completely ignored the barked warnings of half a dozen house dogs along the way, ones Ryan figured Bones would eat for breakfast if they actually tried anything.

They moved from the neighborhood into a small wooded area that separated the residential subdivision from the nearby schools (an elementary and junior high sharing the same large parcel of land). A well-worn footpath had been cut through the stand of trees and crossed a narrow creek before emptying out directly onto the practice field behind Ryan's new school. Bones trailed along a few feet back but still shadowed Ryan pretty closely. As they crossed the creek, the shepherd inhaled the various scents of the animals that used the creek as a source of water – raccoons and possum, mostly. He was still sniffing at these when Ryan reached the edge of the woods, just at the edge of the practice field, and stopped. He looked down at Bones, whose whiskers were still twiddling in the air, and then kneeled beside him.

"You could jump the fences at Uncle Norman's house like they were nothing," he said quietly. "But you think you have to keep looking out for me."

Bones just stared at Ryan, panting quietly.

"If you want to stay, that's fine," Ryan continued. "I'll see you at home when I get back from school. But if you don't…"

Ryan reached into his backpack and retrieved a battered strip of cloth, Bones's Pittsburgh Bureau of Police collar with his name on it. He reached around Bones's neck and put the collar back on, snapping the little plastic clasp in place.

"This is so nobody thinks you're a stray and everybody'll know your name."

Ryan petted the area between Bones's ears, his wounds now as healed as they were going to be, but then he hugged the German shepherd close to him. Bones didn't like this and tried to squirm away, but Ryan held him tight for only a moment longer before letting him go. Ryan started to tear up.

"Well, I love you, Bones."

Ryan got back to his feet, looked at Bones one more time, and then turned and walked across the practice field. As he went, his footfalls gently creasing the closely cropped grass, he fought the urge to cry. His eyes became glassy with tears and his nose began to run, but he wiped off both with his sleeve. Only when he reached the other side of the field did he allow himself to look back, half-expecting Bones to be three steps behind him, having not understood what Ryan had told him.

But Bones was long gone.

Bones had stayed within the trees as he walked, following the creek as far as he could, but about a mile down it stopped at an underground drainage pipe, and that was the end of that. He'd ostensibly been following the scent of a raccoon, but wasn't hungry and wouldn't have done much more than tease the thing if he'd caught up to it. Climbing up the sides of the creek bed, he saw that the trees had momentarily fallen away as the pipe ran under a rural, four-lane highway that cut through the woods. On the opposite side from where he was standing, Bones could see that not only did the trees start up again, but there were also no signs of houses or businesses or people for a ways, just the endless thicket of a state forest.

Bones waited until a lumbering tractor-trailer, the only vehicle on the road, passed by, then took a tentative step onto the road. After another second, he galloped across, disappearing into the trees on the other side. As he ran, the exhaust and oil smells of the highway faded away and were replaced by the sweet scent of mountain laurel and rhododendron. It wasn't long before he found another creek to follow that was weaving through the chestnut trees. He played with a frog, urinated against a picnic table, barked at a chipmunk. Took a nap in the afternoon, raided a trailside garbage can for dinner, and then slept under the stars.

When he woke up the next morning, he found another creek.

SHEPHERD

Lupus in fabula

Prologue

There is an old joke in high-end real estate that compares selling a space in Manhattan to Los Angeles. A New York realtor will show a loft to a perspective client, pointing out the view, explaining the history of the neighborhood, who may live in the building, what's close by, but will ultimately always close with, "It's the total New York experience."

In Los Angeles, it's all trees, hills, canyons, high fences, and privacy, where the potential buyer is finally told, "You won't even know you're in L.A."

Los Angeles is a city of isolation. In New York, the subways, the buses, and the sidewalks force a sort of egalitarian integration among the classes. In Los Angeles, cars are king because of how far everything is from each other, making it easy for people to stay within their self-selected residential pocket. You're East Side, West Side, Valley, the Hills, Culver, downtown, LBC, the Marina.

During the Rodney King riots, LAPD officers in riot gear enforced these divisions by forming a shoulder-to-shoulder human barricade on Wilshire Boulevard to prevent looters from crossing north into Beverly Hills.

This at a time when law enforcement was letting other parts of the city burn. Families will live in an area they can afford but then rent a cheap apartment elsewhere to establish residency in the school district they want to send their kids to. Micro-cities within Los Angeles like West Hollywood have seceded to make certain that their tax dollars only go to their own services and not to pay off the city's burgeoning debt, making for wealthy, crimeless duchies throughout the disparate megalopolis that only consider themselves Los Angelenos when the Lakers are in the playoffs.

Then along came a great equalizer.

When it arrived, it was hardly a surprise. The City of Los Angeles regularly posts bus shelter ads and billboards begging its citizenry to prepare for emergencies by creating "earthquake kits" just in case. These were recommended to contain important documents and cash, with water and nonperishable food not far away. Even more so, in the eight months leading up to the quake, water mains routinely broke around the city, and cautionary stories floated around the Internet that this was the result of a trembling along the famed San Andreas Fault, where the Pacific Plate rammed up against the North American Plate, resulting in unending tension. About a hundred magnitude-1 and -2 earthquakes began rattling California throughout the winter and into the new year.

But even then, Los Angelenos were dismissive along local lines.

"It'll probably hit out in Pasadena," someone would say. "We won't feel it in Los Feliz."

"Luckily, we're right on the water, like *right* on the water. It'll suck for everybody crammed in downtown, but we'll be okay."

"Good thing we're in the city proper, because it's not the quake but the fires that will break out in the hills when all the gas lines snap that is really going to do the most damage."

"It'll be the worst for the poor. Those buildings they live in haven't even been retrofitted. They're going to flatten, and you know there's like twenty people living in each one. Jesus."

"Man, the beaches. When aid rolls in, they're the furthest out. They'll be cut off."

In the end, everyone turned out to be right.

I

There had been a point in the winter when the hikers quit coming, which forced Bones to switch from his diet of trash-can leftovers to a steady stream of wildlife. He'd assiduously avoided what some of the animals of the Ohiopyle woods did when the snows came, an ever-closer march towards civilization, whether rest stops or winter cabins, in order to continue scavenging off man's leftovers. Instead, Bones pushed even deeper into the forest, happy to be shy of people for awhile. Mice were easy enough to catch, but not filling. Rabbits became a staple. He'd killed a turkey once, but when the feathers poked at his gums and took root between his teeth, he had decided to stick to mammals in the future. Having become a keen hunter relatively quickly during his time in the woods, Bones even found himself going after the odd lynx or bobcat from time to time.

Long thought extinct in the area, a pack of timber wolves was active in the woods as well, but Bones knew to avoid them. If a confrontation became unavoidable, he could probably use his superior size and strength to fight off two or three of them, but the four or five of a hunting party would easily overwhelm him.

Thus far, there had really only been one incident, and it was easily resolved. Bones had been snoozing under a rocky outcropping during a light snowfall. He hadn't eaten for a day or so and was starting to get hungry when a year-old buck walked by, all alone. Its horns more resembled thin sticks than a rack of antlers, which seemed to indicate that it had only lost its fawn spots a few months before. Still, it stood three and a half feet at the shoulder, which gave it more than enough meat to satisfy a ravenous German shepherd.

Bones waited until the deer crept past his impromptu blind, the snow playing havoc with the deer's sense of smell, which typically would be effective against predators that close. The young buck moved with caution, as if realizing that another large animal had been in the area not so long ago. Still, it seemed to be banking on the fact that whatever-it-was had since moved on.

Wishful thinking.

Bones crouched low, his eyes focused on the buck's ears, eyes, and tail to see if anything was setting off its internal alarm bells, but everything proceeded as normal. The buck's reactions indicated little trepidation.

Once it had moved a few feet downwind from the outcropping and was investigating a small patch of grass in a neighboring clearing, Bones made his move. Moving swiftly and low to the ground, the one-time police dog launched himself off the rocks and directly onto the buck's back. At the last moment, the larger animal seemed to realize what was happening and whirled around to bolt, but not in time. Bones wasn't as fast as he'd been as a younger dog, but he made up for it with the viciousness of his attack. Knowing that the buck would fight back for only as long as it thought it had a chance at survival, the shepherd knew to come on strong and in a dominating manner. An older buck, arrogant in its size and standing in the woods, would fight back even with catastrophic wounds bleeding it out onto the forest floor. A younger one feeling mortal fear for the first time would sooner submit.
In this case "sooner" equaled less than a minute.

It was still barely alive when Bones tore open its soft belly and began stripping out the hot organs on which he feasted first. That's when the shepherd's well-tuned ears picked up a new presence in the area. Like the deer, Bones's nose had been adversely affected by the weather, but his sense of hearing was as good as ever, and even in the soft snow he heard the footfalls of several hunters.

Bones turned around, instinctively blocking his kill with a tough defensive stance, and saw that the hunters were wolves, six in all, that seemed to have been tracking the buck when Bones interrupted and brought it down on his own.

Bones growled, the blood on his maw sluicing onto the snow as he bared his teeth. He'd had his first taste of blood for the day, was hungry for more, and wasn't interested in being interrupted.

The wolves, which could have easily torn him apart as a group, stood their ground but refrained from coming closer. This infuriated Bones. He growled louder and then began to bark, loud, threatening noises filled with violence directed mainly at the closest two wolves. One of the others in back began to whine, and Bones turned his savage barking on that one in particular, as if indicating that that wolf would be the first to die by his jaws.

After a couple of seconds passed with no movement, Bones simply turned and went back to eating, showing the wolves his tail. His back was still rigid as if ready to fight, but he allowed it to gradually relax. When Bones then heard the wolves resuming their approach, he tensed and stopped chewing, but the footfalls weren't stealthy this time. In fact, they were as tentative as the buck's.

In response, Bones whipped his head around and barked sharply at the three approaching wolves, startling each and making them recoil in their tracks. But just as quickly as he had turned, Bones angled his head back to the food and continued eating/ignoring them.

After another moment had passed, a single timber wolf stepped up beside Bones, sniffed the buck and inched its nose closer and closer to the food. Bones turned and growled at the wolf, but this only made it hesitate. It moved a little closer to the fallen deer, saw that Bones wasn't going to kill it for doing so, and then opened its jaws to sink its teeth into the newly dead flesh.

As the other wolves slowly gathered around the kill, Bones kept his peace, and soon the buck was torn to pieces. Each wolf took a chunk for itself, but also kept some back to deliver to the rest of the pack, doubtless nearby.

Bones ate his fill, gorging on the choicest pieces of meat without a care for the rest of the wolves. When one moved too close to a piece Bones wanted, the shepherd didn't make a sound but simply reached over and tore it away from the other animal. The wolf responded with a growl of its own, but Bones didn't engage, and soon the wolf had wisely moved on to a different piece.

A few minutes later, Bones was finished. Continuing to regard the wolves as if they were little more than crows begging at the trough, he spryly hopped away from the kill as the wolves watched and then disappeared into the woods without looking back. Once he was out of sight, he lifted his leg and peed on a tree. Then he moved on.

"It says we're right on top of him, but I don't see shit."

It was three months after the incident with the timber wolves when Bones had detected the first humans of the season. He'd been asleep, but their harsh scent filled his nose when they were still half a mile away. There were a number of them and they made a lot of noise as they walked, making it easy for Bones to get moving and keep a few hundred yards ahead.

After only ten minutes of the humans staying tight on his trail, Bones realized he was being pursued.

"Bones! Here, boy! Bones!!" cried a voice.

Bones started in the direction of the voice, some deeply embedded bit of training unexpectedly rising to the surface. This quickly faded and he bounded away, heading higher into the hills around Sugarloaf Mountain.

As he went, he continued to hear the men behind him. Though he was upwind, the men were dauntless in their ability to track him, never missing a turn, as if they had his scent and good. Bones wasn't tired, however, and just kept running. He was enjoying the pursuit, his mouth open as he galloped away, as if playing a game. He never imagined he'd be caught.

Thupp...thupp...thupp...thupp...thupp...

Bones heard the sound of the helicopter only seconds before it crested a nearby hilltop, a man hanging out of it, holding a pair of binoculars. The wash of the rotors kicked dust and needles off the aspens, creating clouds of debris that affected the shepherd's sense of smell. Momentarily unable to tell which direction the men were coming from, Bones made like an arrow for a small crevasse only a few hundred yards away.

"Bones!"

This time, Bones stopped in his tracks at the sound of a very familiar voice. He turned and looked in every direction, but saw no sign of the speaker. He woofed a little as if to invite the person to announce his presence, and on cue the voice came again, though blended with feedback.

"Bones. Stay right there, buddy. We're coming in after you."

Bones suddenly felt a sharp pain in his neck and yelped. He whipped around, barely able to glimpse the little red feather fletchings of the dart already pumping a sedative into his bloodstream. He could feel his shoulder numbing when he turned to escape, and this caused him to stumble awkwardly and plow his snout into the dirt. He attempted to pull himself up on all fours, but both of his front legs were weakening.

Snuffling, Bones slid to the ground, eyes darting all around in panic at his sudden vulnerability. This did not last for long, however, as his panic was soon replaced by a dull numbing of his senses that resolved itself with sleep.

Bones awoke as he was being hauled through the woods on an Indian-style travois, two posts crossed at the head with a plastic tarp tied up between. Bones's mouth felt as if it was full of cotton, so swollen was his tongue. He was groggy and glanced up at the people hauling him in. They were in typical cold-weather gear, like the hunters he occasionally saw from a distance.

That's when he noticed one pair of eyes looking down at him in particular, a grim smile under them.

"Hey, Bonesy," said former police sergeant Lionel Oudin. "You've put on weight. You're looking real good. Guess outdoor life agrees with you."

Bones looked up at his old trainer, a man he'd known since he was a puppy but who had also become his partner when he became a police dog, first for the Doña Ana Sheriff's Department in Las Cruces, New Mexico, and then the Pittsburgh Bureau of Police. When Lionel retired, Bones had been assigned a new trainer, but that man had been killed in the incident leading up to Bones's eventual escape into the wild.

Lionel leaned over and poured some water from a bottle into his hand, allowing Bones to lap up the liquid as the travois bounced along.

"Hate to tear you away from the woods," the old man continued. "And I wouldn't have, either, 'cept there's a national emergency, so much of one that they didn't blink when I suggested using that whirlybird to track you down. Bet you were wondering how we did that, huh? Well, that's a Pennsylvania state-thing, embedding you with a tracking device like they use on soldiers nowadays. I'd forgotten you even had it when I got the call looking for you."

Lionel reached down and touched a raised spot under Bones's left leg.

"They put that in right after we got here from New Mexico, but you were knocked out," Lionel explained. "Guess they figured you're too expensive a piece of police property to let get away. Still can't believe it worked after all this time."

Bones listened awhile longer, drank water when Lionel offered it, but then looked out over the disappearing treetops. The farther they went, the less he smelled the wilderness and the more he smelled what the men had brought with them: oil, beer, tobacco, plastic, guns, deodorant, sweat.

Bones glanced back towards the woods one last time and saw a single curious timber wolf just within the trees. He stared back at it for a moment, wishing he had the strength to clamber off the tarp and go after it, but he didn't. Resigned, he sank back onto the tarp and stared up into the sky.

The next few hours were a blizzard of activity. Bones was brought first to his old haunt, the K-9 school attached to the police training academy on Washington in Pittsburgh, where a police veterinarian gave him a clean bill of health.

"I'm surprised," the vet admitted to Oudin. "He's in tip-top shape. I don't know what he's been eating out there or how much exercise he's gotten, but I'd say he's fit for service."

Bones could detect a hint of disappointment in Lionel's face, but then the former police sergeant turned to the dog and smiled, scratching him between the ears as he led Bones off the examination table.

Two hours later, Bones found himself on a platform alongside four other enforcement/detection dogs, two German shepherds like himself and two Belgian Malinois, all younger. They were lined up at Pittsburgh police headquarters behind the chief of police as he prepared to give a speech to an assemblage of local press. Lionel was in attendance, too, standing just behind Bones with the other dog handlers, though he was the only one out of uniform, favoring a simple polo shirt with a Pittsburgh Bureau of Police badge embroidered on the chest.

"Because of the recent tragedy in Los Angeles, Pittsburgh is sending five of its best search-and-rescue dogs to aid in the city's recovery efforts," the Chief announcements. "These animals have a combined thirty-two years of service to our community and are of the very best trained in the country. Along with the number of Pennsylvania National Guardsmen and women already en route to the devastated city, we hope that our contributions will continue to help lead that city back from the brink."

A reporter raised his hand, and the chief nodded his direction.

"Are these dogs going to be used on a short-term basis to look for survivors, or are they going to be part of a longer process to look for the remains of the estimated four to five million dead?"

The Chief hesitated a moment.

"As I understand it, these animals will be asked to participate in a three-pronged process utilizing their skills at search and rescue, but also as enforcement animals used to control looting and criminal activity and, yes, also as cadaver dogs to help recover the deceased."

Bones noticed Lionel bristling at this list of tasks, his hand tightening on the leash as if momentarily regretting sending his friend into this maelstrom.

"Good-bye, Bones," Lionel was saying, leaning down and stroking the head of his old partner when they reached Pittsburgh International Airport with the rest of the team. "I'm sorry to say that I'm not going with you on this one. They asked me to, but, well, all those years of no smoking, no drinking, and healthy eating have caught up with me, and I've managed to pick up a nasty case of cancer. But you know what they say, you live long enough, you're going to get it. I just didn't think that meant sixty-one."

Bones stared up at his old friend, knowing something was worrying him but having no idea what it was. He nuzzled his snout into Lionel's hand, and the former police sergeant pulled close to him.

"You be careful out there," Lionel admonished the shepherd. "It's full of crazies and that was even *before* the quake."

Lionel chuckled, coughed, then chuckled again.

"Anyway, keep your head down. You never know when there'll be another aftershock."

Bones and the other dogs, as well as their handlers, were loaded onto a C-130 military transport plane, along with a large cache of supplies gathered from local merchants and bound for the devastated city. Bones was knocked out for the flight and slept in a large carrier alongside the other animals. He woke up an hour before the plane was to touch down and stayed awake, his snout resting on his paws as he looked around the inside of the massive plane. He smelled gunpowder and gun oil in the air, but also a different scent, one he recognized from the same incident of the previous year that had claimed his handler. It was a harsh chemical smell of almost a thousand biodegradable polyvinyl body bags that were stacked in the back and had the distinct odor of an old children's swimming pool that had gotten musty in the garage.

Bones had been around crime scenes in his career long enough to know that where those smells were, there would soon be others, including the souring stench of rotting corpses.

The plane landed at Edwards Air Force Base, the longtime military aircraft proving ground with a runway so long it was where the space shuttle landed when inclement weather clouded the Kennedy Space Center in Florida. Northeast of Los Angeles out on the high desert of the Mojave, Edwards was still far enough away from prying eyes to host the occasional top-secret craft but was mostly used in modern times to test unmanned and transport vehicles.

The C-130 bucked and bounced along the runway, but if the passengers found that unusual, they didn't say anything. It was only when the ramp was lowered and they saw the condition of the base that their looks turned to astonishment.

"Dear God," said one of the Malinois's handlers, her face falling as she saw what the quake had done to the base. "It looks like it was bombed."

In truth, the base looked less bombed and more like it had long since fallen into disrepair, maybe fifty or sixty years before. Most structures were still standing but with giant cracks through their walls, broken windows, partially collapsed roofs, and, in some cases, large chunks of concrete and metal cracked off and smashed onto the ground nearby.

But then there were the hangars.

Rather than an earthquake, the row of seven massive hangars alongside the runway looked more like they'd run afoul of a hurricane, a great wind having twisted their steel frames, wrenched away their walls and roofs, and then started a chain reaction that sent whatever was left over tumbling to its foundation and crushing whatever planes were inside. The hangars were so big that it seemed almost impossible that something had been able to pulverize them in such a way.

"Looks like God Himself came down and did a few cartwheels," another of the dog handlers joked. "We pretty close to the epicenter or something?"

A mechanic who'd been dropping blocks around the plane's wheels grinned over at the newcomer.

"We're just past the 100-mile mark. You ain't seen nothing yet."

II

The mechanic wasn't lying.

The dogs and handlers were driven by Humvee from Edwards, down the devastated 14 Freeway towards a staging area at the Burbank Airport just on the valley side of the Los Angeles basin, and got their first taste of the devastation. Before the quake, it was a trip that took twenty minutes without traffic. Now, with broken vehicles, trees, dirt and rocks from landslides, utility poles, and everything else strewn out across the highway, it took two hours.

The closer the convoy got to the city, the more pronounced the damage. Apartment buildings, houses, professional buildings, grocery stores, shopping centers -- they had all been driven into the ground, including modern structures that had likely been built not only up to code but to actually withstand even larger quakes, depending on the building owner's insurance rider. None of these things mattered, though. There had never been a recorded 10.2-magnitude earthquake in California history, and the likely reason for this was because it was so outside the realm of possibility that it meant there might no longer be a California.

But that's what had happened.

"All right, everybody in line!"

A tall, drill sergeant–looking fellow in digi-pattern camo fatigues and combat boots named Dalton was waiting for the Humvees as they arrived at the Burbank Airport. Though the dog handlers were all from various law enforcement agencies, they were technically in Los Angeles as civilian advisors to the Los Angeles Police Department. While they were in the air, things had changed.

"All of you are now under the umbrella of Pentagon 'total force,'" the sergeant announced. "You will not be subject to the military's chain-of-command, but you will have the enforcement authority of the Defense Department. The president has designated Los Angeles, Orange, Imperial, San Bernardino, and Kern Counties as disaster areas and has declared martial law."

A nervous reflex resounded through the dog handlers. Dalton noticed.

"I know what you're thinking," Dalton said. "No matter the situation, 'martial law' is just one of those boogeyman terms that can make its enforcers as nervous as those its meant to protect. But for the survivors here and especially on the other side of the hill, it lets them know that we're here and that we're doing something about the situation. There are fires, there's no water, no electricity, no way to move food, nothing. Because of that, you've got folks going to bed praying that somebody doesn't come in all 'Straw Dogs' on 'em in the middle of the night. If the ACLU wants to watch over my shoulder for abuses of power over the next stretch of days, they're more than welcome but should be ready for a diet of MREs and iodine-tasting water."

This made the handlers laugh.

For his part, Bones wasn't paying much attention. Since they'd arrived in Burbank, his nose had been going into overdrive. All around him he could smell the dead, both the bodies that had already been recovered from the surrounding area that were awaiting identification in the one standing hangar, but also the dozens still buried in the surrounding buildings, particularly a large hotel just off the airport entrance that was now little more than a pile of rubble.

Bones had been assigned to a female handler named Elizabeth Acho who had come down from Portland, where she'd been a civilian dog trainer for the local sheriff's department. For years now, she had traveled the country, delivering seminars to law enforcement on how to better utilize a dog's natural desire for play and exploration to make the animal an even more effective detection dog and a healthier, happier animal in general.

She had a German shepherd of her own that she was training named Charlie, but he was still young, and she'd left him behind in Oregon. When she'd heard that Bones, a semi-legendary dog in police circles, was being shipped to Los Angeles for quake duty but would need a hander, she put herself on the next plane. She hadn't known if she'd be lucky enough to get assigned the shepherd but hoped that if she put herself in the right place at the right time, she could make it easy for whoever was to make the decision.

"You have experience with this kind of animal?" the head of the K-9 unit, a Marine MP up from Camp Pendleton, had asked.

"Absolutely," Elizabeth replied. "In fact, he's something of my specialty."

And just like that, Bones was hers.

She'd been there when he'd arrived in the convoy from Edwards and knew from the moment he'd stepped out of the Humvee that he was different from the animals he rode in with. The other dogs paid attention to the people around them, while Bones, though not entirely oblivious, already had his nose in the air and was actively assessing his new surroundings. His was obviously an independent spirit accustomed to working alone, but also one inculcated with enough training and routine to accept his mutually beneficial affiliation with the humans.

Once Dalton had finished his address, Elizabeth went over and introduced herself to Bones by holding out her hand and squatting down until he could see her eyes. The shepherd seemed to understand immediately that this person would be taking on the role of his handler, but if he cared that much, he didn't show it.

"I'm not here to get in your way," Elizabeth said, knowing that though her words were meaningless, her tone was what mattered. "I'm just along to expedite what you're already here to do."

Bones stared at her for a moment but then looked back towards the collapsed buildings ringing the airport. Elizabeth found herself strangely envious. In a situation as grave as this, two dozen humans were useless compared to a single search-and-rescue dog. A person could spend days digging on a single site in a search for survivors, the same task being accomplished by a dog in a matter of minutes. A couple hundred dogs spread out in a grid pattern over the city would theoretically be able to locate any survivors within a forty-eight-hour period.

"We're going to do some good, Bones," Elizabeth said. "Mark my words. We'll be on CNN before sundown."

This prophecy proved untrue.

The earthquake happened on Sunday. Elizabeth had arrived by Tuesday and had hit the city with Bones for the first time Wednesday morning.

By Friday, she was regretting her decision to come down, as the emotional toll of seeing the horrific destruction up close was weighing down on her like a broken promise.

Since she and Bones had been helicoptered into their assigned search zone, the neighborhoods around Dodger Stadium, including Echo Park, Angelino Heights, and Elysian Park, they hadn't uncovered a living soul. Though they had a small military escort coupled with diggers and paramedics never more than ten minutes away, Elizabeth and Bones were mostly on their own as they picked across endless collapsed houses and businesses. She kept praying for the shepherd to stumble across one single survivor, but the devastating realization that there probably weren't any was beginning to sink in.

Instead, they found corpses.

As they had started in a more easily accessible business district off Sunset while army engineers cleared the impassable roads that wound through the residential areas, the bodies were limited to a handful at first; mostly homeless people, a few clerks and stock boys, a couple of other late-night denizens. The quake had hit at just past five o'clock in the morning, which was why the military had given it the provocative nickname "The Big Sleep," as so many had been killed in their beds. The media had picked up on it but had decided it was too ghoulish for prime time. In only two days, there were already more than 200,000 confirmed dead, though indications were that it was easily ten times that, with twenty or thirty not ruled out.

"What did you find?"

Elizabeth watched as Bones circled a spot atop the roof of a collapsed barrio-style house they'd climbed a gravel-strewn path to investigate. Try as she might, Elizabeth couldn't determine if what they were looking at had previously been a one- or two-story house.

Bones circled again, whined, then nosed around near a shattered piece of roofing. Knowing about what to expect, Elizabeth gingerly picked her way over, having learned her lesson after stepping onto seemingly stable surfaces that then gave way twice the first hour.

"Hello?" she called into the house as she pulled a flashlight out of her pocket.

She shined the beam down into the hole and looked around for signs of life, but that's when the smell hit her. Stinking of rotten food, feces, and cooked flesh, made worse by the hot sun that had turned many of the crushed houses into pressure cookers. The stench just about overwhelmed her, and she took a couple of quick steps back. In doing so, she stepped through a pile of broken glass that had once been a skylight.

"Shit!" she cried, hopping on one foot to avoid shards piercing up through her soles. "Shit, shit, shit, *shit!*"

She looked over at Bones, who seemed to be eyeing her with incredulity. *Why was his handler acting like an idiot?* indeed.

"Sorry, boy," she said for the umpteenth time in the past two days.

She regained her balance, pulled an aerosol paint can from her knapsack, and was getting ready to spray a large "X" over the front of the rumble with a "best guess" estimate of the number of dead inside based on smell when she heard movement coming from within.

"Oh, my God," she said, clambering back onto the roof.

Bones yipped excitedly, having heard the sound as well.

"Bones? Where's it coming from?"

Bones, understanding perfectly what was being asked of him, nosed around the break in the roof and then circled a spot a few feet away from it on the roof. Elizabeth grabbed her radio, having almost forgotten the code for survivors.

"Hello? This is Dog Team Alpha-Michael," she exclaimed. "We have movement inside a house…"

She quickly checked her GPS to give the search team precise coordinates now that everything from road names to address numbers had been rendered obsolete.

"…1500 block of Sargent Place, cross street is Lavetta Terrace," she said. "Again, we have movement."

She pocketed the radio after hearing the quick-return call from the search-and-rescue squad announcing they were sending a four-man, quick-insertion team that would be there within minutes to start the digging. Though they admonished Elizabeth not to attempt the extraction herself, she thought that if the person below was on their last legs, hearing that a rescue was on the way just might pull them through.

"Move over, Bones," she said, dropping to her knees as she tried to pick apart the roof tiles. "Hello?!?"

With her heavy gloves on, she made quick work of the shattered tiles, tossing them aside as Bones bounced around behind her, happy to have done well. Though part of the reason she was digging so quickly was elation, another driving force was guilt. She and Bones had worked the hillside below Lavetta Terrace the day before, and it had been her decision how to break down the grid, figuring houses on the lowest part of the hill presented the greatest likelihood for survivors, given they were mostly small, single-story affairs, whereas the houses farther up were larger, two-story buildings. How many people had she let suffer or even die because of this decision?

"Hold on!" she cried, adrenaline fueling her hysteria. "We're almost to you!"

That's when she heard the movement again, as if the person underneath the rubble had heard her and was trying to signal back. This made Elizabeth dig faster, literally throwing chunks of tiles behind her as she went. The smell got worse the deeper she dug, and she realized with horror that whoever was down there had possibly been trapped with at least one or more corpses. This disgusted her, but she knew that the person's ordeal would soon be coming to an end because of her.

Well, and Bones, she thought.

She glanced over at the shepherd and was surprised to see him with his ears pressed flat against his head, his teeth bared. After another second, he even began to growl.

"Bones!" Elizabeth reprimanded. "What's wrong with you?"

This only seemed to make Bones's growl deepen as he stared at the hole Elizabeth was digging in the roof.

Elizabeth looked at the dog with incredulity for a moment longer, but then reached down and found a large flat chunk of ceiling panel under the last couple of tiles. Realizing the person must be trapped underneath it, she squared up her feet and bent down to grip the edge of the wood.

As her gloved hands coiled around the edge of the plank, she suddenly felt something reaching out and grabbing onto her fingers.

"Shit!!"

She dropped the plank but quickly regained her composure. Fearing she might have injured the very person she was trying to save, she grabbed the panel again and this time was able to force it up. As soon as it was even part of the way up, she could see the face of a middle-aged Hispanic man.

It took a second to realize she was only seeing half of it.

The other half, the bottom half, had been completely eaten away by rats, of which there were at least half a dozen running around underneath the plank.

"Oh, no!!"

It was a silly thing to yell, but it was how she felt. The rats had scattered when she'd raised the board, but were now back looking at her as if waiting for the human to recognize that the man was dead and should be left for them to deal with.

That's when Bones moved in. With a growl, the shepherd launched himself at the rats, grabbing one in his teeth and shaking it so hard that it was quickly torn in half, the rodent's blood drooling down Bones's lower jaw as he dropped it and went for a second rat. This one he bit in half immediately gulping down the head.

"Bones! Stop it!" cried Elizabeth, but to no avail.

Bones stepped down into the hole in the roof, careful with his footfalls, and tore apart a third rat. As he did, Elizabeth looked at the men's corpse and realized there were at least two more bodies lying next to it, that of a woman and, Elizabeth realized with growing dread, that of a small child.

When the search-and-rescue team arrived, they comforted Elizabeth as best as they could. She expected derision or, at least, a couple of sidelong glances, but things had been going so drearily that even the idea that there might have been someone still alive had recharged a couple of spirits. The rush of adrenaline, the launch into action -- it had been good for morale, no matter the outcome. But this did little to alleviate Elizabeth's melancholy.

"It's all right," said one of the paramedics, a Las Vegas–based RN named Chris Wieneke. "You're not the only one out here needing a win."

"I know, but it's the rats, too. It was…shocking."

"Yeah, we're hearing they're everywhere," Wieneke said, nodding. "It's like they saw an opening and decided the city was theirs for the taking."

"They can have it," replied Elizabeth, miserable.

Elizabeth and Bones spent the rest of the day doing more of the same, though Elizabeth worked harder to distance herself from what she was seeing. She accepted the fact that there wasn't going to be a happy ending, no camera-ready rescue from deep within some crushed house revealing thankful survivors. And as the day went on, experience proved this out time and time again as she and Bones located another thirty to forty victims buried in the rubble, her spray can eventually running out of paint. To take her mind off it, she let her thoughts wander as she walked. She'd only been to Los Angeles once before, to give a training seminar to West Hollywood sheriffs and had only seen the city from the airport to WeHo and back again. She hadn't even stayed the night.

Still, she knew enough to know just how devastating the earthquake had been. The views had changed as completely as the skyline. Where once on the hills around Echo Park she figured she would have been looking down onto apartment buildings or telephone poles or houses or churches, with all the flattened buildings she could now easily make out the contours of the land that formed the L.A. basin and could even see as far as the ocean. She tried to imagine who the last person to see the Pacific from her unelevated vantage point might have been and decided whoever it was had probably been dead a century. She'd seen a number of collapsed Victorian houses in Angelino Heights at the end of the first day and had asked a local law enforcement officer about them. When she'd heard that it was only the second neighborhood ever built in the city and dated back to the late 1800s, she wasn't surprised. There was no telling how many minor quakes these houses had weathered through the years, but with a seismic event on the level of the Big Sleep, these old buildings had crumpled under as if they'd been made of toothpicks and held together with Elmer's glue.

It was while she was thinking about all of this that Bones barked to get her attention. And then barked again. And again. And again.

Unlike with a corpse, Bones was genuinely excited and pranced around on top of a house that seemed only half-collapsed. The garage was still standing, at least partly.

"What did you find, boy?" Elizabeth asked as she wandered over.

Almost immediately, she was rewarded with a beeping sound that came from the other side of the garage door.

"Hello?" she said, not expecting a response. But then the beeping returned with two quick beeps in a row. "Okay, hold on! We're coming in!"

The familiar rush of adrenaline pumping through her, Elizabeth grabbed her radio and called in a report, but this time she tried not to get anyone's hopes up and muted her enthusiasm. After putting her radio away, she started in on the aluminum garage door, which had been bent all to hell when it was compacted down onto the cement driveway by a collapsing roof.

"*Gnh!!*" she cried, trying to bend it back but finding it immovable. "Shit!"

That's when she heard Bones barking from the rear of the garage. She got to her feet and went around the building, seeing that the back door was on the left half of the garage, which hadn't seen as much damage as the right and therefore was mostly intact. Despite the fact that the doorframe was slightly crumpled, Elizabeth thought she might be able to break the door apart and create a hole.

Using her boot, she kicked at the door with her heel and managed to crack it across the middle. Two more kicks, and it caved in. She immediately reached in and pulled out the broken pieces of door, tossing them into the yard. Getting down on her stomach, she looked inside the garage and knew this wasn't going to be easy. The garage must've been a mess already and then the quake just threw everything into the blender, as even with her flashlight, she could barely see in due to the piles of trash. It looked like a landfill in there. It was obvious she wouldn't be able to stand up inside, much less move, but she figured if she had a pathfinder that didn't have to solely rely on his eyes, it might be easier.

"Bones," she said, turning to the shepherd. "Get in there!"

Bones didn't have to be asked twice. He'd been standing nearby watching as Elizabeth worked on the door and was obviously very happy to finally be allowed to explore the hole. He slithered under the top half of the door. For a second or two, just the last half of his tail was visible, but then it also disappeared.

"Okay, wait for me!"

Elizabeth got down on her hands and knees and crawled after Bones, pulling herself into the garage. She was fairly thin, but her height made such close quarters awkward. But as soon as she was a few feet inside, she discovered that there was more space than she'd initially led herself to believe.

"Bones?" she asked, shining the flashlight ahead. As her eyes adjusted to the dark, she could see the sun creeping in through a few breaks in the roof and from under the broken garage door, which increased her visibility.

She heard something moving up ahead of her next to what she thought was a station wagon. She reached out to find something to steady herself on and realized she'd grabbed the heel of a man's shoe, the man's foot still in it.

"Jesus!!"

Beep...beep...beep...

"Sir? I'm right behind you. Are you okay? Can you speak?"

Beep...beep...

With all the debris, it took another couple of minutes for Elizabeth to get closer to the man's face to check his vitals. When she finally did, she saw Bones's snout illuminated in the dim light of a cell phone as the dog's tongue lapped gently against the face of an elderly man, the fellow's fingers wrapped tightly around the phone.

It took about ten minutes for the search-and-rescue team to pull the old man out of the garage, and by then the news cameras were there broadcasting images.

"After five days and little to rejoice about in the devastated city of Los Angeles, a ray of hope for those hanging on to the belief that loved ones may still be alive in the rubble has been uncovered," announced a female reporter up from Melbourne into her rolling camera. "A man whose identity has still not been released has been discovered in a demolished house where he was trapped in his own garage since the earthquake of last Sunday..."

Elizabeth found this idea so strange. This isolated little spot miles and miles from what anyone would consider civilization was at this moment being seen by millions, and soon would be seen by tens and maybe even hundreds of millions of people by the end of the day. The man's name, Victor Romo, was known, but it had been decided that it shouldn't go out until at least a cursory attempt to notify relatives was made. Elizabeth's name, however, was getting a ton of play. She was interviewed by one camera crew after another and did her best to explain point-by-point what had happened, knowing that a "Hero Dog" story would go over even better than a hero-person one. Even though she was a civilian, her team encouraged her to do as much press as she felt able to do, not only to help the morale of her fellow workers but also to spur on the much-needed donations the various service organizations were already starting to solicit.

Happy for a break from all the misery, Elizabeth settled into a routine of spelling her name, explaining who she was and what she did, and then writing out the URL of her dog training business so that each outlet could run it over her interview in case people wanted to learn more.

Only a few camera crews had arrived in time to actually watch Victor Romo get extracted from his house, but there were several in attendance when the search-and-rescue team brought out the dead body of the elderly man's wife, who had been found crushed in a bedroom. At death's door though he was, the old man had refused to be taken away until her body had been removed, and the press had dutifully turned off their cameras as his body quaked in anguish at the sight of her being hauled out on a stretcher.

As the reporters hung around, perhaps hoping more gold might be mined from this unexpected vein in Echo Park, Elizabeth found herself again with the paramedic, Wieneke. They were now tasked with loading the old man onto a Humvee that would drive him to an open enough area that had been determined safe enough to attempt a Medevac.

"Why don't you just drive him out of here?" Elizabeth asked, a little puzzled. "Wouldn't it take about the same amount of time?"

"It's all about symbolism right now," Wieneke answered. "Every morning, everybody sees those Medevac choppers out there on the runways, fueled up and waiting for a call that never comes. Seeing one of those birds lifting off, seeing it overhead, it will just do so much for morale. Everybody's going to be talking about it. You know, 'well, if they found somebody alive maybe we can, too.'"

Elizabeth smiled and nodded, and then let Wieneke patch up the cuts and scrapes she'd acquired getting to the old man. In the course of this, she found herself surreptitiously gathering intel on where his base station was. She thought it might be nice to get good and laid that night, since she'd seen him checking her out more than once that day.

Something to look forward to.

Soon, however, the paramedics, the reporters, and the search-and-rescue teams were all gone, and it was just her and Bones again. The team had fed the shepherd, and he had been resting comfortably under the one still standing tree on the block when Elizabeth walked over and slumped down next to him.

"We're going to keep going, Bones," she said, as if trying to convince herself more than the dog. "If some old guy can survive five days under all this, you'd better believe there's somebody else out there."

Bones spent the rest of the day mostly on his own, as Elizabeth was off in her own head. He went from house to house, often locating multiple corpses in each, some old, some young, men and women alike. The smells got more distinctive and easy to trace as the afternoon sun continue to cook the rotting human meat for yet another hour, until Elizabeth couldn't take it anymore and wrapped a bandanna soaked with water around her mouth.

Of course, this didn't bother Bones. He had a job to do. When he smelled something dead, he went to it and alerted his handler by moving in a circle, pawing at the area where the smell was emanating from and barking. Elizabeth had long run out of treats to reward Bones with, but she had realized early on that he was one of those rare service dogs who didn't require one every time. His training was so ingrained that when surrounded by the smell of this many corpses, locating the dead superseded all other interests he might have pursued.

But every time Bones moved into a collapsed or semi-collapsed building, the same thing happened. He'd take a couple of steps in, his own scent would hit the air, and he'd suddenly hear the skittering of tiny feet.

The light galloping gait of a rat.

He'd seen more than a few rodents as they moved away from his approach, and he found even more of their fecal matter, sometimes all around the dead body it was eating but more often, particularly in the newer homes, around the walls. In these homes, the rats appeared not to be eating so much the people, but gnawing on the insulating layer between the drywall and the outer stucco, a tart-smelling, poly-fibrous material that had been laid between the interior rooms.

Everywhere they went, Bones would see the material, the exposed sheets being silver on both sides with a third sticky red-colored sheet in between, each time pockmarked by rat bites.

At one point, Bones took a couple of sniffs of the material, gave a chunk of it a healthy lick-and-chomp but found that it just gummed up his jaws. He tried to spit it out, but it instantly clung to his teeth, and with each breath the tiny fibers were pulled back towards his windpipe.

With a yelp, Bones took a couple of steps back and did what came naturally: he vomited.

A healthy torrent of the contents of the shepherd's stomach hosed most of the insulation out of his mouth and onto the floor of the room. Sniffing over what he'd just puked out, Bones resisted the urge to lap it back up and moved into the next room to hunt for the dead body he'd initially scented out in the house.

There had been almost constant aftershocks since the initial quake, but as almost all of them were relatively minor, it quelled the fears of both survivors and government officials alike. Seismologists, however, were becoming increasingly alarmed by the erratic nature of these additional quakes and, too late, it turned out, began to suggest that they weren't aftershocks at all but a precursor to a second major event. Generally speaking, an earthquake *was* the event, a buildup of pressure between plates that was alleviated when the tension reached its peak and an earthquake resulted, and after which the plates were allowed to settle. In this case, however, scientists were beginning to believe that a second earthquake was pending.

A so-called double earthquake wasn't uncommon. One had happened in New Brunswick in 1982 when a magnitude-5.7 earthquake struck on Saturday, January 9th, to be followed by a second quake on Monday, January 11th, that measured 5.1. As the Los Angeles earthquake had measured 10.2, the idea that the first quake could have merely been a preamble wasn't even discussed. A double quake indicated that the job was only half done the first time, and as a 10.2 was the strongest recorded earthquake in modern U.S. history, it was inconceivable that something twice that size could even occur.

This opinion was revised when powerful aftershocks started hitting every hour on the hour five days after the event. It was revised even further when the aftershocks began hitting in the upper 4s and even the lower 5s on the Richter scale, making them substantial seismic events in their own right. The opinion was completely thrown out the window and the very field of seismology was altered forever by what came next.

III

About an hour after her shift was up, Elizabeth found and fucked Wieneke in what was once the visiting team's dugout at Dodger Stadium. The locale was hardly romantic, but as the stadium parking lot had stayed at least somewhat intact, it had become base camp for the search-and-rescue units assigned to the eastern recovery zones and was handy. They had looked for somewhere better than the dugout, but there was no privacy in the camp itself, and beyond the guarded perimeter it had been whispered that gangs of looters operated with impunity by night.

So they ended up slipping into the off-limits stadium, off-limits because half the building had collapsed in Sunday's quake, including the entire home side of the park. The upper decks had come down on the mezzanine, which had collapsed on the field level, and all of it together spilled out onto the field. Half the bleacher seats in the outfield had collapsed as well, and if seen from above, the park would seem to be like a great, haunted maw with an intact upper jaw whose lower one was little more than a pile of twisted metal and shattered concrete.

The dust of the crushed cinder blocks still hung heavy in the air, and as Elizabeth gasped for breath in time with Wieneke's thrusts, she wondered if she was unwittingly making herself a candidate for the same kind of health problems faced by World Trade Center first-responders, who spent a few weeks inhaling all the pulverized asbestos and a few years on were suffering from cancers of many stripes.

As Wieneke dug his teeth into her neck just a little too much, Elizabeth pushed this thought aside and gently suggested to the paramedic that he should find a more constructive way to get out his aggression.

It was at this very moment that the second quake, soon to be dubbed "Omega" (renaming the initial quake "Alpha," half-assed, media-friendly allusions to the Book of Revelations), arrived, though it came slowly at first. She flinched and knew immediately the bad joke Wieneke would make, as she had learned to her distress over the last hour that he was the king of such things.

"Yeah, you felt it, too, huh?" he smirked without a hint of irony.

Elizabeth rolled her eyes but then closed them. Aftershock or no, she was determined to focus on the sensations in her pelvis and not the idiot that was causing them, as she just wanted an orgasm. Because of this, she didn't see the gigantic concrete block fall off the roof of the dugout and crack him on the head. The blow sent him reeling backwards as the block continued to roll until it came down on his foot, breaking several bones, though he was already well on his way to unconsciousness.

As soon as she felt his body go limp, Elizabeth opened her eyes and saw not only that her partner was now heavily bleeding from a gash in his skull, but also that their surroundings were beginning to shake in earnest.

"Oh, shit!!" she cried and leaped forward off the dugout bench. She bolted for the guardrail and swung under it up onto the field, hoping that she'd be safer out in the open.

It was then that she looked up and saw the second half of the stadium beginning to come down. Large chunks of concrete crushed the media booths and bounced down through the seats like boulders aimed directly at her. With nothing in their way, they simply accelerated with every bounce and didn't stop when they reached the field, tearing up the turf as they kept going.

Elizabeth had a feeling of helplessness in the face of the hailstorm of mortar. She didn't want to believe, but she couldn't escape the idea that all of these events were literally bigger than she was and that it would be seconds before she was pulverized and, perhaps, forgotten against the backdrop of the larger tragedy.

But as she turned and ran, leaving behind Wieneke without a second thought, she allowed herself the fantasy that maybe she and Bones had bonded enough over the past few days that he wouldn't allow himself to be used by another handler until he had located her broken body in the rubble, maybe even still barely alive. The longer the quake went on, however, the less likely this seemed, and in her distraction she tumbled forward and skinned her knees.

She looked back at and saw through the gray darkness that at least forty Honda-sized chunks of concrete were hurtling themselves at her and creating new, albeit smaller boulders as they came.

The reality of her situation was overwhelming. It would all be over soon.

Bones and the other search-and-rescue dogs knew about the second quake a good thirty seconds before their human counterparts did. They had been kenneled outdoors in a fenced-in pen complete with hard plastic doghouses and a small area over grass where they could do their business. They were fed in it and had some room for exercise, but only as much as a 10-foot by 10-foot space would allow.

When they felt the coming quake, they whined like they did for every aftershock, which signaled the nearby National Guardsmen, who had by now realized what the in-unison protest represented.

"Aftershock coming!" they called out, and a few people responded by passing the announcement along.

But when the quake erupted in earnest, the already cracked parking lot ruptured and bowed, knocking everyone off their feet and collapsing many of the temporary structures that had been set up to house the unit's command and communications personnel. Seconds later, the remnants of Dodger Stadium began to come down, and both soldiers and civilian workers alike panicked and ran for open ground.

The dogs were among them. The pen gates weren't very high to begin with, but Bones and the others sprang lithely over them, and they raced out to flat ground, yapping and yipping like dogs playing in the rain.

For reasons unknown, the fuel dump where supplies were kept to gas up the Humvees each day was probably the least secure area of the temporary base, set up more for ease of access than to guard against future earthquake damage. That is not to say that even if precautions had been taken they would've included the possibility of a second magnitude 10-plus quake anyway, so perhaps the breaking open of so many barrels and the saturation of the area with fuel was an inevitability.

The dogs paid little attention to the humans, happy finally for a little freedom. They raced out towards the woods of Elysian Park and over a small hill that took them directly into the backyard of the Los Angeles Police Department Training Academy. Interestingly, the very place they were traversing was the "secret" burial location of the LAPD K-9 officers that had died in the line of duty. As the cemeteries where human officers were buried weren't about to let animals be interred there, enforcement dogs or not, the K-9 unit had a long tradition of taking their fallen comrades to a spot in the hills behind the training academy and burying them there in a reverential service marked with tradition. No one outside the unit actually knew the precise location of the spot, and as so many members of the current and previous LAPD K-9 units had been killed in the first quake, the chance that the spot would be lost to history was good.

Leaving the woods behind, Bones led the other dogs over the hill and into the devastated training facility. They raced past the outdoor shooting range, the Daryl Gates Cafeteria, and the three-tiered and tree-shaded waterfall and reflecting pool that stood as a memorial to fallen human officers. As they passed the pool, a couple of dogs stopped for a drink, but then the group carried on out into the parking lot and down towards the shattered 101 Freeway, which served as an ad hoc border between East L.A. and the rest of the city.

Despite their roving, the dogs were easily rounded up the next morning by the search-and-rescue team. Miraculously, including Wieneke, there had only been four deaths in the base camp, though there were a couple dozen minor injuries reported. The National Guard would later be commended for their selection of Dodger Stadium as a staging ground, but as soon as they had re-established communications with the superiors at the Burbank Airport, they learned that they were one of the only groups so unaffected. All across the broken city, other search-and-rescue teams hadn't been as lucky and were reporting casualty rates of seventy to eighty percent. At the Burbank Airport itself, the rate was around fifty percent, with a majority of their vehicles rendered inoperable by Omega.

"The long and short of it is that our situation has become untenable, and we're being forced to pull back to Edwards," the high command repeated over the radio to each of the search-and-rescue team commanders in the field. "As that means we will no longer be able to provide support to your team, you are to be extracted as well."

A couple of the team leaders protested, but their hearts clearly weren't in it. The surviving members of the teams were demoralized and were ready to leave. The fear was that the ground had just become so unstable that no one could predict what might happen next.

No one was more surprised by the events of the day than Elizabeth. To her surprise, she had survived Omega with barely a scratch, having made it to the rubble of the already-collapsed home side of the stadium and finding there a narrow path between what had been the Dodger bullpen and the field seats behind the foul pole. As the ground continued to shake, she slipped between spears of broken railing, fearing they could impale her at any moment, but then reached the parking lot beyond and managed to escape.

The only problem was that she had left her pants back at the dugout and was completely naked from the waist down, being forced to pick her way across the broken-up pavement of the circular parking lot to get back to base camp in her bare feet. In the darkness with aftershocks hitting every ten to fifteen minutes, it took her an hour and a half to make the journey, tripping and scraping her knees as she went, which was why she practically burst into tears upon finally seeing the generator-fueled lights over the camp. With everyone else distracted by the hubbub of repairing the camp, she was able to make it to her temporary shelter, grab new pants, shoes, socks, and underwear, and reclaim at least some of her dignity before going to the head of the paramedics.

"Wieneke was in there," she said, pointing to the devastated stadium.

The paramedic didn't have to ask why she knew this, but Elizabeth burst into tears anyway. She was given a sedative and led back in her shelter to ride out the night. The next morning, the news of their extraction was music to her ears, as all she wanted to do was get out of California and go back home.

She went to check in with the soldiers who had rounded up all the escaped dogs, placing them carefully in their travel crates for transport, and that's when she noticed the one absence.

"Wait, where's Bones?"

The night before, Bones just hadn't stopped running. When the voices of the soldiers started calling out for the other enforcement dogs, the others had all stopped and eventually trotted back towards the stadium. Bones, however, ignored the cries, as he was busy exploring a cracked culvert that ran alongside the highway. Though the quake had hit at five in the morning, the 101 had still been busy with cars and trucks utilizing the stretch of road as one of the many NAFTA highways that connected Mexico with all the major cities of the California coast and beyond up to Canada. When Alpha hit, most of the drivers didn't even feel it at first, the swaying light poles alongside the highway being their first indication. But then the long network of bridges and overpasses that ran from south of downtown all the way to the Valley began to domino downward, as their earthquake-reinforced columns were only tested effective up to an 8.5 quake.

Due to all the new technological advances made in strengthening a vehicle's "roll cage," many people actually survived the initial collapse. Their vehicles may have hurtled downward, and oftentimes engine blocks were forced backward, resulting in crushed legs and spines, but the roll bars kept people's upper torsos intact. Instead of being killed instantly, several hundred drivers and their passengers found themselves in the unenviable position of being slowly bled to death in excruciating pain, whereas in a bygone era they would've been put out of their misery immediately. Some had even survived all the way until Omega.

It was over these broken overpasses that Bones now wandered as he made his way out of East L.A. The stench of death rose from below Bones's feet, and though it was easy for the shepherd to differentiate between those who had died a few days before and those who were in the process of dying just now, he still couldn't get to them. He whined a little, looked around for a human handler he might alert to the situation, but then moved on.

"Hey!! Heeeey! Is someone up there?"

Bones stopped short and looked around in the dark, but saw no movement. He nosed around a little and then discovered a crack out of which he could inhale the scent of a still living, breathing man.

"Hey!! Who's that? Who's there?" came a voice from about fifteen feet below. "Hello?!?"

Bones whined a little and heard a sigh in response.

"Oh, Jesus, a fucking dog? My legs are crushed, I'm starvin' like Marvin, and you're a fucking dog?"

Bones sniffed through the crack, smelling bread and other baked goods, an incongruous scent certainly, but it seemed to be in abundance. The smell overlapped with oil and gasoline, but there was enough of the bread-scent to tell Bones there was at least some kind of food supply below, which kept his attention.

"Come on, boy. Go get help or something. Do you have a master? Are you search and rescue?"

Bones ignored the man's voice as he circled around, trying to determine if there was some way to he could get down to the food source. The collapsed overpass appeared as solid as a tomb, and Bones whined a little in frustration.

But then Bones heard something echoing up from below. At first it sounded like somebody was spilling ball bearings out onto the concrete and they were rolling closer to the injured man. As the sound neared, a new smell appeared attendant with it, but with all the oil, food, shit, and corpses below and the dust from the collapsed buildings and the on-and-off fires in the nearby hills clogging the air above, it wasn't the easiest thing in the world for Bones to fix in on the new scent and identify it. Whatever it might be, the scent was nothing if not powerful.

"What is that?" asked the man below, more to himself than the dog he'd identified up on the surface.

The sound grew louder and louder as its source drew near. The man below didn't speak, but Bones could hear him shifting around, trying to get into a better position to see what was going on.

That's when Bones finally recognized the scent: rats.

Lots of them.

"Oh, my God!" shouted the man as the herd of rodents finally reached him. He sounded as incredulous as he was scared. "What the fuck?!"

Then he started screaming.

Bones took a couple of steps back as the man's terrified high-pitched squeals were soon joined by the sound of others beneath the broken overpass, indicating the fellow in the bread truck was hardly the only to have survived so long. One sounded like a small child, another like an elderly man. As the smell of the rats became omnipresent, the screams rose to a crescendo, only to then go silent one by one. Bones could smell the blood of the man directly below him as it was drawn out through multiple wounds, the rats chewing into him from dozens of different spots. His screaming was cut off and his breathing got ragged, but then both were strangled.

Bones woofed a couple of times in the direction of the rats but then began moving away. As he looked down the overpass to the south where the sound had originated, the shepherd noticed movement in the dark, as if the night sky itself had touched down and was rippling over the roadway like a black tide. It didn't take long for Bones to realize it was more rats.

Bones woofed an alert to any humans in the area, but the rats kept coming.

Normally, rats only moved as one when fleeing. Sailors reported watching herds of rats sweeping up from the bowels of a ship when it was sinking, having had no idea such a pulsing mass of creatures had been living among them during the voyage. This colony, however, was traveling in that way in pursuit of something, which was wholly unusual. These animals were like army ants in their single-minded mission. A mission that, at present, appeared to involve a German shepherd staring at them from only about a hundred yards away.

Bones woofed a third time and then pranced around as if to assert his unquestionable dominance on the food chain. The rats didn't seem to notice, as they were moving without fear. The closer they got, the more Bones could pick up on the oily odor that emanated from their skin, which was much more pungent than the rats he'd encountered even earlier that day. He could also tell that they had picked up another scent: blood.

Blood was in the rats' fur, in their claws, and dripping from their teeth. And it wasn't just human blood, either, but all types of animals. It was such an eclectic mix that it was as if they had stopped off at the Griffith Park Zoo before descending on the 101 Freeway.

Though they were only rats, Bones knew better than to stand and fight. He could've easily gone up against a dozen or so at once, but something about the new smell bothered him. It was a reflex like the kind an animal has to alcohol. Bones knew something wasn't right about the rats and didn't stick around to discover what it was.

Instead, Bones turned ran north on the crushed highway, leaving Echo Park behind and heading in the direction of Hollywood. As he ran, he could hear the rats behind him but soon heard the sound of other rats rising up from below, joining the chase.

Deciding on a detour, Bones made a lateral move and leaped over the broken median, crossed the southbound lane of the highway, and ran up a grassy embankment to what had once been Sunset Boulevard. The street was littered with abandoned and demolished cars, but Bones flew by the old CBS complex and through the rubble of collapsed buildings away from the highway. For cars, the avenue would be hopelessly impassable, as it wasn't only the shattered buildings that blocked the road but also everything inside them that had been vomited out into accidental roadblocks. For a dog like Bones, however, this was easy enough to hurdle, and he simply jumped over this pile of cinder blocks and that busted billboard as he fled the rats.

The trouble for the shepherd was that scent worked both ways. His blood was pumping and the rats could smell it, which egged them on. Bones's nose informed him in no uncertain terms that he would soon be overtaken. His tongue lolled out of his jaws and he was just beginning to feel winded when a new sound entered the fray, followed quickly by a man-made light source cutting through the night from the north.

In his peripheral vision, Bones could see a dozen or so motorcycles, followed by two garish yellow civilian Humvees, weaving their way down to Sunset on a side street. The Humvees bounced over the rubble on the streets like it was nothing.

"It's a dog!" came a cry. "What the hell's a dog doing setting this thing off?"

Bones stopped short when one of the motorcycles got close enough to almost run him over, and then he smelled cordite from a recently fired gun. With a *clank*, two turret guns, typical of a military Humvee but hopelessly incongruous on a consumer model, were readied and aimed at the oncoming rats.

"Light 'em up!"

With a tremendous burst of muzzle flash, hot lead screamed out of the twin guns and chewed through the incoming rats. The bullets moved so quickly and the targets were so near that it looked like a sci-fi movie laser beam was being used to sear through Bones's attackers.

Bones turned and barked at the spectacle, though his voice was easily blocked out by the tremendous *THRRUUUUMMMM* of the mounted machine guns. Satisfied that he was no longer being pursued, Bones wheeled around to run off, only to have a harness thrown around his neck by one of the motorcyclists.

"Where do you think you're going, *puto*?" the biker, a large Latino wearing a sweatshirt and ball cap, asked as he reeled the shepherd in.

Bones struggled against the leash every inch of the way to the motorcycle until the biker produced a cattle prod and jammed it against Bones's shoulder. As 9,000 volts coursed through Bones's body, the shepherd dropped to the deck, unconscious. As the hail of bullets continued shredding the air around him, the last thing Bones smelled was the oily-scented blood of a thousand dead rats.

Bones awoke a few hours later in great pain and found himself the subject of a surgical procedure. The tracking device that had been placed in his left leg was being removed by three people he could not see, and the pain had jarred him out of unconsciousness.

Naturally, he wheeled around and sunk his jaws into the would-be surgeon, the iron-flecked taste of the man's blood quickly oozing across the shepherd's tongue.

"Holy shit!! Zap him, man! Zap him! He's awake!!!"

The cattle prod was quickly brought around and jammed into Bones's side. Bones shuddered and sank back into unconsciousness after the second recharge.

When Bones woke up a second time, his muscles were sore to the bone, and his skin was burned wherever the cattle prod had touched. On top of that, his leg was in tremendous pain from the impromptu surgery, and despite the expert way that his fur had been shaved away before a careful incision had been made, no painkillers had been administered to ease his transition into consciousness.

So when Bones immediately stood up, the other four people in the room, folks who only showed up as smudges to Bones's bleary eyes, all jumped as well.

"He's awake!" said a twenty-something man in a gray suit, clearly terrified.

"Don't worry," said the younger of the two women in the room, who appeared dressed in business casual. "He's chained."

"My neighbor had a Siberian husky when I was growing up," said the older woman, who wore sort of green pajamas. "That thing bit right through its chain. They bought another one, and it bit through that, too."

"Yeah, well, this a German shepherd," said the fourth man, an older fellow in a sweat suit.

"I knew a guy who had the rear tire of his Volkswagen chomped into by a German shepherd," said the older woman. "He had no idea that it had happened, so he drove away and pulled onto the 134. His tire blew and he had to pull over, but got plowed into by an eighteen-wheeler. His widow sued the owner of the shepherd and won."

Bones had been looking from person to person and hadn't noticed the chain they'd been referring to until he took a step and felt himself jerked backwards. He tugged at it, found it sold enough, and decided to voice his disdain for it with a huge torrent of barks that echoed all around the room and scared the hell out of the four humans.

"Jesus Christ!" shouted gray suit. "He's pissed!"

Bones tugged at the chain a second time and discovered that it was wound around an unused, many-times-painted-over radiator under the one window in the room. Angry, Bones grabbed the chain in his jaws and tried to chew through it.

"See?" said the older woman. "He's going to bite right through it!"

But Bones took a couple more snaps at the chain, didn't like how it felt against his teeth, and promptly lay back down on the floor, to the surprise of his fellow prisoners. He had given them something of a sniff-over, detected nothing but the scent of abject terror in their sweat, and decided he couldn't be bothered with anything else. Moments later, he went back to sleep.

It appeared that Bones and his fellow captives were being held in a small office in what must have been one of the last still standing buildings in all of Los Angeles, a multi-story Deco design that was likely apartments at one time, now converted into office space. Though one wall was marred by a gigantic crack and the glass of the window had shattered (though it was mostly still held in place by wire "quake-proof" mesh), those were the only signs of the recent seismic event.

Though the group had talked earlier in the day, they now fell mostly silent in hopes of not riling up the snoozing German shepherd. They stayed that way for an hour until someone finally opened the door.

"Bathroom break," came a guttural voice that, unsurprisingly, belonged to a bulldozer-sized, biker-looking type with an intimidating shaved head and mustache combo and least three visible Iron Crosses tattooed on his neck and shoulders. "Anybody?"

"Me!" said the gray-suited man.

The biker grunted at the man.

"Me, too," said the younger woman. "Is there a ladies room?"

In response, the shave-headed man shrugged but then turned to make sure that the group could see the gun in his belt to know that questions weren't welcome. He waited for any other takers, but when there were none, he looked over at Bones, who was waking up.

"Bet you need a walk, huh, boy?" the biker said. He nodded towards the gray-suited fellow. "Unchain him. Bring him with."

"You're kidding...."

The pistol was out of Chris' waistband and aimed at the younger man's face so fast that everyone in the room save the tattooed man gasped.

"Turns out I'm not," grunted the gunman. "You gonna get him or what?"

A couple of minutes later, the group was walking through the crumbling building. The biker had said his name was "Chris," so the young woman introduced herself as Sharon Wiseman and the gray-suited man as Gary Loeb. As they walked, the trio passed first a ladies room, then a men's room, and Gary got a little nervous.

"I thought you were taking us to the bathroom," Gary said, trying to sound tough.

"The building's intact, but the plumbing ain't," explained Chris. "You piss in there, it goes all over my friends downstairs. You might not have a problem with that, but they would. There's a latrine outside."

Once they'd gone down the three flights of stairs to street level, Gary's initial fears fell away as he became preoccupied with the building around him.

"So why this one?" Gary was asking to no one in particular. "I mean, it looks like what, 1920s? We're in Hollywood, right? It's not like this area wasn't affected, but was this one just built a little stronger? Retrofitted after the Northridge quake slightly better than it should've been?"

Sharon rolled her eyes and Chris caught it, grinning back despite the fact that he'd threatened to murder her as recently as the night before.

Once they were outside the building, Gary's point was driven home. Every other building at the corner of Hollywood and Vine had collapsed or at least lost a major part of its super structure: the new hotel, the new condominiums, the old theaters (the Montalban and the Pantages), the Metro station, the old office building in the northeast corner, and almost every other piece of architecture in sight, right up to the once space age–looking Capitol Records Tower up Vine that had pancaked down on itself.

For anyone who might have seen the area in years past, it was now unrecognizable as even being in the same city. In fact, it more resembled post-war Dresden or Nagasaki, a forest of multi-story corners or facades of buildings with no floors in between, the contents of each poured onto the sidewalks, which were now covered in everything from broken glass and office furniture to file folders and ducting.

"We dug a latrine behind the parking lot," Chris said, nodding to a spot behind the Deco building. "Unisex."

Sharon nodded, but like Gary she was taking in the sight of the numerous armed men who came into view, patrolling around the building and the adjacent streets. Some were using piles of rubble to elevate their vantage points, while others had created blinds in the other buildings despite many looking as if they might come down on themselves at any moment.

Abandoned vehicles had been rolled from nearby streets to create defensible barriers at the end of each block, disallowing any kind of transport from getting close to the men's base of operations.

"Worried about looters?" Gary joked as he nodded towards the road blocks.

"It's for your protection, not ours, asshole," Chris scoffed.

"From what?" Sharon asked.

Chris paused as if the answer was self-evident but then shrugged, turning to Sharon first.

"Sharon Wiseman, some muckity-muck with a banking giant out of Baltimore, right? In charge of a large number of accounts, apparently a genius at picking stocks on the international marketplace."

As Sharon looked surprised, Chris turned to Gary. "And you, your father is the CEO of an aerospace giant in Colorado doing the real work while you blow all his money telling nineteen-year-old wannabe actresses you're looking to finance movies."

"How'd you know all that?" Sharon finally asked.

"You're both on the list."

"What list?"

"Bounty list," Chris explained. "Everybody knows L.A.'s fucked. Millions are dead. *Millions.* It's unprecedented. But as soon as it happened, a bunch of companies and a bunch of rich guys started putting bounties out for people. Most of them were for family, but some are for business people like Sharon whose companies can't move forward without knowing the status of certain employees and starting a chain of succession in earnest. The U.S. government's our biggest client but also the easiest, as a lot of military guys now have to get those GPS tracking implants in their wrists like our friend here."

Chris looked down at Bones, who had gone mostly unnoticed for a couple of moments and who hadn't waited for the latrine to urinate, having just whizzed on a nearby pile of broken cinder blocks.

"We even thought this guy was one of 'em," Chris continued, nodding at the dog. "He had a tracking device, was on the move and there's a $20,000 reward from the government per trooper, so we went for it, and it turned out to be some kind of enforcement dog. Hell, we're still trying to figure out what kind of money we can get for him."

"But you're holding us against our will," Sharon said, her agitation level rising. "How can that be legal?"

"Let me assure you, it's for your own protection," Chris countered. "I don't know if you have a sense of just how feral it's gotten out there. Lotta crazy gangbangers picking through the rubble, lotsa thieves who'll knock over anybody who gets in their way, and those are just the humans. L.A.'s also got this big rat problem now, too, isn't that right, boy?"

Chris looked down at Bones and rubbed the shepherd's snout.

"So you've got me on a list and you're probably talking to my dad," Gary asked. "When do I get out of here?"

"Soon as he deposits a million dollars in our company's account," Chris replied. "He went into the press all earnest about finding you, but the more days go by, the more it looks like he figured a pussy like you wouldn't be able to survive."

Chris led the pair to the latrine, taking Bones's chain from Gary. Parking himself on a nearby pile of broken bricks to wait, Chris stared out towards the south as Bones lay down.

"You're a good boy, aren't you?" Chris asked before reaching in his pocket and producing a candy bar. Bones angled his head up expectantly. "Oh, now I've got your attention, huh?"

Chris unwrapped the candy bar and took a small chunk for himself but then tossed the rest to Bones, who wolfed it down in one gulp.

"Guess you were hungry," Chris said.

Chris talked for a moment longer about how happy he was to have a dog around, but Bones wasn't really listening. Instead, he was focused on a large flock of pigeons that seemed to be circling overhead as if guided by a dervish waving a sword. They'd duck low, roll, sweep back around, then race skyward again in an elaborate pattern, always perfectly in unison.

That's when Bones spotted a red-tailed hawk sitting atop a nearby outcropping, a single surviving corner of an otherwise collapsed six-story building. The hawk was watching the pigeons as closely as Bones but seemed to be intimidated by their movements, even though it was the predator. Though the pigeons would normally regard the raptor with fear, their swirling flock moved closer and closer to the hawk until it finally took flight. As it did, the pigeons swarmed towards it, engulfing the large bird in their midst and tearing it apart. Unseen by Chris or any of the other men, the hawk's shredded corpse soon fell from the sky, dropping soundlessly into the rubble of the Montalban Theater.

Disinterested, Bones turned away and saw Sharon returning from the latrine.

"That was a most disgusting experience," Sharon said.

"Yeah, well, everybody else still alive in L.A. is pulling water from whatever they can find, not realizing most of it is run through with human piss and fecal matter. We've got about a day and a half before cholera wipes out anybody left alive out here."

"Why don't you rescue them, too?" Sharon asked. "Or is this simply a mercenary operation?"

"Oh, absolutely a simple mercenary op," Chris replied. "We have enough manpower to rescue and defend the elite and that's it. The rest is the government's responsibility. Bet you're glad to be important, huh?"

Sharon didn't say it, but she had to admit that she was.

IV

Chris brought Gary and Sharon back to the room on the third floor of the Deco building, where the pair quickly brought the other two (the older man, Arthur Nguyen, and the panicky older woman, Barbara Kuhn) up to speed.

"What's the name of your company?" Arthur asked.

Chris hemmed and hawed but then replied: "I guess you could say we work for an umbrella corporation called Mayer, but we're mostly freelancers getting paid by a middleman Mayer hired."

"Is this like a Blackwater thing?" Gary asked.

"A lot of us are ex-military, ex-special forces, but we get hired on a mission-by-mission basis. Blackwater couldn't afford us full-time even if they wanted to."

Chris waited around for a moment, didn't answer any more questions, and then took Bones out with him.

"You stay in there too long and you'll walk out a bitch, am I right?" Chris asked Bones, who just seemed happy to not be cooped up.

Chris brought Bones back out into the courtyard to walk the perimeter, which consisted more of the handler stopping to shoot the shit with a number of his comrades as they went. The big topic of discussion was the rat encounter from the previous night. Everyone had a "the rats are going nuts" story to tell from the last couple of days; one with a sighting of hundreds of the creatures devouring the still living residents of a well-built nursing home, another mentioning a "shower of rats" endured by a fellow when the ceiling above his head collapsed and four or five dozen rats tumbled through, and a third who had seen a pile of skeletons literally covered with tiny little rat bites from where it'd been picked apart by dozens of the beasties. No one ventured a guess as to whether the victim had been dead or alive during the encounter.

Throughout the stories, there was another constant. Though the rats were primarily focused on devouring people, they had also been seen gnawing on the walls of buildings. From what Chris and a couple of the others could recall from their limited knowledge of rodents, rats gnawed on walls not out of hunger but out of a desire to sharpen and whittle down their teeth or enlarge a living space. But as Bones had observed, the rodents had a taste for the material found between the interior and exterior walls of newer buildings.

"What's worse is then you see it in their shit," one of the guys, a fellow named Rodney, exclaimed. "They can't digest it, but they can't get enough of it. What is that stuff?"

"It slows fires," an older guy named Eswin explained. "It's this high-tech fibrous material that's got a really, really high flashpoint. Think it's called Nivec. So if there's a building fire, it takes longer for it to move from room to room, as it really has to cook the walls to finish the job. It won't completely contain a fire but just slows it down for awhile, like wet wood."

"How come the rats like it so much?"

"How the hell should I know? Maybe it tastes like rice pudding."

Chris snickered. "We're going to see a lot of shit worth writing home about before we pull out, I'll bet. That's just the tip of the iceberg."

Everybody nodded in agreement at Chris's statement, not realizing they'd all be dead by morning and wouldn't be writing home about anything any time soon.

Bones found patrolling with the Mayer-hired mercenaries boring.

He missed being out on in the broken city doing his job. Though he was classified as a work dog by law enforcement, his training made it so that the retrieval of bodies registered in his mind as instinct. Rather than being a hunter-gatherer like his ancestors or the timber wolves, Bones's brain told him his job on the day was to look for the dead. Being tied down to Chris in and around the Deco building almost felt like punishment in contrast, particularly with the heavy chain the men insisted on keeping around his neck. In the evening, Chris went on break and took Bones up on the roof to finally deliver on the big meal he had been promising the dog since sunrise. It was mostly canned beans and tins of meat, but Chris had liberated all his two hands could carry from the mess hall, so it was in abundance.

"Mr. Loeb's lawyers are getting antsy about the money," Chris told Bones with a laugh. "Apparently, the quake really fucked the market, and when you add up the son's insurance policies, stock portfolio, and pieces of his would-be eventual inheritance pie, Daddy's suddenly realizing his boy's worth more dead than alive. Neither side wants to say it, but they're both dancing around the same thing. 'Cut him loose.' Hell, they'd probably pay us a little something just to do that and look the other way."

Chris and Bones had come across Chris's boss at one point, a rugged-looking, deeply tanned Britisher named Gerson. Gerson looked permanently annoyed as he tried to lock down bounty payments so that at least a few of his "charges" could be sent east in a pre-dawn helicopter evac the next morning to free up more of his men to go after further contracts. It sounded like Mayer had been the only game in town for a couple of days, but that was changing.

Time and again, Gerson was tasked with convincing the hopeful wealthy that his team was the best and that by contracting them they were most likely to get their loved ones out of the quake zone.

"You have to understand what it looks like on the ground here," Gerson would say. "The first quake was bad enough, but then the second one hit, and even the military pulled out. You can deal with the cowboy organizations, sure, but we've been handling private search-rescue-secure operations dating back to Hurricane Andrew. This is what we do, and we're the best."

More often than not, this would do the trick, and the Englishman would close the deal, giving a thumb's up to whoever was closest while waiting for a satellite-delivered image of the to-be-claimed package or information on the person's possible whereabouts.

"Oh, shit," said Chris after seeing the accompanying address on one of the pictures. "We went by there when we pulled that Kleiner fellow. Everything within ten blocks was rubble."

Gerson shrugged. "Next best thing to a reunion is closure. Find me a body, and I'll see what I can negotiate."

At some point during the day, Chris had decided to give Bones a name and started calling him "Butch." He talked to his newfound companion about the last three days, how he'd been helicoptered in from offshore to a relatively untouched airstrip in Long Beach that had been deemed unsafe for some reason by the military. He lived in Tucson but split his time between Arizona and California working as a trainer for the Navy, having been a SEAL himself. He'd established his digs on the fourth floor of the Deco building and had his kit all laid out, one that contained a full two weeks' worth of supplies, and at the end of the day he took Bones up there to settle in for the night. It was pretty spare with a cot, some clothes, a lantern, and a bag, but perched in the window on a bipod was what Chris referred to as the most important part of his kit, an SR-98 Accuracy International sniper rifle complete with flash and noise suppressor, folding stock, and five-round magazine.

"There are looters for sure, but they know to leave us the hell alone," Chris said, nodding out the window to the dark, rubble-strewn streets of Los Angeles, where distant sounds indicated that they weren't quite the only people left alive in the city. "But still, gotta be ready in case the skinnies get brave, you know?"

Bones didn't seem to care all that much, so Chris fed him another candy bar, which the shepherd happily devoured. They hadn't been down five minutes before one of the other guards knocked on the doorframe.

"Hey Chris. Some woman's asking for you down in 310."

"Young one or that old broad?"

"Older broad."

Chris sighed but then nodded towards Bones. "Beggars can't be choosers, right? You don't mind bunking down a flight, do you?"

Chris led Bones down to the empty office where he'd woken up that morning and found that Arthur, Sharon, and Gary had each eked out a corner of the room, where they'd set up the cots the Mayer men had issued to them. The group seemed surprised by Chris's appearance, having been ready to turn in for the night. All of them, that is, except for Barbara, who looked up at Chris expectantly when he opened the door and poked his head in.

"You wanted to see me?" he asked nonchalantly.

"Can we talk a minute? It's about my husband and this 'bounty' that he may or may not be trying to raise."

Chris nodded but walked Bones across the room first and re-chained him to the radiator.

"Oh, come *on*," cried Gary. "You can't leave him in here with us all night. I have allergies."

"Company wants us to make sure everybody's protected," Chris reported sternly. "Somebody unauthorized gets within a hundred feet of you people, and you'd better believe that dog's going to let everyone in the building know."

With that, Chris escorted Barbara out and closed the door behind him. As soon as he was gone, Gary leapt to his feet.

"Shouldn't we have tried to stop her?" he asked, sounding pissed. "This is textbook Stockholm Syndrome, and he's taking advantage. He's abusing his power."

"And what have you been doing all afternoon with me?" Sharon dryly retorted. "'Hey, we're stuck in here, shouldn't we try and make the best of it? C'mon, baby.' I mean, I'd call it flirting, but I've never seen it so one-sided."

Arthur chuckled at Gary's reddening face.

"Oh, fuck you," Gary snapped. "Like you weren't doing the same thing. I saw you two huddling over there in your corner."

Arthur and Sharon looked at Gary with incredulity.

"Keep me out of this," Arthur chortled, laying back down on his cot. "If you had been listening carefully, you'd know that Miss Wiseman and I were actually playing a rather strident game of chess."

"Without a board or pieces?" Gary scoffed. When Sharon just rolled her eyes at him, the young man realized that was exactly what they meant. He scoffed a second time and flopped down on his cot.

Bones, for his part, had fallen asleep five seconds after Chris had left the room.

The reason the Deco Building hadn't even partially collapsed during either quake was actually both complicated and secret, at least outside of a handful of people in the Los Angeles City Planning and Transportation Services Departments. When the Metro Station at Hollywood and Vine was being built, the tremors from the digging equipment had produced massive cracks in the building's foundation that had gone completely unnoticed by its owners, a consortium of cardiologists who lived in Agoura Hills and owned a number of east side apartment buildings as well as a handful around Hollywood. After it was quietly brought to their attention, the city planners debated doing nothing about it at all but feared that if the building subsequently fell in a quake, the inevitable liability lawsuits might spur the cardiologists to hire powerful enough lawyers to get to the bottom of it, and once they did, the city would be sued.

After two closed-door consulting meetings with the city's legal team, it was decided that the amount the city would likely be made to pay out in damages would just surpass the dollar figure of repairs, as long as the repairs were done in secret. If the cardiologists and subsequently the media were alerted to this accident, it would likely create a frenzy in the press as reporters, concerned citizens, and just about anybody else looking for handout began sniffing around for cracks in other buildings that might have been created by the never-ending Metro dig. This might lead to court actions, which could lead to the most feared word of all: injunction.

So the necessary repairs were clandestinely made to the Deco Building, and the planners were assured that even the strongest earthquake on record wouldn't be able to bring it down. As it turned out, that boast was not only correct but also surpassed all expectations. Unfortunately, none of the planners or the contractors who mounted this quiet achievement would ever know of their success as, to a man, they were all dead.

The fact remained, however, that Metro tunnels were running under the building. And in a city that stank of nothing but dust, oil, rotting food, and rotting corpses, the attendant smells of the living: freshly cooked food, fecal matter, sweat, etc., stood out like a beacon in the night.

The rats, including the main army that Bones had encountered, had already begun to utilize the underground routes to travel across the city en masse and had recently picked up on the smells from the Deco Building and were endeavoring to determine their source.

At one point, the rats had been a group numbering in the dozens, but that had swiftly become tens of thousands within the first forty-eight hours after Alpha. By the time Saturday night arrived, a mere few hours before the one-week anniversary of the first quake, the number of rats assembled into a single pack was numbering right around six million, a sea that stretched almost a mile. If it had been seen from the air, the rat army would appear like a great black snake winding through the city, searching for a substantial food source to feed its Herculean number. But the rats stayed underground and out of sight, since when they did surface, they became easy prey to the various predatory birds now encircling the city.

It wasn't as if any of these stragglers fed to the birds were mourned, however. The rats were in a state most similar to rabid. They had a poison running through their system, but in the way rabies manifested itself with insatiable thirst, this poison from the Nivec did the same with hunger. The rats would never be able to eat enough, and this would eventually kill them. But while they were alive, it meant that no living thing in the Los Angeles basin was safe.

Just past midnight, Bones awoke to screams and gunfire.

He got to his feet just as Gary, Sharon, and Arthur all did the same, staring bleary-eyed at one another as what began as sporadic incidents of shooting quickly became a fusillade of bullets echoing up from below as if a war was being fought two levels down in the building.

"Shit, shit, *shit!*" cried Gary, freaking out. He leaped up and started pounding on the door. "Hey! Let us out!! What's going on?!"

Arthur raised a hand. "Did you ever think it might be better to stay be locked in here in a situation like this? Maybe even keeping quiet?"

Gary turned and was about to unleash an expletive-filled rant at Arthur, but then realized what he was saying might be true and stepped away from the door. As he did, the massive Humvee-mounted cannons in the courtyard began firing over the other gunfire, and the trio of humans raced to the window, only to be surprised at what they saw.

"Why are they firing *into* the building?!" Gary asked, his eyes going wide.

It was a bizarre sight to see so much firepower blazing away into the very structure they were being housed in, but they could also see a great number of men running away from the Deco building, obviously terrified. For a moment, the group thought that looters might have taken over the guns and there was a battle going on between the mercenaries and locals. But soon they could see that those mounting the Humvee cannons were the same as had been standing guard earlier.

Bonea heard it first, a single sound rising so high in its intensity that it even dulled out the gunfire. It was a low rumble that echoed as it traveled up the walls, sounding not unlike the coming of yet a third earthquake. Arthur heard it next, then Sharon, and finally Gary, all three of whom initially believed it to be an aftershock, though a couple of seconds later they began to realize it was something else entirely.

"It's everywhere!" Gary said, stepping away from the window.

The rumbling came up from the stairwells, down from the ceiling, over from within the walls, and beneath them in the floors. The room began to vibrate. In a panic, Bones barked and tugged at his chain so hard that it finally unraveled off the radiator and clinked around the room.

"Quiet!" Arthur yelled at the dog, but to no avail.

The noise of the rats got louder and louder, sometimes a rattling, sometimes a scratching, sometimes a pounding. Sharon thought it was as if she had suddenly found herself inside an echo chamber surrounded on all sides by an enthusiastic phalanx of snare drummers who couldn't decide a rhythm, so they had simply agreed to play louder and louder.

Just as the noise reached its apex, Gary disappeared.

More accurately, the floor beneath his feet disappeared, crumbling away and carrying the man and about four dozen rats down into the office full of unused furniture below. Gary screamed the whole way down until he landed amidst a cluster of wooden chairs with a sickening crack, the bones of both his legs splintering as he landed, one of which produced a spur that shot out through his flesh.

"FUCK!!" he cried, tears instantly welling in his eyes.

Sharon and Arthur gazed in horror at the sprawled-out young man and saw that though he was already partially covered in rats that had come down in the fall with him, even more were now racing across the floor towards his prone body. He screamed in horror as they dug their teeth into his skin, but when one ran straight to his face and sunk its incisors into his left eyeball, causing a geyser of blood to shoot a good two feet up into the air, Gary's screams became even more high-pitched.

"Oh, God," Sharon said.

As she spoke, rats began emerging from the edges of the broken floor and were now looking up at her, Bones and Arthur.

"This isn't going to be pleasant," said Arthur, as if describing an unappetizing piece of salmon.

The rats spilled out from the broken floor, but as they launched themselves at the humans, Bones playfully leaped towards them. He kicked a few over, nipped at this one or that, but when one of the rats had the bad manners to bite the shepherd on the foot, Bones snatched the squealing rodent up into his jaws and bit it in two. The other rats didn't seem to notice and continued moving at Sharon and Arthur, but Bones decided to involve himself. Without a thought, the large German shepherd jumped into the fray and began tearing the rats apart, but with an almost genteel touch. Bones would lean down like a mother cat, gently pick up the rat in his mouth, but then bite its head off. At the same time, he would use the great claws on his forepaws to tear open the soft flesh of other rats' underbellies, killing them just as easily. Within fifteen seconds, Bones had killed at least fifteen rats, and the driven little bastards were beginning to get the message and were stopping short at the edge of the hole in the floor.

"They're not just going to stop," Arthur said, shaking his head in disbelief.

Sharon was about to respond when the wall behind them broke apart, pouring literally hundreds more rats into the room, some immediately sliding to the hole in the floor as if it were a drain and being dropped onto their comrades devouring Gary below. As Sharon screamed, the rats massed together and then turned towards the other occupants of the room.

But just as Sharon prepared herself for a most horrific death, a noise like nothing she'd ever heard tore the room.

Well, to say she "heard" it is a misnomer. More like her ears momentarily sealed themselves up to allow a dull, hollow throb to pound incessantly within her skull, so much so that she felt as if she'd been deafened by a blow to both temples. She and Arthur both dropped to their knees and saw that Bones seemed to be affected by it even worse than they had been, since he shook his head violently and then battered it against the nearby sofa as if trying to shake something free.

What Sharon saw next shocked her. The rats fled as if the building was on fire. They escaped into the wall and into the hole in the floor where Gary had fallen, and a few even exited through a small space in a corner of the ceiling that Sharon hadn't noticed before. They vanished so quickly that Sharon had to remind herself that they'd been real in the first place and not just a terrifying figment of her imagination.

As she contemplated this, she felt a hand on her shoulder.

Turning to look, she saw a man in full body armor and military-style urban night camos looking down at her. he uniform had no insignia or distinguishing markings to it, but she still recognized the pattern as that utilized by Israeli special forces. She had done her two years of service in the IDF and had hardly been part of any elite unit, but she'd seen the digital blue and gray she was looking at now once when a special forces team had temporarily bivouacked at her base in Mishmar Ha Negev. The special forces team hadn't fraternized with the regular IDF soldiers as much as some of the female soldiers had wanted them to, but that only added to their mystique.

"Sharon Wiseman? We're here to rescue you."

Finer words, she had never heard.

The special forces troopers, led by a tall, olive-complected lieutenant named Paul ("Just Paul"), would not listen to Sharon when she demanded that both Arthur and Bones be extracted with her.

"Our mission is to retrieve you and you alone," Paul said. "We don't have the resources for an additional player, much less a dog."

"Then I'm staying here," Sharon replied.

"Then we'll remove you by force."

"Do you know who my father is?" Sharon shot back. "And who my grandfather was and what he meant to the nation?"

Paul was about to rip right into her but then held his tongue. He could hear the Mayer soldiers regrouping downstairs, and the last thing he wanted to do was be discovered.

"Just the man," Paul said.

Sharon looked at Bones but then reluctantly nodded, despite the dog having saved her life. "All right."

Sharon and Arthur were brought over to the window, where they saw how the special forces team had breached the room, coming across Vine on a wire connected to the last standing corner of the shattered hotel across the way where Bones had earlier seen the hawk. The team hooked a harness around Arthur and sent him across. Once he was safely away, Paul harnessed Sharon into a similar apparatus.

"Wait a sec," she balked. She moved over to Bones and unhooked the chain from around his neck so that he was completely unfettered. She then rubbed his snout.

"Take care of yourself," she said to the shepherd. She then allowed herself to be harnessed and zip-lined across the street. Paul, the last one in the room, glanced back at Bones, who was now sniffing around the bloody hole in the floor.

"Don't make me regret not shooting you," Paul said, though Bones didn't seem to notice.

With that, Paul exited across the zip-line, and seconds later the rope was cut as Bones watched. As if on cue, the door to the room was kicked open by four of the Mayer men.

"Where the hell'd they go?" barked Gerson, the leader of the group.

Bones galloped over to the window and began barking up a storm. Gerson and his men raced over and immediately saw the group of Israeli commandos retreating through the broken building across the way.

"Fuck!" shouted Gerson, who instinctively pointed his AR-15 tactical carbine out the window and began spraying the hotel with 5.56 NATO rounds.

Almost immediately, one of the Israeli commandos took a million-to-one shot to the neck, spun around, and fell four stories down to the street, where he landed with a dull thud, not unlike the hawk before him. The rest of the commandos immediately formed up and fired back, but with much heavier fire power.

High-powered rounds arrowed through the walls, easily tunneling through the midsections of Gerson and the other Mayer shooters despite their heavy plate body armor. It took a fusillade of less than a dozen bullets to silence the four men.

Having been just below the head- and chest-level shots taken by the commandos, Bones avoided getting shot, only to then have to dodge a falling mercenary who had taken three rounds to the stomach and was staggering backwards towards the hole in the floor. Bones ducked out of the way and let the man fall (directly onto Gary as it turned out, who seemed to groan upon the merc's impact), but then skittered out the door.

Instead of going downstairs, Bones followed the scent of Chris up to his squat on the fourth floor. He discovered both Chris and Barbara absent their clothes on Chris's cot but also absent most of their skin, having had it chewed away by the rats. Still clinging to one another, it seemed as if they'd been taken completely by surprise when the rodents swept in and, rather than fight, had allowed themselves to be devoured in coitus.

Bones sniffed around for a moment but then descended downstairs. When he reached the lobby, he saw that there were only a handful of the

Mayer men left, and they were all too preoccupied with trying to get back in contact with the outside world to notice a lone dog.

"We've got a real emergency here!" shouted one of the men. "We need an extract!"

"How many of the clients have been affected?" came a voice on the other end.

"We don't know. Too difficult to assess. You have to understand the gravity of the situation here on the ground! We have been breached, and we're at almost 100-percent casualties!"

There was a long silence on the other end of the line, but then a weary voice came back. "I'm afraid any attempt at extraction could be compromised by the current instability of the city. You're advised to sit tight or attempt your own extraction via a southeastern, overland route…"

The man smashed the radio receiver at this point and shook his head. "Those fuckers! When I get back there, I'm going bring their goddamn company down to its knees. They won't even know what hit them. Pricks."

This man's name was Richard Uhlmann, and he would unwittingly destroy mankind two hundred and forty-two days from this proclamation.

Bones padded out of the Deco Building and found Hollywood completely dark now that the generator-fueled lights set up by the mercs had been mostly extinguished. On the street and sidewalk directly in front of the structure were the corpses of thousands of dead rats shredded into mincemeat by the quick-thinking men in the Humvees, but also more than a few dead humans. Skipping through the carcasses, nose filling with the scent of the recently dead, Bones wandered north to Hollywood Boulevard, picked up a new scent, and began walking west.

The devastation along one of the most storied streets in the world was remarkable in its consistency. Very little was left standing, as the buildings had come down on both sides of the street, destroying the palm trees, signage, and even the "walk of fame," granite stars placed in the sidewalk emblazoned with the names of media stars, many long dead before the quake, far more dead after the quake.

Bones kept moving, as he found himself hungry and had picked up the scent of food. He tracked this to a warm spot on the street five blocks down from Vine where he detected the smell of gasoline and cordite, the place where the Israeli commandos had parked their vehicles before beginning their operation. Bones sniffed around this for a moment but then kept moving.

A few more blocks, and Bones found a hot dog stand storefront that had been demolished by the quake but seemed to have proved impenetrable to looters, though it was obvious some had tried to get in but hadn't managed to. Bones, however, was a very determined animal, and got down on his stomach, scratched his way forward, stretched out his spine, and finally edged his way into what had been the kitchen of the hot dog stand, now little more than a crawlspace filled with rotting meat. Bones immediately began feasting on the leftovers, scarfing down hot dog after hot dog until he couldn't eat another bite. He almost fell asleep right there, but started to feel queasy and struggled back out onto the sidewalk.

Once he was out, he staggered forward, threw up, and then shit all over the sidewalk. It was a disgusting evacuation to be sure, but Bones immediately felt a little better. At the very least, he wasn't hungry anymore.

As he walked, Bones looked up to the grassy hills above Hollywood most recently ablaze due to broken gas lines, but now only smoldering. He could see a couple of spots of orange that indicated fires that could have either been survivors or still burning homes. It was impossible to say.

His nose started picking up something else at this point, neither smoke nor rats nor gasoline nor people. It was a threat, and he scanned the darkness for its source, though this time the odor was coming off another canine.

Yipe...yipe...yipe...

The chilling, high-pitched call of a coyote pierced through the otherwise silent night, and Bones spotted his first would-be attacker: a skinny, gray-red coyote hurrying across the street towards him on spindly legs. No sooner had he see the first than he spotted two more on the way, called by their scout. They were skinny little animals with long, fox-like snouts, bushy tails, and incredibly sensitive ears that had been able to pick out Bones's approach, even if his scent might have been obscured by every other smell in the air.

Unlike the timber wolves he'd encountered in Pennsylvania, this pack was desperate for fresh meat and could tell that Bones, still suffering from a myriad of injuries, wouldn't be anywhere near 100 percent in a fight. Recognizing this himself, Bones began preemptively barking and barring his teeth, but this didn't even slow the coyote's pace. Though it seemed the pack hadn't decided which of its number would lead the charge, they didn't appear to be expecting much of a fight.

Bones backed up three steps, acting the wounded gazelle just enough to get one coyote out in front of the others. When it was far enough away from its pack, Bones launched forward. He caught the surprised animal off-guard and tore out its throat in one smooth motion. To drive his point home, the shepherd then lifted the fresh coyote carcass over his head, shook it around in his jaws a moment, but then let go. It flew a couple of feet before dropping lifeless onto the broken, rubble-strewn street.

But the coyotes were only momentarily put off by this display. They saw it for what it was: the one card Bones had to play. Now that it was on the table and the advantage had passed back to the pack, they quickly encircled the shepherd with their teeth bared.

Bones began barking, but the coyotes barked right back and snapped their saliva-dripping jaws. Bones stamped his feet a bit to show off his impressive claws, but the coyotes didn't slow their advance. Not even when Bones dropped his shoulders and opened his mouth to allow the dead coyote's blood to sluice through his bottom teeth onto the pavement did the coyotes seem to notice.

Realizing he wasn't going to be able to bluff his way out of this one, Bones spread his front legs to give himself an open stance and waited to be attacked.

Suddenly, three shots rang out from above Bones's position, fired straight into the air. The coyotes immediately sprinted away. Bones, a second later, did the same in the opposite direction. The shepherd only got a couple of yards before a man holding a rifle leaped down from the rubble of the building alongside the dog and blocked Bones's way. Instinctively, Bones barred his teeth again and barked at the man.

But then another man jumped down behind Bones, slipped a choke chain around the shepherd's neck, and pulled it tight.

"Out of the frying pan and into the fire," said the man standing in front of Bones. He stepped forward, revealing himself to be Paul, the Israeli commando team leader. "Sharon told us that you were some big fancy cadaver dog. Lucky for us, lucky for you."

Bones continued growling as Paul walked up to him, extending a hand. But as Bones leaned forward for a sniff, Paul punched him in the snout. The shepherd reared back, snarling in anger.

"The man your friends killed back there? My wife's youngest cousin. When we get done here, I'm going to eat your fucking heart, dog. But until then you're on the team."

Bones continued bucking at the choke chain, lunging forward and snapping at Paul, but the commando had already turned and walked away.

V

"So you *do* have a name."

Sharon was walking over to sit next to Bones as the sun rose over the mountains way out past Pasadena and the Angeles National Forest. The Israeli team had pushed on through the night, creeping down what was left of Sunset Boulevard until they turned south on Doheny, went down a steep hill, and established a base camp at the intersection of Santa Monica and Doheny in a park opposite what had once been the Troubadour. Most of the buildings along Santa Monica had only been one or two stories high, so when they came down, there was so little rubble compared to everywhere else that it simply made the area appear as it did before the city was even established. The park had been chosen due to its location at a major intersection but also because it afforded clear lines of fire both up and down the hill, as well as the fact that because of the park's fallen trees, it was easy to camouflage the two trucks the commandos had brought with them. It was also chosen due to its proximity to the next day's target.

"Bones," Sharon said, sitting next to the shepherd and handing him a piece of fruit.

Bones's stomach was still torn up from eating the rotten hot dogs the night before, but he readily accepted the food, swallowed it whole, and then expectantly looked up at its provider for more.

"You saved us back there," Sharon continued. "Paul claims his team had been waiting for the right moment and knew the rats were on their way, but I was there. We would have been toast if it wasn't for you. Sounds like your military is still looking for you, as you're presumed missing in action but not dead."

Bones continued waiting for another apricot.

"I just wanted to say 'thank you,'" Sharon said. "And I know what Paul said, but I won't let him do anything to you. We do need your help, though."

Bones nuzzled his snout into her hand, and she smiled. "I knew I could count on you."

The shepherd pushed his nose through her hand to her pocket, discovered the three remaining apricots, and deftly removed them with his tongue, slurping them down as Sharon ran her fingers across the hair under his chin.

Sharon was a mid-level executive for the nonprofit wing of a massive foundation set up by a multi-billionaire, Ivan Stephane, whose money came from two sources: yogurt and privatizing the world's sources of fresh water. Many felt he was one of the world's most effective villains when it came to subjecting the poor to further hardships. A notorious example involved Chinese peasants who had been farming the same land for generations. They suddenly found themselves forced to pay for the water that irrigated their fields as the government had sold a controlling interest in the nearest river to the multi-billionaire's corporation. In order to rehabilitate his public image, he had set up the Stephane Foundation with a substantial endowment to contribute millions to worthy causes around the world. Because of this, every negative article written would almost be forced to acknowledge the irony of his oppressive business practices due to his great (and tax write-off-able) philanthropy.

After each fiscal year, the culmination of the foundation's annual charitable endeavors was an international conference held in Los Angeles to promote ethical and "green" business practices that gathered the controllers of almost 20 percent of the world's GDP, or $10 trillion, in one place. This conference invited finance ministers from the world's leading economies, governmental representatives from emerging nations, well-heeled captains of industry, and barons of the world markets in order that all could be brought together to discuss how they might work to better society and the human race.

Of course, what the gathering had become known for were the endless negotiations between those with the money and those with the natural resources, leading to deals in which public and private money from wealthy nations was passed along to their less fortunate neighbors, but in a way where said money could only really be spent on that which would directly benefit the donor nation in the first place. Money for roads was donating, but the roads would run between a foreign oil company's refineries and bases of operation. Hospitals would be invested in, but only if long-term contracts were negotiated with western corporations that would supply the hospital with everything from surgical masks to Q-tips. Public utilities were constructed but were loans, not donations, and the terms of the deals made it so that the lucky country would be paying back those who built the dams, the power plants, and the electrical grids for decades to come.

With interest.

It was basically six days of extraordinarily high-end extortion and exploitation that left the attendees wealthy and those who the contracts were meant to help anything but.

Sharon worked for the foundation as a financial advisor to those responsible for not only maintaining but growing the endowment. Sharon's primary interactions were with representatives of the Israeli government on one side and then a number of the world's largest financial institutions on the other. A number of these institutions had majority stakes in the Boursa, Israel's Tel Aviv–based stock exchange, which listed not only 600 some-odd companies, but also numerous government and corporate bonds, hundreds of mutual funds, and then an ever-fluctuating number of ETFs, or exchange-traded funds.

While the Boursa was hardly the world's largest stock exchange, it was one of the fastest growing and had recently signed memoranda of understanding between it and the Shanghai Stock Exchange, as well as the London Stock Exchange. Those seeking to expand their wealth and influence on the Boursa were the exact type to be attracted to the Stephane Foundation's annual conference, and it was Sharon's job to make sure all interested parties not only were invited but were treated like royalty while in attendance.

Unfortunately, this year's conference, held at the Beverly Hilton Hotel, fell on the same weekend as the twin earthquakes, and the Boursa had all but crashed, losing investors hundreds of millions, destabilizing the Israeli Finance Ministry and the government at large, and creating a fiscal emergency that the world hadn't seen since 9/11. For the sake of their nation's economy, the Israeli commandos had been sent to rescue survivors and identify the dead in order that temporary reassignments of control of government finances could be made permanent and the deceased brought back to Israel for burial. To an outside observer, such a mission might seem mercenary and even cold, but with the world's markets already trembling due to the destruction of its fifth largest economy, the city of Los Angeles, desperate measures were called for.

"Though the U.S. government cannot officially recognize the legitimacy of our mission, it has given us access to both satellite photos and heat detection intel from the initial military flyovers, which indicated there were a number of survivors still inside the hotel," Paul explained to the team as they assembled Monday morning to go over the day's plan. "Admittedly, that intel is now days old and reflects a pre–Second Quake reality. What we do know is that the Beverly Hilton, while not intact, did not receive the level of structural damage of a lot of the city's other buildings, which suggests there may be survivors. But again, those survivors might not have stayed at that location. We are going in primarily to identify bodies if we can find them, extract survivors, and gather intel on the location of any that might have moved on. Additionally, we're to recover and destroy anything confidential or otherwise potentially compromising to the Israeli mission at the conference. Are we all on the same page?"

Everyone was. Even though Arthur was semi-retired, he'd been a lawyer for decades, and whereas many might find a mission like this surprising, he understood from the get-go. His only problem with it, in fact, had been when he learned that Sharon's rescue had little to do with her, but more her convenient ability to identify all the players, living or dead, they might encounter in the hotel.

"Isn't that dangerous?" he had asked her. "What if the building comes down around you?"

"If it wasn't for my position, those mercenaries wouldn't have picked me up, and these commandos wouldn't have saved me from the rats," Sharon had replied. "I'm not above singing for my supper."

An eight-man team led by Paul would go in with Sharon and Bones, while a two-man team would stay outside with the vehicle, where Arthur would be sequestered. Arthur had tried to stay out of the commandos' way, but Paul seemed to bristle every time he saw the older man.
One more mouth to feed, one more potential liability if a fast escape was called for.

For his part, Bones had been mostly ignored. One of the youngest commandos, a man named Nashon Sahar, had fed and provided water for the shepherd and that, coupled with the apricots from Sharon, had the dog feeling better than he had in days. He was also glad to be away from the mercenaries and back in the field. He recognized and felt comfortable with the martial attitudes of the soldiers around him, though he didn't know what would be required of him by the men.

When everyone had struck their campsites and loaded up their gear, Paul walked out of cover and onto Santa Monica Boulevard, taking the morning's temperature. When he felt he had a good sense of it, he turned back to the men and nodded.

"Let's move out."

The two trucks were empty except for their drivers and the civilians, Sharon in the lead vehicle, Arthur in the rear. The commandos crept alongside the trucks as they slowly made their way down Santa Monica into Beverly Hills. They passed beautiful but decimated houses on the right and brutalized office buildings as they went. A long stretch of twisted chain-link fence looked less like it had been in an earthquake and more a tornado, as it had been wound in on itself to the point that it had gouged great holes in the ground around it.

The commando team kept moving, passing the intersection with Beverly and then coming to a relatively undamaged stretch of road that probably survived solely because both buildings and trees had been pulled back far enough away from the street to leave it unaffected. They soon reached a sign that announced the Beverly Hills Police Department on their left, but they could see nothing of it. The police headquarters, the library, and the courthouse had not only been flattened, they'd also crumbled down into the multi-level parking garage below, leaving little trace.

"That it?" asked Nashon, who was on point.

Paul looked up ahead and saw the Beverly Hilton rising on the right, obscured only by the bell tower of an Episcopal church that had somehow managed to say upright. From that distance, the Hilton looked as if it had suffered a bomb blast that had shattered all its windows and generally made a mess of things, but it also looked relatively intact.

The Hilton was actually a series of buildings that included the main hotel, a ten-story, V-shaped building that contained 570 rooms, but also two additional buildings that housed innumerable ballrooms and conference rooms that extended out from the main structure, bordering on either side a long, U-shaped driveway/turnaround that could accommodate the countless limos and town cars of the hotel's most famous annual event, the Golden Globes.

Unlike the sheer devastation seen elsewhere in Beverly Hills, the miraculous sight of the still intact Beverly Hilton would give anyone reason enough to believe that someone inside during the quake may well have survived.

As they reached the hotel, Paul switched from speaking seldom to hand signals only. He signaled for the two trucks to stop at the mouth of the driveway but still out of sight from anyone passing on Santa Monica.

In Nashon's care at the end of a makeshift leash, Bones watched as Paul went first down the Hilton's driveway, his eyes everywhere at once, looking for movement. The team leader looked like a gunfighter in a movie stepping through a quiet Old West town he felt sure was teeming with the enemy on both sides. He walked with his hands wrapped tightly around the Heckler & Koch MP5 submachine gun, swinging it in different directions as if hoping any would-be sniper might flinch and give away his position if finding himself on the wrong end of a gun barrel.

There were actually a handful of bodies lying around the driveway, which only added urgency to Paul's caution, but when he got closer to them he could see that they'd died of severe trauma, likely after falling or jumping from the windows above. Disturbed by the sight, Paul moved on and tried to shake the images from his head.

Through all of this, Bones remained completely still. He understood what was required of him and maintained his rigid composure.

It was about a hundred yards from the mouth of the driveway to the hotel entrance, ground Paul covered in a little more than a minute. The hotel lobby appeared open air until one realized that all the glass had been blown out, and the flapping curtains and splintered marble weren't simply evidence of a crazy architect's mad aesthetic. Paul peered into the dark recesses of the building for a moment, but then turned back to his men and nodded.

"Let's go," Nashon whispered to Bones.

The commandos, Sharon, and the shepherd now moved down the driveway to join Paul. They were just as careful as their team leader, knowing that some ambushes simply hold their fire until the point man has passed, but no attack came. As the soldiers' boots crunched down on the broken glass of hundreds of different windows, Bones stepped lightly to avoid getting shards in his pads. For his part, Nashon couldn't help but stare up into the wall of potential snipers' nests above them, all empty hotel rooms, all with wind-carried curtains to mask the movements of a rifleman.

After they reached the hotel's entrance without incident, Nashon and the others could immediately see that visibility would be spotty at best. There was some breakage that allowed light in here and there, but the group could see that large chunks of the ceiling and walls had crashed down, smashing through the floor into whatever was underneath, which would make for treacherous going. It would be impossible to tell how stable the ground beneath their feet would be.

Paul turned and nodded to Nashon.

"Let the dog go."

"Just like that? What if he wanders away?"

"This is his job. If he wanders away, then he's no use to us anyway."

Nashon nodded and unchained Bones. The shepherd looked up at Paul.

"Do your thing," said the team leader.

Bones looked inside the building and knew what was expected of him. Taking a couple of tentative steps forward, pieces of glass still crunching under his paws, Bones entered the hotel, his head low and back stiff as he kept a suspicious eye on the ceiling. He kept moving, seeing and smelling no sign of life. When he was about fifty feet into the lobby, Paul nodded to the others and they began to follow.

Bones's eyes were the weakest part of him. It wasn't the fact that he was in his eighth year and they were hardly as sharp as they'd once been, but more that his nose and ears were just that much better. This meant that he'd learned to over-rely on them, so the darkness of the hotel did little to halt his advance. He listened as he stepped and, more importantly, continued to inhale the cornucopia of scents wafting through the lobby.

The floor had been marble but was now jagged and broken due to the falling ceiling. Bones stayed away from the holes, as the floor was more unstable around the cracks, even though it was through them that the smells of the dead wafted up. Bones could tell that despite the building having survived mostly intact, there were still several corpses both in the floors above but also below.

Amidst all this and combed through with the now-familiar stench of pulverized concrete and rotting food, Bones could also detect the scent of the living, and there almost as many of them throughout the building as there were dead. However, they weren't making their presences known yet.

"If he's anything like the dogs we used in Gaza," one of the commandos, a man named Zamarin, began, "he's going to be responding to the living first, then the dead. Not sure why it works that way, but it seems to be how they're trained."

Bones didn't hear this, having turned his attention to a broken door leading to fire stairs. He poked his head in, took a couple of deep sniffs, and proceeded inside. The stairwell was completely intact, with no real sign of earthquake damage on the first couple of floors, so Bones ascended the steps with ease, only vaguely aware that he was doing so in abject darkness.

"Lights," Paul said, turning on the rail-mounted tactical light attached to his MP5. The other commandos did the same, except for the weaponless Sharon. She looked at the stairs but then back at Paul, a querulous expression on her face.

"What is it?"

"If the stairs are so easily accessible, why would anyone still be up there? Don't you think the fear of a second quake would empty the place?"

"If there's anything I've learned, it's that you can't underestimate the stupidity of people under duress," Paul replied before turning to head the steps. "We'd need to sweep these rooms anyway, and no one's coming out of the woodwork to welcome us, so wherever they are, we're going to them."

Bones kept moving until he'd reached the eighth floor. He smelled living things on the other side of the door but also a heavy acrid stench like phosphorus or nitrogen. Bones tried to get through the door, but it was shut tight, and he had to wait for the humans.

"The dog has stopped on eight," Zamarin, currently in the point position, called back down to the team. Paul and the other commandos hurried up the steps as Bones whined at the closed door.

"Pull him back," Paul ordered Nashon, who quickly took Bones's leash and moved him away.

"Breaching in five…four…three…," said Paul, going silent for the last two, then swinging the door open for Zamarin to head in first.

"Oh, God…!" were the first words out of Zamarin's mouth, words that were followed by a torrent of vomit, the entire contents of his stomach.

Hearing this, Paul nodded to Nashon. "Send in the dog."

Nashon released Bones, and he bounded up the steps and out onto the eighth floor. Actually, it was now the eighth and ninth floors of the hotel, as the ninth had collapsed down a level, giving the floor the feel of a cavernous rooftop atrium with two-story walls and windows. The outer walls had held so the framing was still in place. It just seemed the ninth floor had buckled and spilled everything out onto the eighth.

But that wasn't what made Zamarin lose his breakfast.

There were at least four or five dozen human corpses on the level, likely hotel guests from both the eighth and ninth floors who had been killed in the initial quake, but the corpses were in no way "intact." In fact, it was as if the bodies had been hooked onto the back of a vehicle and dragged around for a few days, allowing them to slowly be torn apart over time, the entrails consumed, and nothing but desiccated skin and muscle tissue left behind on scattered bones. In addition to the human bodies, there were also amongst them the torn and ragged corpses of around a thousand rats.

Like the humans, the rats had been torn apart. Their bodies had been opened and their organs ripped out, but it wasn't as a complete a job as what happened to the humans. Whereas the human carcasses were only identifiable by surviving skeletal structure, the rats often still had their fur and heads and tails attached, their attackers hardly licking their plates as clean as those who devoured the humans.

Bones barked a couple of times as the Israeli commandos looked around in horror.

"What the hell are we dealing with here?" asked one of the commandos, a fellow named Levy, staring around the room.

"No idea," replied Paul. He turned to Sharon. "We had people on these floors, correct?"

"We had two suites on the ninth floor," Sharon said.

"You're not still thinking of 'retrieval,' are you?" asked Zamarin.

"We knew the bodies might not be intact," Paul said, then nodded towards Bones. "He did his job. Now it's time to do ours. At the very least, we need to make an attempt at identification."

The team split up, half starting at the far end of the level and the other the near in hopes of meeting in the middle. Sharon tried to indicate which rooms the Israeli delegation had been in, but it wasn't easy.

"Sorry, I'm getting a little turned around," she admitted as she tried to imagine where the elevator bank had been. "We had 912 and 914, I think, which were on the far side of the elevators, wherever they were."

"Southwest corner," Paul said, indicating a floor map.

Sharon nodded and tentatively stepped down the hall, only to have her feet squish through a pulverized rat corpse. "Oh, *shit*."

Bones walked over, sniffed her shoe, and padded ahead, deftly springing over this corpse or that to get to the end of the hall.

At the opposite end of the building from the stairwell, Paul indicated into the rubble where suites 912 and 914 had landed, but it was clear to everyone that the collapse was total, and any human who might have been in either room was now squashed under tons of concrete.

"Oh, no," cried Sharon, seeing something she recognized.

She clambered over the rubble of the combination of rooms 812 and 910/912, having spotted human remains near the edge of the building. More of a skeleton with hair now, the corpse was that of a woman who seemed to have been pinned by chunks of ceiling in the calamity but had been unable to get free. From her outstretched arm, it appeared that she might have died reaching out to the now nonexistent window to try to get help.

The rats had then come and eaten all of her skin off. There were bite marks up and down her bones, and the only conclusion one could draw was that this person's last hours or, worse, last days were in agony. Her jaw seemed to be frozen in a scream with bite marks even there, covering her teeth and nasal cavity.

"Do you recognize her?" Paul asked quietly.

"Keren Paransky, the Finance Minister's wife," Sharon said, then added simply, "We were close."

Paul nodded, silently bringing out a list and making a notation. Bones walked over, glanced up at Sharon, and then regarded the semi-skeletal remains with a quick sniff before wandering over to where the floor ended and the wind was gently blowing in the curtains. Bones looked down the eight floors to the driveway below.

"Hey, boy, you okay?" asked Nashon, walking over to the window and squatting next to the dog. "Want some water?"

Nashon poured a little water from a canteen into the canteen's cap, and Bones slurped up three helpings. Nashon was about to pour him a fourth when he noticed something out the window.

"Um, sir?"

Paul looked over. Nashon pointed down to the street. "They're gone."

Paul hurried over next to Nashon and scanned the driveway. The two trucks were in place, but there was no sign of the drivers or Arthur. Paul hefted up his MP5 and looked down the scope, which only revealed, to his horror, a single severed human foot glistening red out in the morning sun.

"Did anyone hear any shots?!" Paul roared, calling out to the entire team. "Anybody?!"

No one had. Suddenly, Paul got a bad feeling. Sharon could see his entire body tense.

"What is it?" Sharon asked.

"I think something got to them," Paul said.

"Why didn't we hear shots?" Zamarin asked, hurrying over. "If it was those fucking rats again, they would've opened up. No way we wouldn't have heard them."

"Yeah, but the rats are moving at night, not day," said Paul. "This is something else. Pass the word. We're out of here in one."

Two rooms down, Bones had wandered over to a different ledge and nosed through the curtains until he was looking out directly over the decimated buildings of Century City. Though there hadn't been as many buildings in that direction as, say, Hollywood or the Wilshire corridor, all of them -- hotels, offices buildings, hospitals, an outdoor mall, etc. -- had been these truly massive structures. So when they all came down, the rubble made the district look like a quarry.

Their absence, however, now afforded a view from the eighth floor of the Beverly Hilton directly to the Pacific Ocean. Though pollution might have still made this difficult in the past, in the week following the first quake the sudden lack of ongoing air pollution seemed to have changed the color of the sky. There was still a smoky gray haze from where the wind picked up concrete dust and carried it on the wind alongside the smoky embers rising from the Hollywood Hills and Santa Monica Mountains fires, but the yellow, the orange, and the toxic green hues that were part of everyday atmospheric life in the City of Angels were already fading away. Eight days without people, and already the place looked better.

Bones turned and looked out towards the northwest, over towards the Pacific Palisades and Malibu beyond, and saw a thick black cloud of smoke rapidly making its way across the blue sky, as if a great conflagration had just been ignited and was consuming everything in its path. But then the cloud's tail broke free from the earth, and it just became a wandering black splotch on the horizon following the coast down towards Santa Monica.

Only, the wind was blowing northeast.

Bones started barking but wasn't sure why. He was definitely barking at the cloud, particularly now as it seemed to be changing direction again and moving less towards Santa Monica and more in the direction of Beverly Hills. Then something even stranger happened as the sky darkened behind the hotel as well, casting the floor in shadow.

Bones began barking in earnest.

"Bones! Keep quiet!" Nashon cried, hurrying over to the dog, a shushing finger to his lips. "We're getting out of here."

But the shepherd couldn't stop. Something was clearly terrifying it. As if catching a scent on the wind, Bones bolted around and headed out of the room, across the hall and towards the east-facing side of the structure, where he began barking even louder just as the shadow over the sun began getting more and more complete, dimming the light in the already dark hotel.

Paul and Sharon hurried out of the "room" they had been in and watched Bones, the dog's panic quickening their pulses.

"Shit, what does he know that we don't?" Zamarin asked.

Paul, a little scared to do so, strode quickly over to Bones's side and looked out into the sky towards where the shepherd was directing his alarm. Upon seeing what the dog was up in arms about, Paul immediately knew the casualty rate of the coming encounter would be large.

In the eastern sky, blocking out the sun, was a collective mass of literally hundreds of thousands of birds, possibly millions, flying in from the ruins of downtown. Paul was amazed by the sight, as he'd never seen so many birds outside of a documentary.

"Sir? We've got birds incoming."

Paul turned and saw Levy pointing out towards the west.

"What do you mean? They're over here."

But then Paul saw through the building that an equal number of birds were coming in from the ocean side of the city, as if to marry up with the complementary fleet from the east at the Beverly Hilton's brunch buffet consisting today of Israeli commandos, one young woman, and a German shepherd. Paul turned and looked around, finally recognizing that the phosphorus and nitrogen smell, coupled with what he'd wrongly written off as some kind of chemical powder from the building's fire extinguishers, was actually bird guano.

He'd never been to Los Angeles before but understood that it, like many a metropolis, was overrun with pigeons and seagulls. It had never occurred to him that birds would have interest in devouring anything as large as a rat, much less meat off a human corpse.

"Back to the stairwell – now," he ordered.

Paul didn't have to convince anyone. The other commandos saw the approaching flocks and recognized malevolence in their movements. What they didn't realize was just how quickly they were approaching.

Sharon surprised herself by being the last to move, as the previous week had found her exercising reflexes and response times she didn't know she had. She'd been in bed in her Wilshire Corridor apartment when Alpha hit and was up like a shot. Her girlfriend had not been as fast, figuring the quake to be as mild as any they'd ever felt, but within seconds had been crushed under the full weight of their collapsing ceiling. From her vantage point in the living room, Sharon had just glimpsed this but had had a clear view of the panic on Emily's face when she realized too late the mortal danger. Sharon had successfully avoided calling that image to mind for eight days now as she'd fought to survive, first to get food and water, then when having to fight off would-be rapists at Memorial Stadium on the USC campus, where a number of survivors had initially gathered but then when hunted down by the Mayer men, who seized her about half an hour after she had found a working satellite phone and had called the Stephane offices in New York.

But she found something hypnotic about these birds. If she'd had the wherewithal to write it down, she'd admit that it looked like something out of a 3-D movie winding its way towards her from the screen. She actually loved birds, and a couple of weekends before the quake had spent a morning with Emily photographing them at a bird sanctuary in Griffith Park. As she'd never seen birds exhibit anything remotely like this behavior before, naturally she was enraptured.

"Come on!" shouted Paul, this time snapping Sharon out of it and making her run.

The humans were all at different distances from the stairwell door when the birds coming in from the east slammed into the building first. It was a tremendous sound as several of the flock collided with the building itself both above and below the open-air eighth and ninth floors. Still, thousands drove in through the windows at the commandos, and within seconds, two of the commandos had been pounded so ferociously that they fell off the edge of the building, while another two had been similarly driven to the ground, their eyes bloodily torn out.

"Shoot 'em!" screamed Paul, who turned and blasted into the birds with his machine gun.

This proved disastrous for the team leader, as the flock was moving way too quickly and as soon as he fired, he found himself pelted with just as many severed beaks and claws from the ones he'd killed as from the living. Gallons of bird blood splattered against his face as a gull reached his head, dug its claws into his temples, and tore out his eyeballs.

Nashon didn't even bother firing. He hit the deck immediately and landed nose-down in a dead rat's stomach. He retched, but kept his head down so that the worst he got from the birds racing by overhead was hair torn out of his scalp and his clothes shredded.

Sharon actually managed to get behind a large chunk of rubble and survived without a scratch, save a gash she gave herself as she scraped her leg when she'd ducked down. A number of birds smacked into her temporary barrier, but those flying by overhead didn't even see her.

"Help me!! God, help!!"

She looked over and saw the commando named Levy as he appeared to be less pushed and more physically *carried* over the edge of the building. It was an unbelievable sight, a man being carried by birds. Even though he was flailing mightily against his attackers, Sharon felt the commando looked downright angelic, as if he was being held aloft by some unseen Heavenly protector.

But the moment passed and, like Icarus, Levy became all too aware of his limitations, and that knowledge seemed to break the illusion and cause his body to fall. As with her girlfriend, Sharon managed to make eye contact with the man as he began his descent. He looked terrified but did not scream the entire way down to the concrete below.

It suddenly occurred to Sharon that that explained the bodies down in the driveway.

Well aware of what was coming, Bones had simply lain down on the ground behind a crushed piece of flooring and watched the birds pass over with amusement. At first, he made a couple of snaps at them, even pulling a mourning dove out of midair, which he promptly killed, but the action brought the attention of some of the other birds, who came and tore into his fur as they flew by. Realizing it wasn't worth it, Bones knelt back down and sat out the action.

It took the entire ocean-borne flock less than fifteen seconds to make their aerial maneuver through the hotel and come out on the other side, where they faced off against the flock from downtown.

"What the *fuck* was that?" screamed Zamarin.

Sharon looked over at the older commando and saw that though he had managed to secret himself behind a broken concrete slab, his left eye had been torn from its socket and was now hanging down his cheek.

"I don't know," she said, clambering to her feet. She looked around and saw that two commandos were dead on the floor, three were missing and, she presumed, had gone over the ledge of the building, and that Paul, who was being attended by Nashon, had been at the very least blinded by the birds. She moved over next to him and saw that he was sitting upright in a massive pool of blood surrounded by empty cartridges and shredded birds.

"Who's alive?" Paul croaked, his commanding voice intact but sounding punch-drunk from blood loss.

"I am," reported Zamarin. "Ms. Wiseman, the dog, and then Corporal Sahar."

"No one else?" Paul said, though he didn't sound that surprised.

"No, sir."

"And what are the birds doing?" Paul asked.

Sharon looked out towards the sky and saw that the two flocks had merged, but rather than turn and blast directly back into the hotel to finish the job as she expected, they appeared to be killing one another. The corpses of literally hundreds of birds were cascading down to the rubble-strewn wasteland of Beverly Hills in a torrent.

"They're fighting...or something," Sharon said. "There are birds dropping out of the sky. They're killing each other. It's the craziest thing I've ever seen."

"I think they're infected with whatever got into the rats," Paul suggested. "Either that or God's decided to take pity on us for a moment. Either way, let's not spit in His face by wasting it."

VI

With the birds momentarily preoccupied with tearing each other apart, the survivors of their initial assault helped each other to the stairwell and shut the door. Once there and safe, Sharon pulled bandages from Paul's woefully under-stocked first aid kit and wrapped them around his head, covering his empty, still bleeding eye sockets as well as the numerous cuts on his face and scalp. Nashon started to do the same for Sergeant Zamarin, but there was a question as to what could be done with the still attached eyeball hanging from the end of the optic nerve.

"You can have that reattached," Sharon said, though she was loath to actually look at it. "It's not that uncommon a procedure. Just try and pack it back into the socket in some way, and then we'll pad it with bandages."

"You have any idea how quickly it'll get infected?" the sergeant asked. "Minutes, not hours. And that close to my brain? Thank you, no."

Zamarin pulled a knife out of his belt, snipped through the optic nerve, and caught his now severed eyeball in his hand.

"Oh, I can't believe you just did that," Sharon said, turning her head. Nashon looked as if he might throw up.

A bit delirious himself from blood loss, Zamarin clearly enjoyed the attention.

"If this is to truly be one of my last days on earth, there's something I've always been curious about," Zamarin began, a whimsical tone in his voice as if reciting a children's rhyme. "What does it look like, the inside of a dog?" With that, the commando fed his severed eyeball to Bones, who swallowed it in one gulp. "Oh, dear God," Sharon said, her mouth agape.

"Did he just feed his eyeball to Bones?" Paul asked, surprisingly matter-of-fact.

"He did."

"You are one sick bastard, sergeant," Paul said, shaking his head. "You take the prize."

Zamarin shrugged, but then looked down the dark stairwell. "Be that as it may, I'd imagine the plan couldn't go much more topsy-turvy. We can't stay here. God only knows what's waiting for us below, and if we step back out onto one of these floors, chances are the birds will come right back to play another Hitchcock number on us."

"Well, it just doesn't make sense," Paul said. "We got intel as recently as yesterday that there were survivors in this building. There were heat scans, they were moving and alive. Where could they be?"

That's when a thought occurred to Sharon and she looked down the stairs. "The conference was being held in the subbasement ballrooms, which are right off the kitchen. If they stayed intact, wouldn't that be the place to go?"

Paul nodded.
"Only one way to find out."

With Zamarin taking point and Nashon leading Paul, the group slowly made their way down the stairwell back to the first floor. Bones took his lead from the surviving commandos, staying close and not straying ahead. This allowed Sharon to keep a hand on the shepherd as they walked, the darkness giving her a sort of vertigo on the way down she hadn't experienced on the way up. Even with the dog, she found herself stumbling every few steps when she missed the handrail.

"*Shit!*" she cried, tripping but then catching herself on the wall. "Fuck."

"You all right?" asked Paul.

"Fine, fine," Sharon scoffed. "I don't know what's wrong with me."

"You're dehydrated, you're overloaded with adrenaline, which has contracted your blood vessels and exploded your heart rate, and you're probably in shock, at least mentally," Paul explained. "What's worse, you keep demanding your body move forward. This is it reacting."

Sharon exhaled sharply, knowing Paul was right but not willing to concede that she might not be fit for this kind of duty. "I'm fine."

"We all need rest," Paul said. "I'm near a full system collapse."

"Then why don't we abort the mission?" Sharon asked. "Turn ourselves over to the U.S. military, get extracted."

"I don't know if you heard, but the American military has suspended all operations inside the Los Angeles basin," Paul stated, groaning as Nashon slipped a little and bumped the team leader against the railing, confirming to Sharon that he was more hurt than he had wanted to let on. "They're not coming in here, no matter what. We're on our own. We have a boat in Venice that's fueled and ready to go. That's our extraction."

"You really think we can get out all the way out there?" Zamarin asked. "Rats by night, now birds by day. Los Angeles is getting pretty feral. Never seen such aggressive birds."

"Those birds weren't being aggressive," Sharon said. "That was some kind of defensive behavior, as if protecting a nest, only – no nest. It's what the Mayer guys said about the rats. The rats are poisoned with something that affected their sympathetic nervous system, and now it's been passed on to the birds."

"That doesn't make sense. It's all over the city, so that suggests it could be picked up from multiple sources, which suggests it's either airborne or waterborne. If that was the case, we'd be infected. And if doesn't affect humans, then Bones would probably be affected."

"Could it just be animals with simple nervous systems? In both of these cases we're looking at animals that are prone to hive-mind activities."

Paul was about to reply when he realized that Bones had gone completely silent. "What's Bones doing?"

Sharon looked over and saw that he was staring expectantly down the stairwell, his ears perfectly erect.

"He went rigid," Sharon said quietly. "I think he hears something."

Paul got to his feet with Nashon's help and picked up his machine gun. "I'm not crazy enough to fire this thing blind, but in case it's someone that can be easily intimidated…"

That's when they all heard what Bones had heard, a distant *creak* from below. Paul bent over, felt around for the shepherd, and then leaned in close to the dog's ear.

"Go get 'em, Bones," Paul whispered.

Bones leaped to his feet, zipped down the remaining four flights of stairs, and was out in the lobby in seconds.

"What if it's a friendly?" asked Sharon, incredulous.

"Then we'll know soon enough. But I've never had a problem with the idea of pre-emption."

When Bones reached the lobby, he quickly looked around for the source of the sound, only to hear it again coming up from the stopped escalators leading to the lower ballrooms. He wheeled around, raced down the escalators, and immediately found himself in another dark part of the building.

The sub-level was filled with dead bodies, the corpses of about thirty people lying in the hallways, though it looked like a few had been carried down by collapsing ceilings and columns rather than having been in the sub-basement for the quake. But though the stench of death hung heavy in the air, Bones was able to immediately pinpoint that one scent distinctive from the others: *the living.*

Leaping across the bodies, Bones made his way down the dark hallway to where a thin slit of light was framing a door.

"Someone's coming!" came a voice from the dark. "I hear them!"

"Is it the rats?" came a second voice.

"No, I don't think…"

But before this person could finish, Bones reached the door and with very little effort forced it open. The man who had been standing behind it, a fifty-something named Sebastian Zobrist, was knocked backwards, and Bones immediately stood on top of the fellow, drooling in his face as he gave him a sniff-over.

"Christ, get it off me!" Sebastian cried. "It's going to kill me!!"

Bones glanced up and saw that there were about as many living people on the inside of the ballroom as there were dead outside. He looked back down at Sebastian and licked his face for good measure.

That's when Bones sensed something coming towards him and looked up in time to receive a broadside in the form of a metal chair that a middle-aged woman swung against Bones's ribcage, sending him sprawling.

"Jesus Christ, you'll just make him mad, Greta!" Sebastian said as he scrambled to his feet. "You should've killed him!"

"With what?" Greta asked, nodding around the room.

"We have those knives," someone offered from the back of the room.

Before Greta could reply, Bones was back on his feet and pissed. Rather than growl, he kept his head low to the ground, his spine straight as he wasn't "threatening," more slipped into about-to-leap-up-and-tear-your-throat-out mode. The humans saw this and flinched backwards.

"Oh, shit," Sebastian exhaled. "Now what?"

"That's enough, Bones," came the voice of Paul, stepping through the door and into the ballroom, his machine gun surprisingly well-aimed directly at Sebastian's rotund middle.

Bones quieted as Nashon walked over and put the leash back on the shepherd, pulling him back to the group as Paul and Zamarin stepped forward.

"Who are you?" asked a woman in a thick South African accent.

"Tzva Hahagana LeYisra'el," Paul snapped back, returning to martial mode.

"Israelis!"

Nashon, Sharon, and Zamarin looked in the direction of a man, obviously of Arabic descent, who stepped forward. "If anybody was going to get to us, it would be *katsas*."

"I'll take that as a compliment, but we're not Mossad, we're Army special forces," Paul said. "Your accent is Lebanese?"

"Your accent is the West Bank?" the man replied, challengingly. "Perhaps even Gush Etzion? Bet you wouldn't have come all this way if you knew there was a chance you'd be saving an Arab life."

"That situation can change," Zamarin said, voice mixed with threat and sarcasm.

Sharon raised her hand. "Please! Let's see if during this Apocalypse maybe we can set aside our differences for even a moment. Given the gravity of our situation, can't we see each other for a moment as fellow human survivors and not avatars of our governments?"

The Lebanese man shrugged, then nodded towards Paul. "He's the one with a machine gun aimed at unarmed civilians."

Paul sheepishly lowered his weapon, but Zamarin kept his raised. "Unarmed? Didn't I hear somebody say something about knives?"

A young woman in the tatters of a catering uniform held up a stack of breakfast silverware, hardly a threat to anyone, and Zamarin lowered his weapon.

"I know you," said Greta, nodding towards Sharon. "You work for the Stephane Foundation."

"I do," Sharon replied. "We're here to rescue you."

"We're here to rescue the Israeli contingent," Paul corrected.

Murmurs went through the ballroom. The Lebanese man scoffed, as if Paul was confirming everything he'd ever believed about Israel.

Sharon wheeled around on her heel. "The Israeli contingent, if we had found all alive, would've been around forty people. We are looking at thirty. I believe we can accommodate them, given the situation."

"Are you forgetting that we are down two-thirds in force?" Paul hissed back.

"Are you forgetting that you're blind and that you guys need us more than we you?" Sharon said, then spotted the half-grin, half-sneer on Paul's face before turning back to the assembled group. "First of all, we need to know how many of you are injured."

It turned out that a tiny slip of a woman, Lisa Nong, who had grown up in St. Petersburg, the child of Japanese diplomats, was a doctor, having come to the Stephane Foundation conference as the representative of a large Asian medical consortium to lobby for economic partnerships in other countries. She had patched up the injured as best she could in the ballroom, which had at one time incorporated a number of local Beverly Hills residents who had made their way to the hotel once they saw it was still standing.

"After the first quake, we probably had a good one or two hundred people in here, maybe more," Lisa told Sharon and Paul as she cleaned up Paul's wounds and re-bandaged his eyes. "We had food, we had candles, we had some lanterns, and we even had a couple of generators that we knew to use sparingly. As survivors made their way here, we were afraid that we'd be over-capacity within hours, but that just never happened. And after the second quake, a number decided to try and get out of the city."

"Where did they hope to go?" Paul asked.

"Over the Hollywood Hills and into the San Fernando Valley. They thought they'd be safe, despite the fires and the landslides. A few said they were going to try for the ocean and said that if they found rescue, they would send people back. We haven't heard from any of them. You've encountered the rats?"

"Last night," Paul nodded. "We were going overland into Hollywood to retrieve Ms. Wiseman here, and our satellite linkups kept showing this massive heat signature that had been building around the city for days. We thought it had something to do with burning gas lines, but then we saw the tribe of rats for ourselves."

"We saw rats within hours here the first day when we started making the first meals. They were curious and seemed to be going after the food in the kitchen, but they weren't as feral as the ones that started coming by a couple of days later. We noticed they were getting more aggressive, and, worse, they attacked a couple of people that went out on a supply scout. Then on the third night, they swarmed into the hotel and killed six people, and we had to beat them back with torches. That's when we sealed ourselves in this one ballroom. The fourth night, we were pretty well sealed in here in case they came back, but then there was the second quake. The people you see out there in the hall? They bolted when it struck, and the rats were waiting."

"And the birds?" Paul asked.

"That's new," Lisa sighed. "We only started to see them a couple of days ago. Somebody came in here and told us that they'd seen large swarms of birds patrolling around downtown, including gulls feasting on corpses, but we didn't believe them. There have been a lot of rumors. But then they attacked a supply party yesterday, and that's when we stopped sending people out. That's when we decided it was just no longer safe to leave this room. We've been here ever since, driving each other crazy."

"Have you had any contact with the outside world?" Sharon asked.

"Couldn't get a single phone to work," Lisa said. "We saw all the military helicopters the first few days and figured they'd get to us eventually. But then the second quake came and the over-flights ended. Any idea when they're starting up again?"

Paul shook his head. "What's worse is that once they get wind of this rat and bird situation, that's going to delay them even more. I don't think they've ever had to deal with something like this."

Bones was lying down nearby, his eyes following the conversation as Lisa spoke, turned to Sharon, and then turned back to Paul. He even noticed when Lisa casually rested her hand on Sharon's leg when making a certain point and similarly noticed when Sharon didn't push it away.

"So what's the plan?" Lisa asked. "Are you planning to take us out? Or was your earlier sentiment the most accurate: Look for Israelis, realize not a one survived down here with us, and slip away in the middle of the night when we're not looking?"

"Well, it's a risk either way, and not just for us," Paul stated. "As their food supplies begin to run out, the rats and the birds are going to get even more desperate, which means they'll find a way in here, believe you me. But if you come with us overland, we'll be attracting a lot of attention and the chances of being overrun are high. Either way, it's not going to be a picnic."

"So what do you suggest?" Lisa asked.

"I think that decision should be left up to you and your people," Paul said. "You've been savvy enough to survive this long, so that's a major indicator towards your instincts. Also, you've been negotiating this city post-quake longer than we have and have a greater sense of the risks."

It didn't take long for Lisa to explain the options to the others and even less for a vote to be decided on.

The group in the ballroom consisted of Lisa; Sebastian, who was an English real estate baron but who had inherited everything from his father; the woman who'd struck Bones, Greta, who was an Austrian finance minister; Shahin, the Lebanese man who turned out to be the vice president of one of the largest construction entities in the Middle East; and Sally, the catering waitress with the knives, who had originally come from Tennessee.

Additionally, there were two other members of Lisa's medical consortium; a four-man Malaysian news team covering the conference who had been sharing a suite on the tenth floor and were, in fact, the level's only survivors; an Australian finance minister named Garth Trenchard and a woman he referred to as his "secretary" named Kathryn, but who was obviously a highly-paid escort; a Hollywood agent named Jeremy who hadn't been at the hotel at all but at an agency across the street when the quake hit;, eight Latino hotel workers - four women and four men - all employees of the hotel who had been working around the kitchen and sub-basement when the quake hit and had survived entirely unscathed (though they had originally been a much larger contingent, as a number of the hotel employees were the ones who had decided to "brave" the outside after the second quake); a lecturer on investment opportunities in heavy manufacturing of electronics in Taipei named Gregoire; and then there were two kids, an eleven year-old named Tony and his older sister, Heather, who was fifteen. They'd been staying on the sixth floor of the hotel, their mother having been an attaché to the finance minister of Ecuador and whose room had been crushed, leaving no question as to the fact that their mother was dead.

Tony hadn't spoken since they'd arrived in the ballroom.

But now with this motley crew assembled, Lisa got them ready to vote.

"All in favor of holing up here for a little while longer until the military arrives?" she asked.

Trent raised his hand first, followed quickly by each member of the Malaysian news team. One of Lisa's colleagues at the medical consortium raised her hand, but the other did not. Kathryn, the Australian escort, raised her hand but, upon receiving a dirty look from her lover, lowered it. Gregoire raised his hand tentatively for a moment, but after seeing how few others were of this mind, he lowered it.

"Okay, all in favor of making a run for the ocean?" Lisa asked.

Sebastian's hand shot up, followed by Trenchard and Kathryn. Shahin's hand raised next in unison with Sally's and, from the grinning look they gave each other, it would be obvious to anyone paying attention that this pair had been getting it on, albeit discreetly, over the last couple of days.

The others in the room followed suit, including the hotel workers, who first conferred amongst themselves in Spanish before deciding on an option. The last to vote were Tony and Heather, and they seemed as swayed by a desire to vote with the majority as Gregoire.

After making sure it was a clean majority, Lisa surrendered the floor to Paul, whom Nashon had kept abreast of the raised hands.

"All right," Paul began. "First of all, anyone who wishes to stay can still do so. We won't make anyone leave. That said, I firmly believe there is strength in numbers and would strongly invite you to change your mind. Both the rats and the birds have proved willing to sacrifice large numbers when they attack, and they can move quickly, making them a foe you cannot fight, only elude. Whether we leave during the day or during the night, our scents will travel the second we leave here, and whichever predator is about will move on us and might spring unexpected. The *one* thing we have going for us is this dog, Bones. He's an enforcement animal and could buy us a few minutes to get to cover, as he'll pick up on any attack before we do."

The ballroom survivors looked at Bones with new eyes, most having figured him for some kind of companion or mascot.
Potential savior? Not really.

Paul waited a moment, sensing the feeling of dread creeping over his audience, all wondering if they chose poorly when voting for the escape. But then he continued:

"Personally, I think we have a better shot against the rats. There are more of them, possibly millions, but we'll be fighting on an X-Y axis. With the birds, it becomes X-Y-Z, as they'll be above us, and that's a hard variable to overcome. Also, there's that slim chance that the rats will simply be too far away to get to us by the time they catch on, and we can outrun them to the beach. The birds, of course, can cover that same amount of ground in a tenth of the time."

The feeling in the room was obviously going Paul's way now, and Nashon whispered as such into Paul's ear.

"All right," Paul concluded. "If you've decided to come with us, we'll leave at dusk. Be ready to go."

Paul's pronouncement had come around noon, so there was plenty of time to prepare. Weapons were fashioned from broken chairs and the sharper edges of kitchen implements, what little food was left was gathered, and a couple of items that perhaps no one had considered as being easy to weaponize had been acquisitioned by Nashon on Paul's instructions. Almost more important than all of these things, routes were determined. Gregoire and Trent, despite both having initially voted against the excursion, were key to this last point, having been on several of the scouting excursions out into Beverly Hills and down to Century City.

"You have to understand how fucked up it gets the further west you go," explained Trent, indicating along a map to Zamarin and Nashon as Paul listened. "There were fewer tall buildings to topple over and create obstacles, but it becomes about the road itself. Santa Monica Boulevard was under construction and got hit pretty hard. The road becomes almost impassable just beyond Century City. You won't be able to drive vehicles."

"Wasn't planning on it anyway," said Zamarin. "If anything's going to invite the rats in an otherwise quiet empty city, it'd be the trucks. We're on foot."

"Good point," agreed Trent. "But that still puts us on the ground for two or three hours at least. You're going to have people climbing over broken concrete in the dark, and not everyone here exactly in the best shape."

Trent nodded over his shoulder at Sebastian and Trenchard.

"Yeah, we'll be shouldering them through, I'd imagine," suggested Nashon. "It won't be easy."

"That's where natural selection comes in," said Zamarin. "Some will be fed to the enemy so the rest of the pack can survive. It's like ballast for a balloon."

"You can't be serious," exclaimed Gregoire.

Zamarin got right up in Gregoire's face and sneered. "You want to hear me say that every last one of us is going to make it to the beach alive and well, and tomorrow we'll be doing this big happy joint press conference in San Diego about our harrowing escape? I mean, I can tell you that, sure, if you need to hear the words. But I'd be full of shit."

Gregoire thought about this but then shut up.

In the kitchen, Sharon and Lisa gathered food as Bones padded alongside. The shepherd occasionally got underfoot and poked his nose where it didn't belong, but Sharon had realized that in this whole mess the only time she felt any sense of safety was when Bones was near.

"So you're from here?" Lisa was asking. "Where were you when the quake hit?"

"At home," Sharon said. "In bed. Not far from here, actually. Westwood."

Sharon fell silent, and Lisa sensed that she didn't want to talk about it. Instead of pressing the matter, Lisa moved on with the preparations, only to hear Sharon exhale.

"You don't have to talk about it if you don't want to," Lisa said.

"It's like a superstition," Sharon said. "If I don't say it aloud, it didn't happen, you know? I lost my partner, my girlfriend, of four years in the quake. It could've been me that died, but I was just faster."

Lisa nodded but then put her hand on Sharon's shoulder as the younger woman stared glumly at the floor. It was such a depressing thought, life without Emily. She'd so successfully put it out of her mind, but here it all was.

"What was her name?" Lisa asked. "If you don't mind me asking."

"Emily," Sharon replied, her voice cracking on the third syllable, making it almost sound like a question. "She was a student. We met when she was seventeen at a club, but I didn't pursue anything for propriety's sake until she was eighteen. I needn't have worried, though, as she was far more mature and worldly than I ever was. I'd been married when we met, but my husband and I both knew something hadn't been right for a while. So we finally packed it in, and after he moved out, he went back to Tel Aviv telling everyone I threw him out for cheating on me."

Sharon chortled a little, shaking her head. "I've never understood how that was better than admitting the relationship didn't work. Even worse, he made it sound as if the accusation had merit, which has always made me wonder if something had been going on and I just never noticed. Anyway, I had kept in contact with Emily and we went on a date. True to stereotype, she moved in *maybe* three weeks later. She was eleven years my junior, but we were absolutely in love."

Sharon looked as if she might cry. Lisa put her arm around her shoulder, and Sharon continued, "The hardest part of this is, well, we were moving out. We'd bought a house out in Agoura Hills. But when the Stephane conference hits, it takes over my whole life for the months leading up. So Emily had been packing on weekends, the new house was being painted, and we were all set to move…"

Sharon hesitated, trying to remember the date. When she realized when it was to be, it gave her pause. Even Bones, who had sat down at her feet, looked up, sensing her distress.

"…tomorrow morning."

Lisa hugged Sharon, drawing her close as Sharon began to cry, her body quaking a little with the tears.
"It's okay," Lisa said. "I know it's hard, but we'll be out of here soon enough, and you'll be able to grieve for real."

"I'm not worried about me," Sharon said, shaking her head. "It's just, how long is Emily's body going to be in the rubble of our apartment? Weeks? Months? A couple of years? She's not buried, and even though we're not the most traditional of relationships, in my culture you're supposed to bury someone within three days of the death. It bothers me a lot, like I failed her. It makes it hard for me to want to leave."

"I can only imagine how you feel," Lisa replied softly. "But if she loved you as much as you love her, you have to know that she would want you to survive and carry on. Hold that close."

"I do, but it doesn't make it any better."

"All right," Paul said, addressing the group at fifteen minutes until six, the agreed-upon departure time. "We'll be going straight down Santa Monica Boulevard to the coastline, no stops. We're going to be as quiet as possible, doing nothing to give away our position. If we encounter any enemy, we will only engage this as a last resort. We're trying to escape, and we're not prepared to fight. Understood?"

No one replied. Paul nodded to Zamarin, who raised the one-shot sonic disrupter.

"I don't know how many of you are familiar with our crowd-control methods, but this is what's known as an LRAD – long-range acoustical device – or just sonic disruptor, which admittedly sounds more sci-fi. It emits a piercing blast of intense acoustic energy that can momentarily stun anything with a sense of hearing. On the low end, it can burst a human's eardrum if jacked all the way up. On the high end, it can do similarly to the rats. That said, it has a very limited range and, like a taser, has one shot in it before needing to be recharged. We only have one, but it just might buy us some time. You see the sergeant or Corporal Sahar raising it, you stop, cover your ears, and open your mouth. Got it?"

Incredulous as some of the people looked, they all nodded and agreed.

"Okay. We leave in ten. Be ready to hit the ground running."

They left in eight.

Trent had been stationed in the lobby and alerted the group just as the sun set over the distant ocean. The entire group of survivors were up the broken escalators in a flash, led by Zamarin and Nashon. Paul hung back with Sharon and Bones, who acted as something of a seeing-eye dog even though he was too excited to do anything but gallop.

Following behind were the rest, a mob of people desperate not to be left behind but also terrified of being out in the open. Greta was the last one out onto the driveway, and as she looked back at the hotel, a gallows smile spread across her face as she nodded at Sebastian. "I feel I'm stepping out of my grave to run off to my funeral."

"I know the feeling well, my dear, believe you me," he replied, already sweating. "But whatever happens, you can count on me to be by your side."

Up front, Sharon kept an eye on the skies. She didn't see any birds, but she kept telling herself that the absence of anything flying overhead didn't mean they weren't there, waiting. She looked down at Bones, the only member of the party that didn't seem to have a care in the world, and wished she shared his optimism.

Running through the night, Bones was thrilled to finally be out of the hotel, as the smells were really getting to his sinuses. The corpses, the fine concrete powder hanging in the air, the sweat of the living, the rotten food, the myriad odors of asbestos, plastic, and various chemical cleaners all mixed together in a toxic brew had done nothing but give the shepherd a severe headache. But now that he was outside, these horrible smells that the humans seemed only vaguely aware of now absent, he inhaled deeply and bounded along beside Paul.

"Slow down a little, Bones," Paul said, angrily yanking back his leash.

"You still planning to shoot him at the end of the mission?" Sharon asked.

"He's not coming on the boat, if that's what you mean. Shooting him would be doing him a favor, given what we'd be leaving him with."

Sharon scoffed but kept going. She planned to revisit the issue once they were at the boat. Maybe give the dog another couple of chances to save Paul's life and he'd change his tune.

The group had raced away from the Beverly Hilton and onto Santa Monica Boulevard as if it was a sprint, but then Zamarin and Nashon had slowed the pace to something that could be maintained. The sun had almost completely disappeared over the horizon now, and everything was colored in shades of gray, purple, and black.

When they reached the toppled buildings of Century City only a few minutes later, it began to get treacherous, but Trent's knowledge of the jumble of rubble helped immensely as he showed Zamarin a path he'd taken earlier. Bones's keen senses helped with this as well, and soon the group had crossed over the worst of it with only a minimum of twisted ankles.

Once they were on the other side of the fallen buildings, Trent's admonition proved true in that the road was in utter disrepair and there were more stumbles, but part of this was because the farther away from the Beverly Hilton they traveled, the less likely it would be to race back there in retreat should something happen. More and more, they were at the mercy of the city.

For Sharon, this was the part of the trek she was dreading. She watched as the familiar streets passed by: Avenue of the Stars, Century Park West, Beverly Glen. Sharon had driven this road home from work for years and had taken it back from the Beverly Hilton the night of the first big quake. These very roads, now long gone. She looked up ahead, and even though nothing was standing, she knew they were within a few hundred yards of her collapsed apartment building and Emily's broken body somewhere within.

She forced herself not to cry and ran on.

Closer to the ground, Bones found it easy to navigate the rubble and therefore hadn't suffered the mental fatigue of the others, either. Paul, who was beginning to tire, yanked back more and more on Bones's makeshift tether.

"Come on, Bones," Paul said. "Stay with me."

But that's when a different scent entered Bones's nose. The buildings were farther away from the street on this part of Santa Monica, so he'd been light on smells for a while, fresh air cutting through the rotting trees and concrete, but now there was something new.

Bones slowed and sniffed the air, recognizing the oily odor of matted fur and blood that he'd first picked up on a couple of days ago now on the broken Hollywood Freeway. As Bones slowed, Paul knew immediately from the break in the shepherd's stride what he'd picked up. He leaned down to the shepherd, feeling his snout, and could tell Bones had picked up a scent.

Paul hesitated, feeling cold and alone and isolated in his new blindness, practically naked out on this desolated rubble-strewn street in the middle of nowhere. Icy shivers ran down his spine as he realized just how disastrous this plan might turn out to be.

"Here they come!"

VII

The Mayer men had been dead-on.

It was the Nivec that the rats had been chewing on which contained a chemical compound called methylstinine that caused a rabies-like reaction in rodents when they ingested it. But Paul's idea that the birds brought it into their systems by eating the rats was completely false. Instead, when the buildings and houses fell and exposed the Nivec to the air, it released massive quantities of the already broken-down synthetic alkaloid that the birds then aspirated into their lungs, causing the same sort of mutation.

While the humans and every other animal in Los Angeles were breathing it in as well and often in just as heavy concentrations, the behavioral changes were expressed quickly in the lesser mammals and in birds. The rats got sick, Bones did not. The birds got sick, but the humans did not.

Yet.

Scientists were just beginning to understand the carcinogenic properties of Nivec, and the effect of methylstinine on the survivors of Alpha and Omega would have provided conclusive proof that even limited exposure caused incredibly aggressive cancers such as had never been seen before.

"Would have provided" because there was a separate, albeit tangentially related event on the horizon that was to have an entirely different effect on humanity in general. No amount of medical science could have prepared mankind for this, so something as comparatively simplistic as cancer would have seemed downright quaint in comparison.

If, of course, anyone had been around to make the comparison.

"Where do we go?!"

This scream came from the Australian Kathryn, who seemed determined with her high-pitched squeal to drive the rats directly to them.

"Do you see anything?" Paul asked Nashon, who was moving alongside the team leader. "Do we even know if they're in front of us or behind us? Could we be walking straight towards them?"

"There's no telling," Nashon replied. "Bones seems to be indicating they're behind us, but it's gotten dark pretty fast. We can't see anything, and there doesn't seem to be anywhere to hide."

"How far to the coast?" Paul asked.

Nashon turned to Sharon, who shook her head.

"Nowhere close. We're just at the 405 Freeway. On the other side of that is Santa Monica, and then we'll still have about fifty or sixty blocks to go."

"Where are the bastards?" Zamarin asked, looking around. "Shouldn't we see them by now?"

That's when Paul reached down and touched Bones's head. The dog's snout was investigating a manhole cover. With a heavy heart, Paul raised a hand and stopped the group's progress.

"We won't see them if they're still using the sewer," Paul said to Zamarin. "I think they're under us."

"Oh, God," Sharon said. "Can't we get to some kind of high ground?"

"Not any the rats can't climb," Paul replied.

"Then what's the plan?"

"We fight. Try to make a big show and buy ourselves some time. At least if we stop now, we get to pick the battleground. Might mean all the difference."

Sharon looked at Zamarin, who looked unconvinced. To his credit, the sergeant raised his submachine gun and waved to the group.

"Everybody behind us. Looks like we've got company, but we think it just might be a couple of them."

Everyone knew this was a lie but did as the sergeant asked. The 405 passed over Santa Monica Boulevard, but the bridge had collapsed onto the street during the first quake. The group began taking positions on the rubble to, at the very least, be up off the ground, however futile it felt.

"Keep going," Zamarin said. "Try to get to the highest points."

Bones trailed Paul up onto the broken bridge, but then stiffened. The shepherd jutted his nose into the shattered concrete and then immediately started barking. That's when Paul came to a realization and turned to Sharon.

"If the sewer ran under Santa Monica Boulevard…"

"…then the weight of the bridge collapse might have smashed through the road and broken into the main," Sharon concluded. "They were waiting for us."

Sharon turned to the bridge, her eyes training around from human to human. She was just about to shout a warning when the black silhouettes of the rats began erupting out of the holes and fissures of the broken bridge like a burst pipe.

Within seconds, the humans were outnumbered 67,000 to 1.

Nashon and Zamarin's barrels were almost to overheating as they blazed away at the rats, firing at anything that moved. The sonic disrupter had been used right away and had, in fact, driven away a few thousand rats, including several with ruptured eardrums. Some of the survivors had looked ready to celebrate, but every injured rat was replaced by a hundred more. It was soon looking like a no-win scenario.

"Everybody get to the other side of the bridge!" Paul yelled, grabbing Sharon's arm to hold onto. "They'll hold them off long enough for us to get…"

But Paul's words were cut off by the screaming of one of the hotel workers, who was suddenly being swarmed by rats coming from behind them.

"They're all around us!" yelled Sebastian, hurrying over to help the worker and his companions as more and more of the rats scurried over to their position.

Sharon did a 360 and saw rats coming at them literally from all sides but up. There were rats flooding up from beneath them, rats coming from both ends of the broken bridge, and then rats flooding up from sewer grates and breaks in the road on the east and west sides of Santa Monica Boulevard. It was as if the humans were at the bottom of a bathroom sink and the rats were being poured in over the lip from each side and were accelerating down to them just as fast as water.

"What're we going to do?" Sharon asked, terrified.

"Plan B," Paul said, then turned to Zamarin. "Plan B!!"

Zamarin nodded. Sharon looked at Paul with surprise.

"Plan B?"

"Plan B," Paul replied as Zamarin, still blasting away at the sea of rats, ran over and grabbed a pack from Paul and set it on the ground. Sharon finally got a look at what Paul had ordered Nashon to retrieve from the kitchen as Zamarin extracted five plastic-wrapped six-packs of Sterno and quickly tore them open.

Sharon started at them in surprise. "Explosives?" she asked.

"Not on their own, no," Zamarin replied. "But with a little help…"

The sergeant next plucked a pack of thin, flashlight-sized propane tanks out of the bag, the kind utilized by the Beverly Hilton on the crepe station grills during Sunday brunch, and set them next to the Sterno cans. He immediately opened the first can and smeared the denatured alcohol jelly on the outside of the propane tube and nodded at Sharon.

"Last ditch. This can go all ways of wrong, including killing us."

As soon as he had one done, he nodded at Nashon. "You ready?"

Nashon nodded, and Zamarin threw the makeshift firebomb in front of them. "Don't fucking miss!!!"

As the tiny tank arced over the rat-swarm, Nashon fired a burst into it. As a bullet caught the tank, the little bomb exploded, creating a small fireball with a six-foot radius, igniting a handful of rats.

"That's not going to do much," Trenchard, who had stumbled over to the commandos, announced derisively.

"Oh, ye of little faith," Zamarin replied.

What Trenchard hadn't noticed was that when the tube exploded, tiny burning droplets of the sticky Sterno had landed on literally dozens upon dozens of rats. Rats that were now erupting in flames and setting other rats on fire as they tried to get away. These rats then set other rats on fire, which then set other rats on fire, who then set still *other* rats on fire. It was a chain reaction of burning fur and flesh racing through a living sea of black.

"Oh, my God!" Kathryn screamed. "You're cooking them."

"Here comes another!" shouted Zamarin, smearing Sterno on a propane tube. He tossed it in a different direction and, after Nashon blasted that one, too, another couple hundred rats burst into flame and began evangelically passing it on.

By now, Sharon, Lisa, and Trent were helping Zamarin smear the Sterno on the propane tubes as the other survivors hurried over to see if they could assist. Two of the Malaysian television crewmen, with much better aim than Zamarin, began throwing the completed bombs out in front of Nashon, who gladly blasted them to pieces.

"Uh, oh," said Nashon, noticing something.

The flaming rats, in their confusion, were running every which way, and that meant some were coming straight at the humans.

"Look out!" Nashon yelled, nodding at the incoming rats.

But that's when Bones, who had been dancing around near Paul enjoying the spectacle, moved in. Though naturally averse to fire, the shepherd went after the rats with zeal, snatching up the burning creatures in his mouth, snapping their necks and flinging them aside. He stomped on a couple with his claws, bit the heads off others, and in general tore through them as you might think a playful, fun-seeking, middle-aged dog would do. Soon the rats, even in their addled states, began choosing any direction to run but at the humans.

"Do we have enough to try and break through?" Paul asked Zamarin.

"Got seven left," the sergeant said after doing a quick count. "We should be able to get to the other side of the bridge and maybe put a nice wall of flame between us and them."

"All right, then. Let's light them up."

Zamarin signaled the survivors, and everyone gathered round to make a break for the other side of the bridge.

"Now!!"

Everyone began to run towards the west side of the bridge as the two Malaysian TV crewmen picked up the last Sterno-smeared propane tubes and threw them into the sea of rats. Nashon blasted into them with his machine gun, the subsequent explosions creating a path as if he was parting a Red Sea of rodentia.

"It's not pretty, but we've got a hole," Zamarin shouted.

"Let's go!" Paul roared, rising to his feet as Sharon and Bones led him forward.

As a rolling mass of tens of thousands of burning rats ran in circles around their feet, some getting kicked out of the way and others outright crushed underfoot, the Beverly Hilton survivors followed Paul and Zamarin across the bridge, over the smashed chunks of guardrail in the direction of the west side of Santa Monica Boulevard. One by one, they made it and ran as quickly as they could away from the seemingly endless fountain of rats.

Nashon pulled up the rear, switching out the magazines of his gun in a fluid motion as he continued to blast at the closest rats. With the scent of burning fur and flesh heavy in the air, most of the rodents had actually seemed to forget about the humans and were primarily focused on escaping the flames. Worse, there were still others that Nashon noticed, to his revulsion, were using the opportunity to feast on members of their own species. Rats convulsing as they died a terrible death in the flames hardly noticed their brother and sister rats nibbling away at their legs or even face as it was too late to fight back.

"Disgusting," Nashon said, not for the first time that day.

But then Nashon turned to follow after the rest of the group and found a small group of curious rats moving into position behind him at the edge of the bridge.

"Oh, shit," he said, pulling the trigger on his machine gun.

The rats splattered all over the concrete as Nashon leapt over the broken guardrail that demarcated the median of the highway bridge. He'd only gone a few feet before something made him trip, the "something" being three rats that had emerged from a crack in the bridge.

"Gnh," he exhaled as he smacked into the concrete, just able to catch himself with his hands before a sure-broken nose would've made his face explode with blood. He clambered back up, but not fast enough, as a large group of rats emerged from under the bridge and swarmed up his legs. "Sergeant!!"

Zamarin looked back in time to see all the blood drain from Nashon's face, cast white against the gray of the concrete before disappearing completely under about three dozen rats. The sergeant immediately wheeled back as Nashon started screaming, the rats dragging him back under the highway through a crack. The survivors could hear Nashon's bones beginning to break as he went.

With a heavy heart, Zamarin raised his machine gun and fired a single burst into the swirling mass of rats, and Nashon's screams abruptly halted. The rats quickly dragged the corpse under and disappeared.

Zamarin shook his head as he turned back to Paul and Sharon. "All right!! Double-time it!"

The propane tube bombs had done enough to clear a path and buy the group a few seconds, but now the humans were once again on the run. Though the fires had certainly slowed them down, the rats began to regroup. The humans were only about a thirty yards away from the bridge when the rats regrouped and began the chase all over again.

Sharon looked back and saw that the entire boulevard appeared to move as the rats extended back like an endless tide, a creeping darkness that extended from one side of the boulevard to the other that was now washing towards them.

"There are just so many of them," she cried out to Lisa. "We kill a couple thousand and there's ten thousand more!"

Lisa said nothing, but Sharon could see the terror in her eyes as they ran.

Bones ran alongside Paul, his nose filled more and more with the smell of the ocean only a few miles ahead. The taste of the dead rats in his mouth strangely lingered, an oily aftertaste sliding down the back of his throat like a stream of thin caramel. But Bones kept running, licking his lips for more of the oil as he went.

Then a rat jumped on the shepherd's back and he wheeled around, sending Paul tumbling as Bones's jaws sank into the rat, bit it in half, and dropped the two pieces to the concrete.

Sharon and Trent hurried to help Paul get back to his feet as Bones killed a second and third rat, some now emerging from the collapsed buildings on either side of the road.

"They're catching up," Sharon whispered to Paul. "Got a Plan C?"

Paul shook his head. "Just keep running."

But it was quickly obvious that the couple dozen humans on two legs were no match for the million rats behind them on four. The rats, driven by their blood-need to sink their teeth into the flesh of the humans, pressed harder and harder, seemingly indefatigable. The humans, some of whom hadn't had a decent meal or night's sleep in days, were the opposite. Once the adrenaline had cycled through their bodies, it was as if they had nothing left in the tank and were willing themselves to fail as surely as Bones's buck back in the Ohiopyle woods. The inevitable was the inevitable, so why fight it?

This was the case with Sebastian and Greta, who were in the rear and the closest to the rats. The rats reached Sebastian first and scurried up his legs as he was in mid-stride. Within seconds, a dozen rats were charging up the backs of his legs, up his back, and onto his shoulders as if the pets of an eccentric.

Sebastian's steady stride came to an end as he tried to swat the rats away, resembling a man beset by bees. "Christ, he's on my ear!" Sebastian grunted, a rodent turning an attached ear lobe into a detached one.

"Hang on," Greta said as she reached over to bat it away. Unfortunately, the rat simply grabbed her hand in mid-flight, bit into it, and then ran up her arm directly to her face, where it bit her nose.

"*Aaaah!*" she screamed, trying to get it off.

Members of the Malaysian news team and a couple of the hotel workers slowed down to help the pair. But this all-too-human impulse proved to be a grave mistake as the rats simply swarmed them as well. A rat bit into Sebastian's carotid artery, and he bled out within seconds. The moment a second rat bit into her, Greta gave up and slid to the ground as well, resigned to their killing of her, to which the rats happily obliged. Two of the hotel workers were next, the rats moving up their bodies like cartoon army ants, and then one of Lisa's colleagues at the Asian medical consortium who, mistakenly, thought Sebastian could still be saved.

Though he hadn't made the mistake of slowing down to aid his fellow man, Trenchard, the Australian finance minister, was next, as years of living high on the hog caught up to him as thirty rats leaped onto him.

"Kathy!!" he cried, reaching out to his mistress.

She looked back at him, shot him a sort of conflicted look, but then kept running without a word.

Sally and Shahin were way out in the lead, but even they seemed to know that the end was nearing. They looked back at the rats and then each other.

"I'm pretty sure I love you," Shahin cried.

"Yeah, me, too," Sally replied. "I never would have made it this far without you, and you know it."

Shahin smiled and kept running. "Race you to the beach."

"Last one in is a rotten egg."

They kept going, but Sally could feel the burning sensation in her legs and side and knew that she wouldn't be able to complete the race.

Sharon looked over at Lisa and saw that the rats were now running alongside them, swirling around like dirty water. She was barely able to watch where she was running, the constant fear of twisting her ankle and going down, smashing her face on the concrete, going through her head.

"This is it," she said to Lisa for no reason in particular. Lisa nodded back just in time to see another of their number fly backwards, multiple rats on their back, and sprawl into the piranha-like miasma where they were quickly torn to pieces.

Of the runners, Bones was actually faring the best. Rather than simply trying to bat the rats away, every time one landed on him, he made sure to kill it and toss the corpse aside. Seeing this happen, a number of the rats seemed to stick with bringing down the humans first, which suggested that if the shepherd had so desired, he could have used this opportunity to flee. Perhaps he could have more of a fighting chance away from the group, as the rats didn't look too ready to divide their number. But Bones was too loyal, simple, and endlessly rat-hungry to consider making a simple turn up a side street and disappear from view. Instead, almost blissfully unaware that each moment could be his last, he continued casting his lot in with the humans.

A new sound suddenly cut through the night, and it took the survivors a moment to realize it was coming from above them. Sharon was the first to look up as lights pierced through the night sky and rapidly approached their position.

"What is it, sergeant?" Paul asked. "Choppers?"

Zamarin looked up into the dark but couldn't believe his eyes. "Looks like, sir. The cavalry has arrived."

Two SH-60 Seahawk helicopters with U.S. Navy sigils lowered themselves over Santa Monica Boulevard, hovering as if seeking out a flat enough surface to land on, but then deciding to take action from the air as they realized how dire the situation on the ground was. They lowered themselves to about thirty feet off the ground, the wash from the rotors so tremendous that it knocked a few of the survivors off their feet, though it had the same effect on the rats.

The side doors of both choppers slid open, and a pair of National Guardsmen began firing at the rats with heavy door-mounted machine guns as the helicopters came around and began blasting at the same with nose-mounted Vulcan cannons.

The muzzle flash illuminated the street as if it was the middle of the day, but the sound was more deafening than the sonic disruptor the commandos had used. Sharon clapped her hands over her ears but kept running, slightly hunched over, as she stepped into the pool of white light created by the helicopter's high beams.

The helicopters continued blasting away at the rats, the white hot bullets racing over the humans' heads as they ran, chopping the rats to millions of little pieces. The rats continued to surge forward regardless, but the door and nose gunners had more than enough ammunition to answer them.

It took a steady stream of fire that didn't cease for well over a minute to finally turn the tide, but not until more than a quarter-million rats had been torn to pieces.

As the helicopters landed, several guardsmen hurried off the helicopters to the survivors as Sergeant Zamarin pulled Paul to his feet. Bones seemed to have lost a step or two to the rats but was recovering. Sharon, her clothes torn and her body bleeding from two dozen cuts, got to her feet in a state of disbelief.

But then she looked down and saw that the rats had chewed through Lisa's stomach and had dragged out her entrails as they fled. Sharon bent down and could tell from the blank-eyed look on her friend's face that, perhaps thankfully, Lisa was already dead.

Along with Lisa, Sebastian, Greta, and the Australian finance minister, the two other members of Lisa's medical consortium, Gregoire, three of the hotel workers, and Shahin were all dead. Sally had actually survived, but had her hands chewed down to the bone, as Shahin had been the one to fall behind first and she had been trying to save his life when the helicopters arrived. This left a dozen survivors, albeit severely traumatized ones.

The guardsmen approached Paul and Zamarin, looking over their weapons.

"Where did you get those?" a captain asked, "Feliz" on his uniform's name stripe.

"Found them," Zamarin replied without blinking.

"Where?" the captain continued, sounding as if he didn't believe Zamarin.

"Back of a truck. Same place as we found these clothes. Looked like the owners had been killed by the birds. Mercenaries, I think. Mayer, maybe?"

The captain looked from Zamarin to the others in the group, waiting to have the man contradicted, but when no one did, he sighed.

"Well, this was just meant to be a flyover, not a rescue," the captain said. "I'm sorry, but we don't have room for all of you."

"That's a shame," Paul said, piping up. "My friend and I will be the last ones on. If there's no space for us, we'll do what we can."

Captain Feliz wasn't expecting this response, but then nodded. "We can see about sending back a relief helicopter, but we were under strict orders not to land or engage anyone on the ground."

"We're glad you countermanded that order, captain," Paul replied. "But even if you did come back, we're not really planning on staying in the same place."

"I understand," Feliz said. "Good luck to you all the same."

One by one, the survivors divided themselves amongst the helicopters and climbed on board. Once they were on board, one of the guardsmen looked expectantly at Sharon, but she shook her head.

"You won't considering taking the dog, will you?" she asked, knowing the answer.

"Are you serious?" the guardsman asked.

"The number of times he's saved my life, I can't just leave him behind," Sharon explained. "Thank you, though."

Paul turned to Sharon like she was crazy. "You need to get on that helicopter."

"I cast my lot with you guys. You've gotten me this far."

"Yes, but that's mainly because we know who your father and grandfather is and was."

Sharon grinned and nodded, moving away from the helicopter.

"Lieutenant?" Captain Feliz said. "Relieve them of their weapons."

The sergeant stepped forward, but then Sharon stood in the way. "You can't leave us defenseless!"

"I absolutely cannot allow weapons like that to remain here in such a hostile environment," Captain Feliz said. "If they should fall into the wrong hands, terrorists domestic or foreign, I would be in dereliction of my duty."

No one missed the implication of Captain Feliz's emphasis on the word "foreign" as he made it clear that he knew neither Paul nor Zamarin were locals. The lieutenant indicated for the pair to hand over their weapons, so they did so. The guns were then loaded onto the helicopters with the others.

As the choppers began prepping to take off, Captain Feliz eyed Sharon.

"You're staying behind? Despite the dangers?"

"Absolutely."

Captain Feliz turned to Paul and Zamarin. "I don't know who you people are, but I have a good idea, and something tells me that I don't want to know more. I don't wish you ill, but I will be reporting your descriptions in my report and will recommend the new military authority locate you and possibly take you into custody. If your business here is concluded, I'd suggest you bug out at your earliest convenience."

"Understood," Paul replied.

The captain nodded and headed back onto one of the Seahawks. A few moments later and the helicopters were aloft, sending a storm of concrete dust all down the street. But Paul, Zamarin, Sharon, and Bones were already gone, taking the captain's advice and hastily beating a path to the ocean.

Though they had one eye over their shoulder the entire time, the rats never returned. The night passed swiftly, but now that it was only the three humans and one dog, they made excellent time. The streets were even relatively clear of debris -- that is, until the last blocks before the ocean as the buildings got higher and the familiar sight of massive chunks of broken concrete sprawled across their paths returned. It was when they reached 16th Street, though, that the impassibility became laughable, as the road was completely blocked by a tall hospital structure that had collapsed across Santa Monica Boulevard for several blocks.

"What now?" Sharon asked the sergeant.

"It's too dark to pick through, so we'll have to go around," Zamarin said.

"The side streets are a mess, too."

"What do you want me to tell you?" Zamarin replied, shrugging his shoulders. "We either backtrack or pick our way down. Simple as that. Paul?"

"I don't want to sound too confident, but I think the rats have found something better to do," Paul suggested. "I think we can afford a detour if that means saving time in the long run."

Sharon nodded and Zamarin turned Bones's leash, aiming his nose south. "What's your nose telling you, boy?"

Bones sniffed the air a little, didn't seem to be picking anything up, and Zamarin nodded. "Let's go."

Though the side streets were littered with broken buildings and cars, Sharon's belief that they would be just as impenetrable as Santa Monica proved untrue, and soon they had found a much more passable route.

"Guess a stopped clock really is right twice a day," Sharon said. Zamarin scoffed and kept going.

A few blocks later, Sharon saw something rising on the horizon. She didn't think it was any kind of structure, but whatever it was hadn't fallen in either quake.

"What is that?" she asked.

Zamarin peered ahead and grunted. "Looks like trees. A park. Some kind of oasis in the desert."

"Intact?" asked Paul.

"Yeah, appears to be. Quake brought down every goddamn tree from here to Christendom, but decided to leave this little group alone."

The survivors moved ahead, and as they neared the park they saw how right Zamarin had been. There were a couple of tennis courts and a children's soccer field, but then there were rows and rows of live oak trees left to grow wild in and around a winding walking path. All in all, the park covered at least three acres of land that appeared, at least cloaked in darkness, to have avoided the brunt of the quake.

They moved ahead and stepped into the park. The feeling of grass and soil beneath her feet was surprising to Sharon. It really was like discovering some Garden of Eden that had already grown up amidst the ruins, a more believable scenario than to think somehow the quakes that had devastated the city simply weren't felt in this one perhaps acre-sized patch of trees.

"You'd think this would be the one place any other survivors would come to camp out," Sharon suggested.

They'd seen the evidence of other survivors in Santa Monica as they walked or, more accurately, smelled it. Cooking fires were distinguishable from accidental ones mostly by the rich scent of the food being prepared over them. Though they didn't see anyone, there was a part of Sharon that was allowing her brain to imagine that Emily was among these people, having somehow, miraculously, survived the initial collapse and found herself separated from Sharon. She knew this was unlikely, but it made her happy.

"Seems like someone has," Zamarin said, nodding at a pile of belongings leaned up against one of the trees that included a pile of empty food wrappers.

Bones moved over to the wrappers and began nosing around in them. He found two miniature donuts and immediately scarfed them up.

But then, Paul stopped and raised a hand.

"What is it?" Zamarin asked.

"You don't smell that?"

"I don't smell anything," Zamarin replied cheekily, but then saw Paul was deadly serious.

That's when Sharon smelled it, too, something she hadn't smelled since the hotel, the same acrid phosphorus and nitrogen of the eighth floor. She tried to look around in the darkness but knew what she'd find.

Guano.

"Oh, God," Sharon said under her breath. "The birds."

Sharon looked up into the trees above and watched as a bird shifted its wings a little as it rested on a branch. Even in the dim light of early morning, she could see that there were literally dozens of birds just above her, which led her to believe there were hundreds, maybe thousands throughout the trees in the park.

Paul, sensing her distress, leaned over next to her. "What is it?"

"The birds are in this park. This is where they sleep."

Paul froze. Zamarin moved over, having heard this, and took Paul's arm. "It's dark. Let's keep going. We'll stay quiet."

Paul nodded but then leaned down next to Bones.

"You're going to need to be quiet," he whispered, gently holding Bones's jaws shut. "Absolutely silent. Do you understand?"

Paul removed his hand and Bones licked his chops but didn't bark. Sharon took Paul's arm, and the group slowly made their exit. The park wasn't particularly sizable, but given how few structures were standing as well as how few trees, it might have been the one place in the entire city that a flock that large could bunk down together. The irony that it just happened to then be precisely in the path of the survivors was not lost on them.

Bones did his part by not making a sound. He could tell that the humans were being stealthy and he copied this, keeping low to the ground and quiet. He hadn't smelled the birds, as his nose was still awash in the stench of the burning rats, obscuring all else. But after poking his nose into the ground under the trees, he could at least inhale the smell of the nitrogen and phosphorus of their shit.

Stepping lively, the group made it out of the park in under a minute and were soon on their way again. Sharon looked ahead and realized that she could see the ocean. Well, not precisely the water, per se, but where it was meant to be on the horizon with no more obstructions.

"We're only about eight blocks to the beach," Sharon said. "We're as home free as we're going to be, I think."

"You want to jinx us?" Zamarin snarled. "Watch. We'll get to the pier and the boat will be covered in birds."

Paul chortled at this. "Well, let's get there first. How much longer until the sun comes up?"

"Fifteen minutes?" Zamarin suggested.

VIII

The boat, a converted cabin cruiser that wouldn't attract much attention if discovered, was anchored just offshore in a marina surrounded by a number of sailboats. It had been painted white, but if someone knew what an LRAD looked like, they might be able to identify the large version mounted to the front deck. Originally designed to be attached to the top of a truck, the mounting had been modified to fit on the boat and painted the same color before being shoved in the bag of a transport plane and brought to the American West Coast with the Israeli commando team.

Zamarin climbed into a skiff and made the quick journey out to the boat, powered it up and then drove it to the pier, where Sharon helped Paul get aboard. Bones stood on the dock, looking uncertain, but then Sharon turned to Paul.

"We're taking Bones, right? No more you're going to shoot him?"

Paul shrugged as if he didn't care. Sharon reached out to the shepherd, and he hopped on board. Within seconds, Zamarin had the boat turned around and was leaving the shore.

Sharon stared back at Los Angeles as the sun began to rise over the hills. There was a part of her that felt this was not what was meant to be and that her lot was cast with the City of Angels. But here she was, leaving, Emily still buried in the rubble some miles away. She was leaving with unfinished business.

She felt the Bones's head moving under her hand, the shepherd nuzzling up next to her. She kneeled alongside him, stroking his ears, then glanced back to Paul to see that he had already fallen asleep on one of the benches. She looked over at Zamarin, who grinned.

"Yeah, passed right out. Hopefully that'll be us soon."

"I'm running on adrenaline myself," Sharon said. "When I crash, it'll be for hours and hours and hours."

"Sounds good to me. Except, the moment we're in safe waters, I guarantee the U.S. military is going to swoop in and demand to debrief us."

"Let them try."

Zamarin snorted and turned back to the wheel as Sharon looked back over at the city. She saw the birds coming, the entire flock from the day before, and chuckled. Her brain told herself that it was an optical illusion, that it was smoke, that it wasn't aimed anywhere near their direction, but she knew all of this to be untrue. She wasn't in a nightmare, like her subconscious was also trying to convince her of. No, she had thought she was going to escape, and here came the engines of her destruction.

She turned away and sat down, staring in the direction of the ocean. She watched as the waves approached the boat, and then glanced to her right and saw the white water of the boat's wake churning through the green of the Pacific.

She vaguely heard it when Zamarin shouted in alarm when he, too, saw the birds, and Paul rocketed awake. Bones began dancing around the deck as the birds moved closer and closer, but Sharon didn't care to look.

Instead, she sat as if meditating on her life. She closed her eyes but continued picturing what had been directly in front of them moments before: the never-ending expanse of ocean. She remembered seeing footage of a group of Mahayana Buddhist monks burning themselves alive in protest of the persecution of Buddhists by the South Vietnamese government in the early sixties, and she imagined the supreme concentration and focus that act must have taken. She remembered seeing one of the burning monks topple over and out of his lotus position, only to quickly right himself in the flames. Their composure had been unbelievable. She was determined to follow their example, and as her body was torn apart, she wouldn't flinch and she wouldn't flail. She would embrace the experience and disregard the pain.

Her eyes were closed when Paul ordered Zamarin to wheel the boat around and face the birds head on. The sound of the boat engine practically blotted this out, but she felt the boat come around and realized what Paul had said. She heard an electric whine as the LRAD on top of the boat was charged and magazines were inserted into submachine guns.

She heard Zamarin coaching Paul on where to aim, his voice filled with naked terror as the birds neared. She could hear them now, clucking and crying as they flew, though they didn't sound like birds. Their "voices" were strained, and they struck Sharon as sick.

"Come on, goddammit!!!" Zamarin was shouting. "Motherfuckers!!"

"Sharon!!" Paul cried. "Help us out!"

But Sharon didn't move. Bones tripped over her feet as he continued his circuits of the deck but righted himself. He barked and barked in answer to the cries of the gulls.

The sound of the birds got close enough that they couldn't have been more than a couple dozen feet away, and that's when all the sound was sucked out of Sharon's ears and replaced with an impossibly high-pitched whine. She felt it in her head but also her throat, stomach, and bowel. Unlike the handheld disruptor, this was something else entirely, and Sharon found herself vomiting across the deck.

The birds screamed, and she heard what sounded like hail as the animals smacked into the ocean and the boat, several dead.

This broke her trance, and she turned around to see what was assuredly a bizarre sight. As the LRAD continued to sound, birds tumbled dead out of the sky. Carried by inertia, they spun out of control and splashed down into the waves. The effect in the sky was similar to the earlier parting of the rat sea, only this was mass death on a different scale. Dots of black and white were suspended against the hazy white and blue of the morning sky, but as they hit a certain spot in the sky, the radius of effect for the disruptor, they tumbled down like lemmings over a cliff straight into the water.

Hundreds upon hundreds of birds soon lay dead.

But then the LRAD shut off and Zamarin shouted to Paul. "All right. Steady…three…two…one…"

As the disruptor recharged, Sharon watched as Paul and Sergeant Zamarin blazed away into the sky with their guns. She was shocked at how well Paul did, given his blindness, but she supposed he'd been able to lock in at least a little bit on the sound. He and Zamarin fired out a magazine, tossed it out, and reloaded in quick succession, sending several more birds to a watery grave.

When Zamarin activated the LRAD again, Sharon realizing that the ringing hadn't left her ears in the first place, so when it began anew it had little effect on her.

Then she saw something that amazed her. The flock, sensing the device's range in some way, shot out to the west, angled upward, and flanked the boat.

"SHIT!" Zamarin cried as he spun the wheel so quickly that Sharon and Bones were both knocked off their feet.

But the birds were too fast. They came around the craft at a perpendicular angle and swooped in, cutting the distance in seconds. Though Zamarin turned and got a couple of shots off, the birds quickly reached the boat and tore into Zamarin's face.

"Sharon, jump!" cried Paul.

Without thinking, Sharon did just this, abandoning ship without a second thought. She hit the water and turned to get her bearings, only to have the boat, which was still turning, smash her in the face.She was knocked unconscious and immediately began sinking beneath the waves into the depths of the dark, cold ocean.

Sharon woke up with the midday sun bathing her in warmth. Her clothes were almost dry, but her hair was still damp. She was lying on a beach, her face cupped in a shallow divot of sand. After a moment, she pulled her legs up, brought herself up on all fours, and then threw up. She had so little in her stomach that it was nothing but acid and bile and tore at her throat as it came up.

She leaned back on her feet for a moment and then sat up, staring out towards a row of ruined beachfront houses. As she looked up towards Ocean Avenue, her low angle afforded her a view straight to the bluffs of Temescal and Rustic Canyon but prevented her from seeing any of the ruined houses on the cliff side or the hotels and apartment buildings down below.

The coastline as it was and now would probably be again.

Sharon slowly got to her feet, took a step, and kicked something. She looked down and saw that it was a dead seagull, its stomach ruptured and its feathers waterlogged. Glancing around, she saw that the entire beach was covered in dead birds, literally thousands of them washed up on the shore. She looked back down at the one at her feet and saw that there was a pair of dark red streaks burnished into its beak just below the nostrils.

She stood there idly for a moment, but then realized that one of the corpses on the beach about fifty yards to her right was human.

"Oh, God, no...."

She walked over to it but found that her legs were borderline unresponsive. They were stiff as if they were asleep, and the lactic acid churned inside as she walked. When she finally reached Paul's body, she could tell that he was long gone. She leaned down next to him and saw that he was already being feasted upon by an army of sand flies and rove beetles. She looked at his bandaged face, bloated from being in the water but could also see that he had burns on his arms and torso, implying there had been some kind of fire on the boat.

She couldn't remember a thing. She had hit the water and then...nothing.

As she regarded Paul, a sand crab emerged out from under the bandage wrapped around his empty eye sockets and she almost vomited. She had a vague notion that she wanted to bury him but didn't think she had the strength to pull him all the way up the beach and onto dry land where there'd be soil instead of sand.

But then she decided that that was exactly what she was going to do. What else? This man risked his life for her without a thought. She could at least do for him what she couldn't do for...

Her train of thought froze as she looked up to a bicycle path running parallel to the ocean up by PCH and saw a certain German shepherd sitting there watching her, its tongue out and panting in the heat, giving it, like all shepherds, the appearance of a grin.

"Bones."

She marched across the sand directly to the dog and immediately dropped to her knees and put her arms around him when she reached the path. The dog whined a little and tried to break free, but Sharon held him tight. His fur was still damp, and she knew that he must have dragged her to shore.

"You saved my life. Thank you."

Bones finally broke away from the human's embrace and looked up at her for a moment. She stared back into Bones's deep black eyes and smiled.

"We're going to be good friends, you and me."

As she thought it would, the burial of Paul, whose last name she didn't know, took hours. His kit and uniform had been too heavy, so she'd eventually stripped him almost naked on the beach and tossed his clothes and weapons aside. In doing so, she kept thinking she'd find that one identifying card or letter or picture, but Paul was a professional and must have judiciously left all such things behind. Angry at having their meal taken away, the sand flies bit at Sharon's arms and legs, but she eventually was able to drag him as far as the bicycle path.

She saw the ruins of a bicycle rental store nearby with rows of perfectly intact bikes and carts and buggies alongside the shattered building. It turned out that the bicycles were all chained together, but with a little doing she was able to wrench one of the trailers meant to carry children off the rear of one of the bikes and roll it back to Paul's corpse. It wasn't much easier to go up the hill with Paul on the trailer as opposed to simply dragging him, but she knew she wouldn't have been able to get him even halfway up the steep incline without the wheels.

It took her a good couple of hours to find the right place to bury him, finally deciding on a spot at the end of what had once been San Vicente Boulevard, overlooking the ocean. She had nothing to dig with until she found a bent "No Parking" sign and used it to at least start a hole. Once it was about a foot deep and roughly the size of a man's body, she found herself using her hands more than the sign.

It was late afternoon before the grave was as complete as it was going to be, Sharon's hands raw and bloody from clawing the earth out of the ground. About two feet short of the requisite six, Sharon had continued digging more out of a sense of fear than duty. She had no idea what she'd do once Paul was buried.

Throughout all of this, Bones kept her company but aided neither in the transport or burial of Captain Paul Harazi, born in Ashgelon, died at the age of thirty-six, leaving behind an ex-wife and three children. But Sharon couldn't have made the trek without the shepherd. After she'd noticed that no birds were coming to kill her, she kept an eye on the sky regardless, but none came. She didn't know if the rats would come with nightfall, but something told her all of this was over.

When night did come, she realized that neither she nor Bones had eaten yet, so they tromped up San Vicente in search of food. When they reached their first convenience store, she was afraid that there'd be nothing left, as it was sure to have been ransacked by previous scavenging survivors, but then she found that virtually nothing had been touched. Bones had quickly discovered the dead clerk in the stockroom, likely having been refilling the trays of Marlboro and Camel Lights as the quake hit, but there were corners of the store that looked pristinely unaffected.

Avoiding all refrigerated goods, Sharon filled bags with bread, Spam, chocolate, trail mix, water, breakfast cereal, and anything else she thought they could use, loaded it onto the Day-Glo red and yellow trailer, and moved on.

They bunked in for the night in a park across the highway from the vast Los Angeles National Cemetery, where thousands of the war dead from the Pacific Campaign of World War II had been buried, and waited for the rats. They never came. By midnight, Sharon had even managed to fall asleep, her head resting against Bones's stomach as a pillow.

When morning came, Sharon felt a real sense of exhilaration. She had survived the quakes, she had survived the rats, she had survived the birds, and she had survived the ocean. There was nothing she could not surmount.

Ever since she had buried Paul, she knew what direction she intended to go with Bones. It only took half a day to travel from the cemetery back to the Wilshire corridor, where the pair turned south and moved down what had once been Westwood Boulevard. Throughout the previous day and now this morning, there hadn't been so much as a flyover, and Sharon began having visions of the earthquake "spreading," devastating the entire country until the only living things were herself and her dog. She found this a ridiculous thought but enjoyed it nevertheless.

But then they reached her old apartment complex, the ironically named Shamrock Village. It was a mountain of broken concrete and splintered drywall, with broken pipes and pieces of furniture jutting up at odd angles from within the rubble. Her apartment had been in the northeast corner on the third floor, but as the building had been so hopelessly crushed, she thought Emily could be anywhere in there.

"Bones? Ready to go to work?"

Both the birds and the rats had begun dying off the morning that Sharon, Paul, Bones, and Sergeant Zamarin were on the water. By noon, they were all gone and began to rot along with the rest of the Los Angeles dead in the hot sun.

The U.S. government did not know what to do about Los Angeles, an understatement of ridiculous proportions, but the American people didn't have anywhere near the sentimental attachment to the place as they had to post-Katrina New Orleans (coupled with the fact that there were only a tiny handful of survivors ringing the bell of "rebuild it!"). The same magazines, i.e., *National Geographic*, *Time*, that had listed all the reasons to rebuild New Orleans now ran similar cover stories explaining why it was pointless to rebuild L.A. Scientists and the military had moved in to explore the area and remove any last survivors, as well as to investigate the reports of massive tribes of killer rats and birds, but came away with very little in either department.

Everything in the Los Angeles basin was dead, it was determined. Any survivors living in the broken city had likely been so traumatized by the events that they were hiding out and refusing extraction and probably wouldn't survive more than a few months.

There had been a push by the military to bomb Los Angeles or use it as a testing facility, but that was where public opinion had stepped in. So many had died there that leaving it intact was memorial enough for now. Also, scientists from around the world were extraordinarily curious to analyze what would happen next in the city as nature reclaimed the land. A real memorial was constructed outside the Presidio in Golden Gate Park a few hundred miles to the north in San Francisco, and when the president and state governor dedicated it, more than a million people were in attendance.

When asked why San Francisco took this tragedy so to heart, the answer was simple: "It could've been us."

And that was the fear for much of the rest of the spring, into the summer, and then into the fall -- that another massive earthquake would strike somewhere, causing a similar disaster. But the truth was, the double-quake of Alpha and Omega had actually brought to temporary rest the more major incidents of seismic activity around the Pacific Plate. A correction had been made, and now the planet could live on in the peace for the time being.

But for Los Angeles, this was cold comfort. Almost immediately following the earthquakes, the city had begun to decay. The few remaining buildings began to fall, the last trees died off, and when the spring rains came, new plant life began to push out through the acres of concrete to start the long process of wiping the place off the map forever.

It had taken a month, exactly thirty days, for Sharon to uncover Emily's remains. Like one person working a quarry, Sharon had taken apart the broken site brick by brick over several days until it resembled an archaeological dig. After the first couple of days proved difficult to even begin, Sharon had gone on a hunt for a hardware store, and when she finally found one, had retrieved picks and shovels galore, knowing that many would break when working against concrete rather than dirt.

On the eighth day, she had seen a helicopter but had ignored it. When one returned and called to her through a bullhorn, she ignored that, too, but then one landed up on Wilshire, and a detachment of soldiers came to talk to her. She explained her situation, showed them her food and her dog, and asked them to leave her alone, as they were now standing in her home. The soldiers understood the desire not to leave someone behind and, to their credit, did not report the day's incident.

There had been a couple of false positives during the dig where Sharon had uncovered a desiccated corpse, only to have it turn out not to be Emily, and she buried those, too. But on the thirtieth day, she had had a feeling that her hunt was over, given the number of personal items from her old apartment she was discovering, coupled with Bones's insistence that a corpse lay under the next chunks of flooring.

And then there she was, identifiable only from her tattered hair and tattered pink pajamas. Sharon wept for almost an hour as she slowly pulled Emily's remains from the shattered apartment and laid them out on a blue blanket that she had retrieved expressly for this purpose. She had made a meal for herself and Bones and then sat with the wrapped body for the rest of the day, praying to no one in particular but really trying to send her thoughts out to Emily in the great beyond. She had done what she'd set out to do, but it gave her no pleasure. Instead, it extinguished any figment of Sharon's imagination that suggested Emily might have been injured but not killed, had survived, was in a hospital somewhere. Was already recovering. Was waiting for her. Missed her. Still loved her.

All of that went away with the discovery of the corpse lying a couple of feet from Sharon by the campfire.

Across the thirty days, the only animals that had bothered Sharon and Bones were coyotes, which Bones scared off, and a few rats that had begun to reemerge. Unlike the massive, rabid tribes, however, these rats scurried away when so much as a brick was tossed their way, and the shepherd made quick work of those that didn't. Sharon worried, though, that having an unburied corpse with them overnight (she'd buried the other corpses nearby within hours of their discovery) would bring the animals out in force, but then she realized there was hardly anything on Emily's bones worth feasting on.

The thirty-first day came, and Sharon loaded Emily's body onto the trailer for the hike back to the ocean. She fed Bones, drank some rain water, and then started walking back to the spot where she buried Paul, where she had decided she would bury Emily as well.

Bones walked alongside her as they left Westwood, the shepherd picking up on Sharon's somber mood. With a complete absence of other humans, Bones had taken to Sharon and accepted her as his new partner and handler of sorts. Her moods affected his mood just as much as her determination and drive had egged him on over the last month as they attempted to excavate the corpse.

But when they reached the end of San Vicente Boulevard where they'd so recently buried the Israeli commando team leader, Bones found Sharon in such a state of distress that he didn't know what to do. He tried to nuzzle her hand, but she pushed him away. He stayed close to her as she began to dig a new hole, but every time he stepped into the hole himself, he got shooed away.

"C'mon, Bones," came Sharon's quiet voice, the most she seemed able to manage.

Finally, Bones lay down on the ground, put his snout on his forepaws, and simply watched as Sharon dug Emily's grave. She had a pick and shovel this time, so it went much faster than when burying Captain Harazi.

When the hole was finally almost too deep for Sharon to climb out of, she finally stopped digging and moved the blue blanket next to the mouth. She lowered herself back into the grave and then brought Emily's body down with her. But she knew how much Emily weighed, how she felt in her arms. This wasn't Emily. The person was long, long gone, and Sharon momentarily wondered why she had gone to so much trouble for something that wasn't much more than a token reminder.

She laid Emily at the bottom of the grave, considered staying down there with her for a few more minutes, but then climbed out and began covering the body.

Sharon had plans for what she was going to do next. She and Bones would follow the broken 405 Freeway to the Valley, where the soldiers had told her, if she ever changed her mind, a sprawling command post had been set up. There she'd contact her parents, fight tooth and nail to keep the shepherd with her, and then head east, maybe to New York, maybe to the Carolinas, which she had decided sounded nice.

But as she stood her looking at Emily's grave, the tears came all over again, and she realized that she couldn't leave her lover all alone here. Just because her body was buried didn't mean that it wasn't just another faceless victim of the quake.

There'd been a part of her that had considered this and had kept a rope with the materials. She looked to a nearby tree and eyed what she thought might be the strongest branch.

Bones watched as Sharon retrieved the rope and tied a makeshift noose at the end, little more than a loop set with a strong knot. She climbed the tree easily enough, secured the free end around the branch, and placed the noose around her neck.

Time froze for a moment as she felt the rough twine around her neck. She remembered the last time she was at death's door out on the boat when the birds attacked for the last time, and she wondered why she couldn't be as Zen about this moment as she had been at that one.

That's when she realized that this was unnatural. This wasn't what humans did. She'd survived all that she'd survived for what, to kill herself? Hey, last one to die in L.A., don't forget to turn off the lights!

She looked down at Emily's grave and forced herself to remember who she was without her. She was an individual and would continue to be even now. She would endure.

Bones had watched Sharon climb into the tree and was now watching as she scooted back as if to come down. She was working apart the knot when she slipped off the branch and fell.

"Oh, God!" she cried as she fell, managing to grab the noose with one hand and the rope with the other. When the rope went taut, she had just managed to arrest enough of the force that it didn't snap her neck. Instead, she found herself hanging in midair, desperately trying to pull herself back up to the branch. "Bones!"

Sensing Sharon's distress, Bones hurried over to the tree but found himself a good three feet or so below the dangling woman.

"Please, Bones," Sharon whispered, barely able to breathe. "Help me, find help. Jesus, c'mon…"

Misunderstanding, Bones leaped up and grabbed Sharon's foot, giving her a tug. Sharon yanked her foot away but the force caused her to swing away, making it harder and harder to keep from strangling.

"No, Bones!! No! No more!"

This Bones understood. He stayed on the ground, looking up at Sharon as she steadied herself, coming to a rest after a few seconds. She took a deep breath and worked to undo the knot, trying hard this time to keep her cool and proceed methodically.

As she did so, she looked down and saw the shepherd watching her, eyes full of curiosity. He didn't seem to understand what was going on but knew she was in trouble and was standing by to help in any circumstance.

"Don't worry, Bones," she said. "I'll be down in a second. I got myself into this. I can get myself out."

It took two and a half hours for Sharon to die.

It was in increments, one arm weakening and then the next, the strangling being so slow that, if asked, Sharon would have likely reported that she was feeling sleepy, when in reality the oxygen was being gently choked off from her brain. With the fingers of one hand keeping the rope from touching skin, Sharon felt safe, not realizing that the noose was pressing her own hand into her windpipe with enough force that it would soon kill her.

During the entire struggle, Bones had not left Sharon's side. She found herself staring into his eyes more and more as she fought against the rope.

"Shepherd," she had said, thinking about for how many people this dog had been the last living thing they'd ever seen. In her already deoxygenated state, she wondered about this as the true origin of the breed. *Shepherd.* She recalled the twenty-third Psalm, "the Lord is my Shepherd, I shall not want. He maketh me to lie down in green pastures, he leadeth me beside the still waters. He restoreth my soul. He leadeth me in the paths of righteousness for His name's sake."

But then she spoke the next lines aloud, her voice a whisper. "Yea, though I walk through the valley of the shadow of death, I will fear no evil: For thou art with me."

She looked down at Bones, her shepherd, and smiled to herself. Emily would've laughed at the idea of a lost cadaver dog standing in for God. She'd heard the Psalm read at many a Jewish funeral and wondered if there'd ever be one for her and if it would be read then.

She looked down at Emily's grave, her vision losing most of its color, and was happy that she would soon be reunited with her lover in death. She wanted to bargain with God to allow her to be cut down from the tree so that she could crawl over to the grave and bury herself in the same ground, but then she died.

Bones stayed with Sharon's body as it swung in the wind for the rest of the day and on into the night.

When morning came, Bones looked up at Sharon's blackened hands and legs where her blood had pooled and up to her completely ashen face, her pale pink tongue barely peeking out through slightly pursed lips. Bones took a sniff, smelled nothing but shit and death, and moved away. The person he had been so loyal to was now absent, which vacated Bones's feelings of responsibility.

Bones went for a long walk, ranging over miles and miles of ground. He reached a grocery store at one point and ate his fill from the racks, tearing into bags of everything from chips to bread to rice, but then kept moving.

He reached the collapsed 405 Freeway and saw soldiers in Humvees scouting around as a group of civilians workers took readings off some sort of various instruments. Bones flinched as if readying his legs to hurry over and greet the troopers, but something kept him back.

Turning around, Bones trotted back into West L.A. He thought he had sniffed something worth eating a few blocks before and backtracked to pounce on it before it got away from him.

By the afternoon, Bones was back at the ocean, the thousands of dead bird corpses having rotted away. He ran the length of the beach, barking at the brown pelicans that had come up from San Diego and even catching one that flew too low to the ground, quickly tearing out its throat and devouring the bird's organs and muscles in seconds. When he discovered fish inside the pelican's throat pouch, he ate those, too.

He took a nap under the remains of the Santa Monica Pier at nightfall and then decided to go on a night hunt once darkness fell. The beach was as quiet and dark as it hadn't been for a hundred years, the glow of the moon and stars being the only illumination, the waves lapping on the shore the only sound.

Bones padded along at the surf's edge for a moment, hopping out of the water as the night tide rolled in but then playfully jumping back in. He swam out a little ways, felt a fish investigate his foot, and promptly dove his snout into the saltwater to grab it in his jaws.

After devouring the fish, Bones trotted a few hundred yards further down the beach, but after a moment, broke into a run. He ran and ran and ran, the scent of saltwater still in his nose and the feeling of the unbroken sand sinking lightly under his paws.

By morning, he'd gone a mile. By noon the next day, he had gone six. He found an overturned boat in the early afternoon and took a nap underneath it. When he woke up, he started running back in the direction he'd just come, sometimes in the water, sometimes on the sand.

He didn't see a human being the entire time, and he was happy.

ALPHA

Lupus non mordet lupum

Prologue

Bones woke up from a nap and felt a chill down his back that reverberated all the way to his marrow. It built into a dull, throbbing sensation that continued to crescendo throughout his body for a full thirty seconds and then just as suddenly disappeared.

The German shepherd, a proud, strong animal, knew what the extended spasm meant, however, and got to his feet. The pain was visited in order to send him on a journey, but it would be a long one, so he immediately set out for the east.

He was soon to die, and he would die where he was born.

I

The world had ended.

Well, it had ended for the humans, at least. An angry group of mercenaries of the Mayer Corporation, disgruntled with the way they had been treated in the wake of the Los Angeles earthquake disaster that had killed millions and thrown the economy of the United States into chaos, had broken into the Anniston Army Depot in Bynum, Alabama. They were in the process of raiding the armory with the vague hope of committing a string of bank robberies with their haul when something unexpected occurred. Though Anniston was one of seven depots in the U.S. that stored chemical weapons, the mercenaries couldn't have known that the CDC was additionally using the facility to house surviving biological fragments of a large mutated sea anemone that had killed tens of thousands in Pennsylvania a few years before. So when they ran into sentries tasked with guarding said fragments with their lives, they figured they could get by with the kind of threats and bluster they'd made copious use of thus far.

Instead, the sentries immediately drew down per standing orders, a massive gun fight erupted, there was an explosion, followed by another within minutes, and a toxic cloud was released. The minutiae of wind direction, weather conditions, barometric pressure, and the proximity to water sources would be studied closely over the next few days by desperate scientists looking for a way to stop this new airborne killer, a further mutation of the Arctic-originating anemone that was now aspirating into people's lungs at a tremendous pace, where it simply killed them rather than turning them into flesh-hungry monsters, as had happened previously. Unfortunately, these scientists were fated to fail.

Within minutes, everyone on the entire base had been killed; within hours, most everyone in the surrounding counties of St. Clair, Etowah, and Talladega had joined them; and within days, the entire southeastern United States had been similarly decimated. When winds carried the plague out to Cuba, Haiti, and Jamaica, delivering a devastating toll to their nations, the world powers and their respective citizenry realized that this was it, and anarchy began to break out the world over.

A violent coup erupted in Pyongyang, rioters took to the streets of Moscow, London burned, and Paris was swept by mass suicides that soon became contagious across Europe. In many places, the larger cities rapidly depopulated as residents led themselves to believe that they stood a better chance of surviving away from others. Johannesburg lost a third of its number in two days. Rangoon was a ghost town in three. In Stockholm, the people took to the sea and spread out to the many islands of the Swedish archipelago, but were no safer there in the enclaves of their Norse ancestors. In Canada, many headed to the northern territories. In Sao Paulo and Rio de Janeiro, a number of Indians whose families had spent generations transitioning to urban life left their homes and vanished back into the Amazon.

Some went underground. In Rome, the catacombs and sewers beneath the city were opened, and thousands took their possessions and hid there. In Hue, the vast dormant tunnel systems utilizing during countless colonial wars were filled with a terrified but strident group of locals who eventually sealed themselves in, leading to armed confrontations with those who tried to get in later. In Athens, many fled to the old crumbling temples of the past, begging long-dismissed gods and goddesses to save them. Deities whose names hadn't been called out with any real meaning for centuries were suddenly being voiced in earnest from Norway to Cape Town, Kyoto to the Rocky Mountains.

And then, little by little, these voices went silent.

As the inevitable set in, people found it hard to comprehend. How could something like this have existed on the Earth for centuries beneath the ice that, once dredged up so easily, could turn around and kill every member of only one species in particular? Why were there to be hundreds of millions lying dead, stinking under the noonday sun, an entire race erased, but a carefree flock of starlings was allowed to whiz past unmolested? Pet owners stared helplessly from their death beds as the family dog, cat, hamster, and goldfish looked on in perfect health while their meal ticket expired. Those who took to the sea, which were many, thinking it would save them (rightfully so, it turned out, at least in the extreme short term) watched as the entire ocean-borne ecosystem continued to flourish unabated in the waters around them. Many had prepared themselves to stumble across massive fish-kills, gulls pecking the corpses of bloated sperm whales and other scenes of horror but were to be disappointed, as it was business as usual in the animal kingdom.

Basically, the question on everyone's mind was why were just Homo sapiens being shown the door despite being the most evolved, most capable, most prevalent species on the planet? The fact that this was specious reasoning at best, as humans were none of these things, occurred to few, and humanity slowly died off before accomplishing all of those many things it occasionally announced it was hoping to achieve.

Except.

Except for Frank Flores, a Pensacola man who was the first to be identified by the Centers for Disease Control as an actual survivor and who had been quarantined in Toronto, where it was soon discovered that he wasn't even a carrier, had never even fought off an infection, as he was immune. The plague looked at him, didn't recognize the man as a target, and passed him by.

Cases like this began appearing in various places of the world in a wide variety of concentrations. A handful in Africa, a great number in Korea, an even larger number in Norway, some in Russia, virtually none in South America, same with Australia, and then several scattered across the United States, though the majority were concentrated in the American Southwest.

Frank Flores, who had lost his wife and five children in front of him, learned that he had lost all of his friends and many relatives except a handful on his mother's side out in Oregon, and thought that, as they would be next, why should he hang around?

As people in the Toronto facility began dying, Frank approached a sympathetic Army Ranger who allowed him access to his sidearm, and Frank Flores put a bullet through his soft palate.

Frank Flores would have been wise to stick around and investigate those maternal relatives, as he would've learned that though the plague came to Oregon and slashed its way through many, it also spared an aunt, two cousins, a niece, and a favorite nephew. He would hardly have been alone. Death would continue to follow them in the coming months and years, but this was the scourge of privation and other disease. They, too, were immune from this plague.

II

It had been a while since Bones had smelled a fresh corpse.

He had spent about two-thirds of a year mostly alone in the devastated city of Los Angeles, the victim of a double earthquake dubbed "Alpha" and "Omega" by the nation's papers (though when it was believed to be a single quake, Alpha had been tagged with the less Biblical "The Big Sleep," as so many had been killed while in bed and, after all, it was L.A.). After his involvement in the "mutation incident" in Pennsylvania, Bones had been free to run about the Ohiopyle woods for much of the winter, only to be hunted down by the Pittsburgh police, who recognized what an asset he would be in the City of Angels due to his abilities as a cadaver dog. While assisting a team in Echo Park, Omega had struck, and Bones found himself helping a small group of survivors make it across the city as flocks of rabid rats and birds tried to devour them, driven mad after ingesting chemical residues from the flashing of more recently constructed buildings.

The lone survivor, a middle-aged woman named Sharon, had used Bones to help her locate her dead partner in their collapsed apartment building and, after burying her, she (somewhat accidentally) took her own life, leaving

Bones to fend for himself in the broken city. Bones had returned often to the woman's body as time went on, though he spent most of his days in search of food. The mania that had driven the rats and birds of Los Angeles to madness had also swiftly killed them off, but the U.S. government didn't take chances and regularly dusted the L.A. basin with poisonous pellets to eradicate any that were left behind. Bones had learned to avoid eating any bird or rat that carried the scent of poison in its belly after a particularly harrowing night of shitting and vomiting endured by the shepherd, who almost died from a toxic pelican he'd caught in Marina del Rey.

Bones had seen plenty of living people over the course of his time in Los Angeles, but he'd assiduously avoided them. Scientists, military and governmental officials, and eventually federally funded teams of archaeologists entered the quake zone, always heavily fortified against the possibility of contamination, as literally millions of bodies continued to decompose. It had become an issue of national debate: What was to be done with Los Angeles and its dead? No one seemed to know, and before a definitive decision was to be made at the Congressional level, the rest of the country joined the dead of L.A.

Bones, though a creature of habit, still did not notice the absence of planes flying overhead nor the sudden drop-off in vehicles entering the area when it happened two months previously, but as he now left the city, he found bodies that obviously hadn't been part of the earthquake dead. Rather, these people were in an almost uniform state of decomposition and had been feeding the bands of coyotes, ravens, and rats (normal ones) that had rapidly multiplied in the hills around the city at unprecedented rates after the quakes. Bones sniffed around these fresher corpses for a moment but quickly moved on to their packs of belongings, which seemed to indicate a misguided hope of hiding out from the plague in the quake zone.

Though he found no food on the persons of the dead, the shepherd got lucky at a nearby camp site, where he discovered bags and bags of non-perishable food stuffs that were still in edible shape. Using his claws, the shepherd tore apart a few of the bags, gorged himself on beef jerky and Twinkies, and then kept moving, leaving the eight-week-old corpses to continue their slow return to the earth.

Denny Edwin Tallchief, as was occasionally pointed out, hardly lived up to his last name. Never growing past a squat five-foot-five and shoveled food by an over-protective mother who used same to express love, Denny spent elementary school and junior high as a short, fat kid who no one would ever mistake for a class leader. As unexceptional in sports as he was in his school work, Denny learned to hate just about everything school-related, with the one big exception being the school's library. His mother worked in downtown Bullhead City as a secretary for a construction company, and with school out at three-thirty and Sheila Tallchief getting off at five on a good day, this left at least a half-hour drive before Denny would get picked up. Denny's father, Gene, had never married Sheila, which was just as well, since he was in prison for armed robbery at the super-max facility at the Arizona State Prison in Florence, but this meant almost every dime of Sheila's paycheck went to living expenses with nothing left over for after-school care.

But Denny's principal, a kindly old man named Mr. Heiden, who had started his teaching career in Mohave County after returning from the Pacific theater in World War II, often did things to help his students and their families and was considered more akin to a pastor than a school administrator at times. He struck a deal with Sheila to let Denny camp out in the library after school if he helped the current librarian, a revolving parade of part-time substitute teachers, shelve returned books. Denny took to this task with relish and soon was entrusted with a key to not only the library but also the school building. So efficient was he that the temporary librarians found it easy to fudge their time cards, knowing Denny was more than happy to take on all the after-school responsibilities of keeping up the library, from writing up the overdue notices to mending broken spines with just the right amount of book tape.

Additionally, Mr. Heiden began letting Denny borrow books from his own voluminous library that he kept in the principal's office. His shelves were filled, but Denny noticed early on that the vast majority of them were focused on World War II, particularly actions Mr. Heiden had been a part of: Kwajalein and Engebi in the Marshall Islands, Ormoc and Valencia in the Philippines, and then Okinawa, where Heiden had been wounded and shipped home.

Denny never forgot Heiden's personal touch with his students, and after surviving his school years, he went to Arizona State University with the intention of going into teaching himself. He'd slimmed down in high school, was still no one's idea of attractive but ended up dating a handful of girls who were as socially awkward and prone to spending Friday nights in the campus library as he was.

He fell in love for real one day with a woman named Jennifer Baker, who organized study groups in the library for the blind, herself legally blind, though she still had some limited sight in both eyes. Having been burned more than a few times before, Jennifer was dubious of Denny's attentions at first but soon fell for the gentle young man whose most animated discussions came when describing, no, *monologuing* about what kinds of innovations he hoped to use in his future classrooms to keep even the most disaffected students engaged and interested.

They were married in a simple ceremony eight weeks after graduation. They moved to Flagstaff, as both had been offered jobs in the same school district (he at an elementary school, she as a roving administrator dealing with issues relating to the handicapped), and set up housekeeping in a tiny apartment that they decided to endure in order to save up for a down payment on a house. Three years later, one week after Denny's twenty-fifth birthday, Jennifer announced that she was pregnant. Twelve days later, they watched on the news as the first information about the plague that struck Florida began making its way into the media, and three days after that, Jennifer was dead.

Denny had heard some people on the internet refer to the disease as the "sepelio" virus and believed, like many, that it was a technical term or referred to a specific ailment that had been identified as the cause, which meant a cure was forthcoming. In point of fact, a doctor in Cincinnati named Kuhn had dubbed it "sepelio," the Latin for "to bury" and took the additional, colloquial meanings of "to overwhelm" or "to annihilate" in a series of initial findings he posted online eight hours before he died. As such research was in short supply and his outlined the progress of the disease (first came a fever, followed by intense difficulty breathing, as if the victim was having a heart attack that resulted in capillaries exploding in the lungs, which drowned the patient in their own blood), it was treated like gospel by the world media as they desperately sought an answer before it was too late, which is why his name stuck.

But in truth, no one had actually named the disease, and it wasn't even a virus.

After Jennifer died, Denny waited in his apartment with his wife's body in anticipation of the moment that he, himself, would pass. After twelve hours, he fell asleep, and then at twenty-four, he began to wonder what was going on. He let another half-day pass by and finally ventured out to commiserate with other survivors, only to find that his entire neighborhood was dead. His internet was still up and he checked on the plague's progress, seeing that it had continued on into California and that most people in North America had died. The "most" came because there were those exceptions like the oft-mentioned, quickly legendary Frank Flores, who many believed was still alive in Toronto.

On the third day, when Denny realized that he had survived something that had taken the lives of just about the rest of the world, he broke down and cried tears of self-pity.

III

The ease with which Bones took to living off the land as a hunter and scavenger would not have surprised various handlers of his through the years, since they had detected something that seemed to suggest the shepherd was never fully domesticated in the first place. There was always a certain quickness to violence, a deep sense of territoriality, and a keen hunter's instinct that seemed out of place with the dog's ferocious loyalty to his handlers even when it didn't feel earned; something that made more than one trainer wonder if the loyalty part was artificial in any way.

One such trainer of his in the Pittsburgh Police Department worked with Bones for a single day before the shepherd had apparently decided that he would defend this man with his life, something the man hadn't observed in an enforcement dog before. Wondering if there was some sort of vestigial closeness the shepherd felt to male handlers based on his loyalty relationship with his original partner, a Doña Ana County Sheriff named Lionel Oudin, the trainer teamed Bones with a veteran female handler to see what would happen. The woman reported the same experience as the male trainer, finding Bones remarkably quick to accept and defend his trainer.

No one seemed quite sure what to make of this until a visiting ATF agent observing at Pittsburgh's K-9 training facility remarked that he'd worked with a dog like that before.

"It's a rarity in an animal," the agent explained. "The dog I worked with like that had an equally unusual response in a pack situation with other dogs. It couldn't identify and bond with a canine alpha or pack leader, so it never settled into the traces. But with humans, it was just like your dog here."

When it was asked if that meant Bones would lack the qualities of great enforcement animal, the ATF agent replied that it "actually quite the opposite" and that Bones would make an excellent addition to the force, as he would take commands readily and execute them without fail.

"Don't think of him like a partner in the traditional sense," the ATF officer said. "Imagine yourself as king or shogun, and he's your faithful knight or samurai. You want something done? You won't get questions, and there'll be no debate. Some dogs, even the best trained in the world, hesitate when their instinct tells them something's dangerous and they, and possibly their partner, can lose a step. That will never be the case with this animal. He won't question the notion that your commands are gospel and won't think he might know better. He will simply execute."

But Bones was no longer the same dog he was back in Pittsburgh. He'd now gone through two long periods away from having a human alpha where he'd been forced to fend for himself, hunting, gathering, and killing when necessary to stay alive. He proved an adept enough hunter on his own, though going it alone against large game, particularly ones that ran in herds, was never simple. In his encounters with timber wolves in Pennsylvania and then packs of coyotes in Los Angeles where he might have become a member of that grouping, or, potentially, that pack's new alpha despite a difference in species, he never did. His instincts kept him solitary, so he remained on his own.

In the L.A. quake zone, whenever a live meal went scarce, Bones simply turned to foraging for food amongst the vast stores of packaged goods in shattered grocery and convenience stores, people's homes and offices, and everywhere in between. He was able to find food in a buried car, in piles of trash, in semi-collapsed buildings, and even left behind on the side of the road by wasteful soldiers and scientists who came into the city. He did not go hungry.

All this had changed once he left the city. In the vast nothing between Los Angeles and the eastern horizon, Bones encountered fewer and fewer human outposts. There would be gas stations and the occasional neighborhood with its attendant services, but as he neared the Mojave Desert, these dwindled in number or had already been ransacked. Again, he was discovering more and more human corpses, all of which had been dead for about eight weeks and long picked over by other scavengers, which meant that even if he'd been willing to sample human meat, there was none to find. Instead, Bones found himself heading out into the desert at night to find his food, feasting on wood and kangaroo rats, the occasional rattlesnake or jackrabbit, a bighorn sheep that Bones had tracked for hours, and even an unlucky badger who had emerged from his hideout directly in front of the hungry shepherd and didn't even have time to react before Bones had viciously snapped its neck.

But other than these few forays into the wilderness, Bones stayed on the main roads, keeping near the scent of humans. The stench of the dead hung heavy, but every so often, Bones caught a whiff of the living that had ridden the wind out to the desert. Also, the roads were simply easier to travel on, and Bones had a place to go. Every test of his muscles seemed to increase the strain he felt deep within his body, giving his travels a sense of urgency.

Typically, the shepherd chose to move at night and into the morning, rested during mid-day in whatever shade he could find, and then continued on in the late afternoon or evening, generally seeking out sources of water that he would drink heavily from before seeking out his first and often only meal of the cycle before continuing on.

A few days after his wife's death, Denny began a series of forays around Flagstaff and soon found that he wasn't as alone as he thought. A small group of survivors, fourteen in all, he would soon learn, had gathered downtown in first the hospital and then the Flagstaff Sheraton on West Route 66 in the historic downtown district, where they had hung sheets off balcony guard rails with writing on them to alert others to their presence.

But on that first day out, Denny had driven around Flagstaff for much of the morning and seen no one. He surprised himself by having little trouble adjusting to the depopulated city, breaking a window to slip into a neighbor's house to retrieve the truck keys of the young man he knew had lived there, as he had one of the newer and best-suited for Denny's purposes vehicles on the block. While he was in the house, he went on to help himself to the fellow's stores of bottled water, food, and even the cash he'd had in his wallet, sixty dollars, before realizing that he probably would have nowhere to spend it.

He took the truck to get gas and found an ancient service station with non-automated mechanical pumps that had apparently been left open and accessible to anyone by the charitable station owner. He collected and filled up every one of the red plastic gas cans the owner had put out for sale likely only days before, and then drove the fuel back to his apartment. He stole a second truck that afternoon and was driving around in search of a second gas station to drain when he saw the sheets hanging out of the Sheraton. He went to investigate and was shocked when he saw two people standing on the roof, smoking cigarettes.

Believing he might be met with suspicion, he did nothing to quiet his approach, parked outside the chain-link fence that had been erected around the hotel grounds, and walked up the long driveway to the entrance. He was halfway there when he realized that maybe he should have brought a weapon in case the "welcome" messages on the sheets were a ruse. When he entered the lobby, he found two women, a mousy-brown-haired twenty-something with what appeared to be a shy demeanor and then an older, black-haired femme with sinewy (gym-hardened?) features and a pinched smile. They gave him a casual nod when he entered, as if this was the third or fourth time they'd seen him that week. What he noticed immediately about both women was that, like him, they had the features and skin tone of American Indians, specifically Apaches.

"Are you alone?" a tall, thin man in his mid-forties who soon would introduce himself as Lester Ingram asked, coming in from the manager's office.

"Yes, sir," Denny said, noticing a pistol tucked in Ingram's belt that couldn't have been more obvious if he'd been twirling it in his hand.

Lester nodded as if mentally checking a box and nodded to the women, introducing the younger as Carrie Millsap and the older as Anna Blackledge before getting Denny to tell an abbreviated version of his story, the four of them standing in the lobby as if they had just met at some seminar and were looking for a new topic to pass the time. Like Denny, they appeared to be shell-shocked but finding ways to adjust to the new reality. Also, everyone seemed to have made the same assumptions that most everyone in the government was probably dead, that no help was coming, and that any other survivors there might be were in about the same boat as they were, surrounded by strangers and figuring they might be the only people alive.

After Denny told his story, he learned that Lester had been a real estate appraiser in his former life, was divorced, no kids. Carrie had been a housewife with a three-year-old son and a husband who had been her high school sweetheart. Anna had, at one point, been a city planner with four children, all of whom she had buried forty-eight hours before alongside her husband, an auto mechanic who owned his own shop. She described the business and insisted Denny must've at least seen it if he wasn't a patron.

"Huge place, big sign that read Big Mike's, over on Humphreys," she explained. "Started on one lot but then just bought out the three adjacent and kept right on expanding. American cars, Japanese, even had an old Romanian fellow who could fix European cars, Andreas."

Denny went along with her illusion and agreed that he'd seen it a number of times. "On Humphreys, right?" he said, earning a blink-and-you'll-miss-it smile from Carrie.

"He was a good man, a good father, and our kids were the best," Anna explained passionately, though Denny thought it sounded rehearsed to maximize sympathy. "I barely got to say goodbye."

Denny looked over at Carrie and could tell her mind had traveled to her own losses, but he didn't say anything.

"The good news is, if we're alive, then there are others alive," Lester summed up. "Others are probably gathering in their respective cities, and we'll hear about it. Right now, I figure it's our job to get everyone in the Flagstaff area together. We have to be smart about boiling water and using the generators only for essentials. For now, we also have plenty of food, and if we're smart, we should be okay in that department. What I would ask, if you want to put in with us, is that you bring any supplies you've stockpiled to be shared."

Denny nodded but said nothing about the gasoline he'd taken back to his apartment. A part of him, the part that had preferred the school library to the classroom as a youngster, wanted to keep something in reserve just in case things got bad and he came to the conclusion that he'd have a better shot back on his own.

IV

In Las Vegas, two hundred and fifty miles to the northwest, two men and one woman, who had discovered each other alive the day after everyone else in the city died, were racing through the fourteenth floor of the west tower of the Venetian Hotel and Casino.

"Shit, where are they coming from?!"

"I don't know! I thought they were all upstairs. We have to get to one of the other rooms!"

The noise echoing in from the stairwells grew louder and louder as a strong feeling of dread set in, accelerating their heart rates even more than the running. As a dull throb began pulsing behind the eyes of the woman, Judy, she realized that so soon after narrowly evading death she was now going to die, horribly, and there would be no escape this time.

Unlike their counterparts in Flagstaff, the trio of Las Vegas survivors had reacted to their survival of the plague by indulging in the kind of Bacchanal the city was known for, though it would still be considered extreme in anyone's book. The men, Greg Stokes and Damon Mebane, friends since their kindergarten days in San Jose, had been in Vegas together with four others (all dead) when the plague came, and got caught in the gluts at the airport and car renters and were unable to get home. Greg was in finance and advised several wealthy clients, while Damon was always bouncing from this start-up to that, given that he knew a variety of software suites but didn't have the business savvy to self-promote himself into any kind of career permanence. Greg was the good-looking one and Damon the one who looked like he spent most of his day hunched over a computer lit by fluorescents.

Judy Albert lived in Las Vegas, was originally from Florida, and worked at a gift shop. She didn't have the kind of looks that drew glances from even the drunkest of her shop's patrons, but after she ran into Greg and Damon, she found herself being competed for by two men ten years her junior, and a tension emerged almost immediately, a tension made worse when Judy selected Greg to sleep with a few nights later. Any hurt feelings that erupted were just as quickly erased, as the primary activities of the trio involved getting drunk, getting high, and treating the Las Vegas strip as their personal playground.

That was, of course, until the dogs showed up.

Damon had spotted a group of them wandering the Strip one day when he went to retrieve more water bottles from downstairs at the Venetian where they'd been staying. They'd seen plenty of birds around, including the various exotics that had escaped the enclosure behind the Flamingo; had visited the Mirage, where they saw that the lion keepers had had the decency to euthanize the famed white lions there when it looked like no one would feed them anymore; and even gone to check out the aquarium at Mandalay Bay to see if the keepers there had done similarly (they had not).

"If they didn't, I'll bet it's a feeding frenzy, sharks against all the other fish and then shark versus shark," Greg said, soon to be disappointed when they arrived and found that the lack of electricity meant the water temperature had dropped severely, killing all inside.

But now, here were dogs.

Damon thought at first they were coyotes or even wolves as they were so large, but then realized they were domesticated pets of a variety of breeds probably from the vast suburbs that had sprung up around the city in recent years.

"Hey, pooch, you hungry?" he called out, though the dogs hardly looked starved.

But rather than regard him with any kind of friendly recognition, dog to human, the animals immediately halted, their ears standing straight up in alarm. This reaction was puzzling to Damon, as if they'd never seen a person before, but he pressed on.

"Hey, we've got food," Damon continued. "It's okay. We're not gonna eat you."

He bent down on one knee in a sort of supplication, extending his hands to call over the dogs, and they sprang away as if he was a predator. That is, except for one of them, a light brown Rhodesian ridgeback that kept its gaze glued on Damon. It didn't growl, it didn't bare its teeth; it simply regarded Damon appraisingly for a moment and then trotted away.

The next time Damon saw this dog, it would be trying to kill him.

In the days following the first encounter, more dogs started coming around the Venetian and, Damon having related his experience to the others, the three agreed that they were just taking Damon up on his offer and were scavenging around for handouts. From their windows, they'd see them scurrying around on the sidewalks below. When they'd go down to the casino floor to retrieve supplies or wander to another hotel, they might catch the sight of a tail, encounter a pile of shit in a corner (or, far more common, the stench of urine sprayed on a slot machine or gaming table), or spy a couple racing across the street as the sun went down. They tried to make friends and left food out for them, but it was never touched. With so much else going on, however, Judy, Greg, and Damon paid the dogs little mind.

It was only one afternoon when they'd come in out of the pool, the only of the Venetian's amenities that they made even passing attempts at keeping up, and were about to make the long slog up the stairs to the penthouse when they discovered that though they might have been paying little attention to the dogs, the animals were paying plenty to them. Every encounter having been a test, every venture into the casino a scoping of geography as sure as when wolves became aware of a herd of deer in a certain patch of forest and were moving in to pick the area clean.

The dogs were hunting them.

Judy saw them first: a pair of dogs approaching from the cashiers' cage but without the skulking deference they typically showed the humans when they'd been stumbled upon.

"Oh, shit," Judy exclaimed, at first more amused than scared. "Dogs."

As soon as she pointed, she caught a flash of movement behind them and then saw a dog standing on a table watching them from a little ways away. She glanced back and saw that a couple more animals were trotting around behind them, closing a circle.

"Guys...?"

Greg turned and was just becoming aware of the warning in Judy's voice when he saw one of the dogs approaching from the cage spring at Judy. Without thinking, he lunged forward and pushed Judy towards the open stairwell door, only to catch the brunt of the dog's attack as it sank its jaws into his arm.

"Fuck!!" Greg shouted, trying to bat the thing away. "Damon, give me a hand!"

Damon was already moving to do just that when he saw that the dogs that had moved behind them were readying their attack. "Judy!! Run!!"

Judy didn't have to be told twice and disappeared into the stairwell as Damon rushed to Greg's side, flailing violently at the dog biting into his friend's arm as a second one leaped forward and bit his foot.

Greg screamed and violently rolled to his side, which shook the second dog off as Damon kicked the first one in the side, sending it sprawling. Unfortunately, this forced Damon to turn his back on the other dogs, which was when he caught a glimpse out of the corner of his eye that the ridgeback he had first seen out on the street was immediately to his left and was about to spring at him. He screamed and turned, but it was too late, as the dog was already in flight. But that's when he saw a brass pole swing around and smash into the ridgeback's side, batting it away. Damon looked and saw the bikini-clad Judy standing over him, thinking he'd never seen a sexier sight in his life.

"Come on!" she yelled, and the two men clambered to their feet and followed her into the stairwell.

As soon as they were inside, she slammed the door behind them just as several of the dogs hit the door at once, snarling and attempting to claw their way through.

"The door will hold," Greg said with confidence, and they all hastened up the steps.

When they reached the penthouse, the most glaring problem was that they didn't have that much food stockpiled. The long trek up the stairs may as well have been Annapurna to the oft-drunk survivors, so it was an unenviable task to be sent for food. When it was Damon's turn, for instance, he would go down to the casino floor, tool around for awhile, and then eventually raid one of the numerous gift shops or bars for booze, chips, jerky, nuts, or candy before wandering by the kitchen to see how much canned food he could fit in the couple of gym bags and wheeled suitcases he would then have to drag up the stairs, since the electricity and hence the elevators were long dead. He had never been angrier than when he caught Judy and Greg throwing cans out the penthouse window to see what they would look like when they exploded on the concrete below, given how much energy he had expended getting them up there.

It was bad enough to know that every time he went down, the other members of his survival party were using his absence as an excuse for a fuck.

The dog attack had come at a time when they were running particularly low on food. Greg had, in fact, planned to go down with Damon to retrieve supplies that afternoon to relieve him of some of the burden and make up for the four or five days that there hadn't been a run. They'd never simply dragged everything up, as it had been thought that they would get bored with the penthouses in the Venetian after awhile and they'd move on to another hotel, but in the end, the Venetian was where their drugs were stockpiled, so they stayed put.

"Were those fuckers rabid?" Greg asked as he used one of the first-aid kits they'd brought up in their first, less drug-fueled days to bandage his wounds.

"I don't think so," Judy said. "They weren't foaming at the mouth."

"Then what the fuck was that about?"

"They were hungry," Damon suggested. "We were lunch."

"Those weren't fucking *wolves*, man, they were dogs - *pets*," Greg countered, reaching for an unopened bottle of Jack Daniels. He slipped a fingernail under the black plastic seal and stripped it off in one move before taking a long drink.

"Didn't you just take a handful of pain pills?" Judy admonished, eyeing the bottle.

Greg was about to lash out at her but then realized she was right and put it aside. "Fine. But what do we do?"

"We could go down and try and kill them," Damon suggested. "We have a few guns."

Which they did, liberated from dead security and police officers. The only problem was that they hadn't figured out how to undo the trigger locks on all but two of them. These lucky two, naturally, were out of bullets, as one particularly drug-fueled night led them to firing them into the city from the roof.

"They're moving pretty fast, and we're pretty fucked up," Greg retorted. "Next idea?"

"We could just wait them out," said Judy. "They'll probably move on once they realize we're not coming back down."

"How long do we wait?"

"As long as we have to. I know it's not much, but we never raided the honor bars of the last penthouse suite down the hall. With what we have in here combined with that, we should last for awhile. Maybe even a couple of weeks if we're smart about it."

This seemed the best idea, so they agreed to it.

Twelve hours later, Greg was half-asleep, half-unconscious on the sofa, having given up on Judy's advice and drained the entire bottle of Jack. Damon and Judy had both slept a little themselves, but when Judy woke up, she realized that they still hadn't made good on their plans to grab food from the other room and woke Damon. As they walked through the pitch-black hallway to the other penthouse, Judy realized that the idea she'd been toying with, that she needed to have sex with Damon, would happen right now. She didn't like the way Greg treated him but also thought it would be good to have him in her pocket now in case things got bad.

"Come here," she said to him as they walked into the room, already unlocked, since they'd broken in to make sure there were no bodies in it the day they took over the floor. Damon knew exactly what she was after and, three minutes later, Judy began to regret her decision, as it turned out that he couldn't fuck half as well as Greg and was actually a quite terrible lover.

"Come on, just go a little easier," she said, a gentle request, getting firmer by the minute.

"Sure, sure," Damon said but changed nothing about his Yeti-humping-a-cedar-tree approach. "Is that what you tell Greg?"

Great, this is a hate-fuck, Judy realized and hoped he'd finish soon.

She was trying to think of something to reply when she suddenly heard something in the hall. Terrified that it was Greg, she pushed away from Damon and the wet bar he had bent her over, and grabbed her clothes.

"What the hell?" cried Damon, his erection shriveling.

"*Shhh...*," she whispered.

But that's when she saw the first dog sniffing its way into the dark penthouse. It bobbed its head twice, spotted Damon and Judy, and immediately it curled its lips back into a growl. Illuminated only by the stars outside the window, Judy could plainly see its bright white teeth cast in a dull blue.

"Oh, shit," Judy said.

Back in his room, Greg woke up when he heard screaming from down the hall and clambered out of bed. He went to the door and swung it wide, only to see that he had surprised a pack of about a dozen dogs creeping towards the far penthouse. They registered his presence immediately and as two lunged back for him, he slammed the door shut.

"Holy fuck," he whispered to himself.

"GREG!!!!" screamed Judy from the other penthouse. "GREG!!! Wake up!! They got through the door!!!"

"Where are you?!" Greg shouted back.

"In the last penthouse! Damon and I were getting supplies!! The dogs are trying to get into the bathroom!"

Greg looked around the dimly lit room for Damon and knew, with a roll of his eyes, what the dogs likely interrupted.

Hearing smashing sounds coming from the far room, Greg considered abandoning them and striking out on his own, but then heard dogs scratching on his own door and realized this might be easier with some ballast he could cast off in an escape. He wandered over to the bar, where they kept the guns in an empty refrigerator. There was one pistol that he thought he might be able to crack the trigger guard off in a pinch by utilizing a wine opener. He fumbled around for the right gun and then set it up on the counter, positioning the tip of the corkscrew between the two plates on either side of the trigger. Raising his hand, he smashed it downward to break off the panels and succeeded, but then the corkscrew slid under the trigger guard and sent its point into the soft flesh between the thumb and forefinger of his left hand.

"*Shiiittt!!*" he screamed as blood gushed out of his hand.

Fuming, he grabbed a towel, stiffened with his blood from the first dog attack of the day, and angrily wrapped it around his fist.

Fucking Damon and fucking Judy, he thought. *I should be high.*

He went to the door, took a deep breath, clicked down the safety on the gun, and wondered, for a moment, if he should fire off a test shot to make sure it was okay before figuring that would just mean one less bullet for the dogs. Closing his eyes, he swung open the door, popped his eyes back open so that all he'd really see was movement in that blurry quick second of pupil adjustment, and fired the gun at the first dog he saw.

Back in the other penthouse's bathroom, Judy and Damon heard the shot and knew Greg was on the way. The pawing at the door continued as the shots got nearer but then finally subsided after about the seventh or eighth bullet as the dogs retreated.

"Greg?!" Judy cried.

No answer.

"Oh, shit," Damon whispered.

"GREG?!?" Judy yelled out again but then heard something padding towards the bathroom door. She raised the toilet's tank lid to bring down on any dog's head, but then the door handle rattled, and she realized it was Greg.

"You assholes okay in there?"

Judy breathed a sigh of relief and then opened the door to see Greg standing there in his boxer shorts, holding a gun.

"I don't mind if you fuck," Greg said. "Just don't be bitches about it and try to hide."

Judy looked down, feeling bad about her decision. Damon attempted a look of defiance, but it seemed pretty silly as he stood there flaccid and naked opposite a man with a pistol.

"Come on. We should get back to the room and try out the other guns," Greg said. "Guess dogs can get through cheap-ass casino doors, huh?"

The trio made a beeline for the refrigerator back at their home base and spent half an hour trying to break the trigger guards off further guns, with only limited success.

"We should've prepared better," said Damon. "What if we're the last three people on the planet Earth and we're about to get fucking killed by dogs?"

"That's why I suggest you take a few of these, my friend," Greg said, handing over a pile of pale brown amphetamines. "You don't want to know what it'll feel like if these things really do get a hold of us."

Judy stared at the pills and then realized she wanted some, too. She'd been curbing her drug use the last couple of days but knew that she didn't want to feel the flesh torn from her bones by animals. Besides, the only reason she'd been holding off was because she figured they might need her womb healthy at some point, but now she thought that was just not going to be in the cards.

"Give me some, too," she said, and Greg complied.

The dogs returned within the hour, and despite the weight of all of the penthouse's furniture against the door, the dogs managed to crack through and then wriggle between two sofas to get at the humans. Greg had a plan for this and put it into action, which had the three move from their balcony to the one teasingly close next door. They were a little off-balance as they climbed over one guardrail and onto the next, but Greg had been just sober enough to help the other two.

Once they were in the room, they fled out the door and down the stairs, only to find dogs waiting in the stairwell.

"Holy shit," Greg exclaimed, incredulous that the animals would leave guards almost as if expecting a flanking maneuver, as they bolted onto the fourteenth floor.

As they ran, Judy could hear the dogs coming from behind them but also ahead of them in the stairwells that ran down the center and far corner of the tower. It wouldn't be long now.

"I'm sorry, guys," Judy said, having no idea what else to say.

A few minutes later, Judy sobbed her eyes out from a second locked bathroom as she listened to the dogs tearing through Greg and Damon's bodies in the next room. The morning sunlight was just starting to come through the windows of the bedroom, and she could see the shadow of a dog standing at the bathroom door and lowering its nose to sniff under it. As the dog began pawing at the frame and whining to the others, Judy began to scream hysterically, violently shaking her head as the sound at the door got louder and louder.

V

It took Bones a week to walk into Arizona. He couldn't have known it, but he was on Interstate 40, which ran from Barstow, California, all the way to Wilmington, North Carolina, crossing several mountains ranges and states along the way. Bones had been on the Albuquerque to Oklahoma City section of the road once before when he and Lionel had packed and moved to Pittsburgh after a call for enforcement dogs had gone out a few years before, but he didn't know that, either.

As he went, Bones was continuing to survive on whatever he found along the way, which often meant whatever he could catch. This was becoming an increasingly unreliable method of getting by, exemplified by a moment when he was stalking a bobcat and gave up his position when his legs buckled and he brushed against a bush. Hearing this, the cat immediately sprinted away, but Bones gave pursuit, having chosen his ambush location after first determining the exact spot on the bobcat's nightly constitutional with the fewest avenues of escape. Quickly, Bones cornered the animal, but the bobcat seemed to realize that its attacker was hardly in tip-top shape and fought back like a lion, bloodying Bones's face and right front haunch with its claws.

Angered at the situation, Bones managed a second wind and threw his entire weight on top of the bobcat, surprising the smaller animal as it made the shepherd's soft underbelly a perfect target to inflict even greater damage. It immediately went to try to tear out Bones's entrails, not realizing that the dog had exposed himself on purpose in order to get a clean shot on the bobcat's neck. Though the bobcat tore three deep gashes into his ribcage first, Bones's jaws were soon around the bobcat's neck. He sank in his teeth and then shook the animal violently, killing it in seconds.

Once the bobcat was dead, Bones collapsed in a heap, bleeding and panting. He licked his wounds for a few minutes but then tore open the flesh of his kill to feast on.

It was a meal well-earned.

It had been just over two months since Denny had joined the Flagstaff survivors, a group that now numbered forty-eight, and he was still adjusting to his place in the new and still growing community. Though Lester had become the de facto leader, Denny was the man people turned to when they had internecine conflicts. With his mild, non-confrontational stance and teacher's patience, folks found it easy to like Denny, and he was often called in to play peacemaker between the harsher Ingram and the leaders of incoming groups, who sometimes found it difficult to learn they would no longer be the unquestioned top dog.

Because the pair spent so much time together, many of the newcomers thought that Carrie and Denny must have known each other from before the catastrophe. The duo always teamed up for work details and took their meals together in the makeshift mess hall that had been established in one of the hotel's ballrooms, and when there were forays out into the city for supplies, they inevitably went together. The truth was, whereas many of the other survivors got through their own pain by "talking about it" with others, Carrie and Denny did not and respected the other for discussing almost any topic other than those concerned with loss.

They kept busy, they continued to help each other out, and they quite naturally fell in lust, but just as naturally (for the two of them), hated themselves for being able to so quickly put their spouses behind them and didn't act on it for weeks, when it all boiled over. In fact, the first time they had sex was on the first day they kissed. They had been on a mission to find a department store that carried cold weather gear, as so few did in summertime in Arizona summertime, but with fall upon them and winter around the corner, everyone knew such items would be at a premium.

The actual event happened soon after they found themselves wandering through a Sears furniture showroom and Carrie made a comment about how difficult she had once found it to pick out a sofa in a store, as the department had been in a sub-basement and she found it impossible to get her husband's opinion remotely, since her cell phone got no service. As the memory of her late husband began getting the better of her, Denny stepped in and kissed her, an act she gladly reciprocated. They made out for less than a minute before their clothes were half off and they were having what would inevitably turn out to be guilt-inducing sex on a nearby chaise lounge.

When they finished, they dressed quickly, hoped no one back at the hotel would miss them/make assumptions, and then loaded up the back of one of the many brand-new pickup trucks they'd "requisitioned" (a word the group now used for everything, almost as a survivor joke – "we're heading off to requisition water," "I've got a hunting party together to see if we can requisition a couple of cows or a deer," etc.). They had climbed into the cab to head back to the hotel when they started kissing again.

They had sex a second time then and there in the truck, but it was much faster and furtive, both keeping an eye out the window in case another vehicle pulled up with some of the others out looking for them.

But by the time they got back to the Sheraton, dropped off the clothes to the hotel's one-time laundry room that was set up as a community "wardrobe," and checked in with Ingram, who was working with two newcomers to repair the pumps that were pulling water into the now six working stalls of the basement locker room showers, it was all they could do to keep their hands off each other. Once the truck keys were turned in, they headed straight upstairs to Denny's room, made sure no one saw them as they went in, and had noiseless, but richly passionate sex for most of the afternoon. It wasn't the best sex either had ever had, but it was probably a moment where they both needed it the most. But far from being about personal pleasure, it was much more about trying to feel needed by the other person.

"That was just about perfect," Carrie said after. "If I'd known how good it would be, I would've tried to get you in the sack earlier."

Denny grinned, but both knew this wasn't true.

"Think it'll be weird downstairs?" Denny asked. "I'm not saying people will know, but we sure will."

"Nah," Carrie replied, shaking her head. "Most people think we're together already anyway."

Denny laughed. "True."

They were lazing around and talking, slowly getting their clothes back on, as Carrie had a shift to take down in the kitchen, when they heard a commotion from outside the window as a group of vehicles arrived out front.

"Those don't sound like ours," Carrie said, the slightest warning in her voice.

Denny walked over to the window, where he saw six trucks with at least three or four dozen people in them at the makeshift front gate. The driver of the lead vehicle spoke quickly to whoever was on guard duty there, and the man or woman immediately swung open the fence and let the trucks race down the driveway towards the front entrance. As they arrived, Lester and others of the Flagstaff group hurried out to meet them.

That's when Denny saw the blood.

Carrie and Denny were downstairs in five minutes, just in time to watch as eight horribly wounded individuals were brought into the lobby. It looked as if they'd been shot or in car accidents, as each had multiple wounds on different parts of their bodies. Denny shot a quizzical look over at one of the more recent arrivals, a fellow named Riley who'd come up from Yuma with a twelve-year-old girl and an elderly woman.

"Dog attack," Riley said quickly. "They were camping outside the city. Said there was something like two hundred dogs."

"Two *hundred?*" Denny exclaimed.

Riley nodded. "Yeah, and they keep saying, 'They weren't wolves, they weren't coyotes,' they were just fucking dogs. People's pets gone ape shit."

Riley hurried on as Denny looked over at Carrie, who appeared similarly incredulous.

"Jesus. Let's see if we can help."

On the afternoon that the wounded arrived at the Flagstaff Sheraton, Bones was still a few miles away from the city, taking a nap on a dog bed inside the office of an Arizona Highway Patrol station. Bones didn't know why, but there was something nice, cozy, and familiar about the place. Recognizable smells like gun oil, coffee, cigarettes, and boot polish had soaked the fiberboard ceilings with their unique brew over the course of several years, and for Bones it was like coming home.

He'd found the dog bed in one of the offices and curled onto it for a nap that lasted hours, and when he woke up, it was dark outside. He searched the station for food, only to find that even the vending machines had been previously ransacked, and went about on his way.

He hadn't gotten a mile before the smell of slaughter entered his nose. At first he thought it was close, but then after raising his nose for a fresh sniff, the shepherd realized it wasn't that it was nearby but instead was a substantial kill site with more than one victim. Bones kept walking, but strayed off the highway and kept his nose in the air. The odor of death grew heavier in the air, but then he smelled something else as well, an animal other than human. Cautiously, Bones crept ahead through the dark until he reached the first human corpse.

The body had been torn to pieces, a leg here, an arm there, the head ignored but the torso shredded and the entrails stretched in multiple directions. Judging from the smell, Bones could tell that it had actually been the work of several dogs and that this was hardly the only carcass.

As he nosed around, he discovered at least seventy corpses on the ground next to a collection of tents, extinguished cooking fires, and a few vehicles. There were also guns among the dead and a smell of cordite hung in the air, suggesting that at least a couple of the humans got off shots at the dogs before being killed, though Bones found no dog carcasses.

The shepherd was about ready to head away when he heard a growl coming from out of the darkness. He peered into the black and saw a single animal trotting towards him through the abattoir-like surroundings

Bones woofed a warning of his own but was unwilling to bark. He wasn't alarmed and didn't want to suggest as such. The dog came into view and Bones saw that it was a female, a bitch Rhodesian ridgeback. As he stared at her, trying to collect her scent, he realized that due to the sheer amount of blood in the area, his senses had been dulled and that there were a number of other dogs around as well, likely watching the encounter.

The ridgeback stopped and stared at Bones for a moment as the large shepherd lowered his head, ready for a fight. At the same time, Bones heard the other dogs circling around him, getting into position on either side. Though the ridgeback was in front of him, Bones knew the first attack would come from either his right or left to distract him and that the ridgeback would probably wait and go in for the kill when the shepherd was distracted.

But Bones wasn't going to wait.

As his two would-be flankers got into position, Bones suddenly bared his teeth and moved as if to charge the ridgeback. Instinctively, the bitch took a step back, only to have Bones change his course and lunge at the animal to his left, a wolf hybrid – seventy-percent wolf, thirty-percent Siberian husky. The dog was taken completely by surprise, and Bones tore out its throat in a single, vicious move. Beside the wolf hybrid was an Australian shepherd who immediately turned, wanting no part of Bones, but the shepherd launched himself at this animal, too, and ripped out its throat as well.

Now the ridgeback's entire pack began moving backward, as if realizing their quarry wasn't quite the lackluster specimen they initially thought, and regarded Bones as a group of well-armed hunters might a wounded, yet capable grizzly bear despite their superior numbers.

Bones didn't stop there. He wheeled around and went for a Rottweiler that had been circling around on his right despite the dog outweighing him by a good forty pounds, with layers of fat and muscle around its neck, both things making it far more difficult for the shepherd to use his typical attack throat-gouging attack. Instead, Bones leapt up and used his claws to jab at his opponent's eyes until he had managed to gouge out the left one. After this, he proceeded to tear off the Rottweiler's left ear.

Panicking, the dog moved backward, but Bones merely launched forward like a wrestler and grabbed the Rottweiler's front left leg in his jaws. He plunged in his teeth and quickly tore it off, yanking the bone from its socket and then tearing the epidermal layer away before tossing the whole thing aside. As the Rottweiler limped away, mewing and crying like a wet cat, Bones turned back to the ridgeback and was ready to kill it, too.

However, the ridgeback had a different idea and was already backing up, bobbing her head up and down and woofing a little in supplication. The dog then moved over to one of the human corpses that hadn't been completely devoured yet, tore off a chunk of meat from a ragged, bloody thigh, and dropped it a few feet in front of Bones.

The shepherd eyed the ridgeback but didn't move towards the meat. After another long moment, the ridgeback simply turned around and walked away in the direction she'd come from. Within seconds, Bones's nose told him that the many other dogs of the pack that had been just out of sight were now gone as well.

Bones waited a moment longer but then approached the chunk of human thigh, sniffed it over, and proceeded to gulp it down in four quick bites.

VI

At the same time in Flagstaff as night continued to shroud the hotel, Denny, acting on behalf of Lester, who was helping the wounded, finally got the whole story out of a couple of the attack survivors.

"We're from the Jicarilla Reservation out near Moenkopi," one of the middle-aged survivors, Norman Devers, told him. "When the plague hit, we fully expected to die as so many in the towns had but then a good fifteen, twenty percent of us survived. We buried our dead and, like your group it seems, began collecting supplies. We had no intention of leaving reservation land, but after we had to go further and further to locate fuel for our generators, we voted, and it was decided to strike out for Flagstaff. We hoped that if we weren't the only ones, we would find more of our people here."

Our people. Denny nodded when the fellow said this but was still amazed by what it implied. He kept waiting for the one white person, the one Mexican or Latino, the one black person to show up, only for it to always be the same: Indians.

More specifically? Apache Indians. More specific than that? Apache Indians of the Ypandes tribe.

There had been many discussions of this abnormality, and it was pretty quickly decided that just like certain races showed a more marked susceptibility to certain diseases, blacks to sickle-cell anemia, Jews to Tay-Sachs, etc., the Ypandes-Apache Indians appeared to have a sort of genetic resistance to the plague, at least so far. Denny knew the other survivors had all sorts of theories about this, many of them relating to their own spiritual beliefs and thoughts that God might have spared them for some greater purpose, but Denny had another theory, one he kept to himself as the most recent arrival continued his tale.

"We saw the dogs here and there as we traveled but never that many of them. We imagined they were content to pick through our trash, but we didn't have enough food to try and feed any of them, even if we thought one or two looked like they would make good watch dogs."

"Were they ever aggressive?" Denny asked.

"Not really. At least not that we talked about or was discussed, I guess. When we got onto the road, crows and vultures were following us, too. Thought of them the same as the dogs. Just scavengers."

"Then what happened yesterday?"

Norman took a deep breath and then described something that sounded incredible even to the young schoolteacher, who was accustomed to the fanciful stories of elementary school kids. The day had apparently started like any other. They'd camped the night before just outside of town and when dawn came, they sent a group on foot into Flagstaff, a dozen all told, to scout for any potential dangers.

"We ran into a problem with a couple of aggressive hoarders outside Cameron who fired a couple of shots in the air to show us how tough they were," Norman said. "It was a silly reaction. We wanted to say, 'Hey, bet we know something you don't know' and then show that we were Ypandes, too, but everybody's got to make their own way through this, you know? So the scouting party came back and said that you guys had these sheets out the windows here and didn't seem to be looking for trouble."

Denny nodded. The sheets now had writing on them, a massive painted message in English and Athabascan (Apache) that both said the same thing: "You are welcome," though the Apache phrase suggested something greater. Not just "you're welcome here," but carried the implication that if you did come in, you would also be protected, almost like the Pashtun notion of nanawatai.

"We were happy to know there were more survivors but also glad that we might have access to water and more permanent shelter after being on the road for a time," Norman said, slowing his narrative as if trying to make sure he had the details right. "When the attack came, we were packing up our supplies and loading the trucks. We weren't in any real hurry as, after all, we thought we had reached our destination. Then somebody shouted. I don't know who. I was with my sister, and we were packing her son in the truck we'd been using. I thought it was a fight or somebody hurt themselves on their truck or maybe spotted somebody else on the road. But then we saw the dogs, and they were coming fast. I didn't think. I shoved my sister inside the truck next to her boy and slammed the door.

"Anyway, the dogs were hunting us like any kind of pack predator moving on a herd. They had us circled and were just picking us off, a few dogs coming in at a time in small groups, all coordinated against one person at a time. They were organized, as if they were lions more than dogs. It was like something on the Discovery Channel, but instead of going after the young or old or weak or sick, there didn't seem to be a plan. We had a few guns, but it took a minute or two for people to react. We still thought we were looking at dogs. One of the biggest guys in our group was laughing his ass off as one of the dogs bit his arm because it was this little bitty thing. He didn't see that there were three others behind him."

Norman shook his head, frustrated in hindsight.

"We kept thinking we could scare them off. People were honking horns, waving towels and T-shirts, firing guns into the air like they were sheep, but it did nothing. The dogs kept coming, more and more and more of them. Every time we thought we'd seen all of them, another dozen or so would show up to block our escape. I've only ever seen crows do that. A group of crows will harass and herd a hawk away from their nests that way, driving the bird of prey to a stand of trees where four more crows are waiting to join the chase, just to make the hawk wonder if there are crows at every turn. The dogs were doing it like this.

"I'd say it took us a whole five minutes to wake up to the situation, but twenty people were already dead. By the time we started fighting them with guns, we'd already lost the fight and the dogs were on the run, having done the damage they'd set out to do. We knew they'd be back, so we took off, even though we didn't have enough room in the trucks for the dead."

Norman looked down for a moment and exhaled a long troubled breath before he finished up. "When I got back to my own truck, once it was obvious things had gotten completely out of hand, I saw that the front windshield had been completely smashed in and knew I wouldn't be seeing my sister or nephew again. You know what kind of glass they use in a truck windshield? Big heavy shit, shatter-proof. It's supposed to withstand just about anything. Tell me you think a dog, a fuckin' *dog*, is supposed to get through that."

Norman finished his story and looked around the room as if seeing it for the first time. Denny didn't have any words, so he simply reached out and put his hand on Norman's hands. "I'm really sorry."

The man started shaking, and Denny realized that he was crying.

Back at the city limits, Bones finished his meal and turned towards the city of Flagstaff still a few hours before the dawn. He had picked up the dog pack's scent and knew they were heading north, though the smell of exhaust told him that the most recent human travelers on the road had gone south. Bones turned to follow the humans' trail, which was made easier by the fact that the drivers had been going fast, just choking out the fumes, which lingered heavy in the air.

But as soon as Bones entered the city, the stench was almost entirely muffled by the overwhelming stench of corpses still left unburied in city whose population had, at one time, been over 60,000. The worst was likely over, the organs having long since decomposed, with the muscles coming next and then the hair and skin beginning their long decline into dust, but the stink had infected the walls and carpets and ceilings of where the person died, and without so much as an open window, the odor took weeks to slowly air out. For the average human nose, this smell wouldn't be much more than that of passing a garbage dump with its mountains of decaying food, plant waste, and other organic material. But the shepherd's nose picked up everything else as well, the uncovered waste and rotting sewage that lay just under the smell of tens of thousands of unburied carcasses.

Through all of this, though, Bones could still detect the unmistakable scent of the living. It was faint, like a faraway radio signal near impossible to locate on the dial, but the shepherd kept at it, determined to follow it to its source.

He turned on West Route 66 Drive, and the distant smell suddenly got stronger until he was finally able to zero in on its location, the large, fence-ringed structure of the Flagstaff Sheraton. As Bones got closer to the front fence, he could see two men with guns standing at the gate but could also smell the blood of the dying. An instinct told him to hold back, so he followed the fence around to the back from a few dozen yards away to get the lay of the land. He didn't smell any of the dogs, but that didn't mean they weren't there.

At the rear of the building, Bones caught the twin scents of the hotel's outdoor latrines and then a large garbage pit that had been dug just on the other side of the back fence. The pit itself was twenty feet by twenty feet and an impressive thirty-five feet straight down. Though it was within the fenced-in grounds of the hotel compound, a second, three-foot-high fence topped with barbed wire had been erected around it as well. Trash was then dumped in, but securely tied in paper bags that were then periodically covered with dirt.

Bones, who was trained in such things, quickly scaled the chain-link fence and hopped into the yard before moving over to the pit. It took him less than a minute to dig under the three-foot fence, squeezing through the tight hole, and then bounded down the slanted pit wall to the piles of trash.

When he reached the first bag, he tore it open to get at the fish smell he had detected, only to find a couple of empty tuna and sardine cans that were already so clean it seemed they had been washed before being thrown away. Bones licked the last remnants of oil from the cans and then moved on, hardly sated. He tore through the rest of the accessible bags and found only more of the same, hardly enough to satisfy the hungry dog.

After fruitlessly wandering through the now strewn-about trash for a few more minutes, Bones discovered a dirt-covered corner of the pit out of the way from the rising sun and settled in to take a nap.

"See? Told you we found a dog. It's right there."

Bones opened his eyes and looked up to see a handful of people looking down at him in the trash pit. The sun was now up, but the shepherd was still very much in the shadows of a far corner of the pit.

"I saw the hole under the fence but didn't think whatever dug it would still be there," the youngest man of the group, a twelve-year-old kid named Joseph was saying. "Then I saw the dog."

Denny, who held a rifle, stared at the animal before raising the gun and lining the shepherd up in his sights. He had never killed anything before and had only recently become proficient with a gun, but he knew what he was willing to do to preserve the Flagstaff group. This was a dog, and Norman's words about the great suffering that came from underestimating the species were already ringing in his ears.

"Might be others around," Denny said to another of the recent arrivals, a fifty-something fellow named Gutierrez. "Why don't you get Joseph and the others inside?"

Gutierrez nodded and the group wandered back in, except for Carrie.

"Where's the rest of the pack?" Carrie said. "This one looks pretty harmless."

"Yeah, but we don't know what he's been through or if this is some kind of trick. You heard what they were saying. The dogs were doing all kinds of things to draw people out."

"Yeah, but this guy? Look at him. Hardly looks like a killer."

As if on cue, Bones rose to his feet and began trotting over to where Denny and Carrie stood. Finding a path up to the fence line (cut into the sides to allow those who dug it easy access to the pit floor), Bones wandered up to the surface, tongue hanging out as he stretched a little. He felt a real stiffness in his bones, a likely result of the coldness of the ground he had settled onto.

Though he detected no threat from the shepherd, Denny kept the gun on Bones as he continued his ascent. When the dog reached the fence, he began sniffing around the air, inhaling the scent of the two closest humans. Dissatisfied, he then stuck his nose through the fence, obviously seeking an extended hand.

"See? He's just a dog," Carrie said. As if to prove her point, she held out her hand, and Bones first sniffed it and then gave it a couple of quick licks. Denny remained skeptical.

"Is that blood on his snout?" Denny asked, eyeing the dog's mouth.

Carrie looked but shrugged. "Could be from a mouse, Denny. He's not acting like a killer. He's acting like somebody's pet."

That's when Denny finally noticed Bones's frayed collar. There was barely anything left of it, but Denny could see that it at least appeared military. He lowered the gun and squatted down to get a better look as Bones edged closer to sniff the young man. Denny raised his hands to show that he meant no harm, let Bones give him a quick lick, and then reached through the fence and turned over the collar. Immediately, he saw that it showed not only the shepherd's name but also that he had been attached to the 11th Armored

Cavalry, a holdover from when the animal had been utilized as a cadaver dog in the ruins of Los Angeles.

"Jesus, he's some kind of military dog, maybe worked with the MPs," Denny said. "His name is 'Bones.'"

Upon hearing his name, Bones stood upright and eyed Danny.

"That's morbid," Carrie scoffed.

"If we bring him in, we'll upset a lot of people," Denny said. "I think we have to shoot him."

"If there's some kind of feral dog pack out there capable of sneaking up on even large groups of people in broad daylight, don't you think having a dog around might be useful?"

Denny had, in fact, thought of that as he ran through what he might say to Lester about why a dog, particularly a German shepherd that had some military experience in its background, would be a good addition to their group. But as soon as Carrie said it, he realized that he didn't want to have to make excuses. The truth was he wanted to keep this dog because he didn't want to kill it. After all that had happened, the idea was downright abhorrent to him. He understood the need for survival and had certainly taken part in hunts with the other Flagstaff survivors into the surrounding desert, but pointing a rifle through the fence to shoot a defenseless animal wasn't something life had prepared him to do.

"All right," Denny said to Carrie, but then turned to the shepherd. "Don't make me regret this."

VII

There was another reason Denny wanted to save the dog, but it wasn't something he found easy to articulate. He knew something of the history of the Ypandes-Apache people, despite having grown up with a mother and grandparents who had about as little interest in imparting such information to the young man as possible. Instead, he found the answers in books, and one of the things he learned early on was the relationship between the Apache and dogs.

There was a school of thought that suggested dogs would have been marginalized, possibly even extinct, if it wasn't for the establishment of domestication ties between humans and canines, likely during Neanderthal times. Dogs became hunting companions and watch animals while humans protected and fed them as an essential part of the tribe. This continued as both species evolved through the millennia and dogs were eventually brought over the land bridge that had once existed over the Bering Strait, known to native locals as Imakpik, and settled across North America.

Dogs quickly became an essential part of several Native American cultures, used by nomadic tribes to haul things just as mules or horses would later be. The dog was a member of the family, and some tribes caught wolves to crossbreed with their dogs in order to make them more effective for hunting. Dogs ate with their masters at every meal, dogs were part of many Indian creation myths, and dogs were given some of the same burial rituals and rites as their human counterparts.

For the Apache, dogs were as important to the tribe as they were to several others in the American Southwest, but it was the detail about the tribes bringing them across what had come to be known as Beringia that had Denny thinking these days.

The Ypandes-Apache tribe was not known for having participated in famous battles or sired chiefs renowned for their abilities as killers or diplomats, but in the late twentieth century, something had been discovered about the Ypandes that put them on the map regardless. Their language was very distinct, different from many of the others in the area, and had sparked some interesting comparative research that had identified similarities between it, some early dialects of Korean (Proto-Korean/Buyeo), and then a Laplander language spoken in the Arctic nether regions of Finland. Blood tests were taken and genetic testing done that showed a common ancestry shared among the three ethnicities. Scientists postulated that during the last Ice Age, which sent several of the northern tribes south, a group of the northern tribesmen headed east, with a large group breaking off and going south when they reached Siberia to end up in the Korean peninsula, while the others continued on into North America, similar to how many believed the Altaic language groups were proliferated. In both cases, the various clans intermingled (read: interbred) with others, producing larger clans, but traces of the blood line survived to the modern day.

As the Flagstaff survivors were only of these people, Denny thought that if the plague was tied to this deeply buried genetic strand, that could mean there were other pockets of survivors in Korea and Scandinavia. While yes, that also suggested a Korean or Finn or Ypandes-Apache living in Argentina or Tunisia might have survived as well, it was difficult to imagine such isolated numbers being able to link up with enough other survivors to do much more than attempt to survive in the hostile new world, much less establish and populate a new society.

Denny figured he'd be long dead before his theory might be proven or disproven, but it was an idea that gave him hope.

"You're telling me this as a roundabout sort of way to suggest we get pregnant?" Carrie had asked when Denny laid out this theory one day. "I mean, I'm all for it, but don't you think it could be a little dangerous giving birth these days?"

As the conversation was mostly in jest, they had left it there until a middle-aged woman named Lucille Amaro arrived with one group of survivors and explained that she had worked as a doula. Carrie and Denny had then had a second conversation, came to a conclusion, and then began having regular, unprotected sex. Denny wondered if it was the kind of thing they should bring up with Lester first, but both decided that the decision was theirs and no one else's.

But now, here was Denny leading Bones back into the Flagstaff Sheraton on a makeshift leash, another decision made outside the purview of the group that he thought might not go over all that well.

"You couldn't just shoot it?" snarled someone Denny recognized from the Jicarilla party who, like the others, must have been waiting to hear a rifle shot.

"He's a police dog," announced Carrie, as if that was enough to silence any critic. "He's too valuable to be killed."

Denny said nothing but simply led Bones through the lobby to the manager's office, where he knew Lester would be.

"Denny," Lester said heavily as he regarded the trio. "You need to get that dog out of here. You don't want to shoot it? Fine. Let it go. But you've got a group of people here who just watched all their friends and relatives survive one plague, only to get massacred by dogs. On top of that, you've got a second group who just heard that story and are jumping at every shadow."

"He was a military dog," Denny said but knew from the look on Lester's face that wasn't going to carry much water with him.

"Be that as it may, you have to get rid of it. These people are looking for a reason to let out steam, mix it up, get a little violent, and here you come, throwing a cat among the pigeons. This just isn't what we need right now. I'm pulling rank."

Denny heard the challenge in Lester's voice loud and clear. Old dog, young dog, alpha dog, team dog. But Denny knew that Lester's words rang true.

He nodded and turned, but Carrie shook her head. "We need this dog. If we've got a dog problem, he'll bark…"

"How do we know they won't just come up, trade a couple of sniffs with your friend there so he lets them waltz right in?" Lester asked, now sounding exasperated. "Having a dog is one thing, trusting our security to one is another. If this was yesterday morning, I might have a different thought, but I've never heard of any dogs acting like the ones that attacked those people on the road. Yes, this dog looks perfectly fine to me, but I'm not willing to give much of anything the benefit of the doubt these days."

Carrie was about to protest again but caught a look from Denny and silenced herself, following him out.

"This is a mistake," Carrie said as Denny walked Bones out of the front of the hotel to the gates.

"Maybe it is and maybe it's not," Denny replied. "Some things you can't know."

Bones looked up at the two humans with confusion as they took off his leash, led him out beyond the gate, and then let the two guards close it behind him. The shepherd pranced around a little as they turned their backs on him and headed back towards the hotel. He then stood there for a long moment, waiting for their return, before ambling away into the city again.

"Guess we know which side you're on," said a stern-faced woman, another Jicarilla survivor, as Denny and Carrie walked back inside "Gotta be stronger than that to make it in this new world."

Denny gave her a hard stare, and she looked right back at him with a scowl. Denny later found out that she'd lost her great-uncle and a cousin to the dogs and regretted the confrontation.

Bones spent the rest of the morning wandering around Flagstaff. He stayed relatively close to the Sheraton, as now that he found people, he knew he'd have a semi-consistent food source from what they threw away, but he also scouted around in search of more food on his own. The grocery and convenience stores in the immediate area had long been picked clean, so Bones ended up slipping into this house or that office building as he had done in Los Angeles, following his nose to vending machines and pantries full of non-perishables that only required stepping over a few corpses to get to, something that the residents of the Flagstaff Sheraton were still avoiding due to potential contamination. As Bones didn't consider such things, he feasted on precisely what he was hoping to: beef jerky and chips in a suburban utility room.

It was while he was eating this that he caught the scent of a feral cat outside and decided to make a run at it. He slipped out the door he'd come in through and spotted the cat feasting on a dead mouse in the garage. The cat didn't seem to notice the shepherd in the slightest, so it was easy for him to slip over to only a few feet away and then spring at the animal, slaughtering it before its heart rate had time to quicken. On top of that, the mouse had been freshly killed, so he ate that, too.

It was while he was chewing the mouse that something inside him seemed to rupture, sending Bones's entire body into spasm, and he loosed his bowels. All of a sudden, Bones found himself sitting in a puddle of his own blood and shit as his vision began to cloud. He tried to stand up, but felt too weak and toppled to his side. As he panted for breath, he found himself urinating down his leg.

That's when the pain came, a tremendous throbbing sensation in his bowels that quickly traveled up his entire body, causing him to quake and whine. After another moment passed, he drifted into unconsciousness swathed in as much agony as he had ever felt.

Back at the Sheraton, Denny found himself ostracized by the other survivors, so he figured he'd make himself useful and push it out of his head. He went to help in the makeshift infirmary that had been set up in the hotel's kitchen and learned that two others from the Jicarilla massacre had died in the night and a third was just barely hanging on. Though they had plenty of medical supplies, an early priority for Lester, they still didn't have access to fresh blood, which was a real problem, given how much the victims had lost. No matter how skillfully their wounds had been washed, disinfected, stitched, and dressed, their bodies could not make up the difference with blood.

But even if they had been able to conduct transfusions, they also had no way of typing blood, so it would be a crap shoot unless someone just happened to know they were O-negative, but no one was.

"I'm sorry," Denny found himself saying time and time again to folks as he tried to bring them something to alleviate their pain, even if it was only the itching from their stitches.

Additionally, the lack of refrigeration meant that several drugs they'd found in this hospital or that were now useless and, to no one's surprise, the morphine and codeine supplies around Flagstaff had almost been exhausted by those in the medical profession who attempted to ease the suffering of the quickly dying, which in many cases meant euthanizing their patients and then themselves.

Something would have to be done.

"You're the guy who brought in the dog, right?" one of the wounded Jicarilla men asked. "I'm not blaming you, as I would've probably done the same. But if you had seen what we had out there, you would never want to see another dog for the rest of your life. It was like sharks. All teeth and instinct."

Denny nodded and offered the man a glass of three-hundred-dollar Scotch, which he readily accepted.

When night fell, Bones awoke knowing he was in really bad shape. He was cold all over and could sense that his bowels had let go at least one more time that day while he was out. He struggled to stand up, and when he finally got on all fours, he discovered that he wasn't alone.

Just outside the garage on the driveway, he could see the six dogs watching him. He got their scent and knew immediately that they were of the same pack he'd run into the night before.

Bones also knew that they could smell his weakness and lowered his head, baring his teeth. He struggled to make a deep, guttural growl to suggest that even if they came at him in this weakened state, he wasn't about to make it easy on them.

But the dogs didn't attack.

Perplexed by this, Bones stepped forward challengingly, suggesting – basically - that he would come to them if they didn't have the balls to attack him, a move that from the various smells sluicing through the air was painfully obvious false bravado to all concerned. But the shepherd didn't know any other way and started limping through the garage to confront the waiting animals.

When he got to the edge of the garage, though, new smells suddenly filled his nose, and he didn't even have to look up to know that others of the pack were directly overhead on the roof, ready to pounce down on him like wolves. The problem was that Bones's own stench was some great that it had temporarily diminished his abilities to scent out the others.

Bones growled but then saw the Rhodesian ridgeback appear alongside the house. The other dogs seemed to be holding back, waiting to follow their pack alpha's lead. Regardless, Bones bared his teeth, ready to battle the animal to the death…

…until a *new* smell filled his nose.

It had been awhile since he'd taken in such an odor, but he knew exactly what it was. The ridgeback whined a little and slunk closer to Bones, whose own instincts in the matter began to take over. He was sick, he was dying, but he was still the male of the species, and when the ridgeback wandered into the garage on the far side of an old '76 Mercedes and "presented," Bones complied with the unspoken request to the best of his abilities.

VIII

"It's a necessity. We have guns, they don't have the element of surprise anymore if they're even out there, and we'll be in vehicles. We need supplies and we know where they are. This will be fine."

Everyone listened as Ches Marzan, a survivor from Cottonwood who had come in with two others a month after Denny, addressed Lester and a number of the others in the ballroom that night. The lights dimmed as one of the generators outside the fire exit sputtered as if to emphasize the seriousness of Marzan's words, but then glowed back to life when Lester appeared to be in agreement.

"All right," Lester said. "But in two groups: one for the medical supplies and a second for the guns. You guys leave first thing in the morning."

It had never been a question in Denny's mind that he'd be in one of the next day's requisition parties. He'd always been a part of them, he knew the streets, as he'd been a resident, *and* he had seniority, so it came as a surprise when he went out to the loading docks the next morning and found Ches shaking his head when Denny went to climb into the back of the truck he was fueling up.

"We've got enough people, man, but thanks," Ches said.

Denny stared at Ches incredulously. "Are you kidding? Who knows where all the good pawn shops are? Me. Who knows where the sporting goods stores are? Me."

"And me, because you showed them to me. But that's precisely why we need to be showing other people the routes, too. We've got new folks, and there's no telling what happens next, you know? We've got to get everybody up to speed."

It was a good enough manufactured reason to show Ches wasn't going out of his way to show up Denny, the former school teacher thought, but he saw the looks on the faces of the men already loaded into Ches' truck and could see the truth. Each held a rifle and regarded Denny the way his classmates once did in elementary school. He was the one going unpicked for this assignment, his position on the delicate pecking order sliding downhill due to his inability to kill a defenseless animal that morning. He supposed none of these men would've thought twice about it and this made them better suited, but he disagreed.

He turned and walked over to the group seeking medical supplies, this one led by Anna Blackledge.

"Do I have to beg?" he asked her.

She shook her head and nodded to the back of the SUV. He clambered in, and the two small convoys left the hotel grounds.

When Bones woke up for the second time that day, he was still feeling weak but was better able to stand this time. When he looked around, he saw that the Rhodesian ridgeback and the rest of her pack were gone but had left behind half of a deer carcass that Bones could tell had only been killed a few hours before. He sniffed the dead animal, realized he had no appetite, and left the garage without taking a bite.

There was only a slight chill in the morning air, but Bones felt it all through his body. His fur was getting stiff and the skin beneath it loose, as he had lost some weight over the course of his journey. But he still knew which direction he had to go and began moving that way, wandering towards the rising sun.

His gait had accumulated a serious limp, his right rear leg quivering every time his right rear foot touched the ground. He hopped along for a few steps, found that even worse, and continued limping.

When he heard trucks, he didn't care so much and made to slink down an alley to avoid detection. But as he did so, Bones caught the scent of the dog pack. He moved down a side street, around the back of a small strip mall, and spotted a couple of the dogs – two Belgian shepherds – in a resting position just alongside a small staircase leading to the second floor of a one-time Mexican restaurant. About two hundred yards away were the trucks Bones had heard, now parking in front of a large building.

Though Bones could only see the two shepherds, he could smell a great number of the others. They were in the area and were watching and waiting, none moving. The strange thing was that he could tell it wasn't the whole pack, as he caught no scent of the ridgeback.

"I used to have eighty guns all told, three gun lockers around my place," Ches was telling the man in the passenger seat, an older fellow who went by Pepe, as his last name was Pepoy. "I got with this girl who had a young son, and I really had to keep the guns locked up tight around him. But you know every time I opened one of those lockers, he'd just stare in there like I had all the treasure in the world behind that door. So I took him out shooting while his mom was at work, and would you believe it, he was a natural. Guns got demystified for him real quick, he saw that they weren't like on TV or video games; they were just tools. Anyway, I had just gotten him NRA-certified, which is when we were going to tell his mom, and we came home and found her *in flagrante* with one of my long-barrel revolvers…"

"Oh, bullshit," Pepe said, his first words in twenty minutes.

"I shit you not," Ches said, holding up his hand as if swearing on the Bible. "She had a condom on it so it looked like it was in one of those World War II movies where that's how the soldiers keep their muzzles dry, and I didn't have the heart to tell her that lube was just about the worst thing possible to get rubbed into a gun. Anyway, she freaked out, demanded to know where we'd been, and when I told her, the argument became all about me – you cretin, you dipshit, you asshole - and what I'd been doing behind her back. She split that very night and I never saw either of them again, but part of me feels like I did my good deed teaching that kid about guns. One more person out there who knows his way around firearms. Oh, well, shit – he's probably dead now, but whatever."

Ches finished his story right as they parked. He swung open the door of the truck and hopped out, glancing up and down the street before nodding at the others.

"Think we're good to go."

His requisition party was ten men strong, all armed, but Ches was still cautious. He'd been in the Navy at one point and felt that put him in a natural leadership position. Some of the survivors at the Flagstaff Sheraton knew how to fire this piece or that, but he knew how to fire *all* the guns they'd come across, which gave him a leg up, especially now that it looked like firepower might count for something. No more being led by a school teacher or a real estate appraiser, whatever-the-fuck that was. For Ches, it was time to treat an apocalypse like an apocalypse.

"What're we looking for in here?" one of the party asked.

"Easy, light rifles for the women and some of the men," Ches said, pausing for the laugh. "And then whatever you feel comfortable with for yourself. Now, I don't want to see a bunch of compound bows and big game guns that require fancy ammunition we're never gonna see again. Be smart. Load up on cartridges like it's the last time you're ever going to see any, and then let's move out quick as we came."

Everyone nodded and moved into the store, where an entire rack of shotguns and rifles waited at back of the shop.

"Oh, yes," Ches added. "Look for hunting and scaling knives. Probably could use a couple of those, too. Maybe even some fishing line if they've got it. Think like a soldier, 'cause that's what you are."

Across town at a medical supply warehouse they'd found in the phone book, Denny walked along with Anna as their group, also about ten persons, gathered up everything in sight. Occasionally, someone would wheel an oxygen tank or portable defibrillator over to Anna, who would have to judge if it was worthy to bring back ("no" to the tank, "yes" to the defibrillator, given that its battery could be recharged by the generators), but there were few things they couldn't imagine needing.

"I have to admit, I'm a little jealous of you and Carrie," Anna said, her back turned to Denny as she swept boxes of medical tape off a shelf and into a basket. "Yeah, I'm probably too old to have any more kids, but I think I'd really enjoy the regular sex part, the excitement of the time. It's not like I don't get propositioned, but you guys seem to have a nice thing going on. Am I right?"

Denny shrugged. This wasn't a subject he would like to discuss with anybody, but Anna Blackledge least of all, knowing how she talked.

"It's hard enough being alone," she mused. "But physically alone is a different story, especially when you're surrounded by other people who feel the same but for some reason just can't make that connection." Anna looked like she was getting ready to cry. "What I'm trying to say is that you have an open invitation. If it makes more comfortable to bring Carrie in on it, I don't have a problem with that, either."

Denny fought hard not to laugh at the absurdity of what he was hearing but accidentally let out a snort, which Anna couldn't have missed in any circumstance. She reddened, turned, and walked down the aisle until she was out of sight and left Denny feeling truly uncharitable.

He shook his head, wondering what she must have thought his reaction would be. That's when Denny heard the barking of a dog.

"Shit," he whispered as all the humans in the warehouse suddenly became extremely alert, like deer who'd heard that distant twig snap.

He hurried to the front of the store and grabbed his rifle, slinging it over his shoulder as he peered out the front window. Anna and the others quickly joined him and saw that the barking had come from a familiar German shepherd who was now dancing around in front of the closed doors of the supply warehouse. Bones paused for a moment, glanced inside at his audience, and then continued to bark.

"There's no way that's the same dog," said one of the men who had been at the edge of the trash pit the day before.

But Denny caught a glimpse of Bones's collar and shook his head. "That's him," he said simply.

"He's going nuts," Anna said. "Think he's just excited to see us?"

Denny didn't think this at all. There was real alarm in the dog's bark, and as he scanned around the street, he spotted a couple of other dogs racing straight for Bones.

"No," said Denny, his pulse starting to race. "He's warning us."

"And yeah, there's that one chick, Anna? Holy shit, is she hot for it. Never seen a chick so much in heat, particularly an older broad."

Pepe, cradling four shotguns in his arms, considered what fun it would be to just shoot Ches to shut him up but knew he'd get busted by the others. Ches was popular. Shoot him, and there'd be consequences even for an old convict like himself, a fact he'd been keeping on the down-low. Still, it was a nice thought.

Pepe was contemplating this very thing as the gun group exited the sporting goods store to an empty parking lot. They had checked it out pretty thoroughly from the windows and had seen no sign of any dogs or other threat, but now Pepe was hearing a sound coming from above him. As he stepped out from under the store's porch roof, he saw an angry-looking Rhodesian ridgeback looking back down at him.

"Oh, shi…," he started to say, but in the time it took him to get those two words out, the ridgeback had already leapt off the roof and had Pepe's head firmly in its jaws.

Ches whipped around in surprise as dogs started coming around both sides of the building.

"Oh, fuck me," Ches cried as he fumbled around for his pistol just as a wolf hybrid clamped its jaws on his wrist and violently snapped the bones within. Ches screamed as his hand was torn from his arm while a second dog went for the meaty part of his right calf.

The attack was over in seconds.

Back at the medical warehouse, Denny's first attempt to shoot down one of the dogs coming at Bones failed when the shot went wide, the dogs moving too fast. He fired a second time, missed again but then remembered something he'd heard a million times about shooting a moving target: lead the animal with the muzzle, keep the barrel a couple of feet out ahead. He did just that, pulled the trigger, and the dog's skull exploded in a lingering mist of shattered bones and blood, looking like he'd shot a watermelon rather than an animal.

He turned the gun on the second of Bones's would-be attackers and shot that one clean through the chest.

"There are more coming!" cried Anna.

And sure enough, there were. What looked like a hundred dogs were now coming at their location from every direction.

Denny thought fast. The dogs were in hunting mode, and even if the group of surviving humans stayed in the warehouse to weather any potential siege, the dogs would assuredly find a way inside. Worse, if they were missed back at the Sheraton, Lester would probably send a search party that wouldn't be any better prepared for a fight against this number of dogs than they had been.

Basically, this wasn't going to end well for anybody unless they moved out *now*.

"Come on," Denny exclaimed. "Into the trucks. We're leaving before they can get pin us in."

Everyone remained still for a heartbeat, but Denny was already halfway out the door. He was still lugging a couple of bags of medical supplies and quickly threw them in the back of the nearest SUV, which had been left unlocked. He then climbed up on top of one of the SUVs and began shooting at the incoming dogs.

Seeing what he was doing, Anna led the others to the SUVs, where they quickly threw in the harvested medical stuffs but then clambered in and shut the doors. Riley, who had been in the group as well, got up on top of the second SUV with a rifle and joined Denny in his turkey shoot.

As the men blasted away, dog after dog after dog went down in a halo of blood. Denny exhausted three five-round clips in a row, each bullet finding flesh. Riley, who had claimed to have learned to shoot in the Boy Scouts but hadn't fired a round in the thirty years following, was almost firing with the same level of accuracy, putting down dogs one right after another. Some flipped over in the air like a marlin on a fishing line, such was their forward velocity when hit.

For his part, Bones stayed between the two SUVs and barked his head off. He could smell the blood of the pack as they were killed only feet away, but he knew where he would be safe and stayed there.

And then, as suddenly as it had begun, it was over.

Though Denny had fully expected to drain himself of ammunition and then be forced to drive through a mess of oncoming dogs, the animals ended up retreating after about a third of their number had been slaughtered. He thanked Providence for small favors and then nodded at Riley before climbing off the roof.

"Okay, everybody in?" Denny asked as he got into the passenger seat of the SUV he'd been standing on. "They might be coming right back."

He found everybody staring back at him with a new level of respect. It was a surprising reaction, but he liked it nevertheless.

"What about the dog?" one of the women asked.

Denny looked out and saw Bones still standing there on the other side of the vehicle. He hesitated for a moment, but then nodded before clambering out and opening the back of the truck.

"You know I'm the one who threw you out earlier, right?" Bones just stared up at Denny with a confused look on his face. "Well, I thank you anyway."

IX

Back at the Sheraton, everyone listened in disbelief to the stories from Denny's party. Carrie had almost passed out when she'd heard but kept herself from sending "I told you so" glances to everyone that had earlier pooh-poohed bringing in Bones.

"He saved our lives," Anna said. "We wouldn't be here if not for him."

Lester praised Denny, Lester praised Bones, the group accepted the dog, and Denny got more than his share of reappraisal from those who had earlier judged him so harshly.

But Denny's redemptive makeover was becoming increasingly overshadowed by the fact that Ches' team was staying gone for longer and longer. Lester and a couple of others went to the roof and tried to raise him on the battery-operated walkie-talkies that had been issued to the parties beforehand, but everyone knew in reality that the range was barely even four blocks. They were unable to get any kind of response.

By the middle of the afternoon, the prevailing belief was that they had either skipped out, however unlikely, or been attacked by the dog pack and were somewhere between the sporting goods store and the Sheraton, possibly in need of assistance.

No one was sure what to do, least of all Lester, but then Denny came to him with an idea.

"I'll go find them," Denny announced. "One truck, a couple of guns, and Bones. We'll drive there and back. Won't even get out of the truck. We get into trouble, we floor it right back here, but we'll know what happened."

Lester thought about this for a moment, but then shook his head. "It's going to be dark soon. Then what?"

"That's why we have to go now," Denny pressed. "If they're injured, they're not going to make it through the night. If they've been killed, we need to know."

"And if they've gone rogue and are thinking about coming back here to shoot up the place or some silly shit, we'll know that, too, right?" Lester replied making it sound like he hadn't completely dismissed that as a possibility.

"Right."

Lester sighed. "If that's the case and you see them, feel free to shoot them. But after what befell you guys, I'm pretty sure I know what happened to them."

Bones was with Carrie in back of the hotel when Denny came out.

Bones had had a big meal and was currently drinking a second large tub of water. Having been around dogs most of her life, Carrie knew that despite his healthy appetite, something was the matter with the shepherd. His teeth seemed fine, as were his ears, but when she went to stroke his back, he moved away, obviously tender in a couple of places. She could see traces of blood dried in the fur near his haunches and had a good idea where that had come from, and even his tear ducts were leaking pus. Even worse, she saw him limping around a little, all of which added up to a dog that wasn't in great shape.

"I don't think you should take him," Carrie said, nodding up to Denny. "He's sick."

"Sick, ate something bad sick? Or, sick-sick?"

"I think he's an old dog. I think something happened to him after he left here yesterday maybe."

"Really? Like what?"

"I don't know," Carrie replied. She stroked the hair between Bones's ears and looked him in the eyes. "I'm sorry, Bones," she said.

Bones, as if understanding her words, gave her a quick lick on the hand. But then he glanced up at Denny, saw the look of uncertainty on his face, and left Carrie's hand to rise to his feet. He squared his shoulders and faced Denny as if literally rising to an unspoken challenge.

"He looks okay to me," Denny scoffed. "Or, at least it looks like he's not ready to throw in the towel."

Carrie eyed the dog and had to agree.

Moments later, Denny and Bones were back in one of the two SUVs they'd taken to the medical supply warehouse. The sun was setting and there'd be no telling what was out in the night, but Denny cracked the window a little anyway to allow Bones and his impeccable nose access to the various scents passing by outside the vehicle in the hopes he'd get an early warning if there was trouble ahead.

All the way to the sporting goods store, Denny kept an eye on the road to make sure he didn't drive right past one of the trucks Ches and his guys used, but seeing nothing only confirmed what Denny felt he already knew: They were all dead.

He knew why he wanted to prove this, though, and it only partially had to do with an attempted rescue. A real rescue, a rescue where there was any belief whatsoever that folks would be found alive, would've likely required at least two people. But Denny had taken up the mission to prove to himself and everybody else that, in the end, he was better equipped to survive out in this world than Ches. Yes, this was petty and small, and if it wasn't for Bones, he probably would've been with Ches' group, and if it wasn't for Bones, there'd be two groups out here dead, so he felt he'd been more than proved right.

But a small, primal part of him couldn't let go of the fact that Ches had insulted him, and now Denny would be standing over his dead, arrogant body, able to literally piss on the man's grave if he so wished. He did not wish and he didn't even like to admit the impulse, but there it was, and here he was driving to the scene.

When he reached the sporting goods store, it was just dark enough that Denny had to turn on the headlights to see the two trucks. As he got closer, he saw that the front door of the store was wide open, suggesting that no one had managed to get back in and attempt a barricade if they were attacked, but a second later he saw the remains of one of the dead men on the ground.

It looked exactly like what the dogs had been trying to accomplish at the medical supply warehouse. The men had gone inside, collected their weapons, and were on their way out when the animals attacked. The surprise had somehow been complete and the men were all dead, probably without getting off a shot, as Denny didn't see any sign of blood out in the parking lot, only up by the human carcasses. He looked for Ches but couldn't differentiate one fallen man from another in the dark.

"Should we get the guns while we're here?" Denny asked Bones.

The shepherd hadn't so much as woofed on the drive, so Denny figured the dog pack might well have been long gone. He eyed the guns spilled out in front of the store and was starting to think that maybe he'd take his reputation up another notch by bringing back the weapons.

Ches? Oh, yeah, he had ten armed men and couldn't manage to get the guns back to the hotel in broad daylight. Denny Edwin Tallchief? Went out alone and got them at night.

Denny parked alongside one of the SUVs and glanced over at Bones, who was sniffing the fresh corpses from the window.

"Is it safe out there, Bones?"

Bones glanced over to Denny at the sound of his name but didn't bark, so Denny took this as a positive sign and slowly opened the truck door with one hand as he awkwardly held up his rifle with the other. He took a cautious step out of the cab and glanced around, aiming the gun in every direction. So far, so good.

"C'mon, Bones," Denny said, and the shepherd hopped out of the vehicle as well, sticking close to the human as they both carefully walked over to the front of the store.

Denny peered into the building but almost lost his footing when his shoe began to slip around on the slick surface below. He looked down and realized from the color of the shirt that he had inadvertently stepped on a chunk of Ches' body that had fallen directly onto the store's welcome mat.

"Oh, man, I'm sorry," Denny said, without thinking that he was apologizing to a corpse.

He took a step back, reached down and grabbed two of the shotguns that had fallen alongside the man, and piled them in the back of the SUV. Still hearing nothing out in the night, Denny got a little braver and started picking up more weapons and then baskets full of ammunition, which he loaded into the truck as well. The men had spilled some of the bullets and shells onto the concrete when they'd fallen, but Denny scooped those up as well and soon had an SUV full of enough guns and ammunition to supply a full company of soldiers.

"All right, Bones," Denny said finally. "Let's go home."

Denny opened the driver's-side door, and Bones tried to jump up onto the seat but slipped and fell backwards onto the parking lot.

"Oh, shit, are you okay?" Denny asked the dog before helping him back up.

Bones snapped at Denny's hand when he accidentally touched Bones's throbbing right rear haunch, but it was only a warning. Denny angled his hands around and tried a second time to help the dog up, and this time he made it.

Denny grinned and patted Bones on the snout. "We make a good team, you and I."

At that moment, Denny heard a new sound from behind him, something clicking out a fast rhythm on the parking lot, and knew it was a dog. Cats retracted their claws, dogs didn't, a lesson taught to him by his grandmother at one point when pointing out tracks in the mud. This was clearly a dog.

Having been distracted while attempting to climb into the SUV, Bones had not immediately picked up on the new scent in the air. The shepherd turned, saw the Rhodesian ridgeback racing full-tilt for Denny, and started barking as he wheeled around. He awkwardly tried to launch himself forward from the seat to defend Denny but slipped again, this time smashing his snout on the dashboard as his legs went out from under him.

Denny had set down his rifle to help Bones but now turned his head and was frantically looking for it as the large dog grew closer. He had just spotted it leaning up against the back door of the vehicle when he sensed movement in the air behind him, and before he could react, two hundred pounds of muscle and claws slammed into him, smashing his body down onto the driver's seat of the car. He felt the hot breath of the snarling ridgeback at the back of his neck just before the animal began tearing into his flesh with its claws.

"*Fuuuuuck!!*" Denny screamed.

He fought against his canine attacker, trying in vain to lift himself up enough to shrug the heavy animal back out of the SUV, but it was just too heavy. The ridgeback's powerful front paws were pressed down against his shoulders with his left arm curled under him and his right straight out in front, making it impossible to get any lift as the animal's claws shredded his skin. He felt so helpless in the face of his own death that he became furious, his face reddening in frustration as he pushed with all his might but was still unable to move his body up a single inch.

Meanwhile, Bones worked hard to regain his footing on the cab floor. He was dazed from the dashboard-inflicted shot to the snout, but he could tell Denny was in real trouble. With a tremendous effort, he finally found the strength to pull himself back up onto the seat and lunged for the ridgeback. The ridgeback, having believed Bones incapacitated, staggered backwards in surprise just as the shepherd lowered his head, ducked under the ridgeback's snout, and clamped his jaws directly onto her throat. Terrified, the ridgeback lifted herself off Denny and thumped back down on all fours, effectively dragging Bones out of the truck, as the dog's teeth were still embedded in the ridgeback's throat. As the shepherd slid over Denny and onto the parking lot, he relaxed his jaws, and the ridgeback yanked herself free from Bones's grip.

But no sooner was Bones outside the truck than the female lunged straight for Bones's weakened hind leg and sank her teeth into it. Bones yelped but then quickly swung around and bit into the ridgeback's ear, tearing into the soft flesh. The ridgeback yanked away, losing much of the ear in the process, but then clawed into Bones's underbelly.

Bones rolled away from the ridgeback but was already winded. He had given everything he had to his first attack and was now almost drained after less than half a minute. He bared his teeth as the ridgeback prepared to spring one last time, knowing he wouldn't have the energy to fight back.

The roar of a rifle echoed through the empty parking lot, causing Bones to flinch. The ridgeback had been in mid-spring, and the bullet had cut across her back, cooking the fur, burrowing through the flesh, and exiting out the other side after chipping bone.

The ridgeback hit the ground with an agonized yelp, and Bones sprang to his feet to go in for the kill, only to have his legs buckle out from under him. Denny turned the rifle on the ridgeback's head as it slunk away behind Ches' truck, but then he saw them.

While they had been distracted by the ridgeback's attack, the entire pack had moved into the parking lot, forming a horseshoe-shaped ring around the three vehicles, hanging back ten to twenty feet.

"Oh, shit," Denny whispered. "Oh, *shit.*"

He fumbled with the rifle as Bones joined him on the side of the truck. The ridgeback was whining now, attempting to lick its wound but having little success. Bones moved next to her and, to Denny's surprise, began licking at the wound himself.

But then his attention turned back to the rest of the dogs. None were growling or making any sign of attack, but they were skittish and confused by what was going, which made the one human in attendance believe they were seconds away from simply tearing him and Bones apart.

That's when Denny got an idea. Below his feet was a Heckler & Koch 9mm that one of Ches' men had dropped and beside that, a pump-action shotgun. He slowly bent down and picked up the automatic, dropped the safety, and stepped in front of Bones and the ridgeback.

"GET THE FUCK OUT OF HERE!!!" Denny roared, pulling the trigger.

The pistol kicked so hard that Denny almost dropped it, but when he regained his stance, he fired another flurry of rounds into the air. When the gun was empty, he raised his rifle and emptied that into the air, and when that was drained, he picked up the shotgun and did the same.

From the first shot, the dogs started moving away, though their eyes were still on their fallen alpha. When Denny had switched to the rifle, the dogs were already beginning to scatter, but after the final empty shell had been ejected from the shotgun, the only dogs left in the parking lot were Bones and the ridgeback.

Denny looked down at the two wounded canines, then pushed every bit of advice he'd ever heard about dealing with injured animals out of his mind as he opened the back of the SUV and grabbed a towel. The ridgeback had lost some blood, but he thought he could still manage to lift her into the truck if she would let him.

"Bones," Denny said as he walked back around to the dogs. "Get in the truck."

At first, Bones wouldn't leave the ridgeback's side, and Denny was incredulous at how instantly devoted the shepherd was to an animal he was fighting to the death moments before. Feeling a stabbing reminder of his own battle with the dog as his shredded shirt brushed against his shoulder wounds, he pointed out to himself that he was doing the same thing.

However, his reasons for requisitioning the bitch were far different from Bones's.

X

"That's it!" Norman was shouting. "That's the fucking dog that attacked us!"

Denny was lying face down on a kitchen table as Carrie and the doula, Lucille, cleaned up his wounds while a young woman named Beth did what she could to disinfect the ridgeback's wound through the bars of an animal cage that Denny had picked up from a giant pet food retailer on the way back, though she continued to circle and snap at her as she did so.

Bones sat nearby on a pile of towels. Denny looked over at one point and was sure Bones had fallen asleep, but when he looked back, the dog was wide awake and paying attention.

As Norman ranted, Lester looked from Bones to the ridgeback to Denny, appearing like a man harassed to the edge of sanity. He finally raised a hand to silence the Jicarilla survivor and turned to Denny.

"You brought this dog back, why?" Lester asked.

"She's the pack's alpha," Denny explained. "She's the key to stopping these dogs from attacking us and, hopefully, other packs in the future."

Lester let this soak in, realized it didn't make sense to him, and eyed Denny. "What are you talking about?"

Denny tried to raise himself a little, but Carrie just pushed him back down. "Hold still."

Denny nodded but then looked over at Lester. "These dogs were pets two months ago. How many dogs you think there are in America?"

"I don't know. A million?"

"Almost a hundred million," replied Denny, happy to surprise the group. "Some student every year would do a science fair project involving their family pooch with that factoid glued to their tri-fold display board, though I think the real answer was closer to 77 million. How many humans do you think are left in America? Optimistically what, a few thousand? Let's go as high as 100,000. Do the math. Two hundred dogs killed seventy people in fifteen minutes two days ago. One hundred dogs killed ten people earlier today. One hundred dogs almost killed another ten at the same time, and the only thing that saved them was another dog."

The room did the math and didn't like what they came back with. Lester looked over at Bones a little dubiously but then nodded. "It sounds like you're getting ready to make a point."

"Say a third of those 77 million dogs died in the plague because they were locked up, couldn't find food, whatever," Denny continued. "That's still 500 dogs to every one human. We are no longer the dominant species here, and these feral dogs have proven that they're extremely capable of making us go extinct very quickly, and if not in this generation, then in future ones. But you see how Bones reacts to us. He recognizes that there's this tie of domestication between humans and dogs, and he respects that. The other dogs, well, they respect and follow their alpha, this other dog here. Somewhere in her mind, this dog and the other dogs remember that they were domesticated at one point. But a generation of dogs from now isn't going to have those memories. We have to take this opportunity and try to re-establish ties of domestication between our two species the way our forefathers did. If we don't, the human race may well be on its way towards extinction."

The room had gone quiet after Denny explained what he hoped to accomplish, but this was broken by Norman shaking his head at Denny with a scolding glance.

"We have bullets. We have *guns*. We can wipe them out. This is absurd, specious reasoning."

"You think we can wipe them out for good?" Lester asked. "Fifty million dogs breeding other dogs? Chasing down deer like wolves out there away from where we are? We're going to have bigger fish to fry than exterminating dogs."

Lester waited for a response but continued when he got none. "They always said we didn't have many predators in North America. Snakes, bears, a few wolves," he said, shaking his head. "We never thought we were cultivating a damn army in our own houses. We can't kill all of them. It's that simple. We're barely able to survive right now, and it's not like that's going to get better. We're having to teach ourselves how to gather food and water, basic necessities. How soon until we run out of grocery stores and medical warehouses and pawn shops and we have to start fabricating what we use again? We're at the beginning again. Luckily, we still have our books and our memories of how a light bulb works or how a battery works, so we can get there again, but we have to get moving. It's not going to work if we're looking over our shoulders the whole time waiting to get attacked."

Lester turned to Denny, a serious look on his face. "If you have some way to fix that, you've got my support."

With that, Lester exited the room. It was obvious that Norman and some of the others who had gathered still thought Denny's plan was insane, but they eventually walked out as well to leave Denny to be patched up.

When Lucille finished stitching up Denny's back, she glanced from Carrie to Denny and smiled. "You're planning to get pregnant, aren't you?" she asked matter-of-factly.

"We've talked about it," Carrie said.

"Well, get to it! You heard the man. We're at the beginning! Your child will be one of the first born 'after,' a little baby Jesus." The doula laughed, though Denny thought it sounded more like a cackle.

Nobody talked much beyond that, and Lucille took off when she was done.

As soon as they were alone with the dogs, Carrie looked at Denny with concern. "Do you intend to domesticate all 50 million yourself? That's the part I can't wrap my head around."

"No," Denny said. "In fact, I'm sure there are a bunch out there that haven't joined a pack yet. We can feed them, bring them into our pack. We'll probably have to put down some of them, unfortunately, but I think we have to try to domesticate this pack at least. If there are a couple hundred of us and a couple hundred dogs working with us, we'll be better hunters, be safer. There's the emotional centeredness that comes with it. There are reasons our ancestors did this. Good ones."

"But you're also asking dogs who are out there leading their own packs, fending for their young, and surviving in the wild to effectively enslave themselves," Carrie replied. "It just sounds impossible."

"So does everything these days. There aren't so many alternatives. But if we just start with one dog and move out from there, we could make this work."

Denny looked over at Bones, who had settled in next to the ridgeback for the night, and knew that he was right.

During the night, Bones stayed beside the ridgeback as she floated in and out of delirium. She had lost a lot of blood and hadn't allowed anyone to really stitch her wound, so it still bled periodically. Bones, however, pressed his body up against the bars of her cage, and eventually the ridgeback lay down next to him and was warmed by the large shepherd.

Slowly but surely, the ridgeback seemed to accept Bones's presence, so when he passed food to her from his own bowl to the cage a few hours later, she was as much grateful as grudging. Eventually, she went to sleep.

Though he desperately needed the rest, Denny just couldn't find his way to sleep that night. Aspirin helped the pain, but nothing could make the stitches not itch. He struggled to get comfortable in the bed he shared with Carrie until finally she awoke.

"I'm sorry," Denny said. "I didn't mean to wake you."

"Yes, you did," Carrie replied. "But it's okay."

She looked down at him in the dark and kissed him.

"What was that for?" he asked.

"I'm just happy," she said. "I know we're supposed to be suffering through this, mourning the dead and our past lives, but you make me very happy. I'm lucky to have found you."

Denny knew how Carrie felt, though he, too, had been reluctant to voice it.

"I loved my husband, we had a great wedding, we had a fantastic honeymoon, and then we had Scott a few months later, but I was still getting to know him," Carrie continued. "For spouses and then parents, we were still strangers on certain issues. That's not the case with you. Just think of how much we've gone through in only two and a half months. Forget how much I've learned about you, I've learned even more about myself. I thought my life was going to be all Little League games, company picnics with my husband, a second kid, a third, maybe. Making ends meet. Cooking and baking. I thought a couple of weeks ahead, sometimes a month. Now, we're thinking a lifetime ahead. I know what's important to me now and what doesn't matter in the slightest. I like that feeling."

As Carrie talked, she was stroking Denny erect under the sheets. "There used to be such a pecking order to things, everything so civilized. I knew what I was supposed to want and what I wasn't, and now that's all different. I can spend the day working on the water supply system and feel like I accomplished something at the end of the day. If I want to celebrate by getting a little drunk in the evening, I do." Her voice became mischievous. "And if I want to be filled with your cock in the middle of the night, I roll over and convince you that that's what you want, too."

With that, she inserted him into her, and he sighed.

"That take your mind off your stitches?" she asked, gently rocking backward.

"It certainly does," he replied.

"Good," Carrie said. "Then take your time."

Out in front of the hotel compound, Anna Blackledge was engaged in much the same activity with Gutierrez, who had her bent over an unlit "No/Vacancies" sign that stood just beside the long driveway up to the hotel.

"If you stop, I'll kill you," Anna said. "And you know I have a gun."

Gutierrez, having not expected Anna to come onto him when they took their turns at guard duty, had jerked off earlier and now felt like he could shag Anna for hours. He'd had a thing for the sharp-featured, dark-haired forty-something since he'd arrived (well, he'd had a thing for every woman he'd seen since the plague came and took away most of them) but never thought it would result in something like this.

Ten minutes later, Anna was starting to regret this interlude, as the older man was now sputtering and panting, so she turned around to quickly relieve him with her mouth and a couple of well-placed fingertips that left him wondering why he'd never considered doing or having someone else do something like that to him before.

"Wow, you're really good," Gutierrez said as Anna jerked up her jeans and re-buttoned them. She smiled knowingly and nodded. Though she extolled the virtues of her husband at any opportunity, he'd actually been a bit of a drunk who would come home from a bender and demand sex. After years of enduring his fumbling frustration at being unable to keep an erection long enough to ejaculate, she'd learned about the trick she'd just used on Gutierrez, forced herself not to think about the less than sanitary aspects of it, and went to town. Her husband became downright docile after that, to the point that Anna began referring to it as his "off switch" in conversation with the friends of hers that she shared such details with.

"What now?" Gutierrez asked, snapping Anna out of it.

"What do you mean?"

"Are we going to be public about this? Tell others we're together?"

As Anna stared at Gutierrez, she realized that even though the man was easily in his mid-fifties, he was as smitten as a sheltered nineteen-year-old. "No, I think we should keep it to ourselves for now. Don't want to upset any apple carts. I've seen how the girls look at you."

As Gutierrez's face filled with surprise, Anna internally rolled her eyes. Plague or not, men could still be controlled with a combination of flattery and a finger up their asshole.

"We should take a look around," Anna said. "I haven't heard anything, but just in case."

Gutierrez agreed, and they walked towards the front gate. That was when they heard the first distant yipping out in the night. It wasn't a howl like you'd hear from a dog but a quiet, coyote-like baying, as if calling out to a friend.

"Oh, shit, they're here!" Anna said with surprise, suddenly embarrassed at the idea of having to explain herself to Lester, who she'd also slept with, or any of the others.

But as the pair peered out into the night, neither could actually see any of the dogs.

"At least they're on the other side of the fence," Gutierrez said, looking around.

"You don't think they can get in?"

"It's fenced, right?"

"Yeah, but dogs can…" Anna trailed off as she saw a single dog approaching the fence a little ways down to her right. She raised her rifle and wondered if she should shoot it. It was on the other side of the chain-link, of course, so her fear was that if she shot it through the fence, it might just rile up the other dogs and stir them into action.

But as the dog got closer, illuminated only by the generator-fueled lights that had been rigged overhead and then the handful of stars, she realized there was something strange about it. In fact, it wasn't on the outside of the fence at all, its movements being an optical illusion.

No, the dog was already inside the gates and trotting right for them. Anna had instinct enough to look behind her and saw the silhouettes of three more dogs approaching, and knew it was too late for either of the two humans.

"Dammit," she said, raising her rifle and firing off four quick shots into the air to warn the others as Gutierrez stared at her in surprise. When she'd stopped at the fifth bullet, the last in the magazine, she looked at the man querulously. "I don't know how you feel about being torn apart, but it isn't this lady's cup of tea."

With that, she placed the muzzle of the rifle between the teeth, the heat from the iron just beginning to burn the roof of her mouth in the half-second before she pulled the trigger.

XI

When Bones heard the gunshots, he scrambled to his feet. The ridgeback was still out cold, but Bones knew that he was needed elsewhere. Though the door had been closed to the kitchen where the dogs were sequestered, Bones knew how to get out of it fairly easily and made haste through a side door leading to the ballroom whose broken latch pre-dated the plague.

He hurried through the room and was soon out in the lobby, where he came face to face with a rifle muzzle.

"Don't shoot, that's Bones!" cried Denny as he came down the stairs.

The rifleman, one of the survivors from the reservation, looked as if he might shoot anyway but then turned and headed out of the hotel in the direction of another round of gunfire. Bones hobbled out to the lobby with Denny close behind until the pair could see what was happening outside.

What was happening was madness.

What looked like an entire army of dogs had descended on the grounds of the hotel and were tearing through the human guards like they were made of cheesecloth. A number of the Flagstaff survivors had begun shooting at the dogs, but this time the animals didn't flinch, much less run away. Instead, even as their comrades went down around them, the surviving members of the great pack kept running at the humans without fear.

"Bones, get back inside," Denny whispered, figuring the wounded shepherd wouldn't stand a chance.

But Bones didn't hear him, as he was already out in the courtyard, heading for the fight. He neared a Doberman that was mauling the face off one of the young women who had shown up with the doula and, without thinking, launched himself at the animal and tore its throat out in one move. Within minutes, Bones had repeated this action four more times, the blood of his victims soaking his snout and pooling at his feet.

It took the other dogs a few moments to realize that one of their own was tearing their numbers, but once they did, they turned on the shepherd. At first, it was a couple of Akitas that attacked, but after Bones tore the two dogs in half, several of the others began prioritizing the one-time enforcement dog in their attacks.

"Look out, Bones!"

Bones turned in time to see a mastiff coming at him from the left side of the building. He pulled himself into a confrontational stance, but just as the dog leaped, a bullet whined through the air and entered the animal's right ear and blew its brain out the left. Bones glanced around and saw Denny standing nearby with a rifle.

"Yeah, you're welcome. We've got a lot to go."

Denny continued firing his rifle while Bones kept going for throats. The human had a handful of magazines in his pants pocket but still endeavored to conserve his bullets, while the shepherd just got angry and sank his teeth into everything that moved. But as far as Denny could tell, even then they were barely making a dent. Dogs seemed to be coming in from every corner of the yard, far more than they had seen outside the sporting goods store.

"How they'd get in?" cried Lester as he made his way out of the hotel, still barefoot but carrying a pump-action shotgun.

"Hell if I know," called Denny. "But there are a lot of them!"

That's when Denny saw a number of the dogs racing inside the hotel itself. "Carrie," he whispered.

Bones caught a glimpse of Denny hurrying back into the building from the corner of his eye and wheeled around to follow, springing away from one fight to get into another.

Denny entered the building and just realized that the screams he'd been hearing for the last minute or so weren't solely contained to the exterior of the building. There were dogs in the lobby, dogs on the stairs and in the offices, and, Denny had to assume, dogs wherever Carrie was. He slammed a fresh magazine into the breech of his rifle and was halfway to the stairs when he heard Carrie's voice calling from the kitchen.

"Denny!!! DENNY!!!"

Bones caught sight of Denny as he made his way back towards the kitchen and went to follow even though several dogs were already close at his heels. Lester and another of the survivors were following in after them, shooting their guns at the dogs, but Bones also felt the hot breath of the bullets as they whizzed by overhead, chips of plaster splintering out of the walls upon impact.

When Denny got to the kitchen door, he found it blockaded but managed to push his way through, only to see a gun pointed at his face. "Carrie, it's me!! Don't shoot!"

He stumbled the rest of the way in and saw that Carrie, Lucille, and a couple of others had locked themselves in with the still caged ridgeback who, detecting the members of her pack, was bounding about in her cage. Denny quickly went to re-blockade the door but then saw Bones coming, too, and allowed the shepherd in before slamming the heavy kitchen tables Carrie and Lucille were using as barriers back in place in front of the door.

"What about the ballroom entrance?" Denny asked.

"Closed that one off, too," Carrie said. "There's more than two hundred dogs out there. I looked out the window. I think there's at least twice that."

"They're just tearing through everybody out there," Denny said, catching his breath. "And now they're inside."

As the humans discussed their next move, Bones moved over to the ridgeback and saw that she was actually substantially better. She calmed herself for a moment and exchanged a quick couple of sniffs with Bones, who sat down next to her. The shepherd sniffed at her wound and gave it a few licks, though his tongue could barely reach through the bars.

Denny watched all this, knew the time had come but was reluctant to act.

"How is this supposed to work?" Carrie asked. "We just take her out of her cage and kind of hope she doesn't tear us to pieces?"

"I have no idea," Denny said as he walked over to the cage.

Upon seeing the man approach, the ridgeback immediately jumped to her feet and bared her teeth at Denny, growling low. As if hearing their alpha's distress, the sound of the pack scratching and beating on the kitchen door only got louder.

"Easy, girl," Denny said, but the ridgeback only backed up and lowered her head, increasing her look of ferocity.

"Shit," Denny muttered, the memory of an attack at the hands of this dog still fresh in his mind.

That's when the ridgeback, cage or no cage, flung itself forward at the bars as if figuring they would give way under her assault, and she was almost right. The cage rocked forward as she hit the metal, and the hinges of the cage door buckled with the vicious hit. Denny did a quick calculation and decided it would only take two more strikes like that for the ridgeback to break through.

"Okay, so maybe this was a stupid idea," Denny admitted as he raised his rifle and prepared to shoot the ridgeback.

The caged dog moved to the back of her pen to launch a second attack, but it was at that moment that Bones came around and stood in front of Denny. Just as the ridgeback was about to spring, Bones began barking like a demon. He bared his teeth, which could plainly be seen under his curled lips throughout his vocal assault. The ridgeback halted her attack but then began barking back at Bones and then growling at Denny.

That's when Bones did something that no one in the room expected. He suddenly *stopped* barking, yawned, and lay down at Denny's feet. The ridgeback continued barking, but Bones didn't seem to give a shit. His eyes were still on the ridgeback, but his head was now resting on his front paws. Outside, the rest of the pack continued their angry cacophonous roar, punctuated by the occasional blast of gunfire or human scream.

But Bones just lay there. There was a break in the ridgeback's vocal assault, and that was when Bones made a small woofing sound. The ridgeback looked as if it might start snarling all over again, but then it didn't.

After a moment of quiet, Carrie looked over at Denny with a questioning gaze.

"Fuck if I know," Denny said.

Slowly, the ridgeback began moving towards Bones. The shepherd held back for a second but then slipped forward a little bit as well. When the ridgeback's nose reached the cage door, Bones took the last step and touched his nose to the other dog's nose. Then the ridgeback lay down, too.

Denny looked at this and then up to the ceiling. He thought that if they could climb up onto the stove, they could reach the crawlspace between floors and get into the higher levels of the building from there. He hastily suggested this to the others, and though they weren't sure of his plan, they agreed that the kitchen was soon to evaporate as an option, so they had to go somewhere. The dogs in the hallway were already starting to claw through the door, and their combined weight would easily push aside their hastily stacked kitchen equipment.

"Let's do it," nodded Lucille as if they had simply decided on which color to paint a bathroom.

With a little bit of help from each other, the assembled group climbed up and out of the kitchen, with Denny being the last to go. He hadn't taken his eyes off the ridgeback the entire time but now he moved towards her cage. She leaped to her feet and began snarling at him, but he didn't flinch. He just kept staring at her, reached his hand down to the door latch, and unhooked it. He then turned his back on her and walked over to the stove, hearing Bones getting to his feet to defend him as the ridgeback nosed her way out of the cage.

Denny didn't take his time, but he didn't run, either. He was no prey to be run down, and he had the added confidence of a pistol in his hand that had been handed off by one of the others who had gathered in the kitchen with Carrie and Lucille.

As soon as he was in the ceiling, he looked back down at Bones to see the shepherd staring straight back up at him. Denny knew Bones was sick and wondered if this was the last time he'd ever see the animal that had saved his ass a couple of times now. He didn't think the ridgeback or the others of the pack would kill him, but he didn't think Bones's own body would let him see many more days.

"Thanks, Bones," Denny said to the dog. "Thanks," he said again, then disappeared after Carrie and the others.

XII

Through a couple of signals and more than a few yells, Denny, Carrie, and the others directed the survivors of the pack attack up to their barricaded hideout on the top floor of the hotel. It had been a controversial idea, but Carrie suggested lighting controlled fires in barrels at the top of the stairwells, utilizing trash cans and laundry bins to block the paths of the dogs. After bashing out a few holes in the ceiling and in various windows to allow the smoke to ventilate, Denny set the fires himself, and the dogs did steer clear.

It turned out there were more survivors of the assault than they had initially believed. Lester had led several folks out of the compound, around the back, and to the trucks, where they took off, circling the grounds and firing at the pack to draw them away from the hotel and back into the city, though this meant leaving many wounded behind.

Denny knew this decision must've killed Lester, knowing how much he cared about the survivors inside the hotel, and it had been his idea to get on the roof with some blankets at dawn to do a Warner Brothers cartoon version of an Indian smoke signal to communicate to the others that some had made it.

By then, the pack had receded, and Lester and the others returned mid-morning, joining Denny on the top floor of the hotel after a careful reconnoiter up the stairwells. Over the next few days, small, heavily armed groups were sent downstairs, where doors were nailed shut, entrances and exits sealed, and supplies brought back up, but no one ventured outside and the groups only stayed down in the building for an hour or less at a time, generally during the heat of the day.

It was a full week before they stepped out onto the grounds.

On the seventh day, Lester and Denny led a small group out to the trucks to bring up ammunition that had been left in Denny's SUV. When nothing happened, when there wasn't so much as a single dog sighting, a slightly larger group composed of an armed escort and the strongest of the survivors went out to bury the dead in the same plot of ground just outside the gate, where those who had only lived long enough to reach the hotel after the massacre of the reservationists were buried.

The next day, a day Denny told Carrie "felt like a Monday" even though nobody except Lester really kept track of the calendar, the survivors moved back downstairs and began repairing the damage to their various "public works projects" in an attempt to pick up from where they left off. They were still very much mourning the recent dead but were similarly determined to move forward.

That afternoon, Lester, Denny, and a couple of others climbed into a truck and went on a scout of the city.

Again, no dogs.

Instead, they found a small herd of deer in Thorpe Park eating the grass, about fourteen all told. The men readied their rifles, aimed, and killed the entire herd. The deer were all does and what looked like a handful of juveniles born in the spring, and had barely turned to run when they were cut down.

The men brought the hunt back to the hotel, skinned and butchered the deer, prepared the pelts for tanning, and cooked the meat over three great fires in the courtyard. Soon, the scent of roasting venison was all anyone in the hotel could smell, a rich, inviting aroma that eased its way through the windows and walls of the building but also rode the warm evening updrafts out and over the surrounding neighborhood.

Denny saw the first dog about forty-five minutes after the meat had been placed over the flames. It was one of the many wolf hybrids that were a part of the pack, snowy white fur with a handful of black patches dotting its haunches and coloring its snout and ears. Even in the dim light, Denny could make out the paleness of its eyes.

Seeing the same thing, Lester rose to retrieve his rifle, but Denny held up his hand. "Give it a minute. No sudden moves."

Lester nodded and sat back down by the fire, using a broom handle swaddled in towels soaked with makeshift barbecue sauce (more tomato paste than anything) to baste the meat as it cooked. Another minute passed, and the survivors began to see more dogs. When the meat was deemed ready and taken off the fire a few minutes later, there were now at least a hundred dogs outside the fence line.

The next part, Denny knew, would be tricky.

Donning gloves, he collected half the roasted, still warm meat in a wheeled laundry tub and then wheeled it over to the fence. With Joseph's help and a couple of riflemen waiting in the shadows, Denny tossed large chunks of their kill over the fence to the dogs. At first, the dogs flinched back as if under attack, but quickly reversed gears and tentatively approached the inviting meat. It didn't take long before the meat drew more and more dogs out from the surrounding area to the human-made feast.

Denny waited a little while, knowing that the meat would hardly be enough for the dogs, and then settled into a large communal meal with the other survivors. Some were so nervous that they cried as they ate. One, from the Jicarilla reservation, prayed rather than ate. As the dogs finished their meat, a couple of fights breaking out here and there over scraps, they all pressed close to the fence, but none attempted to come in.

When the humans were done eating, there was plenty of meat left, and Denny loaded up the laundry tub a second time, rolled it to the front gate, and tossed it over the fence. The dogs dove in and ate the leftovers. When the meat was done, the dogs disappeared again.

As Denny watched them go, he realized that he had seen no sign of either Bones or the ridgeback.

A few more days went by, and when a hunting party was sent out to "requisition" deer, an animal to be found in some abundance in the silent city often seen grazing on subdivision front lawns instead of eking out an existence in the nearby deserts and valleys, the dogs appeared, too, trotting alongside the vehicles. They were obviously allying themselves with the hunters but kept at least a block away.

In cases like these, Denny had a standing order. Half the kill goes to the dogs.

Day after day, this went smoothly. The dogs would sometimes even chase the herd towards the riflemen, coming by their half of the prize honestly.

It was on one of these outings that Denny finally saw the ridgeback again, right at the head of her pack. Her injury looked well on its way to being healed, leaving behind a healthy-sized scar but nothing more. Still, Denny had hoped to see Bones with her, but the shepherd was nowhere to be seen.

It was only three days after that when he was listening to the stories of a group of incoming survivors that he learned where Bones had gone.

"Yeah, we saw dog packs up in Denver, big, crazy fuckers going after everybody, but we got outta there," a Colorado woman, Ines, was saying. "They were like wolves. Before coming here, we dropped south into New Mexico and took the I-10 west. Saw more dog packs down there but managed to avoid them. Didn't see any more dogs until we were camping one night right near the border, and a lone German shepherd showed up at our campfire, some kind of military collar. He stayed a little out of sight, but we threw him some food and soon he got close. He stayed near the trucks that night and when some wolves showed up, he barked like hell. Earned his keep as far as we were concerned."

"Where did he go after?" Denny asked.

"We were perfectly willing to take him with us, but in the morning he was gone. We saw him up the highway heading east, I guess. Hate to say it, but he was looking pretty thin. Was he your dog?"

Denny took this information straight to Lester with a request to go after him. Lester told him he was crazy and that it was a complete waste of resources, but let him have a truck anyway. Denny then went to Carrie, who understood but was also violently opposed. Sure, the group had talked about trying to send somebody out to see if there were groups like them in Santa Fe, Tucson, Albuquerque, and even El Paso-Juarez, but no one had ever suggested it be one person.

But Denny was adamant and soon got his way. Most of the Flagstaff survivors figured he'd earned the opportunity to be a little wasteful and reckless through his repeated acts of heroism over the past few weeks anyway.

He set out at nightfall and drove without stopping to the Arizona-New Mexico border.

As he went, Denny listened to a CD on the truck stereo. Music hadn't been any kind of priority to the group, but Denny had often passed a library on his various excursions into the city and had later suggested it as a place for Lester and him to retrieve books on carpentry, plumbing, and electrical work. He'd seen the baskets of compact discs and remembered them when he went to go look for Bones.

When he put in a disc of Soviet-era film music by Shostakovich, a rival of Prokofiev and one of his favorites, as it had been one of his wife's favorites, he found himself weeping behind the wheel. It wasn't so much that the music was beautiful or so surprising to hear after so long, it was more that it immediately put him in the mindset of where he was when he last heard it, sitting alone with Jennifer in their living room, trying to place themselves in the lives of the Minsk Chamber Choir when they recorded it (not realizing that their CD was from a more recent recording of the score). World War II was over, the Cold War was just beginning, and the never-ending putsches and purges of the Stalin era kept the citizenry on their toes, Shostakovich himself being denounced the same year he wrote the score Denny was currently listening to. But here they were, singing like angels for the soundtrack of a film neither Denny nor Jennifer had ever heard of, much less seen.

The couple had talked about what their lives had been like and whether any of them could possibly still be alive. He knew the answer to that one now. They discussed the Orwellian hardships much of the citizenry faced, both mentally and physically, and wondered aloud if having found one another as Denny and Jennifer had done would be enough to make life worth living.

Denny cried because he missed his wife but also because so many of the things he had wanted to do in life were now gone. He would never go to Europe, he would never sit on the school board, he would never watch his children go to a better college than he did, he would never win any kind of awards for his teaching or possibly coach his students into awards of their own. He would never see any of those same students graduate. Now he had no goals other than those directly tied to his survival. He had mourned his friends and wife before but now, selfishly he thought, he mourned the loss of his own life as he knew it.

He reached what was pretty obviously the campsite of the Coloradoans (they had left notes for other travelers explaining the size of their party and where they were heading) well before dawn and then kept going east, though at a greatly reduced speed now, down to twenty from seventy-five. He debated halting his progress until daybreak so he wouldn't miss spying Bones but then realized the dog, having had a day on him, was probably at least a few more miles down the road, so he'd be okay.

Just as the sun got a little higher in the sky, he pulled off to the side of the road to urinate, did so behind a tree though the likelihood of anyone coming along at the moment was next to none. When he turned around to walk back to his truck, he got the scare of his life, as he found Bones sitting beside the passenger side door, looking at him.

"Jesus, Bones!" Denny cried. "I didn't even hear you come up."

Bones woofed in acknowledgement, but weakly.

Denny walked up and knelt beside the shepherd, only to see that he was little more than skin and bones now. "Ah, jeez, Bones," Denny muttered as he stroked the animal, the fur even stiffer than it had been. "Glad I found you."

Denny opened the passenger side door and pulled out the fresh meat he'd brought for the dog, but Bones barely touched it. The shepherd whined a little, got up on its feet and pranced a bit, and Denny understood.

"All right," he said, tossing the meat away and helping Bones up into the truck.

XIII

Even with Bones in the car, Denny drove along slowly. He had the windows down, and Bones kept his snout to the wind as they went. They had only gone sixty miles by midday, but Denny had enough fuel to take them all the way to Florida if need be, though he didn't imagine that would be the case. No, something told him that the dog's destination was closer than that, or he wouldn't have been walking it. He got the idea that the shepherd knew exactly how bad his condition was and that he chose his time to leave the Flagstaff pack carefully, not too late, not too soon.

But then they reached the exit that would send them to the town of Las Cruces, New Mexico, and Bones began whining, which soon turned to barking. Denny didn't know if it was a smell or a sight that had alerted Bones to their position on the map, but the dog couldn't have made it clearer that this was where they going.

Las Cruces, "the City of Crosses," was about the size of Flagstaff and was located in the southern part of the state, surrounded by mountains. None of the buildings were very tall, a common sight in New Mexico, as there were ordinances about blocking views of the horizon. Church steeples were high, apartment buildings were not. As Denny rolled into it, he found it eerily silent and filled with the stench of death.

Having no idea where they were going, Denny drove around a little, circling the downtown mall area off Main Street until Bones indicated this direction or that. It was mid-afternoon by the time Bones had finally decided on a neighborhood, and after trolling up this street or that, Denny finally decided that the easiest thing to do would be to let Bones out on foot, and he'd follow in the truck.

This easily proved to be the better plan. Though the dog was hobbled by illness, Bones's nose seemed to instantly grab onto a scent, and he made a beeline down the sidewalk, crossed two lawns, and took a side street down to a row of modest, single-story houses at the very edge of the neighborhood where the back fences abutted the arroyo. One of the houses didn't have a back fence, its backyard invitingly open to all comers. It was to this lot that Bones ran.

Denny parked the truck in the driveway alongside an old Chevy Blazer and climbed out as Bones scratched on the front door. Self-consciously, Denny glanced around but saw no sign of people, and was about to try to force the door when he discovered that it was unlocked. He swung the door wide, and the shepherd immediately ran inside.

Denny had feared that they would be greeted with the scent of a rotted corpse, but this wasn't the case. A heavy, musty smell permeated the air, but even the always attendant stench of spoiled food was absent from this place, as if it had been cleaned out after being abandoned.

As he walked through the small den, kitchen, and dining room at the front of the house, Denny realized that the house likely belonged to an older man, a belief confirmed when he went into a home office of sorts and saw the kind of jumbled, paper-strewn mess that no woman he ever knew would tolerate. On the wall were plaques celebrating the law enforcement career of a man named "Lionel Oudin," and there were several photos of him in uniform.

And then there was a photo of Oudin in uniform alongside Bones.

"Oh, my God," Denny whispered.

But he didn't know what he was most reacting to, the fact that he was being given a window into this dog's past or that Bones was able to navigate himself back from wherever he came from all the way to his master's house.

Denny looked over a few more of the awards and photographs, Oudin clearly having had a particularly distinguished career, but then exited to find the shepherd.

He didn't have to go far, as there were only two more rooms in the house: a dusty, unused guest room with a four-poster bed in it surrounded by dust-covered boxes and then the master bedroom, which looked more like a hospital room. A large semi-electric hospital bed with heavy bed rails and an over-bed table was set up in the middle, surrounded by medical equipment that suggested someone quite infirm lived here.

The only thing was, the bed was empty and there was no sign of its one-time occupant.

Bones was going over the room with his nose, as if he'd picked up on the slightest of smells but couldn't for the life of him find where it emanated from. He moved from the bed to the dresser to the closet where an old man's clothes hung, the floor littered with boxes and shoes.

On a chest of drawers, Denny saw photos of Lionel with a young woman, probably a daughter, and then a few more of the woman alone through the years. A very young Lionel stared out of a wedding photo with a young lady who favored the daughter in the other pictures, further confirming Denny's belief regarding their relationship, though the wife appeared in only a few other photos in the room, all from younger days.

"You okay, Bones?" Denny asked the shepherd as the dog snuffled around in the closet with greater and greater intensity.

Denny walked over and looked at the dog as he made his search, until he finally figured out what the shepherd wanted. In the back of the closet hanging from a hook was an old leash that appeared to have been used in an official capacity, as it had the logo of the Doña Ana Sheriff's Department on it. Denny took it down and placed it on the carpet in front of Bones.

"Is that what you wanted?"

Bones replied by sniffing all around the thing, circling it over and over. Denny waited a couple of minutes, but then walked away and left Bones alone with it.

A few minutes later, as Denny sat in the living room wondering what to do next, Bones wandered in and moved directly to the sliding glass door that opened out to the patio and scratched at it for a moment. Denny rose and slid it open, allowing the shepherd to scamper out and nose around the yard. Though he knew there was no fence and Bones could just walk away, he didn't look on the dog as "his" in any way and didn't think he'd ever feel that way about any animal again.

In fact, Bones going right to the leash surprised him. He thought of it as a symbol of subjugation, and why would a dog like Bones want to be subjugated? Then he realized that he was thinking of it as a human might, which had little or nothing to do with how the dog saw it. For Bones, the leash was not a symbol of subjugation so much as an indicator of his close relationship to this man who obviously meant the world to the dog. Denny wondered where the man's body was, as it seemed clear that he was sick well before the plague came.

He sat back down in the recliner in the old man's living room and, having now been awake for more than twenty-four hours, promptly fell asleep.

Denny woke up about ten hours later in the pitch dark. The first thing he grabbed for was his gun, finding just where he'd left it. He hadn't seen any dog packs roving Las Cruces on the drive in, but that didn't mean they weren't watching him.

That's when he remembered Bones.

He went quickly to the patio door and slid it open, terrified that he might find the butchered carcass of the shepherd lying there, savaged by those very unseen dog packs while attempting to get back in. But there was no sign of the animal.

"Bones?" Denny asked, in case he had just walked out a little ways into the field beyond. When there was no response, he tried again. "Bones?!" Still nothing.

Denny went to the kitchen to see if there was any non-perishable food worth eating that might save him a trip to his truck and found only powders, vitamins, and prescriptions, Lionel clearly having been on a mostly liquid diet. Glancing through the prescriptions, he saw several related to the side effects of chemotherapy and realized that Lionel had been dying of cancer.

When the sun finally rose, Denny walked out in the backyard with his rifle and looked around for Bones some more. He called the shepherd's name repeatedly, but there was no answer. Nothing moved but the birds.

Undeterred, Denny got behind the wheel of the truck, drove around to a dirt road that ran behind the row of houses and continued searching for the dog, slowing to call out his name while being careful not to drive anywhere too dangerous for fear of breaking an axle. While he figured he could easily trade in the truck for Lionel's Blazer, there was a lot of ground to cover between the scrub behind the houses and Lionel's back patio. If there were any dogs around, Denny would be greatly exposed to predation. This was the new mindset, Denny realized.

At midday, Denny began running out of fuel, decided that would be the moment he'd give up the search, and, half an hour later, stopped the truck to gas up from one of the many cans in the back.

"BONES!!!!" he cried one last time.

But the dog was long gone, having disappeared into the wilderness of his youth behind the home that had been the first and only place Lionel had ever owned, rented out during a couple of years while in Pittsburgh, and then returned to for his retirement, "to be close to his daughter," he told friends.

After a long moment, Denny nodded to himself, tossed the empty gas can in the back of the truck, climbed behind the wheel, and began following the setting sun back to the west. He glanced into the rearview mirror but continued to see no sign of the German shepherd, though by now he didn't expect to.

Epilogue

The moment Denny had opened the back door, Bones got the scent he knew he would. It was faint, now months old, but it didn't matter, as this was what the shepherd was trained for, his specialty. He headed out through the scrub and mesquite trees, and within the hour he'd made it into the Organ Mountains east of the city.

Bones had grown up walking the various trails of the Organ Mountain National Recreation Area and knew the slopes well, the smell of pine and mahogany filling his nose as he headed across the lower steppes and into the higher elevations. He could tell the trail he was following now would take him through the Needles Range and into the distant canyon, one that had a stream through it certain times of the year, which included now, due to the recent rains. Rain in the desert can make a nasty habit of erasing any sign of a tracker's quarry, something many a lawman discovered in the Organ Mountains, dating back to the time of Pat Garrett and Billy the Kid, but this was precisely why Lionel had chosen the place to train the shepherd.

"Just keep walking," Lionel had said to a group of trainers and their dogs brought to the mountains for training one day. "If a scent came from that direction a moment ago, don't decide the trail has gone cold just because your dog has lost the scent. He's got 200 million scent receptors in that nose of his to all five million of yours, and that means it takes a lot more than just rain or cold or other animals to wipe your fugitive away. Humans are surprisingly foul creatures whose stink and oils can be more definitive and potent than a skunk; we've just grown accustomed to them. On top of that, you add deodorant, toothpaste, shampoo, cologne, cigarettes, junk food, and everything else your target came in contact with in the last twenty-four hours, and you're damn right there's still a trail. For a human, the desert's a hard place to find somebody. For a dog, it's like looking for a needle on a white floor. It's not obvious from every angle, but you can't miss it if your eyes are open."

Bones had been a puppy the first time he'd heard Lionel give a variation of this speech, but it meant as much to him as Sanskrit to a roof rat. What Bones took away from this was how the other humans regarded Lionel and how the dogs regarded their trainers. He knew where the target, a Doña Ana reserve deputy named McCaffrey, was hidden, a cave some six miles away where he'd been camping for three days without fire. Bones had been with Lionel and the reservist two months ago when they'd selected the spot and then spent the next six weeks intermittently walking different trails with the young man to drop latent scents. Then Lionel had the fellow change everything else about his routine, which meant different shampoo, toothpaste, a scentless deodorant, and even a new diet.

It didn't matter, as the dogs located the man within five hours, deep within Fillmore Canyon.

Bones had been along for the ride, mostly, though Lionel was also using him and his scent as an ongoing distraction to the training dogs, two of which were female. Bones performed his role with flying colors, but it would be another eight months before he was involved in an exercise as a trainee.

Now the shepherd was heading back to that same canyon, the scent of his master faint but that of the only human who had been this way in months. The farther away from Las Cruces Bones walked, in fact, the fewer human smells he detected at all. Lionel's neighborhood had been a veritable curtain of death, each house on the old man's street containing at least one or two bodies alone. But now, out in the wilderness, as the trail got ever clearer, Bones knew his master wasn't far away now.

Bones found Lionel an hour later next to a stream. He was in pajamas and a bathrobe, seated in a red and green beach chair with thick wool socks and hiking boots on his feet. By his side was four-footed quad cane that had been slightly overgrown with moss, the Organ Mountains famous for this type of fast-growing botanical life.

Lionel's fingers, folded in his lap, had been chewed away, and his eyes had been pecked out by this creature or that, likely the work of birds and possibly a fox, but they had soon discovered that through his body ran a manmade poison meant to slow the progress of the disease that was killing him, which had the additional side effect of rendering his meat inedible to wildlife. The only thing the old man had brought with him other than the chair (no easy task) and the cane was a leash. Unlike the more martial leash Denny had retrieved for Bones in Lionel's closet, this one was cloth, made for a puppy, and was clutched in his hands.

Bones padded silently around the old man's chair, taking in his scent and nuzzling his hands. For about an hour, the shepherd sat alongside the dead man with his head resting on his knee, listening to the stream and the occasional bird call coming from overhead.

As the sun set, Bones lay down at Lionel's feet, inhaled deeply the scents of the nearby juniper and stool, and then closed his eyes to take a rest.

BIGFOOT
An Apocalyptic Interlude

Prologue

"Five bucks! Man, you can't get *anything* for five bucks anymore! That was awesome!"

In the back seat of the white Mazda 3, Jess rolled her eyes. Patrick had repeated this for the last ten minutes. Yes, the park ranger had let them in after dark and only charged five dollars. But she'd also seen the potbellied man with the gray, bushy mustache in the too-small uniform and ridiculous hat slip the bill in his back pocket even as he'd made no real attempt to hide his ogling of her chest through the window.

"I thought they were going to kick us right out, or there'd just be a locked gate," Patrick continued, motor-mouthing like the stoner he was.

"Can we drop it?" Ruthie asked, seated next to Jess. "We know how bad you'd feel if your inability to get out the door this afternoon screwed up our trip."

Patrick finally fell silent. It was true. When Dan, Jess, and Ruthie had arrived at Patrick's doorstep to pick up the last of their number for a camping trip over the long weekend, the first-year associate not only wasn't packed, he was completely naked, his ornate glass water bong in his left hand, an Xbox controller in his right.

"Wait, what day is it?" he had asked through bleary eyes.

One of the cases Patrick was on had been settled in the firm's favor earlier that week, so most of the team was on mandatory vacation. Meaning, even though they could accumulate no billable hours, they were expected to work on their other cases, on so-called "Approved Office Projects," which typically meant researching and writing articles for legal journals that a partner would then put their name on, or shepardizing/blue booking the legal briefs of others to make certain the laws being cited and the citations themselves were bulletproof.

Somehow, Patrick had dodged all of this. By telling all comers that he was doing last-minute due diligence on a deal being closed or that he was in the middle of compiling exhibits for a senior partner or was helping a friend by holding the file on another case, he managed to convince the entire firm he was buried in a hurricane of work. In truth, he rested comfortably in the eye of the storm.

At first, Jess had been impressed and looked forward to picking up a few tips over the weekend trip. But now all she could think of was the ham-fisted way Patrick had tried to pick her up at a company party when they were summer associates, only to vomit across a partner's lawn and pass out seconds after being rejected. Even then, he'd managed to cast suspicion on a junior partner and dodged blame.

A born lawyer, Jess thought.

Which made it even harder to rationalize that person with the jabbering pothead currently occupying the front seat. Why was he so quickly taken in by the ranger, when all Jess saw was a slightly scummy creeper making a quick buck?

"I think that sign said the C and D sites were up here to the left," Dan said, breaking the awkward silence following his girlfriend's remark.

"Which one are we looking for again?" Jess asked.

"4C," Dan replied, glancing to the ticket he held against the steering wheel with his thumb. "Everybody keep their eyes peeled."

Jess did as requested, staring into the darkness that seemed to engulf the narrow dirt road leading to the state park's camp sites. The trees on either side of the car were so close they brushed against the doors and windows, as if they'd made a wrong turn and were blazing a new trail through the woods.

But then they rounded a corner, and the Mazda's headlights illuminated an elderly couple parked in lawn chairs alongside a bus-sized mobile home. A roaring fire blazed in a pit at their feet with a kettle alongside it, which Jess surmised held either coffee or hot chocolate. An inviting light glowed from within the camper, promising a night in a cozy bed with an electric heater as opposed to a moth-eaten sleeping bag on the cold ground.

To say nothing of its proximity to an indoor toilet.

"Really roughing it, huh?" Patrick scoffed, and rolled down his window to make sure the old couple heard him.

Jess shrank in her seat, hoping they hadn't heard. But then the old woman looked directly at the car, making eye contact with Jess instead of Patrick. Luckily, she appeared more confused than offended, as if the words had been lost on the wind.

As Ruthie chuckled, Jess caught a quick look from Dan in the rearview mirror. She rolled her eyes, and he grinned. She'd thought he had a nice smile even before she found out he was dating Ruthie, one of the second-years who had already positioned herself in a sort of mentor role to Jess. And in an office where everyone scrambled pitilessly over everyone else, it was nice having someone on your side even if that most often meant helping to shoulder caseloads when Ruthie got swamped.

They passed two more occupied campsites before the road split off, C sites to the left, D to the right.

"*Finally*," Patrick groaned. "I'm starving!"

But there was something in the way he said "starving" that made Jess realize Patrick was planning to make a move on her that night, this despite numerous assurances from Dan and Ruthie that this wouldn't be the case.

I wish Scott was here, Jess thought. *Dad was right. He was the one.*

They found 4C, little more than a short gravel driveway, a fire pit, and a square concrete slab that a single tent might be pitched on. Jess knew it would go to Dan and Ruthie but didn't mind so much. Even though it was summer, the ground would be colder. Despite this, Jess knew she wouldn't feel like they were actually in the great outdoors unless she felt the bumps and ridges of small rocks, twigs, and the uneven ground beneath her tent floor.

The idea of this, half a recollection of times past times spent in the woods, banished all previous thoughts of aseptic beds in claustrophobic, overheated mobile homes.

The wind picked up as they unloaded their gear, the tops of the nearby trees swaying against the backdrop of a vast star field. Jess threw on her fleece and dragged her tent to an area upwind of the eventual fire. Patrick, who clearly had never been camping before, began setting up his almost at the edge of the fire pit, directly downwind.

"We need to get a fire going, *pronto*," Ruthie suggested, pulling a grocery bag of plastic forks, knives, and plates from the Mazda's trunk. "It's freezing out here."

"No, let's get these up first," Dan countered, hauling his four-person tent out of the trunk. "Once we get a fire going, we won't want to move, and then we'll be tired. Two minutes later, we'll be debating whether or not we can crash in the car overnight."

Jess stifled a chuckle. Throughout undergrad, every time a friend of hers or Scott's invited themselves along on one of their camping weekends, she'd get a refresher course in the "ancient arguments of the tenderfoot," as her father had called them.

"They don't want to elevate the food supplies, they don't want to carry their trash out of the park, they think the best way to start a fire is to use more lighter fluid, they get hungry and immediately want to eat instead of finishing the task at hand, and on and on," he would say. "The good news for you is they'll be the ones eaten by the bear or consumed by the forest fire while you're hightailing it out of there."

Jess smiled at the many memories of camping with her late father that came flooding back. He'd been an avid outdoorsman like his own dad, so the disappointment he felt when Jess's older brother, Rich, showed no interest in "hitting the trail" was palpable. When his daughter, on the other hand, would stand at the back door and cry until somebody let her play in their wooded backyard, this from the time she was one year old, a special daddy-daughter bond was quickly forged.

"Won't putting up the tents take forever?" Ruthie pressed. "We could have a fire going in no time."

"These tents are easy," Dan said, shrugging off the remark. "A bitch to get back in the box later, but setup takes five minutes."

Ruthie was dubious, but Jess, who had the two-person model of the same brand as Dan, knew he was right. The eight tent poles were connected by elastic cords and, when unfolded, snapped rigidly into place. These were then inserted into narrow sleeves along the tent seams to form the tent's exoskeleton: four eight-foot poles to stretch out the square base and four twelve-foot poles to give the tent its arching shape. As the edges of the sleeves were color-coded to match the rods, even a novice would have no problem putting the tents together.

As Jess pulled her tent from its box and laid out the poles, she saw Dan eyeing her progress. There was an unspoken challenge in his gaze.

Accepting it, she quickly stretched the canvas over the ground, putting stakes at each corner. Dan did the same, unfolding his tent poles and hastily slipping them through the sleeves like a fencer's thrust. Jess pulled ahead, but then mistook an eight-foot pole for a twelve and had to draw the rod out again.

"What, are you guys racing?" Patrick asked, having dumped the tent he'd bought off Amazon the previous week, scattering the pieces everywhere. When neither Jess nor Dan replied, so focused on the task at hand were they, he burst out laughing. "Okay, now that's pathetic!"

But the two kept at it, and soon Jess found herself four stakes from victory. She pounded the first two down with her rubber mallet, but then heard the impossible.

"Done!" cried Dan, holding up the empty tent box.

Shit, Jess sighed.

"Wait, you didn't have to put in stakes since you're on the slab," Ruthie interjected. "I think Jess won."

Jess was surprised that Ruthie had her back over her boyfriend, but then heard the hint of jealousy over their little competition.

"Oh, whatever," Jess conceded. "Given how bad his team is about to lose the Reyes case, he could probably use the victory."

Ruthie laughed as Dan scoffed. But then all three caught a familiar sweet scent on the air.

"What?" Patrick asked, puffing on a newly rolled joint. "You're telling me you're not going to want some of this later?"

In the end, it took an hour for Patrick to erect his tent, which Jess took for metaphor, and this was even with Dan's help. By then, a fire crackled in the fire pit, and Ruthie had already started a second round of veggie burgers.

"Mmm, don't these smell good?" she taunted Patrick, who'd already expressed his dismay at the absence of real meat.

"Come on, Ruthie," Patrick whined. "That can't be *all* you brought?"

Ruthie just shrugged as Jess passed her another hamburger bun.

"How many emails did I send around this week, asking you guys to send in any special food requests? And how many did you reply to? And of course, you could've brought your own food. But you'd rather complain."

This shut Patrick up for a while. A few minutes after Ruthie cut him down to size, however, the smell of another joint wafted over to the fire. This time when Patrick asked if anybody wanted some, the other three campers partook.

Four hits in, Jess remembered why she didn't smoke marijuana. Rather than offer a relaxing high, it made her melancholy, like a sorority girl after two glasses of red wine. As happened so often these days, this made her think of Scott and all that gone wrong.

There'd been a plan, and it had gone swimmingly. They'd gotten together freshman year of undergrad at Drexel and stayed together all four years. They ended up at Penn State for law school, and though there had been rough patches, mostly born of the intense pressure and stress exacted by the elite and highly competitive program, they made it all the way to graduation then, too. Even better, they'd both accepted coveted summer associate positions at Jankis, Leonard, Whitehead, and Clarke in Pittsburgh the summer before their senior year and had been among the twenty who'd received offers at season's end. They were going to finish up at Penn, find a place in Pittsburgh, study for the bar, then start at Jankis, Leonard as first-years when they passed.

After that? A decade of hard work, a hoped-for move from an apartment to a house, the inevitable wedding, a hoped-for partnership, maybe kids, and the building of a beautiful life.

But soon after they started at the firm, something changed.

On their first case, Scott, Jess, and several other first-years were tasked with sifting through thousands of boxes of medical files in a documents warehouse. A group of clever doctors had determined how to over-bill for simple procedures by tricking the very computer system meant to root out such malfeasance. And it had worked for going on thirteen years before, unbeknownst to the users, the system was updated by the insurance company and suddenly, every instance of fraud, however minor, was illuminated like a slaughtered sheep on a bed of snow.

Jankis, Leonard took the case knowing that the discovery period would likely be longer than a year and would require a great deal of work done by hand.

Which is precisely why they took it.

"We're all happy now because we just started at a big prestigious firm and are making six figures for the first times in our lives," Scott had announced to the group during a fifteen-minute lunch break (brought in, of course, as there was no time to go to a restaurant), three weeks into the project. "But if you break down how many hours we're putting in on this case, we're making $18.25 an hour. The firm is billing the client over $100 *per associate*. Let's say we're good for $20 apiece in overhead costs — that's still $60 in pure profit for the firm. Who pockets that? The partners, still riding their fat contracts, those fat contracts they signed in the eighties. And they've already told us it's eight years before anyone here will even be considered for a junior partnership, which means twice that or longer for partner. They expect us to quit and be replaced by a fresh crop next year. This is a sweat shop designed to weed out any non–true believers. We drank the Kool-Aid."

At the time, Jess had thought Scott was simply venting his frustration, the twelve- to fourteen-hour days getting to him. But that Sunday, while they worked across the table from each other at a breakfast place near their apartment, Scott put the file he was going over back into his backpack, sipped his coffee, and smiled for the first time in days.

"I'm going to quit," he said.

"What're you talking about?" Jess scoffed. "We knew it was going to be hard. Let the other people quit."

But the look on Scott's face told her his decision was final. The conversation devolved from there, Scott reiterating how this wasn't why he'd gotten into law, Jess telling him that the firm was a means to an end, the thing that would allow them the security and lifestyle they wanted.

"In a time when everybody else we went to high school or college with is just struggling to find work or figure out what to do with their liberal arts degree, we're in the catbird seat."

"It's just not what I want out of life," Scott had replied.

Their relationship ended in that moment, but both parties lived on in denial for the next couple of months, seldom seeing one another except late at night or for a few hours on weekends. Scott tried out the nonprofit sector but soon realized this wasn't what he was looking for, either. Then, after they hadn't slept together for a good month, he announced that he'd met someone, or more accurately, reconnected with someone from his old high school online, and he was going back to Philadelphia to take a job at her father's lumberyard in Berwyn.

Even though he suggested he'd be coming back, Jess knew this was a permanent change. Six weeks later, when he called about driving out to Pittsburgh to pick up his things and maybe "have lunch," Jess made sure it fell on a date where she'd be working and then hired a moving company to box up all of his things so he'd only spend a minimal amount of time in their old place.

When she'd informed him of this via email, he wrote back thanking her and saying that "Laura" would be coming out with him to help load the U-Haul, so he thought they'd be in and out in less than an hour.

Whether the mention of the girl he'd so suddenly abandoned her for was simply informational or a parting shot, Jess wasn't sure. She hadn't responded to the email and didn't hear from him again. Only when she came home one Friday night and the boxes that had been stacked in the hall and living room, as well as a few pieces of furniture, were suddenly gone did she realize he hadn't even confirmed his move-out date.

Rather than bask in the apartment, which suddenly felt twice as big with all the new empty space, she turned on heel, drove to a coworker's birthday party at a bar downtown despite having earlier declined the invitation, and hooked up with a married junior partner from the Denver office in town for business, staying the night in his hotel room.

Anything to avoid spending that first night in the emptied-out apartment alone.

This was ten months ago. Since then, Jess had thrown herself into her work, rocketed her billable hours into the stratosphere by working long hours during the week and on weekends, and tried to take on only projects that would matter during her every-six-months performance review. She'd passed her first one with a "leading the pack" designation, a consulting firm's version of an A, which was somehow better than the "ahead of the curve" grade given to almost everyone else, and she'd celebrated by embarking on a six-week affair with a newly divorced senior partner. Contrary to most men she'd encountered, this one was loath for anyone at the firm to find out about their relationship, likely for fear he'd be seen as jeopardizing the firm's financial position by leaving it open to a potential harassment lawsuit, and this was just fine with Jess. When she'd ended it a month and a half later, mostly due to lack of sleep and its impact on her work, he'd looked downright relieved.

But now, taking yet another drag on Patrick's joint as she warmed herself by a fire instead of in the arms of her one-time "true love," she couldn't help but wonder if she'd made a grave error in judgment by allowing Scott to slip away so easily.

"Are you going to take a hit or just let it burn all the way down?"

Jess snapped out of her ruminations long enough to pass the joint to Ruthie.

"Sorry," Jess mumbled, reaching for her bottle of water.

The winds had picked up, blowing through the tops of the trees with even greater ferocity. As Jess glanced through the nearby trees, she could see the flicker of far-off campfires that illuminated only those closest to the flames. All else was cast in darkness.

"When we were kids, I remember going camping with the Boy Scouts in parks just like this and discovering you could only see firelight from other campsites at night," Patrick slurred, his half-shut eyes suggesting he was stoned beyond recognition. "Figuring if we could see them, they could see *us*, so we'd get naked and see who could jump over the fire pit. I singed a few ass and ball hairs then."

"Christ, Patrick," Dan sighed, even as he stifled a laugh.

"It was worth it the next morning. Our troop would be hiking, swimming, or just hanging out, and every other camper came by, giving us dirty looks. There was this one Scout Camp alongside some kind of girl's camp, maybe cheerleading. Anyway, we did that there, too, but they called the cops. They couldn't bust us because they couldn't identify us off our asses alone. I mean, we were a bunch of skinny teen boys. So the Scoutmasters picked out the only troublemakers on their collective radar and sent them home."

"Let me guess," Ruthie snarked. "It was this grave injustice that sent you into law?"

"Not at all!" Patrick shook his head. "That night, all the girls did the same thing over their campfires, and we started signaling back at ours. Eventually, a rendezvous was arranged, and we had, like, this total orgy in the woods."

Patrick chuckled at the memory, but Jess shook her head.

"I call bullshit on that story. Not that you dumb-ass guys didn't jump over the fires, but that the girls did it the next night. Or that you guys had an orgy."

Ruthie fell silent as Dan sent Jess a funny look. Patrick took Jess's measure for a moment and then shrugged.

"You can think whatever you want to think," he sniffed, unconvincingly. "I know what happened. Just 'cause you wouldn't be up for that kind of adventure…."

"All right, all right," Dan cut in, waving his hand. "Let's take two steps back, okay?"

Jess was about to chide Dan, telling him she could fight her own battles, when something appeared in her peripheral vision. There was a flurry of movement beside one of the campfires to the northwest of their site. As Jess peered through the trees, she could just make out several large shapes racing in front of the blaze. This was followed by distant screams.

"Wait, what was that?" Ruthie asked, suddenly alert.

"Something's going on over there!" Jess said, leaping to her feet.

But the words were barely out her mouth before there was a great crash and the fire was doused, as if by a fallen tree.

"Holy shit!" Patrick exclaimed. "What was *that* about?"

"Over there!" cried Ruthie.

Everyone turned in time to see the same rush of silhouettes pass another campfire, this one closer by, followed by more screams. Again there was a large crash as a tree trunk snapped from its base and collapsed on the fire, extinguishing it in seconds.

"Get in the car!" Dan yelled, grabbing for his keys. "We've got to get out of here!"

Of course, Jess knew he was right, but in her stoned condition, she lost a step, worrying that they should put out their own fire first. She glanced between the campsite's fire pit and Dan's Mazda, as if unable to comprehend which was the more urgent move.

"Come on, Jess!" Ruthie yelled.

As she said this, the surrounding forest came alive. Though the trees had been swaying in the wind, they now quaked and shuddered, as if an earthmover was bashing them aside as it neared the campsite. Two more neighboring campfires were snuffed out by trees as cries of anguish echoed through the night.

Something finally clicked in Jess's head, and she broke for the car. She had only a couple dozen feet of ground to cover, but before she could reach the vehicle, a giant figure lumbered out of the woods, grabbed Ruthie, and lifted her off her feet.

The beast was easily nine or teen feet tall, covered in stringy, matted hair, though the color was hard to discern in the low light. At first glance, it could be mistaken for a bear standing on its hind legs. Only, it had long humanoid legs and arms. Instead of a bear-like snout, its nose was pushed in like a pug. It had wolf-like ears peeking out from behind the shaggy mass of hair hanging from its head, but its eyes were completely human.

And at the end of its feet and hands were great claws, a point driven home by the blood pouring from each currently driven into Ruthie's scalp as she was held aloft, screaming at the top of her lungs.

"Ruthie!" Dan roared, his eyes filling with terror.

A second monster emerged from the woods and grabbed at Ruthie. It caught hold of her feet, and a savage game of tug-of-war began. As Ruthie's shrieks rose to an inhuman octave, her body was torn in two like a piñata struck in the middle. As her entrails rained down onto the campsite, the creature with her legs whipped them over its head as it whooped in victory.

Jess stared into Ruthie's eyes as the life drained from them and her pupils rolled up into her head. Jess forced herself to turn away and climb into the front passenger-side seat of Dan's car. He threw himself in next to her as Patrick leaped into the back seat. The beasts were now coming out of the woods from every direction, tearing at the nearby trees as if to bring them down upon the car.

"What're you waiting for?" Patrick cried. "Let's get out of here!"

But all the color had drained from Dan's face.

"What is it?" Ruthie asked.

"The keys," he began, his voice wavering. "They were in Ruthie's pocket."

"What?!" shrieked Patrick.

Jess looked out the window to the creature still waving Ruthie's lower half over its head. It shifted gears, slamming the legs on the ground like a knight trying to pulverize an opponent with a flail. Only this animal seemed to do it solely for the joy of hearing the wet slap the severed limbs made each time they struck the ground. The chances that such violence hadn't knocked the keys loose, sending them flying into the dirt, the nearby trees, or even the fire, were slim.

"Release the parking brake!" Jess yelled to Dan. "And put the car in neutral!"

"Wait, what?!" Dan asked.

"You've got one of those keyless remotes. When Ruthie drove your car, I'd see her unlock the car, hit the power button, put the key in her pocket, and drive like that. She said she was always forgetting to leave it in the ignition when she had to valet."

Dan realized what Jess was suggesting and turned to stare at the monster pulping his girlfriend's legs, a loose femur already beginning to show out of the top of her blood-soaked jeans.

"You're crazy! You know how close we'd have to get for it to pick up the sensor?"

"No, I don't," Jess retorted. "And neither do you. But I don't see what other options we have."

She pointed out the window. The bipedal monsters had toppled a tree onto their campfire and were celebrating by tearing Ruthie's arms off her upper torso. But they were being joined by several others of the towering beasts, who had concluded their business at the other campsites and were meeting up with the main group. These newcomers, their maws dripping with blood in some cases, weren't content to rest on their laurels. They peered into the Mazda with eyes half-hungry, half-angry. Whatever their motivation, the one closest to the car opened its mouth to reveal strips of human flesh hanging from its canines as its lips twisted up at the corners in a sick parody of a smile.

"Oh, shit..." Patrick whispered.

The beast raised itself up to its full height, stomped its feet, and issued a mighty roar. A moment later, it charged.

Jess didn't wait for Dan to react. She kicked her foot past his, released the parking brake, and jerked the gearshift down to neutral. The Mazda was on a slight incline, but it didn't move.

"Now what?" Patrick bellowed.

"Hold on!" Jess cried.

The car was actually struck by two of the monsters at once, once from behind and the charging beast on the driver's side. The side impact was so great that without the attack from the rear, the car would've surely rolled on its side, imprisoning its occupants. Instead, the blow struck to the Mazda's rear balanced the two attacks, causing the vehicle to lift off its left wheels, only to be shoved forward at the same time. This pitched the front end ahead, slamming it down on its front bumper. Though the collision threw Dan, Jess, and Patrick around the inside of the car, smashing Patrick's face into a window as Jess's forehead smacked into the dashboard, it also rolled the car forward a few feet.

Jess recovered enough of her senses to see they were that much closer now to the creature waving Ruthie's legs. She jammed her finger onto the car's power button to see if it would come to life, but the symbol of a yellow key was illuminated on the dashboard instead.

"Shit!" Jess exclaimed. "We have to get closer!"

"*Jess*," Dan snapped. "If we stay in the car, we're sitting ducks!"

As if to drive this point home, the Mazda was hit again, this time from three sides at once. Jess's door was bashed toward her, the window showering the front seat with broken glass as it exploded inward. The rear window shattered as well, but as it was safety glass, it landed in one heavy piece on Patrick's head, opening up a gash over his left eye.

"Goddammit!" he shouted, trying to push the broken pane aside. "Somebody help me!"

Patrick looked up in time to see one of the monster's fists flying straight for him. Aimed at the center of a bull's eye created by the splintering windshield, the punch cratered both the glass and Patrick's face, shattering his nose, right eye socket, right cheekbone, and upper jawline. As his head flopped backward, he felt pieces of his shattered teeth sliding toward his throat on a river of blood.

"Aw, fubbbb…" Patrick gurgled.

Dan jabbed his finger onto the power button, only for the yellow key to reappear. The car had slowed to a stop again, but worse, the monster carrying Ruthie's legs had wandered farther away.

"Turn the wheel!" Jess shouted, even as she grabbed the wheel herself. "Get us rolling!"

But as soon as they jerked the wheel left, it locked, and they couldn't move it anywhere.

"Shit! What now?!" Dan asked.

"Heeeelb me!!" Patrick yelled from the back seat.

Two of the creatures fought their way to Patrick, shoving each other aside in order to claim the prize. Jess wheeled around in her seat, hitting at the closest monster's paw as it tugged at the safety glass blanketing Patrick. Without a hint of anger, the creature backhanded her in the face, smashing her head into the roof of the car. Stunned by the blow, Jess knew exactly the emotion behind it: *Wait your turn.*

That's when a curious thing happened. The fight at the rear of the car sent both creatures slamming into the rear bumper. This moved the Mazda forward, as if by design. But as they kept at it, bouncing off the vehicle as they seemed to forget about the humans' presence altogether, the car continued to roll.

Dan took a breath, and then punched the power button again. Still nothing.

"Come on, come on…" he whispered.

Jess felt eyes on her and looked right. Standing beside the dying fire was the largest beast yet, easily twelve or thirteen feet. Given its hairless, pendulous breasts, Jess guessed it was a female and, perhaps, the leader of the group.

And it stared daggers into Jess.

"Um, Dan?"

Dan's eyes went wide as the beast let out a guttural war cry and charged at the car.

"We're dead," he sighed.

The other beasts joined in, abandoning their current tasks to focus on the three people in the car. Jess thought she heard Patrick crying and saw in the rearview mirror that the monsters behind the car had stopped fighting and were now staring directly at the young lawyer, saliva dribbling from their open mouths. The other creatures at the campsite lumbered closer until the car was surrounded, their eyes staring in through the smashed windows.

All the other creatures, that is, except the one holding onto Ruthie's legs. This one continued to bash its trophy against the ground, thoroughly amusing itself in the process.

"This is rich," Jess groaned, but then got an idea. "Hey, motherfucker! You done playing with yourself?!"

"Jess!" Dan protested. "What're you doing?!"

"You really think it understands English?" Jess snarled.

She honked the car's horn and flashed the high beams.

"HEEEEEY!!!" she cried, smacking the horn over and over.

The other creatures looked confused at first, but their fury grew. The large female gritted her teeth in anger, raised her fists, and brought them down *hard* on the roof of the car. The other beasts followed suit, raining punishment on the little compact, each blow denting the steel frame.

"Jess…?!" Dan whimpered, rattled to the point Jess thought she smelled piss.

"Wait!" Jess demanded.

And then it happened. The monster holding Ruthie's legs got to its feet and lumbered over, staring blankly not at the humans, but at the blinking headlights. It pushed past a couple of the other creatures until it stood directly in front of the car. Its eyes became slits, focusing on the bright lights as if trying to blind itself.

"The rocket scientist of the bunch," Dan muttered.

Jess ignored him, reaching again to honk the horn. It took only one blast of the horn to enrage the beast. It raised the severed legs and slapped them onto the hood with tremendous force.

"Hit the button!" Jess cried.

Dan pressed it over and over again, but the legs were already aloft again.

"*Shit!*"

Jess punched the horn again, hitting it over and over until the monster raised Ruthie's legs again.

"Get ready!" she said to Dan.

But he responded by screaming. The horn honking had enraged the other creatures, causing them to break ranks. The one nearest the driver's side had grabbed Dan through his shattered window and was actively trying to yank him out. Only his seatbelt kept him in place.

"Dan!" Jess cried, grabbing for her friend.

"Grab my hand!" he said, gripping the belt tightly in hopes that it would stay in place while reaching for Jess's arm.

Jess coiled her fingers around Dan's wrist as she hit the hazard lights with her other hand and continued to pound on the horn. The pissed-off behemoth now beat the car with abandon, Ruthie's ruined lower half spraying its remaining blood on the windshield, thankfully obscuring the sight of torn flesh.

But Jess had a new problem. Every time she released the horn to try for the power button, it threw off the monster's rhythm. It momentarily broke away, taking Ruthie's jeans with it. Jess tried to come up with a solution, but between the roars of the monsters outside the car and the screams of Patrick and Dan on the inside, she felt as if she were being driven out of her mind.

Letting go of Dan's wrist wasn't a decision. One minute her fingers were tight around his arm, and the next they were jabbing the power button. In that half second of time, two surprising things happened. First, the perfectly timed strike turned on the car, Jess's mad gambit that the remote key in Ruthie's pocket would activate the vehicle's sensor paying off. But when she turned a triumphant grin Dan's way, she saw that his head had been torn from his body.

"What the *fuck?!*" Patrick screeched from the back seat, giving voice to Jess's thoughts.

Jess glanced out the window, the she-beast still staring back at her, a triumphant look of her own on the monster's face. Jess stared back a moment longer, then shot a hand over to Dan's seatbelt. Unsnapping it, she opened the driver's-side door and kicked the headless corpse out of the car, much to the surprise of the gathering creatures. She hopped into the driver's seat, slammed the door, threw the Mazda into reverse, and stomped on the gas.

Three of the hairy demons standing directly behind the car took the brunt of the attack, at least one tumbling to the ground on newly broken legs. But the trio was large enough that their bodies still stopped the lightweight compact in its tracks. Jess had anticipated this, however, and threw the car into drive before spinning the wheel, aiming directly for the big female. Again, Jess put her full weight on the accelerator, plowing over the creatures as she raced toward their leader.

The she-beast glowered at Jess, but had the wherewithal to leap out of the way rather than face certain death. The Mazda crashed through the rest of the campsite, clipping other beasts, almost plowing into the downed tree that put out the fire, and running over Jess's immaculately erected tent on its way back to the main road.

But then it was over.

Jess held her breath as she watched the woods on either side of the car, waiting for one of the monsters to come barreling out from the thicket, but none appeared. In fact, the others had disappeared so quickly in the rearview mirror that Jess momentarily wondered if they had existed at all. The sight of Dan's blood smeared down both sides of the driver's-side door shook Jess back to reality. The car was a wreck, and she worried that it would break down before they got to safety. But with every passing second, she put more distance between herself and the ruined campsites. Survival felt less and less improbable.

"You okay back there, Patrick?" she asked as he pushed the spider-webbed glass aside and sat up.

Jess didn't expect the look of death Patrick shot her in the rearview mirror.

"You let him die? Just like that?!"

"What're you talking about?" Jess asked, incredulous.

"You let go of his hand. To save *yourself.*"

Jess couldn't believe her ears.

"I did it to save all three of us!"

"Uh-uh," Patrick said, blood pouring from several wounds across his face. "You got scared and you sacrificed Dan. That was some cold-blooded shit."

Jess whirled around so she could look Patrick in the eye as she delivered her retort, but knew from the second she did so that it was the wrong move. Before she'd even opened her mouth, Patrick's eyes filled with white as they expanded in shock and horror. She turned to see what had sparked such a reaction, fearing the worst.

The Mazda was hurtling down the dirt road at fifty miles an hour when it struck the tree trunk stretched across the track. A pignut hickory, the tree had reached a circumference of twelve and a half feet and weighed over 5,000 pounds. This was more than enough to arrest the car's motion, then send it flipping end over end into the air, getting at least a baker's dozen feet off the ground at the apex of its trajectory.

Jess, however, had been launched from the car a second after it hit the trunk, having neglected to fasten her seatbelt. She still hadn't processed what happened when she impacted with a second pignut hickory, this one upright and alive.

Everything went black.

I

Bones was willing to wait all day for revenge.

He'd woken early to a strange smell and tracked it for half a mile before discovering its source, a female porcupine and her brood of porcupettes. The German shepherd recognized the sow's quills and guard hairs as a threat but decided to toy with it anyway. But as Bones playfully hopped in front of it, the porcupine spun around, swinging its tail at the dog, quills at attention.

Before the larger animal could leap aside, two dozen quills were lodged in his snout. Bones yelped in surprise, tossing his head from side to side. This jogged loose a couple of quills but drove the others deeper. The adult porcupine hastily ushered the juveniles toward a hollow tree trunk and waddled inside. Bones continued to jump in a circle, bleeding and whining as the quills only dug further into the soft flesh of his nose. He dragged his face across the ground and then a nearby tree, but this only exacerbated the problem.

Recognizing the futility of his efforts but still lathered into a fury, the shepherd charged the tree trunk, jammed his snout inside, and barked furiously. The mama porcupine responded by swiveling around again and stabbing yet more quills into the dog's face.

Yipping in pain, Bones backed up, banging the top of his head on the trunk as he did. He repeated his attempts to clear the quills with as little success as before. He kept at this for a few more minutes, at least until the pain became bearable, then crept back to the trunk. As blood and drool trickled down his face, the shepherd flopped down onto his belly to wait out his nemesis.

The previous night, he'd startled a rabbit and, after a brief chase, caught and killed the thing, so it would be some time before he would be hungry again. He could wait all day for the family of porcupines to show.

Midway through the morning, however, the sun became too much for the shepherd, and he fell asleep. When he awoke again a few scant hours later, the scent of the porcupines had somewhat faded. He rose to his feet and moved to the hollow trunk, his eyes confirming what his nose already knew: His quarry had vanished.

Sniffing around the tree, Bones picked up their scent. The trail led northeast toward the river falls. The shepherd was just about to follow in pursuit when he heard a weak voice calling from the nearby brush.

"*Help…me….*"

It had been a while since Bones had heard human speech, and he was momentarily curious. Only, the scent of the porcupines lingered in his quill-filled nose, luring him to their trail.

"*Please, I can hear you,*" the voice continued. "I need *help.*"

Bones turned his head and, in doing so, banged his nose into a nearby bush, tweaking his injury. He yelped and shook his head.

"Hello?" the person queried, now confused.

Bones finally picked up the scent of the human, who was upwind and covered in dirt. But slowly the smells of blood, traces of perfume, deodorant, hair products, and even marijuana drifted over to him. He followed the aromatic cornucopia a few yards from the hollow tree, finding Jess splayed out on her back. She stared up at the imposing animal in fear, her knees and hands grass stained and caked in earth as if she'd already crawled a great distance.

But as the dog lowered its head and sniffed around her body, she breathed a sigh of relief. The beast appeared to be domesticated.

"Where's your owner, boy?" she said, having easily determined Bones's sex from her low angle. "Can you go get them?!"

The shepherd eyed her with confusion for a moment, which was when she glimpsed the quills. She also noted that he wore no collar. Though a little boy named Ryan had put a collar on the shepherd before sending him out into the wilderness a few weeks back in the hope that strangers would recognize the dog as domesticated, Bones had torn it off in a matter of hours.

"Oh, shit. You're alone, aren't you?"

In response, Bones stick his nose in Jess's face and gave her a couple of quick licks, grazing a couple of the broken quills across her cheek. She shrieked and rolled away, but the dog kept after her, thinking it a game.

"Cut it out!" she cried, shoving him away.

But the second she did this, the movement spawned a ripple effect of searing pain through her muscles and nerves. She gasped in indescribable agony, trying to hold her body perfectly still to prevent the feeling from returning. As the tormented internal shockwave ebbed into a throb of manageable misery, she exhaled and looked back at the dog.

"I could use some help on this one."

Jess had woken up at first light and knew immediately that she was in bad shape. She was covered in blood from a myriad of contusions that began at her scalp and ended at her shoeless feet. Her mouth was numb, and a quick check with her tongue revealed a handful of chipped teeth. A gash had been opened on her left shoulder, and her arm looked like it had been painted a reddish-brown. Every breath felt like a heart attack, which Jess took to mean that she had either broken her ribs or pierced a lung, or both. Her back ached as if she'd fallen downstairs. Her legs were cut, but appeared the least damaged, though it seemed like she'd broken a couple of toes.

She was disoriented and dehydrated, and being out in the sun didn't help. She brushed her hair aside and found it was matted with dirt and a large amount of blood that she tracked back to a cut in her forehead. She worried that she had a concussion but had no mirror to check her pupils. She'd risen to her feet and limped along a little, but couldn't keep her balance. Crawling turned out to be the best alternative, despite the wear on her already tormented joints.

Her first move was to try to return to the road to check on Patrick. But the tree trunk and the surely wrecked Mazda were gone. There wasn't a single sign of the accident, not even a pebble of windshield, much less the other law firm associate, which made her wonder how she escaped detection by whoever did the cleanup.

Worried that that "whoever" might soon return, she slowly spun around on her stomach and crawled off into the trees. The ground was littered with rocks and fallen branches, but as her shoes had come off when she'd been thrown through the Mazda's windshield, every time she considered limping along on broken toes instead, she remembered why she'd chosen this method of travel.

But at one point it had just become too much, and she'd collapsed. She'd meant to rest only for a moment or two, but had swiftly sunk into unconsciousness. Hours later, it was the whine of the stricken dog that lifted her back to the land of the living.

"So, what's your name?" Jess asked, realizing immediately that such a question suggested she was worse off than she imagined. "Well, whatever it is, we should be moving on. We need to find something to get those stickers out of your nose, and I need to get to a doctor."

This time when she touched his neck, it was to pet him. Bones let her, making no move to give her a lick in return.

It took the awkward pair two hours to find a trail and another forty-five minutes to reach a map. Jess hoped there was some quick route that would take them directly to the ranger station at the front of the park, but it appeared that her late-night escape had driven her farther into the park rather than closer to the exit.

"There's no way I can do ten miles on all fours," she grimaced, eyeing the map.

At first she'd imagined that once they were on a trail, she'd simply flag down the first hiker she saw, who would go get help. It was a three-day holiday weekend, after all, and any state park within driving distance of Pittsburgh would be packed with tourists. But after an hour had gone by, a bad feeling began to take hold in the back of her head. What if, due to the slaughter at the campsites, the park had been closed as first-responders and cops cleaned up the mess?

Would they know to look for her?

Heck, were they the ones who had towed the car while she slept?

As her panic level rose, she noticed the symbol for a fire tower on the map. It was just off the trail, about half a mile north.

"There's got to be some kind of radio in there," she announced to Bones, who rested nearby. "Think we can make it?"

The shepherd sprang to his feet.

"I'll take that as a 'yes.'" Jess smiled.

It took another hour to get to the fire tower, but on the way, Jess found a large branch that worked perfectly as a crutch. Once the tower appeared over the trees in the near distance, Jess forgot her pain and hopped along faster, Bones dashing ahead and around her, as if in encouragement.

"If you don't have an owner, you can certainly come home with me," she advised the dog. "I wouldn't have made it this far without you."

This was proven again when Jess missed the unmarked path to the tower altogether. Her eyes had been so glued to her objective and the smaller trail was so unkempt that it was easy to miss.

But not for Bones.

Likely scenting off the tower's previous tenants, Bones alerted to the trail head and circled back to Jess until she finally turned. When she saw that it really was a path, she shook her head in alarm.

"Wow. You deserve a medal."

The narrow path through the woods brought the trees and bushes claustrophobically close to Jess and her companion. Before, they'd been on open ground in broad daylight. She'd told herself that if the monsters that killed her friends returned, she'd at least see them coming. But amongst the trees, she wasn't so sure, and freaked herself out imagining every branch to be a hairy arm swinging for her head.

She hadn't wanted to say, much less think, the word "Bigfoot," but this was clearly what had come into the campsite. She generally had no opinion one way or another on the supernatural. She didn't *really* believe in ghosts any more than she did angels, but if pressed to specify why she felt this way, she would've had a hard time with her answer. But Bigfoot? It wasn't even a consideration, as she just assumed everyone knew they were made up, right?

But if presented with compelling evidence, she might've had just as hard a time explaining why she didn't think they existed, either. That evidence had tried to kill her the night before, so all questions were off the table, replaced only with thoughts of survival. Any consideration as to the "how?" or "why?" or "what?" would have to wait.

"Oh, Jeeeez," she sighed as she and Bones finally reached the fire tower.

Her relief at the sight had been replaced by horror as she counted the rungs reaching up to the tower's metal base. She'd known a climb was in store even when she saw it from a distance, but she'd guessed it would be no more than a dozen steps. Fifty-two — she'd counted twice to make sure — seemed downright impossible.

She reached out to grip the first rung and already earned the first jolt of pain, one which spread throughout her entire body in less than a second. She gasped, but was punished by her broken ribs or collapsing lung.

"There's just no way."

Ignoring her remark, Bones moved past her and skittered straight up the ladder. Jess couldn't quite believe her eyes as the dog ascended higher and higher, expecting him to lose his nerve and come back down or slip and fall. When he instead reached the top, put his head against the trapdoor, and pushed upward, she realized this was not the first time he'd made the climb. That hardly made the feat less amazing to witness, but still.

"Okay, Jess," she said, psyching herself up. "If the dog can do it, we can do it."

She soon discovered that going up the ladder was much easier than crawling across the ground or limping with a crutch. By placing the arch of her foot on the rung, she was able to climb without knocking into her toes. She slipped a couple of times, but this simply necessitated the removal of her socks, which she pocketed. The remaining problem, her back, ribs, and shoulder, made it near impossible for her to raise her arms, much less pull herself up. But this soon seemed not such a monstrous problem as she learned to lean her torso against the ladder and only use her arms and hands for balance.

The one time she began to fall backward, she instinctively grabbed for the ladder, squeezing it tight. The misery that followed was so great that tears streamed from her eyes and her body quaked with sobs, making the pain in her chest that much worse.

But as it had before, the agony subsided, and the throbbing numbness slowly replaced it. She waited until her breathing became shallow again and continued.

When she reached the top of the ladder, she tried to lift the trapdoor with her head as the dog had done, but it didn't give. She momentarily panicked, fearing that it was latched from the inside. She tried it a second time and it opened right away, Bones standing beside it now, eyeing her with surprise.

He'd been asleep on top of the trapdoor.

"That offer to come live with me when this over? Consider it rescinded," Jess snapped.

Bones moved to one side as Jess climbed the rest of the way into the tower and let the trapdoor fall back down.

"We made it!" she exclaimed, feeling safe and unexposed for the first time all day.

Four walls, a floor, a roof, and a trapdoor with a latch will do that for a person, she thought.

The fire tower was fairly spartan, like an empty cabin where even the furniture had been removed. What remained was a table nailed into the floor on the west wall of the tower, with a wooden rolling chair, its cushion long since frayed away into nothing, sitting under it. Windows making up the top half of the walls provided a wraparound view of the entire park. In any other circumstance, Jess would have found it almost unbearably beautiful. What looked like an emergency escape ladder, made of yellow nylon rope and plastic rungs, hung from hooks on the ceiling. As Jess stared at it, she realized that, stretched out, it would be nowhere near long enough to reach the forest floor below. That's when she saw the ceiling panel alongside it and realized it allowed access to the tower roof.

The only place in the tower where the windows were obscured was in one corner where what Jess first took to be a large wardrobe stood. Only when she wheeled herself over to it in the rolling chair and opened the door did she see that it was a cramped chemical toilet, like the kind found on construction sites, with no running water, only a dispenser of evaporating hand sanitizer on the wall.

But across from the toilet was a large wooden chest painted green with a metal first aid kit resting on top of it.

"Oh, thank Christ," Jess exhaled.

She opened the first aid kit, finding it fully stocked with Band-aids, packets of painkillers, sunscreen, a bottle of hydrogen peroxide, and a tube of Neosporin. She wheeled this away from the tiny bathroom and came back for the chest. When she opened it, she found four large liter bottles of water. But even better, under the water was a treasure trove of unopened cases of trail mix, energy bars, and beef jerky, alongside large sealed packs of dried mangoes, banana chips, nuts, and even potato chips.

"This isn't for you, is it?" she asked the German shepherd, who had come over to inspect the contents of the chest. "Well, take your pick."

Bones dug his nose into the unopened box of jerky.

"That? Okay," Jess said, tearing open the cardboard and removing the plastic wrap from a few sticks.

Bones devoured everything she handed him, so she unwrapped five more sticks of jerky and dropped them on the ground. She then opened one of the bottles of water, but, finding no bowl, emptied the contents of the first aid kit into the chest and poured half the water into the tin box. The shepherd momentarily eschewed the jerky for the water, lapping up the entire contents of the tin in seconds.

"You must've been thirsty." Jess grinned, pouring the rest of the bottle in the tin before worrying that she might regret her decision later. "*Shit.*"

Turning her attention to her own wounds for a second, she popped the lid off a second water bottle, torn open three of the packs of ibuprofen, and popped six pills right away. She washed them down with a long drink of water, stopping herself before she finished the bottle, but then finishing it anyway. She opened the box containing the energy bars and ate two of those, opening the third bottle of water to wash them down, but this time was careful to only drink about a quarter of the contents.

Taking quick stock of her injuries, she attended the cuts first, pouring liberal amounts of hydrogen peroxide across them, and holding her breath as it bubbled and stung. She then used the hand sanitizer to clean away as much of the dried blood as possible before smearing a topical antibiotic on the wounds to keep them from getting infected. Bandages and Band-aids were next, though she took a quick break to open another half dozen jerky packets for Bones. Returning to her wounds, she used up the Band-aids on her legs and stomach alone, using the bandages on her shoulder and head.

When all of this was done, she eyed her broken toes, already bruised black and yellow, and considered taping them to the middle toe as she'd seen done once to her little brother after he broke his toe playing soccer.

Can't really do much for a broken toe, the doctor had said.

But Jess was worried that she'd do it wrong and the bone might begin to set in a way that would them to be rebroken and reset later. She decided to take her chances that a rescue was soon in the offing. As for her ribs and/or lung, there was nothing to be done there except continue to pop painkillers. By the time she'd finished with the bandages, the ibuprofen had kicked in, and even the thudding headache she'd taken for granted began to ease.

The one unfortunate side effect of all this was that it allowed her mind to wander back to the night before. She thought of Dan, Ruthie, and Patrick; two she'd seen ripped apart in front of her, and the third she assumed dead as well, with a definite case to be made that it was her fault.

For a moment, she thought about what it would be like to face those charges in court and how her white-shoe corporate law firm experience and training would either be a help or a hindrance. At the end of the day, she doubted any prosecutor would pursue such a case, but then remembered her explanation of events would sound like the ravings of a crazy person.

She might be in trouble after all.

Jess had fallen asleep less than five minutes after she'd finished bandaging herself up, having forgotten all about the quills in Bones's nose. After he'd gorged himself, the shepherd had settled in to sleep as well, but found the needles too sharp to get comfortable this time and tore into a couple of energy bars instead. After these proved less than appetizing, he moved on to a bag of potato chips, popping it open with one stomp of his left forepaw before digging in. He wolfed down the entire bag within seconds.

He'd also managed to unscrew the cap from the third water bottle, which Jess, in her haste, hadn't sealed tightly. As the contents splashed across the tower floor, Bones quickly lapped up as much as he could before it dribbled between the slats to the ground below.

Now he was ready for sleep.

He settled again on the trapdoor, the one place in the tower that seemed to draw sunlight no matter what time of day it was, and rested his head on his paws.

But that's when a new smell invaded his nose. It was something he'd encountered more than once out in the woods, a heavy, dank, odor that combined the sweaty musk of a human with the thick fur of a bear. The shepherd had instinctively known to avoid this creature's path and stayed away, though he'd never come face to face with one. That wasn't hard, however, as the man-beasts tended to keep to themselves far to the north in the densest part of the wilderness. To pick up their scent this close to the human campsites was rare indeed.

Bones got to his feet and circled the trapdoor, sniffing around the edges. Opening it was an easy process the shepherd had learned ages ago; claw the worn area near the latch until it raised up, then jab a snout into the opening. But he didn't do this now. Rather, he continued to pace, alerting to the new odor without making noise.

This changed when he felt the tower gently quake, the vibration of someone or something putting weight on the lowest rung.

Bones began to whine.

The intruder either didn't hear or didn't care as it continued to ascend. Bones circled faster now, prancing left and right in giddy anticipation of the newcomer poking their head up through the trapdoor. He yipped as well, then added a couple of low woofs. Behind him, Jess didn't move a muscle, her face suggesting it might take a lightning strike to pull her from slumber-land.

Now the metallic ping of a shoe or claw on the steel rungs echoed up to Bones. The intruder was only a few yards down. The German shepherd inhaled, taking in the full bouquet of the creature's aroma. In addition to the scents the police dog had smelled before, urine, blood, raw meat, and shit were added to the mix. The shaking of the tower had grown in earnest, the ladder-climber's weight being obviously greater than the sum of Jess and Bones.

When it was only a couple of rungs from the trapdoor, it stopped, as if listening, perhaps smelling as well. The hair on Bones's back rose, and a growl so low it almost couldn't be heard rumbled up from the blackest pit within the shepherd's torso. It was a sound of anger, sure, but also one filled with violence, assuring whoever was unlucky enough to hear it that they were seconds from having their throat torn out by a vicious canine that didn't make threats it couldn't back up with horrific savagery.

The cessation of movement now felt less like a quick investigative beat and more like a hesitation or stall. The intruder had plainly not only heard Bones's growl, but had received the message within it. Though by now the shepherd had smelled the several other members of the intruder's party waiting down below, this did nothing to assure the one on the ladder that it would be anything but dead the second it raised the trap.

A few seconds more, and the smell retreated. Bones could hear the would-be invader descending back down the rungs to the forest floor and relaxed a little, retiring the growl even as his stance remained tight as a coiled spring, all potential energy waiting to be launched at an opponent with a barbarity the shepherd reserved only for moments of life and death.

When even the scents on the ground had returned to the woods, Bones finally calmed, sagging back down to the floor to lie down. The dog's eyes were soon closed, but he'd always been a light sleeper. If so much as a mouse passed by within twenty yards of the fire tower's ladder, the shepherd would be on his feet all over again, ready for war.

II

Jess was having one of the strangest dreams of her life when she was violently awakened by the sounds of vicious barking. In it, she was in some kind of affair with Dan, but couldn't figure out at what point in their relationship timeline it was. Her dream self had slept with Dan and regarded the experience as positive, one she'd like to repeat. But even as they walked down the street or the farmer's market or the outdoor mall, whatever the dream location was, she could only see the back of Dan's head. He was wearing a gray sweater, jeans, and a baseball hat. When she said something, he turned around, and she found herself suddenly reliving his decapitation. He would begin to turn, a sly smile on his face, but the flesh around his neck would tear like a popping seam, the head would fall away, and she'd be regarding the bloody stump.

Only, it wasn't bloody, not like in real life. No, in her dream, it was as if his body was perfectly whole and animated, just with a horrific wound between his shoulder blades that looked like the round slabs of lunch meat waiting behind the deli counter. Instead of being cut by an impossibly sharp blade that allowed turkey to be sliced so fine it was translucent, this looked like someone had taken a ragged chainsaw to the bologna log. It was a mess, a dog's breakfast, and as she looked at it, the little flaps of torn flesh around the windpipe blew up and then fell back as the body continued to inhale oxygen into its lungs and exhale carbon dioxide back into the air.

Every time she saw it, she was alarmed, but something in her mind told her she had to play it cool, not call attention to her boyfriend's odd appearance. She'd smile and say something she couldn't hear, and, after slowing to take in the comment or even reply, Dan would face forward again, and the back of his head, ball cap on top, would reappear in her line of sight.

Inexplicably, she inspected the skin around his neck for signs of scarring or even stitches, but saw nothing. The head had completely regenerated.

She was just trying to come up with some way to negate any further attempts at communication between the two, which began with considerations for the bedroom. She guessed he could fuck her from behind, but it wasn't like she'd forget what was back there, the little flaps of skin bouncing up and down as his breathing increased with a nearing orgasm.

She had just come to the staggering realization that the man in her dream wasn't Dan, but Scott, when Bones's bloodthirsty barks woke her with a start. At first she mistook the sound for a rifle shot. As her eyes adjusted to the low light and saw the German shepherd jumping up and down on the trapdoor, its lips angrily pulled back to reveal rows of bright white teeth, the memory of her horrific circumstances washed over her like a cold wave. Was she really in the woods, her body a wreck, her friends dead at the hands of something that didn't exist, and her one companion a dog she'd just met?

Indeed.

"What is it, boy?!" she cried.

But Bones didn't stop. There was a wild look in his eye, as if the dog had just realized that his barking was useless. The intruder coming up the ladder wasn't retreating. In fact, as Jess could just now make out its steps above Bones's oral assault, it kept coming.

Jess climbed back into the rolling chair and pushed herself to the supply chest. The fire tower hardly maintained an arsenal, but she hoped to find *something* to use as a weapon should one of the creatures pop up through the trapdoor. A fire axe would've been ideal, but with none forthcoming, she looked for a hammer, a screwdriver, a spade, a flare gun, *anything*.

Still nothing.

In the first aid kit, however, she spotted an EpiPen, designed to shoot epinephrine into anyone having a serious allergic reaction to a bee sting, for instance, or going into anaphylactic shock. Realizing this would be her best bet, she stripped the wrapper off the auto-injector, twisted the cap off the needle, and placed her thumb on the trigger button. Climbing out of the rolling chair, she crawled to the trapdoor and cocked her right arm, ready to fire the needle into the creature's neck. She wasn't sure what would happen and was leaning toward "nothing at all," given how hard she imagined it would be to pierce the beast's thick hide. Still, she hoped it might at least throw the creature off balance, off the ladder, and to the ground below.

Jess's ears rang, so close was she now to the raging German shepherd. She'd never heard a dog bark that loud, and certainly hadn't been so close to one so angry. What she did know was that without him, she'd be curled up in the bathroom, terrified for her life. That she was instead fully prepared to fight for her life even if that meant taking another was due to the courage the animal lent her by example.

Then something unexpected happened.

"Hey!! Is anybody up there?!" The voice was accompanied by a rapid-fire knocking on the trapdoor. "We need help! *Please*! Open up!"

Bones's verbal barrage didn't change one iota, which threw off Jess. He hadn't reacted like this to her, had been downright friendly, in fact. Did he sense something she didn't? Or was this just his way of protecting what he saw as his territory and, perhaps, his wounded human companion?

Jess made a decision. She pushed Bones aside and looked him in the eye.

"Quiet! Stay back!"

But Bones was in no mood to comply. He kept barking, and a bad thought occurred to Jess. If the person on the ladder was, perhaps, another camper in trouble, couldn't the shepherd's volcanic uproar unintentionally serve up their location to every Bigfoot in the woods?

"QUIET!" Jess said, shushing Bones with a finger. "No barking!"

The shepherd woofed a couple more times, but retreated a few feet back toward the bathroom.

"Who's there?" Jess asked, EpiPen quivering in her hand. "I'm armed."

"Good!" returned the voice. "My name's Alex! I'm with my girlfriend, Christy. There are all these *creatures* in the woods. They already killed…a member of our party. We need *help*."

Jess hesitated a single second longer, then unlatched the trapdoor. It was immediately pushed upward by a dark-skinned twenty-something with close-trimmed black hair, a chinstrap beard, and a dim LED headlamp illuminating his face from a clip on his backpack strap.

"You're a lifesaver!" he exclaimed breathlessly, climbing into the fire tower. He turned back to the starlit emptiness below the trapdoor. "Christy! Come on!"

A second later, a brown-haired girl with a dark tan and athletic frame appeared at the top of the stairs. She had a wide, wicked gash extending from the bottom of her short shorts all the way to the top of her sock. When she saw Jess staring at it, wide-eyed, she shook her head.

"It looks worse than it is. I was under a fallen tree and they got a claw into me, but Kenji distracted it."

Christy looked down at the voicing of the name, and Jess knew he'd A) been her boyfriend and B) was likely dead.

Not wanting to embarrass her, Jess turned to Alex, only to see that his eyes were fixed on the German shepherd standing at attention nearby, peering inquisitively at the newcomers.

"Is your dog cool with this?"

"Not my dog." Jess shrugged. "But he's calmer than he was, so that's a positive."

"Holy shit," Christy suddenly said, kneeling beside Jess. "They got you, too."

"Not quite. Car crash trying to get away. But I sure know what you're talking about. First aid kit has bandages and hydrogen peroxide."

"Thanks," Christy replied, walking over to it. She stopped at Bones, offered her hand to sniff, and then stroked him between the ears. "Hey, boy. It's okay. We're friends."

She reached into Alex's backpack and extracted a stick of beef jerky. She held it out to Bones, who slurped it up in one bite.

"That's a good boy!" Christy said, petting him some more.

Traitor, Jess thought, then realized she was jealous of the attentions of a pretty girl to a dog she barely knew. *You really need to get back to civilization before you lose that other half of your mind, too.*

"He loves that stuff," Jess offered.

"Thought you said he wasn't your dog," Alex retorted.

Jess pointed to the empty wrappers next to the food locker. Alex nodded in understanding, but Jess had already decided he was a prick.

"How'd you find the tower in the dark?" Jess asked.

"We passed it while hiking," Alex explained. "Spent most of the day backtracking and looking for it, as we didn't think we'd get out of here until dark."

"But as we wanted to keep off the main trails, it took a while to orient ourselves," Christy added.

Staying off the trails would've been smart, Jess thought. *Somewhere my dad is shaking his head at his dumb daughter.*

"What's your story?" Alex asked.

"I was with three friends. We'd arrived maybe two hours before, set up camp, were just eating, and then the..."

"Sasquatches," Alex interjected.

"Sure. The *sasquatches* erupted from the woods and tore everybody apart. I was lucky enough to be near the car when it happened, but it went down so quickly. My friends were dead before I could even get over to them, so I got behind the wheel and raced off. They chased after me, but I guess I got just far enough away that they gave up. Then, like an idiot, I hit a fallen tree and got thrown from the car."

In the dim light, she searched Alex and Christy's faces for any sign of disbelief, praying her story passed muster. Alex nodded appreciatively.

"We saw a couple of fire roads on the way where they'd dropped trees, obviously to keep people from escaping. You were probably lucky to get as far as you did."

Jess fell silent. It was morbidly vindicating to think Patrick's death was probably orchestrated by the sasquatches.

Christy poured what little hydrogen peroxide was left over her wound and went to work bandaging it up. She fed Bones two more sticks of jerky, which he gratefully accepted. Alex, meanwhile, used his shoulder lamp to investigate every corner of the tower in search of an electrical outlet. Jess didn't remember seeing one when she arrived, but admitted that she hadn't been looking for one regardless.

"There are antennae on the roof, so they may have been connected to something, possibly near the ceiling."

"Doubtful," Alex countered. "Any radio they had probably ran on batteries. If there's a wire running up the post, the outlet should be near the floor."

Jess was just mentally reasserting her opinion that Alex was a prick when the young man let out a victory whoop.

"Here it is!" he announced, pointing to a spot on the wall mere inches up from the floor. "Throw me the pack."

Christy tossed the backpack over to him, and he shook out the contents. From the ensuing pile, he extracted a cell phone and a cord, which he quickly plugged in. Immediately, a green light burned to life on the phone as it charged.

"You have a phone?!" Jess exclaimed.

"Don't get your hopes up," Christy said. "We haven't had reception the entire time."

"But it's better than nothing!" Alex added. "And we're up high now. A whole different story if we're above the tree canopy. Now we see how long it takes to charge."

It turned out that Alex and Christy were brother and sister and American Indian, not Hispanic, as Jess had initially surmised. The late Kenji, in fact, had been Christy's boyfriend, a young Japanese foreign student that she'd met at Princeton, where she was an undergrad in molecular biology. Alex was on academic probation from Michigan State, something Jess was surprised he was so open about.

"It's fine," Alex said, shaking off Jess's attempt at a pitying look. "The professors ganged up on me. I'm part of a number of different actions, particularly ones that work against the logging in the U.P., and those are the guys who buy and sell every public institution in the state. So, a few protests, a few arrests, and a few court dates later, my profs aren't letting me take make-up tests or hand in late assignments. I drop below a 2.0, and they send me a letter saying I'm on probation. If I don't improve, then I'm out."

"So you came to Pennsylvania?" Jess asked, perplexed.

Alex nodded to his sister.

"He was two days from leading some new protest," Christy said, looking tired and drawn, hardly as interested in this line of conversation as her brother. "We, Kenji and I, suggested he come camping with us."

"An intervention," Alex added.

Jess idly wondered if, in his last moments, Kenji had regretted reaching out a helping hand to his ne'er-do-well, possibly future brother-in-law.

"Are you a big camper?" Alex asked, the question sounding surprisingly like a come-on.

"My dad used to take me all the time. He died a few years back...."

"Sorry," muttered Alex.

"No, it's okay," Jess said, meaning it. "He was a lawyer, so he'd been fighting all his life. When he got sick, I could see it in his eyes. Fight it, and maybe you'll make it a year or a little more, but it'll be nothing but misery. Take nothing but pain medication, and you're looking at maybe two months and a really painful last week. He chose the latter. It ended up being four good months and three painful weeks, but I didn't leave his side the whole time. We hadn't been that close since I was a little girl. We went to D.C., we went to New York. I delayed the start of my senior year, but the school was cool about it."

Alex scoffed. Jess wondered if his anti-logging campaigns were strictly about the environment or hinted at class rage as well.

"What about your mom?" Christy asked, trying to cover up her brother's response.

"She and my dad split when I was six. I didn't know at the time it was unusual for a father to get full custody. Even if he was a lawyer. I found out later that my mom was just a black-out drunk and really abusive. My dad started wondering why I had all these little red marks on me and realized that my mother used to slap me in ways that wouldn't leave a *big* mark, but she'd still get out of her system whatever was bottled up in there."

"Wait, like how?"

"Instead of one big hit, she'd slap me on both sides of my face over and over and over again, but these light slaps that just made me cry and cry and cry."

Jess suddenly fell silent. She didn't understand why she was telling all this to total strangers. This was something she'd barely talked to her father about and only mentioned to Scott the night she learned her mother, then a born-again Christian, was pregnant with another daughter. She'd cried a lot that night. She wondered if being so close to death was just bringing everything back now.

"Sorry," she sighed. "I don't know why I'm talking about all this."

"It's okay," Christy said. "I don't think any of us know how to react to all this."

Jess nodded and ran her fingers through Bones's fur for comfort. The dog had been mostly quiet since he'd slipped down the stairs to relieve himself, an action Alex was against at first even as the shepherd pawed and whined at the trapdoor. The fear was that he would attract the sasquatches, but Jess assured the two others that, given his familiarity with the tower, he'd probably been in the woods for some time, ignoring and being ignored by the creatures. While Jess secretly worried he wouldn't return, he was gone only ten minutes before they heard his claws clinking back up the ladder.

"Maybe it's good to have his scent down there," Alex admitted. "If the sasquatches think he's on his own, maybe it'll cover us up."

Doubtful, Jess thought, but had nothing to base her doubts on.

She was just massaging the base of the dog's neck when his ears suddenly perked up and he raised his head.

"Does he smell something?" Alex asked, heading to the window.

"No, he sees your phone," Christy replied.

Sure enough, Bones was staring right at Alex's cell phone. The red light indicating the dead battery was now green.

"Holy shit!" Alex cried, grabbing the phone. "Time to get out of here."

But as soon as he held it up, he was reminded of the earlier issue.

"No bars. Dammit."

"What about the roof?" Jess suggested.

"Oh, yeah!"

Alex sprinted over to the ladder and rolled down the coiled-up rescue ladder. He climbed it gracelessly, the lightweight frame pitching and twisting under his weight. But a second later, he pushed up the trapdoor on the ceiling and disappeared onto the roof, his heavy footfalls echoing down into the room below.

"Still nothing!" he moaned, moving from one edge of the roof to the other.

"Be careful!" Christy admonished him. "Don't slip!"

Not wanting to miss the excitement, Bones leaped to his feet and raced to the ladder. Jess thought this one would give the dog more trouble, but the shepherd ascended it with ease and joined Alex.

"I wonder if he's some kind of military or police dog," Christy offered. "I've never seen a dog do that before."

"Me, neither," Jess admitted.

"Wait, I think I've got something!" Alex called down. "Holy...yeah! Two bars! Calling 911 now. Have to put it on speaker so I can hold it as high as possible."

The phone beeped three times as Alex punched in the number, then waited.

"Holy shit. Busy signal. Holy *shit. And*, I just lost reception again."

Bones's footfalls were excited, as if happy to be out in nature again, if only through his nose, as he inhaled the various smells of the night.

"Try the ranger station!" Jess suggested.

"You have the number?"

Jess wheeled over to the supply chest and opened it. On the inside of the lid were several phone numbers, the ranger station being up top. She read it out to Alex, who punched it in immediately.

"Ranger station. Is this an emergency?" came a sleepy male voice through heavy distortion.

"Yes," Alex intoned, his voice turning grave. "There have been several injuries and deaths in the park."

"Wait, where are you calling from?" the ranger said, suddenly not so sleepy.

"A fire tower. I'm on the roof."

"Is there a number on the roof?"

There was a pause.

"Yeah, a big black seven."

"What's your name, son?"

"Alex Hazares. I'm with my sister, Christy, and another camper."

"What are the nature of the...you said *deaths*?"

"Yes, injuries and deaths."

"I'll give you one warning. If this is a prank, that's the kind of thing that goes straight to the State Police. We don't fuck around."

"No prank," Alex said, maintaining the strictness in his voice. "There's been an attack. Bears, big cats, *something*. It killed a member of my party and attacked and injured members of the other camper's party."

Good, Jess thought. *Don't say "sasquatch." Anything but that.*

"Well, I wonder if that explains why Chuck and Laura weren't on post when I came on for my shift tonight," the ranger drawled.

Jess suddenly recognized his voice.

"Alex! Tell him the other camper is the girl he let in for five bucks the other night. We were in a white Mazda."

Alex related this, and the ranger's tone changed again.

"Ah, yes. The blonde or the brunette?"

Yep, that's him, Jess thought.

"The blonde," Alex replied, flabbergasted as to the turn in the conversation.

"Okay. You guys sit tight, and I'll be out as quick as possible. If there is a bear or some kind of cat or, more likely, a pack of wolves coming over the bridge from Sault Ste. Marie, we need to get Fish & Game out here *pronto*. You're in a safe place?"

"For now," Alex replied.

"All right. Look for me in about thirty minutes. You're *way* the hell out there."

The call ended. Alex came back down the ladder, followed by Bones, and plugged the phone back in.

"It's already dead again," he explained.

Jess nodded as Bones returned to her side. She knew the next half hour would be the longest of her life.

III

No one spoke much as the trio of humans and the one German shepherd awaited the arrival of the park ranger. At one point, Christy started crying, a memory of Kenji floating to the surface before she could sink it back down. Alex sat next to her, putting his arm around her shoulders. Jess wished for the umpteenth time that night that Scott was there to do the same for her.

Forty minutes in, everyone got nervous, and the stories flowed again. Alex and Christy talked about growing up as "Yoopies," slang for the denizens of Michigan's Upper Peninsula.

"But you actually hear two things – 'yoopies' and 'yoopers,'" Christy explained. "Down state, Lower Peninsula, call us both, but I've never really heard anyone from the U.P. call themselves anything but yoopies. So, I'm a yoopie."

"The short version of growing up in the U.P. is that you're outdoors a lot," Alex added. "*A lot a lot.* They give up on school buses in the harshest parts of winter, and everybody shows up on the backs of snowmobiles. It's crazy."

"Did you ever see a sasquatch up there?" Jess asked.

"Nah," Alex snorted, shaking his head. "There are dozens of 'spirits' in the Potawatomi religion, and they all have some tie to animals, but seeing a sasquatch? Didn't even think they existed until last night."

"Grandma Lil believed in them," Christy said.

"Yeah, but she believed in stuff that was Ottawa, Anishinaabe, Noquet, and Wyandot, too, but not because she was an Indian. She just watched all those cable shows that investigated that shit, and she bought into it. I remember her telling some Canadian that Potawatomi Indians believe in Wakinyan and Unktehi. I was like, 'Grandma, you're thinking of the Lakota, and we sure as hell ain't Lakota. Come on!' But she just started saying that her grandfather told her all about it and she remembered it like it was yesterday. But you'd check the TV listings in the paper, and whatever she was talking about would've been on one of her shows a day before."

For the first time all night, Christy laughed a little.

"Remember that time you ended up feeding a pack of wolves?" she asked.

Alex laughed.

"I believed in recycling food," he explained. "We put the lawn garbage in the green barrel, recycling in the blue, trash in the black. Food was *supposed* to go in the black, but it just felt wrong to me, stuffing it into a garbage bag that would have to biodegrade first. So I just took it to the edge of the woods behind our house and threw it out there."

"Composting without any of the necessary ingredients to actually compost," Jess offered.

"*Precisely*," Alex enthused. "I wasn't so stupid as to put meat out there, but fruits and vegetables, old bread, so on. I didn't know this, but pretty soon we had a substantial population of Norwegian rats out there. Sure, I saw more hawks in the area and heard more owls at night, but I didn't put two and two together. But then some of our neighbors started reporting seeing actual *wolves* in the area, not a common sight in the U.P., and I figured out what happened. I thought Dad was going to skin me alive."

"Mom wanted him to, but he couldn't stop laughing," Christy interjected.

"What did you do?!"

Alex's arms were raised and mouth open, primed for the enthusiastic punch line. But whatever he was about to say was interrupted by an outburst of sudden and feverish barking from the resident German shepherd. Everyone in the tower jumped, but collectively realized who it must be.

The dim glow of headlights whitewashed the corner of one of the tower windows as Alex galloped to investigate.

"It's a Jeep. I doubt those monsters can drive, so this is a good sign."

He turned to the trapdoor, but Jess raised a hand.

"I know we want to think this is over, but we told him it was a bear or a big cat. It's cold-blooded, but there's a chance they followed him right to us."

This stopped Christy and Alex in their tracks, surprising themselves at how quickly they came around to Jess's way of thinking. There lingered an unasked question: Should they even warn the ranger, at their own peril, now that he was here? But they all answered it for themselves, a unanimous decision made without a word spoken.

Bones, however, didn't get the memo, and continued raising a clamor.

"You guys gonna shut that dog up?!"

The voice of the ranger sounded both bemused and knowing, as if campers scared shitless of things that went bump in the Big Frightening Woods were hardly worth climbing out of bed for, much less driving out to some distant fire tower.

"Hey, quiet down," Jess said, signaling Bones.

The shepherd obeyed, sitting down on his haunches to watch what the humans did next.

"Safe to come up?" the ranger asked, though they could already hear him coming up the ladder.

Christy opened the trapdoor and was relieved by what she saw.

"He brought a gun," she murmured to the others.

A moment later, the ranger appeared. He was just as Jess remembered him, a short, paunchy, mustached weirdo who kept the top three buttons of his shirt buttoned, in strange contrast to the lowest three, which looked ready to separate from their buttonholes and fire across the room. A fraying patch on his shirt announced his name as Tom, something Jess hadn't noticed on the drive in. As soon as he was off the ladder and up on his feet, the ranger's eyes went straight to the German shepherd.

"You didn't mention a dog. Who does he belong to?"

"None of us," Jess said. "He found me on the trail. Helped get me this far."

"Well, you're going to need to leave him behind. If we're dealing with wild animals, having a dog in the mix just increases the likelihood of a confrontation."

"He's been a great watchdog through all this, though. He knew you were coming long before we did."

The ranger shook his head, turning dour.

"You know how long I've worked parks? Almost thirty years. What you don't want is to stick a wild card into an already volatile deck. We can always come back for him in the morning."

Jess eyed Bones, preparing a response, but thought better of it.

"Okay," she relented, turning to the shepherd. "You're going to have to stay here."

The dog looked back at her without comprehension, though Jess couldn't decide if he didn't understand or didn't care.

"Can you get down the ladder?" Tom asked Jess, nodding to her injuries.

"I got up here, didn't I?" she snapped back, still unhappy about leaving Bones.

The ranger put a hand on his hip and scowled like an old woman. It was a comical sight, a man put out by a child, but Jess still felt bad.

"I'm sorry. I'm still a little out of it."

"That's okay," the ranger replied. "Let's just try to remember we're all on the same team here."

He glanced from Christy to Alex.

"Ma'am? I think it'd be best for you to go first, maybe stay a few rungs below your friend here and talk her down."

"Don't you think I should go down first?" Alex asked.

"No," the ranger said, shaking his head. "The injured girl...sorry, what's your name again?"

"Jess."

"*Jess*. Tom Winters. *Ranger* Winters. Anyway, she's going to take the longest to get down. If there is some kind of threat out there, the last thing I want is the three of us standing around by the Jeep waiting for her when your wolves or bears or *wolf-bears* decide to attack. Make sense?"

It took Jess a moment to process what the ranger was saying before realizing it was a karmic quid pro quo. She hadn't been any more willing to expose herself to risk when the ranger arrived than he was now.

And from the look on Alex's face, there'd be no protesting the arrangement by him.

"Can I have it?" Christy said, nodding to Alex.

Alex stared at her, as if trying to force her to take back words already said. But she held out her hand instead.

"If I'm going down first, it's the least you can do."

Tom and Jess looked from one sibling to the other, unable to crack this code. Finally, Alex reached into his backpack, took out an automatic pistol, a .38, and handed it to Christy.

"Holy shit!" Jess exclaimed. "You had that the whole time?"

"For emergencies," Alex insisted. "A last resort. We're down to only a couple of bullets."

"Whoa, whoa, whoa," Tom protested, putting a hand on his rifle. "You fired that in the park? I'm sorry, but that's got to come with me."

Alex got to his feet. He was easily a foot taller, if not more, than the ranger. His body language wasn't particularly intimidating, but his size did the talking for him.

"We haven't been completely honest with you," Alex said. "It's not wolves out there, not bears. It's sasquatches. Bigfoot."

The ranger scoffed, then looked to Jess, as if checking to see if she was in on the joke. Only, Jess stared back, deadly serious.

"I saw them, too."

"Oh, come on!" Tom replied. "What is this? Are you people criminals? Just dehydrated? This isn't funny."

The ranger backed up a few more steps until Christy grabbed him. He whirled around, unshouldering his rifle in a single fluid motion. That's when he saw he had almost backed himself right down the open trapdoor.

"Look, if it helps you, just think of them as bears or people in costumes playing some kind of horrible, murderous prank," Christy stated flatly. "Our injuries are real, and we need medical attention. We're not criminals. We just need your help getting out of here."

Tom relaxed a little and nodded.

"All right," he said, then turned to Alex. "But yeah, she should take the gun."

Christy descended the ladder at an even pace, keeping an eye on the tree line even as Alex, Jess, and the ranger did the same from the fire tower. With no moon, the visibility was almost nil. But Christy's eyes had long since adjusted to the dim light and could at least see that nothing was moving directly below her.

When she reached the bottom, she crouched low, taking out the gun and turning in every direction. The coast was clear.

"Okay," she called up to Jess before climbing halfway back up.

In anticipation of the climb, Jess had popped a handful of ibuprofen and even had the bottle in her pocket, anticipating its need later. Rather than shooting pain as she lowered herself onto the ladder, she felt absolutely without strength. Her arms, legs, and back were completely numb and would barely respond to her commands. She would take a single step, and the rest of her body would sag, content to simply fall to the ground rather than balance her frame on the step.

It would have to be all mental.

"You all right?" Christy said, creeping up a couple more steps.

"Yeah," exhaled Jess. "I'd better be."

Slowly but surely, the pair descended a few more steps. That's when Jess got an idea.

"You set the pace. Let me watch you."

Christy was confused at first, but did as requested. She dropped her left foot down a rung, and Jess, watching carefully, mimicked the act exactly. Christy then followed with her right leg, which Jess again repeated.

"Good?" Christy asked.

"Yep. Keep going. Taps into some other part of my brain, and I just follow like a trail dog. Don't stop this time."

Christy nodded and began her descent. It took half a minute for her to get to the bottom. To her surprise, Jess was right behind her.

"Almost here!" Christy announced.

But by now, Jess was completely spent. She had no more energy. As her left foot touched the ground, her body finally gave up and fell backward into Christy's arms.

"Hard part's over," Christy smiled. "Let's get you in the Jeep."

Jess was about to reply when, up in the tower, Bones began barking all over again with the same level of barbarity he'd aimed at any of the newcomers.

"Oh, shit," Christy whispered.

The two women looked into the woods beside them but still saw no movement. But that's when Jess noticed a couple of the trunks didn't look like the others. They were mottled and hairier. When her gaze traveled upward, she saw a pair of eyes staring back at her.

Seeing the same thing, Christy whipped out the gun and looked around for more of the creatures. This didn't take long, as they were surrounded on all sides.

"Oh, *God*," Christy exclaimed, sounding as if ready to pass out.

"Tom!!" Jess called, looking up to the tower. "You've got to get down here!"

But instead of a response, they heard more barking and what sounded like a scuffle. The ladder shivered and shook, and Bones's woofs sounded more and more alarmed.

"Alex! What's going on?" Christy yelled, no longer caring how far her voice carried.

"Christy!" Alex said, sounding fraught. "Get in the Jeep! Go!!"

Christy was just about to voice her confusion at this when a rifle shot echoed across the woods. As the sound bounced off the trees on one side of the clearing around the tower first, it took both women a moment to realize it had emanated from the tower itself.

"ALEX!"

Jess thought Christy was screaming out of concern. But when Alex's body, which Christy had seen being shoved through the open trapdoor, landed a few feet away with a grotesque snapping of limbs, neck, and ribs, she also screamed. Alex's face was caved in as well, but not from the impact. There was a clear entrance wound on the right side of his face and a horrific exit wound on the left side. What was left of his face still had the symmetry to suggest he had been human, though the ragged meat on one side versus the relative intactness of the other gave it a distorted, funhouse-mirror appearance.

Before they could react, however, the sasquatches moved in from the trees. Christy had the presence of mind to swivel around and fire the gun at the nearest monster. It went way wide of the thing's head. She pulled the trigger a second time, only for the gun to jam. As she stared at it in horror and frustration, the beast grabbed her wrist and snapped it like a toothpick. Christy howled in pain, dropping the gun to the ground.

Jess staggered backward towards the Jeep, hoping to get inside and figure out some way to blockade herself within, but the doors were locked. Two of the sasquatches approached her, grabbed her by the biceps, and heaved her face first into the grass in front of the vehicle.

"Goddammit! What the hell...? Hey! Help me up here!"

It was the ranger, calling down from the tower. Jess couldn't see what the problem was, but then heard the vicious growl of her now-favorite German shepherd in the world. Clearly agitated by Alex's death, the dog had decided the park ranger was the enemy and attacked.

"Come on! Hurry up!" the ranger called, more terrified by the second. "He's gone crazy!"

One of the sasquatches hurried to the ladder and climbed up. It did so with such ease and dexterity, as if the ladder had been designed specifically for it, that Jess wondered if Christy's "men in Bigfoot suits" theory was that far off.

The creature had only gotten halfway when the ranger tumbled through the trapdoor, screaming all the way. He landed directly on top of the sasquatch, pulling the beast off the ladder. Together, the two fell backward through space. Seeing that they were heading directly for her, Jess quickly rolled aside as the sasquatch landed beside her, its head striking the front bumper of the Jeep with such force that its neck snapped. The ranger hit the ground next to Alex's body, but as the sasquatch had broken his fall, the portly fellow only snapped his ankles upon landing.

"Aw, Christ!" he spat. "Oh, Jesus Jesus Jesus, this *hurts*!"

A female sasquatch, though Jess didn't think it was the one she'd seen earlier, crossed the clearing to stand over the fallen ranger.

"No, I'll be all right!" the man said, quickly changing his tune. "Look!"

The ranger fought his way to his feet, grabbing the ladder to hold himself up. But as he stood there, grimacing in tremendous pain, there was a second, sickening snap. As he sank to the ground this time, a sharp shaft of bone extended from his ankle.

That's when Jess noticed that there was a *baby* hanging onto the back of the female sasquatch. Only, it wasn't hairy like its mother. In fact, it more resembled a large human baby, maybe an eight-month-old, but one that had already grown to a disproportionately large size, maybe two and half a feet tall. It stared back at Jess, smiled, and then waved.

"What in God's name is *that*?" Christy whispered, aghast.

"I have no idea," replied Jess. "And I don't want to know."

"Please, let me be!" Tom begged, tears and perspiration streaming down his face. "Just leave me here! I won't say anything to anybody! Just let me live to see the end. What if I'm one of the blessed?! One of the survivors? I can *help* you!"

But the female sasquatch was unmoved. With a roar, she kicked the man down, stomped on his neck, and twisted her foot, snapping his neck. With this accomplished, she let out a war whoop of triumph. The other sasquatches joined in, as if momentarily forgetting their other captives. Jess turned to try to crawl away, but suddenly felt the ice cold foot of the female sasquatch on her neck as well.

She looked up and saw its black eyes staring down at her, not in anger, but in challenge. Did Jess wish to fight her for the privilege of escape?

Jess did not. She sank back onto the ground, and the sasquatch stepped away. As she did, Jess caught sight of something falling off the ladder in her peripheral vision. When she looked, she saw that it was Bones, who had somehow crept a little ways down from the tower and had launched himself at the nearest sasquatch.

"Oh, boy," Jess muttered, doubtful at the dog's prospects.

But the sasquatch whose shoulders Bones landed on was taken completely by surprise. It raised its arms in anger, swatting at the dog and roaring its disapproval. This second action was its downfall, as Bones sank his teeth into the creature's lower jaw, yanking it until it was dislocated from the sasquatch's skull, hanging limply on one side. As the monster groped at it with its fingers, Bones bit four of the digits off its hand and, with a quick second chomp, bit into the brute's throat.

The man-beast's eyes went wide as blood spurted out of the wound, splashing on the ground, the tower ladder, and the pile of corpses, which the sasquatch would obviously soon join. The strength of the fountain of blood ebbed quickly with the dying of the creature's heart, and it keeled over, spread-eagled on the ground.

By the time this happened, Bones was already on his way to the next sasquatch. This one the dog attacked awkwardly, trying to climb up to its neck by leaping straight up its body. The sasquatch managed to get in a glancing blow, which tipped the shepherd off balance. But it wasn't a total loss, as Bones managed to sink his teeth deep into the monster's abdomen. The sasquatch twisted and stomped, but the dog hung on, even with all four feet swinging in the air. Rather than shake the canine's teeth free, the monster only succeeded in forcing Bones to tighten his grip.

Unfortunately for the creature, the shepherd's razor-sharp fangs soon cut deep enough into flesh to pull away everything they had stabbed into. Bones tumbled away from the sasquatch, yanking fur, skin, muscle, and pieces of the creature's large intestine with him.

Worse, the dog hit the ground running.

A second later, and the newly disemboweled sasquatch joined the other dead on the forest floor.

"You just found that dog while walking around?" Christy asked Jess, incredulous, as they watched Bones tear the genitals off another sasquatch.

"Yeah," Jess whispered. "Glad he didn't eat *me*."

Bones had just sunk his teeth into the tender inner thigh meat of another sasquatch when an elderly woman flanked by two other sasquatches stepped into the clearing. She was tiny, barely four feet tall, had almost no hair, was so tanned her skin was the color of dried blood, and wore buckskin clothes.

"*Enough!*" she roared in a voice surprisingly threatening for someone with such a meek appearance.

The sasquatches all turned to her, save the one whose eyes Bones was currently tearing from its skull. The old woman nodded to someone behind her, who stepped forward. It was a young boy not more than nine or ten, wearing similar clothes. The child raised a wooden bow and strung an arrow. The boy stared straight at Bones and loosed the arrow. It made a whistling sound as it flew from the edge of the woods into the soft meat of Bones's haunch. The dog was thrown off the dying sasquatch's head, propelled a good ten feet by the arrow's impact.

"Oh, no!" Jess cried.

She tried to get to her feet, but the female sasquatch shoved her back down. She struggled, but soon found her face being ground into the dirt. When she couldn't breathe anymore, she stopped fighting. The sasquatch took her foot away. Jess glowered at her, tears of shame and helplessness glassing her eyes.

"Let me go!" Christy yelled. "What're you doing?!"

One of the sasquatches had lifted Christy off the ground and thrown her over its shoulder. It moved amongst the trees lining the clearing as others gathered the dead. The old woman and the young boy moved to Bones's side. The shepherd was trying to stand, but blood sluiced down his leg and through his toes, pooling on the ground beneath him. The arrow was in deep.

The old woman kneeled beside the shepherd even as the dog grew woozy from blood loss. Her hands shot out, grabbing Bones around the neck. He pawed at her but didn't even have the strength to push her away.

"I am sorry, *erhar*," she said, then nodded to the young archer.

The boy leaned down, put a cloth around the arrow at the point where it entered Bones's leg, and pulled it out. The arrow was a bolt with a small pointed tip as opposed to one with razor-sharp notches meant to ravage flesh when pulled out. When he took the cloth away, more blood poured out, and Bones's lethargic yet bloody maw opened and closed listlessly. A second later, and he slipped into unconsciousness.

Jess felt a pain in her heart unlike when Patrick, Ruthie, or Dan were killed. They died panicked and afraid, as she had been. The shepherd had died defending his new friend, risking his life over and over until he was shot down.

"I'm sorry, boy," Jess whispered as another sasquatch lifted her onto its shoulder.

As she was carried into the woods, Jess stared back at the only member of the party left behind, the German shepherd, until she couldn't see him anymore or even lie to herself and imagine that he was staring back.

IV

By the time the sun came up, the walk had become excruciating. Jess had passed out at some point in the night, but wasn't sure when. It couldn't have been for very long, however, as when she woke up, it was still dark. The ibuprofen had worn off, and now every step the sasquatch took sent a ripple of pain through Jess's body.

But as much as she wanted to cry out, the young lawyer refused to give the clan of sasquatches and humans the satisfaction. Besides, she figured the gruff beast that had her over its shoulder wasn't being punitive as it roughly stomped through the woods, causing Jess to bounce against its (she couldn't tell the gender from this angle) hairy back or slam into a passing branch. A protest would likely fall on deaf ears.

Jess counted at least a dozen sasquatches, with twice that number of humans. The sasquatches dwarfed the people, some barely coming up to the monsters' waists. As their clothing looked like a Hollywood director's idea of American Indian apparel, she was predisposed to believe that was what they were. But that wasn't the case. Rather, they looked like Caucasians to her eyes, albeit ones who had grown up outdoors, earning deep tans that leathered the skin of even the youngest members of their party. Instead of feeling like a frontierswoman taken hostage by those whose land her family had encroached on, Jess imagined she was being hauled off by some cult of sun worshippers out in Central California.

Albeit ones that had established some sort of alliance with sasquatches.

At one point, the sasquatch carrying Jess stopped to urinate. When it did, the creature carrying Christy *and* the corpse of Alex, one body over the left shoulder, one over the right, moved past.

"*Christy!*" Jess hissed.

But Christy's eyes, which were open, remained fixed on her brother's corpse. In only a few hours, his face had become puffy and bruised, but Jess realized that was because of all the blood that had drained into his head in the absence of a pumping heart. He was virtually unrecognizable.

"Christy," Jess repeated, knowing she taunted fate.

"He's dead," Christy whimpered. "He's really dead."

She couldn't see Christy's face, but her voice told her the whole story. She hadn't slept, she'd been forced to stare at Alex's body for hours and hours, and she'd about cracked.

"Christy, listen to me…" Jess blurted out, but the sasquatch carrying the other girl was already out of sight.

Jess sighed, having figured that once the adrenaline wore off, Christy would crash. She wondered if she'd be able to try to pull her out of it once they reached their destination.

Wherever that was.

At first light, she'd glimpsed Mount Whittlesey. From the fire tower, it had loomed large to the northeast. Here, it was only a few hundred yards away. But as the sasquatches climbed what appeared to be old game trails through the rocks, Jess noticed they'd stopped ascending at one point and were simply traversing the cliff side. When they came down the other side, she saw a vast forest stretching all the way to the horizon, likely the Allegany, which continued up into New York State. She wondered what kind of range the sasquatches must have, given they'd already traveled several miles.

Then, around midday, the group stopped. They didn't seem alarmed, just at the end of their journey. The waiting continued until an odd noise, like the honking of the world's largest goose, echoed out to them. One of the sasquatches raised its hands to its mouth and returned the call, but in a short series of squawks that almost sounded like Morse code. A single long honk in return, and the party kept moving.

Jess had glimpsed a large hill in the distance at some point while rocking back and forth over the sasquatch's shoulder. She kept trying to catch a look at what lay ahead, generally through glimpses past the monster's swaying arm. At first, the distant hill looked like any other ridge or promontory, but the closer they got, the more Jess could make out what appeared to be a loose grid of cave entrances. Only, as each was situated under rocky outcroppings or in crevices, strategically obscured by shadows, trees, or scrub, she realized they were manmade. Sure, to a casual observer on land or in the air, they could pass for natural formations. But when carried toward them by a notoriously secretive cryptozoological phenomenon most agreed was a myth, their true nature became obvious.

They were only a couple hundred feet from the base of the hill when the old woman, who rode on the shoulders of one of the sasquatches like a child, raised a hand to bring the caravan to a halt. As she did, several other humans and sasquatches emerged from the caves to see what the party had returned with.

A man in perhaps his late twenties and wearing not a stitch of clothing materialized from one cave, sprinted over to the old woman, and embraced her. At first, Jess thought he was her son or grandson. But then she kissed him back in a way that suggested a very different kind of relationship.

"Thank you, my love," the old woman said, patting the young man on the cheek. She turned to the sasquatches carrying Jess and Christy and nodded. "Put them on the ground."

The sasquatches did as requested, and Jess thudded to the hard-packed earth with a shriek of pain. She scrunched her face, trying not to betray just how badly she was hurt, fearing an end similar to the park ranger's. Two buckskin leashes were thrown around the two women's necks, and their hands were roughly brought behind their backs to be tied as well. Jess gasped as the rope was tightened at her wrists, aggravating the gash in her left shoulder.

The two were then shoved forward and forced onto their knees.

The old woman approached, giving each an appraising look. Jess thought the woman spent an inordinate amount of time eyeing her breasts and hips, barely looking her in the eye. It was as if she was a cow at the State Fair rather than a recent victim of a kidnapping. When the old woman finished giving Jess the once-over, she eyed both.

"Have either of you had children?" she asked.

"No," said Christy.

"No," replied Jess, wondering if she should've said the opposite.

"Don't think, simply answer," said the old woman sternly, reading Jess's mind. "This will be easier on you if you comply."

"If I don't have children, does it make it easier to kill me?" Jess retorted.

"If you hadn't noticed, it would be the easiest thing in the world to kill you," the old woman replied matter-of-factly. "But if you answer my questions to the best of your ability, I can offer you so much more than you could ever imagine."

Jess eyed the woman with incredulity, but saw only a gentle earnestness in the woman's eyes as she stared back, definitive proof that she was completely insane.

"May I continue?" the old woman asked.

"By all means," Jess replied evenly.

"Have either of you ever had an abortion?"

"No," said Jess.

"Y…yes," Christy replied.

"When?"

"When I was seventeen," Christy admitted, though she was staring at the ground.

"Was it healthy?"

"I don't know. I terminated it when it was still in the first trimester."

"Were there complications during the abortion?"

"Not that I remember."

This seemed to satisfy the old woman, even please her.

"I know that couldn't have been easy to admit, but I appreciate your candor," she said. She then plucked a small blue plastic case from her pocket. "Does this belong to one of you?"

"Not me," Jess said, recognizing it as a birth control pill case.

"You don't use birth control?" the old woman asked.

"I've had a violent reaction to every type of pill I've tried," Jess confessed. "I eventually gave up."

"But remained sexually active?"

"I did. But I kept a pretty close eye on my cycle," Jess continued, the back-and-forth having reached the plane of the surreal. "And I tend to stick with partners I trust to wear a condom."

This seemed to satisfy the old woman, who turned her attention to Christy.

"Those are mine," she said.

"Are these new?"

"No, I've been on the pill since soon after my abortion."

The old woman signaled one of the sasquatches standing behind the women. It stepped forward, gripped Christy's head under the chin and beside her left ear, and bloodlessly snapped her neck before the girl even realized what was happening.

Screaming at the top of her lungs, Jess launched herself sideways as Christy's body dropped limply to the ground. Pain exploded from points throughout her body, but she ignored it all, wriggling in the dirt as she crawled away on her knees and shoulders. Dirt kicked up into her eyes, nose, and mouth, but even then she forced herself forward.

The sasquatches and humans reacted as one, propelling themselves after Jess, ready to fling her back at the feet of the old woman. But their leader again stopped them with a lift of her hand and moved a few feet ahead of Jess.

"What you need to understand is that you, your friend there, the people you grew up with, your family, everyone in your day to day life, is about to die," the old woman calmly explained. "Humanity is on the precipice. A great apocalypse is on its way, and very, very few will survive."

The old woman paused, giving the young lawyer a moment to absorb this. Jess could have had a thousand moments, however, and barely scratched the surface of why what she was being told was just about the most ludicrous nonsense anyone had ever tried to shove down her throat.

"The good news is, by a quirk of fate, or actually genetics, you're looking at what will likely be one of the larger pockets of survivors."

"You're some kind of 'chosen people'?" Jess scoffed, spitting dirt. "That's what you're telling me?"

"That would imply a choice was made," the old woman said. "And that is the opposite of what happened. But for us to survive in the next world, and by that, I mean our children and children's children, we must become strong. We are being caught almost unawares at a time when we have allowed ourselves to become weak in ways we didn't even know."

As the old woman continued, Jess let her eyes travel up to the caves. It was only then that she recognized one of the pairs of eyes staring back at her.

"Oh, my God! Patrick?"

The crows had arrived at first light. There was only one at first, but its calls, a guttural clicking in its throat, soon brought over a dozen. Each lighted on a branch above Bones's body, which lay on its side in the clearing, for a few seconds, but then glanced around, as if waiting to see who might go first. The stench of blood hung heavy in the air, as far more had been shed alongside the fire tower than had issued from the German shepherd. The flies had beaten the crows, as they always do, and buzzed from drying pool to drying pool, unable to differentiate or uncaring as to which had flowed from human, sasquatch, or dog.

In the end, two crows flew down at the same time. The dog's eyelids weren't completely closed, revealing the tantalizing prize: two watery orbs that were as much delicacies to the birds as the testicles would be to a passing fox. The first crow had landed about three feet from Bones's snout, while the other had chosen a spot just beside the dog's tail. This one cheekily clamped its beak on the spiky clump of hair on the tail's tip, trying to spark a reaction. When there was none, it hopped closer.

The first bird was faster, however, jogging along, then flapping its wings to go airborne for the last several inches or so. When it landed directly in front of Bones's face, it lowered its head to stab its sharp, 6.5-centimeter beak directly into the dog's retina. This would cave it in, allow for easier extraction.

But before it was able to do so, Bones rolled onto his stomach, opened his jaws, and fired his snout forward, biting down hard on the bird's neck and upper torso. The crow's hollow bones splintered like a handful of dry pine needles, its ribcage piercing its heart to deliver the death blow.

The second crow hopped backward and spread its wings. Unlike smaller birds that could get aloft relatively easily, it usually took a crow a few flaps to gain even a couple of inches of altitude. The great black bird was hovering a foot off the ground, a flap away from beginning its ascent in earnest, when Bones whirled around and caught its wing in his mouth. Violently jerking his head back and forth, the shepherd soon tore the wing off the crow's body, then pinned the rest of the dying bird's body to the ground. Another flash of teeth, and the bird's head was severed from its body as well.

The crows in the trees watched in relative silence. A couple on lower limbs fluttered upward but soon landed again, their black eyes fixed on the carnage below. They would soon lose interest and move on, but not before waiting a few minutes to see if the large mammal below would collapse from his wounds again, making him a valuable prize all over again.

Bones devoured the birds quickly, tearing off the feathers, spitting them aside, them ripping in the meat. It was hardly enough food to satiate the dog's hunger, but it was better than nothing. Once every edible piece had been consumed, Bones turned to the tiny bits of crow blood staining the soil and lapped them up as well.

The pain in the German shepherd's back leg was tremendous, worse when he tried to put weight on it. He whined for a few minutes as he attempted to walk, staggering around the clearing with the haunch raised, limping along on three legs instead of four. Unfortunately, the uneven ground and the occasional rock made this near impossible, as time and time again the dog's brain told its body that balance could only be achieved if the injured leg touched the ground. Six or seven jagged needles of pain being stabbed directly into Bones's spine later, and he learned to keep the foot aloft.

He smelled food up in the fire tower, but could barely get up four rungs of the ladder before hopping back down to the ground. He whined a few more times, but then stuck his nose in the dirt and sniffed.

The scent of the sasquatches was all around him. They'd left a while ago, but their smell was so distinctive that it was impossible to miss, particularly for a dog like Bones. He sniffed some more and smelled the humans as well, both the dead and the living.

The crows followed the shepherd from above as the scents led him north. As he hopped along, the wound in his leg began to bleed again, a thin trickle that the dog barely seemed to notice, but whose odor excited the nerve endings in the birds' noses.

They would be patient, wait for the dog to falter, then swoop in as he lay dying.

Patrick had broken a ridiculous amount of bones in the car crash, over a dozen, but they were all contained within his right arm. His fingers had been twisted and splintered, his knuckles shattered, and his wrist snapped. Both the radius and ulna of his forearm were broken in multiple places, and his humerus was fractured as well. Even worse, the humeral head had been chipped and yanked from its socket.

"It was the craziest pain," Patrick told Jess. "It felt like I was wearing this heavy plate armor over my arm, like something that over weighed two hundred pounds, and every time I moved, it pressed down on me as if trying to crush my arm flat. The car had crumpled when you hit the tree, and somehow my arm got caught between the door and the roof as they crumpled together. No other part of me was scratched."

"That's awful," Jess exclaimed. "I'm sorry about that."

"Like it was your fault?" Patrick asked. "Don't be. Besides, I could've been killed, and I wasn't. That's a bonus in my book."

After her back-and-forth with the old woman, Jess had been led into one of the caves. Since they were barely lit by beeswax candles, the young lawyer had the feeling of descending deep into the ground rather than into a mountain. In a large cavern lit with dozens of candles, the ceiling scorched and yellowed by what looked like centuries of the practice, Jess was made to sit, provided with food (corn, roasted deer meat, cranberries, and squash), and told to wait. A moment later, Patrick was ushered in. He sat beside her and was also handed a plate.

Then, to Jess's surprise, they were left alone.

"So what happened when they found you?" Jess asked, continuing her line of questioning.

"I thought I was stuck in the car, but they tore it apart like it was nothing," Patrick explained. "They put something under my nose, and I was out a second later. When I woke up, I was here. The food's fine, so you know."

Patrick pointed to Jess's plate. She hadn't touched a thing.

"It's crazy to say it, but I'm not hungry. Not after what they did to that girl out there."

"I hear you," Patrick said. "But they probably did her a favor."

Jess nodded, but then realized Patrick didn't mean it the way she initially thought.

"Patrick…?"

"The old woman, Orenda, has seen the future," Patrick explained. "The end of the world is coming. Not the whole planet, mind you, but a correction. Humans will no longer be the dominant species. Not by a long shot. In fact, we might not even survive in the new world. What *can* survive are these things, these *sasquatches*."

Jess stared at Patrick as if he'd gone mad. He sighed.

"I know what you're thinking."

"Oh, do you?" Jess asked, bemused.

"'The Stockholm Syndrome kicked in fast with Patrick,' right?" he joked. "But then you'll spend some time here, start to see things that don't make any sense whatsoever, and you'll begin to believe, too."

"Believe what? In the end of the world?"

"Oh, yeah. And a lot more."

Patrick related the story as he'd been told it. The sasquatches were of a tribe that predated most Native Americans. The Indians knew about them but stayed away for the most part, allowing them to occupy the remotest areas. This was just fine by the sasquatches, who wanted nothing to do with humans anyway.

Then at some point in the seventeenth century, other humans arrived. The sasquatches were warned of these people by intermediaries, mostly among the Iroquois. Then the invaders moved farther into the country, and the sasquatches were pushed into even smaller pockets, leaving the woods for the hills and, depending on the region, the mountains to the far north. A number now, apparently, existed north of Hudson Bay in Canada, almost in the Arctic Circle. Another band existed in the Rocky Mountains. Still another was rumored to have gone south and now lived along the remotest parts of the Amazon in Brazil.

"But what about the humans here?" Jess asked, now eating while actively wondering how this would tie into a foreknowledge of the end of the world.

"That's the fascinating part to me," Patrick admitted. "Apparently, in 1692 during the Salem Witch Trials, a handful of the accused from three or four of the villages closest to the frontier decided to escape into the woods and face the Indians rather than the persecution of the witch hunters. To hear them say it here, some of these witches actually did have some powers in the realm of hedge magic. The Indians they encountered had no interest in sheltering them, but suggested they might find a home amongst the sasquatches, particularly as neither had an interest in being discovered. The groups met at the Susquehanna River, apparently an almost formal event, and an agreement was arrived at. Orenda jokes that it was the one treaty made between Indians and white people in North America that's still good."

"Wow. So Orenda is a descendant of Salem witches?" Jess said. "This will totally help make my witch costume this Halloween that much more authentic."

Patrick didn't grin at the joke.

"You understand that, now you're here, you can't leave."

"That's bullshit!" Jess joshed, feigning indignation.

"*Jess*," Patrick said, leaning in. "I'm trying to tell you that you and me? We've got less than a year to live. Things are falling apart. Those sasquatches that attacked the campsite? They were led by a female named Onatah who had split from Orenda to lead the raiding party. She knew time was running out and drastic measures had to be taken. They think she wanted to try to kill all the humans before they could infect the tribe. They have rules about exposing the group to the outside world, but she seems to have gone bonkers and taken a number of her compatriots down with her."

"Is she still out there?"

"No, they hunted her down and killed her and her compatriots. There's no way these killings can be covered up for long, not even with the most sympathetic of park rangers selling stories about gas leaks or toxic clouds of concentrated CO_2 erupting from a nearby lake."

"So why do they keep killing?! I watched Orenda and her band kill a park ranger *and* Christy."

"Christy was collateral damage. What they need are people like you and me."

"For what?" Jess asked. "To be their slaves until we all die on the Day of Armageddon?"

"They need me to impregnate their women, both humans and sasquatches," Patrick said evenly. "They need you to carry the baby of one of their champions, this guy Tadodaho."

At first, Jess didn't think she'd heard right. This was clearly the punch line to a long and elaborate joke Patrick had spent the past five minutes laying out to her. But then she saw that he was dead serious, and she felt all the blood drain from her face.

"They want us to have *sex* with them? What the *fuck* are you telling me?"

"I'm telling you that buried in their DNA is this one gene that gives them immunity from the coming plague. But after centuries of inbreeding, the rest of their collective gene pool is getting fairly weak. They need an infusion of new blood or, in this case, foreign strands of DNA to keep their species alive past the apocalypse."

That's when Jess realized just how calm Patrick had been throughout this explanation. He was popping pieces of roast meat in his mouth in between gulps of water and bites of corn on the cob. There was a cocksureness to him that she hadn't seen in the young man in any of their previous interactions.

"Holy shit," Jess whispered. "You've already had sex with them. You've *already* had *sex* with...*them*!"

Patrick nodded as if admitting to nothing more than nabbing the last donut from the break room.

"I have, and was honored to do so."

"How many?"

"Only four, three sasquatches and one young woman. One's actual sperm count goes down in between too much to count for much, so I have to rest in between, eat, and recover, and so on. Then they'll bring the next one who is ovulating to my chamber."

"Then what?" Jess asked, incredulous.

"We copulate."

Jess felt like throwing up.

"Jess! If you bear Tadodaho a child, they'll treat you like a queen. Don't you understand? They've got five or six other women here, runaways and lost hikers mostly, who are trying for the same thing, but they're not having much luck. Time's running out for a human to bring a baby to term before the end of mankind. I'm telling you. This is a good thing!"

Jess's feeling became a reality. The entire contents of her stomach launched from her mouth and landed on Patrick's lap. As she coughed and choked, he merely patted her back.

"My first reaction, too. I mean, in the beginning, it's like having sex with a Wookiee. But then it becomes so much more, and you realize just how lucky you really are."

Jess felt dizzy, the room spinning as she tried to raise her head. But some things were just not meant to be, and she passed out on the table.

It was late afternoon when Bones came across the yearling, just upwind. Its herd was about thirty-strong, but the young male had strayed, staying too long at a berry bush even as the rest had moved along. As the shepherd neared, the yearling raised its head and turned its ears half a dozen times, as if sensing the dog's presence. But after a few seconds, it returned to its meal. At one point, it even took a few steps to follow the others, but then ducked its head to the ground and lapped up a few fallen berries.

Easy pickings.

Bones closed the distance between himself and the deer in seconds flat. The animal didn't even have to look up to know danger was approaching. One moment, its nose was to the earth, the next, it was galloping off through the trees.

But the shepherd's injured leg meant a chase was out of the question. Though he'd normally prefer to strike his prey in the neck, hoping to snap it and prevent a drawn-out fight, the yearling was too fast. Instead, Bones got as close as he could before the deer managed to get up to speed and lunged for its leg, knowing he only had one chance to get it right. His jaws found the deer's right rear leg and bit down hard, snapping the bone. In the same beat, the shepherd threw his weight to the ground and twisted his head, halting the deer's forward motion as he dislocated its leg.

Once the deer was on the ground, Bones leapt to his feet just as the yearling twisted its head around in an attempt to gore the dog with its short, albeit spike-covered horns. The shepherd rolled left and shot forward like a wrestler, gathering the deer's throat in his mouth before pulling it out in one move. The yearling shuddered twice, its blood steaming off Bones's maw, and died.

The shepherd stripped flesh from bone and began to feast.

V

When Jess came to, she was in a different chamber altogether, this one smaller than the one in which she'd met Patrick. There were also far fewer candles, giving the place a more haunted feel. Rather than feel like a cave, though, Jess, on a bed of animal skins, imagined herself in a medieval castle. She looked up and saw that the ceiling had been painted as a star field, like something a child or developmentally arrested college freshman might have above their bed.

She couldn't see past the tall doorway into the tunnel beyond, but soon realized that was because one of the sasquatches sat there, blocking almost all light.

"You are awake?" the sasquatch asked.

"You can talk?" Jess replied, realizing it was the first time she'd heard a voice emanate from one of the beasts.

"Yes," it said simply. "It is not something that comes natural to us. We communicate in other ways. Actual speech feels antiquated."

"Ah."

The sasquatch smiled in what looked to Jess like a self-deprecating way.

"How are your injuries?"

Jess started. She knew instinctively that she should be in pain, but there was none. She moved around, even sat up, but felt fine. The sasquatch nodded.

"It was in your food. I'm afraid some of it upset your stomach, but it also served to heal you."

"No, I'm pretty sure I threw up for other reasons," Jess assured the sasquatch. "But maybe that's why I passed out. You are Tadodaho, aren't you?"

"How did you guess?"

"I was told I'd be having sex with someone, and I wake in a bed," she said, then drew back the animal skins. "Also, I'm naked."

Tadodaho nodded, then pointed into the corner.

"If you're cold or would simply be more comfortable, your clothes are over there."

Jess looked. Sure enough.

"Does that mean we've already…copulated?"

"No, in fact," said Tadodaho, getting to his feet and nearing the bed. "Your clothes were covered in blood and bile. I washed them for you and dried them over burning rocks. You should find them in good condition except for the damage done out in the forest."

This wasn't what Jess was expecting. Tadodaho moved closer, saw the incredulity in her eyes, and looked down again.

"What is it?" she asked.

"It will sound horrible."

"More horrible than what I've witnessed already?"

"Possibly not," Tadodaho replied. "This is just difficult for me."

"The slow buildup and self-rationalizing you have to conjure to force yourself on me?" Jess offered. "Or trying to talk me into believing it's not like that?"

Tadodaho snorted.

"No, the act itself. It's not something I can comprehend."

Wait…what?

"The act of what, precisely?"

"Having sex with a human animal. I am attracted to members of the opposite sex of my own species but have never found a human arousing."

"Oh," Jess managed, another conversation having taken the turn for the surreal. "You don't *want* to have sex with me?"

"It's more complicated than that," the sasquatch replied. "There's less of a choice than you make it sound. It is important to the survival of both our species that we do. We *must* copulate in hopes of creating offspring. And my genes have been deemed superior by Orenda and the rest of the tribal elders. I am soon to begin a cycle of impregnation attempts on the human females. It is this that so upset Onatah that she launched the attack into the park."

"The sasquatch that was killed? That was your mate?!"

"My 'mate'? We had not 'mated,' but we hoped to do so one day. But after it was decided I was to mate the human females, she went on a rampage."

My sasquatch is a virgin, Jess thought. *And his beloved killed my friends. Forget law, I'll be selling this story to the tabloids and talk shows for years.*

"Couldn't you have done both?" Jess suggested. "Have it off with her and the 'human females'?"

"And continue to weaken the gene pool?" Tadodaho scoffed. "'One more mouth to feed is one too many,' Orenda says. I fear she's right."

"And that bitter taste in your mouth will affect your ability to father our future child how?"

The sasquatch laughed long and hard, as if he needed it. Only at first, Jess thought she'd pissed him off, and the raising of his head and the opening of his mouth was preamble to a vicious attack. When his body shook, his eyes closed, and his lips curled into a smile, Jess couldn't suppress a grin.

"So, when's this copulation to take place?" she asked.

"Right now," Tadodaho replied straightforwardly. "Orenda says that you're ovulating right now, in fact. She also said that she thought you were the most fertile of our newcomers."

Jess's eyes flitted down to the sasquatch's nether regions for the quickest of moments before she forced herself to look away. She hadn't seen anything, as there was too much hair, but she disgusted herself with the very impulse.

"It's okay," said Tadodaho. "I remember being curious the first time I ever glimpsed one of the females of the human tribe bathing in the river. It was a completely foreign sight and, well, repellant. But as I suppose it called to mind the genitals of the females of my own species, it was still alluring."

"We're never going to get anywhere," Jess admitted, surprising herself by saying "we." "This is just too crazy."

That's when Tadodaho stepped back into the tunnel and returned with a bucket that appeared to be filled with liquid.

"Apple wine?" Tadodaho offered.

Jess laughed.

"Oh, my God! You're like every guy I met in college. It's that easy, huh? Two sips of that, and I'll forget all my inhibitions?"

Tadodaho shrugged.

"To hear Orenda tell it..."

"You rely on her wisdom a lot, huh?" Jess interrupted. "Does she really know magic? It seems more like you sasquatches are the muscle around here and these little descendants of witches tend the crops and keep you happy."

"To hear *Orenda* tell it," the sasquatch continued, more amused than irritated, "this is what fueled the very first cross-species pollination between our two peoples hundreds of years ago, and the practice has continued ever since. It is, in fact, what other members of my tribe have resorted to with the other females of yours and vice versa."

"Patrick?"

"Actually, no. It was explained to him, he met the first he was to copulate with, and they went at it almost immediately. I have heard that it was not a pleasant experience for the female, who advised the others to partake before approaching him, but your friend seemed satisfied."

"Again. Like all men."

"If that is how your species is reduced to organizing the process of intercourse, I'm not surprised overpopulation isone of the primary drivers of the coming apocalypse."

Jess chuckled and reached for the apple wine. She sniffed it, lifted it to her lips, and took a drink. It was warm, but good, like apple cider that reveals its alcoholic content only in the aftertaste.

"This is good," she said, taking another sip. "You want some?"

"Thank you," the sasquatch replied, taking the bucket.

They passed the bucket back and forth that this for a couple of minutes, peppering their conversation with gallows humor and wry observations about the differences in their bodies. Jess shed the animal skins at one point to tell a story and was shocked to see that the sasquatch had an erection poking through the copious amount of hair covering its pelvic region.

"Wow. That didn't take much. My genitals reminding you of those of another of your species?"

"Are mine?" Tadodaho shot back, with a grin.

Jess took another swig from the wine bucket and nodded.

"Yes, but it's slightly larger than I'm accustomed to. You'll make allowances?"

"Of course," Tadodaho replied, as if offended she'd even ask.

Jess rolled over and blew out a few of the candles, and the sasquatch climbed onto the bed.

"Maybe not *too* many allowances," Jess revised as she rolled onto her back. "But let's take things slow."

It took Bones most of the night to reach the sasquatch's mountain encampment. The scents of the multiple sentries positioned on platforms in the trees reached him from a hundred yards away. There was no fear in their smell. They clearly were not expecting company.

As the shepherd neared, he wound around the various manmade traps and trip lines designed to alert the tribe to large animals and outsiders. But the dog had been trained from early on to be exacting in his steps and navigated around until he found an unobstructed path through the tribe's cornfields that led him to the base of the rocks.

A sasquatch had just emerged from one of the lower caves. It looked out into the night as if considering an evening constitutional. When it spied Bones, its lips curled back in a snarl and it bent low, baring its teeth. It extended its arms, its clawed fingers silhouetted in black against the flickering torch light coming from the cave.

By the time it bellowed out a howl of warning to its compatriots, the shepherd was only a couple of feet away. The cry was cut off almost before it began as Bones collided with the beast's upper torso, his teeth grinding into the sasquatch's voice box. The monster gurgled a little, then collapsed.

Several more sasquatches and human tribesmen and women emerged from the caves, and moved toward the dog even as arrows flew in from the sentries on the platforms. Rather than be daunted, Bones merely lowered his head, growled, and charged the nearest biped.

In moments, the body parts and corpses of several of the tribe were strewn on the ground.

Jess had an acquaintance in college named Vicky Albrecht who she'd thought, at first, was a lesbian. She showed no interest in the opposite sex, didn't associate with anyone at the university she'd gone to high school with (which wasn't uncommon for those wanting a fresh break), she lived off-campus freshman year in her own apartment paid for by her parents when most students were clamoring to live in the dorms, and she'd once petitioned the administration to allow her dog, Mickey, to be allowed to come to class with her every day. Her reasoning was simple. He was the same as a medical assistance service dog, as she suffered from severe anxiety. Mickey made it possible for her to function more or less normally.

Her request was denied. Her request for an appeal was denied. And she learned to deal with it, going to classes with a stuffed dog that was weird, but within the rules.

At some point during junior year, Vicky got a boyfriend. His name was Emmett, he was a library sciences major, and he loved films. He took Vicky to endless on-campus screenings, and though she had never professed any previous interest in the cinema, she never missed a one. In fact, everything seemed to be going smoothly for the couple when Jess heard, out of the blue, that they'd broken up.

"What happened?" Jess asked Vicky after running into her in Ross Commons one day.

"I don't know." Vicky shrugged evasively. "It ran its course, I guess."

Six months later, Jess got the story from Emmett himself at a party.

"She called me by her dog's name during," Emmett said simply, after taking a deep draught off his bottle of beer.

"That's it?" Jess asked. "She probably says his name a hundred times a day. It was an accident, no?"

"Sorry, I should clarify. That was her 'thing.' The first time she did it, she pretended it was an accident. But when I made a joke about it the next morning, she was genuinely hurt. We didn't talk about it for a while, until one day in a moment of sharing and utter vulnerability, she asked me if it had really offended me. Realizing the answer she clearly needed to hear, I said, 'No.' A few days later, she did it again, but knowingly, looking me right in the eye like it was a challenge. What could I do? I went along with it. It's not like she asked me to bark or wear a leash or eat from a dog bowl. But after a few more weeks of that, I was over and heard her call Mickey by my name. She gave me the same kind of knowing, winking smile that told me she'd been doing it for as long as she'd called me Mickey."

That was all Jess needed to hear. She told Emmett that she was totally on his side. Later that night when he made a mild pass at her, she considered it but knew she wouldn't be able to resist calling him by his canine *nom de plume*.

She didn't see Vicky much after that. It wasn't like she purposely avoided her, but before, she'd had to go out of her way to see the girl, who'd been little more than an assigned partner on a Psych 101 project.   She started to wonder why they even became friends in the first place. When Jess heard she'd gotten into some exclusive grad program at Northwestern, she thought, *Good for her.* And meant it.

But that was probably the last time she'd given Vicky Albrecht so much as a second thought.

Until this night, of course, wrapped in the arms of Tadodaho after what she conservatively believed to be the single greatest night of lovemaking in her young life. What she'd anticipated would be a simple attempt at insemination, a couple of clumsy thrusts and an ejaculation, turned into something richly and *impossibly* satisfying. This would have never been the case with a human virgin, but as Tadodaho's size and strength continually reminded her, this was no human. At the very beginning, the monster had been shy, which brought out Jess's coquettish side. But after a while, his natural instincts took over, and he brought a passion and vigor that surprised Jess by how much it turned her on.

Then she remembered that that was how Scott had once been, just a monster in the sack that couldn't get enough of her no matter how often or for how long they made love. That was the Scott she missed who had vanished those first few weeks at Jankis, Leonard and never returned, replaced by someone too lost in their own mind to be worth a damn in bed.

As she lay on her side, wrapped in Tadodaho's arms, however, her thoughts inexplicably moved from Scott to Vicky. Did she really fantasize about her dog? Or was this some kind of twisted, Emmett-specific sex game? She tended to believe it was the former, which made her wonder if she would be interested in other dogs, or if it was about her connection to Mickey?

Basically, would this be her definition of pure bliss? Jess wondered. *Or would she be as panicked as I was initially? And maybe most importantly, would she be able to let herself go and enjoy the experience?*

On this last point, Jess figured there'd be no way in hell. But as she nestled back into Tadodaho's body, she really hoped Vicky would. Her bed mate shifted, likely fading in and out of sleep like Jess was.

"Are you all right?" he asked quietly, nuzzling the back of her head.

"Never better," she whispered back. "I still can't believe that was your first time."

"Did I say that? I meant my first time with *you*."

Jess laughed, Tadodaho unable to even properly feign being some kind of sleazy jerk.

"I know you're kidding, because you froze up every time you thought you did something the wrong way. It was cute, actually. Glad you eased up after a bit, though."

"Oh, that?" Tadodaho continued. "Yeah, another thing they said you'd find 'charming.'"

Jess scoffed, but her thoughts turned serious for a moment. She was glad her father didn't have to face whatever apocalyptic nightmare was apparently soon to consume mankind. But there were other relatives and friends she wished she could see one more time or at least warn that things were at their end and that maybe they should prepare in some way. With every passing moment, however, that life felt farther away as she accepted there would be no going back.

"How long do I have?" Jess asked quietly.

"We don't know. Perhaps a year. The planet makes signs to us that most have long forgotten how to read."

"Except Orenda?"

"Except Orenda. She says it is soon and that she won't make it, but that many of us will."

Jess nodded.

"If I become pregnant sooner than later, I might actually get a chance to know my baby a little, yes?"

"We would hope so, yes," Tadodaho replied. "Similarly, the baby would get to know you, too."

Jess had never thought much about children. It was this far-off *maybe someday*. But as it looked like "somedays" were in short supply, the idea was growing in its appeal. A baby would be something, a sign that she'd been there. Though she wouldn't be around to raise it, the very thought of the child continuing on in her absence gave her a real feeling of peace in a moment of panic and upheaval.

She rolled over, putting her hand on Tadodaho's face.

"You ready to try again?"

"The chances that I'll already have enough viable sperm to make it worthwhile are slim."

Jess grinned and slipped a hand down below Tadodaho's waist. When his body responded to her gentle strokes, he kissed her on the lips. She could feel his urgency.

"Tell me again how not worthwhile this is?"

He groaned and bit Jess's lip as she slid onto her back, spreading her legs. She was about ready to guide him into her when he suddenly stopped, cocking his head toward the doorway.

"What is it?" she asked.

"I think I hear...*barking*. Could that be?"

The fight in front of the mountain was not going well for the sasquatches or their human tribesmen. Bones had thus far evaded every attempt to capture him and, worse, had killed and maimed well over a dozen of the mountain's inhabitants in the process. Working methodically, the injured shepherd let the attackers come to him, his limp giving them false hope. When they got close enough, Bones aimed for the closest limb, sank his teeth in, and held on. He suffered tremendous blows to his back and head, but won victory after victory by shredding flesh and, in some cases, severing fingers, forearms, and even legs. Because of his injury, the dog couldn't leap very well after a while, negating his more standard throat-slash.

Still, if he got an enemy on the ground, the rules changed, and he went for the face, neck, entrails, or genitals. In short order, the number of sasquatches and humans willing to try their luck against the murderous dog dwindled to almost nothing.

Bones was just biting through the cervical vertebrae of a fallen sasquatch, chipping apart its spine as he did, when a familiar voice cut through the night.

"Oh, my God!"

The shepherd looked up as Jess stepped out of one of the caves, half-dressed in her now clean clothes. Even in the dim light, she recognized the large canine.

"What're you doing, boy?" she asked, horrified at the bodies littered around the base of the mountain. "You have to stop!"

Bones eyed her querulously, but as all others were at a remove, there was nothing else to attack. Jess took this opportunity to scramble down the rocks toward the dog. At first, the shepherd took three steps back and lowered its head, as if ready to attack. But when the girl slowed and showed him her hands, allowing him to get her scent, he softened and sat down, soaking his haunches and hindquarters in freshly spilled blood.

"Are you okay?" Jess asked, kneeling beside the shepherd.

Despite his recent injuries, however, Bones looked one hundred percent.

"Jess? You need to move away."

Jess glanced back, seeing Tadodaho a few yards behind her. He nodded up to the trees and rocks, where she saw a handful of archers waiting with bows and arrows. She turned back to Bones and sighed.

"You came all this way for me, didn't you?"

The dog gave her a friendly lick on the mouth.

"Then I'm really sorry."

She stood up and stepped away, allowing the archers their target.

"Wait!" thundered the voice of Orenda, who approached from the darkness. "Don't shoot!"

Slowly but surely, she came around the boulders until she was only a few feet from Bones. She stared at him for a long moment before nodding.

"I am sorry that we didn't recognize you, Tawiskaron," she began. "You have come here to show us what we face in the coming world and teach us how to best prepare. We are woefully unready. Thank you for your concern, and we honor your judgment and training."

As she spoke, she moved in close. Bones responded as he had with Jess, backing up and lowering his head, but he added a growl now.

"No, you have nothing to fear from me," Orenda said, extending a hand. "Come."

Bones hesitated, so Orenda sat down in the same bloody muck. So small was she seated that the dog towered over her at his full height. He finally padded over to her, sniffing her fingers before giving them a playful lick.

"Thank you, Tawiskaron," Orenda said. "We owe you our salvation."

But as the shepherd stepped backward, his legs faltered. He suddenly appeared drunk, and swayed back and forth. His tongue lolled out of his mouth, and his eyes watered.

"What did you do?" Jess asked urgently.

Orenda held up her hand, revealing a greasy substance on her fingers.

"It's temporary. Will last just long enough to get him inside."

At this last word, Bones toppled over, landing on one of the dead before rolling right off, unconscious. Orenda signaled a couple of the sasquatches, who hurried over and lifted the dog from the ground.

"Take him to the arena," Orenda ordered. "We have much to learn from this spirit."

As Bones was whisked into the mountain, Jess helped Orenda back to her feet. But as she did, a strange smile formed on the old woman's mouth.

"Already?" she intoned.

Jess reddened, but nodded.

"Oh, no. I wasn't talking to you," Orenda replied.

She placed her ungreased hand on Jess's stomach. The young woman felt the warmth of the touch and realized what Orenda implied. A feeling of great joy swelled within Jess's body. She couldn't remember ever feeling so happy or so at peace.

VI

"The new world will be overrun by the mistakes of the previous one. Some of these will manifest themselves as residual devices that continue to pollute after they're no longer tended to, while others will reveal themselves over time. Plants that have been so genetically altered that consumers of their fruit will suffer cancers for generations. The same with various strains of farm animal. Then the shifts in the weather as the planet recalibrates to an earth without fossil-fueled machines or factories. What man has installed to hold back the tides and the rivers – dams, levees, breakwaters, berms, and so on – will eventually crumble as well, and we must be ready for those changes, too, sudden as they might be upon us. But there is one shift that will come unexpectedly in the form of this."

Orenda paused in her speech to point to Bones, emerging from unconsciousness in a nearby cage. The old woman stood in the center of a vast underground amphitheater ringed with benches carved into the rock. Every sasquatch and human, aside from a handful of sentries, was assembled in the room, staring down into the circular pit in the middle.

"The dog will go feral within a couple of days of the fall of man. They will form great packs and sweep across the land, preying on whatever they might find. Though man has neutered or spayed millions of the domesticated variety, there are so many more than that, which will lead to a population explosion. Within a couple of years, they will be the dominant species, replacing humans.

"While they can be slaughtered by a variety of weapons, as we have seen through this gift from Tawiskaron, even one can spell disaster for our people. Now, this one is a special case. He is completely fearless and brutal, and has experience with the hunting and killing of man, as we've seen by the way he attacks our numbers. He knows the weak points and sets upon them, killing a person with the smallest amount of expended energy possible."

A low rumble passed through the throng. Some preferred to think of Bones as one of the white dogs of Tawiskaron, capable of impossible feats. How else could he have killed and maimed so many of them already? But others were terrified, recognizing the shepherd as indicative of the unknown terrors they would face in the coming world. If they could be undone by a single dog, what chance did they have against a pack?

"So, we will train with him," Orenda announced. "You will know the experience of facing a creature like this, one who doesn't at all feel threatened by the presence of man like the wolf or bear."

In the stands, Jess was seated alongside Patrick and the other so-called newcomers, humans who had grown up in the outside world but were now part of the tribe in hopes of strengthening the gene pool. As Patrick had suggested, the ways they had come to the sasquatches were all over the map. All had been taken against their will, most had watched their comrades be slaughtered for refusing to join, and, to a person, they'd become convinced as to the sanctity of their mission.

"I was a cardiologist," one of the men, a thirty-something who introduced himself as Ramin, told Jess. "My life was an endless stretch of surgical suites interspersed with boring dates, meaningless sex, girlfriends frustrated that I was permanently on call, breakups by text, the occasional golf game, the out-of-town conference, then more chest cracking and heart massage. I didn't choose anything, as my life was laid out, hour by hour, by circumstance. But when my car broke down out on the 86 coming back from Buffalo and I met these fine people, it was as if I was accessing part of my mind I didn't even know had lain dormant for so long. My compatriots, the three other doctors driving back with me, understandably wanted no part of it and paid for their choices with their lives. But I've never felt more alive. I'm a part of something important. I never had time for kids before, but now I'm a father of two, with four more on the way. Sure, I'm to die next year, but I'll die having *done* something. Something that *mattered*. Not just transplant the hearts of unlucky young motorcycle drivers into the chest cavities of rich old fucks after a lifetime of red meat."

Jess understood completely. As Ramin, one of the men who had decided to eschew all semblances of the outside world and go about naked, spoke, Jess found herself inexplicably aroused. She was enjoying this very experience herself and was amazed to find someone else who understood precisely how incredible it was. The incredible infusion of self-worth. The intense feeling of responsibility. The *perspective*.

How do you tell somebody that things you believed your whole life to be of the utmost importance were suddenly without meaning? Unless, of course, they'd gone through the same thing.

But Ramin sensed her ardor and smiled sheepishly.

"Any other time, I would absolutely couple with you," he said. "You are young and astoundingly gorgeous, with perfect hair and breasts. But I must preserve myself, just as you have to. We cannot confuse paternity. Your womb has a reserved sign!"

He said this last thing as a joke, but Jess knew he was right. She almost commented on the absurdity of his rejection, given that he was sitting there with an impossible-to-miss erection, but refrained.

The women, on the other hand, seemed to take an altogether different view. As there was no question of pregnancy, Jess realized early on that casual coupling amongst the female newcomers was seen as a positive, something that drew them together in shouldering the attendant burdens of their new lives. Jess had never had any kind of homosexual feeling, much less experience, but found herself unwilling to rule it out as a future possibility.

As she listened to Orenda speak in the arena, her eyes drifted to a self-proclaimed hippie chick named Faith from San Diego who'd actually followed rumors all the way across the country to the tribe. She showed up one day dehydrated and half-starved, but claiming to have been guided to their doorstep by the stars. After spending a few days meditating with Orenda, she was accepted. She was so well-liked that her inability to conceive after five months of trying with various males didn't result in a death sentence. She even offered to take her own life to reduce the number of mouths to be fed, but after this was unanimously voted down, she vowed to redouble her efforts, beginning that night with a marathon of partners, even though she knew she wasn't ovulating at the time.

"It just felt like the right thing to do," she'd explained to Jess when they met.

Jess wondered if she'd ever get to the mental space where a gang bang "just felt like the right thing to do," only to banish the thought for fear of the answer.

"Did that dog really kill all those sasquatches by the fire tower?" Patrick, beside her on the bench, whispered.

"Yeah," Jess nodded. "It was like one of those karate movies where the hero just goes down the line, knocking everyone out. Except the dog killed them all."

"That's fucked up," Patrick said. "As if they didn't have a population problem as it was."

"Well, Orenda seems to think it was some kind of blessing, right?" Jess replied, lowering her voice to a whisper. "Like he's some of god-dog sent to teach them how to fight?"

"I guess we'll see," Patrick sighed. "But what does it say about her visions if all this planning and procreating will be undone by the first pack of feral dogs that makes it this far into the wilderness?"

Jess was about to respond when four sasquatches rose from their seats near the edge of the arena and climbed down next to Orenda. She nodded to them, and they bowed reverentially to her. They moved to the opposite side of the pit, where several tribesmen and women offered them various weapons to choose from. One of the sasquatches took a club, another a spear. The third took two long knives, with the fourth selecting a primitive sort of bolo.

Once each had nodded in satisfaction at their chosen weapons to Orenda, she stepped out of the pit and indicated for Bones to be uncaged.

The shepherd was still a little woozy, but had watched the sasquatches enter the ring and take up their arms. They had formed a semicircle around the dog and waited for it to attack. A sasquatch turned a gear that, in turn, wound up a length of hemp rope that ran to the ceiling of the arena, through a pulley, and down to a hook on the top of Bones's cage. Before it had risen six feet, the sasquatches had already closed on the dog.

But Bones appeared nonplussed. Sure, four massive, hairy beasts, two carrying weapons meant to tear his flesh and the other pair with ones to bash him into a pulp, would have made for an intimidating sight to most. But Bones wasn't most. He saw it for the lazy threat that it was and waited. There was no malice in these monsters, only fear and reluctance.

When the sasquatch with the bolo lowered the heavy stone balls to spin them in a deadly circle, Bones leaped for its leg, biting into its kneecap with such force that the kneecap separated from the tendon, sending the monster to the ground. The sasquatch with the club wheeled around to bring its cudgel down on Bones's head, only to accidentally strike its comrade on the hip.

Now the melee began in earnest.

As the sasquatch with the spear tried to parry with Bones, keeping him at a distance with the spear's handle, the dog simply grabbed it in his jaws and yanked it away. Weaponless, the sasquatch broke and ran for the edge of the arena. The shepherd gave chase and caught the back of its thigh in his jaws. Tearing away a layer of hair, skin, and meat, Bones dropped to the ground, waited for the injured sasquatch to tumble backward, then bit down on its windpipe, ripping apart its neck as he bolted away.

One down.

The sasquatch with the club ran at the shepherd, club held aloft in its right hand. As it brought it down, aiming for Bones's back, the dog dodged the blow and grabbed the sasquatch's wrist in his mouth. As Bones held on, blood streaming from puncture wounds on both sides of the sasquatch's arm, the club dropped to the ground. The man-beast leaned down to pick it up in its left hand, giving Bones the opening he craved. Dropping the arm, he jumped at the sasquatch's head and tore off its nose, half its cheek, its lips, and much of the flesh on its chin. As blood showered from this ruin of a face, the shepherd snapped at its neck a couple of times before hitting pay dirt. When he punctured the sasquatch's carotid artery, Bones's face was doused in blood from the wound.

As the monster hit the ground, soon to bleed out, the shepherd shook his head to clear the blood from his eyes, and took a few steps back.

The sasquatch with the knives and the injured one with the bolos assessed the situation with greater care. They wisely decided to combine their efforts, the knife-sasquatch indicating for the bolo-bearing one to swing his weapon to draw the dog's attention. When the inevitable attack came, he was to drop his bolo, and the one with blades would swoop in and stab the animal while it was momentarily distracted, claiming victory in the process.

How it worked out in reality was slightly different. Bones was indeed lured by the swinging bolos, but the sasquatch with the knives made a move too soon, anticipating the dropping of the weapon and raising his twin sabers to strike.

Leaving his midsection tantalizingly unprotected.

The shepherd leaped for his exposed stomach and tore out his intestines as the now-unarmed sasquatch watched in horror. As the disemboweled creature tried in vain to gather itself back up, Bones turned to the one cursing its belief in the bolo and attacked its throat with such vengeance that death was caused by a broken neck instead of blood loss.

The dog then turned and tore the eyes out of the entrail-less sasquatch, hastening his death.

The assemblage grew so quiet that the shepherd's shuffling footfalls in the sandy pit echoed with crystal clarity around the arena. Then Orenda got to her feet, hands raised to calm her kinsmen's fears.

"If this does not teach you the importance of our preparations, then I don't know what…"

Her words were cut off by a hundred pounds of fur-covered fury leaping from the ringed pit to the one moving person in his vicinity. Bones didn't even have to open his jaws as the impact of his strike threw Orenda backward against one of the stone benches, shattering her skull, snapping her spine, and breaking her back. Her death was instantaneous.

Blind panic ensued.

Rather than fight the enraged canine, the spectators agreed as one to evacuate and regroup elsewhere. There were four passages through which to leave, and they were soon flooded by humans and sasquatches alike, fighting to get out. A couple of punches were thrown, but the much larger sasquatches easily won out and were first into the tunnels.

Jess stared at the lifeless form of Orenda, heartbroken at what she imagined were all the lessons the old woman would now be unable to impart to her or those who might care for and raise her baby in the future.

"If this is the best they can do, these guys are *fucked*," Patrick whispered, coming up behind her, his arm still in its sling.

"Shut up, Patrick," Jess snarled back. "You heard her yourself. It's some kind of dog-spirit."

Patrick did as commanded, but not for the reason Jess intended. Instead, he stared at the one-time first year law associate with surprise, a silly grin spreading across his face.

"What?" she asked.

"I'm here for the sex, but you're already a true believer. Man, Jess, I never pegged you as the susceptible type."

"Fuck you, Patrick," Jess shot back, elbowing him in the chest.

Bones galloped around the benches, nipping at the retreating tribal members, but doing little damage. They were terrified of him, and this suddenly put him in an impish mood. He leaped and pranced, woofed and licked, but no one would take him up on his jovial offer to play.

Soon, the arena was empty and the shepherd alone.

He hopped back into the pit, sniffed around the corpses of the dead sasquatches, peed on one of them (spear-sasquatch), and then jumped out to investigate the body of the old woman. Orenda's mouth was barely open, as if in a tiny gasp. Her eyelids were half down, however, suggesting someone ready to sleep.

Bones sniffed around her clothes and found a small store of black walnuts and hickory nuts in a pouch on her belt. He tore this open with a claw and quickly ate them. He sniffed around a moment longer, became bored, and made for the exit.

The shepherd ambled down the tunnel unchallenged. He caught the scents of a few retreating humans and sasquatches, but they were giving him a wide berth. He picked up traces of Jess, but nothing strong enough to provide direction.

But suddenly this changed.

Directly ahead of him, he caught the young woman's scent, but also that of one of the sasquatches. Unlike the others, it betrayed no feelings of fear and wasn't running away. Bones advanced cautiously, the cool night air now reaching his nose as well, so close was he to one of the cave mouths.

He turned a last corner and found his path blocked by a large sasquatch, Tadodaho. In one hand, it held a weighted net. In the other, a crude pitchfork.

"Come, Tawiskaron," Tadodaho bellowed. "Your time here is finished. Time to pass back into the spirit world."

Tadodaho barely raised the net, but it was enough to elevate the hair on Bones's back. He lowered his head, growled, and bared his teeth. The shepherd was fatigued, the time between the fight and this current encounter having slowed his heart rate, allowing his body to tire. with Tadodaho slowing his heart rate and allowing his body to tire, but he had about one more fight in him.

"Perhaps you want me to come to you? Is this *my* lesson? I accept your challenge. Now do me the honor you accorded my tribesmen!"

Tadodaho feinted with the pitchfork. Bones took the bait and launched himself at the sasquatch's arm. But the monster quickly pivoted on his left heel, allowed the shepherd to bite down on the pitchfork handle, then swung the net around, delivering glancing blows to the dog's head, back, and hindquarters with the evenly spaced weights.

To the man-beast's surprise, Bones was back on his feet in an instant, his teeth gnashing the air. But fast or not, Tadodaho was ready for this and swung the pitchfork handle around, knocking the shepherd in the side of the head, which sent him rolling to the ground directly in front of the sasquatch. It was then nothing to drop the net over the dog, the heavy weights, about thirty pounds each, keeping the edges in place. This time when Bones tried to right himself, the low net kept him from getting to his full height. As hard as he fought against the ropes, he could neither bite through them or lift them from his body.

Tadodaho raised the pitchfork.

"I look forward to meeting you again, Tawiskaron," the sasquatch said, relieved.

But before he could deliver the death blow, Tadodaho was struck from behind by a fiery club. It wasn't the strongest attack he'd ever endured, but as he wasn't prepared, the force was enough to send him to one knee, dazed. As he tried to stand back up, however, he was struck again, this time feeling the heat of the weapon with greater intensity.

"Fuck you, Bigfoot!" cried Patrick, raising the club again.

He brought the club down again, this time on the sasquatch's back, but could tell the blow did no damage. But it didn't matter much, as Tadodaho's fur had already caught fire, the blaze spreading quickly around his head and neck.

"Why did you…?" the sasquatch roared, raising itself up and turning to face Patrick.

"'Cause maybe you're not the dominant species you thought you were," the young lawyer announced, slamming the club directly into Tadodaho's face. This had the desired effect, crumpling the bones in the sasquatch's face as his mouth and nose exploded with blood. The monster had just realized he was on fire when the blow happened, but now it was too late.

Patrick lifted the net off Bones and picked up Tadodaho's pitchfork with his one good hand. As the sasquatch moaned in pain, smoke pouring off his body like a pyre, a shriek of horror filled the tunnel.

"No!" screamed Jess, seeing her lover in flames.

Patrick eyed her a moment, then shook his head.

"It's for your own good, Jess," he remarked.

He raised the pitchfork and slammed it directly into the sasquatch's throat. A geyser of blood erupted from the double wounds, and Tadodaho choked out his last breath.

"Come on, boy," Patrick said to the German shepherd.

Patrick ran for hours. He didn't know where he pulled the energy from, but he knew death followed, so he had no choice. As the forest was pitch black, he tripped over countless roots, rocks, and bushes, tearing his arms and legs. After seeing the sasquatch tribe panic in the arena, he'd decided he'd hitched his future to the wrong wagon and had to get out. He'd considered getting his belongings from his living quarters but didn't think he had time. The key to escape was the dog, and the dog wasn't going to wait.

So now he paid the price.

"Goddammit!" he cried, receiving three bloody scratches from a leafless branch as he tripped, the kind of thing even a windbreaker would've prevented.

He cursed again when he scraped his shins on a half-buried boulder. Again, a pair of jeans, and he would've been fine.

But he couldn't dwell. He had to get back to civilization, tell the authorities what he'd seen, then bring the army back here and blow the whole place to pieces. As he ran, he memorized his story, knowing he had to keep mention of sasquatches and old women who could see the future to a minimum. He knew enough of the newcomers' names to raise an alarm. And if those in Forestry Service who had clearly aided and abetted the lost tribe stepped in and accused him of being some kind of mass murderer, he'd show them where they buried the girl Jess had come with. No one would believe a hundred-pound weakling like him could break a girl's neck with a flick of the wrist.

And then he'd set about trying to stop this "apocalyptic event" Orenda kept talking about.

He'd tried to keep track of the German shepherd, but it wasn't easy. He'd stop, hear rustling nearby, fear it was the sasquatches, and keep going, only to see that it was the dog a few minutes later. He wasn't sure why the animal was following him, but maybe the thing felt some sense of loyalty to Patrick since he'd freed him from the net.

At first light, Patrick finally slowed down. He jogged instead of ran, but he knew he was dehydrated. He hadn't found any water at night, though he'd expected to come across some kind of creek or river at *some* point, but there'd been none.

But amidst the birdsong and the rustle of the tree canopy in the breeze, he now heard a new sound: running water. The only problem was the density of the thicket. He couldn't see more than few yards to the left or right due to all the trees, so he had no idea which way to turn to get to the creek or even if it was directly in front of him.

As he stood there considering this, he suddenly heard a great crash behind him. He whirled around just in time to see the merrymaking German shepherd bound past him in a diagonal direction, snapping twigs and kicking up leaves as he ran.

"Wait up!" Patrick called uselessly.

He hurried after the dog, slicing his arms and legs and even his right ear now on the nearby branches, but he knew the shepherd was leading him to water.

Sure enough, he found Bones lying at the bank of a small brook a few minutes later. Only about three feet across and maybe eight inches deep, the creek's current was so gentle it could be stopped by a matchbook. But it was water, and plenty of it. Patrick fell to his knees and drank.

"Thanks, boy," Patrick said, petting the shepherd. "Good find!"

After downing his first dozen gulps, Patrick realized he had to pee. He stepped over the river and pissed against a tree on the other side. When he came back, Bones was asleep.

"Good idea," he said, but without any intention of joining the dog.

He took another drink, then washed his feet and the various cuts on his arms and legs. The frigid water stung like hell, and he had no clue what kind of microbes existed in it, but it got the dirt out and stopped any wounds that were still bleeding. He drank a little more, had to pee again, but this time came back to no dog.

"Ugh," Patrick sighed. "Where'd you go, boy?!"

He waited for an answer, but figured the shepherd had either gone off to pee as well or was distracted by a passing rabbit, possum, or skunk. He sat down on the bank to rest for a moment longer before heading on. When he heard the familiar rustle of branches and leaves behind him this time, he barely glanced back.

"Enough play time, dog. Let's keep moving."

But when the rustling stopped and no dog materialized, Patrick turned around.

"Come on, boy! Let's go!"

That's when he saw Jess a few yards away, just within the trees.

"Jess?!" Patrick said, surprised. "You realized I was right, huh?"

She answered by raising a crude bow and stringing an arrow. She loosed it at Patrick and it whistled past his face, missing by a foot.

"Jesus Christ!" Patrick bellowed, clambering to his feet. "You could've hit me."

Without a word, Jess moved a few steps closer and strung a second arrow. Patrick, incensed, stomped toward her to grab the bow away.

"What the fuck are you doing?!" he roared.

He was only three feet away when Jess let the second arrow fly. It hardly had time to get up to speed, but it pierced Patrick's side regardless. The impact was the same as if he'd been kicked in the stomach by a horse. He doubled over, then saw that the arrow was buried several inches into his flesh. As he tried to move, he could feel the sharp tip grind through his muscles and organs.

"*FUCK!*" he cried, sinking to the ground. "Jess?!"

But the young woman had already pulled a third arrow from the quiver hanging at her side. She strung it and fired. This bolt struck Patrick in his thigh, but awkwardly, entering near the top, skating over the bone, then exiting the other side before drilling its tip into Patrick's elbow, which was leaning on his other leg as he was bent over.

"*GNNNHH!*" Patrick gurgled, feeling like he had to vomit.

When he saw Jess stringing yet another arrow, he launched himself backward. The arrow flew harmlessly past him. As she strung another, Patrick limped to the brook and stumbled down the bank, trying to get away.

But as the trees only made aiming difficult, Jess discovered that Patrick had made things even easier for her. He moved in a straight line away, but so slowly that he was still an easy, albeit gradually shrinking, target. She raised her bow, strung an arrow, and loosed. Though she'd aimed at his back, it entered his neck at the base of his skull. He whirled like a cartoon character swatting a bee, then fell face first into the water.

Jess grabbed another arrow and ran over to find him twitching, his muscles seeming to spasm as his body was hastened on toward death.

"Jess…?" he whispered, as if hoping for absolution.

Instead, she roughly pulled the bloody arrows from his body and placed them back in the quiver.

"Sorry. It's apparently hard to make arrows, and we need as many as possible."

Patrick stared at her in horror as she yanked the one out from his leg, taking almost half a pound of flesh with it. She then kicked him over, his head landing face first in the stream, placed a foot on the back of his head, and tore the one out from his neck. As his life's blood gushed out and into the creek, she kept her foot on his skull. Red foam erupted up to the surface as Patrick weakly fought back, but it was over soon.

Leaving the bloody drowned mess in the water, Jess stepped back onto the bank and began the long walk back to the mountain. She knew there would be a time to mourn, but now she had to prepare. She touched her stomach, a little unsure, and inwardly said a prayer of thanks to Orenda and asked for the old woman to continue to bless and guide her from the other side.

A few moments later, as her face filled with the sun's warmth when she entered a tiny clearing in the dense woods, she knew her prayer had been answered.

It took Bones half the morning to find the rabbit that had pulled him away from Patrick. He'd actually picked up its scent, then discovered its warren first, staying close by until the rabbit returned. When it did, it detected the shepherd and bolted for its hole. But Bones was driven by hunger now and easily overtook the small animal.

After devouring the rabbit, Bones returned to the creek and found Patrick's corpse, the young man's hair bobbing up and down the only remaining movement. He sniffed around it a moment longer, then discovered the scent of Jess as well. He tracked it for a few dozen yards, then grew tired and took a nap, settling under a nearby tree.

When he awoke hours later, Jess's scent had grown fainter still, replaced by the smell of the herd of deer Bones had taken the yearling from the day before. Getting to his feet, still a little weak from his injury, the shepherd tracked the scent to the southwest. It would take hours to catch up, but Bones was hungry again.

Epilogue

Jess's baby, a boy, was born ten months later. She named him Tadodaho in hopes that when he heard stories of his father, he would see those qualities in himself. Like a handful of the other babies born around that time, he shared characteristics of both his human mother and his sasquatch father. A couple of the women had had to have primitive Caesarians, as their babies had grown so large in utero that a vaginal birth would've likely killed the mother, but Jess had Little Tadodaho naturally and was back on her feet within days.

The baby thrived and was soon one of the largest newborns in the encampment. When word of the plague finally came, Jess had an optimistic thought that maybe they'd survive, so cut off from the rest of the world were they. But after the first few newcomer deaths, she knew she was soon to die as well and prayed that her child would be spared.

A week later, two days after the disease had struck her with such intensity that one moment she was cooking an evening meal and the next she was in bed wrapped in skins, quaking with fever, she was taking in what she knew would be her last sunset.

Tadodaho was finally brought to her, and she delighted in his healthy appearance. He'd most certainly been around her when she'd been infected, but he showed no signs of illness. She wept bitterly, wishing with every fiber of her being that she could see him grow up, become strong, become the image of his father, but knew this wasn't meant to be.

She finally smiled at her baby and, with her last breath, told him the world was his. It would be almost two hundred years before the grandson of this small child encountered at last the animal that had been so pivotal in bringing his parents together before being just as instrumental in tearing them apart.

Called a "quite gifted storyteller" by *Fangoria* magazine and "an exciting new voice in the speculative, dark fantasy genre" by author Michael (*Enter, Night*) Rowe, Mark Wheaton is the author of the bestselling and critically-acclaimed indie horror novels *Sunday Billy Sunday: A Memoir* and *Flood Plains* as well as the popular *Bones* series. He is also a horror screenwriter (*Friday the 13th, The Messengers, Infected*), graphic novelist (Dark Horse's *The Cleaners*) and children's playwright (*Evita Sassy and the Black Mask's Last Gasp*). His first YA novel, *Finders & Keepers: The Sword of the Realm* is set for release in '13 from ZOVA Books.

Made in the USA
Middletown, DE
01 March 2023